JOURNEY TO THE BLUE PLANET

C. E. HAUPT

Journey to the Blue Planet
All Rights Reserved.
Copyright © 2019 C.E. Haupt
v6.0

This is a work of fiction. The events and characters described herein are imaginary and are not intended to refer to specific places or living persons. The opinions expressed in this manuscript are solely the opinions of the author and do not represent the opinions or thoughts of the publisher. The author has represented and warranted full ownership and/or legal right to publish all the materials in this book.

This book may not be reproduced, transmitted, or stored in whole or in part by any means, including graphic, electronic, or mechanical without the express written consent of the publisher except in the case of brief quotations embodied in critical articles and reviews.

Outskirts Press, Inc.
http://www.outskirtspress.com

ISBN: 978-1-9772-0044-0

Cover Image by Eva Jones

Outskirts Press and the "OP" logo are trademarks belonging to Outskirts Press, Inc.

PRINTED IN THE UNITED STATES OF AMERICA

My first novel of Science Fiction is dedicated to my dad, Charles Edward Jones, who loved Science Fiction, was an extremely avid reader and taught me to love all genres of reading from an early age and use my imagination to dream big. It is also dedicated to all the students over the course of many years to whom I taught writing skills and literature in the hopes that I helped them to open up their imaginations to dream big also. I wish and hope for them the courage to attempt to use those ideas, little and big, and the ability to translate the unreal into reality and the impossible into glorious possibilities. It's never too late!

Acknowledgements

I would be remiss in not recognizing just a few of the people who made my life easier in helping me through the process of wriitng my first novel. First and never least is my husband Jim, who knows a lot more about computers than I do and was there to troubleshoot for the 1st, 2nd and the 50th+ times to bail me out of a difficult place. My gratitude is undying, especially for all the cooking and laundry you did to allow me time to write; my good friend Pam Prosser High who read the entire manuscript in between working and gave me voluminous notes and corrections that helped to get me to the finish line. Good friends are a blessing. A shout out to my Legion buddies at our table, Marlene, Bucky and Audry who are waiting patiently for this to go to print and all the friends and colleagues who are encouraging me to continue with Book Two even before they have read Book One. They are always there to pick me up on Fridays. Last but not least, the publishing group at Outkirts, especially my Author rep Colleen Goulet, who had the patience and generosity of a saint in working with me when it seemed as if I knew nothing after the umpteenth time of helping me through each step. I will miss some names I know, but all the helpers in the chat rooooms to answer my every question no matter how simple; Tina, Alison, Jamie and the other unnamed people who worked together tirelessly to get me to this great place and fulfill a lifelong dream. My golden years will be filled with gratitude that I had so many good people to lead me to my dream and make it become a reality.

Insertion 1

Caldera Yellowstone in Idaho at the Border: Over 12,500 years ago

Three travelers moved quickly through the thick woods as silent as leather foot coverings would allow them. Their faces and bodies were caked in mud to keep the mosquitoes from feasting on their skin. If they stopped moving even for a second, they would be covered as with a swarm of bees. The air was filled with a putrid, sulfuric odor of rotten eggs and slimed vegetation that brought tears to their eyes and bile to their throats. They weren't pleased to have to move in this direction to get to their camping grounds but the known path had been blocked by a rock fall from the high mountains. They had little choice and looked up to the peak as one, almost as if their minds were connected. The sides were steep and few trees were growing, eating slowly away at the rock and gravel, seeking any little bit of moisture to stay alive. They came to the edge of the woods and the landscape before them was stark and eerie. The air had a heavy, moist feel to their skin and the odor became so offensive, one began to gag and swallow, trying to keep down the little food he had taken into his stomach.

Suddenly, ahead of them an open spot of ground showed them myriad colors displayed; ochres and red clay, brown mud with pink edges, green algae and white films over rocks. A thick, yellow sludge covered large puddles and the edges of steaming holes. Streams of water shot up and dropped, shot up again toward the clear blue sky and dropped again. It roared at them and they watched in awe as it rose little by little until it was the height of eight of their huts if not more. They could feel the heat and moisture, the steam weaving its way toward them.

All three began moving back step by step, moving to the woods at their rear. At once, as if summoned by the towering funnels of water all around them, spouts appeared quickly. Some were of bubbling, hot mud in spurts and chunks, others spreading out, covering the rocky ground before them, inching out in a wide circle. The noise was deafening and they looked at each other with terror in their eyes.

This land was 'evil' it was said. No one came here unless they were traveling to their winter camp and could not pass through ice and snow covered hills with their horses and supplies. They were told many spirits were here to watch and hover over anyone who dared to attempt a journey through these forests. Those who returned from travel through these tortuous lands told of shadows and sounds that left terror and fear with them. They believed these were spirits who watched them as they moved, talked to them as they camped for their nights and touched them while they slept. There was something that prevented them from moving or seeing or speaking if they woke while this was occurring. No one who succeeded in reaching home would ever attempt to go this way again. Many never reached home. Those who did had no explanation for when their friends had disappeared and they had lost any trace of them.

Stories would be told of soft, clay-colored, strange spirits with foreign faces who visited them and examined their supplies, themselves, and their animals. Some were returned home in a deep sleep that lasted weeks. Some who were unhealthy in their travels found themselves feeling gradually better. Over time they had regained their good health, sometimes better than they could ever remember feeling. Feeble- minded ones became clear and focused. Those with bent back and weak joints found strength, straight spines and strong- muscled arms and legs.

Little did these tribes realize that they were watched by 'others' unknown to them. These 'others' were observing their habits, their rituals, their music and festivals and recorded all these marks and measures that were the bedrock of their culture. The 'others' sorted out some of their number to take back to the living quarters they had formed. They had done deep investigations into the bodies and their minds of their subjects. They had given them back better health, stronger bones, sharper minds and had altered the DNA of their makeup with subtle changes before they found themselves back at their tribes without knowledge of how they had gotten there. These changes would show themselves over generations to benefit whole tribes and families with traits they required for the future.

The lands and lakes would remain hidden for most of a thousand or more years. The people who roamed there would tell their tales. The ones who had been given 'miracle cures' would pray to their ochre-toned gods who gave them long life and happiness. Those who never returned to their tribes from their solitary journeys would be kept by the 'others', isolated, 'changed' and assimilated into the new 'families' who were seeking a quiet, secret life. These were places few people would even be aware of for centuries of time. Their work and efforts at survival would continue on and their numbers would grow.

For the indigenous peoples who had to suffer through these volatile, changing lands of earthquakes and geyser eruptions, earth-shifting, steam vents and mud pots opening up in unforeseen spots, they continued their existence in a traditional, ritualistic manner. They stored their pots and tools in caves and pits. They buried their refuse with broken shards of pottery and their people with hand crafted jewelry, semi- precious stones and beads as a sign of respect and arrival into their afterlife. Glyphs would be carved in rock falls and on the sides of their pinnacled, soaring hills that became mountains over time. Clean, rushing rivers carried arrowheads, pottery shards and bone fragments miles out of the area to be discovered centuries later. Students would be digging up these artifacts for history lessons or science field trips. Tourist traps would be the end result of all the lives that had worked and played, been born and died on these grasses and plains. The towns of Paige, Bear, Tucson and Mammoth, as well as many others, would make their living taking tourists on rafting trips down the river. They would stop to examine these glyphs and walk in the cool waters of the riverbed to escape the indomitable, searing heat of the desert sun.

For the time being, those who continued their own investigations, experiments and observations into this foreign world they had voluntarily entered, began to build lives for themselves and the children that would be born. They had enough space in this open, far ranging land to live in small communities, making homes that blended into the surrounding areas. They taught their children how to adapt and thrive and use their skills and formidable knowledge to be a part of this world. They had the knowledge to confront and overcome the pitfalls, diseases and dangers that the indigenous people had to suffer through. They increased their numbers but still buried their dead. They clung to the history of their true home and created tomes of information secreted away in files that could not be translated or deciphered. These they passed on to their young when the time was appropriate. They only used their advanced technology to keep hidden and safe. Communication was a continuing, necessary connection to all the 'others' who were spread all over this globe of white and blue skies, sand colored lands and azure and emerald waters. Building councils of the most adept scientists and technicians among their number was the most important move they could make to share happenings, provide secure living habitats and insert themselves into the civilizations across this globe. As each one formed, grew, rose and then fell, the cycle repeated itself generation after generation.

Yellowstone Caldera would be waiting a long time for more recent people to discover it, investigate, examine and commercialize it. Those who needed this secret, mysterious place could continue building their fortifications, performing their tasks and living their lives in continued anonymity. The day was coming when their descendants would have to exit from their cover and join a different time. Their preparations would have some breathing space and some time to be refined. But prepare they could and they did. Uncovering it would be a different story altogether.

Chapter 1

Present time

Sabina Carter stepped gingerly out of the shadow of the doorway leading to a small tunnel at the northwest side of the Akrotiri ruins. Her shoes were rubber-soled to silence the crunch of the gravel and she tried to step on it as silently as she could. Every one she could identify had gone home or off to tourist buses long ago. She had remained in one of the deeper rooms until she could hear no noise, no conversation, and no footsteps. If even one person spied her or even heard her steps, she would leave quickly and regroup her thoughts and plans to find another way to reach her target.

The Sun continued its descent toward more shadows and the crickets began their chirping in the crumbling gaps of the walled stones. A small dust devil stirred the grainy sand around her and sent little devils into the air with a soft whistling. She felt the cool air softly touching her bare skin and involuntarily gave a little shiver. So much depended on her success at this site and she could not fail as others had. There was little time left.

She took a step forward, then another and froze. A footfall sounded on the other side of the broken wall. Instantly, she made a move, "Hello. I thought I was the only one to miss the bus."

He stood still, mouth open, eyes wide and staring. Before her stood a very tall man somewhere between six one and six four, thin and angular, but muscled, a short haircut a shade off military, of a dark brown, with green eyes the color of new sea turtles, looking her over as she did him. There in front of him, was a trim, tall woman around five eight or nine, long legs and tan trousers, a tangle of dark hair to her shoulders and the bluest eyes he had seen since his baby sister, a shade of topaz he couldn't remember on anyone else he knew. "Oh I didn't miss the bus. I'm here by myself, out for a late tour on my own."

"Bummer, that you missed your bus." His voice was a deep tenor with a decided American accent, "You alright?" he asked.

She didn't miss a beat and she thought quickly, "Oh, then you can give me a ride back to town" and thought of how long it would take her to return, finish her search and get out of here with what she needed in hand. "I'm fine, just wasn't sure how I could get back to the hotel. You're a gift."

She held out her hand, "I'm Sabina Carter, here on a holiday and apparently will be late for my own funeral."

Rodane held out his hand and she gripped it with surprising strength and looked over her shoulder, "I guess we better get going before there is little light on the road. It can be difficult even in the daytime."

"Carry your duffle?" he asked, looking at the large bag at her feet.

"No, it's fine." She hefted it and held on tightly as they walked to his car at the other end with hardly a word. The silence stretched out on the drive and became somewhat strained and uncomfortable.

"How's your tour going, having a good stay in Akrotieri?

"It's been pleasant," she answered."I have too little time for all I want to see and do."

{especially with what I need to do}

"Would you like to repay me for your return trip?" He looked over with a boyish grin.

"Oh…of course. How much do you want?" She reached into her fanny pouch for her wallet.

"Hey, hey, just kidding," He was beginning to flush, it was cute. "I just thought you would have dinner with me for repayment and some company. I'm really pretty good company." He surprised himself.

{I haven't had dinner with anyone in over a year}

He blushed a little deeper. They were approaching the outskirts of town and the sun was almost over the edge of the horizon. The shadows were now darker and the buildings were lighting up with returning couples or families from a long day.

She had to think quickly, "I really wish I could but I'm meeting someone and we're going to have a lot to catch up on but I'd be happy to give you something for gas."

Rodane looked at her as he pulled up to the only hotel on this side of town.

"I wouldn't think of it, happy to be able to help you. Have a great time with your friend."

He parked his car in a small lot and they both went up the steps together to the lobby. The inside was very well appointed; tapestries on the walls, sturdy draperies at the floor to ceiling windows and a low watt bulb at the counter where a young girl was filing her nails and looking bored.

Sabina walked to the counter, "Could I have my room key, 217, please?"

Rodane turned as he was walking towards the stairs, "Don't you keep your room key with you?"

"No I'm out in the ruins so often, I would be afraid of losing it among them, then I would really be in a pickle" and she smiled a little.

Rodane looked around for a minute and then turned to her, "I don't see your tour bus here. Are you sure they know you were left behind? Maybe we should call and let them know you're here. How many days are you here for?" His eyebrows lifted slightly.

"Well, the tour continues on to Crete but I decided to stay extra days and I'll catch up to them later. I'll give them a call when I get to my room. Thanks again for the lift."

{ too curious and that won't do}

He took the stairs to his rooms and she followed behind, noticing he continued up one of the flights. As she turned the corner, the plush green and deep purple carpet quashed any sound she might make and she stood outside room 217 for exactly three minutes by her watch. It was very quiet here at this time of night. There was a soft tinkle of glass and silverware from the dining hall on the first floor, with a low murmuring from diners having an early dinner. One thing could be counted on of diners in Greece. After a full day of tours and shopping, most were glad to get back to their hotel and relax over at least an hour or two of dinner and wine.

{maybe a drink of ouzo. I could use one at this point}

She opened her door slowly and quietly as she could. Key cards were a blessing in this age, she mused. It made it much less likely anyone would hear her come and go in the wee hours of the morning and it looked like that would be her return time. She stripped quickly, used the toilet, pulled out a clean shirt, this one with long sleeves, and a fresh pair of slacks from the small closet and changed her sweaty socks for dry ones. She ran a brush through her hair and washed her face and hands in the small sink by the bed.

This room was a 'study', big enough to sleep and dress/undress, with no frills, no luxuries… hell, not even a tub. It had only one small window but it did have a small refrigerator with a microwave on top and a safe. The bed was comfortable enough and it was pretty far removed from the other, more touristy rooms so it afforded her a little more privacy. A small chair was in a corner by the bed. On the way to the door, she slipped a small bag of trail mix and a granola bar into her pockets, grabbed a bottle of water from the fridge, a flashlight, stuffed them into the duffle bag and turned on the light by her bed. Anyone looking at her window would think she was there. The timer she had put on the light would click off at midnight. She put the Do Not Disturb sign on her door.

She listened in the hallway for a moment, heard nothing and made her way to the back stairs. Once out and around to the parking lot, she noticed that Rodane

{that's odd, he never said where he was from and I never asked him}

had parked his car in the end space, away from three more cars.

{doesn't trust anyone not to ding his baby}

Rounding the far corner of the hotel, she started walking back to the ruins, thinking it would take her the better part of an hour to get there. That would leave her with a little more than four or five hours to do what she needed to, almost desperately had to do. She had received news that a team of archaeologists was moving back to her little spot and beginning a new dig into that area based on some new readings on their EMS tests.

{damn why now}

There had been few explorations into the area where she needed to dig and the likelihood of a quick find was negligible but the possibilities left her with no other choice. She had to accomplish this tonight if she wanted to keep to schedule.

{well tomorrow at the latest}

The night air was still rather warm but a soft breeze was bringing the hope of cooler air from the north and she lifted her eyes to a moon that was almost full enough to actually give her some light to walk safely. She passed no houses on this route except far off to the left of her, she could see a few lights of scattered homes, two or three for the entire walk. A couple of crickets were chirping and an owl flew over, startling her when it left out a 'scree' right over her head. Her heart beat a little faster and she picked up her pace. She broke out the trail mix and ate it slowly since it would have to be dinner for the evening. She took a few swigs of water and walked on.

After about forty minutes, she saw the hazy dark outlines of the ruins ahead and it gave her a pleasant little jolt to almost have arrived.

{ye gods, I want a shower and a good night's sleep}

Soon she could breathe easy and return home to put things back on schedule. They could then put long-laid plans into motion. Too many people were waiting on her and would anxiously await her outcome of tonight or tomorrow.

She picked up speed, tried to block out the bad luck she had earlier and hoped that soon, she would be walking back to a warm meal, a soft bed and a successful find. The round, almost full white moon guided her through another journey. Rodane, whoever, would be a small glitch in a large puzzle.

Chapter 2

Akrotieri ruins

Rodane crossed the room he was using to the one window facing the direction of Akrotiri ruins. He stood there a few moments listening to the sounds below him and taking in the parking lot. It was too dark to see very far down the access road but he could see to the end of the lot. He was torn between going to the dining room to have some dinner or following his hunch. The hunch won. His mom always told him, 'Roddy, trust your instincts. They're good ones and they'll serve you well if you listen to them.' He shook his head as if he had an itch in his ear.

{what would you say mom am I nuts or just grasping at straws}

There was just something 'off' about Sabina Carter. He couldn't quite put his finger on it but it felt wrong. She felt wrong somehow, not lying, but not being totally honest either.

{who gets left behind from a bus tour and doesn't bother to call them}

For that matter, he wasn't even sure if she was on a bus tour. No bus, no name tag, no concern for being left behind, no water while touring ruins in baking sun... too much to accept from someone who seemed too smart, too aware, to actually be a left behind tourist. So if his Sabina Carter...

{okay she's mine now}

...wasn't what she led him to believe, then who was she and why did it matter to him? Refusing him dinner was probably a polite way to brush him off. Maybe she was a tourist, by herself and using the excuse of a missed bus to give herself a sense of safety in accepting a ride from a stranger. If she was meeting someone, what about the bus tour?

{who is this girl and why do I care}

Up to now his trip has been uneventful, pleasant but similar to many other tours he had taken over the last two years. Bouncing around old ruins in the Mediterranean, taking various camera shots, Bouncing around old ruins in the Mediterranean, taking various camera shots, cruising up and down the islands had given him plenty of ideas for his lecture series when he returned home to the university for the fall semester.

Having dual interests had made the job offer from the University of Montana impossible not to consider. They offered him a chance to travel to many lovely, ancient sites, to take pictures and gain firsthand experience of the archaeological sites he taught to his students. Bringing home catalogs, brochures and pictures galore, allowed him to produce at least one travel book per year for added income and gave him a further appetite for more. The university only asked for a small percentage of the profits.

One drawback was his daughter, Sophia. They were at opposite ends of the states with her in Virginia but he was able to use Skype frequently and email more often as well. Taking her on his tours was out of the question. Caroline was adamant that she not leave the country. She even had it written into the divorce decree four years ago when things between them were at their worst. It had become better in the last two years since he had set up a special college fund for later and managed to keep all his support payments up to date by writing his travel books. But on Sophia's travels, Caroline put her quite heavy foot down. He was allowed to have Sophia every other Christmas and Easter.

He had her four weeks in the summer, also court decreed.

{love how she allows me time with my daughter}

To be fair, this job kept him at a distance to Caroline and was advantageous in many other aspects, except it also kept him from closer interaction with Sophia.

{does one cancel out the other}

If she would stay interested in her latest 'conquest' as she put it, they might even get to be civil with each other. A little green devil niggled at him when he thought of someone else being the male role model in Sophia's life while he taught long hours, traveled all over, and spent weeks working on his travelogues.

The last time he and Sophia had actually, physically, spent time together was four days in April for Easter vacation. He wouldn't get to have her with him until mid-August and that cut his four weeks summer time to two and a half weeks. Guilt reared its head.

{your choice buddy}

Caroline seemed fine with the short visit but who knew what she complained about to her coworkers and her 'conquests'?

{I'm more the villain here keeping her life from being ordered and comfortable}
Then pictures cascaded across his memory box of arguments
{fights buddy, let's be real here}
…with Sophia, heir apparent to the wagging finger in his face,
{that stopped when she was five and a half}
so he instituted Sophia and Daddy time…and it would be just for both of them,
{ agreed to be nice and not nasty}
and she had thought a little more about the nasty part. It also was because…
{ now be fair here}
Caroline had sat her down and impressed on her how Daddy and she were fine with each other now and they wanted Sophia to love and respect each of them equally.
{yeah, tell that to a five and a half year old who lives with a harpy}
But it did make her trips a little calmer and each year she grew so much, her maturity sometimes seemed to outstrip his.

Lost in these thoughts, he barely registered the shadow that he sensed from the periphery of his vision out on the parking lot at the end. Maybe it was the fact that she passed under a light. He pushed the curtain away and looked deeper into the shadows.
{damn can't see mud here}
He went and switched off the light and rushed back to the window to look again. Yep, he was sure that tall, lithe figure was his girl Sabina.
{christ, she's not my girl}
He looked again and watched and listened for a few minutes more. Ok, his instincts were working just fine. No friend, no tour bus, no taxi or limo and heading out at night in moonlight, back toward Akrotiri.
{should I follow you Sabina Carter or let you go to your secret adventure}
He lost her in the black of night and his stomach rumbled from hunger. Checking his watch, he realized that the night had five to six hours at most of isolated quiet time, either to eat and sleep or lose the night to satisfy his gut feeling.
{why do you care}
He wasn't really sure why this was, but the plain truth was that he obviously did. It might be time to follow up on this whim of his. He had something to prove and he was all in at this point. He made his way downstairs and asked the concierge for a sandwich and two bottles of water on his bill. Then he inquired if there was a bike to be borrowed by anyone at the hotel. The concierge looked at him for a few seconds… then went to check.

{probably thinks I'm balmy}

Ten minutes later he came back with a key to a bicycle lock and told him the bike was around the corner to the left. He also handed him a brown bag with two sandwiches and two bottles of water, "I promise to have it back before morning."

"Yes sir, glad to be able to help. Anything else I could help you with sir, like a light… perhaps a flashlight?"

"No thanks, you've been very helpful." Rodane walked out of the lobby, said hello to two people coming in arm in arm, glanced into the dining room and headed around the corner to the bike.

He wasn't sure what possessed him here, giving up food, sleep and riding a bike into the countryside at night in the dark but he felt the need like an itch. He couldn't remember ever doing anything this precipitous and foolhardy. Maybe that was why he found himself slightly exhilarated and excited by the whole adventure part of this mysterious episode.

{okay Miss Sabina Carter here comes Roddy}

Only family ever called him that.

Chapter 3

Akrotieri ruins

The tunnel at the Northwest corner of the lesser ruins had a flashlight beam peeking through from the inside. Sabina gripped the handle of her small shovel and continued her digging into the fifth of her explorations, into the solid layer of Plinian earth at her feet. It was a combination of pumice, earth and ash, remnants of the outer layer of the volcanic event from 1610 BCE. It was the last of the surges to occur in the second phase of the eruption; rapid moving, dense and very hot, almost 400 degrees, and it was the end of the pyroclastic flow after two days.

If her measurements were even close to correct, she should have found some piece of her prize by now. It seemed like she had been at this for hours. The sweat was running down her face and soaking the clean shirt she had put on.

{should have brought a change or a wet towel}

She sat back against the wall, took a long swig from her water bottle and wiped the sweat from her face with a rag. She had carried in a small duffle bag this morning, before sunrise, well before the arrival of the early tour buses. She had hidden behind one of the lower walls in the shade of a half collapsed ceiling in the very room she was digging in, then covered it with loose rock and dirt. Now she took out her EMS again and redid the algorithm that should have helped her, by now, to unearth the device she was searching for.

{where are you little sucker I need you to show yourself now}

As if connected to her thoughts, the EMS gave off a series of beeps that alerted her to a possible red spot behind the wall where the duffle bag lay. She placed the EMS on the ground next to her and used her shovel to begin another dig. The shovel was specifically fashioned with a pointed tip that was made from Anodized steel that could pierce metal. It only needed to pierce the layer of Plinian earth about one to three feet in depth. She set to work for the sixth time, took in a deep breath, sent her thoughts to all the gods for help and struck again and again. The reverberations from the hard surface caused her arms to tingle and cramp. She kept going, heedless of time or place or her surroundings, hoping against hope that she was close to discovery. From out of the dark a soft voice spoke,

"Sabina Carter, I have a favor to ask." Her hands stilled, her heart raced, her breath caught and her ears became attuned to the spot from which the voice came. She slowly reached for the duffle bag near her feet.

"I hope you don't have a gun or weapon of some sort, because I'm unarmed and I don't intend you any harm but I will protect myself if you attack me." Then he went silent again.

{jesus mary and joseph why can't I avoid the nuts and the perverts}

"Rodane is it?" she asked, "Why are you here?"

He spoke softly, "Same reason you are, I suppose, to solve a mystery from the looks of it or at least to complete one".

She stayed close to the duffle and sat back on her heels, "Did you follow me?"

He came around part of the wall but hugged it close, out of her reach or other means. "Sort of" he looked at her, slowly measuring her, taking in her clothes and her shovel and the duffle.

"What do you mean, sort of? You either did or you didn't!" she snapped at him.

He put up a hand, "I saw you leave the hotel on foot and thought you might want some transportation back to the hotel."

"I didn't hear your car."

"That's because I came by bike." He looked right in her eyes and a smile started at his lips and stopped. She actually broke out laughing.

"You came by bike and you want to provide me with transportation? Are you insane, Rodane?"

When she heard the lilting rhyme, she stopped and shook her head slowly.

"What are we doing here?" Blue eyes took in green eyes, though neither could tell in the semi darkened room with only the light from her flashlight.

"I'm not sure," Rodane answered, "What are we doing here?"

"What I'm doing here is my business and what you're doing here is butting in." She took her flashlight from where it lay and began to rise to her feet.

"Wait!" Rodane moved one step closer. She tensed. "I'm not a threat to you and I have a reason for following you. There may be others who are taking an interest in what you're doing."

A cold touch to her neck made a shiver crawl down her spine, "What are you talking about?"

"I had a hunch about you. I was looking out the window at the parking lot and I saw you pass under the light on your way 'out'." He pointed to the room they were in.

"So?" I could have been getting some air, walking to get some exercise, looking at the moon, anything. Rodane, you are a very weird man, I think. And what's with the 'possible threat'?" She used her fingers in a quote sign, "Do you have a habit of stalking someone and corralling them in a dark closed space?"

"Look Sabina," he put up his hands to ward off her anger and she snapped out, "Don't talk to me like we know each other! You don't have that right." Her voice trembled and she shut her lips tight against an oath.

"Ok, Miss Carter" he was becoming annoyed himself.

"Dr. Carter to you!" she almost spit it out.

"Damn it, would you listen to me woman?" his voice echoed in the small space. She jumped back as if slapped, "Whoa there, Bucko!" she took a deep breath, "How about we tone it down a notch?"

"Doctor Carter", he emphasized each syllable, "when I decided to follow you, even though I missed dinner and need some sleep, it was because there are two people at the hotel who stirred my interest enough to follow you. They were on the road when we left here earlier and when you were heading out tonight in the dark, they were having quite the argument below my window as to whether they should follow you or not. Do they get to call you Sabina?"

When she started to answer, he threw his hand up, "Never mind, that's not the point." Sabina was feeling confused, frustrated and a little afraid, both of him and apparently more than him.

{when will this night give me some hope}

"Ok Rodane. It is Rodane I believe?" He could hear a quiver in her voice.

"Yes, it is," and he pursed his lips a little, "you can call me that."

"Okay, what is the point? How can I be of help to you? Before you say anything, how do you think you can be of help to me with your bike?" The last thing she needed to do was laugh but she felt it trying to come up from some part of her.

{why does this guy tickle my funny bone}

"Well," Rodane relaxed a little "when I left to come here, your two interested parties were heading into the dining area. It seems food was more important to them then to me. It should buy you a little time to get what you came for and then head back to the hotel. You know, 'safety in numbers' and all that. You could take the bike and I could walk back."

Sabina took a few seconds to think, "Or, I could stay here and finish up what I need to and you could go back and have dinner. We could agree to part amiably and continue our separate ways." She found herself holding her breath.

"And you trust those other two not to try and follow you here or do you any harm? They seemed quite agitated."

"What made you come here now? It was no concern to you, after all. You don't know me or what I am or who they were. Why get involved?"

{I really really want to know the answer to that}

"I guess it's that following a hunch I mentioned" Rodane gestured. "Mind if I sit down? My legs are not used to pedaling a bicycle."

She nodded her head, watching him sit slowly in the dirt.

"My name is Rodane Arcos. I'm an Archaeologist. I study antiquities on my tours and I'm very familiar with this area from past trips. I knew you were looking for something as soon as I saw you coming out of this room, earlier. There's nothing here that any tourist, especially with limited time on a bus tour, would even be interested in. This area is pretty much ignored but it's becoming a focus of other teams who have to do some exploring. When you told me you missed your bus and then didn't try to contact them or even show any concern for being left behind, it triggered my instinct mode. What tourist from a bus tour goes off by herself in a strange place, far away from the buses and other people and goes exploring ruins that might be unsafe? None that I know of and…no friend who shows up."

"Okay, that explains your distrust of me but what about the other two?"

Rodane said, "When they argued over you, I remembered seeing them on the way to the hotel. I wondered if they might have been following you. Is that possible? Did you tick someone off from what you're doing?"

"Mr. Arcos, I don't think…"

"Please, Miss Carter…uh, Dr. Carter," seeing the look on her face "and by the way it's Dr. Arcos, if you're interested. It doesn't take a genius to figure out you're searching for something and even a lowly archaeologist can figure out those two were not very friendly. I came to the conclusion you might want to get what you came for and make your way back to the hotel ASAP. Look, if you want privacy, I can bike back and get my car and then come and retrieve you. O…r… he drew out the or…"you can let me help you and we can be out of here sooner rather than later and then you have what you came for. I know you're safe, those two are out any satisfaction for whatever, and I can get some food and sleep." He let out the rest of his breath with a whoosh!

Sabrina sat down in the dirt and wiped her face with a dirty rag, "Dr. Arcos, I find myself in a difficult position here. I don't know you, you don't know me. I have no idea if you're telling me the truth or not and I have no idea who could possibly be interested in me or what I'm doing here."

She saw him wince and beat him to the punch, "But I will meet you halfway. You seem harmless enough."

"Gee, thanks, that's the nicest thing a woman has said to me in a long time." Rodane shifted his seat around and searched her face.

"I'm grateful for your concern, though what I'm doing here is my business and honestly, your concern doesn't change that or leave me to trust you any better. Tell you what. If you really want to help, why don't you be my sentry and I can continue what I was doing while you keep watch for anyone you hear or see? If you give me maybe one hour or less, we could be on our way and you could still get room service if they have it and have a very late dinner and we could both get some sleep from an exhausting day. Hmmm? What do you say?"

She watched his expression, "That's as far as I'm willing to go with someone I just met."

"My curiosity is eating at my good judgment," Rodane managed grudgingly and admitted, "but you're right, and we're wasting a lot of time if I argue with you. I'll be out there" he pointed to the night, "and you can call me if you need me."

"Thank you Dr. Arcos, I owe you one."

"Yeah, whatever that is."

Rodane moved to the outside and climbed up to the night air and a fuller than three quarter moon that gave off quite a bit of light, muttering to himself and taking up his watch beside the best preserved wall.

"That is one stubborn …witch…" he gave her the benefit of the doubt, "but one very interesting lady."

Sabina picked up her shovel pulled herself to her feet and started right in digging where she had left off.

{now what do I do with him if I should find what I'm looking for}

Should she believe him? She didn't need this complication right now and she definitely didn't need someone watching her, who knew what they were about.

{damn this keeps getting worse}

She found herself hitting the dirt with a vengeance and a shovel that was eating away at the dirt inch by inch. She checked her EMS and it was still blinking green though she had switched off the telltale beep as soon as she heard his voice.

Clunk! The shovel hit metal and jolted up her arm. Her breath caught and her head hammered. She scraped some loose dirt away and looked down into her hole. There was a tip of silvery metal, coated in dark, grainy dirt and facing straight up. Using her shovel, she picked carefully away at the surrounding earth till she exposed two inches of metal then three…then her vision actually blurred until she realized it was sweat running into her eyes. Or was it tears? She didn't care, it was here! She used her sleeve to wipe at her eyes then reached down to tug at the small cylinder, gently. She scratched with her fingers to loosen dirt around it, heedless of her fingernails. Then, with one more pull, out it came with a final tug; a six inch, silver cylinder about one inch across with a catch at the top row of buttons. Along the side was a curved depression, where her index finger just fit.

{oh dear gods, I have it, I have it}

She stood up, legs weak and wobbly, leaned against the side and breathed deeply for a moment. She put the cylinder into a leather case the same dimensions as what she held in her hand and put it in her left pocket. She grabbed her EMS, the shovel, the dirty rag and shoved everything into the duffle bag at her feet. She looked for another way out of the room that would take her to the road without Rodane seeing her. Nothing! Damn! Time to go, time to find a way to get rid of Mr…

{Dr. remember}

Arcos, and continue to her next destination. They were going to be so relieved, as was she. There was little time left to complete all this. As she walked out of the room using her flashlight to avoid tripping,

{I can see me falling on it after all this}

and came out into the open air, she couldn't contain the elation in her voice, try as she might.

"Dr. Arcos, we can go now. Thank you so much for your help." Not hearing him, she searched with her flashlight and walked around calling his name.

"Dr. Arcos, I'm finished. We can leave now. Dr. Arcos… Rodane, where are you?" She heard a little groan off to the left, behind a rather large pile of rubble and part of a wall. Holding her flashlight up close to her, she searched around until she spied his feet behind a large stone.

"Dr. Arcos! What the hell! Are you hurt?" She rushed four or five feet to where he lay face down in the dirt, "What happened? Are you hurt?"

Rodane rolled over and looked blurrily up at her then winced when the flashlight hit him in the eyes. "Turn that damn light off! I'm blinded!" He sat up and groaned again and grabbed his head in both hands. "Something or someone hit me! I didn't hear anything. Everything just went black till I heard you calling."

"Dr. Arcos, you're bleeding!" She saw his collar soaked with blood and more oozing from the back of his head. She pulled out the rag from the duffle she had been using and pressed it to his head, "Oof! That hurts!" Rodane inched his way to sitting up and she helped him lean against the wall section.

"You didn't hear anything, see anyone?" She found it hard to accept he was attacked without notice.

{he seems like he notices everything}

"No, I didn't but I smelled something." He saw her freeze just for a second.

"What, that means something to you? What?" He searched her face.

"What did you smell? She stared back and leaned in, toward his face.

"Now just a minute... I got hit and then..."

"What... did... you... smell...?" She asked with infinite patience.

"I'm not sure. It was a combination of smells, sort of blending together"

"Like what?" She looked at the rag and then his head, "It's slowing down."

He tried to separate his thoughts, "Kind of like a mix of mint and cinnamon but with an earthy smell, like fresh garden dirt or a field just mowed. Like that. Is that important?"

"You've saved me a lot of time and trouble. Thank you." She helped him stand up. "Where is your bike?"

"My bike?" He shook his head, groaned softly,

{whoops, wrong move}

"What are you going to do?" She took his elbow and began to lead him away.

She felt him wobble under the lift of her arm, "You're going to take me to your bike and we're going to get out of here and see to your head. I'm going to be leaving shortly."

"So you're taking me up on my offer of a ride?" He managed a weak grin.

"No, I'm giving you a ride. Take me to your bike."

He laughed out loud at that, "Ha ha, sounds like 'take me to your leader'." She didn't smile or respond except to say, "Just get me to your bike and we're getting out of here and back to your car."

They headed into the darkness, stumbling and leaning from side to side.

Chapter 4

Akrotieri Hotel

The ride back to the hotel was a combination exercise of 'Comedy Workshop Meets Two Doofuses on a Bike'. It was a mountain bike, with a light on the front, red plastic flippers fitted into the tires and hand brakes that were very sensitive. She managed to get Arcos…
{he's solid muscle}
onto the handlebars after losing her balance twice. He was still oozing blood and had a monster of a headache.
{probably has a slight concussion}
He was wobbly but managed to hang onto the handlebars as she slowly gained leverage and speeded up to a slow pace. The road was bumpy with loose gravel that caused the tires to slip at least five times on the way. She pedaled her way forward without any talk and he seemed intent on just hanging on. They saw the hotel ahead, about one hundred yards, and she glided into the parking lot. She braked to a stop and Rodane almost fell off. She caught him before he fell and then she dropped the bike along the side. They linked arms and entered the hotel lobby. The night shift had changed and the Concierge was nowhere to be seen.

Sabina smiled at the desk clerk and led Arcos to the elevator and pressed 2. While the elevator made its way upstairs, she took out her key card and turned to Arcos.

"You need for me to check your head wound, clean it, and perhaps put in a few stitches." She turned to look at him behind her in the elevator.

He stood at the bar of the elevator with his head down, eyes half closed, breathing slowly as if he were practicing yoga exercises. He didn't answer her and that concerned her more than his constant chatter. She helped him walk to 217 and she inserted her key into the lock. She opened her door at the green light and stepped into the entryway and froze! She gripped Arcos by the arm.

"Wait!" she hissed, "someone's been in here." She toed the door open and stepped in front of Arcos, holding her flashlight in a defensive stance. Nothing, silence that stretched one minute, two, as she eased her way into the room. The window at the end was open, with the curtains blowing out into the increasing wind coming from the North. The ladder for emergencies was hanging down. As she listened, she heard one set of footsteps, heading quickly out into the dark.

She must have disturbed whoever in their search. Pages were strewn everywhere and her clothes were all scattered on the floor. She checked the bathroom and the medicine cabinet was empty except for band aids. All else was broken. Bottles were floating in the toilet and her cosmetics were scattered all over and crushed underfoot.

{damn, that was a new blush and lipstick too}

She went back to the door where Rodane Arcos was slumped against the wall and doorframe. She brought him in and sat him on the bed. Picking up items as she walked, she went to the bathroom, wet a hand towel in warm water, grabbed some instruments and went back to him, "Let's see what we have here." She used the towel to clean the wound, "Stop squirming, I'm trying to avoid infection. It looks like the bleeding has pretty much stopped. We'll just bandage it after I clean it and apply some anti- bacterial cream. I'm not prepared for fever and infection."

After bandaging his head, she convinced him to lie back on the bed. She covered him with a thin blanket from the closet and picked up the phone. She dialed Room Service and ordered two entire dinners plus desserts from the kitchen. It would be twenty minutes before they arrived so she took the time to pack up her clothes in her suitcase, threw in any good cosmetics and toiletries without any organization, pushed all her papers into her duffle/backpack and sat down in the chair by the desk, waiting for their food. She looked over at Arcos, mouth open, snoring softly.

{boy does this mess up my agenda}

She went into the bathroom and removed her shirt and took off the gold pin from the lapel to keep it from getting wet. She washed off again and went to the suitcase, stuffed the soiled one in and pulled out another. She turned to the mirror and checked her hair and saw Rodane looking at her in the glass reflection. The look on his face was puzzling, a look of interest but not sensual, concern but not personal. He seemed to be looking at her body but not sexually, more like with curiosity.

"What?" She turned to him and said, "It's my room you know. What are you looking at? I'm half-dressed… pretend we're at the beach. How are you feeling?"

"You want the good the bad or the ugly?" He sat up, winced and put a pillow behind his head and sat back against it. "I was looking at your tattoo and noticing its spot. Kind of unusual to have a tattoo under your arm where it can't be seen, isn't it?"

"It's more a personal tattoo than for visual. I've had it forever."

She finished brushing her hair and then walked over to the bed, "Mr… Dr. Arcos…" she began.

"Please…"I think Rodane will do nicely at this point. After all, we've gotten so close these last hours." He grinned at her, winced again, "Ooh, my head!"

"Ok Rodane, what's the good?" she waited.

"I'm not bleeding and I remember tonight just fine."

"What's the bad? I'll bite."

"I have a head that feels like a melon, with a headache that demands a full bottle of aspirin and I think I've gotten into something way over my head."

"So what's the ugly?" She moved to the fridge in the corner, took out a bottle of water, went to her bag and pulled out some Ibuprophen and handed three of them to him with water. She waited for him to swallow them and he downed half the bottle with one swig.

"Well, let's see here. I've met someone beautiful who is a complete mystery, been lied to from the beginning, been attacked by an unknown, and found myself in your room with a head that needs bandaged and no idea what's going on here."

She narrowed her eyes at him, paused a few seconds to think over what he had just said and then answered him, "That's the ugly?"

"The ugly is the way I'm going to feel in the morning and the goon or goons who are loose here, creating chaos and involving me in their dumb ass moves! And what I'm going to do to the one who hit me when I find them. I will find them" he emphasized.

Sabina studied him for a long moment then blurted, "You think I'm beautiful?" and a blush spread over her face and neck.

He narrowed his eyes and thought,

{wow careful bud, this one is trouble}

"That's what you got from everything I just said?"

"I'm sorry" she blurted, "that was quite stupid. I'm just trying to get my head around a night that has been anything other than what I was expecting and hoping for."

"Look" Rodane started to get off the bed, "Ooh, baby, this ain't good" and fell back onto the bed against the pillows.

Sabina rushed to him, checked for his pulse and put her ear to his chest.

"What, you're a real doctor now?" His heart was trip hammering but with steady beats.

"Shut up" she snapped!

She went to pull up his eyelid and he reared back as if burned, "Oh, for God's sake, I'm checking your pupils!"

"How many fingers?" she put up a closed fist.

"Is that to use on me or are you really checking?" his voice wobbly and eyebrows raised,

"Rodane, I think you might have a concussion and the last thing we need is a hospital."

"Why, are they looking for you?" he quipped.

"Oh good God, when will this night end?" she half groaned.

"Ok, Dr. Carter, how about I go to my room, you do what you need to do, do your thing, get out of Dodge, sleep the night away, what's left of it or... whatever. I'll get some sleep and if I feel worse in the morning, I'll go to town and get checked out. Sound like a plan? Then we can go our separate ways."

His breathing had quickened with that little speech and he was holding both hands around his head as if he were holding his brains in.

"Hardly Dr. Arcos...since it's my fault you got hurt." Then she pondered her statement...

{why can't I decide what to call him}

"No, actually, it **is** your fault. If you hadn't followed me, you wouldn't be laying here now, in some distress." She sat in the chair and thought, "Here's what we do. I'll go to your room and bring back any of your necessary things. We stay here tonight and I make sure you're ok, then you continue your tour and I do my 'thing'." Her brows lifted. "Does that sound like an alternate plan? Then you won't be unexpectedly found unconscious or dead by the hotel staff in the morning or maybe in a few days."

She couldn't help grinning at the image in her mind. She looked over at him and saw his eyes closed and his breathing slow. She checked his bandage, his pupils and his pulse. Then she gently reached in his pockets and found his room key in his left front pants pocket, and his wallet in his back right pocket. She opened her safe, placed her gold pin and her leather-bound cylinder inside and locked it, tucked his wallet into her pants pocket, checked to make sure she had her own key card to get back in and went out the door as softly as possible. She went to the middle stairs, glanced down them, saw no one and climbed to the third floor. The same green and purple carpet stretched down the hallway to the right. His key card read 305 on the back so she moved to that number, inserted the card and waited for the green light. Then she opened his door and entered the room very quietly and very slowly then… she realized she had nothing at all to protect herself with.

{I forgot my flashlight}

She took a deep breath and opened it wider.

His room was spacious, with a beautiful chandelier over the center of the room, a big double, maybe queen, bed in the center and a long bureau by the wall with a TV on it. Next to it was a desk with a refrigerator under it and to her left, a bathroom with a full shower…

{ooh, what I wouldn't give for one}

sink and toilet. To her right was a closet with a suitcase rack holding a small suitcase, two suits hanging up and not one thing laid out on the made bed.

{either room service is great here or he's anal}

She made her way to the bureau and checked one drawer after another, just clothes and personal items. She took the suitcase out, opened it and put some of his things in from the drawers he might need for dressing for a day or two. She brought out one suit from the closet, retrieved his toiletries from the bathroom then went to the mini-fridge under the desk. There were a half dozen bottles of water, a Gatorade and a pack of Ding Dongs.

{really Ding Dongs}

She threw it all into the suitcase except for the water. She looked around the room again,

{there have to be personal things here don't there}

spied a briefcase next to the fridge tucked against the side of the desk. Then something occurred to her and she returned to the closet, to the…

{yep there it is}

hotel room safe that probably held any important items he didn't want to leave out in the open.

{dagnabbit there's a combination}

She tried the catches on the briefcase… locked! She needed three numbers, not a key. She wondered if it would be wise to go back to her room and try to look for the numbers in his wallet

{doesn't everyone write them down somewhere when you're in a strange place}

…then remembered she had stuck his wallet into her front pocket looking for his room key.

{good going Sabina}

She opened the wallet and looked in the money pocket, counted the bills and got roughly $300 in Euros without actually pulling them out. He had an

AMEX card, a gold MasterCard and a bank card from Montana's Bank and Trust. In the other pocket, he had a picture of a little girl about seven or eight, an identification card from University of Montana with his picture
{nice pic bud}
and his driver's license, with an honest smiling face.
{why don't we smile for our license }
Maybe no one wanted to look dopey if stopped for a ticket. 'License and registration, please. Sir, you think this is funny'?

A disgruntled traffic cop might take offense to that sunny disposition if he had a rough day. There was a receipt for a shop in town and two sales for jewelry and a mug. On the back of one of the sales tickets was a series of numbers, three of them. Holding her breath, she went to the safe and dialed 22 right, two times, 16 left, one time and 5 right, once. Click! It opened!
{one down, one to go}
Opening the safe door, she spied a mug, a pack of papers in a manila folder, a laptop computer and a small jewelry box of blue velvet.
{eureka this cost some money honey}
Inside was a very thin, delicate necklace with Greek letters, dangling from what was at least 18 karat gold.
{this is for someone special}
She thought of the picture of the young girl in his wallet. Niece... Daughter? There was a plastic bag in a night table and she put all of this into the bag with the water bottles, put the laptop into the suitcase and took everything to the door. She looked into the hallway and moved to the stairs, trying to look casual and headed out. She went one flight down and returned to her room and found Rodane sleeping soundly, a little whistle escaping with each exhale. She checked his pulse again, placed her hand on his heart and listened to his beats, timing them.
{seems like he's doing okay}
Walking to her chair, she sat and pulled out the laptop, opened it and turned it on. She rose, put the water into the fridge and took out the suitcase, opened it and removed the...
{god the Ding Dong cupcakes }
cupcakes and put them on the desk. Then she took out his pajamas, let out a soft chuckle,
{cute little minion pattern}
got out a clean shirt and underwear, briefs and socks. She closed everything up, sat down and saw the laptop had a password. It took her six minutes to break his password,
{when will people stop thinking 0 1 2 3 is so secret}

then got into his files. In ten minutes more, she had dozens of files open. It looked like most of them were teaching files or travel files and one or two personal documents. A calendar listed all the dental appointments he had until 2021, his doctor checkup…

{yep anal}

and legal files pertaining to a divorce.

{aha, being anal drove someone crazy}

Across the room, he stirred, went to turn over and moaned. She quickly came to the bedside, put her hand on his brow and checked for fever, finding his skin clammy instead. She took a hand towel from the bathroom, rinsed it under cold water and wiped his brow. He put his hand over hers and mumbled something unintelligible, like 'mffph', 'Moof'! She removed his hand, wiped his forehead again and covered him over with the blanket.

Returning to the laptop, she went to owner documents and pictures. There were many dozens, hundreds maybe, of ancient sites, temple ruins, monuments, file after file of tours and ruins, statues and beautiful scenes from some of the same places she herself was so fond of. There were seas and lagoons, rivers, people sitting in restaurants having sumptuous meals, sitting by lakes or canals having wine or drinks, laughing, smiling at a loved one, teasing, giggling, beach scenes…she stopped.

{I could waste my whole night on this}

She went to the other picture files and saw dozens more of the same little girl in his wallet. She was also laughing and giggling but there were some of her with tears, pouts, a child's wonder in her eyes at some of the places he had taken her. She watched entranced as she saw this little girl, Sophia, from the file names, grow from a toddler of two or three to the present. That would make her seven or eight in the last shots, a quick joyous trip through five years of growth and adventure, park trips, amusement rides, new outfits.

{he loves to label everything there's that anal again }

She watched her face go from toddler chubby to a thin, oval face with freckles and a long ponytail of hair the color of a ripe chestnut. She was tall and lean for a young girl.

{whoa I just watched the baby turn into a mini Rodane}

She had his gorgeous eyes of sea turtle green. It had to be his daughter, or a niece of a sister who looked just like him. She'd go for daughter unless he lived with his sister and her daughter.

"Water" he mumbled.

She turned, torn out of her genetic queries, "Sorry, what was that?"

"Water" he repeated, "do we have any here?"

"As a matter of fact, we do." She rose and went to the fridge, "I came into possession of a few items of use to you. Here's the water" and handed him a bottle.

"Mmm" he muttered as he drank, "any food?"

"Well, now I know you'll be fine." She sat down on the edge of the bed.

"Rodane, I'm going to go out on a limb here. I took your wallet and room key and went to your room to see what I could do to help you out, as well as myself. I realized that might be a trifle irregular but I felt I had to satisfy myself you were who and what you said you were before we go any further."

He continued to gaze at her, finally making her feel uncomfortable.

{what I'm guilty of something he's the one who interloped on me}

"Did you discover anything that settled those doubts for you?" he stared her down. She told him what she had done, step by step, to when he woke up and asked for water. Then she stared at him. It was her turn to watch him for any sign he made to change her present opinion of him.

"Well I don't really know too much about you yet, but I did glean quite a bit of information about your habits and your present life."

"Woo hoo! Dr. Watson, let's have it. I'm all ears."

"Silly boy that was Sherlock" she retorted.

He paused then said, "Did you know that it was mostly Dr. Watson that uncovered most of the clues to solving all the mysteries that he and Holmes were involved in? Conan Doyle had Sherlock high a lot of the time and Watson was kind of like his sounding board whenever he tried to put clues together. When he wasn't high as a kite, his deductive reasoning was impeccable but that was not much more than one-third of the time, generally. Watson took the clues, put them together, connected the dots and led him to his 'Eureka' moments."

"That was quite a mini lecture. Is that what you teach at the University of Montana in your full schedule? I didn't see your name as teacher or adjunct teacher on any of the course offerings."

She got up, reached for another bottle of water and drained half of it in a few big swallows. The silence behind her caused her to look over her shoulder at his reclining figure. She couldn't decide if his facial expression was one of anger or annoyance or puzzlement.

"Sorry Rodane, I won't apologize for investigating everything I can about you. I have little time or desire to ask a thousand questions you may or might not answer, or for that matter, answer truthfully. It seems I have gotten you involved with me in a little mystery of my own and I'm not high as a kite nor do I intend to use you as a sounding board to solve it. I want… no, I intend, to get to the bottom of it, solve it without you being a part of it and then when you feel better in the morning, which by the way, is only two hours away,

{hell its almost here}

you take your things, go back to your hotel room and I go my way to my next stop."

When he started to respond she held her palm up, "No, I won't be reasoned with or convinced otherwise. I've gotten you hurt for which I do bear the blame and I won't continue to draw you into my personal and professional life. I don't know you, you don't know me and that's the way I intend to leave it in the morning when I go."

"Ok, before you go and before I move on to my next..." the fire alarm sounded, their ears were assaulted and their stomachs roiled. You could hear feet running across the ceiling above them, then feet pounding on the stairs and a Concierge yelling,

"Please leave the hotel immediately, you need to exit at the nearest door and proceed to the outside as soon as possible, please move quickly, please leave…"

They looked at each other and it was almost as if they spoke silently into each other's minds. Both of them began to race around the room, picking up clothes, suitcase, briefcase, stuffing everything into the bags as fast as they could. Sabina threw her clothes into her bag without heed of folding or sorting. She raced to the bathroom and stuffed her toiletries into a backpack with documents, camera and laptop. Rodane grabbed his file folders, his laptop, his one suitcase that Sabina had packed, loaded everything he could into his briefcase and forced the locks closed. They nodded at each other, left her room, and walked down the stairs and out the lobby door to the parking lot.

They stood at the curb, looked up to the third floor and watched the smoke and flames begin to lick at the outside of the building. Fanned by the stiff breeze, the flames spread to the siding and the roof lines. They could hear sirens screaming down the road getting nearer and louder. Rodane moved closer to Sabina, took her by the elbow and leaned in. She felt his breath on her ear and a shiver went up her spine and heat suffused her face.

"That's my room" he murmured, so as not to be heard. He took her hand and pressed something into it.

"Are you sure?" she whispered back, but she knew he was right.

"Yeah, this was what I saw from my window."

Two police cars and two pieces of fire equipment braked to a stop and the firefighters leapt out and stretched hoses so quickly it was hard to see who gave the instructions and who were following them. In five minutes they had a ladder up to the eaves of the hotel. Two men were on top with hatchets, breaking through the roofing tiles and two more were leaning out from the ladder to put a steady stream of water into room 305.

The officer in the police car went to the Concierge. He looked at his phone. They talked for a minute or two, he looked around, followed the finger pointed by the Concierge and walked over to them.

"You are Signora Carter, who has a room on the second floor?" he asked.

"Yes, I am. My name is Sabina Carter and I am in room 217. Why do you ask?"

He ignored her and turned to Rodane, "And you, Signor, are in room 305?"

He waited and looked from one to the other. He looked at his notes, "Rodane Arcos?"

"Yes, that's my room number. As the Signora said, why are you asking?"

"Signora Carter, why is Signor Arcos with you at this time?" he looked at Sabina, "Are you together?"

"Excuse me" she glared at the captain, "you seem to be taking some unusual liberties here, Captain."

"We received a call that this hotel was soon to be torched, I believe is the term, and room 305 was the source of the blaze. Do you know anything about that?" and he pointed to the smoke and flames still licking out the window and upward.

He looked first at Sabina then turned his attention to Rodane, "When did you and the Signora move to her room, Signor Arcos?" He waited.

Sabina took a step forward and the captain put his hand over his pistol at his waist. She stopped and put up a hand, "Doctor Arcos and I returned from Akrotieri earlier today and decided to compare notes on our day. Our interests seemed very compatible so we agreed to meet in my room to view his pictures and notes. We were about to do so when the alarm went off and we moved outside. Does that answer your concerns?"

"Unfortunately, no Signora, I'm afraid we have to ask Signor Arcos to come with us so we can check phone records and check out the call we received about a fire before the fire happened. Curious, is it not?"

"How can this be a problem Captain, if Dr. Arcos has been with me the entire evening?"

"Ah, the Concierge believes Dr. Arcos was not with you all evening as you state, something about a bike and his inquiries into perhaps two of the hotel's guests?" He smiled from the lips but his eyes were cold. Clearly this was no man to be trifled with or lied to.

"Captain, I was returning to Akrotiri to try and retrieve something I lost today and Rodane found I was not in my room. So he came to seek me out and see me home. It was a dark path I was unfamiliar with." She couldn't see Rodane but she felt the tension in the air, like a knife cutting through a very thick curtain. Rodane remained silent.

{what now you can't think of something clever}

She saw the captain's face close down as if he had no more to say and definitely no more to listen to. "I'm sure Signor Arcos can explain why he chose to go by bike to retrieve you instead of his car and why he managed to be in your room when we arrived. I look forward to hearing his explanation at our headquarters. Please accept my apologies for needing to question you. I hope you can still be accommodated here for the evening and you can enjoy your stay here in Santorini."

He turned abruptly and motioned to two of his officers, who approached Rodane and led him to their car. They did not handcuff him or speak to him after directing him to get in the back of the car. Once inside, they headed away from the hotel down the road, toward town. The captain looked over his shoulder at her and then drove away in his car. Her fingers were numb, her breath was short and her heart was racing. She stood a while watching the firemen checking that the fire was completely out and then when the Concierge addressed all the guests, she moved toward the hotel trying to drag two suitcases, a backpack, a duffle bag and two laptops. The Concierge walked over to her.

"Signora Carter, would you like for me to have someone take your things to your room? Your floor was totally unaffected by the fire or any water damage."

He looked pale, sweaty and quite shaken. Poor man! This was not how he must have envisioned his evening.

"Please have someone bring out a luggage cart and I'll follow them to my room." She watched the fire trucks and all the men leave and go toward town.

"Yes ma'am, right away" and he scurried into the hotel followed by the guests, shaking and cold in the night air. They sniffed at the air, now filled with the smell of smoke and fire retardant. She looked at the keys in her hand and realized they were Rodane's car keys.

{what in the god's names have I gotten into here}

This was supposed to be an in and out. She covered her left pocket with her hand then remembered that she had put her 'find' in the safe. Sabina looked at the lightened sky that was showing signs of a beautiful sunrise to the East and the colors were deepening as she gazed.

{what a beautiful country}

The cool morning gave her a spark of energy but her eyes were heavy and all her thoughts were becoming muddled and hazy. She walked to the elevator with the bellboy following, pushing the cart with all her things as well as Rodane's.

{ I'm a babysitter to his things now}

After getting to her room, she locked the door, fell across the bed and went quickly down into a soft, dark tunnel where everything and everyone winked out into blissful sleep and nothingness. No dreams, no thoughts, no worries.

Chapter 5

Αστυνομία, Elliniki Astynomia, (Greek police station)

The windows of the car were so dirty Rodane could hardly see out, along with the fact that without street lights, or even any house lights, the road was so dark it was like following two glowing eyes through a tunnel with no end. He put his head against the back of the seat and rubbed his eyes and his forehead. His headache, which was at one point easing up, had come back with a vengeance. His eyes felt full of sand and grit from being so utterly tired. His stomach gurgled again…and hungry! He figured it had been well over thirty six hours since he had eaten anything. He felt somewhat nauseated even at the thought of food but he knew he couldn't keep going without something to eat.

The officer driving the car was in front of a tempered glass divider but glanced back at him every few seconds as if he were fearful Rodane would up and disappear out the window if he didn't keep tabs. He said not one word, no smile, and Rodane decided to remain quiet as well. No sense in even inadvertently giving them anything to try and trick him up. His thoughts were jumbled and his confusion became more pronounced as he went over everything that had happened since yesterday afternoon.

{was it really only yesterday this began, incredible}

What began as stumbling onto a lone tourist left behind by her bus tour, had somehow morphed into having his head bashed open, treating a gorgeous woman first like a lost puppy, then a criminal or thief…

{what did you do with my files woman}

that he somehow had become a cohort in some cloak and dagger game, at once violent and harrowing. Whatever possessed him to give her his car keys was based on gut feeling as he was led away to the squad car. As to what was happening now, he knew one thing for sure. He knew of absolutely nothing that could make him a target for unknown head bashers and less than nothing about an arsonist out to either burn him in his bed or leave him out in the breeze, with no safety net and no clean underwear. This had to be connected to Sabina Carter. Was it possible for her to have set the fire in his room? She was up there for some time and she had ample opportunity to do anything she wanted if she had the means.

{if I'm not a citizen of the place who do I call }

How would he get out of this mess? His head was again throbbing just as they reached the town and his silent driver opened the back car door and led him inside. The lights hurt his eyes and caused him to let out a groan, "You alright, Signor?"

{he speaks}

"Peachy" He covered his eyes to shield them from the brightness.

"Signor, Signor, your head, it is bleeding!" The officer went to touch his head and Rodane snapped back as if from a whiplash.

"I'm good, thank you. Lead the way please. I want to get back to the hotel and gather up my things if there's anything worth gathering."

They came to a frosted glass door, opened it and the officer ushered him into an eight by ten room with a bare table, a wire enclosed light in a low ceiling, two chairs and a long mirror.

{fellas you think we don't know this is a two way glass}

He took the chair indicated, and his keeper left the room, closing the door that clicked when he did so.

{okay I'm here to visit not stay}

He felt like looking at the mirror and waving but knew it wouldn't do him any good to be cheeky and probably earn him some demerits. Overcome all of a sudden by total exhaustion and hunger, he put his head down on the table, resting on his folded arms and that was that. Gone to la la land! A sharp rap on the table next to his head caused him to jerk away and sit up with a lurch!

{ooh, my head}

He looked up through blurry eyes at the man who had asked him to come here and saw his narrow eyes measuring him like a specimen on a pin board.

"Signor, I understand you have a head wound that might need attention. Is that so?" he waited.

"No, I don't need attention. That is, yes, I have a head wound. Well, it's not a head wound, it's part…" he found himself babbling and stopped in midsentence.

"Yes, would you care for us to have a look at it?" the man's shield said that he was part of the Hellenic Gendarmerie, an officer in the most corrupt police force in the country. This was the police force that had just been investigated for a Trafficker's circuit for bribery and forging documents for illegals just this past June. Apparently, they were going to play bad cop, good cop to show some chops and look efficient.

{easy boy no time to make anyone suspicious or irritated}

"Would you care to tell me Signor, how you came by this 'not' a head wound that appears by the way, to be soaking the bandage you or someone has applied?" He actually looked curious and concerned.

{should I let him know she's a doctor but not a doctor}

"Signora Carter and I were in the ruins of Akrotieri and I bumped my head on the ceiling frame when my flashlight gave out. She tended to it and we were talking afterwards in her room when the fire alarm sounded. We grabbed our things

{partly true maybe not entirely}

…and went out of the hotel with everyone else. Now, could I ask you why it was necessary to bring me down here for questions? I wasn't even in my room when the fire broke out. I know as much about it as you do."

"Oh" the captain brightened visibly at Rodane's words, "you may know much more at this point than we do Signor and we would like to determine what that might be."

He slapped the plastic bag on the table hard enough that it made Rodane's head throb and sat down in the opposite chair waiting.

"Captain, I don't want to sound like a whining child but my head is a set of drums, my stomach is the horn section and my eyes have become the pin cushion that is being stabbed blind as we speak. I cannot think clearly, much less defend my answers at this point so I am exercising my right as a foreign national not to say anything more until I have contacted someone who can help me make sense of all this. I'm sorry if that disturbs you but I really do have to look out for my own interests here. It is clear you will not be so inclined. That's all I have to say."

He sat back, closed his eyes and put his hands to his head again to hold in his leaking brains, or so it seemed at the moment. The next second he was bending over and heaving over the side of the chair. That only caused the ache and throb to go up the scale of 10 to a 15 or 20. The captain jumped out of his chair as though he were avoiding the projectile vomiting of a child and looked at Rodane with disgust. He looked directly at the mirror and yelled, "Nicholas, get the doctor up. I don't care if he's sleeping or not, get him over here now. Bring me a bucket and a wet cloth."

The next few minutes were like a Keystone Cops clip with people running in and out of the room, placing a bucket by his side, slamming the door, going out and coming in.

{christ can't you just close it like a normal person}

The captain left and came back with a cold cloth and applied it himself to Rodane's forehead which was sweaty and clammy at the same time. A man bent over him and put a stethoscope to his chest, dragged his pupils clear, lifted them and shoved the damn light into his brain.

{here come the heaves again}

Then blackout, gone, kaput! Next thing he saw was himself laying on a cot covered by a blanket with three people staring down at him, one being the captain with his arms folded and a sneer on his face and in his tone, "He's not faking? This is real?" he demanded.

"Agnacio...how many times have you faked a dry heaving spell?" The doctor peered at the captain intently, "as well as how many times have you faked a head wound with blood?"

"Okay, okay, so he's ill. I want him to answer my questions and I insist that he do so" he snapped.

"Then have your man let him sleep a while. He most definitely has a mild to moderate concussion. His stomach is obviously empty so he needs some broth or light food. That will decrease the discomfort from his head which I can probably say without a doubt, is probably like ten men playing Rugby right now with his skull as the football. I have stapled and cleansed his head gash. Give him some time to think clearly then try to torture information out of him." He saw the captain's face, lifted his hand and said,

"You sent for me, Captain. I was in my nice warm bed, enjoying a very healthy dream. I'm just giving you my medical advice. Take it or leave it but I can do nothing more here." He left.

They left him alone for the most part. He went in and out of sleep, hearing doors close and the telephone ring, and eventually, one of the officers brought him some soup in a mug and a slice of bread and water, even helping him arrange it on his lap. He tried a little and gave up,

{guess it could be worse they might be pulling on my fingernails}

...then shivered as he pictured just that. The next time he woke up, he realized his headache had become just an irritant that made him squint at the clock. 10 A.M., P.M.? He wasn't sure but it felt like A.M. If that was accurate, when could he expect to be questioned again? Where was Sabina and who else knew he was here? If she didn't stay and just left his car keys at the desk, who would even know he was here, the Concierge?

{that twit turned me in.}

The door opened as if the thought had summoned him and the captain walked in and sat down in the chair across from his cot. "So, now that we have allowed you some time to recover and have been very patient and attentive to your needs, do you think you might be able to answer my questions?" he smiled or sneered, but it felt way short of real.

"I believe I made myself clear before I was taken ill, Captain. I respectfully request that I be allowed to call an attorney and have them here when I am questioned."

The captain slapped his plastic bag on the table and raised his voice.

{ok here we go again}

"You don't have that luxury! Your room was burned till everything was unrecognizable except for this." He stabbed a finger at the bag, "You, my friend, are quite likely to be charged with arson and destruction of property that may keep you here for the foreseeable future with or without someone to come and hold your hand." He flipped his hand in the air, "Take a good look around you. This may be your new accommodation for quite some time." He stood up and walked around to where Rodane was half sitting against the wall on his cot.

"What is it you Americans say when you spend some time in your very gentle jail cells with, what do you say… 'three hots and a cot'? We will not be quite as gentle however, when you have come to our country and committed crimes against our people and their businesses." He leaned closer, his stale breath causing Rodane's stomach to twist and warm saliva filled his mouth.

"I've done nothing of the kind and it's ludicrous for you to be accusing me of this when it was my room that was burned out. I've probably lost everything I came with."

{prick}

He clamped his mouth shut, tried to still his racing pulse and stared down the captain.

"If that is true" the captain replied, as he walked around the table, "then this is one thing you did not count on surviving the fire and it's your 'smoking gun' as they say." He looked positively gleeful as he opened the bag and shook out the small cigarette-box sized item on to the table top. It smelled like smoke even from his cot.

"What's that?" he asked.

"Ah, we play stupid do we?"

{dumb you sick bastard get it right }

"No, I don't play stupid" he raised his voice. "It's dumb. I don't play dumb and I don't know what the hell you have there, so I'll ask again, what is that?"

"Well now, it looks like you and I will be spending a great deal of time here today if that's the way you want to play this. Please, come over and you can get a good look at what you failed to destroy that might very well destroy you."

Rodane rose from the cot, walked over and reached for the black box.

"Don't touch that! It is evidence and we haven't fully processed it yet." The captain reached for it himself.

"Well, if you haven't fully processed it yet, then why are you handling it without gloves or even handling it at all? Your evidence will be tainted now." He couldn't keep the satisfaction out of his voice.

"The captain's face actually grew darker and his eyes became little black buttons in a face that was popping out and jaws that were grinding so hard Rodane could hear the sounds. The captain bent over the table and laid his hands palms down, gripping the edge as if to stop himself from throttling Rodane.

"We know what it is. We know it was in your room and we know why it was not supposed to survive the fire" then spoke slowly, drawing out each word

"You...my... friend... could... be... in...some... serious... trouble." Rodane thought a moment,

{don't say anything just ask questions}

"Well, if...you... know...what... it...is... perhaps you can let me in on your little game."

His pulse was erratic, his heart was hammering and sweat had broken out on his face. He felt light headed and clammy and nauseated. Ignacio studied his face and apparently was aware of his distress. He put up a hand and spoke slowly and calmly,

"Perhaps we can discuss this without all the anger and accusations? You know, innocent till you are guilty and all that? Would you like some water?"

"Please. I need to use the restroom." Rodane waited to see if he would be offered a bucket.

"Of course, please allow me." Ignacio opened the door and let him out to the bathroom. Rodane was led three doors down and the officer waited outside. He went to a stall, relieved himself, washed his hands and face at the dirty sink and used a graying towel hanging on the side to wipe off. He looked in the faded mirror and saw himself as these men were seeing him; hollow eyes, bloodshot, dark circles under them, tousled hair and sunken cheeks.

{I look absolutely craven}

When he was returned to the room, he sat at the table and waited for the captain to return. Another man walked in however, with the plastic bag, opened it and extracted the little black item.

"I am Post Sargent Christoph Acurus. I have something that was taken from your room. This is a timer that was connected to a motion sensor and wired to the electrical box in your room. It was discovered still in the wall when the firemen were cleaning out the burned materials and checking for the point of origin." He looked at the little black box, "It's quite an ingenious little device that I've never encountered before but very clever and efficient. Would you happen to recognize this, Signor Rodane Arcos?" Rodane looked up and realized that Sargent Acurus had been watching him the entire time he had been talking, probably searching for some sign of recognition.

{sorry bud I haven't a clue}

"No, I don't. What is it?"

"What makes it most interesting is that it has to be activated from another remote location, probably anywhere from here to ten kilometers. We've tested this little beauty and surprisingly, we found it has an embedded microchip, never seen anything like it. We have someone from our army base coming out to take a look at it and try to determine its origin."

"Well, I certainly hope you find out where it came from because then you could concentrate on tracing it back to a purchase and then track down the person who set the fire in my room and this whole matter can be put to rest, correct?"

Seeing the little device had Rodane's thoughts whirling, both in confusion and consternation. With all that had been happening in the last two days, something large was happening here that he was becoming increasingly annoyed with. 'Dear Dr. Carter' was into something very dangerous and secretive, which he had been dragged into unknowingly and unwittingly. But now, with the fire and his arrest, he was pretty sure he was in for a penny, in for a pound. He could hardly walk away from this because now he had been targeted and the game had changed. They, whoever they is, had included him in their damn game and he would play but not by their rules. He had never been one to let others decide his fate or his actions and reactions. If you didn't act on your own, you were pretty much at the mercy of other people's wishes and desires. If you only reacted to events around you, you didn't control the events, they controlled you.

{not going to happen}

Whatever he had to do to fix this and get back to a normal routine and complete his work, the first thing he had to do was get out of here free and clear, and get back to Dr. Carter, his car, his belongings, and figure out what to do next to extricate himself from this walking nightmare. Dr. Carter had some very nasty people that were apparently attempting to obtain something they wanted very badly. It seemed they were well funded, well-resourced and very willing to go to some extremely great lengths to get what they wanted.

What would have happened had he gone to his room after they returned to the hotel? He shuddered at the thought.

"Signor Arcos, Signor Arcos!

He was brought back to where he sat, in an interrogation room.

"I asked if you had any reason to be in Signora Carter's room instead of returning to yours."

Rodane shook his head and rattled his brains a little more.

{so you guys have already compared notes and planned your attack}

"We were just discussing our evening and how some things you don't plan for, just happen out of the blue."

"If that is the case, why did we find most of your personal items and your clothing in a suitcase in her room?"

"Whoa, buddy, just what do you people mean by searching her room and my things? Did you have a warrant?"

"It is not played out here as it is in your country. Not everything is talked over, and filed away, and examined before we choose to do our investigations. This was a serious incident and we determine how our investigation goes, so you are..."

A sharp wrap on the door had him look up, annoyed and impatient at the interruption. The officer came and said something in his ear. Rodane gathered in one in every four or five words; thodigite..., katafero...,elefteria... ,avrofrosyini...,...,aid, Arcos. The Inquisitor looked over at him, face expressionless, and the seconds ticked by.

"It seems we may have to take this up at another time. I hope you will forgive our efforts to try and figure out how this all happened. In the meantime, we will be happy to return you to your hotel and we apologize for any inconvenience we have caused you." He rose from the table and opened the door wider. He motioned for Rodane to follow him. Rodane's jaw dropped.

{what the hell}

There were many things he was preparing to hear him say and this could not have been further from anything he expected. He slowly got up from the chair and followed Sgt. Acurus, out to the front room of the station house. They handed him his wallet, phone, loose change from his pocket, and a key chain without a key.

{when did you fellas rifle through my pockets freaking idiots}

They led him to the back door and put him into a plain, compact car and drove down the long alleyway four or five blocks and then out onto a secondary road.

{strange way to get back to the hotel}

His memory of arriving here was hazy at best, so maybe they had come this way. The driver was the same one as the first trip down here. He was just as silent returning to the hotel as he was leaving it. He wasn't sure what he would find or what might have happened with Sabina Carter but he found himself feeling some excitement at the idea of seeing her again, getting his things back and getting out of Dodge. He had quite a bit to discuss with this mysterious lady and he also looked forward to solving it before one of them got seriously hurt.

{you better be there lady I didn't go through this shit for myself}

It might be the last time he might listen to his gut or be a Good Samaritan.

One of the first mysteries he wanted to solve was what had just happened at the jail. No police group who is interrogating a suspect tells them to 'have a nice day' and apologizes for inconveniencing you, then sees you out with a driver to take you back to your hotel. Something or someone fixed his predicament and had enough clout to just say it and make it happen. Was this a connection to Sabina or the ones who were the threats? Going back to the scene of the crime could just possibly be a mistake he might not be able to live with, literally. But his choices were limited and he needed to retrieve what little possessions he had, especially his briefcase and his laptop as well as his camera and his passport.

{maybe my car}

He saw the hotel at the top of the hill and wished for a soft bed, a long shower and a stiff drink, not necessarily in that order. As for Sabina, he wasn't even sure if she was on his radar right now and worse, he wasn't even sure if he wanted her to be there.

Chapter 6

Hotel Akrotieri

A sharp noise had Sabina waking up reluctantly and the light coming in her one small window was a definite sign it was morning... or afternoon. Her mouth was dry and the room was stuffy with a smell of smoke, even through the door. Her neck hurt, as well as her shoulders and her feet,
   {working at digging for two hours and walking for four will do that I guess}
...so she half rolled out of bed and hobbled to the bathroom. Using the toilet, she heard the same, sharp sound that had woken her and realized it was a saw or drill or some sort of construction tool, from above her on the third floor. It seemed to come from farther down the hall above. Otherwise there was no noise coming from the hotel. She opened her door and looked both ways down the corridor and saw no movement or evidence of other people.

There were two covered dinners on a cart outside her room. Her phone showed four hours had passed from the time she collapsed on her bed and there were no messages or texts and no missed calls, nothing from the police or a call from Rodane.
{how could that...oh I didn't give him my number}
She laughed out loud at the thought and looked out her window. The sun was high up and she realized she was hungry, famished actually. She got water from the refrigerator, went to the door, rolled the cart in and popped one of the dinners into the microwave. It took her maybe six bites to eat what was there and she scarfed half of a roll on her way to the bathroom. Cold Salisbury steak, or whatever that was supposed to be, and some white vegetables. She bypassed the lump of what might be mashed potatoes disguised under brown gravy. It would have to do for now. She pulled out her

phone, closed the door, turned on the water tap and placed a call. It took a few seconds for the international code to kick in and the voice on the other end was masked, "Yes?"

"It's Sabina. We're settled in and I'm fine. The walls are thin and the dirt is covering everything. I've cleaned up the place and made a friend from the third floor, although there are a couple of tourists here who don't seem too friendly but I'm going to be happy to be coming home soon. Hope to see everyone and tell them all about my trip. How are things there?"

The nondescript voice answered, "Things are good here. Dad is in good health and we're hoping to get the family together as soon as you return. We think a small dinner party would be nice. Hope you're not too tired to share your trip. Would you like to bring your friend?"

She had been doing this for many years; traveling, retrieving, removing, sometimes destroying evidence, and never had she received a request of this sort. Her life was pleasant enough if solitude was something to be enjoyed. She was affable with those she met on her travels but distance and reserve had been indoctrinated into her from a very early age and it precluded making friends and sharing personal information. Sometimes she yearned for a more stable life, a routine oriented existence, with maybe an animal for a pet, a small house with a garden, somewhere near an ocean or a lake, but whenever she had free time and a set routine for longer than a week or two, she felt antsy, anxious and at loose ends. Before long, she was off on a new trip, to pursue yet another chore that needed to be done and done quickly and thoroughly. It wasn't a difficult life, just a solitary one and she thought she had gotten quite good at it.

"I'm very sure my new friend has his own plans for later on but I am wondering who might be able to send me an item I might need and some extra cash to spend on a nice trinket I've seen and I'm interested in buying." She carried on her conversation using code to explain all the events and her requirements for her journey home.

A long pause told her the translation of her conversation was causing a stir on the other end.

{okay fellas let's see if you're connecting the dots quick enough}

"I'm sure that can be arranged. What items might you need and how quickly? Do you need it hand delivered?"

"Oh I think a phone call to order it would be fine. I'll give you the number and maybe someone could get in touch with the business office and I could have it delivered here in the next day or so? Maybe even express delivery could be arranged?"

Another long pause told her there was now a lengthy dialogue going on as to how much anxiety was building and how crucial they felt the situation to be, "Why don't you send us the name of the trinkets and the prices and we can have express delivery, ASAP? We'll contact the business for you so you don't have to sign for anything, more convenient for you. We'll wire you some funds so you can enjoy your trip more without worrying about running short. Anything else we can help you with?"

"You've been more than helpful and I can't thank you enough."

"Could you use any more company? I'm sure there are some 'family' members who would love to join you for some vacation time."

"No, I wouldn't want to change my plans now to accommodate anyone else at the last minute. Tell everyone I said hello and I hope to see all of you soon." She clicked off and closed her phone.

It had a very clever little blocking device inserted that scrambled everything that was said and rearranged the conversation into an encoded translation to alert the others into their present situation and her needs. She would wait for an answer before she decided what to do next. In the meantime, she decided to see why she seemed to be the only one in this hotel and she wanted to take a stab at checking out the room that Rodane has been in and look for anything that was left to examine. First, she needed a shower, badly.

She locked the door, put her phone on the shelf and turned on the water as hot as she could stand. She washed her hair then stood under the shower head till her skin was rosy and her toes and fingers were wrinkled. Toweling off, she heard her phone, turned off the faucets and answered "Yes?" No niceties here. This was only transferred over to connections to her home base at the moment unless she switched to the other phone. Electronic waves blocked outside communication.

"We're looking into having your two cousins joining you. You won't have to change any of your plans."

She was pleased that her home base had some very swift, smart, translators that had managed to unravel her situation, realized she was with someone, could solve the problem of getting Rodane out of jail, understood her precarious position, and had enough information to begin looking into her adversaries who seemed to be putting both of them more and more at risk. They knew somehow, she had the tool they needed desperately. Her trinket read as her friend. Rodane would be freed, they would spend whatever necessary to get to his jailers and release him. More funds were on their way and she had refused any personal protection for now but it seemed they had their own ideas of her and Rodane's safety. Maybe a couple of shadows might not be such a bad idea after all. They were to get her report to send back to the council and protect her and Rodane as they traveled. She wondered what they'd make of Rodane.

{hell I don't know what I make of Rodane}

They knew now that Rodane and she were both at physical risk even though they didn't know him and that he had then actually been attacked by someone who deliberately targeted them. There wasn't anything else she could do until Rodane was returned and they could try and get out without anyone following them.

What she could do was check out the hotel and see who was here and where. She dressed quickly, brushed out her damp hair, grabbed her key and her phone and left her room. She went to the stairs, not the elevator, and stepped quietly up to the third floor. There were hoses, wires, vacuums, carts, all sorts of cleaning supplies up and down the corridor, mostly at the end to her right. Rodane's room was the one that all the hoses and wires were going into, and not one person was inside. No voice was heard anywhere on the entire floor. She stepped quietly toward the room and stopped at the doorway.

Looking inside, she visibly shook all over when the black and charred remains met her eyes. Everything she saw was unrecognizable; lumps of furniture, walls black with smoke, water seeping from every side, carpet that looked like it had actually melted. She found herself panting, with her hands over her mouth as if to keep from an involuntary scream. She took one step into the room and the sodden mass that had been carpets, squished under her feet and a puddle formed under her shoe. The drawers to the bureau had been chopped to pieces and any clothing that might have been there and in the closet was obviously only ashes now. The smell was acrid and stifling to her nose.

{oh my god if I had brought him up here when he returned he would have been asleep in bed this was not an attack this was attempted murder}

She had some close calls over the years recovering long-buried tools. She had even been followed a few times and it made her itchy and left her skin crawling. This gave her a sick feeling in her stomach, rattled her being, and made her want to turn and run back to her home, out of this country, into a retreat from everyone and everything. She couldn't remember having anything give her this deep seated rush of fear and anxiety, and not just for herself. Whoever was targeting her was now targeting Rodane as well and she had almost gotten him killed, dead.

{of course it did dummy what else is killed except dead}

Her thoughts were muddled, her eyes burning and tearing from the smell. This was not the first time she had faced a degree of danger in her work but it was the first time she had unwittingly dragged someone else into that world with her. It didn't matter that he had interloped on her and her quest. This was because of her and what she did. Never had it hit so close to home, how very dangerous her job could possibly be and how easily others could be dragged into it, even without intent. She thought she understood the dangers. She was prepared to face any obstacle she came across and the goal was directly in the forefront of her mind from start to finish. Everyone connected to Sabina Carter saw her as the epitome of success; the undaunted traveler who always arrived home having solved their problem one way or another but always accomplishing the goal and arriving at favorable results. Until now, this minute, it felt as if a fulcrum had swung unexpectedly to the side and everything became unbalanced in an instant. The game had changed rapidly and someone had changed the rules but not for a game. This was no game! This was a determined effort to destroy, remove any possibility of success, even ending lives to do just that. This was a deathly war now, not a game of chance or the hand of fate dealing a blow to plans and removing players from the events. These enemies… were in deadly earnest and they were acting for keeps.

{that's exactly what they are… enemies we're not playing}

The fine hairs on the back of her neck raised a chill and rolled down her spine. She made an effort not to tense and gently flexed her knees, prepared to turn and attack in one move. The presence behind her was giving off warmth, an odor of sweat and a somewhat familiar, earthy smell that she found somehow pleasing. One second passed and then…

"Ok Carter, what's next?" His voice, so close to her ear, took the chill away and a soft warm feeling of relief replaced it. Her stance relaxed and she turned, almost into him. She had to look up into his face and saw someone with two days growth of beard, circles under his eyes, dark and deep, tousled hair, and skin that actually gave off heat she could feel, like a small heater.

"You could have warned me you were coming. I almost went after you and I have very sharp nails, for the record."

He reached for her hand and held it up and examined the short, unpainted nails on her left hand. She found her hand was trembling and gently extracted it. He watched an actual blush rise up her neck and flushed her cheeks.

"Nice nails, I'm glad my face avoided them."

"Ho…how…how did you get here? I had no idea you had been released already."

She looked out the door, up and down the corridor, "Who brought you here?"

"I was given a ride by our esteemed police department and brought right to the door of my lovely domicile!" he waved to the room opposite them that smelled of smoke and resembled the remains of a college bonfire.

"Wh..wha…, what happened? Who got you out? Do you know?"

She wasn't sure if her contacts were responsible or if something else was at work here…

{stop stuttering girl}

"Well the best I can figure, they were ready to unload both barrels at me, lock me in a cage and lose the key."

He told her about his questioning but left out the little black box that started the fire. He watched her reaction, nothing. "Then, there was a phone call and I only made out a few words from someone speaking Greek. I got a sense it was concerning me, but I only heard every fourth or fifth word; leader… deal… freedom… courtesy… aid… and suddenly, they were falling all over themselves being nice and concerned, got me a ride back to here and told me if there's anything they can do for me, to make sure I let them know. They will make my stay pleasant and do whatever is needed to replace what I lost in the terrible fire that someone else is obviously guilty of setting. Left me feeling rather discombobulated, to tell you the truth."

Sabina's thoughts were flying through her head too quick to keep in order but it clicked into place and she realized Quimby had most likely been contacted to get Rodane freed and had done his magic again. He probably had something on the head of the department and used it for leverage to make all charges go away. At least she was hoping this was the case. He was their 'go to guy' and now she owed him one. They had some issues to discuss and Rodane needed some time to get himself…

"Discombobulated? Is your head worse? What do you need?"

He laughed at her but gently, "No, nothing like that. It's a word that means confused…or… out of balance, which is what I sort of feel like now." He peered at her.

Sabina turned to the room behind her and said, "First things first, where is everyone here at the hotel? I've not seen or heard anyone since I woke up earlier.

{ need to get my own balance back}

Rodane looked up and down the hall, "I didn't see anyone at the desk but there are workers outside eating lunch and lounging around the pool… wow! Look at that room!" He swept his eyes around the destruction and shook his head. "Looks like a shopping trip for some clothes and other personals before I go anywhere."

"I have some of your clothes and your toiletries. I packed up all your items from your safe and your laptop is packed away in your suitcase with some of your clothes, don't you remember? Before the fire alarm?" she waited for comprehension to dawn.

"Sort of…kinda… I guess…" Rodane rubbed his forehead, "Can we go down to your room to sit a little and talk?"

He did look very tired. Maybe they kept him up all night. She took him by the arm and walked to the stairs, "Let's not use the elevator until we know who's here and where. You're going to have a shower buddy, then we're going to find somewhere to get you something to eat and after that we'll talk."

{just not about anything of my little adventure}

When they got to her room, she hesitated to put the key card in and listened at the door. Rodane raised his eyebrows and spoke quietly, "Either you're getting a little paranoid or there's someone you're not mentioning here."

"Paranoid can be good" Sabina spoke in a softer voice, "after what we've been through the last two days."

{it has been only two days right}

"I don't want to be the one who is surprised. I'd rather do the surprising. Paranoia works!" She heard nothing so she slipped in the key and they entered her room. There was nothing out of place, no one in the bathroom or closet and no one outside on the fire stairs. Rodane sat on the edge of the bed and looked over at her. He started to say something, shook his head a little and closed his lips in a tight line. Grim! She wanted to avoid this moment a little longer so she went to his suitcase on the rack, opened it and put the backpack on the bed next to him. "These are your clothes and your toiletries are in your backpack. There's soap and shampoo and lotions in the bathroom. I would suggest making the water as hot as you can stand it and staying there until it becomes cold. You could use the heat for sore muscles and your headache."

"How do you know I have…" he had squinted eyes, "What kind of doctor are you Carter?"

She clenched her jaws, annoyed, "One doesn't need to be a medical doctor to see your color, your dark circles, your squinted eyes or constant rubbing of your forehead to deduct that Watson!" She snapped it out, "Now into that shower and I'm going to go down and find someone to talk to about some food or I'm driving your car into town to get us something to eat." When he began to rise from the bed, she gently pushed him back down.

"One more thing. When I get back, I expect you to be lying down on that bed, clean, relaxed and maybe even asleep. We'll eat and then we'll talk." She handed him three pills to swallow and the leftover half of the water bottle from the night before.

{good god only last night }

He went to his suitcase, grabbed some clothes and went into the bathroom and closed the door. She heard the lock click then she picked up his car keys, her backpack, and headed down to the hotel lobby. Yeah, she was going to get some answers, from someone, but she **would** get some answers. In the lobby, a bellboy was sitting in one of the chairs, playing on his tablet or iPhone,

{never know which one.}

No one was at the desk and it was almost eerily silent. The bellboy looked up, "Signora, you are still here!" He looked astounded to see her.

"Yes, I would like to speak to the Concierge, if he is not busy, please." It's Signora Carter."

"Ah, yes, I know. Sargent Acurus was here earlier looking for you, but I did not know you were still here. Everyone else has left the hotel and taken new rooms in the hotel down in the town. We all thought you had gone also."

She sat down across from him, "Didn't anyone check my room to see if I was still here?" Sabina was annoyed that everyone just assumed she was gone but no one thought to check on her.

Bellboy said, "Roseann went to check your room but came down and spoke to the captain."

"Where's the Concierge?"

"He was fired, Signora. He was asked to leave early this morning and all the other staff went down to help with all the other people who are in their new hotel. They are very happy because it's a much nicer, newer hotel and their rooms are not going to cost them, not even one Euro." He grinned at her

"Fired?" she asked, "Why was he…"

"…because of the fire in the room last night."

"That's insane! How could it be his fault?"

Bellboy was getting anxious, probably to get back to his game, "I'm not sure. It had something to do with letting people into the hotel to wander around without being guests here… or something like that. I heard Sargent Acurus telling Akel that this whole thing could have been avoided if he only kept track of people's comings and goings… and he should be charged with a crime if anyone were hurt in that fire."

Sabina was treading lightly here, to try and get as much information as possible before she left to go into town. "Akel…" she said, "that's the Concierge?"

"Yes Signora. He is very unhappy and also very angry that he is being blamed with the fire. It will cost very many Euros to fix this place and no one wants to fix up a very old hotel and spend money."

She smiled a little at the bellboy, "Aren't you worried about your job? Why aren't you at the new hotel in town?"

"Aha! My uncle owns this hotel and he charged me with watching to see that no one comes in and tries to steal anything of value." He looked around the lobby, "I'm not sure what that would be… but as long as he's paying me, I will sit and watch to see no one comes in." He looked at her, surprised. "But you are not coming in, right? You are going out." He seemed satisfied that his charge was still going well, and he was following orders, a little smug perhaps for his good judgement.

She couldn't help laughing a little, "I think I'm legal here. Also, Dr. Arcos is resting in my room now and shouldn't be disturbed. Please make sure no one goes upstairs, okay?"

She reached into her backpack and he stopped her, "Oh no, Signora, I cannot take money. It is my job." He put his hand up. Sabina reached for his hand and placed the $2 Euro in it.

"This is a tip for being so helpful. I'll be back soon and I'm sure you will still be here, very vigilant."

He puffed out his chest, "Yes Signora, I will be here for anything you might need."

Sabina stopped short, "You cook?" she asked him.

"Cook, Signora? No, I am the bellboy." He looked confused.

"I know but can you cook? Are there any food supplies still here?" she pointed, in the kitchen.

"Oh yes Signora, everything will be removed this afternoon so the workers can continue to try and remove damage and smoke from the third floor."

{aha maybe I can hire two birds with one stone or one bell boy}

"If you were to go and cook up something for Dr. Arcos and deliver it to room 217, and leave it outside after you knock, I would be very grateful. I could also let your uncle know how well you carried out your job and how faithful you have been in helping me out." She lifted her eyebrows and waited.

" Well…" bellboy thought for a minute, brow furrowed, eyes squinted almost shut, "I could get some fruit and cheese together, some of the homemade bread that was made yesterday… it's only one day old." he explained this as if she would be insulted,

"It's very good. There might be some homemade soup left from last night's dinner." He looked so anxious to please, Sabina took his hand in hers, "That would be just the ticket and I'm sure Dr. Arcos would love that!"

"Oh there is no ticket, Signora. I will just make it for him, no charge at all." he grinned wide and she couldn't help laughing, "I'm so sorry I didn't get to know you earlier. You have been a wonderful help here. Your uncle should be very proud."

"My uncle will be happy I could do anything at all for his guests. He thinks I need more 'seasoning'… is the word he used, before I can get a promotion and a raise'. He looked so serious, "This might show him I am getting better."

Sabina asked where the police station was in town. She noticed his frown and hurried to calm his anxiety, "I just want to ask a question or two about Dr. Arcos's room, that's all. We're very curious how everything happened so quickly."

Bellboy looked at her and looked to the ceiling as if he were seeing through it to her room and leaned over for a secret message, "The maids said when they went up to help the guests take all their suitcases and things down to the lobby to be sent to the new hotel, they had never seen such a sight after a fire. They said it was a miracle Dr. Arcos was not there or he would have been a 'sausage in a blanket' was what they said."

"We're all grateful no one was hurt. I'm sure your uncle will do what's best about the hotel. Could you tell me how to get to Sargent Acurus?"

"He would be there now I think" and he gave her directions to the station house.

"Will you be here when I get back?" she asked.

"Yes Signora, I will make sure I am." Back to the iPad he went.

"Uh…food for Dr. Arcos? He looked confused for a second, "Oh yes, of course, on my way." He pocketed his iphone and headed to the kitchen.

Chapter 7

Akrotieri Hotel

Sabina walked out to Rodane's car, got in and drove out and down the road to town, thinking about what she would do when she got there. She pulled over to the side and turned off the engine.

{what am I doing teasing the bear}

She closed her eyes and went over everything she and Rodane had discussed before and after the fire; the conversation, short though it was, with the police captain, the comments told to her by bellboy from the Concierge and Sargent Acurus, and the reactions by the maids, mostly the questioning of Rodane at Police Headquarters and the fact that Sargent Acurus had come looking for her today. Luck would be on her side there, not anything else. Her eyes snapped open!

{this was a set up all the pieces fit}

They all fell into place and it was HER they were after. He was to be the leverage. His room was the target, to erase him from the equation. His death would have just been collateral damage. They couldn't reveal themselves trying to get to her, and they didn't know what connection Rodane had to her, so first they tried to eliminate him. When the Concierge told Captain Whoever, that Rodane was standing there with her, his arrest was a given. What did they hope to get from him? A confession to something they already knew he hadn't done? Or... information from him about her they could use to get what they were apparently after.

Any thoughts she had of questioning the police were gone. She couldn't trust any of the police if she was sure one of them was connected to their enemies. Not knowing which one or all of them were crooked, she could not afford to raise a flag by even asking questions about how Rodane was released. Who was leading who here? Who was the one pulling the strings on the marionettes, and who was the one being pulled?

Then she gasped! Rodane was a loose end. They needed him out of the picture and they had already shown they had no compunction or reservations about violence or murder.

{neither of us is safe now}

She started the car, turned it around and headed back to the hotel, a little faster than might be safe, but road safety was secondary now to Rodane's or her life, and the security of the EMS in her safe. She pulled into the driveway, slammed the car into park and raced into the lobby. Bellboy was not anywhere to be seen, so she headed to the stairs. She came to her door and heard laughing coming from inside.

{can't be too much danger here}

She tried the door and it was locked. She knocked and had her hand raised up to knock again when it was opened by... Bellboy!

"Hello Signora, please come in."

"Well thanks, don't mind if I do." She saw Rodane, sitting at the bureau with a food tray on the top with lots of empties and dirty dishes. Her belly gurgled, they looked at her and both broke out laughing. She realized she hadn't had any food since hours earlier. "Stress always increases my metabolism..." she said, "and I get amazingly hungry." Bellboy

{got to get his name no bellboy is more fun}

...came to her and said, "I will go downstairs now and bring you some food Signora. I will be only a minute! He left and she came into the room, closed the door and walked over to Rodane. She sat down on the one chair in the room.

{ok make this believable}

"I've been thinking. You can stop me anytime you want... but I thought you might consider going with me to a couple of my next stops. You said you were doing a tour guide..."

"Travelogue, little different from a tour guide" he motioned for her to go on, "Sorry."

"Well..." she continued, "you said you needed to get some photographs and..."

"No, I don't recall saying anything about my travelogue or photos, I'm certain of it, or I think...," he grimaced and she could tell he was going over what he could remember.

"Okay, maybe I was thinking of the files I happened to go over when I was checking your laptop"... he stared her down.

"Okay, okay, I was checking out anything I could, to see what I could find out about you. You're a strange man, following me around at night, stalking me, getting into my business…" she stopped, seeing his expression then continued,

"What? It's true and I was protecting myself."

He scoffed, "I'm the one who saw people stalking you. I bought you time, brought you transportation, and I took a blow probably meant for you so I'm hardly the one who has anything to hide here."

"Your bike, transportation? I saved your ass, Rodane!" He quirked his eyebrows at her…

"Yeah, I did. I took care of you, saved you from being a 'sausage in a blanket' or something like that and brought you to a hot shower and food."

He was gaping at her with open mouth, "Sausage in a blanket? Wha…?"

She then caught him up on her conversation with Bellboy and he laughed when she said her name for him in the telling. She left out the part about driving to town and her revelation before she got there that might have just saved them from another 'unfortunate incident'. A knock at the door alerted them to their food arriving. She ushered Bellboy into their room and sat down to begin eating, while Rodane and Bellboy sat on the bed and began an instant conversation where they left off; soccer teams in the World Cup. Boys!

Then she asked Bellboy, "Could you possibly remember what Sargent Acurus said when he came earlier today? I was wondering, did he seem angry or upset or…?"

Bellboy thought for a moment, "He asked if you were still in town and did I see you this morning. I told him no, all the guests were being taken to the hotel in town for the rest of their stay and we were delivering luggage and supplies to the hotel all morning. He asked me if I had seen any strangers, other than the guests of the hotel. I didn't but Roseann was with me and she mentioned there was a couple who had been here the night before and had visited one of the guests. She didn't remember who but she saw them on the third floor on their way downstairs."

Rodane looked at Sabina and asked, "Did he ask her what they looked like?"

Bellboy said, "No, he seemed satisfied with what she told him and then said to let him know if we saw you or if you returned here today to call him. Was that okay? Did I help you? He didn't seem angry or upset, just curious. Roseann might be able to tell you anything I forgot but I can't get her on the phone and her mother said she wasn't home when I called. Do you want to leave a message for her?"

"No, you've been a big help" Sabina said, "We're going to rest now and we'll check in with you later if you're still here."

Bellboy smiled at both of them, "Of course I will make sure you are not disturbed." He left and put the Do Not Disturb sign on the outside of the door as he was leaving with the empty trays.

Rodane looked up at her, "Sooo…what were you saying before about my travelogue?"

Sabina had the grace to blush, "I'm sorry I invaded your private files but I needed to know what I was dealing with here, with everything that's happened."

"And did you find out? About me I mean?"

Sabina let out a little breath she didn't even realize she was holding, "Well, I think you're safe…" He grinned… "and honest about who you are. You obviously make travelogues and travel all over and take photographs of your travels… they're quite good by the way." He smiled again.

She gathered her courage and took a breath, "I thought…"

{keep it business like Sab}

maybe if you're traveling the same way I am, we could go together and keep each other company… till I get to my destination… or you reach yours. I'm going to Vesuvius from here then on to Sorrento. I'll stop over for a day on Capri and then on to Florence, where I'm meeting my 'family'…

{maybe not to you but they are to me}

separate rooms of course." She added, "I know a lot of people along the way and I usually get good rates on rooms and other expenses."

He sat there and it looked like he was really thinking it over, maybe too much.

"It's okay if you have your own plans…," she began.

"No" Rodane said, "It's not that I wouldn't mind the company. I'm just worried that these incidents may be connected and I wouldn't want you caught up in something that seems to be getting amped up."

{oh buddy this is rich you think you're keeping me safe and it's just the opposite}

"Well" she tried to sound confident, "I don't think anything else can happen, do you? You could leave anytime to go off on your own. Why don't you think it over first and let me know what you decide?"

"No, I think it's fine."

"She was startled at how easy it was, "Really, you'll come?"

"I think it's a fine idea and we'll have plenty of time to talk and I get the answers to all my questions…" He raised his eyebrows, "We agreed, right?"

{oh boy I opened myself to that one }

"Yes, sure" she smiled.

Rodane rose from his spot on the bed and rubbed his hands together, "So, when do we get started?"

Sabina thought fast. She had to get out of here with him as soon as possible and they had to do it without raising an alarm, or alerting those who might still be thinking they had them boxed in and unaware. The important thing was going somewhere to meet up with her 'cousins' and find time to contact them. Then she had to choose a route and convince Rodane it was a fun trip without raising his suspicions. Not knowing what questions he might ask put her at a distinct disadvantage, having to wing her answers, handle all his suspicions without making it worse but only until she could get him to Florence. Then, he would be off her hands and she could meet with the Council. By that time they should be able to tell her who was following them, and where they were from.

{gee that's all how simple}

She found herself a little overwhelmed. Suddenly she saw just what she could do and almost solve all those problems in one fell swoop.

{oh I'm good, I'm very good}

"What are you smiling about? Did I say something funny?"

"I just had a wonderful idea! You really need some new things, Rodane, since you lost a lot in the fire. We could head out to a larger town to buy you some new things to replace them and I could go shopping!" She almost clapped her hands and stopped herself. She saw his look… "not a lot of shopping, just one or two things. We could go to Pyrgos. It isn't too far away and they have lovely shops or…we could go to Kamari. It's on the sea and they have quite a few better shops and good restaurants…" she stopped to get a breath and he stepped in with, "Why not go to town here and buy what I need?"

Sabina inwardly slapped her head, "Oh they really don't carry much. I've been there and I'd much prefer to buy you some really nice things in some specialty shops. No Santorini t-shirts. You need shoes too and your good suit needs a new tie…"

"Whoa girl, what's this shopping trip turning into? You're going to buy my clothes and a tie and… no one has bought for me since I got divorced!" He stopped abruptly.

{aha so he is divorced good call Sab}

She tried to look let down but could only sigh inwardly in relief, "I'm sorry… I didn't mean to overstep…" she put her head down and clasped her hands together. He came off the bed and actually knelt in front of her and took her hands, "No, no Sabina, I'm sorry. I didn't mean to be cross or insult your good wishes."

{his hands are so warm}

"I wasn't…it's just…oh, I'm lousy at this!" he said in frustration.

"It's ok," Sabina said in a low voice, even managing to have her voice catch. Actually, it wasn't hard. She found her hands trembling in his and her breath caught, "I don't usually say such forward things to a stranger."

"Sabina" Rodane spoke just as quietly, "I hardly think we're strangers. It's just that we're only now getting to know each other. Of course you can go shopping for my things. Everyone's always saying I need someone to dress me better," Rodane waited.

{and that's the God's honest truth too}

"Are you sure?" Sabina looked up and into his eyes and caught her breath again. Maybe it had only been three days but she felt such a sharp connection with him after all that had happened, "I don't want to take advantage."

"Look, let's pack up, get out of here and you can pick the town where you want to go and we'll get started right away. We've eaten, my headache is almost gone, and I think we've had enough of Akrotiri, don't you?"

She looked at him and couldn't respond for a few seconds.

"Alright...?" Rodane looked concerned when she didn't answer him. Another fine idea had occurred to her. This might be a little trickier.

"I think I've changed my mind," she said.

"Oh no, please don't. I apologize for my rudeness and I would love…"

"No…no, oh no…" she giggled, "not about the trip, about the town. I think we should go to Fira on the coast. It's a really big city,

{like you don't already know that}

…and we could shop. I have a marvelous idea! After we buy your things, we could get on a cruise ship going to Italy and we could cruise to our destination and get to really discuss with more privacy, all the concerns and questions you have." She looked up and smiled at him.

{and it's crazy, but the idea really does appeal to me}

He must have felt the same because his grin widened but then fell.

"I don't know if I have enough with me to buy new clothes and still get a ticket on a cruise ship. Honestly, I don't even know if my credit card would allow for the cost. This has been an expensive trip."

She looked squarely at him, "Now I want you to listen before you say one word. Ok? She waited… Ok? Do we have a deal?"

Rodane paused then nodded his head yes.

"Alright, here it is. I've arranged to have extra funds wired here but I can call and have it rewired to Fira. It's more than enough to take care of anything your card won't cover or even cash." She went on quickly when he put up his hand and started to shake his head… "Now, hear me out. I'll write out my address and information and you send me any funds we use whenever you get back home. It will be a fun time and I've never been on a cruise so it would be something I could check off my travel adventures."

{please, please say yes}
He actually took a minute to think through what she had just said…and she found herself hoping for a 'yes', with mixed feelings as to why.

{oh boy what do I do if you say no}
He looked sideways at her, "On one condition."

"Anything," Sabina said quickly, "well, within reason" she grinned again.

"If we book together on the cruise, we book together." He paused and she waited with furrowed brows "Not together, together… just that we spend our time together, have meals together… you know, like we really are a couple on a cruise." he waited again.

{dude you are making this so easy}
"We could book a suite and each have our own little room for sleeping, with a sitting room and bath…" she giggled, then went on, excitedly "and a deck! I'd love to have a deck."

Rodane saw her face go through so many variations. He was amazed someone could feel so many different emotions so quickly and show them so completely. In only seconds her face was like a video, every feeling visible without her even being aware. There were a couple of times he knew she was fudging the truth or holding something back but he knew she wasn't aware her face gave her away so readily. It gave him pause as to whether he could trust her or her motives but he had his own motives and ideas of where they would go next, so he could give her a little leeway… for now. There was something here he couldn't quite put his finger on and he knew it was right…

"Yes, I accept!"

"Yeeeesss!" Sabina broke his thought and he almost had it. Suddenly she was all business and in charge. She was quicksilver, mercury, a will-o-the wisp except she had legs up to… he looked at her moving around the room.

{wait stop don't go there}
"We have to pack up all our things…" she moved to the safe, put in numbers and opened it, took out the small cylindrical tool in leather and a blue jeweler's box.

"Where did you get that?" He exclaimed. He grabbed it out of her hand, "Where did you get this?" he repeated.

I opened your safe and got out the files and this was in there with a mug. Ok? She sounded very defensive, "I thought you would want it."

He grabbed her and hugged her hard. She was so flabbergasted, she was… gob smacked! She leaned back and said, "You keep me off balance and I don't know what to expect next."

He looked into those topaz-colored eyes and said very slowly and clearly, "Good! Let's go" and started to pack his stuff up.

"Do you have my mug?" he asked.

"Do I have… what is the matter with you?" she asked, exasperated. "Yes, I have your mug. I mean no, it's in your backpack with your toiletries… I think."

"Just checking. It's a gift but I can buy something else. It was only a token anyway."

She really wanted to gob smack him too! "I guess that was for your ex-wife like the necklace is for your daughter, Sophia." she felt a twinge of snide glee at the expression of total surprise on his face.

"How do you… what did you… never mind." he said, "I'm sure we'll have a lot to talk about on our cruise." he looked at her for a few seconds more, and then continued packing up everything without another word.

{did I go too far this time}

And they were doing so well. At least they would get out of here and maybe elude anyone who was determined to interfere with them, no matter what.

Going downstairs, she looked for Bellboy and found him in the kitchen making himself something to eat. It looked like he had used ten dishes and four or five pots and they were all in the sink. 'Uncle' had a ways to go to 'season' him, but he was definitely a sweetheart and really kind.

"Signora, are you leaving?" he looked crestfallen.

"Yes, I am, but I wanted to say goodbye and thank you for all your help."

"Yes, we…"

"Good gods, don't scare me like that!"

"Sorry Sabina didn't mean to frighten you…" as he placed his hand on her shoulder, "We do appreciate all you've done and we'll be going out. Just one favor…" he asked Bellboy.

"Of course Senor Arcos, anything to help."

"If anyone at all comes asking for either of us, you don't know where we are and haven't seen her since last night. Okay?"

"Yes Senor" he smiled, "seen who?" and he laughed out loud.

His car was at the entrance where she had left it. He took his keys from her and they packed all their things in the trunk, except for backpacks. Bellboy had given them a bag with sandwiches he had made, some fruit and bottles of juice he took from the still cold fridge. He even threw in some cupcakes in foil wrap.

{but we have ding dongs}

"I'll just use the bathroom before we go" she said, "be back in a jif."

When she returned, they started out and turned right instead of left onto the highway towards Fira. The first few miles they were content to look at the countryside and just pay attention to the road. He glanced at her from the side, continued driving, with another glance over at her again…

"Okay, what's on your mind?" she asked, "I can hear the wheels turning like the tires on the car. Out with it! We need to start sharing our thoughts and being honest if we're going to be traveling together. Otherwise… it won't be fun or of any help to either of us."

"I was going to begin asking questions…" he said, "but I think it might be better if we travel to Fira, do our shopping, pick up the cruise tickets if we can, and then get into a question and answer game once we are safe on board ship." He looked over and had to laugh out loud at her face, "What, you think I bought your story about fun and adventure?"

She started to answer… "No, let's save it for later. Keep your eyes out for a tail…," and laughed again, harder, when she whistled in her breath and stared at him in consternation.

"Come on Sabina, it can still be fun and it's definitely an adventure, if we can outlive whoever thinks differently."

They drove down the road in silence and she found herself looking in the side mirror for other cars on the road.

{damn! he's too good}

Insertion 2

1610 B.C.E Akrotieri, Greece, Island of Santorini

Lucius rowed as close to the shore as he could attempt safely. They didn't want to alert the people who lived at the boatyard and lose time having to talk to them or explain their presence. The tiny island of Aspronisi was not frequented by people from the larger island but it was a perfect spot for their boatbuilding skills. The entrance to the other islands in the giant caldera started here, where their new boats could be launched to Thera for their maiden voyage before they took to the open sea.

Cordova manned the tiller and Lucius rowed when they needed more power than the single sail that moved them. They made good time with a breezy night. The bag of tools was at their feet between the two narrow seats in the boat, wrapped in waterproof skins to avoid any chance of taking on any water. At this point, any precaution not taken was a possibility of failure and that was not an option. Their oil lamp was turned low to allow for little light. They sat in silence while they moved, gently rocking back and forth.

The boat cut through the water gracefully and only the crescent moon watched its progress. The houses on the island were dark save for a few lights coming from huts where the boat builders were settling in after a long day working on their latest projects.

"Cordova, do you know what I'll miss most after this week?"

"Let me guess" she spoke softly, "the drinking spots on...no, the two women in the drinking spots on Thera at night." She chuckled very low in her throat.

"Well, that, but most of all, the running water that can be heated in a moment from the hot springs and the easy chairs and comfortable beds."

He leaned closer, "You know, don't you, we'll be going northward to some pretty rough accommodations after what we've been used to here, hmmm?" He chucked her under her chin, "Think you can handle that my love?"

"You know Lucius, when you were named after your very long ago ancestor, one would hope some of that "light" would penetrate that brain of yours and allow you to realize how many times we have had to 'start over' as it were, to accomplish what we have. A soft bed is a luxury, not the norm. We're just returning to the norm and it won't kill us to have to stuff mattresses with grass for a while."

"Speak for yourself love. I am very fond of my down mattress and my woven blankets."

"Lucius, if this goes off as planned…" Cordova looked out at the dark expanse of water they were crossing, "we'll be well on our way to Thrace and a new life but leaving behind untold numbers of dead and dying, ruined cities and an end to all the amazing accomplishments we've made over the last four hundred or so years." She swallowed hard and the tears began to well up.

"Wait, wait Cordova, I'm sorry. I wasn't trying to make light of what we're doing here." Lucius took a breath as Cordova broke into deep wracking sobs and dropped her hand from the tiller to cover her face.

"Do you miss home Lucius?"

He stumbled, "Home Cordova, what are…are you…?"

"I mean do you miss home?" and she lifted her tear stained face up to the night.

He thought how to answer that. He tried to speak, stopped, tried once again, "No, Cordova, if you want truth, then no."

Home, he thought, how could he miss it? He had never been there, never seen the land, the seas, the cities, never met his ancestors, never gathered for a family outing. He had never watched a change of season or a cycle of a year, never traveled to some of the wonderful places he had been taught about and seen from Holovids or studied on all the Plastiboards that contained their histories.

Cordova watched his face in the dark by the low light of the oil lamp. She saw many feelings, one after the other, cross over it; longing, wonder, sadness, loss, and finally resignation. She stopped crying almost at once.

She hiccuped, "I'm sorry Lucius, I'm so sorry. I didn't mean to stir up so much especially at this moment. I'm so truly sorry. It's just that I…"

Lucius put his hand over hers and pointed to the night sky. She looked up, watched a 'falling star' at that second, plummeting toward the black sea they rested on and disappearing just as easily as turning out an oil lamp.

"Cordova, I do understand, I do. But you asked me honestly and so I must tell you, this is my home." He swept his arm around the entire bay they were in, "this is the place where I live and breathe and love." He squeezed her hand, "and hope for a long and happy life with my family" He pointed in a wider arc, "here on this sea, with my people, looking at the mountains, this island, all of it, yours, mine, this is home now." He stopped, waiting for her breathing to quiet.

"We move from place to place, city to city, meeting new people, setting up new homes, learning new languages, and for what? To do it over again some years from now, who knows how many, and start again maybe knowing we have left more destruction behind us, more bodies of little children with their life winked out like that" she pointed her fingers at the sky, "I can't even call it what it is aloud…"

She took a deep breath in, "I don't know if I want this to be my home but it is so I guess we need to continue with this and complete our assignment." She swallowed hard, "Ready?"

He nodded and adjusted the oar in his hand, rowed up to the farthest dock and tied up the boat. He handed Cordova the bag of tools after she had stepped up and then followed her. They went as silently as possible through the dark, passing the fishermen's quarters and came to the pathway up the hill. From the top after a long, steep climb, they stopped to take water, wipe the sweat from their faces and then set up the sights. The night was blacker if possible. The only sounds were a thin wheeze, the sigh of a northerly breeze and the soft whistling through the few stunted trees that stood on the rise.

First, Cordova sighted and took measurements then moved over and let Lucius repeat the process. They did this twice and then took out the thin wand from the side pocket of the bag. Cordova flicked open the small stand on the side of the sight and attached the wand to its side. She flicked open her pin from her shirt and used the point of the pin to insert into the bottom button in a line of five. It began a low, slow humming and the blue beam flicked out like the tongue of a lizard. The humming started a cycle; four low tones, three higher, three low tones, two higher, and so on. Then, repeat over and over. They stayed still for three minutes then she inserted the pin into the next button and a yellow beam emerged and started a different cycle; five hums on a low cycle, then six on a higher tone, then four, then three, and repeat. They did this until they had all five beams on a changing cycle and stayed there another five minutes to make sure all the beams were synchronized. Then they silently packed up their equipment, started down the path back to the boat and back to their 'home', at least for a while.

"Cordova, I have to…. I need to ask…." Lucius asked with a note of hesitation "Do you really think…"

"Lucius, it was a moment, a brief moment, where I was overwhelmed. I can only tell you that I love my life, I love my family and I really do understand the need for..." and she pointed up the hill, "this'... sometimes". She hesitated, looked openly into his face and leaned close, her breath soft and earthy like ripening lemons in a grove.

"I wish it didn't have to be like this. I hate the loss of life, the destruction, the 'end' of so many things that our people have worked so hard to give to these people, the accomplishments that might not or might survive just so we can have a new 'beginning'. It doesn't seem quite... balanced," she hesitated, "quite fair".

"Would you make it different if you could?" He asked softly.

A long pause ensued, one that seemed to make his heart slow down and skip a beat. A little shiver of fear touched that heart, spread to his belly. Cordova moved her hand to the side of his face and cupped it in hers gently, "Let's go home and finish packing for our 'new' home." She pressed her lips to his with a sigh. "You think it will be hard to learn another language?"

His eyes filled with tears, "I think a new language will be icing on the cake. How would you feel about starting a new family?" He looked like he was losing color as he spoke. Cordova looked at him, looked across the sea at Thera, only a shadow against a dark horizon then looked to the night sky, now filled with thousands, tens of thousands of stars twinkling.

"If we are about to start so many new things, perhaps we should go home and get a good night's sleep?" she grinned mischievously.

"Yeah I think a good night's rest is in order... eventually!" He chuckled.

They went to the boat and started rowing. A bright streak of light zipped across the heavens and landed beyond the dark horizon like it was trying to find a way to enter the sea or tumble to the ground and take up residence on this turning gyrating mass of earth.

Across the harbor, a grating, moaning sound emanated from the hulk of Mt Thera. Huge bursts of sound thundered into the night and the waves began to build up along the coastline they had just left. A sharp rotting egg smell wafted across the harbor and the birds took flight in a raucous jumble of screeching and wings flapping. Behind them the dogs on the island started up barking and howling. Lights started to wink on in the houses above on the hillside to be soon joined by cows bellowing and donkeys braying. In one week some real noise would begin. There would be terrible, awful wailing and crying of women and children, angry screaming, of men who saw their fishing grounds destroyed and boats scattered, babies fretful and sleepless, crying their last cries and nursing their last feedings. Cordova shivered from head to foot and silently let the tears stream down her face while Lucius rowed toward their home in order to leave it.

Chapter 8

Island of Akrotieri—Road to Fira

The island of Santorini was small. You were able to drive through most of the larger towns in under an hour without stops, and it was walkable along the coast from Santorini to Fira in two hours, the entire island in three. Along the cliffs, the drive overlooks Mediterranean blue waters, with patches of bare earth and paths leading down to the sea and other spots where stunted trees and a few flowering bushes added some color to the landscape. It was disconcerting however, to look over the side of the unprotected cliffs to the rocks and sea below, with a steep drop almost everywhere and a few hair-pin turns around the caldera. There were rocky paths leading to towns like Parisi, Kamari and Prygos, on the way to the airport. Their drive however, along the edge, lent itself to the breeze from the open cliffs and the sound of the waves against the rocky bottom.

Rodane looked over at Sabina as she was reclining a little with closed eyes.

{sleeping or faking my girl}

Her voice startled him nonetheless, "What, something on your mind?" she asked lazily.

"No, just checking to see if you were awake or sleeping."

"Would you like me to drive? You didn't get any sleep as I advised and your night out must have been tiring and stressful." She looked over, "I'd be happy to drive."

"No, I'm fine. There isn't much traffic and the scenery is keeping me awake. It's a shame we have to leave so abruptly. I would have loved to travel this slowly and take some great pictures."

They hadn't seen anyone except for a couple of ATVs, popular for transportation over paved roads, traveling at high speeds, ignoring most rules of the road except to avoid each other. There was an on and off bus that passed them but otherwise they hardly saw more than a half dozen people. They had about twenty more minutes to the town of Fira by the sea and the docking piers for the cruise ships who visited frequently. Many people chose to stay aboard ship so the tourist crush would be minimal.

"Is this the first time you've been to Santorini?" Sabina asked, " Just curious, no Q&A."

"Yes, a few of my travelogues have been for larger cities and only one for small towns. This one is for islands off the coast of larger towns, with the emphasis on the archaeology and antiquity of the islands."

She raised her eyebrows, "Is that what you do as an archaeologist? Write travelogues to these places?" she sounded disappointed. Her phone rang to the tune of 'Rocky' and he looked at it, looked at her, and smiled devilishly, "You going to answer that?" He nodded to the phone.

"Could we pull over, please? I'd like a little privacy…" she smiled as she asked.

{that's always a sign of trouble}

He pulled gently over on the side, as close to the uneven gravel as he could without spitting stones under the tires. She got out and walked away from the car and turned toward the hills, away from his vantage point.

{give her a break nothing suspicious here… yet}

After about five minutes, she turned around and smiled at him as she walked back and got in the passenger seat, "I have good news…for me at least." She turned to him, "I wanted to surprise you so I didn't say anything until I heard from my 'family.' I hope you'll be happy too." he didn't say anything, just waited.

She rushed on, words tumbling, "When I went in to use the bathroom before we left town, I called my cousin to rewire the funds I was expecting, to Fira. They're the best. See, they were dying to spend some time with me this summer and plans have been put on hold because they have been working such long hours and couldn't get away. Helene's job is so difficult to get time off from…"

Rodane put his hand over hers and said gently, "Sabina, it's okay. You don't have to explain everything. Let's keep it as close to honest as we can and we'll have less to explain away?"

She looked at him with her eyes growing larger and that charming blush creeping up her neck, "I was just telling you what we are…"

"What's the bottom line, ok?"

She didn't know whether to be angry or relieved. Rodane watched her war with her emotions…

{sorry, girl, you seem to have met your match}

"Two of my cousins are meeting us at Fira and bringing the money I requested. They're going to join us on the cruise. Isn't that wonderful?" She waited for his enthusiasm to catch up to hers as hers dwindled.

He looked solemnly at her and spoke, "Is this your way of getting out of our together time and the Q&A we promised... each other?"

"No, no!" she exclaimed and grabbed his arm, "No Rodane, I promise!" she stopped, took a breath. Her voice dropped to a soft, pleading tone.

{truth but as little as possible}

"I promised you we would enjoy this cruise 'together' and we would answer each other's questions. We will, honest!"

He thought she was being sincere. Her eyes and face were open and clear, no hint of covering her butt, or making up something on the sly.

"They really are joining us on this cruise. In fact...," she stopped a second, "they have already booked our suite and gotten a discount on the cruise because they had so many points accumulated."

"You mean the two cousins who couldn't get away because their jobs were so consuming?" he asked wryly.

She was getting angry, "Look, I'm trying to be as honest as I can here and everything I'm telling you is the truth, Okay?"

{just not the whole truth}

"Ok, calm down. I'm sorry, maybe it's good they're coming. It will give you some company if we find we need space."

"Yeah, that would be good." Her face fell and he found it more reassuring than anything she could say in words. It changed the tone of his voice.

"Sabina, I really am sorry. I spoke without thinking...or listening. I am looking forward to our cruise and spending time with you. I'm glad you get to see your cousins and I'm grateful you're getting funds to tide us over. I feel awkward, having to take money from you when you really don't know me."

She sounded disheartened when she spoke, "Can we just go and meet them at the ticket office? I'd like to get our shopping done before we board the ship...that's if it's OK with you?"

He took a few seconds to study her face and then did something he had no inkling he was going to do. He leaned over and kissed her softly on the forehead, then turned before she could react and started the car up and pulled out onto the road. Total silence next to him...

{good girl keep you discombobulated}

She settled back and spent the next ten minutes in her own thoughts,

{gotcha you're shocked}

...and when the outskirts of town started to appear, she took a deep

JOURNEY TO THE BLUE PLANET

breath as if she were girding herself for battle. He wasn't sorry he had confronted her. He thought it was high time she realized she wasn't in charge here but neither was he.

Her 'aha' moment to go on a cruise was not a clever idea on her part. He was almost certain it was a way to detour them from the airport where they might be spotted. She knew he was suspicious, he had told her so. She felt that if she came up with a plausible story that included him, he would go for it. In a way he did. He knew she was stressed and worried about his assault at Akrotiri, the fire in his room, the arrest by the police and the about face so abruptly and then everything they learned from Bellboy. He smiled at that. It all pointed to the fact that not just her activity, but his connection to her was being investigated, observed as well and they possibly knew a lot more than he did. What did they know about him? Why him? Then it clicked...

{damn they tried to burn me alive in my bed}

His stomach clenched and he thought he might lose his lunch. She didn't even realize she had let something slip in telling him about her conversation with Bellboy, about Sargent Acurus, and especially the unknown visitors who were walking around loose in the hotel, even gave him all the clues he needed to know what happened in his room. Shame they couldn't talk to Roseann and maybe get some descriptions but it seemed as if Sargent Acurus might be able to do that as well and he had a pretty good idea of their descriptions if he was guessing correctly. Get out of Dodge! That was the goal and it seemed as if she wanted to make sure no one had seen them leave either.

As for the cruise? It was a great idea and he would have jumped at it if it just didn't fall into place so easily. Travel, adventures, a suite together, was a great idea and it meant they wouldn't be separated when she might need him or let's face it, he might need her. It happened too quickly, too easily, conveniently calling cousins without telling him, having the route all planned out instantly, having cousins show up out of the blue and bringing unlimited (maybe not) funds without question, having the cruise booked without one problem,

{never heard of a last minute cruise halfway through its itinerary}

...changing her mind from wanting to go their separate ways in one afternoon to wanting to stay together the next...

{too damn convenient here bud}

Sabina listened to the rumble of the car over the dusty winding road while her thoughts went whirling through her head, jumbled together like marbles in a bag. Why couldn't she get over this feeling Rodane was onto each play she made and even more, every move she tried to get him to make without suspicion? Was she that transparent? This would have bothered her if it weren't for an even bigger problem; her feelings interfering with her usually logical movements, to carry out her tasks and do them successfully. In all honesty, this was the first time she had ever come upon a job that posed actual threats and physical harm to her and others with her. Something here was very different from her other jobs, and very scary. That was just one feeling very different from the norm.

Now she had to be honest with herself and admit her feeling about Rodane's sudden appearance and continued presence was another different variable. That was also new. Rodane had appeared out of nowhere and she had pretty much made up her mind that was coincidence. She didn't trust him completely and could not afford at this point, to tell him what he really wanted to know. She was sure of that but at the same time she had to trust him enough to travel with him and also keep each other safe and look out for any other threats that could be made against them. He was smart and well educated in a field where she had her most secrets to keep hidden. He had sharp instincts, ones that almost seemed in sync with hers.

She had some decisions to make. One was whether to tell him about her 'cousins' if they would be who she was thinking they would be. Another was if she could tell him enough to satisfy his curiosity about the EMS she had taken out of the safe. He had seen it twice now, even if he didn't really get to see it clearly and she knew it was the first thing he would be asking about in their Q&A. The final change from her previous jobs was the insertion of her budding feelings about Rodane, personally. There were many years when she felt she would never be able to form a lasting relationship with anyone for any permanent 'family' unit.

Hers was a loving family, sometimes removed, many times acting as co-workers rather than personal family members but they had common goals, similar histories and closely knit units of people who worked for a greater good over a long period of time. Wasn't that a true family? They cared for each other's welfare and were concerned with the other events and happenings over a long stretch of time. They trusted each other above all others and instilled in their newborns a sense of purpose and educated them to face varied peoples in many different walks of life. They had training and skills that prepared them to enter an adult society everywhere, and knowledge that would serve them well their entire lives. That too was 'family' wasn't it?

Rodane had unknowingly entered that circle when he entered her life at the exact moment he did. She didn't accept coincidence as easily as others did. There was always an element of fate or destiny or having an internal connection. That she did believe in; an instinct, a sixth sense that they all had but few really depended on in every instance. Maybe the fact that her job often put her in positions where she had to use that gut instinct every hour of every day she was working, made the difference between chalking up unexpected happenings to coincidence and looking for connections that tied all those events together.

She felt it now, sitting here next to him in the car. She sensed his thinking of her when she was thinking of him. Some would say proximity to each other would make that a given but she believed differently. Of any and all thoughts that could be going through the heads of two 'almost strangers', thinking of each other would seem to be at the bottom of the list. She looked over at him at the exact moment he did the same with her. He braked and both their faces showed realization, shock, awareness and wonder at the exact same time. Their eyes widened and a sense of something between fear and amazement settled in on them at the same time. He slowed down to a stop on the road side.

Rodane was first to speak "What the hell… I don't understand…" he closed his mouth. Sabina swallowed and cleared her throat, "Rodane, we need to take some time and sit down and work this out. It's bigger than both of us right now and I can't really explain it because I don't know how to explain it. But it's here, so we have to try, but not now. It's too confusing, too new, too insubstantial as of now. Let's try and keep to our agenda and when we can look at it logically and with no stress involved we'll work it out, okay?"

He stayed staring at her face, "Ok?" she repeated. He took one good, deep breath.

"Ok." She let hers out, "Okay."

His hands were trembling but he started the car and in three minutes they pulled into town and found a parking spot in a small lot close to the cruise line office. He came around to the passenger side and opened her door. They got out their bags and backpacks and stood there and looked around. She put her hand on his arm and pressed. He looked where she was pointing and saw two women coming toward them with wide smiles on both their faces.

Sabina broke into the widest smile he had yet to see on her face "Helene, Eugenie! I'm so glad to see you!" They did a group hug for a few seconds then Sabina took Rodane by the arm and pulled him over to them.

"This is my friend Rodane, he's the one I told you about…" and she looked directly at them.

"Glad to meet you" Rodane said, and offered his hand, trying to juggle all their belongings. "I'm glad Sabina will get a chance to spend some time with you. What would your jobs be that keep you from vacationing very often?"

They looked at her, some confusion on their faces and then smiled at him and shook his hand vigorously, "Yes, it's always good to find some time to get together with Sabina, right Eugenie?" She said, "I'm Helene" and her dark eyes, (brown, umber?) and dark hair, plus her olive-toned skin suggested a very different background then Sabina's, and she stood toe to toe with Eugenie, who could have been Middle Eastern by her deep skin tones, her head of curly black hair, and her eyes so dark they almost blended into her pupils. Both were a little shorter than Sabina, but very fit and muscular almost as if they were athletes or weightlifters.

{wouldn't want to cross either of those two in a bar fight}

Sabina cleared her throat, "Mm... have we managed to get everything lined up for our cruise?" Helene handed her a manila envelope thick with papers and a black backpack with Royal Caribbean on the front. Eugenie handed a duplicate to Rodane and they began to walk down the walkway, past shops and small food eateries, taking half their bags to help carry.

"We understand you and Sabina are going to be doing a little shopping before the ship sails..?"

Helene looked at her watch, "Suppose we meet back here in two hours and then we can finalize our trip."

They stopped at the pier where their ship was docked. Men were climbing ropes, pulling cable, hurrying along the outer decks of what was a behemoth with at least ten levels, loaded with bags and linens and carts.

"Jewel of the Seas" Helene said, 'your Royal Caribbean ride to adventure and parts of paradise' "

Eugenie added, "Nice gig if you can get it."

Helene stepped up to Rodane, "We've been advised to give you this for your use and we hope it helps to make your trip enjoyable." she handed him an envelope and stood there waiting for him to open it. He slid the envelope open with his finger nail and pulled out a wire transaction. He looked at it, blanched, and looked over at Sabina. She stood there with her own envelope that Eugenie handed her. It didn't seem to faze her in the least.

{wow where do these people come from}

Sabina, at least, had the grace to look embarrassed. She moved to his side and said haltingly "I know it's a lot but feel free to return any funds left at the end of our trip, ok?" her eyes almost begging him, 'take it'.

{don't make it harder for her}

So he smiled at Helene and Eugenie and said "I'm extremely grateful. I'll be very frugal with this and hope I can repay the favor along with the money. "Thank you" he said simply.

"Okay, here's the thing" Helene said, "you have your car and you're about to board a ship to take you across the sea. We'd like to know if you would be willing to entrust your car to me to take on the ferry over to Athens and you can pick it up there to go wherever you choose. That is, if you're okay with it."

Rodane answered with, "Problem is, it's a rental, from the airport here in Santorini and its due back tomorrow. That's when I planned on flying out, to rent a car there and travel through the east coast of Italy before flying home from Rome."

"Well…" Helene huffed, looking at her watch again, "it's three hours before the ship sails. I'll take the car to the airport. It's only thirty minutes away. I can drop it off and take one of the on and off buses back to here and be back in two hours. That still leaves us plenty of room and time for all of us to board and have drinks in the lounge. Sound like a plan?"

"Why don't you let me do that?" Rodane asked, "After all, it is my rental."

"Oh no, I think not! Sabina is looking forward to strutting your cute self around the shops and playing fashion mogul!" Eugenie laughed, "Besides, we understand you had a couple of stressful days and you could use the time to go aboard and chill for a while before we depart."

Sabina watched Rodane blush and become quite embarrassed. It was cute. She put her arm through his and turned him toward the line of shops on the side street. "I saw some shops I'm sure will do and we can be done in a jiffy. Come on Eugenie, come with us. It will be fun!"

Eugenie studied Rodane for a minute and said, "Size 38 tall, shoes size 11, 11 ½ a longer 36 inch sleeve and likes to have his cuffs rolled up with no tie" she looked at him with a grin.

"How do you women do that?" He exclaimed. They laughed. His discomfiture was evident so he probably didn't shop too often and only when he had to buy something.

Too many men knew what they needed, didn't even need a list, walked into a familiar store, picked out what they needed, paid for it and that was that. Not this trip, Sabina thought. On second thought, they didn't want to stand out and draw attention to themselves for obvious reasons. Oh well, next time.

{next time what are you thinking sab}

Rodane handed over his car keys, told Helene where the rental papers were and which parking lot. She started back to the car with Sabina walking with her for a few minutes. She returned and she, Rodane and Eugenie started toward the shops in the tourist district. Here in Fira, they were pretty expensive and tourists gathered in big clumps to take something classy back home just because they could. He definitely was not buying a t-shirt with 'I love Greece' or 'Santorini' on it. It was a wonderful way to alert everyone you are a tourist. An hour and forty five minutes later, they walked back onto the walkway to the pier, carrying bags in both hands. Sabina insisted on stopping for a fresh-squeezed lemonade and Eugenie had to have a Lemoncello ice.

His feet hurt, he was hungry and the heat of the day was making him sweat through his clothes and give him a headache to boot. Perhaps still a left over from his mild concussion.

"Girls, can we possibly find a spot to sit down and get something to eat? It's been a long afternoon." Sabina looked at his watch and realized most of the afternoon had slipped away and the late hour had left them hungry and tired.

"Why don't we see if we can board now and get something on the ship?" she suggested.

Rodane remembered, "Bellboy made those sandwiches and drinks and I'd be fine with that if I could sit in some shade for a little." He looked around for some tables anywhere.

Sabina was concerned and said, "Wait" opened her backpack and extracted the paper bag she had stuffed in there. She walked over to the side street, went up to a homeless person leaning against his cart and handed him the bag, "Here you go, enjoy." He grinned, toothless, at her. Rodane looked at her in astonishment. She took his arm, hefted her duffle in her other hand, gave her backpack to Eugenie and they steered him toward the pier. There was a sailor at the gate, wearing his pearly whites and he looked up.

"Scusa, we are not ready to board yet, Signoras. We have…" he looked at his watch "…another hour before your boarding" he smiled. Eugenie went up to him, murmured under her breath, pointed to his clipboard and waited while he decided if he would argue or not. Apparently he decided to check his list. Whatever he read had him sharply looking up and almost bowing to them, excitedly opening the gate and motioning for them to walk up the plank laid to the first deck.

"Of course, pardon me, please… go on. They will be expecting you, so sorry… my apologies." he was almost tripping over himself. Rodane didn't shock easily but this was absurd. It was as if they were celebrities or royalty. He stood, eyes wide, amazed at the whole scene. Eugenie and Sabina looked at him lingering at the gate, the sailor watching all three of them.

"Aren't you coming dear?" Sabina asked him. He peered at her, narrowed his eyes and said, "Yes dear, I'm coming" and walked up the gangplank behind two lovely ladies.

Chapter 9

Airport in Akrotieri

They parked their car in the airport's C lot and exited late in the afternoon to walk toward the terminal. Their early afternoon has been somewhat fruitful, from their point of view. They both agreed they would use charm or money or both, to gather information on Dr. Carter and her new friend, Rodane Arcos. They needed to know their plans and their intended ports of call, and soon. It wouldn't pay to have gone through everything they already had, with nothing to show for their efforts, except a newly cemented friendship and a ruined hotel.

Renata looked over at her driver and partner, Tabor, "We need to get moving, get plane tickets and get to the ferry by early tomorrow, so we can try and head those two off at Capri, before they head for Naples. If they get to the city or even further, they can get lost to us in a number of ways and we might never pick up their trail."

Tabor lounged against the car door and said, "Chill a little pet, they don't have more than a couple hours ahead of us and we have a good idea where they're heading."

Renata was exasperated. Nothing about this trip had gone as planned. A simple grab and run had turned into police investigations, a destroyed hotel, an injured witness and an elusive Dr. Carter. That ate at her before anything else...

{the bitch}

It had been a simple operation; watch her. If she found something, get it and return to France. Who was this Rodane fellow anyway? Renata was used to getting her way, accomplishing her goals and receiving her reward with very little energy expenditure. It was certainly not failure but worse yet?

Possibly it might create a police incident that might impede their finalizing their assigned task. Tabor had managed to make their jobs more difficult and most certainly a little more dangerous in a way that excited her.

Not much of anything they had been assigned lately had been fun or adventurous, until now. A simple task of acquiring whatever Dr. Carter was after, had become a little hair raising and therefore not only mysterious but challenging. There was still the question of Tabor being reckless and almost getting them arrested. He was foolhardy enough to attempt some dangerous moves to get what they came for but not circumspect enough to avoid notice. That was something they couldn't afford right now.

Tabor was watching her as she looked around and he could almost see the wheels turning in her head, this wraith of a woman who was his work-partner but also his lover. Their bosses would not be happy if they knew that. To them, it would be a complication in an otherwise professional partnership.

Her hair was cut very short but styled and she looked like an agile gamine, a pixie, one without the wings. That gamine quality was what had attracted him personally from almost the first time he was introduced to her as her new partner. She had looked at him, seemingly bored, with a little disdain and certainly an arrogant attitude. It irritated him at first but then once they had been on a few missions successfully completed, the irritation turned to interest.

He was curious not only to see what made her tick, but also to find out how well tuned she was. It took exactly six months for her to find her way to his bed and then the arrogance was gone and the disdain had become dedication to the job and to him. He had never had another woman who he depended on for both security and physical satisfaction. Certainly there were lots of other women but only for physical pleasure. With Renata, he loved her looks without really loving her. He took and gave pleasure without committing to anything permanent. He loved the softness of her olive-toned skin, the curve of her thin face and upturned nose. He loved to watch her stretch in the mornings, thin and elfin like, with her large amber eyes that were hooded when she looked at him sometimes and piercing with anger or being on the hunt at others.

That first meeting was two years ago almost to the week. Their first mission together was simply to gather information and observe a list of four people in Belgium. It only took three days and when they arrived back in France with their report and a list of contacts they had made in seeking out those four people, Theras called them into his office. "This is your final report?" he asked with raised eyebrows.

"Yes" Renata spoke up.

"No, I want to hear from Tabor, please." He had not taken his eyes off of Tabor.

"Yes sir, we tried to make it as thorough as we could, not knowing exactly what you were looking for. We reached out very subtly to some coworkers and acquaintances to get as much background knowledge as possible. If the report seems incomplete, we can go back and continue to gather more information." He felt himself tense up. He glanced quickly to Renata while Theras went through the pages again. She looked anxious and she nodded slightly and raised her shoulders a little.

Theras looked up and took both of them in at one glance. Studying them, he steepled his fingers and finally said, "I knew I was right to pair the two of you together! My advisors told me I was making a 'damn mistake' as they put it, but I trusted my feelings." He rose and walked around the desk, patting Renata on the arm, kissing her cheek and then clapping Tabor on the back, thoroughly enjoying himself and looking so self-satisfied.

"I was right! You make a magnificent team and everyone will learn from you and it will make such a difference. You have found a template for what I will begin to expect from every one of my agents. Our results will show some very clear improvements, I have no doubt."

Their next few missions went just as smoothly, and Renata thought they would eventually be able to take a break and a short vacation. Their relationship had become physical, Tabor was taken with her and she was gradually letting down any barriers she may have had in working with him. His reputation seemed to put her off at first but they had developed a close working arrangement and it seemed to weave seamlessly into a sleeping arrangement. She asked one thing of him; to not let others know, especially Theras that they had become partners in every way. It would make for some awkwardness and maybe some resentment from others if they knew. She had tried to be politic and explain her reasoning,

"I would like for everyone to feel they could work with either of us or both in any situation and I don't think it wise to broadcast our very close partnership." He understood her hesitations. He had some of the same reservations so it was an easy promise to make.

Then eight months into their working together, Tabor became so enraged in a conversation with one of their 'gentle', questioning sessions, he injured the contact so severely, Renata had no choice but to end the man's suffering. She was the one who had the body hauled to the Thames by one of their helpers and when it was found there was nothing to connect that to either of them. She made damn sure the helper was sworn to secrecy from anyone and it was never solved or at least, not to her knowledge. She and

Tabor had argued well into the night over the risk they had taken and the need for more restraint. She accused him of grandstanding for attention and the lack of self-restraint that could really make problems for them. She paced around the room, wringing her hands, shouting, cursing, throwing a book at him and threatening him with clearing out and going home.

He went to her carefully. She was very unpredictable when this angry… reached his arms around her and murmured into her ear, "Ma cheric, je t'aime…pardonez mois. I… I lost my head! He made me so enraged with his disgust and his sarcastic attitude to me. I swear to you, it will not happen again. You must stop me when I ever attempt to do such a thing again." He kissed her neck, her face, her eyes, and gently led her to their bed and the rest of the evening was 'makeup sex'.

He seemed to love those moments as much as when she took the initiative and enticed him to bed or other strange places. They were a good match. They did good work and she was dedicated to watching out for him and watching his back in all things. She worried that this incident showed poor judgement and recklessness but he swore it was an aberration and she thought so too.

Four months ago, he had lost his cool when searching for someone who had taken off when he had figured out what they were after. The man had made it to the docks, leaving by the back door of the bar, leaving his car and going on foot to alert the ones they were investigating. Tabor had told Renata to get the car and she had followed them till she saw Tabor enter the dockside. She parked the car in a shadowed spot and followed them. She found Tabor standing over the dying form of the man. He was blubbering and bleeding, begging for his life, for the sake of his wife and their two year old son. Right before she made her presence known Tabor bent over him and used his knife to finally silence the other. He spoke softly but the quiet and the breeze from the water carried his voice, "You, my poor bastard, have messed with the wrong man. I send you to your death knowing your son will probably have another father and your wife will share her bed with one or many men but definitely not you." He looked up and saw Renata in the shadows. He looked at her quietly, judging whether to say a word or not. Apparently he decided this time to remain silent. Renata stared at him for a few moments until finally he got up, wiped the blood from the knife on the man's jacket and walked past her to the car. Without a word she dragged the body over to two containers placed close to each other and managed to stuff his body between the two and under the trailer hitch. They never said a word on the way back to their rooms and there was never a report on whether the man has been found or not. They went back to France and Tabor handed in a report that they had attempted to locate their target but could never come up with a single living person who could lead them to him.

{well that much is true he's just leaving out some small details}

Since that time, an undercurrent of distrust and accusations lay between them. They never spoke of the death again or the other one but something subtle showed up in Tabor. He was attentive but impatient. He was sullen when she questioned him over anything and he wasn't worried about dismissing her advice if he disagreed with her. So far it hadn't affected their work.

They still worked well together both on the job and in bed but Renata sensed a shift in their love making. Tabor led the time and place and position and she found herself uninterested and disinterested for those times when she saw him looking at her with his eyes signaling his desire and his hands roaming for familiar spots and soft areas. The one time recently that she had demurred and told him she was tired he had sulked and stayed up late into the night. Then he had come to bed and woken her with lots of attention and had aroused her while she was still half asleep and had taken her rather roughly and quickly then held her, soothing and whispering words of love and passion and need. She had gotten up the next morning and had seen ugly, red bruises on her neck and on her inner thighs.

{maybe I've given him reason and he feels betrayed}

She had tried to hide her disappointment and her anger but it was possible that was the reason for such a drastic change. She tried after that to really squelch any misgivings she might have. She looked to him when making decisions on where and when. Things had become much easier lately and they were very engaged with each other, almost as fervent as their early sexual encounters.

Theras called them into his office and handed them a file they were to study and then make their plans to travel. He handed them an envelope with funds to travel and asked them to contact him as soon as they had located Dr. Sabina Carter and then to follow her closely but not to make any effort to reach or question other contacts or acquaintances. This was to be done as silently and as unobtrusively as possible, no suspicions raised, no contacts made. He was very adamant about that and Renata wondered if he had somehow heard any whispers or rumors of any actions he would be dissatisfied with.

On their way out Theras said, "Renata, may I have a moment with you please? I'll send her right out to you, Tabor" Tabor hesitated, looked from her to Theras and hesitated just another fraction before he nodded his head and left.

"Renata, my dear, is everything going well with you and Tabor?"

"Why yes, everything is fine. Why do you ask?"

"The atmosphere around the two of you seems a bit strained." His tone was not mild but leaving an unasked question.

"No sir, everything is good. We have been very busy for a month and I guess we are both hoping for some time when we can unwind, maybe take a short break or vacation. We know you are very anxious to complete your files so we will have to try and sneak some R&R in when we can."

"He treats you well? You are still working well together?" She smiled at him, "I think our results and reports are the proof you need as to whether we are successful sir."

"You are doing very good work for me, work that I couldn't do for myself but very necessary to our goals."

"Is there anything you are... dissatisfied with either from me or Tabor? Have we done something that displeases you?"

{can't do much but come on out and say it out loud}

He looked at her, took her hand and said, "No, no. I have only good reports of you and Tabor. I am pleased at how you have been working so hard for my interests. You will tell me if there is anything you need or require?"

She looked at him eye to eye and for a brief second thought of coming clean about everything she had been keeping to herself.

{keeping hidden you mean}

"Yes sir, I would not hesitate to come to you if I had any concerns or misgivings." It was his turn to fix her with a questioning face for a second or two. Finally, he let go of her hand and returned to his desk, "Good! I will be eager to get your report and...Renata?"

"Yes sir?"

"Please contact me directly if you are able to get anything at all from Dr. Carter. You have my direct number so don't hesitate if you feel you need to speak to me personally. Understood?"

"Yes sir," Renata answered and went to the door before she could change her mind. Outside the building, Tabor was lounging against the car but Renata had learned to read the subtle undercurrents he gave off when he was disturbed.

"Well, anything I should be worried about?" he asked as if bored.

"No, he was just telling me he thought we might be able to get some R&R time soon and he told me our work was very satisfactory and he was proud of us for our efforts."

Once in the car, he reached over and grabbed her arm till it hurt. "Why just you?" he snarled.

"Tabor, let go, you're hurting me" she exclaimed and jerked her arm away. He let go, fixed his eyes on the windshield and said, "I would not like to think you and Mr. Gallo had anything planned to replace me or interfere with our relationship." He seemed to be mulling something over and then he turned to her and spoke gently, "Cherie, I do not want anything to come between you and me. I care very much for you and I treasure your care and the help you give me so often. I think we make an awesome team and I would hate for someone to try and come between us. It would be a betrayal of everything we have promised each other."

He leaned over and kissed her lips placing his hand on her inner thigh, touching her skin gently and sensuously. She felt heat from his hand and from herself. Their kiss deepened and then he caressed her neck and moved his lips to the edge of her open shirt. She took his head in her hands and he opened the top of her slacks and she lifted her hips while she guided his head to her opened legs. They got lost in the moment and she buried her thoughts as he buried his lips and both felt contented.

At a window on the second floor, Theras looked out at the car parked on the drive and saw Renata leaning against the car window and slowly turning her head from side to side. He watched for a moment and then left them both to their business.

Present time

Tabor asked Renata, "Which flight are we on?" She looked at her watch and said, "One hour from now. We better go and check in. We'll be in Naples by early tonight. We can get settled and begin to do some research on Rodane Arcos. I already contacted a worker at the museum there who worked with him on a recent dig. He's to meet me at 8:30 tonight at the museum."

He peered at her, a look of anger on his face, "What, now you're lining up contacts without me and interrogating them on your own? What gives Renata?" His face was flushed, his hands flexed into fists.

"Wha…t?" she stammered, "I'm just trying to get a jump on the research so we have a place to start. What's the problem?"

"First, you interfere with my methods of questioning our contacts then you meet with Theras behind my back…" Renata attempted to speak, "Shut up bitch! I'm tired of this shit! Now you take it upon yourself to go and make appointments and leave me out of it? You're trying to short-circuit my authority and it seems you are getting the blessing of our boss."

While he was getting fired up, he had been moving towards her and came up to her and pushed his face into hers, "I won't stand for being cut out, Renata." He grabbed her elbow, "Do you hear me? I won't stand for it!"

She realized he was close to rage and decided to try and defuse his anger.

"Tabor, sweetheart, I would never do that to you. We're a team, we work together." She placed one hand gently on his arm, "I only set it up so you would have a chance to prepare your questions for our contact and it would save time. Of course, you're in charge. You always do so much better than me in these things." She watched his flush disappear, and his voice dropped. He let go of her elbow, stood still and let out a breath,

"Of course, forgive me. I'm tired and frustrated at our lack of progress. Yes, let's go and get ready to board the plane. You can share your information with me and we can prepare together." He tugged her hand into his and they took their baggage from the car and headed to the airport entrance and the check in. She breathed a little easier.

Chapter 10

Aboard the Jewel of the Seas

Rodane woke up to a darkened room. It had been light out when he literally fell on the bed in his room and that was all it took. He didn't remember hitting the pillow. He looked around the room, remembered taking the elevator to the 5th level, getting off and carrying their things to suites 510 thru 514. They used their room key cards that had been given to them when they reached level 6 as instructed, and waited to be told their rooms were ready. Sabina went to the bar and brought back three Mojitos, with little umbrellas in them and napkins. They sat at a round table and sipped their drinks then Eugenie came over with three plates. There was a salad, a chicken breast and a roll with butter. Everyone around them looked over with an expression like, 'food, where did you get food?' They ate, while waiting for Helene and when she hadn't arrived by the half hour, the ship's PA system announced everyone could go to their rooms.

Dinner was at seven o'clock in the Angel Room, on level 4. An emergency drill would be held at 4:45 on the open deck at eight and it was announced that their places would be on their itineraries that were given to them at boarding. They looked at each other. They didn't board with everyone else. They were there almost an hour before boarding, and spent their time taking tags off clothes and stuffing their folded new duds into their carry-ons and backpacks .Then they went to the lounge and had drinks and food. Sabina and Rodane went to their suite and told Eugenie to call them on their phones when Helene showed up. They were concerned that she might not make it in time to cast off.

Then Rodane fell onto the bed and that was his last thought. He turned on the light and rolled out of bed. To his right was a double door that led out to his deck. Across from the bed was a settee for two and the desk and chair. To his left was the bathroom by the entrance door and opposite was a door leading into the sitting area. There was a closet next to the doorway to the sitting area and his carry-on and duffle bag were hung on a rack. Inside it all his new clothes were hung up on wooden hangers. He heard no noise from the sitting area but he could hear noise coming from the room behind the bed.

Everything smelled clean and fresh and it was cool in the room with air coming from an overhead vent. The colors were muted and soft pastels, sea colors; pale greens and blues, sand colors on the walls. He went to the double door and pulled back the drapes, looked at his watch and realized he had been asleep for a solid three hours.

{must have been exhausted}

The drapes were room darkening and he opened the door and stepped out onto his deck. Here the sun was at its low, just beginning to make its journey to meet the sea and touch the small, white caps he could see into more endless sea. Rather calm he thought and a light breeze blew across his face. He scrubbed at the bristles on his face and realized he hadn't shaved that morning at the hotel before they took off so quickly.

Now there was something to think about. Why the rush to get out? Why did Sabina come up with her 'aha' moment and delay the trip to the airport? This little trip would cost them at least three days, maybe four, and they had much to do before his week was up. More especially, why did she scuttle the plan to go their separate ways and invite, practically beg him to go along with her? He didn't fall for her soft, pleasing voice which was apparently feminine wiles she wasn't in the habit of using on her opposite sex.

{wait buddy it worked didn't it}

He looked to his left and two rooms over to where Sabina's room must be. The woman was getting under his skin in so many ways. He had to admit he was just as rusty as she was transparently inept, at convincing someone of the fairer sex to bend into his or her wishes without them realizing they were bending at all. She had ways about her that showed him she was not one to have had many serious or current romantic relationships.

{I love how she blushes when she's embarrassed}

She was most definitely an independent soul, used to doing things in her own time with her own methods. Trust was something she didn't take for granted or so it seemed. He got vibes from her that made him restless and stirred his blood. Not to passion so much as to a desire to protect and look out for her. She seemed to be of the same opinion concerning him and he chuckled at the irony of him protecting her while she thought she was protecting him. Bingo! He jolted out of his thoughts to the revelation of… That's why she needed so badly to convince him to come with her.

She knew something he was unaware of. It had to be the arrest…

{no, just a 'questioning' captain said}

The release, the fire, the assault, all of it was happening so fast he barely had time to stop and put the pieces together. But now he did. He was about to confront Dr. Sabina Carter and get to the bottom of what she knew and he didn't. Damn if he was going to let her wiggle out of this conversation that she had promised him.

{and she wiggles so nicely}

He closed the deck door on reentering, went to the bathroom and was about to wash his face and maybe even take a quick shower. They had about an hour and a half before dinner and he was starving.

{time to clean up and maybe go to Sabina's room and see if she…}

Knock, knock! Well, speaking of the little devil.

{softly rapping at my chamber door}

He went to the adjoining door and opened it after fumbling with two locks.

"Hey" she said, holding a bottle of water in one hand and a Mimosa in the other.

"Didn't know if you were awake so I knocked gently, also didn't know what you had here so I brought you a choice" and she held out both hands with her offering. He smiled at her with true enjoyment. The grin on her face was one of enthusiasm and joy. It was obvious she really did feel like she was on an adventure and she had managed to drag him along but definitely not kicking and screaming. He motioned her in and took the water from her hand, "This will do nicely, unless it's your preference."

"No I'm fine with this" and she took a sip from the little straw and umbrella in the Mimosa.

"Ok, Sabina, how about I ask you one question and one question only if you promise to fully answer it?" He didn't want to spoil the moment but he was also very aware how good she was at the deflection and avoidance. Her eyes hooded instantly, transforming that joy and happy face into a closed, guarded stone face. It happened so fast, he wasn't sure he witnessed it clearly. He mentally took a half step back, almost decided to tell her it could wait and then thought better of it. Something as necessary as his safety as well as hers needed to be addressed sooner rather than later. It could be the difference between life and death.

She looked dejected, "Oookay, I was hoping we could spend our first night of the cruise resting and enjoying the sea, but ok." She seemed to gird herself for that battle; shoulders straight, back straight, poker face, hooded eyes…,

"We did promise right?" He waited for her denial.

"Yep"

{she might not be good at feminine wiles but she's definitely an expert at subterfuge}

He took a second to gather his thoughts and find the perfect question to start with,

"What have I gotten myself into and with who?" he looked at her, waiting.

"Can I sit down please?" she asked.

"Oh lord, I'm the perfect host, right?" He looked chagrined, "of course, have a seat."

"Why don't we go to the sitting room next door…" she nodded toward the open door, "It's much more comfortable with a choice of nice, easy chairs." She turned and he followed

{lion leading the lamb}

…and the sitting room was definitely more comfortable and spacious minus a bathroom and closet. There was an arrangement of seating around a faux electric fireplace with a mantle for winter cruises. They chose their chairs and she placed her Mimosa on a side table and folded her arms.

{holding in all her fears or her knowledge}

"First I…" Rodane started…

"I want you to…" Sabina spoke also at the exact same moment. They looked up to each other's eyes and broke out laughing. Rodane picked it up right away.

"I want to have you answer my question and I promise I won't interrupt you until you finish, okay?"

"She let out a sigh, "Honestly Rodane, I've been giving this a lot of thought and I really don't know where to start. So much has happened from only three days ago up to now, I don't really understand it. You can help me out by first listening but if I don't satisfy you with my answer feel free to chime in with anything I don't make clear." She looked up and met his eyes. He considered himself a good judge of character and her eyes were honest. That was the best he could say for what he felt. Then he noticed she had changed to a dress and had a subtle flowery fragrance wafting from her skin. It broke his train of thought and he kept looking at her. Whatever she saw in his face, it made her eyes take on a glisten and a red blush rose from the narrow cleavage of her dress,

{red becomes you}

…to her ears and the tips were bright red to match above the silver hoops she was wearing. Her hair was pulled back and in a relaxed…

{bun chignon how would I know}

"Rodane...," She interrupted his dawdling.

"Yes? Oh, sorry, what were you asking?" She picked up her drink and took a large swallow,

{why do I feel like a kid around him}

"Okay, to answer your question. It's not something you've gotten yourself into. I'm fairly sure it's me that might already know the answer to that and it's me that has gotten us into a 'situation'..." She paused, took a breath, "that I really, as I said before, don't understand." She stopped and the seconds ticked by.

"Go on," Rodane sat and crossed his ankles and steepled his fingers together under his chin. She flicked her head sideways and exclaimed, "God, you look like a professor in class who is giving the third degree to an annoying student. Are you?"

"Am I what, a professor? More like the annoying student I would guess," he answered. "Look, I know you wanted to get rid of me after the first ten minutes we met. I also know you have now decided to keep me close for various and sundry reasons, of which, I hope, you can let me in on those reasons somewhere in this conversation. I must admit that at first I took some things for granted and others as coincidence. I've learned, as the annoying student, that there is much here that you know and I'm totally unaware of but like the professor that I am, by the way, I'm keeping an open mind and letting you help me understand what it is that's happening, hopefully who is making it happen and most importantly, why." Then he waited.

"Ok... ok" she breathed out slowly. She did the opposite of him and leaned forward in her chair, placed her arms on her knees and folded her hands together,

"I'm going to start by telling you I am a Doctor of Science at UCLA, with a degree in Volcanology and Meteorology and I have an adjunct position teaching Climatology and Environmental Science. I teach fall and winter classes only and use the Spring and Summer sessions to travel, work on various archeological sites and meet throughout the summer with both professors of my field as well as archaeological scholars of ancient artifacts to compare finds and investigations."

{all true thank the gods but not entirely}

His expression was widening as she spoke and he felt his eyebrows raised and his mouth agape even as he tried to remain stoic.

{whew roddy who do we have here}

He stayed quiet, waiting. She looked at him, possibly expecting to have him ask her questions but he was still digesting these little... but huge to him, nuggets of information she had laid on him. She straightened her shoulders, and continued,

{girding for battle again}

"My job allows me a lot of freedom to go to places which we're interested in possibly using as sites for grants and student internships to help me with my investigations. Sometimes I travel alone and when I am in places less safe or secure I have support from people like…" she paused, studying him. He finished for her, "Helene and Eugenie?"

Her eyes opened wide, "You knew!" She was gob smacked.

{good grief girl time you found out I'm not lame brained after all}

"No, not knew, just surmised and suspected. I don't want you to think I can read minds or anything but you are obviously in touch with some pretty powerful people who can get things done quickly and spare no expense to make things happen." He stopped at the astonished thought that had just crossed his mind.

"Did you get me released from jail? Was that your doing?" He felt smacked in the face from a left field ball.

"I don't know…," she said in a very low voice. He had to lean in to hear.

"You don't know?" His voice held incredulity, hers held confusion.

"Well here's the thing…," she spoke up, "When you were taken away to town I placed a call after I woke up" she paused, some seconds passed.

"You were sleeping? I was puking in an interrogation room!"

"Rodane, so much had happened from the time I met you at Akrotieri to the alarms for the fire, I hadn't slept or eaten or even rested for hours on end. I was exhausted and worried and… afraid" she said it as if the confession had been tortured out of her. "I hadn't had contact with anyone yet, people were following me as if they knew my every move. I was afraid for you…," she looked up at him, "I felt stressed and tired and confused all at the same time. I was running on fumes and when I returned to my room I collapsed for a few hours of sleep. I'm sorry," she whispered.

He got up from his chair and knelt next to her and put his hand over hers, "No, it's me who's sorry. You didn't have to take me to your room or bandage my head or take care of me." One tear dropped from her bowed head, "You had gone through everything I had, probably more, digging for hours in the heat," She raised her head a little and she started crying in earnest, tears falling to her chin and dripping. She wiped them away furiously, "But that's just it!" she cried, voice choking, "I'm the reason you got hurt, I'm the one who had you taken to jail and…" she hiccupped with sobs now, "I almost got you killed in that horrible fire in your room!"

She grabbed his hand, "If it weren't for me, you never would have had that happen." She looked guilty, regretful, and… adorable! He gathered her to him and she sobbed on his shoulder.

He could feel his shirt getting soaked with her tears, "And it's because of you I found out that I was set up by the police and it was you having me in your room that kept me out of a fire that was meant to kill me." He held her for a long minute while his words sank in and her crying slowed.

"What? You think you were set up, by whom?" Her eyes were wet, red, and puffy but still that beautiful topaz blue color he remembered from his sister.

"Well, the little black box that survived the fire was the giveaway…"

She interrupted, "What little black box? You didn't tell me about any setup…or any little black box" she looked aggrieved.

"If you want honesty, I wasn't sure at that point whether I could trust you or not. You told me yourself you were in my room and you took things out of it. How at that point, was I to not suspect you could have also put something in there as well?" She went to respond and he stopped her, "Sabina, this was before we talked to Bellboy and I was still feeling the effects of the concussion. I wasn't really thinking things through, just reacting to events and covering my ass."

"Fair enough, but when did you decide you could trust me?" She asked, blowing her nose. He made up his mind,

{come clean bucko be a man}

"I guess we can discuss trust after this conversation" and he rose and went back to his chair, "Sabina, what have we gotten ourselves into?"

She looked up and said, 'We'? 'We' haven't gotten ourselves into anything. I've gotten us into something and before this cruise is over, you and I are going to find a way to excise you from their little equation and you can finish your trip with confidence they won't be able to track you or follow you ever again. Whoever 'they' is" she finished.

"Woman do you always shelve and micromanage your emotions?"

"What do you mean?" He stared at her, "Seriously, what do you mean?" She sounded a little angry.

"When was the last time you bared your soul and loosed your tears?" he asked her gently.

"I never meant to break down. I embarrass myself when I allow my emotions to get the best of me." She was trying not to sniffle.

"What, because it makes you human, puts you on an equal footing with us poor mortals?"

"No, because I believe that if I can control my emotions, I can do a better job and use reason to solve my problems and not feelings. They betray you!"

she snapped.

{aha now we get to the root}

"How's that working for you so far?" he asked, chiding her.

She looked at him a few seconds, found a grin beginning to surface and responded, "Not so well."

"Let's look at this from the time I met you. I won't even get into what you were doing there unless it applies." He saw her expression, "Uh, Ok. It didn't start with that day did it?"

"Weeeeell, yes and no… I think." She got up and started walking around the room.

"What's the yes?"

"The 'yes' is I didn't have any idea I had interested anyone in what I was doing. I can usually sense some sort of eyes on me but I didn't catch anything out of the ordinary. When you showed up I thought it might be you. I had to worry about…" she looked chagrined.

"and the no?" He asked.

"Wha…? the 'no'? Oh, I said yes **and** no." he nodded.

"It seems we've been getting some reports of hacking our personnel files and I was one of the ones whose file was compromised. I should have followed up on it. I wanted to follow up on it but I was convinced it was just an aberration. Nothing else happened to alert me to any problems. That was over a week ago and it might not be connected."

"How much do you count on coincidence?" he asked.

"But why go to the lengths they've gone with you and me? Why not just get to me?" After a few seconds of thought, she answered herself, shocked, "You were never part of the problem." She almost shouted, "They didn't count on you being there! You're the X Factor here and it threw a wrench into their plans. If I was by myself…" she stopped. "Those two you saw…"

"If you were by yourself, anything could have been masked as an 'accident' and I would not be here, or possibly you either, working out this puzzle. Whatever they were after…" it was his turn to stop.

Unexpectedly there was a knock on the door to Sabina's room. They looked at each other and that feeling crept over both of them again. They were in sync, total sync. Sabina stopped pacing, went to the door with the chain still on and Helene was on the other side, "Hi folks, ready for dinner? Eugenie sent me here to see if you were up and ready. Dinner is in twenty."

"How fast can you get washed and dressed?" Sabina ask Rodane.

"A few more than ten…" he said. Sabina looked as if her wheels were turning and she lifted the chain and invited Helene in and asked her, "Remember last week when we realized that a significant number of personnel files were hacked?" Helene looked at her and then at Rodane.

"Yeees…?" Helene was hesitant.

"Don't worry, he's aware of our recent problems. Do you have any idea how many there were or where they're located? Who handled the hacked files?"

Helene said, "Why does that matter? It was all cleared up in what, a day? No more problems were detected. They were moved and the site was scrubbed."

"Who, Helene? It's important!" Helene looked from one to the other again. She searched their faces, made a decision and said, "Most likely Egan or Petrus. They're the ones in charge of investigative services and have the resources to do the search and scrub. Sabina, why? Why is he read in?" She looked at Rodane, "No insult intended."

"None taken," said Rodane.

"Someone turned that information over to a hostile site. That's the only explanation for anyone being able to track me, follow me, know where and why I was there." She stared at Helene.

"It could only be done from within, Helene, only inside." Helene thought that over.

Helene asked, "Now what?"

"Now we get ready for dinner even if we're late. We'll come back here after and send off some very interesting insights and information to…" she caught herself, looked at Rodane… "the team leaders and let them know how things are going. They can follow up with a lot less trouble than we could. Since there's nothing we can do to help, I plan on enjoying my cruise!

Rodane, can you be ready in ten? That will only have us miss the appetizer…" she smiled.

"Sure, quick shower and shave. Listen you two, if I pose a problem with your discussing of these…," he cleared his throat 'ahem' 'things,' I can let you handle all this on your own."

"Not a chance!" Sabina huffed. She looked straight at Helene, "He got attacked because of me. He was arrested because of me and he almost died in a fire because he needed to be 'silenced' and a loose end tied up."

Helene looked a little awed at Rodane , "In just two days? Man, you are one lucky son of a bitch! Huh!"

Sabina smiled, "Well, I want to make sure he is aware of most of what we discuss so he is prepared and forewarned if anything else develops. We need to find the 'who' that's involved and why and…" she glanced at Helene, "Rodane has a right to know whatever helps keep him safe as well as we do."

"Ladies," Rodane shook his head a little and left them there to go and shower.

It took him fifteen minutes to get ready. He showered and shaved under surprisingly hot water, found a tan shirt, dark slacks, a black belt and new loafers and socks to dress in. He brushed his hair, slapped some aftershave on and went to the adjoining door and tapped.

Sabina opened immediately and smiled at him. She leaned forward, "Mmm, you smell nice" and then blushed. "I mean… oh never mind! You smell nice!" and she laughed.

They left their rooms and went by elevator to level 4. Entering the dining hall, they saw Helene and Eugenie waiting and motioning them over. They had button-holed a table for four somehow, so privacy was assured and the noise level was made up of low voices, a low laugh here or there, tinkling glass and sharp sounds of silver and dishes being passed back and forth. Rodane and Sabina sat down to their places where a shrimp cocktail was waiting, sitting on their plates, with a side salad and separate dressing.

Sabina said, "I'm starved" and dug in.

Rodane joked, "You'll have to excuse her, she's had a very hectic day and her metabolism is going great guns right now."

Both girls exchanged a look and then told the two of them, "We've heard back from…" Pausing, Helene continued with a sidelong look at Rodane, "our team. They agree with your theory about an insider passing information. I have to tell you they have been thrown for a loop and everyone is on pins and needles now. We've created quite a stir."

"Well good!" Sabina said, "That will make them work harder and keep them on their toes. We shouldn't be the only ones to be going through this." she sounded satisfied.

"If you'll excuse me ladies, I'll be back in a minute." He rose, dropping his napkin and hurried off.

"Sabina, how can we talk about all this with him here?" Eugenie hissed, "He shouldn't be privy to all this information," she stared at Sabina.

Her color heightened, "Do you know what's happened here, Eugenie?" Sabina asked. She pointed in the direction Rodane had gone, "How would you feel if you were in his shoes and no one would help you understand or clue you in to what was going on? What would you feel or think of me if those things affected you directly and I tried to freeze you out?" Eugenie puffed out of breath, "I'd resent it and demand that you…'clue me in' as you say."

Sabina looked at Eugenie and Helene, "You two are sent to protect me. I get that. Now that includes Rodane as well. Actually he has been more assaulted here then I have. Whoever is after me… us… whatever, whoever, he has unwillingly been dragged into it. Except for our 'history'…," she used her fingers to quote the word, "and the names of those on the team we are a part of, he deserves to be kept alert and informed and...," she looked at Eugenie...," protected. Are we clear Eugenie?"

Eugenie nodded slowly, "Clear! So I get to be the one to babysit him?"

Sabina couldn't tell if that idea bothered her or she looked forward to it.

"Yes, but from a distance. Once we arrive in Capri we will be very busy meeting up and sharing our intel and discussing events but Rodane will be leaving on his own to do his job. I have no idea where he will go or what he plans on doing. You'll just have to wing it and call me if anything goes wrong or you get suspicious or sense something is off."

"Hush!" Helene spoke, "He's coming back. Let's talk later in my room, ok?" They all agreed 11 o'clock. "Ok?" "Yes," they said in unison.

"So, is everything settled girls? Can I stay now?" he was assessing their silence and they were speechless.

"See?" Sabina told them, "Like I said, he deserves to know." She smiled at Rodane and motioned him to his seat. After their very good dinner and dessert was finished and they lingered over coffee and brandy, all four of them went to their rooms and Rodane and Sabina both reached their key card toward their room at the same time. They looked over at each other, a thought passed and Rodane spoke to her,

"I'll be in the sitting room in a few minutes if you'd like to join me for a drink?" He waited for her answer.

"I'll have a scotch and water if you would order it, please?" He turned and went into his room.

{what the hell is going on here}

Rodane called down for a bottle of Jameson and two ice cream sundaes, used the bathroom, took off his shoes and answered the door to room service. It seemed as if they must have been waiting in the hall. He took it into the sitting area on a little cart. When Sabina came in she had removed her shoes and undone her hair. She saw the ice cream sundaes and exclaimed "My favorite! How did you... never mind, don't answer that. I'll be spooked for the night."

She took her drink and her ice cream to the deck and opened the door looking over her shoulder at him, "Join me?"

"Most definitely"

They moved to the two chairs on the deck and sat down, sipped their drinks, ate their ice cream and the silence was somehow comfortable and expected. The night was warm, the water was calm and stars were waking up, dozens at a time in a clear sky.

"I guess we should continue our discussion where Eugenie called us to dinner." She sounded disappointed at her own idea.

"Well, we do need to get all this settled before we reach our port and go our own way. I'd like to know I'm leaving you in good hands and I'd also like to have my lingering doubts satisfied," She looked puzzled at him.

Rodane got up and went to the railing to look out at the water,

"You said earlier that you wanted to… I believe your phrase was 'excise me from their little equation'. Before you find yourself trying not to lie to me, I'll tell you that I believe you may be aware of who 'they' might be, maybe not exactly, but a general idea. If I'm wrong, then we're both in the dark. If I'm right, please don't insult me by not telling me the truth. Remember Sabina, forearmed is forewarned," He kept his back to her.

A long, pregnant pause ensued then he heard her chair scrape and she was beside him at the railing. He turned and faced her and she looked up at him and said, "I'll tell you as much as I can. I can't tell you everything because… well, it's a contract and a promise and too much to absorb at once but I will give you…," she crossed her chest, "my solemn promise to give you all the information you need to understand my position, my job and to help keep you out of any more incidents and keep you safe. That's what I can do, but no more."

She stopped, looked long at him and placed her hand on his cheek, "If that's not enough, then let's call it a night," She spoke softly "…and when we reach Piraeus or Capri you can be on your own way and me on mine."

He leaned down and touched his lips to hers. It was soft, gentle and only lasted a few seconds but fire built through both of them and he could feel her pulse as she could feel the heat from his face. They both stepped back at the same time and took a breath.

Finally Rodane broke the silence, "Would you let me see the tool you dug from the ruins, just for a minute?" He was hesitant to ask anything else. She turned to the railing and peered into the darkness as if there were answers out there for someone, to give her permission. Then she spoke hesitantly, "I'll show you the tool if you tell me all about the little black box and the interrogation at police headquarters, all of it."

He led her back to her chair and then he sat and started with Captain Ignacio sending him to the station. He told her as much as he could remember about that next hour or so while they cared for his headache, his head wound, his puking and his in-n-out sleep. He really had little remembrance of who came in and out or how long. He told her about Sargent Acurus, his confrontation and messing with evidence as if it were tourist trinkets, described the black box and finished with the phone call from an unknown that got him released almost immediately.

"So it had a chip and it activated with motion but it was intact?"

"Yes, totally and that's when I knew it was a setup. It should have melted completely, right? Everything else in that room was incinerated and it would have been the first thing to burn if it was in the outlet. If it was really a smoking gun, even the dumbest cop would have treated it with extreme care and I would never have been allowed to get near it."

"Is that is all you can remember?"

"Yes I... wait!" Then he hesitated, "It's small, maybe nothing."

"Anything Rodane... no matter how small."

"When they discharged me or whatever you call it when they spring you, they gave me all my possessions back but there was something there that wasn't mine. I didn't say anything because I just wanted to get out of there and it wasn't anything important, or so I thought. Wait just a minute." He got up, left her there and went to his room. While he was gone she tried to calm herself but kept going back to that kiss on the deck. She put her fingers to her lips and drifted back to it. So short, so gentle yet so exciting.

{what do I want}

She wasn't naïve. She wasn't inexperienced. She had former lovers over the many years she had been working as a team locator and retriever but they were sought after encounters, expected, mutual. They lasted for days, maybe weeks, never longer than that. This felt different, it felt... real like it was not a choice but an event unforeseen, unexpected and she wouldn't have sought him out if they had met on the street or in the hotel or... anywhere... Would she?

Yet somewhere inside, she felt a pull, almost a déjà vu, of synchronicity that couldn't be denied and one she had experienced only once before when she was thirteen, the last time she was with her own family. She covered her face and heaved a shudder that covered her body,

"Sabina are you okay? What's wrong?" He was there at her side, kneeling in front of her, his hand on her arm, tense, gripping,

"I'm okay." She took her hand away, "I'm fine, just a little tired...very stressed, and... that's it. A good night's sleep will do me a world of good."

He rose and went to his seat. He looked at her intently then pulled out something and slid it across to her. It was a keychain without a key. It was gold, had a short chain and a five-sided cap at the end with an embossed bird on the front and on the back, a lightning bolt. At the end of the chain was a triangular piece of metal but he didn't recognize it. He looked up and saw shock on her face, pure and intense.

"You know this? What, you recognize this Sabina?" When she didn't answer him he reached over and gently took the keychain from her hand.

"Would you talk to me?" Rodane pleaded. Her face had lost color and her hands were trembling.

She looked up pleading, "Rodane, I know we made a deal but I have to go see Eugenie and Helene. I promise I'll show you the piece I dug out of Akrotiri, I swear!" Then she saw his face shut down, "But this has to be shared now and I can't explain it to you. I will, but not now." She grabbed him, planted her lips on his, hard, moved into the kiss and felt him harden against her. Then she let go, held out her hand for the keychain and finally spoke one word, "Please"

It held longing, sorrow, regret… and he handed it over to her and she left the room and shut the door gently. He stood there for a minute, maybe two and went out to the deck with the Jameson bottle in one hand and his glass in the other. He sat down and poured a drink and stared out at the black night with myriad stars gleaming down and the whooshing sound of a behemoth moving swiftly through the waters. Then he took a big swallow while staring up at the star-filled, dazzling heavens.

Chapter 11

Jewel of the Seas, Late Evening

Eugenie and Helene were finally settling in for the night. They were both ready for bed, each sipping a glass of Merlot at the small table in their room. Eugenie had described the suite Rodane and Sabina were occupying and bemoaning the injustice of it all, "You should see the sitting area, all soft, squishy pillows, plush sofa. I bet you could even sleep on it. Enough room for a party" she finished, looking around their room. They talked over the day; Helene's trip to the airport, their boarding the ship, their dinner together. Eugenie told her about their shopping trip and 'Bellboy' and got a few laughs from Helene for her description of him and his help. They spent some time discussing Rodane's role in all these events that had occurred in such a short time and his and Sabina's growing connection to each other. They both admitted to some unease in allowing him into their conversations when there was a knock at their door. A ship steward stood outside the door, holding a manila envelope.

"Bonasera, Signoras. Scusi, my being so late to deliver this to you but I was instructed to bring it immediately and even wake you." He was sweating and agitated and they were sure it was because he was worried about disturbing them this late in the evening. Eugenie looked at the clock… almost 11:15.

"Not to worry my friend, it's all good."

"Grazia Signora, Grazia!" and handed them the envelope. "The Captain said to tell you… he took this message himself and printed it out and placed it in this envelope. No one else has access to his quarters Signora," he looked expectantly at them. Helene placed $2 in Euros in his hand. He nodded and left. As they were about to close the door Eugenie said, "Sabina was supposed to be here at eleven. Should we go to her room and see if she's still coming?"

Helene raised her eyebrows at her. They looked at each other and burst out laughing, "Maybe not" Eugenie choked out. Just then the second door down opened and Sabina came out almost at a run.

Helene hurried to her, "What's the matter, did he…" she started toward Sabina's sitting room, fists clenched.

"No!" Sabina grabbed her arm, "He didn't do anything. Come here!" She dragged her toward their room where Eugenie stood at the door. Sabina actually pushed Helene in front of her. Eugenie followed them in and closed the door.

"Look!" Sabina spat out, "Look at this" and held the key ring up to both of them. It took a few seconds to register on both their faces then a very worried two ladies reached out for it. "Is this…" Eugenie began, "That can't be…" Helene began also.

Sabina said, "I just got it from Rodane. He went to his room to get it to show me and when he came back with it I…"

"Wait… Wait!" Eugenie was so agitated she had her hands on her head. "You're telling me that all along, Rodane has been…"

Sabina interrupted her, "No, that's not it. Listen to me! We were having a drink and telling each other our ideas and thoughts about what was going on here, about him being in jail and he said that we were in this together and I agreed and…"

"Sabina," Helene said, looking at Eugenie, "You're babbling and we need to know whether Rodane is…"

"That's just it!" She cried out, "He's not. It's not what you think. He's…" she stopped and took a deep breath. Helene took her by the arm and led her to the chairs. Eugenie sat on the bed and Helene spoke first, "Stop, Sabina. Take a breath, calm yourself. You need to slow down and gather your thoughts." They waited.

Sabina, after quite a few seconds of quiet breathing, looked at Eugenie, "Don't even think about confronting him over this." She held up the key chain, "Listen to how this got into my hand, " and proceeded to tell them everything she and Rodane…

{well almost everything}

had been talking about on their balcony, except for the promise to show him the wand.

{that stays between him and me}

"Then he came back with this," She held it up …"and I came right here with it." She let out a 'whoosh' as if she had just come up for air. Silence… silence that stretched for actual minutes while all three collected their thoughts and their bearings.

Eugenie spoke first, "And you're certain he has no idea what this is?" she asked gently.

"Yes!" Otherwise he would never have told me about it. You know that!" She looked at them both. Helene leaned over to Sabina and touched her hand. Sabina felt like she was a child getting a quiet lecture from a parent.

"Sabina, we were just talking about how you seem…" Helene hesitated, "so involved with Rodane, more so than we've ever seen you before. We're worried maybe this is perhaps a ploy… or diversion of his to gain your trust…"

Sabina cut in, "No, that's not it! It's definitely not!" when she saw the uncertainty on their faces. "You know me! We worked together for ages. You know I wouldn't fall for something like that…" and she stopped, uncertain herself now.

Eugenie spoke up, "Sabina, this is different than any reaction we've seen from you in other circumstances. We're not sure if your assessment of him is accurate or not but we're trying to protect ourselves here and avoid any entrapment. This business is more dangerous and complicated than anything we've done in a long time." She rose and began to pace the room talking and pacing as if it helped her put it in order.

"Okay, let's look at this logically. Rodane came on the scene while you were locating…" she looked up, saw Sabina put a 'thumbs up' and continued with a smile… **retrieving** a wand for us successfully?" She looked her query to Sabina and she nodded yes.

"… and you found him outside with a head wound he said had happened when someone hit him over the head but you saw no one. He followed you back because he said there were two people following you, who you also never saw," Sabina nodded her head slowly, almost unwillingly. "He was taken to jail after a fire broke out in his room but he was in your room so no one knows who set the fire or when." She paused, stopped in her pacing, "Stop me if anything I say rings a bell or gives off a sour note." She continued to pace, "He shows back up at the hotel and tells you he was released unexpectedly and then he agrees to go on this cruise with you when he was ready to walk out and continue his travels alone. You're discussing his jail time so to speak, and suddenly he remembers the black box timer and… that." She pointed to the keychain in Sabina's hand. "Then he goes and brings it to you and that's where we are."

She finished by sitting back on the bed and waiting for a response. "Except for this," Helene said, and held up the manila envelope that they had forgotten about.

"What's that?" Sabina asked. "We don't know," Helene spoke, "It just got delivered and then you came and we haven't even opened it up."

"Open it Helene…" Eugenie said, "Let's see what was so important about this being delivered at 11 o'clock at night."

Helene opened the envelope, flap tucked inside, pulled out one sheet and two pictures clipped together. Eugenie came over and looked over Helene's shoulder with Sabina looking over the other. One picture was of two people, a man and a woman walking down the street in Santorini. The man was tall, looked Middle Eastern or Mediterranean, had a beard and had his arm through the girl's, very possessively. Second picture was of the same two people in front of a low stone building, whether going in or coming out was not clear from the picture. The page was a rundown of all the information that they had gathered on these two from various sources and surveillance.

They read through all the notes written and then Helene took the pictures and went over to the light for a better look.

Sabina said, "Who sent these? How did this message get to the ship?"

Eugenie answered, "I don't know how it got here, except the steward said that the Captain got this and printed it in his private office. I have no idea who took these pictures or who sent them. Have we ever had this many mysteries to solve, this many unknowns to deal with? So many… I don't know, so many of everything all at once?" Sabina threw up her hands in frustration.

Helene yelled out, "Now I know where I've seen them!" They both jumped.

"I knew I had seen them somewhere before but I couldn't place them. He had no beard and I was in such a hurry, I hardly paid attention to anything around me but I remember thinking, 'He's so tall and she's so little'… you know, Mutt and Jeff!"

"Ok, where Helene? Solve at least one mystery!" Eugenie said.

"I took Rodane's car back to the rental lot at the airport. There was a couple returning their car ahead of me. They only had carry-ons and he struck me as 'subdued rage'. Don't know why I thought that but I did. The girl was kind of like Peter Pan's sidekick, you know? Or that's how I saw her, small, delicate but at the same time tough. I only saw them going toward the shuttle to the airport then I booked out of there to catch the bus back to the pier."

"Wow! And that was without any observation," Sabina kidded her, "Wonder whether you would have had their shoe sizes and her bra style if you had really studied them." Helene scrunched her face at Sabina and then stuck out her tongue.

They checked the document again. No names, no info about where and the pictures had no names either, or locations. No film stamp or date or time. It didn't give them much to go on but it was something more than they had before but for what?

"Girls" Eugenie said, "We need to touch base, you know that right? We're in over our heads here and our time is limited.

Sabina looked at them and said, "Before we do that I want to ask you if I can do one thing… just one!" when she saw their skepticism and they looked more than skeptical.

"You can be there. Actually, I need you to be there, to confirm my judgment."

They both said in unison, "What?"

She pointed to the pictures, "Those. I want to see his expression when I show him those people. I think I know but I want you there to substantiate it. Please?" She was plaintive but firm.

Helene looked at Eugenie, "She's kind of got a point. Hit him unexpectedly and see what pops out, so to speak." She grinned and Sabina hit her on the arm and looked to Eugenie for her decision. Eugenie studied both of them and then shook her head slightly.

Sabina's shoulders fell and Eugenie said, "I can't say I agree but… what the hell! It's three against one. Ok."

Sabina went over and hugged her.

Eugenie continued, "I still don't trust him but let's do this so we can check in with the boss."

They picked up the envelope, put everything into it, licked and sealed it closed where it had been opened before and they headed to Rodane's room. Sabina wasn't sure if he would be there or waiting for her in the sitting area.

They knocked, waited, knocked again. They looked at each other and then Sabina took her key card out, went to her door and they entered through her room. The sitting room door was open and Sabina put up a hand to stop them then walked into the room.

Rodane was still out on the deck, and she moved to it quietly.

"Glad to see you decided to return and I hope we can finish our conversation. Do your pals want to come in too?" Sabina looked behind her and put her hands in the air and raised her shoulders. Eugenie and Helene's eyes were wide with surprise. They usually moved like cats on the carpet.

"Hello Rodane," Eugenie spoke first, "Sorry to take up some of your evening."

"Hi Rodane," Helene said, "Mind if we join you for your nightcap?" Sabina raised her eyebrows. Helene was not known to drink on the job, ever.

"Sure ladies, hope you don't mind Jameson or there's more in the minibar" he pointed toward his room. Helene mouthed to Eugenie, "Minibar! He has a minibar!" and Helene looked positively green with envy and made a face.

Sabina stepped to the deck and looked at the bottle. It was three quarters full so she wasn't too worried he would be a little out of it. Both ladies declined to drink and Sabina said, "I'll have one, thanks."

Rodane got up from his chair and brought the bottle into the room. Sabina took her glass from the table and came to join him. The girls sat on the sofa and Rodane and Sabina took the chairs at the desk. He looked at Sabina for some sign, of what he wasn't sure but seemed content with what he saw. After pouring her a drink he said, "Do I get let in on your little revelation Sabina, or am I still incommunicado?"

She held out the envelope to him and said, "This came from the Captain while I was talking to them…" she motioned "and we wanted you to open it with us because we don't know what's in it or where it came from. We thought it might help us figure out what we're up against.

{all perfectly true just not in that order}

"You want me to open it?" Rodane asked skeptically, "Why me?"

"Wellll, you're working with us now, sort of" Helene said, "We want you to feel that we're in this together."

{friends close and enemies closer}

Rodane had a very twisted grin on his face but he took the envelope and slit it open with his finger. He pulled out the document and the pictures fell to the floor. He went to pick them up and his hand was stuck in mid-air.

"That's them!" He exclaimed.

"That's who?" Eugenie asked, eying him closely.

"That's the couple who were in the hotel and coming back the first time I drove to the ruins. They were the ones arguing in the parking lot over Sabina." He was talking faster and faster, "Where did you get these? Who are they?" He looked at all three and swept his eyes from one to the other,

"You saw these already didn't you?" He asked accusingly. "Never mind, don't answer that. I'm sure you have your reasons," he looked directly at Sabina.

"Did I pass your test?" He sounded dejected and disappointed.

"It wasn't her test Rodane, it was ours."

Eugenie added, "If it makes you feel better, Sabina was against our using this underhanded method and we convinced her," Sabina had a blush all the way to the tip of her ears again. Rodane looked at her, grinned and said "It does!" She looked confused and he added…"make me feel better."

He held one document out to Eugenie and she shook her head no.

"Read what it says and see if you make anything of it after reading it." Rodane took his time then looked up.

JOURNEY TO THE BLUE PLANET

"Seems the two people in the picture are one Tabor Doukas and Renata Kappos, origin unknown, residence unknown,

Last known assignment: Toronto Canada, June of 2016. Destination as of August 15th 2019, Capo de Chino airport, arrival August 16th 2019 8 a.m. Further destination: unknown, employer unknown, addendum, possibly Western Europe. Multi-millionaire access, diverse network of interest to MI6 and other agencies connected to banking and munitions sales.

"This is all we got?" he asked.

Helene noticed how he said 'we' to include himself in the team. She smiled inwardly. Eugenie took the document and read over it again. Then she told them,

"Folks, hate to break up this wonderful evening but I'm bushed and we get into Piraeus early tomorrow. We're booked overnight in the city for the festival celebration and the ship leaves the next morning at eight. I'm for getting some sleep tonight and taking this up in the morning. What say you?" She looked at the three of them.

"Yeah, I'm beat" Sabina said, "Maybe we can put in a call to..." she caught herself..."our bosses, and let them know we are ok and give them some idea of when and where we'll meet?"

She looked at Rodane, "We have some business to complete with our team and you have your work to do also, Rodane. "

He knew they were up to something but he was exhausted and that three hour nap was a long time ago. He could use a good night's sleep. Let them play out their act and he would play catch up tomorrow. He went to his room and the three others into Sabina's room and closed the door. He was tempted. It wouldn't be too hard to listen at the door.

{like a girl no, go to sleep}

H shut his door and locked it and got ready for sleep, "Whoops! I almost forgot!"

The time difference would make Virginia about three or four in the afternoon. He took out his phone and dialed an International number. She picked up, "Hello?"

"Caroline, it's Rodane" he said.

"I know your voice, you don't have to announce it!" she snapped.

"Well...and a good afternoon to you, too."

"Sophia's not here. She had a playdate with a friend and had to be there at four. We couldn't wait for you to call or know if you would" a note of accusation in her voice.

{of course it's my fault a play date was more important instead of my call}

"Yeah, I told her I would call today at four and I'm doing it." Pause...,"You there?"

"Of course, I'm here. "You're ten minutes late" as if that would explain why she took her early. He wasn't going to argue. She was too good at dragging him into a useless argument. This was one time he wouldn't bite.

"Thanks Caroline. Tell Sophia, I'll call tomorrow at four. She'll be home?"

"Yes, or sticking pretty close to home. I'll tell her."

He was ready to hang up but she said, "Rodane?"

"Yes?" He waited.

"Nothing…just…jumpy, it's nothing." He could tell by her hesitation and tone it was something.

"What is it? Is something wrong with Sophia?"

"No" Caroline said, "She's fine. We had a burglary in the neighborhood. Well, a break in but nothing was taken. Just jittery I guess!"

"Where was this Caroline?" Rodane tensed up without even realizing.

"Next door actually and during the day. Can you imagine that?" Probably kids looking for drugs."

"You said nothing was missing? Were the police called?"

Exasperated, Caroline said, "Of course the police were called Rodane. What do you think? We live in a very nice neighborhood and we certainly want to make sure our houses are secure."

"To say nothing of your children, correct?"

Caroline used her sarcasm, "Like you're taking care of your women?" she said scathingly. He decided to ignore that remark.

"What did they say?" He moved to his deck.

"No prints, nothing to indicate how they got in, no one hurt, no valuables missing, blah blah blah! No idea why we pay all our damn homeowner's fees for nothing!"

"Caroline, the homeowner's fees have nothing to do with the police. They're a separate department and organization."

"Don't lecture me Rodane. I was just telling you because… I don't know why I was telling you. Well… it's because Sophia…" She paused.

"Sophia…what… Caroline?" Rodane gripped the phone tightly, "Caroline, tell me. I'm her father. I have a right to know."

{damn she has a way of pushing my buttons}

"Rodane calm down! You always get so overexcited about these things. That's why I don't…"

"Caroline" he said sweetly, slowly, "What… about… Sophia? Please?"

No need to get sarcastic" she replied, "Sophia has been jittery ever since the break- in two days ago and she even imagined two people were following her. I swear that child has your rampant imagination."

He felt an icy chill course up and down his spine and he shivered as if he had been immersed in a cold bath. He kept his tone as light as he could, "Why would she think that?"

"You know how a young girl's imagination can be. Well, I guess you wouldn't but Sophia told me she was noticing strangers in the neighborhood and they made her feel funny."

"Did you ask her what they looked like? Where they were... anything?"

"Rodane, you know as well as I do we have security gates and security people at every entrance to this housing development. There's no way anyone could be driving or walking around here without someone noticing."

"So, it had to be someone from the neighborhood who broke in next door?"

{gotcha ms know it all}

"Drugs don't dismiss money or manners Rodane, but we'll find out, I'm sure of it. I have to run. I have an appointment in forty minutes and I need to pick up Sophia."

"Caroline, you don't let Sophia go all over the neighborhood alone, do you?"

"Rodane, I see no need for you to be questioning my parenting when I'm with her every day." Her sharp tone told him the conversation was over.

"Well please, don't dismiss her apprehension so easily is all I'm saying and keep an eye out for strangers."

"Ok, goodbye Rodane. I'll have Sophia here for tomorrow" Click! Call ended.

On board Jewel of the Seas, Midnight

The three women had gone to Eugenie and Helene's room to continue their discussion and make their call. They went over the information on the document one more time to try to figure out how any of this could affect Sabina or Rodane and then Sabina pulled out her pin. It seemed like liquid gold with a shimmer that made it appear as if it were moving. Helene and Eugenie pulled out their exact duplicate and all three placed their pins on the table adjoining each other and they magnetically moved together into one piece. Each pin hooked into the other and formed a triangular shape and the first point on each one began to glow a soft red. The red glow slowly turned white then all three began to blink, first separately and then in sync.

A hologram, standing about two feet in the air above the now joined pins, appeared with a woman's face looking at them in a halo image. Her face also shimmered and waved a little, settled into an oval-faced beauty with jet black hair and a stern look on flawless skin of a deeply tanned, bronzed body.

The face and the body were well-toned and sitting quietly at a small desk. She sat with relaxed hands folded together and spoke clearly, with a deep alto quality to her voice, "Sabina, Eugenie, Helene? She raised her eyebrows, "I take it this is very important," and she stressed the very.

"Suri, we've had a few days of very disturbing incidents. We've gotten some pictures and some very confusing information. We decided you needed to be contacted asap and perhaps even our Committee as well." Sabina looked to the other two and they nodded in agreement.

"Oh, you got the package that was sent to you? Good!" Suri looked to the side and spoke an aside to someone else.

"You sent the package!" Eugenie exclaimed.

"No, Quimby sent the package but we've been in touch. Seems we either have an in-house leak into our affairs or there is a concerted effort to crash our network, very disturbing!"

Sabina said, "Do you know all the events that we have been experiencing so we won't waste your time?"

"Well I know a lot but I would still like to hear from you what you think this started with and then what has happened since. Quimby sent Helene and Eugenie to you for help. Have there been any more confrontations? Are all of you okay?"

Sabina recounted her story from the beginning and when she got to Rodane's unknown assailants Suri interrupted, "We can be pretty sure it was one of the couple you have pics of who probably carried that out, very stupid on their part. It only alerted us to their threat level.

"Tell me Sabina" she asked, "was it Rodane's request to come to your room after the attack on you or was it your idea?"

"He wasn't in any condition to argue with me about that. He was hit pretty hard. Actually, he was diagnosed with a mild to moderate concussion by the jail doctor and right after the attack, I had taken charge for a little. That's how I got my information about him. After he was released, we hashed out the facts until we had a better picture of who and what. That was me leading that discussion by the way."

"So... we know he wasn't playing you and he seems to be legitimate from everything we've learned about him. Egan says he's very well respected in his field and well known for his methods and results." Suri sounded satisfied.

"We think he needs to be kept watch over for the present... from a distance" she said.

"Eugenie and Helene...?" She turned to them, "You decide how to split your duties to cover both Sabina and Rodane until we figure out what's at stake here and how to get to the bottom of it all. If you need reinforcements, let me know."

She said to the three, "Pin me tomorrow and we'll continue this and you can get your work done. Till then, if anything else occurs, call immediately. Goodnight girls, sleep well," and she winked out. They released the common pin, took each one of the three separate ones back and each went to their beds for the night.

Chapter 12

In Flight and on the Sea

The flight from Santorini to Naples was long, boring and uncomfortable. Whoever decided that airlines had to deduct seating space, increase price for said smaller space and then charge extra for each bag that you could no longer fit under your smaller seat was probably flying on a private jet wherever they had need to travel. They most likely were reclining in their leather seats with a private stewardess who served cold drinks or meals and soft pillows and warm blankets. They had their own schedule, didn't need to worry about transportation from airport to hotel or whether the weather would cooperate either before or after they landed.

Renata sat very still. The airplane let down the wheels and the stewardesses and stewards were preparing for landing, rolling carts to the back, collecting trash from drinks and snacks, if you call ten peanuts and eight pretzels a snack, and moving up and down the aisles making sure seats and tray tables were in place, checking to be sure all electronic devices were turned off.

She had her phone under her jacket and was hoping the stewardess would move to the front so she could do her messaging. Tabor was sleeping even after he had to raise his seat and was giving out snorts and sniffles for one third of the trip. Annoying yes, but she was grateful he was tired enough to be out while she made her move. Texting was harder when you had to sneak to type but easier than her having to talk to someone and have them hear her. She sat back and thought about their conversation during the flight. It was becoming very clear that with Tabor, she was in over her head for the first time. He was unpredictable, violent, impatient to the point of reckless, and extremely volatile to the very least criticism or perceived criticism. He had apologized twice for being so unreasonable before the flight and accusatory about her shutting him out. If truth be told, she had made arrangements and set up interviews with people who might be able to help them in Naples because the last few interviews Tabor had been in charge of had either led to leaks from their organization or injured contacts, two of which she knew for sure would never be able to work again.

How had things gone so wrong in the last few months? No, that wasn't true. This began after the death of the witness at the docks. It was like Tabor, realizing she had seen him murder that witness and then heard him laying his own evil curse on the dying man, had woken some vengeful force at work in him that grew with each assignment. Her place in all this was beginning to seem like the dartboard he could use to seek and find his target and take out his rage and almost maniacal need for complete control on someone close at hand. How convenient! His lover could be the focus of his evolving psychosis. Yes, it was convenient for him, but what about her? Could it just be her imagination that he was using her as a substitute for all of his wishes to act with total impunity and with no repercussions toward him? Was she his guinea pig to take the fall for his weaknesses and his unstable actions? Why now?

Then she thought back to when all this seemed to have started. Was it before he was aware of her presence while the witness was dying or even before that? She sometimes sensed not a jealousy but resentment toward her. When did that start? Was it always part of their partnership? If he resented her, why? It wasn't as if she didn't like working with him. She thought he was so good at what he did, street smart and strong, able to extract information from the hardest witness with finesse and charm. She told him often how impressed she was with his clever tactics and his cunning. What could he resent about her?

Yet she also saw a savagery, a cruel streak, and he seemed to revel in how far he could take it before his subject broke. Sometimes he had a look on his face of actual disappointment when they were easy to break, to give in and beg to be allowed to live. They would tell him anything at all, as long as he wouldn't hurt them anymore. He seemed deflated when it was too soon. Blood didn't bother him. Vomit and spittle weren't as disgusting to him as that voice that cried. The tone of whining and pleading outraged him more than when they refused to cry or when they looked at him with loathing and disgust.

The worst beating he had given one of these witnesses was when the man stared at him with no fear or anxiety, spoke softly to him and then turned his head to the side and refused to speak again. Tabor became like an enraged bull, charging the matador who challenged him and teased and prodded him into attack. He used every weapon near him to beat him senseless and bloody; a club, his fists, the tire iron from the trunk of the car they had moved him in. Afterwards he kept saying he 'brought it on himself', 'he brought it on himself' as if ignoring him had ignited some inner demon who must and will be recognized and paid attention to no matter what it took to gain that recognition.

This latest assignment was difficult because it was so unexpected and they had not prepared for the eventuality that it would not turn out as easily as the others. In only two days, Dr. Sabina Carter had, in his eyes, become his ultimate nemesis and he was bound and determined not only to retrieve what he was instructed to obtain but to take her down or make her pay for her obstruction of his planned success. The introduction of another person into the scenario only enraged him further. When they came to the ruins late that night after their dinner in the hotel, Renata expected him to change their plans when they saw a bicycle leaning against the wall and realized someone else was with her especially when they heard voices talking softly inside the room. When Tabor realized there was someone else involved and that Carter was not alone, a change came over his face that terrified her. It was as if he had gotten lucky and had been given a gift and opportunity to go on the attack and he had an actual fire in his eyes...

{always thought that was just hyperbole}

that frightened her more than the other times she had watched him out of control with others.

{I could let Theras know and this would end}

It was possible she would reach that point but not yet. For one thing it would be failure on her part and she was honest enough to know that was a very big part of trying to solve this on her own. She would also admit that she was scared of Tabor possibly finding out...

{somehow he always does}

and that would be far worse than simply being the cream to his rash, the medicine to his fever and admittedly the sex kitten to his rampant desires. Some mornings after he had taken her during one of his fevered outrages, she was bruised and aching with red welts that she covered with long sleeves and make up for bruised eyes. She was a smart woman.

{or I thought I was}

She knew she was allowing him to behave this way. Her physical training could have easily taken him down during one of those brutal sexual encounters. Shamefully, she admitted to herself, she was sometimes stirred and excited when their rough and tumble escapades led to higher and more debased acts that she hated and also responded to. If Theras ever discovered what she was involved with and what Tabor was subjecting her to, he would kill him slowly, painfully, joyfully. No, that wouldn't do.

The final reason for not ending this sorry state of their relationship was not self- preservation but a real emotional tie to this man. She wouldn't call it love, more like a 'misery loves company' relationship. They often cried in each other's arms after one of these recent events some called sex, others would call rape, or sadism or some evil takeover of human emotional acts to those of predatory animals. It always ended with his tears and promises over and over, the giving of gifts as a form of abject apology, the swearing it would be different, he would be kinder, she crying and asking him to love her, take care of her, forgive her failings.

Sitting in an airplane seat waiting to land, she realized her face was so hot it felt like fever.

{from shame or excitement?}

She no longer knew the difference. What she did know was this assignment was very complicated. She knew the police were investigating this whole affair and they had shown themselves to the public more than any other assignment they had ever done together. Would this be the event that would break them... break him... and in turn destroy her? Not if she could help it. She owed Tabor her loyalty and she was deeply, emotionally involved with him. She knew if she just thought ahead she could protect both of them from revealing themselves, protect him from himself and protect herself from serious injury or worse. She'd have to be smart, vigilant, calm and prepared.

Looking out the airplane window, she wiped some tears off her cheeks as if brushing her tired cheeks and eyes, took the phone from under the blanket, kept it low in her lap and typed in her request: Folio for one Rodane Arcos, visitor to Akrotiri, driving a small compact rental from August one and two in Santorini. Possible police report on one Arcos due to fire in Hotel Akrotiri, August 1st, Room 305, in company with Sabina Carter. Request background check, present employment and police report from officers involved. Send ASAP to this number/ classified eyes only, and secure. SN # 110283, Kappos / Doucas.

The steward was coming down the aisle so she turned it on to vibrate only, closed it down, covered it up and put it back into her bag at her feet,

"Madame, could I please ask you to put up your tray? We are about to land."

"Of course, thank you," She closed her eyes and waited for the wheels on the ground. She felt somewhat like they were about to be 'boots on the ground'. One big breath, as the wheels touched and brakes reverberated. Tabor reached over and took her hand in his.

Theras Gallo was in his office when the red button blinked. He picked up the phone and heard "Incoming request". There was a very dedicated, trustworthy system of communicating with all teams in the field. Usually, he had no contact with these communications unless he instructed the command center to report. There were some exceptions, and this was one of them. Generally, everything worked on the pyramid formation of levels of power, security clearances, need to know information, employee levels beginning with maintenance, moving to office staff, investigations, labs, teams of recovery and information and tech employees; Theras' staff, his Chief of staff, and finally Theras himself with his personal secretary knowing as much as he did, maybe more.

Some of these employees had been with him for decades, knew almost as much as he did about the inner workings of his small kingdom, were vetted every year whether they needed it or not. It seemed like a good idea because you never knew when someone could be used as leverage. He had much experience with those tactics himself. Someone might get greedy or have a personal grudge for one reason or another.

He found most were loyal, dedicated and circumspect about their jobs. He paid them well, gave them personal gifts for holidays and their birthdays and their children's births etc… most especially when they were your lover as well.

{pays to have an awesome personal secretary}

Aldora knew him better than anyone else, any other living person, but kept his secrets and his worries to herself. Many a crisis had been run by her because he trusted her judgement and she had repaid him by keeping up with everything that happened in his giant organization. He knew that some of the staff had given her the name of Medusa but he also knew that they respected her and better yet, feared her. He had no fear of her betraying his trust or being unfaithful because he trusted her with everything and she repaid in kind. Plus there were the gifts, the lavish home(s) a nice summer villa and whatever she might ask as far as favors, if it was in his power.

She took vacation days whenever she chose and never left him in the lurch even when she was not there. She ran a tight ship, kept his calendar free of useless requests and onerous businessmen who wanted favors or monetary rewards, sometimes for simply giving him tidbits of information that might or might not be helpful. She ran interference to keep his day light and his nights filled with love, laughter or a combination of both. He loved to watch her walk across the carpet to his desk, her long legs up to her neck, her mane of dark, chestnut hair, lustrous and cut to her shoulders in a soft wave, the piercing blue eyes that weighed and judged each person who tried to have access to him.

Power was an aphrodisiac to some but it could also be a weight around your neck if people saw you as their 'go to' guy or their well that would never go dry. She moved lithely to the desk, picked up the buzzing phone and handed it to him.

"Monsieur Gallo, we have received a request for a folio on an unknown subject from Renata Kappos and she asked for it asap. You left instructions for us to alert you for any of those requests."

"When did you receive it Tonio? Did she send it or did Tabor?"

"Sir, it came directly from Renata from the SN #. They were landing at the airport in Naples from their locator."

"Naples, are you sure?"

"Yes sir, the locator was fully charged and sending a strong signal. They land in approximately 3 minutes 40 seconds."

Theras laughed, "Approximately Tonio, really?"

"Yes sir" he said, and Theras laughed again, "Okay, who is the subject they are trying to get a folio for?" Theras looked at Aldora and she looked to him with raised eyebrows. A request for a folio was unusual while in the process of locating or retrieving. To do so could compromise an entire operation. This one was highly unusual.

"Who is the subject? Theras asked again after a long pause.

"One Rodane Arcos who is with Sabina Carter, the active individual we are following up on and observing. We seem to have lost a location for Dr. Carter at this time." Tonio cleared his throat.

"Aldora, get Acteon here, now!" He managed to add a quick, "please" to the order. She turned, left his office and closed the door. He talked to Tonio for two or three minutes about Sabina's trip and her known movements and told him to keep him apprised of any changes, no matter how small.

Acteon entered the office. He was an older man; tall, elegant, silver-haired, with a deep reddened scar traveling from his left eyebrow, across his nose and down to his chin on the right side of his face. It made him look like a seaworthy pirate except for the fact he was dressed to the nines in a silk suit that had to cost in the thousands. He came to the desk and waited for Theras to speak.

"Acteon, we've gotten a request from one of our operatives, Renata Kappos, for a folio to be gathered on an unknown subject."

"Yes sir, is there something of an emergency to this request?" He knew these matters were not generally handled by Theras himself, so there had to be something unusual here concerning this one.

Theras took a key from his ring, opened the drawer on the right bottom of his desk, rooted through the files and handed one to Acteon. He looked at Theras, stared at the file in his hands for a second and then opened it. His eyes registered surprise but as usual he kept his cool and calm, Here was a man Theras had known for decades and wanted at his back for whatever critical situation he might find himself caught in.

"Sir, this is a file on..." he looked up and caught Theras watching him, "I don't quite understand but it seems fate has decided to laugh at us once again."

{is that a twitch in the devils eye}

"Yes, it does indeed. Our young Rodane Arcos has appeared in the midst of one of our most sought-after retrievals in our long history together, Acteon. It seems we have not seen the last of our Rodane Arcos." He smiled as indulgently as he could, "Take that file and see that it is transmitted to Renata, asap. Make sure there is a copy put into our active files and then return that original to Aldora, please. One other thing..." he seemed to have an afterthought. He walked around the desk and stood at the window looking out at the parking lot. "Find out Rodane's present circumstances, update the folio and bring me the new information personally. Tell no one you're doing this and keep it between you and me. Then send the team to wherever Rodane's wife..." he started again "his ex-wife is now living and have them observe and send me an update. We will decide what we have to do to keep this active retrieval safe and still recoverable. I want two good people on this and by this afternoon, understand?"

"Yes sir, you'll get them. Do you want an hourly or daily update, sir?"

"We'll play it by ear, Acteon. Use your good judgement. I trust it."

"Thank you sir, I'm grateful for that after...," he stopped.

Theras waved his hand, "Water under the bridge Acteon, water under the bridge."

Acteon left quietly and a few minutes later Aldora came into the room, walked over to Theras still looking out the window and wrapped her arms around his waist and placed her hand on his chest. She spoke very softly to him, "Do you think it's wise to involve yourself in this personally? I won't let you...," he interrupted her.

"I appreciate your concern, I really do, and I know you are looking out for me, but... you don't let me do or not do anything..." He felt her body tense against him. He turned and then folded her into his arms,

"My dear, this has never been over. It has always stayed with me and it probably will until I die but I can still be an asset to my own company and I can definitely help out with this particular operation." She looked up at him, her face showing concern, care, and worry about him. He kissed her forehead softly, "Aldora, I'll be fine, I promise. There is a lot at stake here and I'll tread softly but my feet will follow this case and it will be resolved." She kissed him gently on the lips, then turned and left his office to continue her work. He looked after her with affection and satisfaction. She would always be there for him, he was sure.

He went to the corner cabinet and pulled out a key from his key ring with a tag attached. He opened the bottom drawer and took out a black box with a keypad on it. He thumbed the code into it and opened the box. Inside was another pin, an exact duplicate to the one Sabina Carter had as well as her entire team.

{does Rodane have one}

In a little more than two hours, two people left their condo in Manhattan in New York, got into their new BMW and started driving to Washington DC. There they would meet with an agent from Theras Gallo's company, be given all the files available to them and spend part of the night driving to Virginia and their next assignment. Finally, here was some action after an entire four months of boredom and inactivity. They were tired of the gym and movie theaters. Even too much exercise could be a negative. They had gotten the file from headquarters two hours ago and had a packed bag each, all ready for 'go'.

New York City

Zoe Martin drove the car out of the parking garage and let her long, blonde hair blow freely from the convertible they had just bought three months ago. Being inactive but with unlimited funds could be fun but even fun became mundane month after month. She was a small woman, slim and small boned with a thick head of natural blonde hair and hazel eyes on a pixie face. That down time allowed her to practice her art in Jiu Jitsu and Martial arts. She started with partners in the gym until most of them wouldn't work with her. They came off the most bruised, bleeding and sometimes broken. Her reputation had new members keeping their distance and old time members leery of ticking her off over some imagined insult. It seemed like she was always spoiling for a fight. Yet she possessed as well, a ready, quick mind and an incredible sense of detail.

Her loyalty to Lexus Fira, her partner, was well known and the males of the gym didn't try and flirt with her at all. That was after she had messed up a couple of them. They limped away licking their wounded pride and bandaging their actual wounds. Lexus, on the other hand, had no loyalty to her other than to carry out their assignments as early as possible and then receive his pay so he could go out and party. He had regular 'dates' where Zoe was relegated to going to movies, the mall, Rockefeller Center, a Broadway play, the United Nations Museum, Ground Zero… anywhere for three or four hours so Lexus could 'wind down' as he put it after they completed their work. Funny, because she was the one who did the paperwork and wrote out all the reports.

"You have a good way with words, Martin. It sounds better coming from you."

"Sure Fira, I got this!" She would go to her study, do all the necessary work, fax it to a security number for their team supervisor and then go to the online banking center and transfer the funds they had sent her and put them equally into their separate accounts.

They had more than enough money to travel, enjoy fast cars, fine things, and great restaurants but Lexus was cheap and stingy. So they spent their time in a second-rate condo unit, ate carryout and frozen dinners and she only shopped when he was on his 'dates'. However, she believed in her work, she obeyed Lexus' orders and saved her chafing irritation for the gym and took out her frustration on her sparring partners. But she was beginning to run out of candidates and it was no fun just working the punching bag and lifting weights on the mats without a partner. This new assignment looked interesting and if it took a few days of her time, then she was determined to take a few days without her partner and travel to Arizona to see her family.

It had been well over a year since she had seen any of them. She texted her mom, she emailed her friends when they sent her messages or jokes or forwarded something she might be interested in reading. She hadn't seen or talked to her brother in months and didn't know if he had gotten over his little tantrum from the last time she was in town.

It was a real drawback, having a policeman for a brother who was always giving her the third degree about her job or dating life, her cars and clothes, everything actually. Finally after one session during the July 4th parade when everyone was at the ranch for a barbecue, he had cornered her at the barn. The conversation had started out pleasantly enough but then, as usual, had turned to her new clothes, her expensive jewelry, yada yada yada. She had finally faced him. "Ducky…

{where did you come up with that name I'll have to find out}

your interrogation…it's enough. It's really getting tired and old when each time I see you I get the 3rd degree, like I'm a suspect in one of your investigations. Let me make it easy for you. I don't gamble. I don't do drugs. I don't smoke. I drink like any other normal person who isn't on one of the 12 steps. I don't go to church, I'm not married; I don't intend to be anytime soon. I'm not pregnant and I use birth control when I'm in the sack…"

She stopped when she saw his blush turn more and more red, then his eyes sparked and his cheeks puffed out while his lips became a thin line of anger. She folded her arms and then hated that she did so because it was a defensive move and she wanted to be the prosecutor here, not the defendant. She had lowered her voice and looked pleadingly at him,

"Ducky… she saw the distaste in his expression…"no, don't give me that look. You're my brother. That's all I've ever called you my entire life. Mom's the only one that calls you Anthony. I love you, I miss being around you but every time I come home we have the same damn conflict, the same argument and it ends the same way. You suspect me of some criminal activity. You hound me to be more open and I get pissed that you treat me like a child yet you won't accept that I am capable of living my own life and making my own way. It's a pretty good one at that," she finished.

Ducky, (Anthony) actually had tears in his eyes and he turned away, gathered himself together and then spoke, "Zoe, I'm sorry for this distance between us, truly I am but you're my little sister and I'm not sorry I worry about you or sense a …how do I say it…' he turned to her and continued, "a secret or evasive part of you that won't be open to me or even mom. You won't tell us who you work for, you won't bring your partner to meet us or even use his name when you even mention him and that's only when we bring it up. You're too thin, you come home exhausted with deep shadows under your eyes and you don't want to talk about any of it." He paused as if trying to decide whether to continue or not.

He shook his head like he was avoiding a mosquito then said, "I've looked online, trying to get a handle on your job or your boss or your partner and it's as if there is a black hole where you're concerned. Your friends are all from here, your condo is not listed, your phone number is…" he stopped when he looked up and saw her face, "No, it's not spying. Everything I have done is on open Internet access, available information to the public, to anyone who wants to look. I have never used my police powers to do this…," he petered out looking at her.

"How dare you! How dare you!" She yelled and the horse in the paddock jerked his head up and whinnied as he shook his mane, "I have nothing to be ashamed of…

{at least not yet}

I have a legitimate job that pays well and… Jesus Christ!" she yelled again, "It's none of your business what I do or who I work for or who I work with!"

She pushed her hands out when he took a step toward her, "No, don't touch me, unless you want to get hurt." She stood there breathing hard, hot and cold, then hot again, her pulse racing as if she had sparred with two combatants. She took two deep breaths and forced herself to unfist her fingers.

Whatever he saw in her face, he stopped, took a step back and spoke softly, "Zoe, what have you gotten yourself involved in? What work could you possibly be doing that doesn't allow you to talk about it to anyone…" his voice rose again for one second, maybe two.

She was tempted to tell him some, just some of her job and then she thought of the contract she had signed, the confidentiality clause, disclosure penalties if she broke it.

{I'm royally cooked here}

Her throat closed, her eyes filled up and she turned and started away, "Fuck this! Fuck you, and fuck your convoluted sense of fairness and justice! I'm done here! Mom can call me if there's an emergency and that's it. I'm out of this fucking place and away from you!" She stalked to her room, stuffed her things into her bag, threw her toiletries into her backpack and hauled ass out of there.

As she drove away, she looked in the rearview mirror and saw her mother standing at the kitchen door and her brother walking back from the barn. Her mother was wiping her hands on her apron, holding the screen door open and looking back and forth from Ducky to her moving car. That was the last picture Zoe had of her home and her family. She drove with tears running down her cheeks, her breath heaving and hiccupping with her sobs and her rage turning to grief with each tear that fell.

"Damn you all!" and she drove back to the airport and collected herself in the rental lot till she had a hold of her emotions and could go in and change her ticket to the first departure available back to New York and to her 'partner' Lexus.

Now here she was, crossing the George Washington Bridge heading for the I95 interstate, on their way to an assignment that would break the tedium and cure her ennui or at least she had hope. They were heading to DC to pick up files, talk to the agent supervising their assignment and he would send their reports to home base in France. They would be given their roles, their identifications, their reservations for plane or hotel and anything else he decided Zoe and Lexus would need to do the job.

They were to stay overnight in DC and drive to Virginia next day, into the condo that has been rented to them for as long as they had need of it.

She often wondered what the organization she worked for actually did with all the information they gathered. She often mused about fictitious jobs or positions her subjects had that focused the eye of her company on them. Some good guys, some bad guys… it was a kind of screenplay study to move her characters around until she really found out what they did, who they were, and then she stopped thinking about it. She didn't really want to know what these folks did to draw attention to themselves from her company. It couldn't be anything good. She wasn't dumb. She knew how to read and she saw their names in newspapers or magazines after their work was completed and it was never a positive thing. Lots of fraud indictments, illegal activities, jail sentences for various felonies, destroyed careers for sexual indiscretions, blown political careers for misuse of office... so many more she couldn't remember them all but definitely not good.

Then there were the ones who vanished or were suspected of absconding with stolen funds, those whose disappearance was investigated, then after a time the interest waned, their names disappeared as well as them, never to be renewed or revisited. Some were found in ponds, cars upended in lakes, suicide attempts washed up on a beach, under piers, in seedy hotel rooms, after not being heard from for days or weeks, in refrigerators at the dump, in dumpsters at restaurants, alleys..."

{stop this}

She shook herself with a shiver that reached to her scalp, "What is it?" Lexus asked. "You ok? Want me to drive for a while?" She came to complete consciousness and realized they were going through New Jersey, in their warehouse district, with her on autopilot in the car. She would not second guess her job or her company.

{damn you Ducky for putting these doubts in my mind}

"No, I'm fine. How about you take over after we stop for something to eat and get gas?"

"Is something bothering you?" Lexus asked. He looked at her carefully, "You're awfully quiet with this assignment. Anything I should know or be aware of?"

She managed to smile but kept her eyes forward, "No, I'm fine, really. I'm looking forward to getting out and doing something. The last four months have made me itchy and I guess this is just what the doctor ordered."

"The doctor says, get laid!" Lexus laughed, "Cures all ills, solves all problems, works for me!"

Zoe found herself laughing despite her tension, "Well, your 'dates' may satisfy you and I'm glad, but I don't think any of your 'dates' could help me out here. I'm not some social butterfly who has loads of offers and attention."

Lexus grinned, "Never know until you try. My dates are energetic, athletic, and we enjoy lively 'get-togethers', fine conversation, good food and of course, good sex."

Zoe said, "Well, your dates are very handsome and I understand from the ones I have met they can be interested in both sexes. No inequality there but I don't think I would be comfortable with that, no offense."

"None taken" Lexus said, "Different strokes for different folks" he quipped.

"My background is quite traditional and it's taken me a lot of time to loosen up and cut ties with a lot of ultra-conventional ideas and habits," Zoe blushed with the admission.

"You're from where, exactly" Lexus asked disarmingly.

{uh uh I'm not going there}

"We moved all over the states from East coast to West and we've lived in just about all the western states, what about you?" She glanced at him, "Where do you hail from? I remember you talking once about loving the idea of moving back to the ocean, East coast or West?"

"Both," Lexus said, as if that settled it.

It was obvious that neither wanted to get into personal histories or backgrounds. Lexus turned on the radio and tuned to a soft jazz station. After running through the channels more than once he proceeded to doze off and Zoe, left to her thoughts, paid more attention to the road.

They stopped at the Maryland House to get gas and to get some sandwiches and chips that they ate on the way as they drove through Maryland down I-95 and passed a large mall called White Marsh. Zoe looked around them and was pleased at the mix of urban areas with all the over and under passes, next to suburban development and open space. The houses were middle class cookie cutter, two story homes, with noise walls built in front of them on the highway to cut the noise level from the constant moving traffic.

Lexus was now driving and he would mutter under his breath with all the stop and start. The sun's glare from the reflection off windshields and windows was horrific for seeing the road clearly. Anytime a police car was spotted, all the brake lights went on while everyone slowed down. Then they got past and cars sped up again and the road opened up a little. Once they left the city limits and went through tunnels under their harbor, with Baltimore high rise buildings off to the right across the harbor, the road was smooth and they made very good time moving toward DC. Another hour took them to DC and they used GPS to get them to DuPont Circle. They found a parking lot and

{jesus $10 an hour for a lousy parking space}

...they got a phone call to meet at one of the condo high rises that surrounded them.

They walked southwest to the Bristol House Apartments and pushed the number given to them and a buzzer sounded to let them in. They took the elevator to the second floor and knocked on the door of 212.

Lexus said, "Someone is viewing us through the peephole."

A door opened and a short, portly man opened the door. Zoe looked at him and realized that he was wearing a toupee and a fake goatee.

{oh good god a movie version of a spy movie Grade Z}

He moved to let them by and they entered the condo. He went over to the dining table and picked up two folders and a bag and handed each one a folder. The bag he gave to Zoe. He handed Lexus a set of keys,"These are the keys for this unit. There's one key there to the elevator that takes you to the garage and a parking space number is taped on the back. Have a nice day, lock up on your way out..." and he left, wearing a trench coat.

{in july shades of Peter Falk}

Lexus looked over at Zoe, "Why don't you go to the parking lot and bring the car over to the garage and I'll call for some take out and have it delivered. Chinese ok?"

They did know each other well. It always helped when their assignments got dicey and they had to make quicksilver decisions. They were eating their take out. Zoe loved her Kung Pao chicken and Lexus loved him some shrimp and beef with Chinese vegetables. They had the news on the TV and were reading through their folders and checking out their identity cards. Suddenly, Lexus jumped up and yelled,

"A classroom! A fucking classroom?"

"What?" Zoe said, "You mean with kids?"

"Yes, with kids, goddamn it! What else would it be with? I can't stand kids! They're snotty, whiny, they live in their own little clique world with… iPhones and… Twitter and… tablets and… I hate kids!" He got up and moved around the room, not able to even sit still. "What do you have?"

"Actually, nothing specific, just orders to follow with you and your actions, support and back up. Funny! This is the first time one of us hasn't had an actual role to play.

He was irate, "My teaching assignment is as a substitute teacher for a third grade class in a private school. Fuck! How do I do this? I've never been in a classroom with little kids since I was… a little kid! This sucks so much!" he looked at her.

"Want to switch jobs?" he grinned, "You be the teacher, I'll be your backup."

"She looked at him closely to see if he was serious. He seemed to be perfectly serious. She thought about it for all of three seconds.

"No way" she said, "I'm done school, both behind and in front of a desk.

This is your role Lexus. I'm there to support, so tell me what support you need."

"I need you in the classroom with me for support!" he yelled.

"Lexus, they're third graders! They're not monsters and they're not going to attack you. They're just kids for god sake! They still live in a fantasy world and play with Legos and Barbies. Get real! You can do this!"

{maybe not but I won't tell you that}

He walked, he wrung his hands, he actually sweated, "I can do this, I can do this." It was his new mantra, like the little train that could, "Okay, let's think this through. Our job is to get close to Caroline Arcos and her daughter Sophia. The idea is to get them to trust me and let me know what Sophia's dad is doing and where he is. When we find out all we can about Rodane Arcos we send a report immediately to base and get further instructions, should be easy."

"Lexus, have you ever found that when one says it should be easy, it generally turns out to be not only difficult but it has a way of biting you in the ass as a way of achieving Karma?"

"I'm teaching 3rd graders, like you said. How hard can it be? They're kids, I was a kid."

"Ok, Lexus let me ask you, what kind of third grader were you? Good, bad, ornery? Serious, inquiring minds want to know."

His mind did a flashback to Mrs. Reynolds, holding up his paper and telling the students, "This ladies and gentlemen, is how not to write a paper on self- reliance." She proceeded to read it aloud to the whole class. He sat there and listened to them snicker and a spitball hit him in the back of the neck from Bobby Acres, who sat behind him and kicked the seat all during class. He didn't remember getting up out of his seat or slamming into Bobby and pummeling him, until Mrs. Reynolds hauled him off by the collar of his shirt and dragged him to the principal's office where they proceeded to call his mother and have her come and get him for a three day suspension.

"I was a fair student but I managed to get myself into trouble because I wouldn't take any guff from anyone. As I got older, I learned how to make it through without teachers noticing me, so I made out ok."

"In other words, you were a trouble maker who managed to slide through without getting caught," she said.

"Well, that's one way to look at it. I prefer to call it 'gaming' the system."

"Then just put yourself back into the mind of an eight year old boy and apply your charm."

Lexus thought about that a little, "Let's hope this goes smoothly, I get the info we need and we can let home base know and get out of there quickly."

He looked over at her, "You stay behind the scenes but close by, so if there's something we need to do immediately, you'll be able to move and not draw attention to us. Let's figure out what we're going to do and have a timeline in place and try to stick to it."

"Look Lexus, I'm bushed. It's getting late and I still have a lot to digest here in this file. Let's say we go for a good night's sleep and we can start early tomorrow figuring out our game plan and then head for Virginia. We have plenty of time to scope out the neighborhood and the school before you report on Monday morning."

"Don't remind me!" he growled, she picked up her file and her things, giggling at his expression, "I get the master bedroom" she said, and he growled again, "Fine!"

Chapter 13

Jewel of the Seas early morning

Rodane awoke in the dark and had to lay there for a few seconds to get his bearings in the room. Sometimes when you are on the move constantly and staying in different places, you get disoriented upon waking up, not knowing where you are or even what day it is, which direction the bathroom is in, maybe even why you are there. It takes a minute for the brain to realign itself and bring you to the present moment. He felt sluggish, half-drugged and only the need to relieve himself made him get out of bed and head for the head. He snorted! These were the two longest days he could ever remember spending at once. Well, day three was here and he was bound and determined to get some answers before they left the ship at Naples and went their separate ways. He might not ever see Sabina Carter again but he was damned if he wouldn't get his answers before she left his life or he left hers, more to the point.

Her life was too dangerous, too hectic, and too mysterious. He had a revelation! He may not be prepared for being with and working with Dr. Carter but it was one of the most interesting encounters he had been introduced to in ages, if not ever. If he was being honest with himself, it had been a horrible two days, what with his assault, loss of his possessions, his concussion, the fire… but also the most exciting trip he had ever been on, bar none. She was the most mysterious, accomplished, curious, frustrating person he had met and he had found himself entertained, aroused, angry, confused, all the feelings he had put firmly aside for at least four years, probably longer.

Now he had to put these thoughts aside to finish in the bathroom. He took a quick shower and it cleared his head. He dressed in shorts and a tee, slipped into his flip flops and went to find some coffee. The elevator rode him to the fourth floor and the dining hall.

On the 5th floor, Helene and Eugenie knocked on Sabina's door quietly and she let them into her room and checked to see that Rodane's adjoining door was still closed. They took out their pins and connected them. In an instant, the halo formed around a hologram of Suri, the titular head of their family. She looked at them and smiled,

"Good morning! I hope all of you slept well?" They nodded and she continued, "Cruises never appealed to me. I decided after the first one I took, that a cruise was a floating hotel that got you from point A to point B. One advantage, or some could say disadvantage, was you had your choice of eating establishments. But to me, it always felt like you were going to the trough!" she chuckled, "Enjoy yours though. I do think you will get much more from yours than I did mine."

She cleared her throat, "Okay, how goes our Doctor Arcos? And what do all of you have planned for today?" she looked at Sabina.

"We leave the ship at 8 a.m. to go into Piraeus. They have a festival tonight so we're staying over and we board the ship tomorrow to go to Naples. We'll take the ferry to Capri and it should dock at the pier around 9 a.m. the next morning. We'll be in Capri around noon and…"

Suri interrupted, "We decided we can't afford to have many people around where we had previously rented a house to meet. We've decided it'll be better to distance ourselves from any crowds or groups where we can't recognize any one person and they could recognize one of us. When you get to the dock, get on the ferry. You'll be surrounded by Leander, Acacia, Nikos, Evangela and me. Without acknowledging each other, we'll get off the ferry, walk to the Funicular and purchase tickets. When you reach the top, go to the lift at the end of the palisade and take it to Ana Capri. You'll be at the Blue Grotto and there's an office with a large back room. We've arranged to make our way there, where we'll meet. It's a sort of museum and we'll be able to leave at intervals and make our way back to the ferry. Bring all your reports Sabina, and Eugenie and Helene, your report on Rodane." Sabina jerked her head to Helene and Eugenie, and saw them exchange looks and lower their heads in self-consciousness.

Apparently, Suri noticed as well, "Sabina, I'm aware of your position between trusting and suspecting our Dr. Arcos and I have instructed Helene and Eugenie to keep close eyes on Rodane Arcos to monitor his calls, observe his movements and watch who he interacts with. The council members felt it was wiser to learn about Dr. Arcos, than to invite him into the hen house, so to speak. All the coincidences may be just that but better safe than sorry. If we really can trust your Dr. Arcos…no need to raise your eyebrows Sabina, Helene and Eugenie have eyes and ears, dear. As I said, if we really can trust your Dr. Arcos, then we can expect to follow up on your request to test him and his DNA and satisfy your curiosity."

Sabina saw the other two raise their eyebrows at each other. She felt just a tinge of satisfaction at their surprise, "Thank you. It's an inconvenience I realize, but I have a feeling…" she paused, "Sabina, we all know about your feelings. Don't worry. I think we're all curious about Rodane Arcos at this point. It will benefit all of us." She had someone lean over to her and talk out of their hearing.

Then she turned back and said, "Okay, get some sun. We'll see you at the Blue Grotto. Enjoy your morning and your day. I always love their Festivals. They're very raucous, happy Bacchanalias." She smiled at all of them and cut the connection.

They stood up and Sabina opened the door and saw Rodane, sitting out on the deck with coffee and a tray. She nodded to the two women and they left quietly behind her. She stepped out onto the deck wearing her sleeping shorts and top.

"Good morning, Rodane." She looked at the dark sky, "Seems we're all early risers. Hope you slept well last night. You needed it."

"Morning" Rodane looked up at her, "I brought up some coffee from the dining hall and some bagels and cream cheese. Didn't know what you eat in the morning, just a guess."

"A great guess! Did you happen to…yes, cream and sugar. Thank you."

Rodane looked at her as she sat down, spread cream cheese on her bagel and emptied all the containers of cream and sugar into a cup,

"You like some coffee with your cream and sugar?" he asked sardonically.

She sipped at the hot beverage and sighed, "I needed a wake-up call."

"When I heard you ladies talking to someone in your room…

{aha I wasn't supposed to know that}

I thought maybe I didn't have enough for everyone, but here you are…" she looked at him without expression but her chin lifted, "and we have plenty." He drank his coffee black and still steaming.

"Uh, yes, we were on a conference call to a partner. She likes early calls."

"Conference call? Wow! You got some really strong phone service here. It sounded like she was right in the room with you." He watched her eyes and saw what he thought he would… subterfuge.

{not comfortable are you}

"Um…Yes, she talks very loudly." He noticed the fake laugh, "She must think phones need volume to be heard at great distances."

{okay I'll let you slide and add it to the list of questions}

"Sooo, what's the plan for today? Are Helene and Eugenie going to go

JOURNEY TO THE BLUE PLANET

with us? "There's a wonderful tour you might be interested in at…," Rodane cut in…

"…the Archaeological and Maritime Museum?" Her eyes widened when she spoke, "I guess I should realize I won't be able to surprise you with any activities we plan, huh?" One of my questions will be about your career," she smiled at him hesitantly.

"You are full of surprises, Sabina, and I can't wait for the next one," he watched her face take on a fine scowl. "I didn't mean that in a nasty way."

"Okay. After that, we have the whole day to tour and we thought we might hike up to the 'Bowling center at the top of the hill.'

"I guess you've already been there but I would love to visit…" this time she interrupted him, "Kastella on Profites Ilias! I love that place. It has such a view."

Her face fell when he said, "I was actually thinking of…" then he laughed and chided her, "No, I can't do it. I won't tease. That's exactly where I would like to go." They just stared, he at her gorgeous blue eyes, she into his sea turtle green eyes, lost in the moment as if spellbound. Both gave a little shake and tore their eyes away from each other. Sabina spoke first, "This is getting truly weird."

Rodane reached over and took her hand away from her coffee cup into his, "No, more like 'wired' Sabina. It's like, just remove the 'e' in the word and you have us and we are wired together, a synchronicity that exists between us that neither was looking for, seeking, or expecting. There's a lot more I could say about that but it will wait. You look like a frightened rabbit as it is." He dropped her hand and they both looked away to the sky.

The stars had been winking out one by one. She thought how far, how very many…

{thousands upon thousands actually but who really counts}

They were on the starboard side of the ship with a clear view of the horizon. They were facing north at the pier so they had to turn their heads a little to the right, to actually face east. They rose from their chairs and went to the railing. Rodane suddenly turned, startling Sabina, as this show began. She heard him running into his room and throwing things around. She thought to check if something was wrong but couldn't take her eyes off the burgeoning sunrise that had to be one of the prettiest she had ever seen in her recollection. The horizon was taking on a lighter sheen against the surface of a still dark sea and the colors were so subtly transforming from dull to iridescent pink. It changed before her eyes, becoming pearlescent, then darker shades blending with a pale blue above it and softer shades of orange then blended it all together.

Rodane came back with his camera, holding a wide angle lens in his hand and pushed it into her hand, "Here, hold this please. I need to change lenses." He almost pried the single lens off the camera. He tossed that into her free hand and grabbed the other one, rotating it into place. It changed before their eyes, and Rodane was snapping almost as fast as the colors were colliding. The look on his face, as she tore her eyes away from this living video, was intense, focused as the camera lens itself and rapt at what the lens showed his artist's eye. It was definitely an art to look at any view in front of you and see the whole, yet fixate on that one little point of interest that made for quality composition and integrity. Opposed to this were most novice camera holders who did a point and shoot. It was exactly like watching an artist capture a subject and then transfer the reality into a work of art on a canvas.

At this point, the sky was a miasma of color, cloudless, the sun peeking over the horizon. It was a brilliant amber color now, blending with the pinks, magentas, almost purple pieces of the rainbow of color. He lowered the camera and placed his free hand on her own, where she had clasped it to the railing. She was seldom overcome by emotional sunrises when she was not looking forward to the heat of the dig but toiling with each moment that light allowed her. Seldom if ever could she remember moments like these with someone else at her side, as transfixed as she was in watching it all unfold.

She looked down at his hand covering hers and then up at his face. The changing light had somehow caressed his face and left it glowing, yet with a faint shade of the fading pink as if a fire was gradually burning down to golden embers. He must have seen something of the same transfiguration in hers because he took in a little gasp of air and his eyes smoldered as well.

{can't do this}

She pulled her hand gently but firmly free and was sad to see the look of disappointment on his face, "I'm sorry, I don't mean to…,"

"It's ok" Rodane said, "I think we need to go and get ready to go landside, so to speak. I'll take a shower and meet you here if you like and we can get an early start on standing in line at the unloading site. Don't forget your passport," He turned and went into his room and closed the door. She felt…

{how do I feel hot and bothered or just hot}

She went to get ready, for anything. They met for breakfast an hour later after phoning each other to see if all were ready. It was only six thirty and most people were probably sleeping in at least a little, since they couldn't debark until eight. The buffet line was short, made up of mostly older people who had learned to rise early, travel slowly and turn in early as well. No children,

{thank the gods for no fussy babies or racing kids}
...and stewards were serving up omelets made to order, as well as dozens of trays and chafing dishes with as many choices as there were parts of a pig.

All four went to a table after they had gotten orange juice, grapefruit juice and tomato juice, then they went to get food. When they returned with their plates, they had a variety of fresh fruit, dry cereal, Western omelets, pancakes, bacon and yogurt. Helene and Eugenie were digging into the pancakes, stacked three together, with bacon on the side. Eugenie had a bowl of Raisin Bran flakes and had filled a bowl with fruit that they shared. When Rodane and Sabina sat down across from each other, Eugenie and Helene stopped eating and turned to look at them.

"What? Sabina said, and when they didn't speak she said, "What?" again. They looked at her plate and Rodane's and then Sabina looked and realized that she and Rodane had gone to different serving stations and come back with plates carrying exactly the same things on the same places of the plates. Both had omelets with extra veggies, two strips of bacon, home fries and wheat toast unbuttered.

Helene said, "That's weird."

In unison, without a second's hesitation they said, "No, wired!" then burst out laughing at each other. Helene and Eugenie exchanged glances, shrugged their shoulders and attacked their food. Rodane and Sabina did the same and they all proceeded to fill their bellies and enjoy the togetherness at the trough.

Over a second cup of coffee, they talked about their arrangements in Piraeus. Sabina informed the ladies that Rodane was fine with the museum and hiking to Profites Ilias. They all wanted to visit the dockyards of ancient Athens where the Greek warships, Triremes, had been guarded by the goddess, Artemis, for readiness for the War of Themistocles. All of them were up for meeting after dinner and going to the Festival together at Kerishakes Stadium before they visited the old warehouses and factories that had become the 'in' place to be for nightlife in Piraeus.

"If you guys don't want to go, I would like to see the Church of St Constantine and Helena, kind of appropriate, yes?"

Eugenie quipped, "I don't know... you're no saint!" Helene punched her in the arm.

Sabina said, "You know, I haven't been to one beach on my entire trip and the weather has been fantastic. I would like to spend some time, not a lot, soaking up some of that wonderful sunshine. Rodane, are you up for it? We bought you brand new swim trunks. Want to break them in?"

With that they left the dining hall and went back to their rooms until the

PA announced their departure on deck 1 and gave instructions for their return the next day by twelve p.m. sharp; reminders to have passports handy and protect valuables on shore and carrying a backpack for their stayover. They all showed up on deck around the same time and Rodane asked Helene, "What about our rooms for tonight? Are we on our own to book a reservation?"

"No, that's all taken care of. We all have separate rooms at the Hotel Profites Ilias up on the hill. Thought it would be nice to have a view of the harbor and the Saronic Gulf at Bowling Café. I've been here once before in the morning. Sunrises behind the ridge of Mount Hymettes are absolutely gorgeous on clear days. You'll love being away from the noise of the docks too if you want a peaceful night's rest."

After they had left their ship and entered town, they headed straight for the ticket office of the Archaeological Maritime Museum. Doors didn't open till nine but they purchased their tickets and walked a couple of blocks to the Piraeus Open Air Market in the center of town. Helene and Eugenie went off to buy some Greek pastries

{do they ever gain weight... not by the look of them}

…while Sabina and Rodane ambled along the thoroughfare, browsing at jewelry and little tourist trinkets. Rodane had his eyes on a small globe with a dolphin hanging above a wave and Piraeus printed on the front. He picked it up and furrowed his brow, "That would be perfect for Sophia."

Sabina said, "I know. It's just her style from all the pictures I saw." He put it back,

"Rodane, it's okay to spend the money you have. That's what it's for silly" at the look of surprise on his face, "Buy it numbnut! It's only five Euros."

"How did you…no, never mind. Guess I won't be able to surprise you with any of my ideas." They laughed.

Rodane said, "Does it seem to you that it's like weeks have passed since I found you at Akroitieri?"

She giggled, "I was hardly lost…" She looked at him…, "but I know what you mean. I think I know more about you in three days then I know about many members of my own family.

"Many members, how big is your family?" He looked over at an empty bench. "Care to join me?"

"Sure, but let's get a gelato first and we have plenty of time if you want to walk instead."

So they bought two gelatos after Rodane had purchased the globe for Sophia and they sauntered up and down the docks looking in windows closed till nine, and enjoying flying boats in the harbor; hovercraft that took small groups for rides around the harbor and skimmed above the water with air pressure similar to a Hydrofoil. Kids were running up and down the walkways, teenagers were hustling along bare-chested on skateboards and scooters and many couples were doing as they were, just taking in the sights, hand in hand or arms draped around bare shoulders.

As the sun climbed steadily in the clear Mediterranean sky, Sabina let out a sigh, "I've needed some down time for a while. Thank you."

"What are you thanking me for? I'm just the guy who you met spying on you who you had to play nurse to and take under your wing. Seems as if you got the short end of the deal."

She put her arm in his as they walked and gave him a look, the same blue eyes as the sky above them, "My wings are broad enough to handle a temporary adoption. Besides, you saved me a difficult time in the ruins and you definitely earned your keep by being arrested. It alerted all of us to a very dangerous situation with a few people we didn't know about and now we do, thanks to you. Now… if you think you owe me one, how about telling me about your career?" she looked down the pathway to see if Eugenie and Helene might be on their way, "Looks like we've got time"

They sat down on an empty bench right at the water's edge and he took a few seconds to gather his thoughts.

{how much and not enough to scare her off}

"My life isn't boring to me but I think some of my friends and family may feel differently. I was raised in Virginia, of Greek parents, have one sister who, by the way, you remind me of…" He stopped when she looked at him in surprise, "You both have the same topaz blue eyes and same pert chin, and a face that shows every expression of what you're thinking and your eyes show what you're feeling…"

{whoops maybe gave a little too much away there buddy boy}

He cleared his throat…, "Sooo, we were raised in a small community, went to local public schools and my dad would take me on trips with him when he went to buy for his business so I always remember traveling to many different places from a very early age."

"What did your dad do and your mother? It's okay if that's too personal…," she finished.

"No. Not at all. My dad was an importer-exporter and had a large business near Portsmouth on the water near the Navy dockyards. His warehouses were filled with antiquities and beautiful products of the people from all over the world and contacts in just about every Mediterranean, Asian, and Indian country I could name, as well as most of Eastern Europe."

"You must have been very comfortable as a family. That's not a criticism, just an observation."

"I did have a happy upbringing. I got an excellent education and I certainly learned a lot about the world and history with traveling all over. I wasn't spoiled... or at least I don't think I was. My mom made sure I had chores, didn't get everything I checked off in a catalog for Christmas and if I wanted to get something that my parents didn't want to buy for me, I had to pay for it myself, from either doing extra chores or used my own birthday and Christmas money or go without, teaching me some valuable lessons about want vs need."

"Your parents sound like very wise people who were more interested in giving you values and life lessons instead of things."

"Yeah," but then shook his head and a look of sorrow came over his face for just an instant, "I wish I had my dad longer to teach me more of those lessons but my mom did an awesome job by herself anyway."

"Did they divorce or..."

"No, my dad was killed when I was fourteen and my mom had a rough time taking over the business and trying to keep our home together for me and my sister."

Sabina laid a hand on his arm, "I'm so sorry. I know how difficult it is to lose someone at a young age that you respected and loved but never had a chance to finish growing up with them...," and something in her voice had him thinking she was talking from personal experience.

"Your mom, did she remarry or find someone to help her with your business?"

"There was family that stepped up and came over from Greece to sort through the books, take inventory, contact clients, that kind of thing. My mom is a very self-reliant, stubborn, but smart woman. Within six months, she had the business running smoothly and all the workers were still there with increases in pay, some with promotions. She has the most dedicated group of people I've ever seen to help her keep it all going...," He stopped and she turned to him, "What, something wrong?"

"No" he answered, "I just now, for the first time I'm aware of, never really thought about the fact that my mom was never given time to grieve on her own or come to terms with his death. I never saw her cry during that time or even now, if anything is mentioned about my dad. She had no chance to process his death or the aftermath. She was so busy holding everything and everyone else together..."

"Brooding..." Sabina said softly, "sometimes having that much to do to keep everything together is its own form of grieving. It's almost as if the memory of the one lost would dim if you didn't help keep it alive as he would if he were still here. Everyone grieves in their own way and their own time.

No one has the right to expect you to stick to a dedicated timeline as to what stage of grief you should be in at a certain time. Your mom was most likely using her work and her organization of the company as a way to get through, not only the death but the need to save the business and make it thrive to honor his memory as it were. There was also the need to protect and care for you and your sister. I'm sure you were going through your own grieving...," he nodded.

She continued, "How did you and your sister deal with your own grief and loss? How old was your sister?"

"Cassie is six years younger than me. She was eight at the time in third grade and she went into a tailspin. She became afraid of the dark, night lights in every room. She had nightmares for months, her school work was forgotten, she started with temper tantrums and acting out... it was a very hard time for her."

"Let me guess. You took her under your wing and it was you who was the only one she would listen to or open up to."

He asked, "How did you guess?"

"You're Big Brother correct? She's been looking up to you since she was born. Cassie is it?"

"Cassandra," he said, "but I couldn't say it when I was six and had four teeth missing so Cassie...,"

"That was cute. Why do you think she responded to you so well?"

"I think because I kind of became a sort of replacement for Dad. Besides, mom was so busy and each night she came home exhausted and she would almost fall asleep at the table so Cassie got used to me doing for her and being there after school. At night when she had her nightmares, her room was across from mine and she would come crying into my room when one woke her up or I would go to her so it wouldn't wake up Mom. We really helped each other."

"How so?" Sabina asked.

"As much as she needed me at that time, I also needed her. Having her depend on me so much and stepping up to care for her kept me from thinking so much of myself and my life and it helped me stay focused on all the daily things instead of obsessing on Dad's absence."

"Did you get a chance to grieve or deal with his death?" Sabina asked.

"Interesting thing about losing someone you spent so much time with is that in my case, I tried to take my dad's place by using my free time to throw myself into history and archaeology and artifacts found in all the places in the world where my dad traveled and places where our inventory came from. It made me feel closer to him when I was in the warehouse, examining and handling all the semi-precious and rare items we imported. When we shipped the items out to other countries, museums and collectors, I had a chance to study so that I learned so much about their provenance in cataloging them, packing them up and then studying the destinations they were bound for. I think it was the main ingredient in stirring my appetite for my field of study and my love of travel to all those places. Now that I'm trained as an expert in the field…"

"How could you do all that while you were in school and taking care of Cassie and day-to-day activities? That's quite a burden to take on."

"The 'taking care of Cassie' part was easy. I packed two lunches instead of one… cooked dinner for three instead of one…I went to school near her, the bus took her and I got home from my classes before her, so I got her off the bus. My mom hired someone to come in once a week to do the laundry, clean our rooms and do grocery shopping from a list."

"Yes, but you had your own schooling to attend to. Cassie needed time for homework and supervision. How was there enough time in a week to keep up with that?"

"Umm, I have what is known as an Eidetic memory," She raised her eyebrows. "It means…," he began.

"I know what it means. You are one of the rare few who can recall visual information like pages, license plates, books, visual maps in your head etc. But most adults do not have that ability after they begin to mature. It's usually found in young children and fades with time."

"Yeah," he sounded surprised at her obviously knowing about it. She saw his surprise and added, "I've only known one person with such a gift and it amazes me that you fit the bill since it's found in such a small segment of the entire population. Most people confuse it with photographic memory and it's far different." She saw him in a new light.

"You surprise me, you and your wealth of knowledge. No offense. Most people look at you weird when they find out that you're different, and then tend to either see you as a specimen or to be avoided."

"Which were you?" she asked.

"What? A specimen or avoided?"

Sabina rose and looked to her left, Rodane followed her eyes and saw Helene and Eugenie coming toward them, each carrying a bag and a drink in one hand, iced and frosted.

"Hi" Helene said. Eugenie looked at both of them and said, "Serious talk? We can leave for a little if you want…"

"No…" both said. Sabina said, "We were just talking about…" she stopped and looked at Rodane with a question in her eyes.

Rodane was quick to assure them, "It's okay, it's not like it's a secret or anything."

Eugenie raised her brows, "Then give, now!"

Sabina told them what Rodane had told her and ended with, "So we have a small, very small, segment of the population among us here." Impressed, they looked at each other and then back to Rodane. He looked at Sabina and they said together, "Specimen!" When Helene looked confused they all chuckled when it was explained and they finished their cold drinks and headed to the museum.

From nine until eleven, they roamed the halls and rooms of the two-story museum with its collection of excavation finds and antiquities dating back to the Mycenaean heyday, both of war and culture. One room led to another and they made a circuit of displays of commercial and military functions of the earliest days of Piraeus up to Roman times. They moved slowly through the reading and depiction of a highly developed economy using the marketplace and official supervisors with their accounting tools and remnants of their products.

Other rooms held naval history of the Triremes (warships) and various naval artifacts salvaged from wrecks. Two rooms held bronze statues uncovered from the harbor as late as 1959. Pottery, both whole ones and all in pieces, were everywhere. Rodane was caught and mesmerized by the Sepulchral masks, presented from classic art dating from 5th to 4th century BCE.

He turned to find Helene, Sabina and Eugenie, standing in front of the glass cases holding naval artifacts made of various metals. They were whispering, with heads together, from the look of it. They were not in accord for whatever conversation they were having and Eugenie was becoming more agitated by the moment. Helene saw Rodane looking at them and whatever sign she used, there was an instant cessation of words and they turned back to the case and proceeded to examine it.

{yeah right ladies fail}

Sabina walked over to him, "We're going to find the ladies room downstairs and then we're going to go and talk to a friend of ours in the labs. We'll be back at twelve. You could meet us at the entrance or we'll find you here if you're still browsing."

{okay I'll play}

"Sure, I'll just keep wandering and reading. This is fascinating stuff."

They left him and Rodane spent a couple of minutes at a case, actually studying the contents, then he quietly made his way to the stairs and moved down them to the hall at the bottom of the steps. He felt somewhat paranoid but this was open to everyone and part of the museum, so it was perfectly legitimate for him to be here. The silence however, was deafening and he heard a door close at the end of the hall. He passed laboratories that held thousands of pieces of metal, stone, leather and a room marked 'repository' which held archaeological finds still being catalogued and not ready for public view.

He started to go past it to the next room when he heard a familiar voice, "No" Helene said, "we haven't asked him and Sabina is certainly not going to. "Let sleeping dogs lie" is my motto. Besides, don't you think he would have by now?"

Sabina's voice was heard, "Helene, we've hardly had time to breathe much less have lengthy conversations that I've been avoiding the last three days."

A strange, male voice cut in abruptly, "Look, you're out of time here. This information needs to be extracted gently and without suspicion. If he decides you are holding out on him he'll most likely clam up and you won't get anything else out of him when he does have something to relay."

"Ok, can we talk tomorrow or even tonight?"

"Eugenie, you know where I'll be."

Rodane moved quickly and quietly to the stairs and had just reached them when he heard the door open. He spun and took two steps toward them and raised his voice a little, "There you are! I was beginning to think they had added you three to the laboratories for experimentation and cataloging. I'm starved, could we get something to eat?" Sabina gave him an intense glance but he was still able to look her in the eyes and smile,

"Sure," Helene said, "we could use something to eat, right Eugenie?"

They found a small eatery in the middle of a side street that offered Greek salads and Shish Kabobs. After eating, Helene and Eugenie decided to cover the downtown area in order to walk off lunch so Rodane and Sabina took their things to a local beach area, paid their fees, and put their things in a locker/combination bin, changed into their bathing suits and met at the gate of the beach. Sabina wore her thin cover up that she would wear for bed and Rodane came out in just his trunks and flip flops, carrying his sandals. They walked a short path to the beach where servers handed them towels, declining an umbrella but rented two lounge chairs and found a spot near the stone wall that separated this beach from a hotel's beach that was private on the other side.

Sabina carried a loose cloth bag that held sunscreen and a zippered pocket for change and little sundries. "Okay" she said, "I've waited for this since we took off on the cruise. Could you put some sunscreen on my back, please? I don't want to burn for the first day in the sun."

She handed him the lotion and he filled his palm and began to spread it across her shoulders and neck and down her back to the edge of her suit. It fit her nicely, very nicely, and he gently rubbed it onto her skin. He could only compare it to a baby's soft skin like his sister when she was a baby and his baby daughter. This was turning out to be a little different.

Her shoulders were slim yet muscled, the skin tone of a ripening nut and soft as that baby's bottom but he wasn't thinking of a bottom. He found his pulse climbing as well as the heat from his face and more heat wending its way into his lower regions. He knew he'd better finish this or he wouldn't be able to stand up in public.

"Okay, all done!" He went to relax on his lounge.

"It's your turn..." Sabina said, "No sunburn for you on this cruise. I don't want to hear you whining from your room or take care of you if you get sun poisoning." She proceeded and he endured. He seemed to remember other times like this, a few at the beginning of his marriage, but he soon forgot all of them by the time the end of it was near. The sun was close to zenith, and incredibly warm, but the coolness of the breeze from the bay was calming and soothing. Without even realizing they were drifting off, they dozed in the afternoon sun with hands brushing the soft sand below them.

Rodane woke up with his face pressed into the webs of the chair and drooling into the sand. He turned his head and saw Sabina sleeping lightly. In repose, she was more serene than a baby. Her face had a half smile on her partly opened lips. He wondered at her dreams and her memories, wrapped in sleep but held in the recesses of her mind when awake. He found himself hoping to find out enough about her in the next two days so he could remember for a lifetime. This would end too soon but he could relish the time they still had. She opened her eyes and looked directly into his.

His breath caught, she locked her eyes to his for a few seconds then got off the lounge and said, "I'm going to cool off. Coming?"

"Uh, not right this minute, maybe in a few." He watched her walk away toward the water and noticed her legs really did go almost up to her neck.

{not helping here roddy}

He waited, rolled over and breathed deeply for a couple of minutes and watched the flying dolphins out on the bay. He sat up and took in his surroundings; sun, sand, blue skies, people everywhere, and the Siren going into the water instead of out. He got up, threw his towel on the lounge and raced to the water just as she went up to her knees. He caught her by the arms and dragged her squealing into the wash and they tumbled together into the waves that they created.

For the next few minutes, they were kids, frolicking in the ocean, lake, gulf... whatever. Her squeals and his bellows had everyone around them looking and giggling at their antics. They reluctantly left the cooling water and returned to the chairs where they crashed in temporary exhaustion but enlivened by the sea. They stayed a half hour more then they dressed and found the ladies who were just returning from their visit to the Church of Constantine and Saint Helena.

They all agreed to go up to the hotel at the top of Profites Ilias, check into the hotel and then return to town for a tour of the docks and all the trendy shops on the promenade that stretched to the end. They headed to the walking path up the hill. Helene looked at Eugenie, Eugenie to Helene. They shook their heads yes and then started running up the roadway towards the top.

"They do that often?" Rodane asked.

"Yeah, they do. Now you know how they can eat constantly. I should be so lucky!" Sabina giggled,

"Hey, your metabolism is nothing to laugh at either."

They walked up the hill, entered the lobby and checked in at the hotel where they all had rooms with balconies, looking down to the harbor and the Saronic Gulf. It was a beautiful sight in the daytime, with full trees reaching branches out toward the finger of the harbor, surrounding a deep expanse of beautiful blue waters, warmed by the rays of a glorious sun. Sabina looked to her left as Rodane came out to his balcony with camera in hand. He smiled and shrugged at the camera, then started snapping. She looked out at the harbor, put her hands in front of her and said, "Kodak moment" and "Click!" He laughed, "I haven't heard that in a long time."

He walked over to her at the railing between them, "We left off our conversation. Did you want to hold off on more or did you want to continue?" Sabina thought for a moment, "Maybe a little if you're willing."

"My life is an open book," he said.

"Well, school was easy for you with your gift. Were you avoided or a specimen?"

"To answer your first question, yes, I did well in school. We had good teachers so I learned a lot in my high school years. We were close to the navy yards and not too far from the Naval Station so the families stationed there had parents that insisted on, and demanded, a good education for their kids. The standards were very strict and elevated from other schools in other counties."

"What about you as far as social? Did the kids know of your abilities and accept them?"

Rodane laughed, "I made out like a bandit."

"What do you mean?"

"When the kids found out about my 'memory' they offered to tap into it to take exams and write papers, and they offered a price to do that."

"You cheated for them!" she exclaimed.

"No, no!" he jumped in, "It was all perfectly legal and aboveboard. Some of the teachers told them if they wanted to pass or do better, they could learn a thing or two from me and get some hints as to how I connected the dots on tests to help them to develop cues and memory tools to accomplish some of the same results. So a group of them formed an after school study group with me to prepare for tests and to share ideas and notes on papers we were writing in different subject areas.

Their parents noticed right away the change in their study habits and more importantly, their grades. They insisted to the teachers that I be allowed payment since I was acting as a tutor so they thought I should be paid like one. They had a big meeting with the principal and even the school board was involved. The upshot was, I got two days a week tutorial pay for my study group and we worked around my schedule at home." He laughed again, "It was a win-win for everyone, including the teachers. Their test scores were climbing for entire classes, I was making good money..." he looked embarrassed, "for doing what came naturally without breaking a sweat, and my mom was at a point where she found more time to spend with Cassie so we all benefited."

"Well now, aren't you the crafty entrepreneur! Mind my asking how much you earned?"

"Well let's just say that my mom was great to let me keep it but there were rules. Until I turned eighteen, if I dipped into the account I had to tell her what the money was for. Her accountant kept track and I had to put a certain percentage directly into a savings account that was opened with me and my mom on it. Freshman year was hard for me because I was a kid and here was my chance to have anything I wanted." He saw her look, "Well, within reason. By my junior year, when I saw how that money was building up, it helped that I was a little more mature about it as well. When senior year came I had enough to pay for my books for the first two years of college and then some. But...," he looked flustered.

"What, you did something dumb?" she waited then grabbed his arm across the railing, "Tell me! What did you spend it on? Wait! Why don't you come over and we can get drinks and continue this."

"Didn't you want to go to the waterfront shops?"

"Oh, this is more interesting, believe me."

He vaulted over the railing and surprised the hell out of her, "I wasn't... but that wasn't what I was expecting. Do you ignore all doors?" He laughed and they went into her room. The mini-bar was filled but she hesitated to use it, "They charge you for all this," she said.

"Sabina" he said soothingly, "We have or I have, a lot of money left and we only have a few days on the cruise. Let's splurge!" She grinned and pulled out two small minis of red wine and they found two plastic cups and took them out to the small table and chairs on the balcony. They toasted each other and she sighed, "What did you spend it on?"

"My mom informed me that my college fund was already set up. My dad had started it when I was born so she suggested that I leave my fund there and let it build so that I could use it for further education down the road, or on a wedding… or a house… or… something sensible."

"And did you? Let it build?"

"Oy, vey, I wish!" He saw her look, "Okay, I spent it on a girl."

"That doesn't really surprise me," she half grinned.

"I was twenty, madly in love, trying to handle work at home, studying in school, a heavy load… and no time to spend with my girl. She was getting pissed and distant for that reason. She was gorgeous and the bees were buzzing around the hive and I was afraid she would walk. So I planned a birthday party for her and blew $1,000 on a back bar room, food and drink. I bought her diamond earrings and a week later, she left school married my roommate, and she was a mom in six months. There I was, no more money, no more girlfriend and no more roommate, although I did get some extra space in my room."

She chuckled, "I'm sorry, I didn't mean to laugh" and then she did break out in more laughter.

"You have to…," and she laughed harder, till she wiped her eyes from tears. He snickered himself, "Well, all in all, it was probably the best thing that could have happened. I learned quite a few lessons that day and it kept me single until I met my wife, years later. I was a daddy at twenty-eight."

The phone rang and Sabina picked it up and put on the speaker, "Hi, Eugenie, where are you guys?"

"We've been checking out the clubs and bars along the waterfront. We intend to go dancing and drinking tonight after the festival fireworks, you up for it?"

"I don't know…," she turned around and asked Rodane, "Are you up for it?"

Eugenie said, "I just said we were up for it."

"Not you," Sabina said, "Rodane."

"What? He's in your room?" Eugenie sounded excited.

"Mmm we're having a drink and just talking."

Rodane said, "Sure, I'm up for some fun time!"

Eugenie spoke, "Where are we going for dinner Sabina?" She started to answer and then she remembered, "What do you suggest?"

"There's a little restaurant off of Canal Street. It has a great menu and outside tables that are on the bay. Good prices too."

{she's made contact}

"Sure, what time?" she looked at Rodane and he nodded yes.

"Around 6:30?"

"Sounds good. See you then."

Rodane and Sabina talked a little longer, finished their wine and he left to go get showered and ready for dinner. Sabina also took a shower and after she got dressed, she called Eugenie, "What time tonight?"

"During dinner you leave to go to the restroom with Helene and I'll make sure Rodane doesn't follow. It's Nikos you're meeting and he has something for you as well. Take your purse with you to the bathroom."

"Got it, then what?"

Eugenie said, "We can enjoy the fireworks at the stadium and then go clubbing. After all, we go back to the boat tomorrow and you can sleep all you want."

"I'll try but I'm exhausted from sun and sand today."

"And Rodane?" Eugenie asked.

"No, not Rodane!" Sabina snapped, "We really were just talking, nothing else."

There was silence.

"Eugenie!" Sabina exclaimed.

Eugenie dragged it out, "Yeeeees?"

"I'm serious, that's all it was, honestly!"

"Well, then poor you. Mind if I cut in then? Never mind, don't answer that. See you at 6:15 here in the lobby, ok?"

They all met on time in the lobby and the hotel shuttle was called to take them down the hill to the restaurant. The sun was beginning to lower toward the horizon and by the time they were seated outside, Rodane had gotten some great shots of the sapphire sky, edged with a few clouds against the tip of an Umber horizon. The food was good; Greek salad, seafood fresh from that morning's fishing runs, pasta dishes with mushrooms and garlic, sauces hot and hotter, ouzo for Rodane, wine for the ladies. Sabina started her salad, looked at Helene and then got up from the table.

Helene said, "I'll go with you…" and rose also.

"Do ladies always have to go to the bathroom in pairs?" Rodane asked, smiling.

"Excuse me, the restroom beckons." Helene took her bag and they both headed to the back. Rodane was facing the harbor watching the last of the tour boats and ships come into the docks, filled with people hustling from boat to pier, from pier to the restaurant district.

Both women walked back toward the restroom and then turned right into a short hallway. Nikos was waiting for them in a back room with a small table and three easy chairs set around it with a bottle of red wine sitting on the crisp white tablecloth.

"Evening, Sabina…Helene." Nikos kissed them both on their cheeks and offered them a chair. "I thought we might have time for a glass of wine."

"We can't be gone too long or Rodane will begin to wonder. He's too curious by half" Helene said.

"Really" Nikos asked with raised brows, "Why do you think that is?"

Sabina answered by pulling out the leather cylindrical case and handed it across the table to him, "Because of this." Nikos picked it up, removed the metal wand from its covering and looked at it with a sigh and a look of gratitude.

"Thank the gods you recovered it. Thank you Sabina, successful as always."

"I wouldn't call this recovery completely successful," Sabina said.

"Why not?" Nikos asked.

Helene answered with a hint of frustration, "When I said he was too curious by half, it was an understatement. The worst part has been the aftermath of Sabina's recovery and Rodane Arcos is one hard man to keep in the dark or surprised. It's almost as if he's on our heels like a bloodhound, only a step or two behind Sabina. All of us are aware you can't pull the wool over his eyes easily, if at all."

Nikos thought for a second, "So fill me in from wherever you'd like."

They quickly told him about the cruise after Rodane had agreed to accompany Sabina as far as Naples and then they weren't sure what might be next.

Nikos listened attentively to their meeting and then remarked, "I've read your reports to Suri from the ruins at Akrotiri. Quite the dust up there. Lucky he's still with us, correct?"

"Yes and we don't think we're done yet but that may not be accurate. We just don't know." Helene rose, "I'll go back to give you a few more minutes and make excuses for you." she looked at Sabina, nodded to Nikos and started out of the room,

"Helene…" he said.

She turned at the door, "Yes sir"?

"I want you to split your duties so that while Sabina is still working, at least for this trip, one of you keeps track of Rodane until he has gone home by plane. Any idea when that could be?"

Helene spoke up before Sabina could answer, "He has until the end of August before he reports for his first class so at least another week, maybe less."

She saw the look of surprise on Sabina's face and said, "We have a report on him. It was necessary for us to know who we were dealing with, background and all." she saw that Sabina was annoyed.

"Look, I know you trust him and if it will help, Eugenie and I feel the same but precautions must be taken. You understand that, don't you Sabina?"

Sabina slowly shook her head, "Yes, I do but Nikos…" He looked over at her.

"I swear to you I don't get any sense that he is lying or probing for information or…"

"Sabina…" Helene said, "I'm not really sure about the probing part here."

"Okay, yeah…" Sabina said. "That's because of everything he's been through the last few days."

"You're sure about that?" Nikos asked, "Helene, see if you can buy us a few more minutes."

She left and Nikos asked, "What does he want Sabina, really?" She paused then said, "He saw the wand as I was digging it up." Nikos' eyes widened. "He knows it was dug from the Plinian level and he's an archaeologist so right away I was in trouble. He wants me to show it to him and answer his questions. I don't know any more about our hostiles than he does except I can guess why they're all on our trail. Now I don't want him involved but I don't know how to extricate myself."

Nikos sat back and joined his fingers, "I can't let you show him the wand, Sabina." He saw her begin to argue "No, that's a definite but I know you can come up with a satisfactory explanation to appease him…" and he added as an afterthought, "at least for the moment."

"What do you mean?"

"We're very intrigued by this Rodane of yours," He saw her fidgeting…, "Now, don't get hissy! For the moment, he's yours, at least till you dock in Naples. Then he's ours."

"What! What are you going to do, Nikos?" she was agitated, "He hasn't done anything wrong. All that happened was my fault!"

Nikos reached across and patted her hand like a parent, "Don't worry child, we're not going to harm him. We have some curiosity ourselves about this man and we'll be observing and watching him to see where it leads us, then we'll see. He'll be home by then and there won't be any reason to think he could be any more of a problem."

He reached into his briefcase and pulled out a file, "Keep this close and make sure he doesn't see the contents."

"You know… I'm beginning to get the feeling here that I've done something wrong and Rodane is a liability. I would hope the first is a miscommunication between us and the second is not the case," she was angry, her face was flushed.

"Sabina, for now just follow our directions and try hard not to find yourself in a difficult situation. We'll revisit this tomorrow." He rose as did she. She thrust the file into her bag, turned and left the room. He looked after her a moment, sighed and picked up the wand and locked it in his briefcase. He then changed his mind, sat down and poured another glass of wine.

Sabina returned to the table and sat down and put her bag under her feet. The other three were having a cup of expresso and they signaled to the server. He came to the table and she asked for a coffee and a shot of ouzo.

Rodane searched her face, "Everything ok?" he asked.

"Everything's fine! I'm enjoying being the tourist in Greece. Ouzo it is!" she lifted her chin and raised her glass.

"We'll have a good time tonight at the clubs" Helene reached under the table and squeezed her hand.

"I'm not sure I'm up for the clubs, girls," Sabina said. Eugenie kicked her under the table, "We need to party and dance! You'll feel fine after a drink or two." she glanced at Sabina with a smile, "You can sleep in tomorrow… couple of aspirin and your problems will all go away." she looked tellingly at Sabina.

Rodane watched her take a deep breath and let it out slowly. The flush on her face was fading and he could sense her edge softening. His girl ran deep and her emotions, so readily apparent, were now running at full speed, but she seemed to be gradually relaxing and become her more easygoing self.

{wonder who got under your skin my little wild cat}

They declined dessert and after paying the bill, headed to the Kerishakes stadium where the festival was just beginning. As they walked, the crowds thickened and expanded, more and more people pushing closer together to get through the gates. These festivals were free to the public but first come first seated. They slowly moved forward, heading for a row of bleachers that seemed more opportune. Rodane made a move towards Sabina's side but Eugenie came to his side and joined arms…, "Don't want to get separated. You mind?"

"Not at all, hang on!" He kept his eyes on Helene and Sabina up ahead. They turned to the left and the crowd was pushing them to the right. Suddenly a man in front of them stumbled and fell and the people around him moved to the sides to avoid stepping on him. Rodane found himself pushed to the left and then they were entering the stadium and climbing the bleachers. They saw Helene and Sabina waiting for them and pointing to empty seats next to them.

The evening lightened up and they enjoyed the spectacles; the lights, the costumes, all the shouting and singing, voices raised in local songs and the two bands entered and all their entourage, marching in perfect time to the music. Finally, the fireworks went off and there was twenty minutes of varied colors, explosions of white, pink, purple, blues and reds colliding together and spirals, circles, star-shaped sparklers, and layers of color after color.

The noise was intense, the 'oohs' and 'ahhs' were contagious. Walking out much slower than rushing in, they made their way down the main thoroughfare towards the storehouses that were renovated to accommodate the young people who wanted blare, beat and booze in any order. They were heading in the same direction as dozens of others when many of them went into a big open bar. They continued on to the next and finally a third that was somewhat less crowded but still had lots of dance beats and moving lights. They found a booth the size of a garden table where they all fit and it took fifteen minutes to get a server to bring them four drinks.

"Sabina, I have to leave for a few minutes to make a call. I won't be long but it's going on ten and I can't be late. I'll be right back." She looked at Eugenie who got up and followed him out.

Chapter 14

Virginia, Late Afternoon

Caroline put the dishes from breakfast into the dishwasher and turned to wipe off the table, leaning across it when two arms came around her from behind and one wrapped around her shoulders to prevent her moving and one clasped onto her left breast and squeezed. She took a breath, "Adam, Sophia is set to walk in this door in fifteen minutes and I don't think she would understand this position of your hands on privacy parts which I have stressed to her are always off limits to a boy."

He pushed against her so she had to use her hands to prop herself on the table. She found his hardness through her slacks and his hand went from her shoulders to under her shirt and his fingers dipped inside her bra and tweaked her nipple. She gasped and her breathing quickened, "We only need five minutes, maybe less…" and he breathed into her ear as he groped for her buttons and zipper. She used one hand to undo them while the other reached around her and touched his hardness. He moaned softly and pushed against her and she half lay across the kitchen table. She heard his zipper slide and then he pulled her pants and underwear down below her hips and he slid into her, wet and warm. His hands grasped both breasts and both felt the quickened heating up faster and faster. Her breathing rose faster as well and she felt herself melting into a liquid jelly. They both cried out at the same time as she heard the bus come down the road and brake to a stop. He lay over her back, his heart racing against her shoulder.

"Adam, get off! Sophia's coming, get off!" and she pushed him and he stumbled out of the room and into the powder room. She pulled her underwear and pants up and straightened her shirt just as Sophia came in the door and the phone rang at that same moment.

"Mama, phone's ringing!" She dropped her backpack and went to the fridge and pulled out an apple.

"Oh, my very smart daughter, with such excellent hearing!" she picked it up.

"Hello? Oh, it's you! No, just here doing dishes. No, no rush, just housekeeping. You know… that which keeps things going nicely?" she said snidely. She hiccupped and her mouth dropped open in shock at his next words.

"Mama, is that Daddy? Are you sniping again?" and she stood in front of her with her small hand on her hip, munching on her apple.

"Here" She thrust the phone into Sophia's hand and walked away to her bedroom and slammed the door. "Hi Daddy, how's it going?" she listened, "Where are you now?" She pulled up a chair at the table, "Who's with you on this tour? Three ladies? You must think you died and went to heaven! Just kidding! What, you think I don't know that stuff? No, we don't have sex in the third grade! Well dad, you know I have a computer, right? There's this thing called Google, you know?"

She listened for a few moments and they had a back and forth conversation about school, "Miss Cooper is going to be out for a few days, maybe more and we're getting a substitute teacher. I hate when that happens. They never know what they're doing. No, she didn't seem sick. She was upset when she left today. No, I heard her saying a trip wasn't in her budget but the principal told her it was all taken care of for a five day cruise to somewhere. Nope, she's going alone."

Sophia got up and threw the apple core into the recycle bin. She looked out the door "Funny! No, there's this green car that keeps going up and down the street. No, it was parked across the street up at Mrs. Miller's when the bus came then it drove up and down a couple times. Now it's parked down by the culvert. Yeah, mom's real jumpy about strangers in the neighborhood so I can't go around on my bike or even my scooter except up and down the street. It's so lame. No, the cops came by and said, 'nothing shows up Caroline, just make sure your door is securely locked and your windows too'. Like they can get through louver windows! Doofuses! Sorry, didn't mean to diss them. I know, I know, they protect us."

Caroline and Adam came out of the bedroom and Caroline sat across from Sophia. She talked softly into the phone and just listened. She finally looked at her mother and said, "Would you like to talk to Daddy?"

"No dear, I don't need to talk to Daddy." She smiled at her, "Do you want to listen to Daddy?" She spoke into the phone, "No, she's right here, listening to me talk to you." She smiled at her mother again.

Caroline stood up abruptly, her mouth a thin line of anger, "I'll be in the family room." She stomped off and Adam followed her. He grinned at Sophia on the way out and stuck up his thumb and whispered, "Well played!" Sophia grinned back at him.

"I'm good, Daddy, my bus driver lets us off almost right at the door. No I don't talk to anyone. No stranger danger, Daddy, honest! I wouldn't talk to a strange man... yeah... or woman. Ok." She stood up and went to the window, "Yeah, when will you call again? Okay, I'll make sure I'm home by then. Can we do Skype? That would be great! Sit in front of a window so I can see the place where you are. It makes me feel like I'm there, that's why. Yes, I love you too. Talk to you soon. Bye!"

Town of Piraeus

Rodane turned off his phone and walked back to Eugenie, "Hey," he said. "You my babysitter tonight?" He didn't sound annoyed, just curious. She looked at him, weighing her duties against her instincts. She decided to go with the gut. She had spent enough time with this man to think she could make a good judgment as to his honesty quotient.

"Yeah, don't want you getting hit in the head again by some nefarious characters." He looked surprised, "Yeah, Bucko, we want to make sure your head and your body stay connected and in good health. That's our job and for the next few days, you got it? You'll have to make the best of it."

"Anyone who would complain about three gorgeous ladies being at his beck and call needs to have his head examined. I've already had mine done so I'm down with it." He draped his arm over her shoulder and they went back to the club "You're alright Arcos, you're a good guy. I like the way you work."

"Well, thanks Genie. I like your moves too."

"Genie... where'd you get that?" she sounded surprised as she stopped and looked at him. He shrugged, "It kind of fits, you know? Eugenie...Genie."

"My dad was the only person who ever called me that" and she stopped and swallowed "It just struck a chord."

He threw his arm back over her shoulder and gave her a little hug, "Well now, there are two of us so get used to it...'Genie'. You'll have to make the best of it" and they both laughed.

All four of them made it to twelve o'clock then almost as one voice said, "I'm dead on my feet. I think it's time for the pumpkin to take her little pumpkin feet and make it to the hotel. The hell with partying, I'll take sleeping." Those were Helene's actual words but they all agreed with her and walked back up the hill to their rooms to turn in.

"See you in the morning folks" and the two ladies went into their room.

Sabina and Rodane looked at each other and she said, "A nightcap on the balcony?" He nodded and they went into their rooms. About twenty minutes later, she walked out to the balcony and Rodane was there sitting at the small table with two glasses and a bottle of red wine.

"Where did you get that?" she exclaimed.

"Ran down to the desk and paid him to break into the cellar." They were both changed into shorts and t-shirts, ready for bed. She looked out at the night time view of the Saronic Gulf. If the sunrise here was gorgeous, this time of night was enchanting. The view was of the town below them with hundreds of lights sparkling with a glimpse of far off Athens itself. They could see the dark outline of the Acropolis from here and the moon had a heavy glow that sent glimmers across the bay and you could see fish jumping in the shallows. It was a fairyland of light and music coming from below with everything coming together like a midnight painting. She gazed and felt herself relaxing and drifting into a state of drowsiness but every nerve of her body alive and speaking. She came to herself, got up and went to the railing and took a deep breath.

"It's okay, I feel the same if it makes you feel better. Nothing is going to happen that you don't want to happen." She turned to him, "How do you do that?"

"How do **we** do that?" He asked her. Confusion rolled across her face.

"I don't know and I wish we had more time to study it and unearth it but…"

He joined her at the railing and glanced out at the harbor. The breeze was gently ruffling her long, dark hair and he reached up to pull a few strands away from her face. He used that hand to cup her face and she leaned into him. Her lips were soft, pliable and responsive, so they went deeper. He searched for her, standing right in front of him and he found her, both minds reaching for each other in total synchronicity and connecting like a lightning bolt to the earth. She found herself folded into his arms and for a minute they were totally engrossed in the magic of lips touching, pressing, tongues tasting, seeking more heat and more connectivity. Her knees went weak and he held her tighter. She came to her senses faster than he did and she broke that connection and hated herself because she did.

She stepped back, "That's why we can't do this" she was out of breath as if she had been running. "We can't start a movement that only has one ending. I have no choices here, try as I might, to reconcile the feelings with the ending. This is too new, too confusing, too… complicated to let it take hold now, in this place, this time." Tears welled in her eyes and she turned back to the twinkling lights in town.

"Damn it! Where have you been Rodane Arcos?" she almost wailed. She gripped the railing with a strength that her weak body fought to regain, "Why now?"

She lifted her hands to the sky as if chastising the gods and the heavens. Rodane walked over to the table for their two glasses of wine, went and handed her one. They both took healthy swallows of the dry red wine and stood in silence for a moment.

Sabina broke it, "I have something to tell you and you won't like it" her look was almost pleading.

"Whatever happened in the back of the restaurant when you were gone so long, I'm sure your 'family' has come to some conclusions as to where we go from here or more to the point, where I go from here." He arched his brows at her.

"I'm not even going to try not to act surprised Rodane. They're still not sure of you so they're trying to ensure the safety of all of us, you included believe it or not."

"So let's say I get to Naples. It's 'Vaya con Dios' and I think all of this…" he spread his hands out, "goes away. I would imagine I don't get to meet your 'family' and I'm pretty sure most of the questions I wanted answers to are now off limits."

"Yes" she put her glass down, sat and put both hands between her knees, "Yes" she whispered,

"And your promise?" he asked.

"I'll try and answer any that I can but if I can't, I just hope you'll understand it's not my choice."

"Okay, then let's try this. I'll ask my questions and you answer the ones you can and for the ones you can't, just give me a 'pass'. He watched her face and she nodded 'yes'.

He gathered his thoughts, "What was the real reason you were at Akrotiri?" He examined her face and she felt like she was taking a lie detector test.

{tell as much of the truth as you can}

"We had word that a rare artifact had been located at Akrotieri and it was important to get our hands on it before an archaeological team came next week to start digging."

"What about that tool you had in the safe, your 'rare' artifact? How did you discover it at all?"

"We use Ground Penetrating Sonar and electromagnetic waves.

{that's just not all of it}

"We realized where it was, down to yards, so I had to do some digging."

"Okay, who do you work for? Who's 'we'?"

{here's where we go slowly}

"Rodane, my credentials are impeccable. I already told you I teach at UCLA as an adjunct and I'm well versed in Volcanology and Geology. I've been top of my field for years. I don't work for anyone. I am in charge of examining students who apply for grants and internships to help me investigate and uncover rare artifacts and remnants of ancient cultures and events."

"Well then, where would you take your 'ancient remnants and artifacts' when they are found too close to home?" She ignored the sarcasm, "I'll pass."

His eyes narrowed and he paused, then he continued, "If you don't work for anyone, what was that 'power play' with the steward at the pier that gave us carte blanche on the ship before anyone else?"

"I have some very influential people who are in my 'family' and occasionally we ask for favors from them."

Rodane said, "You mean your cousins and yourself?" he was getting very agitated and almost decided to stop questioning her and let it go but then she said,

"We're a tight knit group of members who look out for each other and we have each other's backs before all else. It's been that way for a very long time. We don't generally take advantage of those connections but this seemed to be one of those times."

"Members… That's a funny way to refer to family. How many are in your family?"

"She paused again…, "I'll pass".

He sat up straighter, prepared to respond to that, stopped, took a breath and said,

"How come they want me dead and not attack you directly if it's to gain something from you?"

"To tell you honestly, I would have to just surmise that you were an unforeseen problem. If I was the target, actually the one who is the target, then you got in the way for that. I take responsibility and regret that you were dragged into all this." she looked so despondent that he knew it was time for a break.

"Okay, let's talk about something else, anything but trying to play Inspector Clouseau for the moment.

She laughed, "You remember that?

"Pink Panther was one of my favorite cartoons as a little boy. We'd get the movie out of the library and me and my sister and dad would watch it after school with popcorn. My mom would be yelling 'You won't eat your dinner' and we would say… "I love the way you eat like a jungle animal'

Sabina said, "One of my favorites was, 'I don't know nuuthing'."

Rodane quipped with a very false, French accent, 'Then you must know 'sumetheeng' and twitched a mustache that wasn't there. They spent the next ten minutes talking about cartoons on Saturdays, movies they liked and those that bombed and Rodane sensed that the tension had lessened for the moment.

"Did you take Sophia to lots of movies?" Sabina asked him.

"Well, not when she was little. Now that she's eight, we really prefer to watch them at home with popcorn and ice cream and she gets to jump up anytime she gets bored."

"Kind of like with your dad, huh?" His face took on a wistful look, "Yeah, I wish he could have been there to see her born and now to watch her grow. Nobody for you, no kids?" he asked.

"Heavens, no!" she laughed, "I would not do that job justice."

"I know what you mean. Being away from her a lot of the time makes me feel like I'm a delinquent in caring for her and protecting her, especially now."

"Why now? Is she okay?"

"Yeah" he said, "she's fine. But I wonder at all the strange things happening around her lately and I guess I'm frustrated that I can't be there for her this summer."

{whoa antenna working here}

"Like what?" she tried to keep her voice even and calm, just curious.

"They had a burglary right next door and they live in a 'quote' supposedly safe, gated, community. Caroline says Sophia sees strange people or thinks she does, even swears she thinks people are watching the house. Sophia has a very vivid imagination so you really can't be sure what an eight year old's mind can conjure up. Now she's upset that they're getting a substitute teacher without notice and that always sets the kids off."

"Yes, I know how that feels *{not}* when your regular routine is displaced quickly and no time to adjust to the idea."

{like now myself and the council}

"She'll be fine once you're home and can get a chance to keep in closer touch."

"Maybe so but there are just some strange things happening with them that I wonder, why all at once? Maybe the break in next door has just spooked her. We'll see."

"I'm sure her mom is watching out for her and being especially cautious now that there was that burglary."

"Yeah, funny thing about that... nothing was taken or messed up. Crazy kind of burglary..."

"Maybe they were alerted by a noise or something that made them take off."

"That's the other thing. There was no evidence of broken locks or windows and it was in broad daylight too. Caroline won't be much help if these guys are pros of some kind. She's too wrapped up in her latest 'conquest.'"

"What?"

"Oh, just that when Caroline tires of one man, which is often, it's not too long before she sets her sights on another one who she then sets out to 'conquer' to the exclusion of all else, including Sophia. Those are her words, not mine. It's kind of funny to watch her work but kind of pathetic for me to realize I was one of those 'conquests' also."

Sabina sat up straighter, "Did you not realize it at the time?"

"I had my suspicions but we were hormonally suited to each other at the time" and he laughed.

"You mean you were both catting around at the time?" she giggled and looked at the empty wine glass.

"No, I mean I was a dog in rut and she was a real bitch who became a challenge to me. Sorry, that was not very polite."

"But true?"

"You know as well as I do…" he looked at her and she nodded sagely "relationships can be sticky for the best of couples but Caroline and I seemed to bring out the worst in each other."

"Even while both of you were just dating, or getting to know each other?"

"Yep, she was that challenge I told you about, the beautiful buxom blonde…" he blushed a little more, "with a startling figure and brains to go with it, the perfect package or so my dorm mates told me. I seemed to fall for women who were amazing but also amazingly wily, cunning and scheming."

She raised her eyebrows at that and stayed silent.

"Oh, not you.…" he said and his blush deepened.

"I've had a lot of years since our divorce to analyze myself as to what I was doing wrong and give up that part of my self-destructive behavior."

"Yet you married her, even though you thought she was trouble?"

"I guess we both thought the sniping and the sarcasm was a side effect of our wittiness and our stubborn personalities, both of us a little anal and both determined to show we wouldn't admit failure first."

"What finally did it?" she asked.

"Her parents were quite well off and I was just starting my career and teaching. She convinced me that a big wedding would be just the thing to get all her parent's friends and family to set us up and that those contacts would further my career. I wouldn't admit it at the time but it made me feel cheap even if it did accomplish that and I think I resented her a little for pushing me into it. I blamed myself more for letting her. When Sophia came along, she put on a show for everyone but me. At home, she hired a nanny so she could keep up with her friends and her gym. She was more than content to sleep in most mornings while I got Sophia up, dressed, fed and amused, till the nanny arrived. I took care of bathing and book reading and bedtime…," he stopped and grabbed her hand. "I don't want you to think that I resented it. I loved it all and Sophia and I had the best times together. I was a kid too and it was wonderful, but it seemed the more I did for Sophia and the more time we spent together, the more snotty and callous and bitchy Caroline became. I couldn't back off. We weren't talking about a job here or a friendship or a pet. We fought over stupid stuff like… how I read her too many books at bedtime, or how I dressed her in dresses that didn't match her socks or her hair is terrible to brush because I didn't take time to condition it properly…" he stopped and made an effort to take a breath.

"Was anyone else critical about those things? Was Sophia happy?" she gently pulled her hand away and reached for the wine.

"God no, I knew I was doing a good job because the nanny, Consuelo, couldn't be happier when I was around and she said Sophia was the happiest child she had ever taken care of. My friends used to tease me with Mr. Mom and Tootsie all the time and for some reason it made Caroline furious or more so…," Sabina urged him on.

"I was sick of her jabs and her sarcasm and her put downs in front of my friends. We had gotten into a fight over toys, of all things and Caroline accused me of buying Sophia's affection and turning her against her. She brought her mother over one day and the two of them were going through the toy box and sorting out what was going to donations for Christmas."

"It just so happened that all the ones she had cleared out were all the ones you had bought for her…" Sabina said, "And kept all the others?"

"Yes, exactly!" he studied her. "You probably know what happened next?"

"My guess would be that you had a fight over it."

Rodane was grim, "You'd be partly right, but no."

"Let me guess again" Sabina said, "Her mom and you had a fight?"

"Yep, big blowout right there in Sophia's toy room. She had the mouth of a sailor and I received enough curses to send me to hell on a stick but she told me I was a failure, my education was a waste because I would never have enough to be good to Caroline or Sophia. She… it doesn't really matter, it's all done anyway."

"Rodane…" Sabina leaned over and poured some wine into both glasses, "It does matter, even today. Was Sophia ever there for any of these arguments?"

"No, thank God. I guess both of us had enough sense to try and keep our claws in when Sophia was around and if we fought, it was in our bedroom or when Sophia was at a birthday party or out with Grammy and Poppy."

"Hee hee!" Sabina laughed, "Grammy and Poppy? Were they country folks? I thought…"

"They were from country…" Rodane said "If you're talking about estates and blue ribbon horse stables. No, she and Caroline thought it sounded more affectionate than grandmother or grandfather. There was a big dinner conversation about that…" he grinned.

"How old was Sophia when you split?"

"She was three and I moved in with a college buddy till I got my own place. Caroline immediately filed for divorce and she wouldn't let me see Sophia for months and I couldn't do much about it because I didn't have money for an attorney. It was a very tough time for me…" then he went silent and looked into his glass like an eight ball that would give him the answer he was hoping for. She took his hand and he said, "No… 'your future looks bright here'…"

He looked up at her and a natural blue spark arced up, flashed from his fingers to hers and she jerked her hand back at the shock.

"Whoa Nelly" he said. There was a long pause.

"Somehow I don't think you and I are done here, at least not on my part. I may have to go home soon, Sabina but I'm not going to be satisfied just to say, 'Bye, see you in the next life time' or even 'maybe we'll keep in touch.'" He waited for her to respond.

She was about to say something but then thought better of it. Rodane looked crestfallen when she didn't answer. He got up and took his glass to the sink and said

"I'm going to turn in and I guess I'll see you in the morning."

"Rodane, I want to…" she gulped back her tears but her voice betrayed her. She tried again, "If it were any other time…" Rodane stopped her with a finger across her lips.

"Sabina, I believe in the eight ball. I don't think we're done and it's not because I'll hound you or send loving, begging letters to you
{wouldn't know where to send them anyway}
…or send out an investigator. It's because I think there's something here different than either of us has experienced before and we have to find out what that is. Are you at least honest enough to admit to that?"

She answered him by putting down her wine glass, rising to him and pressing her lips and her body to his. They stood and drank each other in, like the remainder of a fine bottle of red wine. They couldn't have gotten a feather between them but the heat and hardness made them tear apart with what seemed almost like pain.

"Yes" she whispered. He turned away and left her room, closing the door with a soft snick.

Chapter 15

Virginia 9 in the morning

Zoe drove down the street to the house number listed in their file and kept going until she reached the end of the block. It was a good thing their research team had spent a day investigating their neighborhood, the school shopping area, and gym. She decided to go around the block and then go back to the apartment. It was too soon to have any eyes on her car or her face. She didn't want any recognition of either till their job was done and they were out of there. She was hoping for Monday at the latest. The dossier they had been given on Rodane Arcos was slim; date of birth, place, yada yada yada,.., schools attended, high school yearbook picture,

{kind of cute}

…one marriage and divorce, dates, current job position…

{Montana is quite a distance to run}

degrees earned and job experience…that about did it. Virginia lost a voter, and Montana got an archaeologist. Zoe seemed to be the only one who saw the significance of that. Lexus was still wigged out over the fact that he had to teach a third grade classroom on Monday.

Lack of confidence could quickly kill any attempt to be successful at a task you feared. Anyone can tackle a difficult job, even with overwhelming odds against accomplishing it. Zoe was sure every doctor feared that first life/death situation or a scientist feared the results of his new, highly volatile experiments or so many other events that required a leap of faith and step into the unknown where you and you alone, could attempt and succeed, or attempt and fail. Much of that, she believed, had to do with your confidence level as well as your effort level and especially, your level of desire to succeed.

Zoe wanted to succeed so badly! She wanted to prove to herself that she had the guts, the chutzpah to succeed with any tasks she was assigned. She'd take on rolls; be a substitute teacher, a factory worker, a mountain climber, a lab subject, whatever it took to prove she could take on a dangerous or difficult assignment and complete it. She also wanted to prove to her family that she could be whatever she wanted, do whatever she wanted. She wouldn't be relegated to a job chosen for her, a career picked by others, for her to follow. She was a farmer's daughter. She wasn't and wouldn't be a farmer's wife or a farmer.

When she was twenty-eight and had finished two years of CC, she was approached by one of her professors with a proposal and a business card. He had talked a fine talk, and made such a good case, she had called the number and had been put in touch with one of their supervisors. She went for a meeting in one of the conference rooms of the Department of Science and Technology where she met a man who gave her some materials to read and he was there to answer her questions.

He told her how impressed their tech department was with her cybersecurity work, her test results and her professor's Letter of Recognition. She was surprised at that. She didn't ask for any Letter of Recognition. They were always looking for new talent and a sharp mind that could function on the fly which apparently, her professor thought she could. She couldn't remember asking any questions after he told her what her salary and the perks would be. There were bonuses, company cars, all medical and dental, stock options, a 401k, too many to be remembered. She felt like her soul and her body had been set free.

That had been three years ago. She had even been able to continue taking online courses and she would get her degree in two more classes. She and Lexus had worked well together for two and a half years and things couldn't be better, except for Mom and Ducky. If there were times when she had any qualms about her job or the people she worked with, she quelled them quickly and reviewed her life at the ranch and her present life. There was no comparison, absolutely none. As for Ducky, maybe she would go home for Thanksgiving this year and try to make amends. Ducky should have gotten over his hissy fit about her business the last time they saw each other. Her mother called her every couple of months and told her what was going on in town with the other farmers and ranchers, with Ducky.

He was seeing a very nice lady who had a little boy who was three. Her husband was in the Iraq war and had been killed in one of their many skirmishes in some unrecognizable named city, even before she had given birth. Jenny was a doll baby, so well-mannered and so in love with Ducky. When Zoe listened to her mom and occasionally got a word in, sometimes she felt like an outsider or a distant family relative who was reading the requisite Christmas letter with all the news too boring to print.

Sometimes she felt alien, adrift, with a pang of sadness that she couldn't relate, didn't have any true connection now to her past. She did wonder then if there were good cards on the table yet to be shown, a lucky hand that would get her a family, a child, a career she could be proud of like her brother. She could sit around the dinner table on holidays and share stories, work events, funny happenings of her kids. She could hold hands with her husband when going to see the horses, ride into the hills and watch the sunrise on cool, northern Arizona mornings...

{what are you doing girl this is useless fantasizing}

Her mother ended each phone call with, "Come visit Zoe, come let's spend more time together and be a family." Her ending was always abrupt, "I'll see mom, I'm awfully busy now so if I get time...," and she always left it hanging. If her mom wanted to know anything about her job, she was short and evasive so mom hadn't brought that up lately. Another possible connection broken, another chance not taken. She wiped her eyes before she went into the apartment.

They were in an older home that has been converted into three apartments, one on each floor. They had the 3rd floor which had been an attic. It had charm and character and a terrible heating/cooling system. The sink leaked. Even from the closed bedroom door, she heard 'plop, plop, plop', in metric clicks until she placed a dishcloth in the sink each night to absorb the water. Lexus could sleep through a 5 on the Richter scale maybe even a 7. It was warm in the summer up here, which held the rising heat despite a thermometer which said it should feel like 72 degrees. It probably was going to leave ice in the windows during the winter, which she didn't intend to be here for, but it was clean and furnished and Lexus loved the fact that it was $600 a month.

The landlady prorated it by the week though Lexus tried to get her to do it by the day and pay cash. Her sense of integrity held her firm and she was adamant she needed checks for tax purposes. She settled with him on a money order from the Post Office for one week.

They had little luggage. It never paid to have too much to carry if they had to leave in a hurry. That had happened a few times and they had their traveling down to a science; one small suitcase each...

{Lexus can't get his suits wrinkled heaven forbid}

and one backpack. They were well-traveled business people, who used money easily when necessary and held onto it when Lexus felt unnecessarily stingy. Zoe didn't care. She had her own money and if she wanted to spend it she would. She felt a little twinge of hypocrisy because if truth be told, she was almost as tight as Lexus.

{comes from being in debt all the time on the ranch}

She put her key in the door and it startled her when the door was just opened and Lexus hissed, "Where have you been? Get in here" and he reached to grab her arm. She reacted, pulled him out into the hall before she could even think and slammed him up against the wall, "What the hell! Lexus, what's wrong with you?" She had her arm across his throat and her other hand was at his genitals while her leg was between his for leverage.

His eyes were bugging out of his head and he was actually gurgling in his throat, looking down where her hand was ready to crush his treasure. He looked up at her and she said, "You going to try anything stupid, Lexus?"

He shook his head 'no' as much as he could with her chokehold on him. She let him go and he bent over, short of breath and red in the face. After a few seconds, he croaked out, "Damn girl, remind me never to startle you again."

They went into the apartment, her behind him, not sure about that 'trust' thing at the moment, "Okay, what the hell is wrong with you and why are you behaving like a lunatic?"

He turned to her, "The principal. He sent over all these files this morning. He wants to meet with me today, this afternoon, to go over my position, lesson plans, class charts. Pupil Personnel wants to talk to me on Monday morning and the principal wants me to show up early to meet the entire faculty," his voice had risen with each requirement. He was panting as if he had run and she saw panic in his eyes.

"Annnnd…" she slowly formed the word.

"And… and, I'm not ready. It wasn't supposed to start till Monday. I can't get all of that ready in a couple hours!" He was beginning to ramble.

"Okay Lexus, calm down. Let's think. You can do this, just calm down… breathe…!"

He started pacing, "Okay, I'm calm, I'm calm. I can do this… I can do this, they're kids they're only kids."

{good lord man don't be such a weenie}

She didn't know where this Lexus was coming from. This was not the distant, hard man she knew, "Look, it's only 9:45 now. We have plenty of time to read over class lists. You have nurse reports to examine for allergies and medicine, right?

"Yes, how did you know?"

"I used to be in school, Lexus. It hasn't changed that much."

"Oh, yeah, I used to be in school too" as if it were a new revelation.

"You'll have seating charts to go over to make sure that they're in the right seat. Sometimes they like to try and pull the wool over a sub's eyes but that's usually around 6th grade. I don't think 3rd graders are that evolved, but just make sure."

"See, I told you that you should do this. I'm bad at this, really bad! We can still switch."

"Lexus… she tried persuasion, "This is a chance for you to show our organization that you can do anything they can throw at you. This could really give you a leg up with the big wigs at the company, even Mr. Gallo himself."

"Yeah, I'm better than just muscle and enforcement. It's time I got recognition for all the other things I do as well…maybe I'll get a promotion, you think?"

{won't ask you what}

"Good, now let's get to work." She led him to the table and they laid everything out from the files they had. They spent an hour going over class lists, allergy alerts, students who needed meds in school, and a dozen other things to know; cafeteria seating charts, locker lists, class schedules, modified lesson plans for special students… it was an incredible amount of information and class material that had to be learned and used in one short day. Then Lexus spent another hour going over a lesson plan for Monday. He had thirty-two little third graders who were going to be out of whack with a substitute teacher, and he needed to help them and keep them occupied and working. He had never taught a thing in his life so he didn't know where to start.

"Zoe, how do you teach reading to 3rd graders? If they made it to third grade, shouldn't they already know how to read? Same with math. Only thing I can see for 3rd graders would be to learn new history or do science experiments, once they're allowed to handle glass or…"

"Lexus, go back in your mind to 3rd grade. What did your teacher do during reading class?"

He thought back for many moments, "She had us move into our groups. I was a bluebird…" he scrunched up his face. I hated the Bluebirds! We never got to have fun like the Cardinals and the Robins. They did plays and acted out parts and went to kindergarten to read to them. We sat and went over alphabets and spelling rules and reading out loud. I hated reading out loud!"

"Lexus, here's something to remember about classrooms and education today. You asked why you had to teach reading if they made it to 3rd grade. Sad thing is, we push children from one class to another and some did not make the connections. They didn't absorb the lessons, yet they had to keep moving on and they fell farther and farther behind. Their teachers had too many kids in a class, too many who needed extra time. They had lesson plans that didn't allow for that so they just kept pushing them ahead. Those kids became frustrated and they zoned out or they became the 'rowdy' ones, the troublemakers, and still they got pushed ahead. They went through one, two, three grades without getting it. By the time they moved into middle school, they were basically unread, unskilled, and the subject matter was so advanced to them, they couldn't pass if they wanted to.

"That's messed up! That can't be right!" Lexus was astounded.

"No it's not, we all know that but yet that's where they found themselves. Those students passed anyway, maybe some tutoring along the way, maybe some makeup work, but not enough, not often enough, not soon enough. Rare times, they might have a special class for them or some after school program to help them succeed, but the teachers were more interested in getting higher scores on the tests than watching kids actually get better at subjects they found too difficult to learn."

"How could they do that to those kids?"

"Well, what happened to you in your Bluebird class?"

"Miss McCormick!" he looked surprised, "Yeah, Ms. McCormick.

She kept us in at recess two days a week and had a 5th grader come down and work with us and our reading. After a few weeks, we got better. I forgot all that!"

"What about math?"

"Miss McCormick worked with us herself. Saw us after school on Mondays and Wednesdays, I think, and worked with us. My mom was okay with it because she said she could see the difference and I wasn't so mad all the time and even doing homework."

"Lexus, you may find this school is different. I hope it is but if you find there are students who need help, get it for them. Pair them up, weak and strong, make games out of it. Put them in groups to make it go faster and give them more chances to perform."

"Zoe, why does it seem you might have made an awesome teacher?" he was impressed.

"That's not what I want to do. Well… I really don't know what I want to do, but I guess I'll find out in time."

"But I'm only going to be there for one or two days, a week at the most. What can I do in that short time and what difference would it make?"

"What can you do? You do as much as possible. What difference does it make? You'll probably never know but the students will and someday they'll remember your efforts, just as you remembered Miss McCormick's help. We need all the Ms. McCormicks we can get. They're overwhelmed, overtasked, underpaid, disrespected and just plain tired. You okay with this now?"

"Yeah" Lexus answered, "I'm going to go over these lesson plans again. What about our plan to get to Sophia?

"You're supposed to earn her trust in a very short period of time. I'm not sure that's possible but you can start by observing and listening. Find out what she's good at and build on that. Make her feel important and she'll open up easier. Feel out the kids on Monday to see who she's closest to and befriend them. I'm going to go study my file and see where I fit in all this." She went into her bedroom carrying the information that was supposed to give them needed intel on one Rodane Arcos.

{what did you do buddy to bring down these guys on you}

Chapter 16

7 a.m. Piraeus, Greece

Rodane heard the phone ring as if it were under water. Then he realized that it was his head under the pillow and the phone was perfectly dry and fine. He groped across the end table to grab the phone, "It better be good. No human wants to answer this call."

"Rodane, would you like to go to the boat early to have breakfast or would you like to find something in the open market? I thought you might like to spend some time together before you go on to Naples and I head for Capri."

"Are Helene and Eugenie joining us?"

"Would you like them to? They would be fine just going on their own back to the boat."

"Oh, you're setting the watch dogs free, are you?"

"The watch…? Sabina understood and tartly replied, "It was for your protection Rodane. We have no idea how far these two people or if it is just two people, are willing to go to get to you. I'll tell them…."

"No please, invite them. I like Lenny and Genie. They're good people and fine ladies. "Let's get breakfast on the boat, ok?"

"Okay" Sabina said. "Lenny and Genie? Who are you talking about?"

Rodane laughed, "Ask the ladies. Meet you in the lobby packed and ready to return to the sea, in one hour."

His mouth was dry, he had a lingering ache in his head and his gut was warning him he had mixed too much food and alcohol.

In a little under an hour they all gathered in the lobby of the hotel. Rodane narrowed his eyes at his two 'keepers' when he saw how fresh and awake they looked.

"You look positively, irritatingly, in good shape, Genie."

Eugenie laughed, "You need a little advice on your liquor, Rodane? Hydration, before during and after…especially after."

She laughed and Helene came over and looked in his eyes, "Not too bad, must have been some time since you tied one on. You should rectify that. You're one hell of a dancer, big boy!"

He threw his arm over her shoulder, "Lenny, anytime I want a dance partner, I'm hunting you down. My derriere, otherwise known as my ass, is sore from all those gyrations we went through last night. I have muscle aches where I didn't know I had muscles."

Sabina stood there, a little puzzled and confused, "When did the three of you become so chummy and bonded? I feel a little left out."

Rodane couldn't tell if she was serious or kidding. He dragged Helene over to Sabina and put his other arm around her shoulder. "What? Would you like a nickname or maybe another dancing routine?"

"No, but when we get on the boat, I want a good breakfast, a bloody Mary and a hot tub… in that order."

They loaded their luggage into the hotel shuttle and were down at the pier in twenty minutes. When they passed through security, one of the stewards collected their passports and took them over to be double checked under a laser light. He brought them back and they headed to the dining hall on the 4th floor.

Eugenie and Helene put him to shame with the breakfast they brought back to their table. They must have had at least 2500 calories each, on their plates, piled with eggs, hash browns, pancakes, fruit and some kind of fruit filled tarts. Sabina had her bloody Mary and they both settled for an omelet each, toast and good hot coffee. He added hot sauce to his eggs and Sabina loooked sideways at him and snickered. Rodane looked at her in surprise, "You've never had hot sauce on your eggs?"

"Can't say that I have. Maybe I'll try." She took the bottle and sprinkled it liberally till he caught her hand, "Whoa now! The first time, you're a novice. Try it but don't soak them. I'll have to pour cold water down your throat."

Helene and Eugenie were eating yet looking unobtrusively at the two of them joking and eating the exact same thing. Helene looked sideways to Eugenie and they both nodded some subtle agreement that the other two missed. When they had finished eating, they spent some time just talking about the city, the museums, the beautiful sunrise earlier.

"You saw the sunrise!" Rodane felt a flicker of jealousy, looking at Sabina.

"I'm kind of a stickler for sunrises and sunsets when I can work them in. So many sites I've been on don't have work above ground and we start so early, we miss the actual sunrise. But..." she reached over and covered his hand "I took quite a few pictures and some of them are almost breathtaking, if I say so myself. There was the most beautiful shade of violet towards the end. Rays were hitting the Gulf at just the right angle and our balconies are perfectly situated so there was a perfect shot of Mount Hymettes behind the ridge of this city..." she stopped, looking at him.

All three women saw the same look on his face and Helene and Eugenie watched both their faces, a combination of happy intensity, a feeling of connected interest in each other's passion and relaxed intimacy, like couples that have spent time together for a very long time.

Eugenie wondered if this would be something they would see ending in sorrow and wasted wishes.

{you two are really in over your heads}

Returning her mind to the conversations, she realized they were talking about last night. Rodane was talking excitedly, "It made me think of little enclaves, of dance music, cozy restaurants, always around water, renovated sites to draw in the young and the restless... I would like for you to see some of those places. They're a lot newer than anything that holds thousands of years of history...like here, but still quaint and charming none the less."

"Like where?" Helene asked.

"Well, there's a wonderful city in the south, called Charleston, in South Carolina. The old historic downtown has old rehab homes for the most part, dating back to before the Revolutionary War. It's a perfect example of old US history that was saved, instead of replacing them with new modern cubicles with sterile living. Not that they can't be nice too but..."

"I know exactly what you mean. I was in ..." Helene thought for a second, "Savannah I think it was, in Georgia."

Sabina interjected, "It's a marvel of modern rehab, of warehouses and storerooms along the Savannah River, just like Piraeus. It's a club and bar heaven for the young and tourists. Good food, good beer... I loved the Irish pub right along the cobbled walkways."

Eugenie said, "There was a place very like that in Florida, where we stayed for a few days. It was... I can't remember"

"Jacksonville!" Helene said excitedly, "it was a nice little downtown on..."

"The St. Johns River near the ocean, and..." Sabina finished, "Big hotels and lovely beaches, river walks and great restaurants!"

"Wow, you girls know all the hot spots to visit. You must get around a lot for cousins who can't find time for vacations." Rodane put down his coffee cup and looked at all three of them.

They looked back at him, all silent. Sabina broke the silence, "Look

Rodane, we're aware that you know you have 'watchdogs' as you put it. He looked surprised, "Yes, we talk. We have to, it's important that we share information because we need to all be aware of who and what we're dealing with. It's our safety too as well as yours. We can see it's evident you realize we've kept a lot from you. Some of that's on us, a lot on the shoulders of… our bosses."

Eugenie added, "We'll share when we can, we'll keep it between us when we can't. That's the best and most honest thing we can do right now, maybe ever." All three waited for his response.

He held his coffee cup and looked into it, like looking at tea leaves at the bottom, to read your future, "I guess that's what I'll have to settle for, huh?"

Eugenie answered, "Yeah that's what you'll have to settle for. If it makes you feel any better Rodane, we've come to like you and more importantly, trust you. Whatever has happened with you has never happened before so we're all new at this. Let's share info and trust each other, okay?"

"Okay… for now." he rose from the table and asked Sabina if she would like to take a walk on the deck.

"Sure, just let me go back to my room and brush my teeth and I'll be up on the deck in ten minutes, maybe twenty at the most."

On deck ten, there was a walking, jogging track around the outer perimeter. There were two pools in the center, soft blue water with the shallower one for smaller bodies and the deeper one at nine feet with a curling slide. They weren't really too crowded now. People were only just coming on board from town. At the bow of the boat were complete rows of lounge chairs and a table for towels. At the stern was a climbing rock wall, open to anyone over eighteen and with permission, children over ten. They walked twice around the deck and felt like they had allowed their big breakfast to settle.

"Helene and Eugenie should climb the wall if they're itchy for exercise."

Sabina laughed, "As soon as breakfast was over, they headed for the gym. It's got just about every piece of equipment and weight machines you could possibly ask for. Want to go try it out?"

"No, I'd rather talk to you if that's okay? We don't really have too much time left before we part ways." He looked at her a long moment then, "That's if you want to spend time on us. It's okay if you prefer to do something else on your own."

One a.m. in Virginia

"No!" Caroline snapped, "I'm not kidding! If I could fix it so that she would not travel anywhere with him, I would, but he's doing well and if I tried that, I know he would take me to court and you would definitely be a part of his argument that he needs more time with Sophia. I just know he's going to ask for her to join him on one of those fucking digs. He should fall in and then it wouldn't be a problem. Shit! Shit! Shit!"

"Caroline, why is it a problem now?" Adam was talking slowly and softly. When she got on these anger kicks about Sophia, it didn't take much for her to go off the rails. Then the yelling got louder, the words got sluttier and her anger boiled over into a quickening rage, "Come here and sit with me" he said.

They were in her bedroom. Sophia was tucked away hours ago with her school bag packed, homework done and lunch stored in the fridge. She was tired. She had graded papers all this afternoon and that ruined her Saturday and gave her more to complain about. She sat at her dressing table, using lotions to smooth dry skin and to moisturize. She had always taken good care of her skin and her body. She used the gym to ward off her anger sometimes, and it made her feel good to know that when she walked in for a session, all the men looked after her with interest or lust, or both. She had a kitten's smile on her face when they came over to watch her do stretches, pretending they were examining the weights and bells, but their eyes wandering over to her betrayed them. She reveled in her tight abs and her slim hips. She spent a lot of money on gym clothes, yoga mats, nutrition bars, drinks and supplements. She spent just as much time as money, fitting in those yoga classes stopping at the gym for a workout at least three times a week. Adam had been a trainer there when she had met him and dated him for many months.

Finally they had settled into a comfortable routine, at ease with each other, small squabbles settled over meals or walks around the lake near where she lived. She decided it was time to have him meet Sophia. She hadn't done that for most of her 'conquests' as she called them. She never saw the need to have Sophia's routine interrupted with her sexual exploits. She tried to be a good mother and even if it sometimes interfered with her plans and wishes, she made the best of it. She really did do a good job of protecting Sophia and planning ahead to make sure she was involved in outside activities and social groups.

Lately, it was difficult to get her out of her room. There were rules for phone time and computer time. There was a strict policy on homework and chores for Sophia to do and it allowed her to feel independent when she was given her own money to spend on gifts for her father and her friends. Sophia had a later bedtime on Saturdays and all she wanted to do with it was spend more time on Minecraft and do her infernal drawings and stories. That graphic novel shit was too hard to get a grasp, at least for her. She thought good old comic books would do and then found out, in no uncertain terms from Sophia, that she knew nothing about graphic novels and apparently didn't know much about anything else as well.

She rose from the dressing table, creamed, moisturized and softened, lathered and perfumed. She went to Adam and sat on his lap and wrapped her arms loosely around him.

"It's a problem because I have a routine for Sophia. I spend three quarters of the year with her, actually more, now that his digs and travels have started up again. I should be able to tell him when he can have her and how long, but he sees me as the controlling bitch!" Adam looked at her with false surprise on his face, "Stop that! I'm not that bad. Don't give me that look! Adam!"

Adam squeezed her around the waist and moved his hand up to cover her left breast, "Ummm… where was I …" "Stop, this is important."

"Caroline, you realize that if you allowed him to have Sophia more or for longer periods, say the entire summer…" and he put his hand up when she started to protest,

"You know you have all the school year as well as holidays with her, "If…" he continued, "she could spend more time with him, then you and I…" he nuzzled her ear and breathed his lips onto her neck, "would be able to have all the privacy we wanted for ourselves and even be able to travel and have our own vacations… island travels… sounds good to me."

"Huh! I hate the thought of him influencing Sophia to go off on these fucking digs to God knows what places, with disease, and poverty in the towns and all kinds of muggings and thieves and…"

"Caroline, is it the digs that you mind or the fact that they would be having some serious Daddy- Daughter time and you resent that? Be honest here!" She narrowed her eyes at him but then she smiled a little and the tension was broken.

"I am a little of a controlling bitch aren't I?"

He rose, with her coming off his lap, lifted her up and began in earnest to caress her body and kiss her eyes, cheeks and lips.

"Caroline I think it's time for us to begin to think about long term here. I love Sophia, she's smart and funny and talented. She's very mature for her age and I hate to let you in on a little secret, but she pretty much sees through this wall you put up whenever she talks to her dad or talks about him. Don't look at me like that! You know she does. I think, in my humble opinion, it would be good for Sophia to see more of her dad. They really could help each other out more and now that she's getting older, she's not going to allow you to put up roadblocks much longer. That is one issue you may not want to butt heads with her over."

"You wouldn't mind playing second fiddle more?" Caroline asked.

"I'm not her dad, sweetheart, but I'll be here for her if she needs me. Don't look surprised. I plan on being around a little longer than all your other 'conquests.' I'm a keeper!"

Caroline laughed and dragged his face down for a long, deep kiss. She broke away and took his hand and led him to the bed, "Let's talk about this another time. I'll deal with the summer visit when Rodane comes home next week, then maybe the two of us could actually have a very civil conversation and work out a few different arrangements for the coming year. Sophia will probably be delighted and I'll have to sprint around with a smile on my face, and pretend to be so understanding and caring."

The night went deeper and they sank into their own depths and pushed everything else away.

Outside the house, Lexus and Zoe sat in the car and watched the lights go off. The nearest street lamp was three doors up. Zoe had drawn the sketch of the house exits and entrances, backyard fences, and all the other houses backing onto their yards. A little research has shown them that the house to their left behind them was empty for two weeks, with the owners away at a beach resort with two other neighbors. A perfect plan was beginning to form and Lexus was getting itchy to actually get to school on Monday. He would start using his wiles and charms on a little third grader who could possibly give them the information they sought after only one day. They could get out, go home, and collect their sizable pay and continue to enjoy the rest of the summer.

They started the car, a hybrid that had the advantage of moving silently up the street as long as they coasted at twenty or twenty-five miles per hour. They came in like thieves, and they left like ghosts without any loot, but looking forward to an appearance that could net them substantial gains with little effort.

7 PM—Naples, Italy

Tabor came into the small apartment they had rented for a week in the heart of Naples. They had arrived there from the airport after making a secure call and getting the address of the building and the apartment number that was ready for them. He had gone out for some Thai food and had his choice of takeout places along the trolley tracks. Looking out their window, they could see the new dig that had put a halt to further construction. Law of the Land; If artifacts were found in the process of construction, all work by law had to cease immediately. Teams of archaeologists and museum personnel had to investigate the site, take measurements, catalog and identify enough pieces found to enable them to research possible provenance and antiquity. If it was determined that a large dig was called for, a cease and desist was given to the town council until further notice when much of the site could be examined.

It played havoc with the transportation system of Naples at the moment and traffic was congested, drivers were frustrated, taxi drivers were making out very well and the residents of the apartments were now subjected to jack hammers and drills during the day and blinding perimeter lights and scaffolding at night. They covered their windows with black cloth to keep out the light and the apartments appeared to have gaping eyes where window lights should be and balconies abandoned, where clothing flew in the wind at night like headless people dancing on a tight rope hanging down by invisible hands and bodies that jerked, legless.

Tabor got out paper plates and plastic ware from the bags. He spread out the containers on the coffee table and put on a kettle for hot tea. It was one of those habits that had never left him from his growing up in the warrens of London, with a mother who had good manners but no money to indulge them. A good cup of Lord Gray soothed his often frazzled nerves and his edge of anger that always seemed to be right at the rim of explosion lately.

"Renata, are you coming out for dinner?" He yelled to the closed door of their small, smelly bedroom. Too much garlic, too many fried onions and curry, had permeated every corner of the kitchen and odors found themselves creeping into the carpet out to the living room. They were trying to invade her bedroom so Renata kept the door closed and a can of air freshener in every room. Sometimes he would return into a fog of smells hovering over everything after meals were cooked by other apartment dwellers. Most of the smells did not appeal to them but sometimes they made their mouths water and they would salivate till they had found the dish that approximated those smells.

They had two days left till the cruise ship, Jewel of the Seas, was due in port. They had already looked over the file that has been sent to them, more than once. They shook their heads at the irony of it all. This guy, Rodane Arcos, seemed to be legit, a tourist who happened to be at the same place as them, meeting up with Sabina Carter by happenstance. He had no background connections with any other investigations that had been reviewed and his background was very transparent and legitimate. This was the fate of the gods that Tabor thrived on. He abhorred an obstacle to any assignment but especially when it served to thwart his objectives and he was forced to admit failure.

This would not be one of those times. Not only would he catch up to Carter and obtain what they sought, but he would take pleasure in her pain. If she was still with Arcos, he would be extremely fortunate to get another chance to clear the field and maybe permanently.

Renata came out with the file in her hands. Her glasses were perched on her nose and she reminded him of a school teacher, one used to stern tactics and an even sterner demeanor.

"How many times are you going to read that file? What more can you learn?"

"Well" Renata replied, "For one thing I can learn more about his family and who we might need to investigate if we find out there are any connections that might not be listed here. Any stone unturned is a home for more bugs."

He chuckled and sat down on the sofa and began to eat. Renata paced back and forth till he got annoyed, "What is your problem?" he snapped.

"There's something about this that just doesn't sit right. Two persons, who supposedly don't even know each other, hook up by accident, both in the same field, arrive at the exact spot we've been alerted to and prevent us from completing our tasks. How can that possibly be all coincidence? Tabor, I want that bitch! We would not be here after an entire week of nothing if it weren't for her and her... what? Boyfriend, partner, cohort... what? Do you have any ideas here?"

"Renata, he will be here in two days. It won't be hard to see where he goes or where he stays. We have people in every hotel chain watching for him, people at the cruise line office... someone's checking the rental car offices and all taxi companies are alerted to his profile. Is there something I'm missing here, something you would like to do different than the plan we came up with together?"

He got up and approached her, "You wouldn't be interested in diverting from the plan, would you Renata?"

He moved closer, putting his face into hers, "Haven't gotten different plans from anyone, have you Renata?"

He gripped her arm till it hurt. He moved to the sofa, pushing her before him,

"Heard from Mr. Gallo, have you Renata? Got some plans I'm not aware of Renata... partner?"

"No Tabor, no!" She fell down on the sofa and he moved so quickly she couldn't even take a breath. He slapped her hard across the face and grabbed her face in his hands and pinched so hard she felt one of her teeth bite into her cheek.

"Mrff! I didn't talk to anyone! How could I have changed your plan? I just wanted to see if we could maybe speed up this hunt with some new ideas."

He backed off but was not appeased, "Do you think I'm stupid? That I don't make sure I'm at least two steps ahead of you all the time?" his eyes were glazing and his color was rising. She tried to head him off this latest rage,

"Tabor, I swear to you, I haven't talked to anyone. I'm not trying to be smarter than you. I'm trying to help you execute your plan. I just want to make sure there's nothing else I could do to help you…" she was actually in tears. How many times could she talk him down before he seriously hurt her? He stood there, breathing heavily, eyes pinpoints of anger and red-faced. He looked somewhat deranged.

{well you are aren't you}

"Don't ever try to one up me Renata, you'll be sorry. We have a plan, it's a good one and by Monday night we will not have to worry about Rodane Arcos." She saw a sly smile on his face and then his eyes. "Then we keep tabs on Sabina Carter. When we find out her itinerary from him and we track her down, we complete our jobs then it's a trip back to Paris for our money and another job completed successfully!" He threw his arm over her shoulder and led her toward the bedroom, "Let's call it a night." Inwardly, she cringed.

Late Saturday, Jewel of the Seas

The rest of the cruise was relaxing. They all had their dinners together. They all slept in until at least seven thirty. Rodane and Sabina did use the gym that Saturday evening after a heavy meal and later they went to a club room where, according to the boats itinerary, there was supposed to be a band with classic rock. They went to the 6th floor where the club room was and saw two or three couples seated and a four piece group playing songs from the Seventy's and Eighty's. They looked at each other and then turned and went in search of some other action.

They found it in one of the bars where Helene and Eugenie were seated with one other person, getting ready to play Trivia for prizes. The five of them played a very raucous three games of Trivia against two other tables, where they laughingly accused the moderator of padding the questions. Some of the clues they were guessing at were totally useless and if not for the fifth single player at their table, all four would have been put to shame. Their team won and each couple and the single got a choice of a bottle of Blush wine or Cabernet as a prize to take to their rooms. Around nine, they headed toward their rooms to turn in early. The next day was looking very busy and Sabina was sure it would be stressful for her when all the past few days events were completely shared.

This ship would arrive into port at Naples at eight a.m. and they would immediately get to the docks after a short walk from the pier to catch the early ferry to Capri. Most of the people on that trip would be the workers on Capri who used the same ferry for all the supplies that were being shipped over for construction, building projects, and food supplies. There wouldn't be a lot of sleepy workers on that trip and Sabina was told to meet at the stern of the ferry as soon as she boarded. She wanted to get a good night's sleep but she dreaded the short time she and Rodane would have left before he went into the city and to his own business, "Rodane, would you like to share our bottle of wine on the deck of the sitting room?"

He took her by her shoulders and looked into her eyes, "Why are you so tense? You're tight as a drum. After the gym, I would expect you to be very relaxed."

"Because I'm afraid you'll say no and I don't want to leave you without your knowing all the answers I could possibly be free to answer for you and you the same for me."

"I have to call Sophia now and when I'm finished with my call, I'll join you on our deck and we can kill that bottle." He raised his eyebrows and he felt her shoulders relax.

He dialed Caroline's number and it rang four or five times before Caroline picked up. She was out of breath and he heard a lot of noise in the background,

"Rodane!" she went silent.

"Caroline, are you there? Caroline are you…"

"Stop yelling Rodane. Yes, I'm here but this is not a good time. Things are a little hectic and Sophia isn't here. You could call tomorrow and I'll make sure she's back from her friend's house.

"What's going on, what's with all the noise in the background? I hear sirens."

"One of our neighbor's houses is on fire and all the trucks are trying to get down the street. Its bedlam! Adam and I were over there trying to get the dog and cat out of the house….," her voice hitched.

"Are you crazy? You were in a burning house to rescue a dog and a cat? What are you thinking?"

"Shut up, Rodane! I was thinking… I'm thinking I didn't want to look out my back door and see a poodle and a black cat scratching at the sliding doors and listen to the panic in his bark and the wailing coming from the cat…" she burst into sobs over the phone.

"Caroline I'm sorry, really. It must have been terrifying with Sophia there. Is she ok?"

She got her crying under control, "Sophia is fine, she had a playdate with a friend and they asked for her to stay for dinner. Adam and I have spent the last two hours trying to do what we could but everything is nuts here!"

"Do they know what caused the fire? Did you manage to get to the animals…" she started crying again,

"Adam threw a lounge chair through the slider and we managed to coax Max out the door and we got Silas out and into our yard but Max… ran back in the house and we couldn't get past the smoke and…" she was sobbing again.

"Caroline I'm so sorry. I can tell you're really upset at this. I'm glad Adam is there for you and that you were able to save the… what, the dog or the cat?"

"Silas is the little poodle, Max was their cat and…" she was still crying.

{never knew you to be so animal-friendly}

"Sophia loves that cat! She was always going over there after school to pet him and play with him… with his toys… He loves to chase a laser light…" more crying.

"Caroline, could we Skype tomorrow evening? It's been awhile since I've seen Sophia and I still have a week before I'm done with this particular trip. I would really like to talk face to face with her."

"We'll try Rodane. Right now I can't think of anything except to call Mr. And Mrs. Moore and tell them to cut their vacation short and come home early. They won't have a place to go to or maybe they do… I don't know. Everything is so confused and up in the air right now."

"Do you know how it started? Hear anything or smell smoke?"

"We had finished lunch and Adam and I were just enjoying some quiet time after Sophia had been picked up. He thought he smelled something so he checked through the house and found nothing. I was grading papers, the bane of my existence, and Adam was on the stationary bike in the basement. It was getting dark and he thought he saw a flash out back and the lights flickered. So he came upstairs to see if the clocks had gone out for a few seconds. He looked out at their kitchen and he saw…" her voice broke again, "…Max and Silas, scratching furiously at the door. He heard Silas but not Max so he opened the door and smelled heavy smoke. By that time he saw the flames in the kitchen and smoke was pouring out the dryer vents on the side of the house. Oh my God, those poor animals, trapped in that house with no one there! He yelled for me and then picked up the metal lounge and raced to the house and he's still over there with the police and firemen…"

"It's ok Caroline, you're ok, the dog is ok, and you did everything you could, you know?"

"But I have to tell Sophia that Max…Oh my god, oh my god!" She was yelling and sounded hysterical.

"What is it Caroline? What is it? Talk to me!"

"Max, Max… pretty boy! Here Max… come here to me, sweetie."

{are you losing your mind woman}

He heard her laughing and crying at the same time and the kitchen door slammed and she was cooing in singsong…

"Max, you pretty boy, you pretty, pretty boy!" she picked up the phone and sounded deliriously happy. "It's Max, Rodane! Max came to my door. He's here, he's okay. He's dirty and smelly and his fur is all matted and coated with ash but he's alive! He's here! Sophia will be so happy. I'm so happy…" she babbled on and on talking to Max like a baby.

Finally she said, "Rodane, Adam's coming back. I have to go to him… I have to let him see Max. He was devastated and he'll…" She put the phone down and he didn't hear her anymore.

After a few seconds, a dog barked into the phone and he almost jumped out of his skin. Then the phone dropped and the busy signal sounded. He hung up and stood there in a kind of shock. He had never heard this Caroline before; flustered, emotional, truly agonizing over a dog and a cat… this Caroline sounded human and caring and normal with grief and upset. He felt a little put out at her hanging up on him… sort of… while she ran to Adam.

It seemed there was a little more to this present flirtation then just flirtation. Maybe she had finally made a 'conquest' that was genuine and it was a lot more than another notch in her belt. He was gratified that her attention was on a man other than himself because it took the heat off of him but he admitted he was a little resentful that this might be the one she would settle with and he would be the immediate focus in Sophia's life instead of himself.

{hey bucko no more snarking at you eh}

He went to the bathroom, used the toilet and brushed his teeth. He turned off his phone and headed for the deck where someone was quickly becoming his focus and who was much more immediate than anyone thousands of miles away in another world and time.

Chapter 17

Jewel of the Seas

Rodane went out to the balcony off the sitting room and Sabina was at the railing watching the waves wash against the moving boat while the moon was hidden by some low-lying clouds. This was the first night on board where they did not have a clear night with a view of thousands of stars and a warm breeze to face into. Perhaps, she thought, this was a sign of the ending of this part of her life, a temporary hiccup in an otherwise very smooth career. She couldn't blame Rodane for this curling in her stomach or the freeze of her brain when he stared at her without words. He wasn't to blame for the hotel fire, or getting smacked in the head or thrown in jail. This was aimed at her and they still had no idea where those two responsible worked or what their next move might be.

They had names and some details but what could they do with that information to stay safe? She had to keep Rodane safe. He had a daughter, a career. She was determined to stop this here and now. Her family could help, they would be there. But he wouldn't. This short time with a stranger, who was one no longer, was already leaving a hole in the pit of her. She was preparing herself for a clean break and then time to deal with the loss. She hadn't experienced that sense of loss for many years.

Rodane walked to the railing and stood next to her as they covered each other's fingers and intertwined them. They stood listening to the wash of the sea against the hull of the ship and feeling the chilled breeze. She threw out her arm and pointed at the horizon, "Look! I saw a tail and fin disappearing into the dark!" Immediately, another form flew into the air as two or three dolphins took a late night swim in the Mediterranean, a swimming pool that was their home.

"Sabina" she turned her head.

"This might be the finest and last memory of you I will take with me tomorrow. Thank you for putting up with me these few days. I'm very happy to have met you," she looked up at him and studied his face.

{what are you looking for}

"Tell me more about Caroline and Sophia."

He looked surprised. That was not a question he expected.

"Did you work out your differences with Caroline for Sophia?"

He told her about the divorce decree, the digs and times he was limited to seeing Sophia, the move he made to Montana both for his job and to avoid Caroline.

"I wasn't proud to run and leave Sophia behind. I wasn't really there for her and I regret all the time I didn't get to spend with her but we had more time together in the last couple of years and I think we have a pretty special relationship. There were some rough times when I was trying to start a career and support Sophia, with little money. It's been better lately and I'm doing well enough to be able to put money aside for Sophia's college."

"Will you see her this summer?"

"I don't know what's going to happen next. They're going through a rough spot and things are up in the air."

"Something happen?" Sabina asked.

He told her about the fire and Caroline's neighborhood and the traumatic retrieval of the dog and cat.

"Where was Sophia?"

They talked about her friends and her out of school activities, "Her mom isn't very happy with her intense obsessions. I tried to explain to Caroline that all kids go through periods of being totally into a single activity to the exclusion of food or friends or anything else.

"Now" said Rodane, "Time to tell me about you."

"Just one more question about Sophia, is that ok?"

"Sure" Rodane said, "fire away."

"Has she, by any chance, said anything else about feeling watched or seeing strangers in her neighborhood?" He stared at her for a moment.

Rodane asked her, "You can't possibly think anything that has happened here could possibly be connected to my family back in the states? That would be an enormous stretch."

"No, not so much our incidences but didn't you tell me there was a break in during the day right next door to her? That they had no leads? Now there's a fire in the house behind her? Do you believe in that many coincidences so close together?"

He thought for a long moment, "No, I actually don't and I'm embarrassed to think I didn't even put the two together. Perhaps I should call Caroline back and tell her to contact the police and connect the dots... somehow."

"I thought they were going to talk to the police and firemen at the scene..."

"You don't miss a thing do you?" He smiled but it was intense.

"My job is to be observant to uncover clues and do that connecting the dots."

"Well, mine is too Sabina, but it seems I'm not quite adept at it as you are. Your teachers have trained you well. Where was that again?" he grinned.

"Oh, no, you're not tripping me up in a Q&A."

"Oh ho, it's my turn about you. "You said, 'even Steven' yes?" and he waited.

"Who's... never mind. I don't do literal too well. Okay, I'm game, fire away!"

She steeled herself to focus and listen carefully. Her answers had to remain truthful yet discreet enough not to divulge anything that could give away 'family' secrets.

"I must admit I'm very impressed by your educational resume. You put mine to shame just in my field alone." Rodane grinned at her.

"Why do you say that? Your background is just as impressive as mine."

{oops oh my god I failed already}

He caught it immediately, "My background? I don't recall us discussing my background. Sabina...?" He asked when she didn't respond, "Now this is personal. I'm very serious about this. What do you know about my background? Where did this information come from about me?"

She could tell he was actually very angry even though he had himself under total control. "Ok..." she breathed in slowly, "Here's the thing, and don't look at me as if I'm going to start lying Rodane, that's unfair! I've been as upfront with you as I can be so don't judge until you hear what I have to say... unless you'd rather call it a night and you don't have to listen to anything I say, ever!" she turned her face away to the horizon they were sailing toward. He watched her shoulders twitch.

{I'm not going to be swayed}

He felt they had come to a crisis point in their building relationship but he wasn't going to be deterred.

{what am I thinking I leave you tomorrow}

"Sabina...talk to me! We've managed to overcome everything that's been thrown at us over the last four days. I want to believe you, I truly do but you have to open up to me about anything that applies directly to me. You have to agree to that or no, we have nothing left to talk about. I promise I'll listen and I'll try hard not to make judgements until you've said your piece..." she started to say something, closed her mouth and then...

"I'm cold. Can we go in and sit while I say my 'piece'?"

"Yes, of course."

She went in and sat in an easy chair. He brought the wine bottle and the two plastic glasses, raised the bottle and at her nod, he poured two glasses out. He sat across from her and waited... sipping his wine. She took a hefty swallow that caused his brows to rise, in surprise.

"Gathering your courage?" he asked.

She shrugged her shoulders in resignation, "I guess so. I'm not going to ask you to keep this conversation secret but I will tell you..." when she saw his face..."that if you share this with anyone right now you will cause more problems for yourself rather than fewer." He was silent. She waited and finally said, "I'm surprised you didn't question that statement immediately."

"You have no idea how hard I fought myself not to jump in just then." he smiled and was relieved to see a small one from her.

"For those of us like you and me Rodane, digging for answers is a part of our being. We don't give up till our questions are answered when we dig. I don't think this is much different. We're still digging for answers..." she thought it through.

"Look you're smart, you're educated, you know the field of study involved here as well as I. I'll start with telling you that the people who hurt you and the police arresting you were all connected. Those were not coincidences either. You saw the pictures we were sent of the man who was named Tabor Doukas, and the woman was one Renata Kappos. We're still digging... excuse me, investigating them... and their presence in Akrotiri. We've..."

Rodane interrupted "Excuse me for my butting in here, but you keep saying 'we'. Are you referring to Eugenie and Helene and yourself?" he watched her. "No, of course you're not! There's a bigger picture here, isn't there? Would I be more on the mark if I said 'family'?"

She leaned forward "Just as with Kappos and Doukas, it's bigger than a few people on both sides. We're the good guys, Rodane, I promise you."

"That makes them the bad guys, right"

"Yes, it does" she let out her breath, "and we don't know about their organization or where they'll show up next or what their next move is...

{we have some ideas}

but we do know they've shown us by this event how far they are willing to go to achieve their goals. There has not been a threat level like this for a long time. We can't remember having these kinds of encounters for..." she stopped.

"Do you know what their 'goal' is Sabina? "What are they after? That tool you dug up that I'm sure you cannot discuss?" he quirked his eyebrows.

"They're after us Rodane, my 'family'. They're after the things we discover, the places we live, they're after our homes, our children, our jobs… all of it!" and her eyes filled with tears.

He moved to the chair and lifted her from it and folded her into his arms.

"Shush, it's okay. They didn't succeed here, Sabina. They failed. I don't understand exactly what you mean by all that but I know you're telling the truth and I know you're truly scared. I'm not going to let…" she put her finger over his lips.

"Shush yourself!" she kissed him lightly and leaned back in his arms "you're going home and spend time with your daughter and teach fall classes at the University of Montana…" She wiped tears from her face and he kissed it.

"We've been dealing with …well, not this, but the people who have tried for a long time, a very long time, to upend our lives. If they've decided to up their game and violence is now part of their agenda, our plans and safety procedures will be adapted to address these changes and as rapidly as possible. I'm not in any immediate danger Rodane, I can assure you."

"Is that because you always have Eugenie and Helene at your side? What, you figured I couldn't catch them watching everyone who came near to you and me or were watching every crowd we were a part of? They remind me of the other 'men in black' or Secret Service agents watching our president. 'Nobody's going to get by me, sucka!' He said in a hoarse, Southwestern accent. She chuckled.

"Yes, that is exactly why I am safe and you have nothing to worry about either. They will be with me until I return home and you will be safe in your bed as well."

"Your family is quite wealthy, correct?" they moved back to their chairs. She nodded her head.

"That's it? You're not going to give me any details?"

"I'm not going to give you any details that I think you might try to discover more by using the web or internet or other sources of information. That Eidetic memory of yours is very off-putting to people who are used to no one having information on them and especially hard to share any secure knowledge even if you have learned it yourself…if you can use it to learn more than is healthy for you."

"Are you saying I could be a danger to myself and hence a danger to those around me?"

"I'm saying you should leave all this behind you when you go home and leave it behind you for good. Your family is your concern now, not me."

"So your family is so wealthy you can't even talk about it? I'm guessing then they have their figures and fingers in all levels of government, business firms, maybe Wall Street or Nasdaq, whatever. They're probably inserted into contracting firms, banking, real estate etc." he petered off and paused.

"You forgot construction, entertainment, sports..." she caught herself and put her hand over her mouth and her eyes widened.

{damn damn damn}

He came over to her "You're so cute!" and he kissed her on her nose. He filled their empty glasses and killed the bottle then he returned to his seat.

"Can you tell me how your funds can be gotten so quickly and people, read that Genie and Lennie can arrive at a moment's notice?"

"When you have a large 'family' all over the world' you can access the best of the best and you can use your wealth to build a network of many people with varied talents and special skills."

"Is that where you come in, your special skills, your training?"

"I'm just one member of the family who tries to earn my keep and give back to those just growing up and finding themselves, so to speak."

"Tell me about your job, about your education" but she hesitated.

"Hey, it's only fair. Apparently you know my whole life history, probably have more info about me than I do."

'You promise you won't hold it against me?"

"Hold it against... what are you talking about? I was asking about your education, your field of study. How could I hold...?"

"Because" she said, "I'm an overachiever. I never stop trying to outdo myself and I've gotten pretty good at it."

"So? I was a pretty good student too. You had to be, to pass some of the classes I had with those god-awful professors who always thought they would be the next Howard Carter, finding a new tomb."

"Ok, I started at UCLA main campus and I switched schools as I changed my needs. I began in the study of Science which led to my first degree in Volcanology with a minor in Geology. I spread my classes out so I could work at the same time. I got internships on digs in progress and earned credit for them. I got an adjunct position teaching Climatology so I minored in that and got a dual degree."

"Oh, I thought it was in Linguistics."

"Well, that was the second one. I stuck with the Linguistics program and added courses that bled into the Volcanology field and studied the people who lived in areas of ancient destruction, the language component that led to migration and immigration..."

"That's lot of school for you. Finally had enough?"

"No" Sabina laughed, "Remember, overachiever? For each subject area that I took courses in, I went and got a degree in it to add to the list." He looked at her and wondered.

"How many fields are your degrees in? Are they aligned?"

"I'm embarrassed to tell you. You'll think I'm a professional student without real goals or ambitions."

"Sabina, anyone who earns two or three degrees in a short lifespan deserves to be recognized but not for being a professional student. I might be tempted to say 'genius at work.' Don't laugh! I only have two degrees and I'm in the process of completing the application for acceptance of my second doctoral thesis. It will mean a full time position at the university, recognition of my field and my finds and opportunities to publish..."

"If you want the whole truth and nothing but... you know the..."

"Yes, I know the rest. Okay, lay it on me, what is the whole truth?"

"I have seven degrees and I'm almost finished the course load I need for an 8th. I speak five languages fluently and can understand and speak three more passably."

Rodane sat there, floored and speechless. This was definitely a type of woman he had never met before. He was confused but impressed. He saw her as a mysterious, smart, agnostic challenge and yet he was on his way home at the end of the week. She was not about to introduce him to her 'family' so that was a bust. It looked like the best thing to happen to him in years that might have sent him on a life's trip, was slipping away as he watched and he would end up with everything being status quo.

{that sucks big time}

"Can I ask you what you do besides go to classes and teach a course or two during the school year? How can you afford all this education? It doesn't come cheap or else you are a favorite child with the 'family'. Where did you earn all the degrees, all at UCLA?"

"I started out at Berkeley and moved through the campus with each new degree. I studied two years at the University of Madrid and I'm finishing up my current degree back at UCLA campus and that's it."

"What about your job out in the field? You know... your recovery project and the need for your 'family' to keep these projects secure and secret."

"The recent events you and I have experienced will be discussed in detail and examined for any evidence we can discover that might lead us to the head of this group. They're orchestrating this and causing so much chaos and stress among us. It's also evident we have underestimated their personnel and their larger presence than previously thought. It may take some time but the efforts will be made as soon as we can determine where and how. The safety of our people is paramount in this whole scenario."

"I guess the only thing left for me to ask is where you go from this? I know your last stop is Capri but then what? Back home to..."

"France, my home is in France and I'll be heading there as soon as I complete my last two jobs."

"Two jobs, I thought you..."

"I've been instructed to travel to Florence when I finish my work in Sorrento. It shouldn't take long and I was going to ask you about your return home."

"I plan on finishing up my travel in six more days and then fly home to Virginia Saturday, to spend time with Sophia, till I have to report for classes and she starts school at the end of August."

"I thought in the US, they..."

"Don't even go there. Virginia has the strangest school schedule on the East Coast. They start at the end of August and then get out in the early summer, even as early as May. Parents hate it, kids hate it, and the school board ignores them all."

"But that means..."

"Yeah, she starts school while I'm stuck here. I won't be able to have her with me for those two weeks I'm allowed. That's okay. I'll stay there for a few days and we can see each other after school and the weekend. I'll have to be satisfied with that."

"Your stay there, will that be awkward?"

"Don't think so. I've met Adam once or twice and this is the longest she has been with one man. She seems to really care for this one, much more than any other. You never know, this might be the one!" he thought a moment...,"or maybe not. He's a decent guy and he really does like Sophia. She likes him too."

"You're okay with that as her dad? You won't feel shunted aside?"

"Funny you should say that. I was asking myself the same thing when I talked to Caroline earlier" he thought for a few seconds, "no, I don't think I would so..."

"You're not okay?"

"No, no. I meant I wouldn't feel resentful or shunted aside. No, Sophia and I have gotten to a good place with each other in the last couple years. We're rock solid with our relationship and she's getting to be a very smart, wise, young girl."

"When you talk about her you light up and your eyes shine. You two must be very good together..." she sounded wistful, somewhat sad.

"How about your parents, Sabina? What about your dad? Did you have a big family, I mean, besides your 'family'?"

She looked at him sideways, "Digging again, Rodane?"

"No, not at all, just asking out of interest."

"I never knew my father and I only had my mother for a few years. I was very young when I lost her and was taken in by my relatives" she looked up at him, "my 'family'."

"I'm sorry" he said sincerely, "It must be very hard to lose both parents while you're still young. Any sisters or brothers?"

"I don't know..." he watched her face.

"Seriously, I don't know. My father's death was sudden and I never did find out what happened to my mother. No one talks about it and the family that raised me doesn't have any information to share with me so we kind of had to build a 'family' for me. I have no idea who may be out there related directly to me."

"That's tough Sabina. I'm sorry if I stirred up bad feelings."

"No, it's okay. I don't remember my father. I'm not even sure if he was in my life at all. I only have vague memories of my mother. Sometimes I have dreams where she's there and I can see her and when I wake up it...'poofs' she said "So I go back to France."

"If you're teaching a course at UCLA...or are you?"

"Yes Rodane, I'm telling you the truth. I'm going back to France with Eugenie and Helene and..."

"Spend some time with your 'family' I know." he put his hand up, "I wasn't being snide. I know you have to go back to base and share with everyone but would you consider getting in touch with me when you go back to campus?"

She got up, came over to Rodane, took his hand and pulled him to his feet.

She wrapped her arms around his neck, pulled his head down to hers and proceeded to thoroughly kiss him stupid. She breathed in his ear and made his spine tingle, "Write me out your email address or give me your phone number and you and I will definitely hook up."

"How about both, just to be sure?" she laughed and kissed him again and again.

7pm, Virginia, Saturday

Sophia said, "Sit Max!" then she looked over at her mom, "He won't do it! I used treats and toys and he still won't do it." She placed her hands on her nonexistent hips.

Caroline sat at the table making lesson plans and looked up at her eight year old daughter, sitting on the floor with Max lying next to her, looking around and then laying his head on his paws. Adam was on the sofa flipping and channeling from one sport to another. It drove Caroline crazy so this was a time to get something done.

"Kitten, it's time you understand cats," Adam said. "They are a species unto themselves since the days of the Neanderthal and the saber-toothed tiger. They listen to no one except when it serves their purpose and they serve no one except themselves."

"Sometimes Adam," Sophia said, "you sound just like my dad and sometimes you sound like a normal person, but..." she continued, "I know what you mean. On Animal Planet, they have a show where they trained cats and pigs and birds to do all kinds of stuff so I still think I can do it."

Caroline looked over at Adam "Remember when we took Sophia to Busch Gardens and they had an animal show like that with a goat who danced and chickens who followed the trainer around and did somersaults down a chute?"

"Yeah, that was a very interesting show" Adam answered.

"It was awesome!" Sophia chimed in, "That's why I want to work with animals when I grow up… or be an Acheologist like…"

"That's Archeologist Sophia, not Acheologist."

"Well, dad says an Acheologist because when he is done with all his digging he says he aches all over for days."

Adam laughed, "Hmphff! Maybe your dad needs some gym time to buff up a little so that he doesn't ache much." Sophia got up and came over to him "Let me see your muscles" she said.

"Sophia" Caroline chided her, "It's not polite to ask Adam to continually perform for you."

Adam chuckled, "Is that what you call it Caroline, performing?"

"Well, it seems the two of you treat it as a game so what would you call it?"

"Please Adam, then I'll go to bed and you two can get all kissy and huggy and I'll even take Max with me."

"You will not take Max with you!" Caroline retorted, "Max and Silas will sleep out here together where they will be perfectly fine. I'm not having dog and cat hair everywhere in this house"

"No" Caroline saw Sophia put on her little pouting expression, "That's final. Mr. And Mrs. Moore will be here tomorrow and unless they have somewhere else to stay they will be in our guest room for a short time. Max and

Silas will most likely sleep in their room and I don't want that... don't look at me like that. I don't want you trying to lure them into your room, understood Sophia?"

"Ok" Sophia pouted, "Why can't we have a dog or a cat? Why not both? I'll help care for them Mama, you know I will. I help with Silas all the time. Max doesn't do anything but I can even clean out his litter box. Pleeeease!" she begged.

"Sophia you have an hour before bed. Would you like to spend that time arguing with me or doing something you'd like to do? Hmmm?"

Sophia turned to Adam, snorting with frustration, "Adam, please?" she begged.

Adam stood up... pulled his shirt up and made his abs flex back and forth. They were waves of muscle moving up and down. Then he pulled up his sleeves and made a muscle of his biceps. They were well-toned, well-muscled and hard as stones. Sophia reached up and tried to put her hand around one arm.

"Still trying to circle his arm, Sophia?" Caroline looked at the two of them and smiled, "he would have to be wasting away from a disease not to have muscles on his muscles."

"Mama" Sophia exclaimed, "That's not nice. Adam is as healthy as a horse, you said so."

"Look Sophia, I have something for you to try." He took his small flashlight out of his pocket and turned it on. He focused on the wall and began to move it around right in front of Max. Max looked, stared at the moving light and slowly got up into a crouch and began to stalk the light. When Adam moved it, Max swatted at it and moved with it as it changed position, "He's doing it Adam, he's doing it! Can I try? Can I try, please?"

He handed her the flashlight and moved to the kitchen, passing Caroline who lifted her head and smiled at him. They brushed lips as he went to the fridge. He took out a bottle of water and downed half of it in two big swallows. Sophia took the flashlight and coaxed Max into the sitting room and continued their play. Silas lay under the table, content to be lazy and disinterested in everything around him.

"Poor Silas" Adam watched him, "I think he's very homesick for his mom and dad huh?"

"Yes, they're both in a sad place right now, no home and no parents. I feel so bad for all of them. Home is gone, all their possessions are ashes, poor animals scared and lonely for their owners... really makes me appreciate what I have" she looked at him "and who I have" she rose and wrapped her arms around Adam, "I think Rodane might appreciate having Sophia for a

Christmas vacation. He hasn't had her for Christmas since… well I guess he's never had her for Christmas, except when we were together. They weren't all that great either!" she made a face and looked at Adam, "Maybe those islands are a little more doable then we thought."

"Now he smiled, "What were you going to say Caroline, truthfully?"

"I was remembering that last Christmas. We had been fighting a lot. Rodane was still pissed at an incident with toys or something and things were really tense. My mother was encouraging me to kick his ass out of the house or move back home and it was a very uncomfortable atmosphere. Sophia was throwing tantrums and not sleeping and I was exhausted. Christ that was a terrible time!"

"Your mother was asking you to come 'home'?"

"She and Dad thought Rodane was not doing what he needed to in order to give Sophia and me the life we should have so yes, they wanted me home."

"The life you should have? What kind of life did they think you were living?"

They moved to the sitting room. Sophia had gone to her own room and had taken Max with her. Adam saw it but didn't say a word to Caroline. They sat down quietly for a couple of minutes.

She hesitated, thought really hard, and then said, "You know what? I'm going to finally admit to myself a thing or two that I've been avoiding for a long time." He looked at her but didn't say anything.

She spoke, "One thing I've come to realize is that Rodane and I should never have gotten married. It was expected and he was my ticket to a new life, an exciting life I thought, one where my parents wouldn't rule over my every desire and second guess all my moves."

"Did that happen, not having someone second guess your every move?"

"It did at first. We played house for the first year then Sophia came along right afterwards. We got along very well and I guess I saw all my life as more of the same."

"Were you happy?"

"Happy is a relative term. You could say I was satisfied."

"What changed? Why did it end?" Caroline looked around her. She examined the antique furniture, the satin draperies and the pottery and bronze figures. She folded her hands and looked deeply into Adams face,

"I got greedy! Mother said I deserved more. Daddy said his little girl deserved so much more. I listened." her eyes teared up, "I resented the little we had compared to what they convinced me I should have. Sitting here listening to myself, I'm beginning to be ashamed of what I was, how I treated our marriage, of who I was."

By this time she was in tears and wringing her hands, head bowed in sorrow.

Adam walked over to her, placed his hands on the arms of the chair, leaned over on the arms and lifted her chin. Then he leaned in and kissed her lips, gently and softly, then kissed the tears streaming down her face, "Who are you now Caroline? What are you?"

"I'm…" she thought. "I'm a good teacher. I have a good job that I love. I'm a good mother, I think. I try to think of how my life and my actions will affect my daughter and…" she looked into his face and rose up out of the chair to come into his arms. "I'm very much infatuated with a very smart, insightful, wise man, one who brings out the best in me when I seem to be reaching for the worst. I'm selfish, I think too much of myself. I short change Sophia with the time spent with her and I'm too critical of those who happen to see through some of my weaker moments." She breathed a sigh of relief as if she had just gone to church for confession or had finally confessed to her crimes and was ready to sign on the dotted line and give herself up.

Adam put his hands around her face and said, "A journey begins with the first step. You've begun your journey Caroline. You've come a lot farther than the first step and you're well on your way to your destination. What would that be, do you think?"

She put her head on his chest and exhaled slowly, "I guess it would be making peace with all the people I've been at war with; my mother and father, Rodane, maybe even Sophia, the housekeeper I fired because Sophia would go to her before me…Adam, I've been… I've done…" she was again close to tears.

"No Caroline, this is not twelve steps. This is your life. Your daughter is not someone to be made amends to, she is your heart and soul, as you are mine." She looked shocked at that, "You can be sorry for your mistakes, your selfishness, your faults and feelings, but you can't just be those negative things. You are the positives too, the good, the beautiful, the dedicated teacher, the responsible mom, all of those and more. It's okay to be self-aware but not just of your drawbacks. You are also the benefits, the positives, the skills and talents, the good intentions…"

"Oh my God, Adam! How did I manage to find you through all this? How could I be so lucky to find someone who sees me for what I really am, all parts of me and still stays around to watch me fumble and keep being foolish and bitchy and arrogant and…"

"Shush" he kissed her…"and being mine and being Sophia's mom and so much more. I want to reach that destination with you."

Sophia chose that moment to come running into the room to show her what she had taught Max. She held up the little flashlight attached to a feather on a string Adam had given her and flashed it in the air. Max stood up on his back legs and danced in a circle, trying to reach the feather and the light.

"Sophia, that's wonderful!" Caroline exclaimed.

"That's my girl! Adam swung Sophia around in a circle, holding her 'feather light' and Max was dancing around them trying to reach the light, "That's my clever kitten and my very, very clever cat too!" Adam said.

Caroline stood there watching the two of them, heart bursting with love, feeling so blessed, so secure in their love. "What more could I possibly want or need?" Caroline whispered to herself.

Chapter 18

Naples

The Jewel of the Seas tied up at the pier in Naples at 8:15 a.m. pretty close to scheduled time. Everyone had gotten up and dressed for breakfast and had their passports ready at the pier by 8:30. The line of people getting off for the day was long and slow and all four of them were anxious to get to their destination. Rodane was eager to take his photographs of Naples, see the city during the days and get some pictures of the night life for his brochure.

Sabina wanted to go from this pier to the ferry's pier to Capri for the first crossing and get to the meeting that was scheduled at 11 a.m. Helene and Eugenie had their assignment and were ready to do some work for a change. Their trip had been pleasant but the lack of activity had them both raring to go and ready for some action. When they managed to fight the crowd to get off the pier and began to head to the thoroughfare, Rodane turned to Sabina as Helene and Eugenie hung back.

"I can't begin to apologize for your trip up to this point. We've been through quite a stretch in just a few days…,"

"Sabina, stop talking" Rodane moved closer to her to speak softly, "I wouldn't have traded it for anything, well… maybe the knock on the head. On second thought I could have done without the fire, and losing everything… no, scratch that. I didn't lose everything. I think I gained something very important."

He moved to her at the same moment that she moved to him. They met and so did their lips. The kiss was deep and long and heated. She felt his heat and his hardened body and it moved to her and through her whole being. Her heart flooded and his hand on the back of her neck had a racing pulse she could feel through her skin. She looked up at him, the depth of his green eyes and he looked at her, into her startling blue eyes and they sank into each other as if there was a tether connecting one to the other. Her breath was held, his skin was on fire and neither one could make the move to part.

Helene went to Rodane and put her hand on his arm, gently. It was as if a hot torch had touched him. It brought him back instantly and he stepped back from Sabina. The look on her face was one of loss, sorrow, painful separation while they were still together.

Sabina said, "I'll be in touch as soon as I possibly can."

"Shouldn't the gentleman get in touch with the lady first, as a courtesy?"

"Rodane, it's the 21st century and it's obvious you've gotten rusty over the last couple of years but you're cute and I love it. I'll talk to you soon. Keep your phone on."

He touched her cheek, started to speak…changed his mind and went over to give the girls a hug. They said something to him and then he turned his head, smiled at her and started walking off to his left towards the city. He was heading for the hotel Piazza Bellini, a first tier hotel with a second tier cost. It was close to the central train station on a popular Piazza with good cafes and good food with the Dante underground close by. His room had a view of Castel Sant Elmo.

He figured he would walk during the day, visit some tourist spots and then take the underground to a few clubs for some nightlife photos and some good shots of the city lights and hot spots. He decided he would visit the Archaeological Museum first off, since it was in walking distance from the hotel. In writing his travel brochures, he had learned to include a few sites that would appeal to everyone, young and old, tourists and clubbers alike. The easy access to all the sights made this part of Naples a safe place to wander and take in some of those sights while the clubbers were sleeping in from their late night partying. It seemed to work for everyone.

His travelogues were popular and brought a good deal of interest which led to bookings. He got a percentage of each booking by having his email and info on the back of each brochure and he got a flat fee for each travelogue. It was definitely worth his time and travel and it was adding up to a very substantial college fund for Sophia.

Her constant asking for him to take her on some of these trips made him feel guilty for missing out on her time with him. Perhaps when he got home from this trip, he would contact the lawyer to see about revisiting the custody agreement and getting more time with her during the year or he could even take her on his next tour.

{fat chance of that huh Caroline}

JOURNEY TO THE BLUE PLANET

He entered the hotel lobby from SM Constantinopoli and went to the receiving desk. A clerk was manning the desk, a short woman with dark hair mixed with grey, tied in a tight bun that made him think of a school marm. She looked up at him, disdainfully eyed his one rolling case and asked him with a drawling Napoli accent, "How can I be of service, Signor?"

"I have a reservation for one, Dr. Rodane Arcos and I...
{wow looks like I jerked her chain}
have a room in the back, looking out onto the Piazza, I believe?" he handed over his reservation number and his ID. She bent her head over his ID for at least one full minute.

"It's me, I promise." Then she looked up at him and said, "One moment please Dr. Arcos."

She left him to go to the back and returned a few moments later with his ID card and proceeded to check him in, "I'm afraid your room will not be ready until ten, sir. You're welcome to use the lobby or to return at ten. The bar is open I believe."

He was somewhat taken aback. The Piazza hotel usually was right on the ball with service. How could a room, this late in the morning, not be ready? Oh well, he could always take a walk around the Piazza, get some expresso and read the news on his laptop.

So that's what he did. He drank a couple of expressos at one of the many breakfast bars that surrounded the Piazza, sat outside in the early morning sun and read up on all the news he has been missing. Without realizing it, he sat for over an hour engrossed in world news as well as local, political and entertainment. Then he got up, left by the back exit and walked up and down streets too narrow for cars and too busy for bicycles. It was almost like being in a walled enclave and it was the most pleasant experience he could remember since before this particular trip had begun.

He window-shopped and then he stopped so suddenly, someone ran into him from behind and it caused a chain reaction. He turned around to see two or three people untangling their shopping bags and each other's arms. It was so amusing he took his camera off his shoulder and snapped some pictures of people apologizing to each other profusely and laughing at the same time. Early morning Italians were usually a happy people. It was the later heat of the day that brought out the impatience and snappishness that some tourists criticized. He stood at the top of the street and snapped some good shots of the train tracks and the harbor where they had docked. The light was perfect and he thought these might be some really good ones.

It was time to go back to the hotel and as he started walking, the hair on the back of his neck raised up. He kept walking as if he were just strolling along. He looked slightly to the left and still nothing so he stopped at a window to examine the jewelry in black velvet cases. Then he turned right to continue walking, nothing out of the ordinary. He couldn't shake the feeling that someone was very interested in him. He had two more blocks to walk till he got back to the hotel. He took his time and tried not to hurry or alert anyone that he was aware of any strange presence.

When he entered the lobby, the hotel desk clerk looked up and a look of total surprise crossed her face very quickly before she became stone faced. She managed a small smile and nodded to him as he took his things and moved to the elevator. Once in his second floor room, he checked out the room and the mini bar as well as the bathroom.

{a rainforest showerhead sweet!}

He had a balcony which looked out on the Piazza itself and over the roofs to a beautiful sight of the harbor. It would be a restful night.

He thought of Sabina and himself having those late night talks on their ship balconies and all they learned about each other. In such a short time he felt like he knew her better than he had ever known Caroline, yet now that they had shared so many events, he felt like Sabina had opened his mind to some of the behind-the-scenes thinking and acting that he and Caroline had gone through. It didn't explain everything but it sure did shine some light on the motives behind his and Caroline's actions and their reasons.

Did every failed marriage make use of the children as pawns in their battles? It didn't say much about the adults making major decisions but it did say something about him and Caroline trying to make a good stab at having a civil relationship for the sake of Sophia. Maybe that idea about a custody reexamination might have to be reconsidered. He took his camera and went out to the balcony to take some shots from up high with the sun behind his shoulder. He could see the ferry going out and the fishing boats heading to deeper water for the day. Tourists were beginning to multiply and fill the street and the horns of taxis were a mute undertone to the busy life of Naples.

He hooked up the camera to his laptop and downloaded his pictures then he packed his things into his backpack, took water from his fridge and headed out to explore the city. He planned on getting most of his work done near the archaeological dig just begun over by the train yards; old and new, charm and tech, history and 21st century tourism, a contrast in opposites. Good plan for a travelogue. He took the stairs down and went out into the mid- morning sun of Naples, Italy.

Naples Ferry to Capri

Sabina boarded the ferry at 9 o'clock exactly. It was already crowded with workers carrying big bulky tool bags on their shoulders, other workers wearing hard hats and tool belts, waitresses in uniform and maintenance workers carrying cases of fuses and bulbs, duct tape and tool boxes. The seats were all taken. It would be better for her to be outside anyway. She moved to the railing at the aft of the boat and felt the wetness from the wash of the boat. It was a clear day with a hint of the heat to come later. A hand on her shoulder had her jerking and her heart fluttered rapidly for a few seconds.

A voice said, "Try not to turn to me and we can have a very short conversation." Suri was on one side of her and Leander was on the other side. Over in the corner of the deck were Acacia and Evangela talking together. Everyone was here except Nikos.

"Is the meeting still in Ana Capri? Sabina asked.

"Yes. Take the Funicular up and then the lift. When you get there look for Nikos. He will be at the fountain. When he leaves, follow and he'll take you to a meeting room. Try and be there by 11. The tourists for the Blue Grotto will be heading there around noon and we like to be out of sight by then."

"What about Helene? She's here with me."

Suri answered, "I know, I talked to her at the pier." Sabina looked at her surprised. Her eyes showed hurt, "Sabina, I have to get an honest take on what has been going on the last three days. We all do."

Sabina tensed, "You don't think you can get that from me, Suri, after all these years?"

Suri looked at her, this woman who was as close to a daughter as she could possibly be. Their lives had been intertwined since Sabina was three years old. She thought she knew her like the back of her hand but the last two reports were showing her a side of Sabina she had not seen in a very long time. She needed to trust her but she also had to trust her own self and keep her people safe. Better someone not so emotionally invested in this Dr. Arcos, "I'll see you up on the hill Sabina." Suri turned and walked into the cabin of the ferry.

Sabina stood there watching small waves crash against the side of the boat and felt the small shudders of the strength of the sea, warring with the solid planks of the ferry. She wasn't sure if she was the wave or the plank. The ferry continued on to Capri on a beautiful, blue, cloud-washed sky, heading for a natural wonder that many thousands had seen before.

City of Naples

"God damn it woman, where were you?" he had Renata gripped by her arms in a vice hold and the veins stood out on Tabor's forehead like small worms crawling across it. She didn't struggle to get free and she clenched her teeth against the painful grasp to answer him in as calm a voice as she could manage,"I was parking the car like you told me and I had to go around two blocks twice to find a space close to the hotel. The valet wouldn't let me stay in the driveway and I didn't want to draw attention to myself by arguing with him. Now, let… me… go…" she said each word slowly and softly.

His eyes became pinpoints in his face that was red and sweaty but this time she stared him down and she knew her face was a stone mask, despite the pain he was causing her. His hold tightened for a moment. Whatever he saw made him loose his grip and he stepped back, "So, the little elf has a backbone after all" he muttered with a tone of satisfaction. She said nothing.

"We just lost our shot of getting him into the car at the alley entrance of the hotel. Guess we'll have to hope he goes out later and provides us with another chance at him. It looked so easy when there was little traffic. I actually thought for a moment he knew I was there. He seemed to be startled and then he started taking pictures so suddenly I thought he was homing in on me but he just kept snapping so I blended into the crowd.

When you didn't come, I waited by the Piazza entrance and he went straight into the hotel. I didn't think it would be as easy as we hoped. He's managed to shield himself for the last three days and we were lucky we got information on his hotel reservation yesterday or we'd be phoning every hotel in the city."

Renata went over and sat down in the one soft chair in the whole apartment. "He's by himself," said Tabor. "I waited and watched for at least fifteen minutes and no one in their little group showed up unless they were already in the room but the desk clerk would have alerted us if that were the case. She's been paid handsomely to keep us alerted."

When Renata said nothing, he picked up his glass from the table and poured more vodka into it then he looked at her expression, "What's the matter little elf? Are you criticizing my drinking now?" His voice was rough and coarse, he was still flushed and it seemed he was spoiling for a fight and she wasn't going to give him one. She was tired and hot. The air conditioning, if you could call it that, never worked right and her nights were sweaty and miserable. Even the bed sheets were warm even without the blanket.

Tabor had been drinking steadily since the first night they were there. Food didn't seem important to him so she went and bought her own take out or brought a pizza back. Sometimes he ate some, most times not. One day to go and it didn't seem as if they had any edge. It was already late afternoon and tomorrow was supposedly the last day they had to get to Rodane. They couldn't cause a public spectacle and had only hours to extract the information they needed to find Sabina Carter and obtain what their boss was counting on them to get.

Renata knew what she had to do but it made her gut ache and the bile rise in her throat. She felt cold all over for once in the last two and a half days but she didn't welcome it. She got up and went to the kitchen to get a glass. She poured herself a large measure of vodka and came over to where Tabor was, on the sofa. She had a long night ahead of her.

"Darling, let's forget Arcos for now and just take care of each other for a change" she drank and leaned over to him. Of course he would respond immediately.

Four hours later, Tabor was passed out on the bed and Renata had gone to the bathroom. She forced herself to throw up to lessen the effects of the vodka. She ate two slices of cold pizza just to absorb the alcohol in her stomach then after fifteen or twenty minutes, had thrown that up to rid her body of the rest of the poison. She had a monster headache and her guts were rumbling. She felt dirty from head to toe, inside her very soul. Outside, her skin crawled at the thought of his drunken hands on her body, roaming and pinching, his lips on her breast, his tongue in her mouth and entering her, spittle spilling onto her face. She had grasped the rungs of the bed while he grunted and pumped himself so hard into her, battering her head against the headboard again and again. Finally he released and relaxed himself and fell onto her chest, passed out cold.

She rolled him off and now she just wanted to shower till she had scrubbed herself raw and had used up all the hot water. She brushed her teeth until her gums hurt and then stumbled out to the sofa. She found herself huddled in the corner of the sofa, holding in silent sobs, tears rolling down her face unceasingly. She picked up the phone and looked at her contacts. For half an hour, she debated with herself then she dialed the number and spoke at the sound of his voice, "Mister Gallo, this is Renata, sir."

Piazza Hotel

Rodane had a very long, pleasant lunch at a small cafe a few doors down from the Piazza. His stomach was full and his body was tired. His tray of antipasto was devoured, his shrimp Alfredo was sitting heavy in his belly as was half of the third rice dish. He finished his one glass of wine and thought that might be the tipping point but everything settled and he asked for a shot of Amaretto liqueur. Then he decided to use the indoor pool to wear off his bloated stomach and his lethargy. It was either that or take a three-hour siesta which very much appealed to him.

He went back to the hotel at the hottest part of the day so no one was at the desk. He went to his room to change to swim trunks. He reached the pool, grabbed a clean towel off the table and proceeded to do a nine lap set; three crawl; three sides stroke and three butterfly, this done two times. When he was done he felt better; awake and refreshed. He sat in the hot tub for fifteen minutes and finished it off with twenty minutes of the sauna till he was dripping sweat and felt like a dishrag. Then it hit him.

{oh shit I was supposed to try and Skype with Sophia today}

Four there in Va. would be ten his time so a nap was out. He had enough time to visit the Archaeological Museum here, take shots of the downtown and write up a review to send all his materials so far and ask his travel agency for comments and suggestions. He left the pool, went up the stairs to his room and took a nice, hot shower. The bed looked so enticing but he shrugged it off and took his laptop and camera to the desk in his room. He began by taking out his notebook and reading over everything he had done for the last two days. He had the diagram of the Archeological Museum of Piraeus and wrote up a review of all the sites that they had seen Friday afternoon and evening. He downloaded all the pictures he had taken while in Piraeus and he looked at a couple of pictures he had taken of Sabina at the beach and one of the three girls, taken at one of the night clubs they had visited. He closed up the computer, put it into its case, grabbed his camera and bag and headed out to visit the museum.

He spent the next few hours walking all over the downtown and took pictures of the dig in progress at the Dante underground. It seemed like all construction had come to a halt while digging and categorizing was ongoing. He had spent two hours in the museum and took some really nice pictures of the museum's gardens from the outside. Then he visited some side streets and found a few small stores that carried some very nice souvenirs. He bought one for his teaching partner back home, another globe for Sophia and something for his mom and Caroline and Adam.

On the way back to the hotel he stopped for a slice of pizza at a little outdoor cafe and then treated himself to a coconut gelato at a stand across from the fountain. He snapped pictures of some small gardens and back yards of houses on some side streets. When he checked his watch he realized it was already eight.

{well get moving buddy Sophia waits}

He made his way to his hotel and went to his room. He passed the desk clerk, a young man this evening, who looked up when he entered and offered him a "Buona Sera'. He set up his laptop on the table and decided to look at all the pictures he had taken today. Maybe he could sort out the ones he wanted to be a part of the travelogue and get a jump on sending them back home early. He sorted through the areas of the town he had photographed, starting with this morning's walk. He was chuckling at the tumble of arms and bags from the early morning stumble when he stopped… went back and looked again. He dug in his backpack and drew out the all-purpose keychain he carried where the handle to the chain was actually a small magnifying glass. He held it to the screen and turned the laptop to the light to see as clearly as possible.

"Son of a bitch! What are you doing here?"

There in the picture, was one Tabor Doukas, three or four people back, standing along the side looking straight at him in the lens with a look of total focus on the photographer, which would be him! He got up, shaking and pacing the floor, asking himself questions. That was the feeling he got on that street! He remembered the cold feeling he had and the shiver he experienced that made him try to surreptitiously examine people around him.

{why are you here this is not coincidence}

He knew they were the ones who had been in Akrotieri. Why here? Now? To follow him? To follow Sabina? She wasn't here, he was. How long had he been here and how did he know this was where he was heading? Or did he? No matter the reason, this man was here waiting for him and Rodane had to stay alert and aware. For a moment, he was tempted to check out, get tickets on the train to Florence and get out of here, immediately. He even began to close the laptop but his hand stopped him.

{I'll be damned if I let myself be run out by a thug!}

He was doing a job and he wasn't done. He refused to consider this craven surveillance as something that would make him run away. He went to the balcony, looked out at the people in the Piazza. He didn't recognize anyone and he didn't like standing out here where the light would make him a clear target. He went inside, shut down the pictures and set up Skype for Sophia and himself to get a chance to have a conversation together.

The phone rang at Caroline's house and then a little minx showed up on screen holding a…,

{what is that, a cat?}

"Sophia… Hi!" What do you have there?"

"Hi Daddy this is Max. He's the only pet mom will let me have but he belongs to the Moores and they're coming to get him and I need you to ask mom to let me…"

"Sophia honey, slow down and tell me what you are so excited about. How are you and why do you have Max if he belongs to the Moores?"

The conversation took his mind off a very dangerous enemy, who was apparently tracking him.

Island of Capri

The docks at Capri were busy and noisy. All the workers started to stand in the aisles before the boat had even docked. They lined up, some with coffee in their hands, some making phone calls, others just silent. The line moved a few steps at a time to exit the ferry for people to get to work. As Sabina joined the line, she felt herself jostled from behind and a voice in her left ear

"Check your pocket. Then meet me at the Funicular at the top."

She kept moving and when she walked along the far side toward the Funicular, she glanced around at all the tourists. There was no one she recognized. She got her ticket at the kiosk and got in line for the slow trip up the mountain side. She looked out the glass doors and watched the tram proceed past old stone houses, crowded little sheds surrounded by multi colored flowers, all the way up the hill. The boats in the harbor started to look like little fake pieces on a platform for matchbox cars. There were tiny little people stationed at a body of water, seemingly made from blue melted plastic with white glue waves, all moving out of the miniature houses and on the docks.

When the Funicular reached the top, all doors opened and people jostled and elbowed each other to get off one millisecond sooner than the person behind them. They climbed the steps and came out on a gradual incline that led to a courtyard surrounded by fantastic views of the hills of Capri. Benches surrounded the courtyard and people milled around buying lemonade, taking pictures, old men sitting together snapping out Italian so fast she could hardly keep up. She moved over to the side and tried to view the Piazza through the eyes of a tourist. Restaurants, shops and a few connecting buildings met her eyes. The mountain in front of her climbed into the clouds toward Ana Capri and the buildings behind the lift were shuttered and silent. She walked over to the railing and turned right at the corner of the railing so no one was on her side. She reached into her pocket and pulled out a slim piece of paper...

Rodane Arcos is in danger. There are eyes on him who intend to extract information no matter the cost. Get him out of Naples.

She caught her breath and felt hot and then cold. Her eyes took in the sights around her but her brain couldn't process what she was seeing. She gripped the railing till her fingers ached. What could she do here, now? How could she help Rodane to get this message and be warned? She thought of the council meeting here in... she checked her watch, ten minutes. She put the note back in her pocket, took a deep breath and moved to get a ticket to Ana Capri.

At the ticket counter to the left, a tall, slim woman stepped out from the side and looked directly at her. Her dark hair was a few shades darker than Sabina's own. She was taken aback when they looked at each other and she saw the beautiful, blue eyes looking back at her that she saw in her mirror each day. Who...? What...?

"It's you," Sabina stared.

"Yes, I'm guilty as charged. Do you have a minute?" Sabina looked at her watch,

"I have about five. Why did you give me your note? How do you know Rodane Arcos?"

"Let's just say I have a vested interest in keeping Dr. Arcos safe and sound. It was necessary to reach out to you to try and ensure that. There isn't a lot of...ah, time to communicate to the interested parties."

"What can I do? I'm not sure of where Dr. Arcos is at the moment."

"I know. You parted ways yesterday to do your job and he to do his."

Sabina was shocked. Supposedly, this woman in front of her knew a lot about both of them that they had no way of knowing they were telegraphing or making public. Yet still, their movements were tracked and observed. She didn't know whether to be disconcerted that their movements were tracked or grateful that someone was tracking them and now attempting to help them out in a possibly dangerous situation. The woman moved toward her and Sabina took a step back. The woman stopped.

"I mean you no harm. I'm trying to walk a fine line here. I'm between betraying my own interests and giving you a heads up on a possible disaster for all of us."

Sabina said, "I don't understand that. Can you tell me who you are?" She watched her expression.

"Of course, you can't. Can you at least tell me why Rodane is in danger and what I can do to help?"

"You have some very powerful friends and family here who have the resources to help him out. But they may hesitate, thinking that he might be a danger to them as well. As I said, a fine balancing act...for you... as well as me."

Sabina studied her for a moment. Then she hesitated before she spoke, "I feel, I think...this is more personal for you than strategic. Am I correct?"

"It is, in a way. I can't say much more other than to let you know some of what I know that might very well save his life and keep you safe."

Sabina started, "Me? What does this have to do with me? I thought you were concerned with Rodane's safety?"

"Can you honestly say that your interests and Rodane's are not now connected? She waited and watched Sabina's face, "I thought not."

"Ok" Sabina said, "What do I have to do to keep Rodane safe? What and who is a danger to Rodane? I can't really help if I don't know where the danger lies or who presents it."

"You know the where. Your Rodane is there now. The 'who,' you also know if you consider the last few days you've been working together. How you protect him is totally up to you. We've done what we can to alert you to the danger, without involving him directly. That would be a mistake at this point and we're trying to avoid those kinds of mistakes.

Sabina thought this over and considered what was not being said, rather than what was said.

"So I'm to have my resources step up to help Rodane, based on your assessment of the danger he faces, without telling me who, but it's necessary to keep Rodane out of it for your sake as well as ours. Do I have that about right?"

"Perfectly Sabina. Don't be surprised. I think you will find your superiors know as much about us as we do about you. That's really all I can say now and you have an appointment to keep. I hope this works out well for you. I can't be of any more help to you but I hope the rest of your trip is more pleasant than the last few days."

"This danger of yours, toward Rodane... you're a part of whoever is now a threat to him, am I correct?" Her pulse was speeding up and her anger level was rising even though she was attempting to rein herself in.

"Sorry Sabina, I have nothing else to share with you. I've probably said more than I should. Take care."

She turned around and started toward the Funicular to return to the docks. Sabina started to follow her and took a step forward. A hand on her arm stopped her cold.

She turned, prepared to ...what? Helene stood to her side, watching the woman walk away. Sabina's eyes widened at the realization that Helene was aware of the conversation having just taken place.

"Do you know that woman, Helene? Do you recognize her?"

"You're going to be late for your meeting Sabina. You know how the Council hates to be kept waiting. It's also a precarious position to put them in, to show up late and possibly draw attention, to you and to their presence."

Helene watched her, studying her response.

"Fine" Sabina huffed, "but you're coming with me to address all the shit that's happened recently. I have a lot to present, and a lot of questions to have answered."

"Sabina, you'd better get yourself under better control before you face them. Your anger isn't going to help you or your concerns. We're all in this together. You should know that, right?"

Sabina turned and flounced away toward the ticket booth. Helene stepped in front of her and handed her a ticket, already punched. Sabina's color rose and she stopped, clinched her teeth to avoid snapping at Helene and stalked to the lift. Helene followed her onto the two chairs. At the top of the lift, there was a young boy helping people off the chairs and onto the walkway where there were signs leading to the Blue Grotto. To the right of that path was a low building, used for souvenirs and gifts. It was shuttered but the light over the side door was lit. She walked over and was about to enter when it opened and Suri looked out at her. Helene came up behind her, and they quickly entered and closed the door behind them.

Suri waited for Sabina to speak and her face was inscrutable.

"Suri, I have something that needs to be addressed immediately and a concern to all of us I think, but it also involves Rodane Arcos and it's imminent."

Suri said, "Then I guess we'll have to address it first if you're prepared."

"Oh I'm prepared alright, and I need some answers as well, because at this point I'm all sorts of discombobulated."

Suri put her hand on Sabina's shoulder, her expression one of a gentle patience combined with a soft amusement at Sabina's discomfiture.

"It's ok Sabina, we'll do what we have to do and it will be alright. I promise."

They walked into a large room with low lights and there were a number of people sitting around a large heavy rectangular table in the center of the room. Seated were Leander, Nikos at the far end of the table, Acacia and Evangela, sitting next to each other and the three empty chairs at the other end. Suri walked around the table and she seated herself next to Leander and motioned for Sabina and Helene to fill the other two seats. Helene sat down next to Evangela and that left Sabina the seat at the end, looking at Nikos at the other end.

Leander stood and started to address Nikos. Suri stood and cleared her throat. Leander stopped short and turned in surprise to Suri, "Ma Cherie, we discussed…"

Suri said, "Leander, I most sincerely apologize for my interruption but I beg you to give Sabina a few minutes to address all of us before she is required to give her report. I believe she has something of some importance that might require immediate attention correct, Sabina?"

Sabina nodded her head and Suri sat down. Leander looked from one to another then slowly sat down also. Nikos raised his head and nodded to Sabina. Her hands were shaking and sweat had wet her armpits as well as broken out on her forehead. She rose and addressed all of them, one at a time, "If I don't know the facts" she looked from one to the other, "Excusez moi," this was aimed at Leander, "Merci…for allowing me to speak to you but my concerns may affect all of us as I have been told by ah… someone I don't know."

She then proceeded to give them the account of her meeting with her note giver at the Funicular. All eyes were hooded but one could actually feel the tension building in the room as she finished with the woman's last warning. Sabina took a breath, "Does she know more about us than we do her or at least more than I know? If Rodane Arcos is in danger and it could affect us, is there something we could do to help him without his knowing? She was very clear about that."

She stood uncomfortably, waiting for a response from any of them. The minutes ticked by in silence. Finally, Nikos looked up at her and motioned for her to seat herself. As she did, he said, "It seems this whole event has been a lot more complicated than we thought. Let's take a few minutes to process this latest development. Helene?"

Sabina twisted her head so fast she felt a stretch in her tendons and a click of her vertebrae. Helene? How could Helene know anything when she was with them the entire time? Helene stood and spoke, "I've seen this woman before, once in the French ambassador's residence and once in Mykenos when I was on an assignment. She is obviously aware of our events in Akrotieri and she also knows where Rodane is now. She is at least a half step ahead us on this. Dr. Arcos is in a hotel in Naples and last I heard, was visiting museums, walking the neighborhoods, taking photographs and touching base with his daughter but otherwise nothing stands out as dangerous. Would you like me to get an update?" Nikos nodded 'yes,' and Helene pushed in her chair and left the room. Sabina was flabbergasted. What was she missing here? Was she in the dark for a reason or just not being observant?

"Sabina, I think now would be a good time to give us your report on the recovery at Akrotiri and all you can tell us about this Dr. Arcos. He seems quite the unique character from what we've gleaned so far. She touched the file that each one had a copy of on the table, "No, stay seated, please."

It took a while to go over everything and make sure she didn't leave anything out. They didn't interrupt or ask questions or make comments. The whole explanation sounded more and more surreal as she continued laying out the events beginning with the attempted recovery that first afternoon. Going through these events, she stopped when she reached the moment on the cruise when the three ladies went to Rodane with pictures of Kappos and Doukas and he recognized them.

"Oh my god, I know who is after Rodane and why!"

She looked up and realized they all had eyes on her. She examined their expressions for a moment and her shoulders slumped. She almost whispered, "You already know. You've known for some time and you let us hang out in the wind while those two were tracking us, attacking Rodane. They almost killed him. He was jailed when you probably knew he hadn't done anything. Ok…let me breathe… a minute."

Suri made a motion to rise and Sabina put her hand up in protest, "No don't, please. Let me breathe."

Minutes went by and finally she spoke, "You've kept Helene, probably Eugenie also, aware of all you've learned over the past few days but I haven't been made aware of anything. All the time I've been with them and you didn't see fit to acknowledge that I should have known what they were up to? Rodane and I were targets and we had no idea, no way to protect ourselves. Now he's in danger and the person I've never met had to be the one who alerted me to it. You didn't trust me to handle anything that could possibly keep him safe and get him out of Italy."

She looked too depressed and sad and having a hard time reconciling this with 'family' so she slumped in her seat and put her head down in defeat. It was Acacia who rose from her seat and moved to take the empty one where Helene had sat. She moved to take Sabina's hand but it was jerked away as if it had been burned by the touch.

"Ok" She sat back and waited for Sabina to look at her,

"Sabina, you know me. You've known me for years. Do you trust me?"

Sabina looked at her, cheeks still flushed, anger in her blue eyes and a pale face.

"Do you?" Acacia studied her carefully.

"I thought I did. I thought I trusted everyone here, my 'family'…" and her voice broke.

"Sabina," Acacia said gently, "Have you wondered at all why this is the first dig you've had assigned to you where things went south? Did it occur to you that this is your first recovery out of many where things went very badly and you became a liability? Why do you think that is after all this time?"

It took a minute for Sabina to understand, "Are you saying it's Rodane who is… being targeted here, not me? How can that be?"

Nikos spoke, "Sabina, the attack on you was a direct target. It's true. We received pictures of your two subjects from there.

He smiled, "From Roseann's cousin, Stephanos. Seems he didn't take too kindly to being roughed up when they came looking for your Rodane to get information on Arcos. We got this just yesterday from your bell boy…" he smiled, "whose name by the way, is Anthony."

"Why did they want information on Rodane? He was just inadvertently in a bad situation."

"See, that's where we're not sure if that's true or not." Nikos raised his palm… "Wait let me finish. First, Kappos and Doukas. They thought it was just a coincidence as did we but they managed to get a condensed file on your friend and it seemed to set more activity in motion. Your two trackers are somewhat obsessed with the idea of Dr. Arcos being more than what he seems. We're still not sure whether that's an accurate assessment or not but we're going on the assumption that it may be either partly or completely true."

Sabina started to speak but Nikos continued, "No, that's not all. We've done our own investigation into your Doctor Arcos and we're not sure ourselves if there isn't more about him that we're not aware of and it may be why they've turned their attention to him and not yourself. OR it could just be that this Tabor Doukas is acting out of revenge and the desire to have payback for Arcos' interference that destroyed his plans. He seems a nasty sort of fellow with all sorts of issues and a lot of mental instability. Whoever gave you a heads up seems to be attempting to stop this man in his tracks and not because they're doing us a favor. More like they're trying to rein in a possible lone wolf off the reservation that's causing them quite a bit of trouble. Lucky for us! Now we need to discuss what steps to take to keep him safe and safeguard our 'family' in the process. Any ideas Sabina? Do you know Rodane Arcos well enough to know how he will react if we reach out to him?"

Sabina took a moment and then asked, "Reach out to him? For what purpose if I may ask? He's set to go home soon and spend time with his daughter. He begins his teaching semester in a matter of days. If we can provide protection till then it should be fine."

Suri spoke up, "Sabina, if there's more to Rodane and what you've learned… if…no, wait…let me say it. We've been dancing around this since we talked on your cruise. If there's a connection here to our 'family' and our concerns, even a small one, how can we not follow up on it? We've learned much about Rodane since that first report you made and Quimby sent you Helene and Eugenie. They are also of the opinion that Rodane's layers are deeper than thought. We all agree," she looked at everyone around the table.

"And…we are agreed that it is worth the effort. There seems to be something in the works surrounding his ex-wife and his daughter."

"Wait" Sabina almost yelled, "that can't be. There's no way that information is out there."

"Believe that it's out there and there are a few people who seem to be very interested in following up on it from across the pond. He's not insulated, Sabina. He really is a target now for whatever reason, and so is his family. Should we not make sure? Wouldn't it set your mind at rest?"

Sabina put her hands over her face and muttered, "My God, what have I gotten him into?" She sat silent for more seconds. Acacia took her hands from her face and this time she didn't reject her.

"You haven't done anything to cause this. Your job was complete and successful. It seems we have a full blown incursion into our 'family' and there are a few people out there with access to our history and our present and every day activties." All of them exchanged looks with each other.

"Because of me and what I did! How can I help, what can I do?"

Suri said "I'm glad you asked. There's a lot you can do but we need to protect Rodane first, before we can move on. Here's what we do for the moment."

Naples Apartment

Tabor was hung over, really hung over to the point he spent his morning and afternoon between bucket and toilet. Each received equal attention and Renata left him to it. She was hung over herself, though not to that degree. She had gotten a few hours of sleep and had gone out for two hot coffees. She had taken Ibuprofen and chewed a few antacids to cut the acid that threatened to send her into competition with him for the bucket. She was starting to feel partially human and she spent the time watching news on TV and going over Rodane's file again.

Around 6 o'clock in the evening, Tabor became somewhat alive and decided he was hungry. He asked if she wanted anything and when she declined, he went out to find some quick food. While he was gone, she made herself some hot tea and sipped it slowly while she went over all the information given to her about Rodane. As eager as she was to punish Sabina Carter, she could understand why Tabor wanted to take Rodane, torture him, extract information and... what? A dead subject? Theras would not be thrilled with that outcome. For that matter, he wouldn't be too happy if Sabina Carter was eliminated as well.

If she wanted to be honest with herself, she would admit that the reason she wanted to hurt Sabina Carter was because she absolutely abhorred failing at a job and Carter had bested her and Arcos had managed to elude them up to now. It was a new, very uncomfortable feeling, along with the realization she was done with Tabor. She dreaded his attentions, the abuse, as well as the physical... well that was abuse of another sort. Her skin actually crawled when he touched her now. How she was able to conceal it was a wonder even to her.

After her phone call to Theras, she went from relieved to terrified. When Tabor was awake, she went from terrified to being disgusted. She wasn't sure if she was more upset by the thought of Theras knowing what has been happening over the last weeks and months or the possibility of Tabor finding out about her contacting Theras and his reaction. Her stress level was making her light headed and nauseated, even worse than the remaining hangover. She was hot then cold and constantly feeling like she had his eyes on her, testing her, observing her, judging her. She'd go crazy if this wasn't settled soon and she'd be dead if Tabor put his finger on the change in her and the ill feelings she now tried so hard to control.

The key in the lock signaled his return and when he came in with a bag, she was at the kitchen table finishing her tea.

"Feel better?" he asked.

{if you only knew}

Baring her trials and shames of the last months, Theras had lifted a weight from her shoulders she wasn't consciously aware had gotten heavier and heavier of late. Having him know what had become an impossible burden had made it a little easier to finish this job and go home, where matters would then be out of her hands. She could rest and relax, ignore all the stresses of the events that had dragged her down to a very dark place. She would not be working with Tabor, she would be adamant about that. With a new partner or by herself, she would regain her mental equilibrium and her inner balance as well. She could accomplish her tasks without feeling like she was constantly being judged, evaluated, found wanting and yes, raped and demeaned. She shivered from head to toe.

"You ok?" Tabor asked, "You're shaking," he went to feel her forehead and she left her seat and headed for the bedroom.

"I think either I have alcohol poisoning or else I'm coming down with something. I need to sleep."

"We have to plan how we're going to take down Arcos tomorrow. I'm not going another day without finishing this, getting the hell out of here and back home."

She steeled herself to remain calm, "Tabor, sweetheart, I can't think straight now. I feel terrible. I promise. After a good night's sleep and some food, tomorrow we'll work out a plan."

{one that will get both of us what we want and you out of my life}

She looked at him with a true sense of desperation. It must have registered with him because he sat down on the sofa and turned on the TV. He took a beer out of the bag he had carried in and picked up the channel changer.

"Tomorrow then, early my little elf, Eh?"

"Yes, early I promise." she closed the door leaned against it and her legs gave way. She slid down the door to sit shaking, with tears flowing, running down her face. She wrapped her arms around herself as tightly as she could to control her shaking body and put her face into her arms to quiet her racking sobs. The night would be long.

Council room—Island of Capri around 1 p.m.

They had stopped to get some lunch brought in and they broke into three small groups. Nikos and Suri were talking to Helene, Angela and Leander were over in a corner of the room, heads together talking in whispers, and Acacia was sitting with Sabina who had little to say.

{what now I need a babysitter or a guard}

Sabina picked at the food that was in front of her, some pasta dish with a Greek salad and bottled water so cold that condensation covered the outside. She picked up the bottle and twisted the cap open and drank deeply then slowly put the cap back on and placed it on the table.

She turned to Acacia, "Why Acacia?"

As if Acacia could read her mind, she spoke in a low tone for just the two of them to hear.

"…because Eugenie and Helene are fair people. They saw the attraction, the personal investment you were making in a budding entanglement. They certainly didn't mean to shut you out but you were so adamant that Rodane was an innocent caught in a situation by accident. They weren't sure. They didn't trust him at first. There were too many coincidences. We all know what that can indicate. You were a Sabina Carter that we didn't quite recognize and all of us…" she swept her arms slightly around the room,

"They were… well, we just felt it would be safer for the time being if we kept all we know or suspect a little closer to the vest, so to speak."

"But he proved himself to me over and over. He was totally upfront and honest, no matter what I asked him. Helene and Eugenie had to have seen that themselves."

"They did, they do. Rodane has two fiercely protective, involved warriors looking out for him now. I think we have a lot less to worry about with Rodane here where we can observe and place ourselves at his disposal for security and safety."

"Ok" Sabina finally smiled and her color heightened as she thought about his 'girls' being his protectors. She was so far away from anything she could hope to do to help him be safe.

{little jealousy there Sab}

Acacia, continued, "One worrisome thing, Sabina." She waited.

"More than all of this?" Sabina looked around, "I can't remember when we had so many assaults and confrontations so close and so often. Something had to have changed in the equation. Who's behind all this? Is it the same old attempts to recover an experiment… to try and get information on all of us? The level of stress and tension I feel here is enormous now, more so than for decades. What's changed? What's happening?"

"Maybe I can answer that Sabina." Suri was at her shoulder and she raised her eyebrows, questioning her welcome.

Sabina motioned for her to have a seat with them at the table. They made their new circle and Suri looked from one to the other. Sabina noted the slight nod of Acacia's head, whether in acquiescence or in concert, she wasn't sure.

"Sabina, what is it about Rodane that has captured you after such a long time alone? I hope you can be very honest with me here because a lot depends on it." Suri looked directly and searchingly at her face.

She continued, "I know, we all know, you don't give out your feelings often or so completely. It appears Rodane has managed to achieve something so few have been able to accomplish in all your years with us. Can you help us to understand?"

Sabina took a deep breath, gathered her thoughts while the two waited patiently.

She looked at both, she twisted her fingers together, "He's another self," she said so low, Suri had to lean in to hear.

Acacia's eyes widened to round orbs, with a look of consternation.

"He's a…no…what are you saying? How could that be? Maybe you're reaching Sabina, maybe you just want…"

Suri put her hand on Acacia's arm and spoke softly, "No dear, I'm sure he is. It makes perfect sense and it's so logical. Everything fits now. I've had my suspicions but I didn't dare hope…"

"Your suspicions?" Sabina found her pulse racing and her breathing, quick and short "You guessed? You guessed when? I didn't even know till we were leaving Akrotiri! You knew even before we had time to talk to you on board the ship?"

She put her hands to her flaming face then she realized that the entire room had gone quiet. She looked up and saw everyone turned towards them and it looked like statues placed around the room in small groups portraying a solemn scene of interest and somehow, a sense of excitement.

She stood so fast her chair got knocked backwards and the clatter seemed to break a stillness that had settled over them all. Nikos led the others over to them and took Sabina's hands in his, "Sabina, this is a marvelous moment for all of us. It's wonderful for you of course, but for us it's a new lease on our lives here, a start of something so long waited for, so desired by all of us and here it's you." He touched her cheek softly like a father caressing a daughter's cheek with pride, "you Sabina, who has experienced it and we are so grateful and proud. It's so cool!" he giggled, he actually giggled! It released a wellspring of laughter from everyone and rising noises of glee and wonder, and a lessening sense of danger.

"But, I may be wrong," Sabina said, "you said yourself, he might be something more but we don't know yet. How can we be sure?"

Suri looked at her steadily, "Are you sure Sabina? Just you and your own self, are you certain of it?"

Sabina loosened her hands from Nikos, sat down on the righted chair and took a long slow breath, "Yes" she whispered, "Yes, I am. It was such a shock the first time the connection charged and then it happened again and again. He was almost terrified. Neither of us recognized it at first. It was like two minds that just thought alike and we were just getting to know each other. Maybe it was just the situation, maybe just emotions that are heightened but then he asked me straight out what was going on and I knew he was experiencing the same charge I was. Then I knew and it scared me, it scared both of us and we avoided it if we could, until we had an opportunity to examine it further. That chance never presented itself and now I've sent him into clear danger." She looked scared to death.

Up till now, Evangela hadn't said much during the entire meeting. She brushed past everyone and knelt in front of Sabina seated on her chair, her face going pale and tears springing unheeded to her eyes and running down her face

"Por favor, pardonnez moi, por le interruption. Jo habla....Tu es...her emotion was having her split languages as she spoke. She took a deep breath and spoke English after a pause "You are overcome, it is natural but you cannot blame yourself for this or let fear and worry cloud your thinking. We all have an involvement in this problemo. We are all here for you and we will be sure he is kept safe and sound. Sabina, mi preciosa, this changes it all. You have to know we will make every effort to keep you… and our Doctor Arcos from whoever would even think of harming him. Problemo es serioso! Tu problemo es muy problemo, si?"

"Si" Sabina answered, overcome, "Gracias, muy gracias Evangela."

"De nada" Evangela stood and joined her group. They all began to wander off in whispers and muttering, leaving Sabina to Acacia and Suri again.

"What now?" Sabina asked, "What do I do?"

"You continue with what you are doing and you move on to Pompeii as soon as possible. They have three teams coming in on Wednesday of this week and we have to be certain everything is hidden deeply enough or else retrieved. If they do not set up their tables and tents near to where we have our information, our notes and designs, we should be fine for ten or fifteen years, maybe… maybe more. It has to be examined or redrawn or you have to do a recovery. It would require at least three days setting up a reconnaissance and putting legal blocks in their way so we need to move fast and be sure. Right now Acacia and I are going to look into those we have in the states close to where Dr. Arcos' family is living and I'm putting Quimby on notice that we require some help there and soon. By tomorrow late, we'll have people on the way or even there already to ensure their safety. We're going to meet up with you by Tuesday before we head for our headquarters. If anything happens before that I'll pin you."

Helene chose that moment to reenter the conference room and she went to Nikos. They moved aside and had their heads together talking quietly, brooking no interference. Suri glanced over to her and then back to Sabina.

"Acacia, could you excuse us for one moment?"

"Of course Suri, I'll be over with Evangela."

Suri looked at Sabina, with her face hiding any emotions she might be feeling. This girl was, had been, such a delightful but serious little girl. She had kept her thoughts to herself, even when gently prodded to share her ideas and feelings. She had never given them cause to worry or distrust her instincts. Rather, she had led them to a change of attitude over the years concerning their efforts to reclaim their history and recover the proof of their existence. This was despite the danger and the chance to reveal their extensive presence everywhere on this earth of theirs.

Up to this point, the Council had felt they had all things under control and a good handle on the discoveries and new finds they had helped to establish in this age. Now, it seemed things were moving quickly, almost out of their control. All of the current issues seemed to be driven by a concerted effort of more than one person who knew too much, suspected even more, and had resources to seek them out. They had, heretofore, not been aware of these people and yes it was very concerning, very troublesome. Here stood the child of her heart even if not by birth. It seemed Sabina had found her lifelong companion in such a totally unconventional way and at such an inconvenient time. Well, it would sort itself out, she was sure and there were definite steps she needed to walk now without hesitation.

"Sabina, Helene will accompany you wherever your assignments take you. She has my orders and you need to be watchful and extremely observant of those around you. She will remain on the rim of your digging and only show herself if the need arises. Try and complete your work asap, and then we can have you join us in France later in the week…or next week at the latest." She motioned to Helene and she walked over to them, looked quickly at Sabina and then turned to Suri,

"Yes ma'am. I've arranged everything for the next few days. We leave tonight around nine and will be in Sorrento for our lodgings. She should have Monday and Tuesday to get her work done and get us out of there. We have no sign of Doukas and Kappos even though some we talked to recognized them, her more than him. I have someone at his hotel watching Roddy…"she stopped abruptly and flushed.

Suri smiled, "Roddy? My, my, you girls have bonded so well with this handsome, young man. I will have to get to meet him soon, to see how he affects me."

"It's just a silly game and the name that we adopted while a little under the influence but he seems to fit for Eugenie and me. He really is a lot of fun… That's not what I meant!" when she saw Suri raise her eyebrows. She stammered, "No, not good!

He's um…" I mean he's fit in so nicely"… turning redder by the second.

"Never mind Helene, you'd be most surprised to learn he fits in perfectly with all of us. Quite the puzzle we have with 'Roddy' right, Sabina?"

Helene looked at Sabina, saw the glimmer in her eye, watched her nod her head, and she stood there speechless. They watched her face, putting the puzzle pieces together until her face showed her comprehension and wonder, mixed with a very distinct feeling of relief.

"I knew it!" She almost yelled. Chatter stopped for a second, looks exchanged then it resumed, "I knew it! Eugenie told me. We both knew it. It was something big, something event changing. It's the best thing to come out of this uh…"

Watching Suri, she tempered her excitement with an evident effort

"Well, I mean we both thought it would really be nice if Rodane and

Sabina… you know…could actually have…" her voice trailed off.

"It's okay Helene" Sabina smiled and it spread to Helene's face, "To me, it's even more than that. You'll be happy to know all your instincts are on alert and working just fine, same as for me."

Helene suddenly reached over and gave Sabina a huge hug for a few, long seconds. Never one to show her feelings, even less in front of council members, Helene was happy and embarrassed at the same time. It struck Sabina as so real, so honest, she found tears welling in her eyes. She hugged her back and both of them tentatively moved back but continued to smile, excited like new puppies.

"I so wanted it to be right… to have him be one of the good guys."

"Well ladies," Suri said, "he may be even more than that. Time will tell so hold on to your hats because there's a lot more to come if my feelings and suspicions are accurate. Now let's go make plans…" clapped her hands once, twice and everyone stopped their conversation and moved to their place at the table, looking at Suri expectantly.

Chapter 19

11:30 a.m. Classroom in Virginia

"Girls, no, I gave you strict and written instructions how to label and mix all the ingredients you would need for this. There are exactly four steps and you have twenty minutes to complete them."

Caroline looked at the small group of six in the corner and noted they were on step two. The other group of six was in the other corner wrapping up step four and watching the results in their beakers as the flames burned at a mid-level under the four basic chemicals they were using to produce their proper color and consistency. She smiled and gave them a 'thumbs up' and moved toward group two. Out of the corner of her eye she saw Sophia's face at the glass in the door.

{what… oh no not a fever}

She had been expecting a cold or something. The first week of school was when everyone lovingly carried all their household germs to school to share the wealth with all their friends and enemies alike but the first day? Sophia was not one to complain or whine when she didn't feel good. Sometimes Caroline even had to drag it out of her when she wasn't feeling good. The glassy eyes were a dead giveaway.

She opened the door and Sophia hung back and looked down the hall toward her room. Caroline expected to see someone there but it was empty. She looked back at Sophia, "Ae you okay?" she examined her clear eyes.

"Yeah I'm good Mama. I have a break now for study and I was wondering if… could I stay in here and study…" she rushed on, "I'll be quiet you won't even know I'm here, I promise. I have my lunch… I could eat it while I work."

"Your lunch? Why didn't you eat it with your class at 12:30?"

"I was with Mr. Fira and I didn't know how late it was. He wanted me to eat with him in his classroom but I told him I was coming here to eat with you."

"Why would you tell…Sophia what's wrong? This isn't like you. Who is Mr. Fira? Why did he keep you late? Did you get in trouble?" Caroline didn't even realize she was standing with her hands on her hips and a frown had spread over her face.

"No Mama, I… never mind, I'll go eat in the study lounge if Ms. Carpenter will let me" She turned to go but some unknown, small voice whispered, 'wait' in Caroline's mind and it came out in her own voice. She didn't realize she had even spoken it aloud until Sophia turned around and looked expectedly at her.

Caroline shook her head as if at a gnat, flying at her face. She put her arm around Sophia and led her into her classroom. Not sure why, she realized there was a need here that Sophia could not vocalize right now. The expression on her face was one of relief and a lessening of tension.

Caroline could feel it in her shoulders, "Of course you can eat lunch here. I'll call down to Ms. Carpenter to tell her you'll study here with me and… would you like to wait for me and ride home instead of the bus?"

"Yes" she said too eagerly.

Caroline looked carefully at her rosy cheeks and her eyes.

Not sick but… something. They'd have the ride home to talk. This was very unlike Sophia, almost like a frightened rabbit. This was not typical of her. She turned to the clock and then spoke to the class,

"That's it girls. Begin to clean up and replace your equipment. You will have ten minutes to write out your results and your hypothesis. Get to work and not one broken tube or cylinder, girls."

The corner group was standing, still looking at her.

"What's the problem? Jacquelyn?"

"Miss Arcos, we're only beginning step four and we don't have any results yet. Can we have more time?"

They all looked so sure it would be given. Caroline saw these were the same four who had come late to class this morning with the excuse that their car driver was late picking them up.

{first day of school and they're in a car pool instead of the bus}

The other two were followers, the wannabes who attempted to follow this 'clicky' group everywhere, clinging to every word they spoke, laughing at every lame joke that one told. Caroline remembered too clearly as she used to be one of the four. She had to be the leader of a clique, had to 'deign' to allow the wannabes to follow behind, expecting their lavish praise and adulation.

She had so much to tell them now that they wouldn't even attempt to listen to. Eyes would roll and nasty remarks would most likely be said behind her back about the old lady science teacher who didn't have a clue about young girls. She made them wait ten more seconds, a lifetime to 8th graders, before she spoke

"No, you may not have more time."

Their faces fell and Jacqueline began to speak. Caroline was sure it was going to be the beginnings of a debate. She cut her off.

"Don't worry about the fact that you didn't finish" she managed to say politely. "You do have results, girls. You've arrived at an unfinished experiment and you have results of that to record and present. I'm sure you'll have reached a hypothesis regarding the results as you talk among yourselves and go over the steps you took. Now, hurry and clean up, carefully. We need to be finished in…" she looked at the clock… "four minutes"

The time passed…Caroline collected the written results on the worksheets she had handed out and when the bell rang for change of class, she was more than ready to go to the faculty lounge, eat her yogurt and fruit and prepare for the next class. Being the only teacher of Advanced Chemistry, she had small classes and very bright students, sometimes with all the drama and ensuing hormonal friction. She wished for a usual, 'normal' basic Chemistry class or even better, a Biology class. One where dissection was exciting and interesting, the study of hormones of which they were so fond, were led by them and gave them excuses for missed classes, tears, and BFF fights with different BFFs every day.

When everyone had gone, Caroline went over to Sophia at the back of the room. She was looking out the window at the quad and eating or attempting to eat her PB&J and her chips. Most of it was untouched.

"What is it honey?" she asked, "Did I put too much PB on your sandwich? Sorry, but Adam had clients early this morning so I was elected. Would you like to come to the faculty lounge with me and get a yogurt?"

"No" she said it so quickly, it snapped out of her mouth and then she closed her teeth on it in a hurry.

"Sophia, what's wrong? Something is definitely bothering you. Are you sure you're not in trouble?" she said it gently and Sophia put her head down. She spoke just as softly to Caroline, "I feel funny."

"You feel funny, honey?" Sophia looked up, Caroline heard herself and they both chuckled and the tenseness lightened.

"Mama, Mr. Fira makes me feel funny. He asked me to stay after class when the bell rang and talked to me about all the places he's been and all the ruins he's visited and the museums where he works. He showed me pictures of some of them and they were the same places Daddy went. He asked me all kinds of questions about you and Daddy and our vacations and when I traveled with Daddy…I felt funny when he asked me to have lunch with him. I said you were waiting for me to eat lunch with you. I'm sorry I lied to him Mama, but I didn't…"

"It's ok Sophia. I'm glad you came down here to eat lunch. I'm sure he's trying to be friendly for his first day of teaching. He probably thought you would feel special having lunch with him on his first day. Someone must have told him how interesting you are."

{what the hell}

"Mama, I couldn't be that interesting. When he kept asking me questions about traveling with Daddy and vacations with you, I couldn't answer them. I don't know where all those places are or when we went. I'm eight! I sleep on the planes and I sleep in the car or I throw up in the bucket you keep in the car… and then I sleep in the car."

Caroline chuckled, "Yeah, you're not the world's most interesting traveler, are you?" She chucked her chin and leaned over and kissed her forehead.

"No mama, I don't have a fever and I'm not delirious."

"O, my clever, savvy, little traveler, I can't pull one over on you, can I? So, what did Mr. Fira say when you told him you couldn't remember your travels? Were you embarrassed that you couldn't answer them, that it made you feel funny?"

"No he got all pissy with me. Well he did Mama, you say it all the time. He told me I must not be as smart as everyone told him I was and he was wasting precious time, trying to get any answers from an eight year old who didn't know beans."

At Caroline's look, she said, "Well, that's what he said. I was a waste of time and I didn't know beans. Why would I want to eat lunch with him? He's a jerk!"

Caroline started to correct her then stopped herself.

{he is a jerk and what the hell does he think he's doing}

This man was starting to sound like a bully who's using Sophia for his target. It wouldn't be the first time a know-it-all substitute teacher would make an ass of himself.

"Would you like me to go get a yogurt from the fridge and come join you? We have twenty minutes left for lunch and your study lasts until then."

Sophia took a big bite of her PB&J and munched on the chips.

{feeling better aren't you sunshine}

"No, I'll eat it here if it's ok and then do my homework from morning classes. Then I'll have less to do when I get home. Can I have extra time with the computer if I'm finished?"

"We'll see"

Her face was shining now, her usual Sophia, light and laughter. She felt better knowing it was a special time where mom and Sophia connected and she helped drag her out of... well, whatever it was. She stood up and then, on a whim, leaned over and kissed her daughter on the cheek and gave her a hard squeeze.

"Mama, the other kids will think I'm a baby and teachers pet!"

"So... you are. You're my pet and I'm a teacher, so what?"

Sophia laughed and Caroline walked down the hall toward the faculty lounge. As she neared the lounge she saw Mr. Belva, the principal, and another gentleman with their heads together outside the teacher's lounge. They looked up as she neared them and the stranger stepped forward and put out his hand.

"Ms. Arcos, what a nice surprise. Mr. Belva has been helping me recognize the different teachers I will be working with. It's so good to meet you, finally."

She took his hand, gave it a shake and found him holding on just a second or two longer than necessary. She pulled her hand and was nonplussed to have him hold on enough to have her forcibly remove her hand. He searched her face and she found her anger rising for no discernible reason other than resentment that he appeared to be trying to intimidate her. She knew who he was without another moment's doubt. This 'dick' was the one who had made her daughter feel 'funny'. Her first day of school was not a positive experience and Caroline blamed this blowhard for that. She wasn't inclined to be polite or affable.

"And you are..." she said sweetly. She was satisfied to see the look of annoyance cross his face.

"I'm Mr. Fira, the substitute for Miss Cooper in grade 3. I believe that's your daughter's grade?" he waited for her answer.

Mr. Belva seemed ill-at-ease and eager to be on his way. He cleared his throat, "Mr. Fira, I'll leave you here at the faculty lounge. Most of the teachers will be in there from your grade level while the children are at lunch or study. I'll see you at the end of the day." He turned abruptly and walked away towards the front office.

{not too friendly here sport you're batting zero}

She wanted to see what Mr. Fira had in mind and it was evident he was playing her. She had enough of that over the years to recognize fishing when she encountered it. He opened the door and held it for her. As she walked in, everyone in the room looked up and saw them coming in together. She recognized the looks of 'aha' and knew the rumor mill would start as soon as either she or Mr. Fira left or they did. She thanked him and went to the refrigerator to retrieve her yogurt and fruit in the bag marked with her name. He went to the coffee pot and poured a cup and brought it back to the table and sat across from her without hesitation.

She saw him as arrogant and self-satisfied. He was handsome enough, with his blonde short crew cut and his tall lean frame but his dark brown eyes were cold and the sharp angles of his face somehow made her think of a stalking wild dog of the desert of Australia. She watched a documentary of them one time and that image immediately came to mind when she looked at him. He seemed to have every muscle tensed for attack and the half smile on his face expressed cynicism and a waiting… for what she didn't know but he was definitely on the hunt and patiently waiting for something.

She ate her yogurt, waiting for him to talk first, sensing his desire to approach the subject but still hesitant. Finally, he put down his coffee and spoke, "I have your daughter in my class. She's a charming little girl. I look forward to working with her for this week. You wouldn't mind if I wanted to have her help in planning some of my lessons for the week would you? She's very knowledgeable about the subject matter and the other students really seem to look to her for discussion…" he smiled as if it were a done deal.

"Sophia is a very charming little girl, true, and sometimes too polite by far. She is a very astute eight year old who has very good judgement. I'm wondering what Sophia may be able to help you with in planning your lessons. I doubt she knows which direction you want to go here. What are your interests Mr. Fira? What gets your curiosity aroused, your creative juices flowing" she waited and saw his eyes flicker briefly.

{hit the nail on the head did I Mr. Fira}

Mr. Fira took a swallow of his coffee and narrowed his eyes at her. She felt somewhat like a specimen on the corkboard, being readied for dissection and microscopic observation. "I understand Sophia has a dad who she visits, who studies ruins and antiquities. I'm very interested in sharing notes with him. I have the same interest. Would it be possible for you to put me in touch with him with a recommendation that we might be able to exchange emails or addresses and compare our travels and finds? I'd be profoundly grateful. It would be wonderful to communicate with a fellow traveler and archaeologist and I could benefit from his expertise."

He sat back, looking like a cat that had trapped the mouse in a corner and was slowly proceeding to tighten the perimeter around his quivering terrified little critter before he pounced.

She found herself feeling both angry yet spooked. She felt a chill spread from her fingers and toes while a slow heat was building in her skin and rising up her neck. She was just hoping she wouldn't break out into a sweat in front of this man. It would give him somehow she knew, too much satisfaction to see her fear. That's what it was she realized. He wasn't in her face, He hadn't given her any threatening looks. His outward demeanor was calm and personable but beneath the surface she sensed a condescending belittlement of her, a sort of game where she was the prey and he the predator. She placed her spoon down from eating her yogurt because her hands had begun to shake. She would not give him the satisfaction of noticing.

She spoke slowly, "I'm afraid that's not possible. My ex-husband...
{make that very clear}
is on an extended trip right now and he calls us to speak to Sophia when he is able. You could contact him at the University where he works and I'm sure if he can he will get back to you when he has time."

"Oh, that's a shame. My time is limited and I'm sure he's going to be very busy once his classes begin and I'd like to touch base before that starts. Isn't there any way you might be able to let me know where he is so I can perhaps find a way to contact him? You don't have an emergency number to reach him?"
{no not a cat like a snake}
"No, I'm afraid I don't give out his number... to anyone. I'll make sure when he calls again that I tell him you are interested in contacting him. Leave your number with me, why don't you and I'll relay it to him." she swallowed the yogurt that was threatening to rise from her throat and took a pull on her water bottle.

His eyes took on a glitter and his smile was fixed on his face. He rose and said, "Well, I had better get back to my class. It was very good to meet you and get a look at Sophia's mother. She must take after her dad, yes? Are they close? I imagine a young child who only rarely sees her dad needs some time to develop some like interests with him. Being on opposite ends of the country doesn't help does it? That you pretty much are her constant caretaker and companion? Take good care of her. There are so many pitfalls for a single mother and a young girl these days." He turned abruptly and left the room.

She sat still for a moment or two, willing her heart to slow down and the pounding in her skull to lessen. Who was this man who knew more about them than he should? How did he know Sophia's visiting schedule? Did Sophia say more than was prudent about her dad and his travels? Were they subtle threats he made about her and Sophia or was she being totally paranoid? She looked up and realized there was no one else here with her. When did they all leave? How had she not noticed their going? What the hell was happening here that made her feel sick to her stomach? She picked up her phone and dialed Adam at the gym.

Naples, Italy

Rodane tried Sophia at home, dialed in Skype on the chance she might be home. Maybe an early time would allow him to get out later for some night time pictures, some clubs. He tried her number and let it ring for many times.

{guess they weren't home yet}

He closed Skype and started working. He checked the clock on the bedside and realized he had gotten lost in his work for almost two hours. He had successfully set up a PDF file and included a dozen or more pictures in his documents as attachments. He had even begun to organize them to accompany the various descriptions of the sights he had visited. He laid out the first few pages of descriptions and interesting night spots for each site, saved it to his laptop and then backed it up on his thumb drive. He had more than enough pics to complete his trip and take plenty more pictures to use or discard once he had them all on a board. He sent it off to the travel office in Richmond, Virginia. It was 9:30 but seemed later.

He had a very active day and he decided to try and skype Sophia again. If she and Caroline came straight home from school, they'd be home now. Maybe he could still get out to a nightclub or some lights.

{before I hit the sack at 12 or so}

Nightlife didn't seem so appealing to him lately. He was getting older and it wasn't as much of a thrill. He appreciated rest so much more.

This time the screen burped at him and Sophia's face was in front of him.

"Sophia... Hi Sunshine! What do you have there?" Rodane's conversation with Sophia had started out very pleasant. She had the cat... it squirmed in her arms while he asked her about her first day of school. They talked about the Moores and her classes and her new friends...the return of the old ones from last year. He could hear pots and dishes in the background.

Caroline stuck her head in the screen long enough to smile and say 'hi'. Sophia ran to get her latest Manga drawing and returned minus the cat and an eight by ten of some graphic character from one of the manga books. He looked carefully and was quite surprised at how her drawing had improved in such a short time.

{hey buddy it's been over eight months now}

He asked her about her teachers and was shocked to actually see a curtain drop on her face, and a slump in her shoulders instantaneously. Up to that point, she had been relaxed and he was happy to keep her engrossed in a child's conversation of cats and kids and homework. Suddenly things had turned very serious and he recognized a different daughter, one who had once been like this girl, now in front of him, closed, timid, intense. It took a long time to take that slump out of her shoulders and watch her become self-confident and open. He tried to tease information out of her without asking questions that might shut her down completely.

"Is Mr. Belva the principal again?"

That was a safe topic because the two of them got along well, "Yeah, and he has less hair than last year. The kids are starting to call him egghead. Isn't that nasty, Daddy?"

"You bet it is. Does he look like an egghead?" Sophia giggled and looked up at him. She put her hand over her mouth and giggled again, tension broken, "How's the cafeteria? Any better food this year?"

"I don't even care. Mama and Adam pack my lunch and I only get milk to drink or water, but my friends only get pizza and soda. Yuck! that stuff is gross! I know…from last year's cafeteria."

"Let me guess, PBJ, chips and pickles?"

"Daddy! Yeah, Daddy, how'd you guess?"

"Oh, it's just my amazing mind-reading talent. Kind of like I know there's something you're not telling me, and I wish you could share it with me Sunshine."

Sophia looked up and blushed. She turned around and said something to her mother he couldn't catch. Then she squared her shoulders and turned back to him, took a breath and said, "Well, there's this substitute teacher we have this week. Miss Cooper is on her cruise, remember I told you? She went on a cruise, just out of the blue and she's gone for a couple of days." He nodded, afraid to break her train of thought with any remarks or questions, "He's a jerk! Yeah, Mama, he is. You said so yourself." She and Caroline said something else he couldn't hear, and she turned back, "Mama said I should tell you what happened today and see what you think. I think you'll think I'm right and he's a double jerk, for making Mama angry." He raised his eyebrows at that. Must be some kind of day, to set both of them off and have the ire of Caroline turned on you as well. Caroline was pretty affable and friendly with everyone at work. The kids loved her classes and her projects. He had to give her that. She was a born teacher and good with the kids.

Sophia began her tale and then she came to the end of her study period and her lunch, wound down to…,

"Then Mama came in all pissy, sorry Mama, and she had a rotten afternoon with Jacqueline and we both were so glad that day was over. The kids were calling me teacher's pet and I couldn't wait to go home with Mama and then she gave me a lecture about stranger danger and… well, you did. Mama said I can have computer time if you let me so…can I have computer time?"

His head swam at the swiftness of her words and thoughts rushing out like a flowing stream. He gathered his thoughts and said she could go on and do some computer time.

"I hope your next day is great. Want me to call you tomorrow?"

"No" she said, "I'll probably have soccer tryouts or art class after school and Mama is going to stay till I'm done so we won't be home till late, maybe Wednesday."

She blew him a kiss and waved her fingers and was getting up, "Mama wants to talk to you, ok?"

"Sure have fun, love you."

"Love you too. Toodleloo!" and she was gone like a breath of air.

Caroline sat down in front of the screen. He could tell she was flustered and still angry. The color was high on her cheeks and her eyes shimmered like glass shards, a sure sign of trouble.

"What's up? Sounds like you both have had a strenuous first day of school."

She took a breath, placed her hands on the desk and he was shocked and amazed when tears started leaking from her eyes and she swiped them away with the back of her hand. She told him the entire conversation that she and Sophia had and which Sophia had, of course, left out some of the details which had sparked the beginnings of Caroline's anger. She described the meeting in the hall with Mr. Fira and Mr. Belva, the principal and then tried to recount as much word for word as she could of their conversation in the faculty lounge. As she talked, he saw her hands begin to shake and she gripped them together to still them. A leaden feeling began in his belly and his legs felt heavy.

"Are you ok Caroline? What can I do?"

"Rodane, Sophia used the term, 'he made her feel funny'. Well, that goes double for me and I haven't been able to shake the feeling that something very wrong is going on here that poses a threat to both me and Sophia. I know..." she put her hands up..."it sounds crazy."

"No Caroline" he spoke gently, "It doesn't sound crazy at all. You're a good judge of character. No, really, you are. I'm not putting you on, seriously. I think you're listening to your instincts here and Sophia is not the only one who needs to pay attention to stranger danger. What do you think is going on here Caroline? Have you talked to Adam about it yet?"

{can't believe I'm saying this to her}

"No, he's not home yet but I plan to, after Sophia is in bed and we have some quiet time. There's been so much going on with the fire at the Moore's and the dog and cat and the fire investigation. Everything is so quixotic and confusing. Then today... well, I need to wrap my head around all this and it's got me on edge," and her tears started again. Rodane heard her say something he had never heard her express before in all the time he had known her,

"Rodane, I'm afraid and it's crazy because nothing has happened to have me feel that way. Adam is going to think I'm going off my nut and he's probably right." He let her cry for a minute and when she looked up, her face had tear streaks but her shoulders had squared, "but I'm not going to give in to this and I'll kill anyone who tries to harm my baby and I can give some pretty good pay back to someone who messes with me too! I'm sorry Rodane, and I shouldn't have laid this on you while you're over in... where are you anyway? I've lost track."

"I'm in Naples now but I'll be home in three or four days at the latest. I was hoping to come to Virginia and stay there for a couple of days to spend afternoons and the weekend with Sophia since we missed out on our summer visit. I'm sorry about that."

She waved her hand...," It's okay, we've been so busy and things have been so crazy. You'd have walked right into the middle of it all but yes, please come. We can pick you up at the airport and you can stay here, of course. Sophia would love some time with you."

{this woman has been replaced by a pod person}

"Ok. Yeah, thanks. That would be very generous of you Caroline. Adam... He has some self-defense training right? Does he stay there with you?" she started to speak for herself and then answered, "Yes, he's a martial arts expert and yes, he is living here. Is that a problem?" she watched his face.

"No, quite the opposite. I was going to have you ask him to stay there for a while if he wasn't. I feel a lot better knowing he's there to act as your muscle, if you will, in case the need arises."

"What? Do you think...No, forget that. I just told you I was afraid and you're trying to make sure we're safe and have someone here with us. Thanks for thinking of this. Rodane, I'm being a wuss about something that is probably nothing."

"Well, the old adage rings true; 'Better Safe than Sorry'. Do you want me to call tomorrow, just to check in with you?"

"No, Sophia is right. She'll have art class and maybe even soccer tryouts as well. Until I feel this is either my overblown imagination or Mr. Fira is out of there, I told Sophia I'm bringing her home each day from school. She's fighting me on it so far but we'll see tomorrow. Either way, I'm going to watch her like a hawk and make sure Mr. Belva knows how I feel about Fira keeping her for lunch and his comments to her. Not so smart indeed! He should have half the brain she has, the nitwit! Rodane, thank you, you've made me feel better."

He struggled not to show he was shocked, "Caroline, I haven't done anything. I'm stuck thousands of miles away." She said, "You've listened and you haven't dismissed my fears and my hysteria. I feel foolish now having said it all out loud."

"Please don't. I wish I were there. It's not foolish to feel fear and tears are not hysteria. You're handling this very well. Please, tell me you are going to talk this out with Adam when he gets there." He saw her look up and heard the door open and close. Adam came over to her and bent to kiss her. Rodane waited and then he cleared his throat. Adam jumped and knocked the screen. It wobbled and Adam burst out with, "Jesus H Christ! I thought you were working on the computer." He looked at the screen and then at the tear streaks still on Caroline's face.

His expression hardened and he spoke to Rodane, "What's this? What the hell! Have you been…?" Caroline put her hand on his arm and spoke softly in his ear. Rodane couldn't catch it all but he heard…"helping me through a bad day." Adam composed himself, looked back at Rodane's image on the screen and said, "Sorry guy, didn't mean to jump to conclusions there. Thanks for your help… with…whatever."

"Adam, we need to talk after Sophia goes to bed, okay?" Adam looked from one to the other, paused and then said, "Anything I should be worried about? Do I need to find a new place to stay?" He grinned, but half serious.

Caroline said, "No, of course not. It's been a rough first day and we need to discuss some things for the rest of the week, if that's okay?" She looked up at him and the expression in her eyes was so obvious Rodane actually shifted back in his chair. He felt like he was eavesdropping on an intimate moment.

{well screw me that's love}

They both said goodbye. Adam had left to go get water out of the fridge and Rodane disconnected. He sat there a few moments going over everything said by all parties. He found himself becoming more than angry at the situation Caroline and Sophia found themselves in at the moment. He felt helpless and guilty. He was beginning to realize his problems here had jumped ahead of him over the pond and something was brewing that concerned Caroline and Sophia. But what could he do here?

{What would you say to Caroline}

{Oh sorry dear but my bad luck has just rubbed off on to you and I don't have the slightest idea what you can do to distance yourself from it so good luck. Oh and don't forget to protect Sophia while you're trying to figure out who to trust and have to safeguard yourself.}

{fuck me with a stick}

He couldn't sit still. He was itchy and edgy. He wanted to throw something, or punch someone, and he was still contracted for at least three more days to finish his tour and write it up, with photos included. He thought of calling Sabina and talking it over with her, but couldn't bring himself to push his problems on to her. Besides, what could she do? She was busy with her family meeting in Sorrento, and traveling in the opposite direction from him. He made a decision to go out to the nightlife in Naples' thoroughfare and take his mind off back home. He gathered his camera, his notebook and his wallet and headed out. He locked up behind him and took the stairs instead of the elevator. When he reached the lobby, there was some kind of tiff going on with the desk manager and an older lady who was attempting to get on the elevator with a small dog, some type of poodle or something close. The manager's back was to him and he walked past, out the door to the side exit that opened on to a side street. The heat hit him, and even the smells of the docks; rotting fish, salty water, decomposing crabs, and the earthy smell of the tunnel that has been dug at newly discovered ruins. He walked over to the yellow tape and wooden barricades that kept most people out of the site. The spotlights were glaring and he turned his head away from the brightness, to change lenses and snap pictures. Then he walked down the street to the first club where he heard raucous music and deafening drums, pounding out into the night.

He took snaps of outside views, water with the moonlight glinting off it, terraced balconies holding today's laundry, couples staggering, or walking attached at the hip, down the sidewalks. Then he made his way into a doorway and took a wide angle view of the dance floor, the overhead gyrating lights and the gorgeous mahogany bar running the entire length of the bar room, Decades, maybe more, of wax polish had brought the wood to a lustrous sheen that you could see your face in. Every bar stool and open space was taken up by young, younger, and a few older people intent on drinking and having fun in that order.

After ordering a scotch and soda, he found an end stool, blocked by a column, sidled onto it to relax and drink his scotch. He looked up at a girl who stood there with a drink in her hand and a smile on her face. She had less than a yard of material stretched from her chest to her thighs. That was it! Very inexpensive wardrobe if this was a sample.

"Hey handsome, want to dance?" She twisted her hip.

He stammered, "What, you? Dance?...Me? he was startled that she would approach an 'old' man.

"Yeah you. You dance, don't you?"

"Well, yes, I do, but...I'm going...I need to do a job and..."

"It's ok guy, didn't mean to fluster you and all. I saw you sitting here alone and thought you might like a turn on the floor. It's all good."

He put his empty glass on the bar and left a couple dollars tip then rose. She looked up at him and cocked her head, reassessing the possibility of convincing him to stay. He towered over her 5' or 5'2 frame, a snippet of a short haired blonde with earrings that hung almost to her jaw. She had liquid gold eyes, and too much makeup for a pretty face.

"I'm sorry I don't usually get so flustered. I'm incredibly tired and I've been so busy all day, I guess I'm not thinking clearly but I am doing a job and I still have some work to do tonight so I'll have to decline."

She asked where he was staying and he told her…

"But I'm going to go to another club first, then head in for an early night if you can consider it early."

"You're working at going to clubs?" she looked amazed, "Now you're my kind of guy!" and her eyes twinkled.

He told her briefly what he was doing and she was very interested. He checked the time and rose from his bar stool.

"It's getting late and I really want to get a good night's sleep before I have to drive tomorrow."

"Can I go with you to the next club? I'd like to see you doing your job. I won't get in the way, promise! I'm Amber, by the way."

"Sure, come on along…Amber. You can show me what you think a good picture might be for a tourist brochure."

They left the club and started walking down the side street where purple and green lights were flashing against the sky and the noise level was reverberating out the door.

Naples apartment

The knock on the door was loud, hard and sustained. Renata lifted her head from her arms and realized she had fallen asleep on the floor. It felt cooler down here.

"Yeah, what is it Tabor? I'm trying to get rid of my headache."

{you for being the biggest one}

She went and opened the door. He stood there with his hair all mussed, his clothes rumpled and his breath stinking of booze, "We're going now. I'm not waiting any longer. I want this guy and I'm going to get the jump on this before he decides to move on. I won't lose him this time and he'll pay."

His look was a combination of glee and utter hatred. She tried to talk him down

"But we haven't planned this out Tabor. I don't even know what you expect me to do…" he shoved her back a step and she caught hold of the door frame.

"You do what I tell you to do, that's what! Now, get ready and let's get out of here. The hotel said he left sometime after ten but no one saw him go. We start on the street where the hotel is. You park the car at the port down the street and you wait there till I call you. I'll have Arcos with me and we'll put him in the car and take him down to the port's docks, away from crowds. We'll get what we came for and we'll leave him there." his face smiled but his eyes didn't.

"What do you want me to do?" She was hoping to be lookout and driver. Her head really was pounding and her throat was so dry it felt like sandpaper.

"You wait at the car. If I don't call you, stay till you hear from me. If it takes longer than planned, you stay at the car. If anything goes wrong I'll send you a message; #GO and you get out of there and head back to our apartment and I'll meet you there."

"How will I know if everything goes well and how long do I wait?"

"You'll know when I show up with him and you wait till you hear from me…" he shoved her in the chest once, twice, three times with each word… "Do… you… understand…?"

"Yes, I do. I'll wait at the car."

"Thank you so much little elf. It's good to work with you," he turned and muttered "Stupid cunt! Too dumb to answer a phone or follow simple directions…."

They took the car from the parking garage and she drove it four blocks down to the docks, parked in the shadowed area and waited for Tabor to exit the car. He took out a thin briefcase and started walking to the thoroughfare. She didn't look around but she followed his form in the rearview mirror as he walked into deeper shadows. Then she put her head back on the seat and waited. She dozed off.

Chapter 20

Streets of Naples

Rodane and Amber walked to the bar entrance and were told it was a $10 cover charge, each. They both decided they didn't need to pay for buying drinks and using a dance floor so they moved to the next one farther up the street. They talked and shared some history, very little. Amber was named for her eyes by her mother when she was born. She was fascinated by Rodane's job and they stopped at a bench outside, close to a café and he showed her some of his pictures from his tour. She was impressed and also a little drunk.

He saw a whirling light up the street in the next block and started toward it. Amber begged off walking over cobblestones in her heels so he said he'd be back in ten minutes. She sat on the bench and watched the harbor lights outside all the warehouses.

Rodane moved further into the shadows and took out his filter for soft light and leaned against the wall to change his lens. He was about to walk toward the lights when a fist snaked out of the alleyway and clipped him alongside the head. He must have seen the shadow of a hand coming at him. He jerked his head back at the last second and something hard clipped his chin instead of his skull. It unbalanced him however, and a strong arm pulled him further into the alley and wrapped around his throat.

He tried to struggle free and his camera slammed against the brick wall next to them. He heard the glass and tried to jerk away from the wall to save the camera. He got his hand up around his attacker's head and dug his fingers into a mat of hair and felt soft skin give under his nails. Warm fluid ran down his fingers and he began to see spots in his eyes that were blurring. A voice in his ear was hoarse and guttural, "Damn you to hell, you will die before I let you free." But first I will play with you!" A fist clouted him across his right ear and a boot heel stepped hard on his foot. He had knelt on the ground to try and shake the grip around his throat. It was getting hard to breathe and blood was running into his eyes which blurred everything around him. Some part of his brain said 'don't react, act!'

He moved abruptly to stand up and forced his assailant behind him to slam into the wall. 'Oof' was forced from the hoarse voice and the grip lessoned. He felt the tension give and he twisted to the side and slipped out of the choke hold. Another fist got his nose and blood started pouring down his face. He ducked his head and attempted to bulldoze his way into the soft middle but the man moved slightly left and forced Rodane's head into the bricks. Then lights did explode and he heard a rushing in his ears and all other sounds were muffled. He dropped like a stone and a foot got him in his right side and his upper ribs. Pain lanced through his entire chest and those stars in front of his eyes began to whirl. It started to look like he was down for the count, when a shape came barreling out of the street and a voice screamed at the top of the musical scale. The scream became jerky, and rhythmic, unbelievably piercing even if it was muffled in his ears.

He tried to rise, but fell back to the cobblestones and lay panting and choking on blood that was running down his throat. Another form came sprinting from the other end of the alley and launched itself at the attacker. Two bodies collided and he heard grunts and curses and thuds of fists hitting bodies and bodies hitting each other. He tried to look through blurred eyes shot with blood. He made out two figures in fighting stance and saw a glint of light on a silver blade in a hand swinging from side to side, trying to stab into a flurry of hands and arms moving unbelievably fast. One hand gripped the wrist with the knife and in seconds had twisted around and brought the wrist into a backward angle. He heard it snap and the knife slid into the man's side like a carving knife into a side of bacon. Then the slighter figure took the attacker down and his head bounced off the cobblestones. It sounded like someone thumping a melon to test its ripeness. The man lay still but the screaming continued. Abruptly… it cut off and two figures ran to him and laid hands on him. He began to struggle and a familiar voice spoke,

"Shush Roddy! Lay still, don't move till I can see where you're hurt." The voice was out of breath and strained as if in suppressed pain. It was Eugenie but… it couldn't be. How…where did she… he felt himself half floating in and out and heard her voice,

"Would you please shut up and help me get him up so we can get out of here?" The scream cut off and sobs started in their place.

"I came to see what the noise was. I heard his camera against the wall and thought he had fallen. When I got closer I saw there was a man in dark clothes. He had, Oh God! How is he? Is he going to be okay? I've never seen a fight like that before. I…"

"Please miss, please be quiet and help me get him up and out of here. We really don't want to get involved with the police. Do you?"

"No. Oh God, no! I don't want to have to go spend hours in the Politzia and answer a thousand questions. I'm drunk, they'll throw me in the tank and my parents will have to pay to get me out and…"

"Miss, what's your name? Your name, what is it? Eugenie asked

"Amber, my name is Amber. I don't know him. I just met him tonight. I didn't have a thing to do with…"

"I know…" Eugenie cut her off, "I know that Amber. I'm just asking you to help me get him up and out of this alley before someone calls the police, please!" she almost begged.

Rodane tried to talk but every breath was fire and ice mixed together in his chest and blood was still flowing from his head, nose and into his mouth. They lifted him together to a stumbling, halting hobble and between them they moved down the alley to the other end that led to a dark side street.

"Wait here," Eugenie told Amber, "I'll be right back and don't you dare take off and leave him here alone."

Amber watched her sprint down the alley to the prone figure on the ground. She bent down, reached into his jacket and pulled items from him then she grabbed a small satchel by the wall and sprinted back to them, hardly out of breath,

"You're wonderful" Rodane croaked, "Teach me to fight like that" then he groaned, retched to the side and just missed Amber's nice new shoes. He splattered his stomach contents all over the cobblestones.

"Let's go just a little further…" Eugenie lifted his arm and Amber grabbed the other. They hauled him to the edge of the alley and then turned left into dark shadows. He couldn't help groaning in pain.

"Okay Miss Amber, this is where we part company. Thank you for your help. I couldn't have done it without you."

"But… what about that man?" she pointed down toward the alley, "Is he…I mean do you know him? What do you want me to…?"

"Please go back to the thoroughfare. It's only two blocks down and the street is lit. I'll take it from here. Thanks for your help but please just go. He's going to be fine, please?" Eugenie cajoled.

Amber came over and leaned down. She put her fingers to her lips and then touched his that were busted and puffed up,

"Thanks for the company. I hope you're okay. I'll look for your pictures…"

then she stumbled away down the street toward the harbor. Behind them in the alleyway the man lifted his hand to his jacket and pulled his phone out. He'd gasped and punched a key on his phone then sank back down and was still.

Virginia

The screams from the bedroom had Caroline jumping up so fast she hit her head on the lamp close to her in the family room. Adam was off the couch like a shot and grabbed the poker from the fireplace on his way to Sophia's room. It was only 7:30 and Sophia had gone to her room after dinner to finish up her homework and use her extra computer time. Adam flung open her door and she looked up at him, saw the raised poker and started screaming again, louder. He realized he had the poker upraised toward her and he quickly dropped it when he saw no one else there. Her eyes were bugging out, her face was white as a sheet, she was sitting at her desk with the computer on and the rest of the room was dark.

Caroline rushed over to her, wrapped her arms around Sophia who struggled to get away, "Daddy! Daddy... no! Stop! No, don't! Hit him Daddy, hit him back! Damn you man, that's my daddy, let him alone!" Tears were flowing, her sobs and her words were all garbled together and her eyes remained wide-open.

"Get off him you fucker, get off him!" she wailed uncontrollably.

"Sophia, baby, it's Mama. Sophia! Look at me!"

"Help him, someone help him! Daddy! Daddy run, run away!" she kept sobbing and screaming at the same time.

Caroline looked up at Adam in terror. She was crying herself but held tight to Sophia who was struggling to get free.

"Adam, help me, I don't know what to do," she sobbed.

Adam came over, knelt down and put his hands around Sophia's face and turned it toward him. It wasn't easy. It was like her neck muscles were rigid and her eyes were unfocused and wild, "Sophia, look at me. It's Adam, Sophia, look at me..." he kept saying her name over and over... softly, gently, holding her face while Caroline held her body.

This went on through an interminable few minutes that seemed like hours.

"Someone help him! Yes, yes! Help him, get him away, he's bleeding. My daddy's hurt. Get out of there! Thank you for helping him. Daddy go, get away!" then she went as loose as a drink of water and collapsed in Caroline's arms.

Adam picked her up and took her to her bed. Caroline ran to the kitchen to bring back a wet washcloth and wiped Sophia's face and trembling hands. Her whole body was shaking as if she had a fever but her forehead was clammy and cool. Caroline put her coverlet over her and sat on the edge of the bed, holding on to her hand hanging out of the cover,

"Daddy it'll be okay, you'll be okay. They'll help you, they'll get you safe… you'll be okay… you'll be okay…" then she closed her eyes and drifted away as if she were just dozing.

They stayed with her for ten more minutes to make sure she was asleep and then left the room with a night-light on. Caroline turned off the computer and left the door ajar then she went into Adam's arms and quietly cried. He held her tightly and took them both back to the family room. Caroline heard a soft bump from Sophia's room and both quickly went back to check on her. Caroline opened the door wider and there on the bed, snuggled up on the pillow, wrapped around her head was Max the cat. She couldn't help her grin.

When they returned to the family room, Adam and Caroline sat on the sofa together, talking quietly,

"I've never had that happen, Adam, never. I can't imagine what that was about."

"She was having a nightmare, Caroline. Kids have nightmares."

She looked at him a few seconds and said, "You don't believe that any more than I do, Adam. That was no nightmare. She wasn't even with us, she was…" and she burst into crying again.

He held her, both rocking back and forth to calm each other. They decided to let her sleep and they would check on her during the night. If she woke again they would ask her if she remembered what she was dreaming about but not press her. Adam fixed them both a drink of bourbon and water and they stayed up till ten talking and cuddling.

Caroline tried to read but couldn't concentrate. They looked at the TV but would have been hard-pressed to tell what they had seen. Adam asked her, "Should we call Rodane… you know, just to make sure everything's okay?" He sounded a little anxious.

"Adam, it's after two there in Naples. He's got to be sleeping. What would I say? 'Rodane, Sophia had a vision and we wanted to make sure you're still alive and well. Have a nice night and go back to sleep'?"

"I know, it sounds crazy but do you think… could Sophia actually…"

"No don't even go there, that's too scary and fantastic. I'll call him as soon as I get a break at school and make sure he's all right, just to have Sophia reassured."

Naples at 2:00 PM

At that moment in Naples many things were happening at once. Renata opened her eyes, realizing she had dozed off. She looked around to see what might have woken her. The dashboard clock said 1:45 and there were no lights where she was parked. She rubbed her eyes and opened a window to get some air in the car. Mistake! Only air warmer than the stale, fetid air in the car rushed in, and the smell was overwhelming. She was too close to some dumpster or the harbor waste or something rotten but it made her instantly gag. She closed up the window again and then saw her light blinking on the phone. She touched the return and #GO sprang up on the screen, back lit by a blue ocean wave and one palm tree for her screensaver.

"What? How can..." she was disoriented and it took her a few seconds to realize what this meant then she sprang out of the car and started to head in the direction Tabor had gone. Wait! She told herself... can't go rushing into an unknown. Where would she find him? He told her to stay. He said she had better be by that car. But it was the emergency message hashtag.

{go something went wrong I'm supposed to get out of here}

She couldn't leave him here without any way to get back. What if he was injured?

{he'll kill me if I disobey}

Her panic rose and fell like an express elevator; one minute taking steps to follow Tabor then back to the car to head out and back to the apartment.

{christ what do I do}

Her problem was solved when she heard a piercing siren coming from the North toward the town district. Her inner gut told her that any hesitation would be unwise so she jumped in the car, turned toward the bar district and started slowly following the sound of the siren. At least she was leaving that god-awful smell.

Amber stumbled down the street and finally stopped long enough to take off her shoes. Her stilettos had tripped her up twice and she had twisted her ankle. She was so overwrought she even ignored the pain of the mild, sprained ankle. She walked over cobblestones in the middle of the street rather than chance broken glass on the darkened sidewalk. When she reached the bench where they had talked, she felt under the seat for the button she had pressed there.

The woman had met her two days ago at a bagel stand. She had bought her a Mocha Cappuccino and a bagel and given her a picture. It was of a tall handsome man with a day's growth of beard wearing a t-shirt and shorts near the harbor. He was standing by the yellow tape that kept people out of some dig or excavation. He had a camera around his neck.

"Here are 50 Euros now and you'll get 100 Euros more when you use the button and it has to be by Saturday at the latest. You start looking now and if you find him then you find a way to become part of his day or evening or both. I don't care how you do it, just do it by Saturday."

"How do I get in touch with you? Is there a phone number I can call?" Amber looked at Renata.

This person gave her the heebie-jeebies. She was tiny and looked to be delicate but Amber has been around a lot of women just like her. She might be young but she knew a paid hunter when she saw one. Renata had answered her question

"The button does all the locating you don't have to do anything except activate it by pushing this…" she turned it over and showed her the red button on the back.

"Then put it in the last place you are with him. We'll take it from there. Don't let it be out in the open. Then we'll meet you the next morning in the bagel shop and you'll get paid. Simple?" She tried to smile but could only nod her head.

"Good. Glad to work with you. We'll see if we can use you regularly. The pay's not too bad for some simple flirting, right?"

She hadn't seen her since and that was a good thing. Each day she would walk up and down the harbor, walk through town close to the hotels. She visited cafes and gelato shops. She'd sit on benches for hours just watching people go by. She took many pictures of men she thought looked something like the snapshot she had been given and then she would compare them later and delete them when they turned out not to be him.

Then this evening she started her early tour of the bars like she had been doing the last two days. She almost missed him because he was behind a column but she had to pee and she was walking to the ladies room in the back. There he was, finally! She saw Euros in her mind. He was very pleasant and now this!

A siren broke out and she thought 'it's for him' not sure which of the men 'him' was. She wasn't going to wait around for anyone to question her and she didn't give a damn about the money anymore. She walked down to the edge of the water at the wharf and threw the button as far as she could out into the oily blackness. Maybe some fish would lead them on a merry chase. She started home with her last thought for Rodane to be okay. She tucked his picture into her small clutch bag.

Naples—Club district

Eugenie came out one street further over where a car was idling against the curb. When the driver saw her struggling to hold up Rodane, he jumped out of the car and then they both got him inside and laid him across the backseat,

"Good Christ and Mother Mary, what truck ran over him? Where to doll? "

"Where is the last place you've taken someone who needed medical attention without it being a hospital and it has to be kept under wraps, close and quick."

"Got just the place, be there in a jiff!" he set out on the street, made a phone call as he was taking turns from one ally to another and turned left just as a police car was turning down one block west.

"Guess I know where that bloke is going. Does he look as bad as our guest?"

"Worse" Eugenie answered, "It should be a meat wagon." She was bitter and he could hear the anger in her voice,

"A meat wagon, why would a butcher be heading to…"

"A hearse my friend, I should have finished him."

"Oh now doll, our gentlemen friends would not be likin' so much telltale evidence of an attack right in the open now, would they?"

"How much further?" Eugenie asked. She looked back at Rodane who was too still…

{too long to get there, too long}

…then he choked and sputtered, followed by a low moan. She couldn't see his face in the shadows of the backseat but she already knew what he looked like. He was not going to be pretty tomorrow.

{dear god, let there be a tomorrow for him}

They drove a short alley and pulled up behind a narrow house with a tiled roof and a low shed with double doors. He jumped out, pulled the gate open and maneuvered his way into the shed then he pulled the door closed and turned on the light inside. There was a connection to the house and a bell pull next to it. He pulled the cord and waited. A voice came out of the speaker next to the light switch,

"Please look at the lights," which he did.

"So Scalia, what the hell are you doing back here? I told you I didn't want to see your face again till I was looking at it in your casket."

"Evening Doc. Had a bit of a ruckus tonight and brought you some good red meat ready for a steak or two. It's rare and you can supply the wine."

The voice said, "Come ahead and be quick about it," as he was muttering about the middle of the night and being rousted out of bed.

The door to the house clicked open and Scalia and Eugenie got Rodane out of the backseat and into the house.

{good christ almighty, this bloke is heavy}

Doc was waiting inside with a wheelchair and a lady wrapped in a house coat with a turban wrapped around her head and a scowl on her face. He was a dapper looking man with a head full of curly black hair, a dark skin and black eyes. He too, had a scowl on his face but when he saw Rodane, it turned to real concern and he became all business.

"What chugon' do with this sick man in my house tonight Doc ? He get blood over everting." Her accent was of the Atlantic Islands near the South American continent, Pigeon and Barbados combined.

Doc snapped, "Flossie, get towels and basins of water. Bring out my instruments and lots of gauze and bandages and some ether…Now Flossie!"

When she stood and looked at him, arms folded across her ample bosom, she slowly turned and let out a disgusted 'huh!' and headed away. They got Rodane into the wheelchair with his head rolling and blood still seeping from his head, nose, ears onto his shoulders and chest. They wheeled him to a closet door. Eugenie looked anxious and stared at Doc before she looked in the closet. It was an elevator!

{oh boy safe house}

They rode to the top floor not the basement that she expected.

{movies it's always the basement}

When Doc entered the first bedroom on the left it was a small surgical ward. They got Rodane on the table under bright, white lights and Doc proceeded to cut off all Rodane's clothes. All three got them off of him and into a plastic bag and a trash can. He came over to Eugenie just as Flossie came out the other door with an armful of material and she looked at Rodane, "Lawd Almighty, this ooone poor mudder fucker who met up with a real badddd muder fucker. Seen worse but not by much. Maybe we should say a few prayers over him while he can still hear them."

Eugenie glared at her and Doc said, "You should wait next door and let us do our work. We're going to be a while and even though Flossie talks rough, you'll never find a better surgical nurse or a compassionate human being. Trust us, you came to us."

Eugenie looked at Scalia and he nodded his head. She let out her breath and moved to the adjoining door.

"When we're done here my dear, we'll take a look at you. You could use a little TLC Too."

"Hmph!" she said.

"When they entered the room, it was a sitting area, bedroom, office, TV room, almost as outfitted as a hospital waiting room. She saw herself in the small bathroom mirror and gasped. Her hair was streaked with blood, her lips were puffed and purplish, left eye almost swollen shut and her jaw was puffy on the right and taking on a ripe plum color. She had blood all over her top and under her fingernails, two of which were hanging loose, one on each hand. She gritted her teeth and pulled them the rest of the way off. Her right arm was swollen up to the elbow and her fingers were misshapen sausages on both hands.

She saw deep scratches on her shoulders when she removed her shirt and her face had scratches from cheek to ear on the left. She turned on the cold water and ran it over her fingers. Scalia came up behind her but not close. She was giving off vibes of rage and pain like a wounded animal in a trap. You don't go close to that.

"Need help?" he asked hesitantly.

"Not yet." she breathed in and out slowly, bringing her anger under control to deal with her pain, "but if anything happens to him, we're finding that other guy. If he's not already dead, we're making him that way for sure." Silent tears rolled down her swollen cheeks.

About a dozen people were at the end of the alley trying to get a view of what was going on further in. A policeman was standing there making sure no one went any further. A police car blocked the other end where the prone body was being treated by one of their EMTs and an ambulance off to the left had the lights on and the back doors open. The small crowd was making small talk and establishing a right to be there as witnesses, though apparently not a one of them had seen anything till the siren drew them to the alley.

There was yellow tape around a portion of the alley where pooled blood was spread from the brick wall out to the center where the fight had evidently taken place. Another officer was putting tape at each patch of blood and marking prints left in the grime and dirt of the alley floor with chalk. Two more officers put their notes together and determined that the prints were of three, maybe four people. They took pictures of all the prints they could find and would examine them at the station lab. It looked like a mugging gone terribly wrong or a drunken fight that turned ugly. Whichever it was there were definitely one or two people who were in bad shape and only one of them was here. Where the other two or three people were had not been determined but it would be a long night for patrol; cruising the streets, checking out bars and walking the harbor area.

They loaded the man on a gurney, hooked up to tubes, IVs, and wrapped in bandages so thick you couldn't see much of any part of him. It was one hell of a fight that much was clear. He was wheeled to the end of the alley where the ambulance driver waited, lifting the gurney inside, doors closed and the attendants drove off with a screaming siren and a sporadic horn to move traffic. One of the lookers removed herself from the crowd and walked slowly away.

    Renata got in her car and rode around the block to the street the ambulance had driven down. She followed at a distance as it led her to the Napoli Medical Center. She was quiet behind the wheel, her thoughts swirling, emotions jumbled and her body half in shock. She had phoned Theras as soon as she realized the body in the alley was Tabor and not Rodane Arcos. He had given his instructions and now she was carrying them out she had to admit, with mixed feelings and a sense of relief. For what, she wasn't sure.

Chapter 21

Doc's safe house, Naples

His nose itched. It wasn't a big itch, just a small one but it needed to be scratched so why couldn't he get his hand up to scratch it? And his eyes… they didn't seem to want to open. The itch continued. He listened and heard no sounds, no voices.

{okay where am I}

For that matter, who was he? All his thoughts refused to coalesce into any kind of symmetry. He couldn't remember who… where… when…

When was it, day or night? He couldn't tell because he couldn't see. A small niggling panic began to set in, a shadow of doubt. Was he alive? Was this what being dead was? Nothing but jumbled thoughts that he had no answers for?

{what do I remember}

He waited and could see nothing in his mind take shape then he saw a small girl wailing, struggling to be free of people; crying and screaming,

"It's okay, Sophia, I'm going to be okay. Please honey don't worry, Daddy's going to be fine. Sophia, it's okay.

{I'm daddy I'm… Rodane}

Well that was settled at least. Maybe if he just let the thoughts come to him it would be easier.

{damn got to itch got to}

"Rodane, open your eyes. Stop struggling and open your eyes. Rodane, you're okay, you're safe. You need to wake up and open your eyes. Dammit Rodane wake up!"

"Okay, is this how you handle your wounded subjects? It must be wonderful to work with you."

"Doc, you said the longer he won't wake up, the chance of more damage. That's not going to happen, not on my watch."

Rodane tried to raise his hand to let them realize he was awake but his hand wouldn't rise up.

{tied down I'm tied down}

He tried harder. Maybe if he tried to talk…"S..a…b,"

{that's a start keep trying}

"Rodane! He's waking up. Rodane, open your eyes. Now damn it!" He forced one eye open, the other one was stuck. Maybe it was tied down too. The room was too bright, antiseptic white, glaring and painful. He tried again. He squinted with half an eye.

{can you have half an eye and still see}

A face hovered over him; dark skin, curls, black eyes. Eugenie! He remembered! Many things passed through his mind then; a dig… ruins… people at a harbor… in bars… a fire in an open window, with ladders being pulled up… a ride along the coastline… a ship… He knew they weren't in order somehow but at least they made some sense. He had an image of Caroline, a tall lean man coming at him in a dark alley… a young girl in a very short dress holding on to his arm to keep from tripping in a pair of stilts… then he saw Sabina. Sabina? Who is she? Then he saw himself bending to kiss her.

{gotta figure out this one Roddy}

Eventually a voice penetrated his concentrated thinking and he listened harder.

"Roddy, open your eyes and I'll help you put it all together, I swear. You're okay!"

"Light," he croaked.

"Light? What… What light? You're probably just dizzy from the anesthesia."

"Light-Bright!" he said.

"What's he doing Doc, making nursery rhymes?"

"Hey doll it's going to be okay. I've seen a lot of patients like this waking up from anesthesia. It's tough for some. He's been pretty beat up. It'll take a while to orient himself.

Doc said, "Let's turn down the lights a little and see if it makes a difference."

Rodane garbled, "Thanks"

Eugenie brightened, "There, see? He's making more sense already."

He forced his eye open and the room was much better. He let out a sigh.

Someone put a straw to his lips and said, "Drink this lucky man. Be just de first ting you have in your new life." It was alcohol! He sputtered and choked and widened his eyes. "Yeah, dat's de ticket! See? He know what it be alright! Wake up de dead, right lucky man?"

Over his face hovered a woman with coal-black skin, glistening with an oily sheen, holding a cup and peering at him from six inches away.

"M...more" he croaked again.

"He gon be jus fine! See how quick he recover? Dis lucky man only lost one life tonight. He must have at least three, mebbe fo more. Damn lucky!"

Over the course of the next half hour, Rodane was able to return from that deep, dark place. His other eye was swollen shut, not gone. His hand was tied down and the other as well because he was trying to struggle and get off the table. 'Doc' didn't have a lot of time to waste finding out where all his wounds were so they made him immobile. His mind grew clearer with another sip of brandy and they wouldn't give him any more for fear of putting him back to sleep.

An x-ray machine showed no major broken bones. Plenty of deep tissue bruises were beginning to purple up and turn various colors as well. Doc thought he might have another concussion to join the remnants of the first one but there was no evidence of brain bleeding or fracture. He had a bruised kidney, his nose was broken, and his face had fingernail gouges at least a half centimeter deep. His collarbone had been cracked. His shoulder was out of joint so Doc fixed that before he worked on his nose or the numerous cuts on his head that required shaving and stapling. His right ear was a lump of cauliflower that made him look like a welterweight who unsuccessfully tried out for a heavyweight match. Doc had given him one pint of blood generously donated by Scalia who turned out to be a universal donor.

By the end of an hour they had him sitting up sipping on ginger ale and listening to how he had gotten here and why.

"So you don't know who it was or why he chose tonight to come after me? Did he hurt a girl?"

"Amber" Eugenie said, "No, she helped me get you out of the alley. After I called Scalia I sent her on her way, scared and shaken but fine."

Doc said, "I'll let you folks talk to him for a few more minutes then I'm making him rest for a while. I take it you won't be wanting him to stay here?" he sounded hopeful.

"No. We owe you big time but I'll be leaving here with him as soon as he's rested a while longer. I have a room for us and he can recover there. I have a couple of people coming to help out and he will be fine, thanks to you."

Eugenie walked over to Scalia, "You have part of his soul now as he does yours. You are brothers by blood, forever bonded and beholden to each other."

she touched her head to his and he stood there, bashful and subdued. He nodded to her.

Later that long night, close to daybreak, Rodane was taken downstairs and Scalia Flossie and Eugenie got him comfortably settled in the backseat of his car and he drove them north. It was only a few miles outside the city but it was secure and under guard. It was one of many safe houses they used to do business or hide someone for a short time, stocked and comfortable with no neighbors in hailing or watching distance.

Flossie asked him, "You want me come sit wit Lucky Boy for tonight? Keep watch? You got to be one tired girl, doll!"

Eugenie laughed but then cringed when her face hurt, "Thanks Flossie, but I have a feeling Rodane and I will be sleeping for hours with no chance of anyone else being anywhere near. You're the doll… no don't scowl at me. I've seen a lot of nursing care in my short life. I know when it's good and when it's awesome." She gave her a big hug even though it hurt her everywhere to do it.

Flossie pushed a half bottle of brandy into her hands, "Flossie to Lucky Boy when he able. You two stay alive. That's better den what he almost did."

"I want him to hang around for a little longer."

Sorrento Farmhouse in the hills

"Can he travel?" Eugenie almost told Sabina he was lucky he was able to breathe but stopped herself, "Not yet. Doc wants us to keep him near in case something happens that he needs to return for immediate care."

{wrong answer Genie dumb}

"Like what? What could happen?" Eugenie heard her voice rising along with tortured emotions,

"Sabina I'm not going into this now, it will only make you crazier. You'll have to trust me that he looks worse than he is and he'll be much better tomorrow after he's gotten good sleep, food and rest. We have pain meds for him and me and a good night will be just what both of us need."

"Are you sure you're telling me everything? I can…"

"No Sabina I'm lying! He's comatose and I'm in last stages so we wanted to say our goodbyes but he can't talk!" her voice became gentler,

"Sabina he's going to be fine. I wanted to prepare you, not scare you."

"How are you really?"

"Gee, thanks for asking… just kidding. Sabina don't cry. Sabina… please." she waited a few seconds,

"Okay girl, listen. I'll be bringing him to our Sorrento Farm house sometime in late morning if he can travel. If not, I'll call and we'll figure something out. You need to be ready to transport him, get an extra guard to the farm and make sure the medicine cabinet is stocked with bandages and plenty of ice, okay?.. Okay!?"

Eugenie went into Rodane's room and checked on him. She had given him pain meds according to Doc's schedule and he was off in la-la land. Doc had fixed her up as well and pressed a pill bottle into her hand. She protested, "Doesn't matter whether you want to take them or not. You won't do him any good if you're in so much pain you can't be aware and awake. Take them!" he barked. She took them. Scalia was dozing on the sofa in the front room with his gun handy and Eugenie took the opportunity to go into the bathroom, filled the tub up with really warm water and then soaked until the water started to get cold. She toweled off and looked at herself in the mirror. She did look like she had gotten run over by a truck. She wondered what Tabor looked like, wondered if he was in a shroud and the bitch, Renata? Where was she?

{the gods help you if you survive you'll wish you were dead both of you}

She laid down in bed in the room next to Rodane with the door cracked open and it was lights out! When Eugenie woke up after four hours of sleep she felt better even though her reflection even threw her off. She went out to the kitchen, put on a tea kettle and opened the fridge looking for food.

{sure sign of getting better}

Scalia came in from the front room, stretched and yawned,

"Need some sleep?" Eugenie asked, "you want me to spell you?"

"No, I'm good for another few. What's the plan, can you tell me?"

"Around three this afternoon we're driving to Sorrento and meeting up with someone. Rodane seems to be resting comfortably so I think we're safe in moving him. There's a farmhouse in the hills that we use and we'll stay there today and tomorrow. Then I guess I'll find out what my next job is and what they will do with Rodane. I'm just glad there is a Rodane to do something with. I think it was touch and go with him for a little."

"Yeah, he was one hurting bloke was he not? And you, how do you feel?"

"If I said 'as good as I look', would you send me to hospital?" she tried to grin and winced when her face hurt.

"You're a tough cookie doll and a foolhardy one at that." He saw her expression,

"Yeah, yeah I know…you can fight. The guy in the alley proved that but what if you hadn't been able to turn it around? I would have been there waiting for two dead bodies. Do you know how long that might have lasted?" he grinned at her.

She poured herself a cup of tea and added sugar. Then she leaned against the sink and sipped while thinking. She motioned to Scalia and the teapot and he shook his head 'no'. "I need to know what happened to Doukas because the hospital won't give out information and we'll be leaving here soon. I can't leave it at this…" she looked crestfallen, "It was because I wasn't there soon enough that he's in the state he is."

"Okay now, there's no need to be takin' on the blame for another man's life. How could you know? You were close enough to save him, doesn't that count?"

Before she could answer there were god awful squeals from the bedroom and they both barreled down the hall and into Rodane's room. He was standing by the bed, leaning against the mattress, trying to pull a t-shirt over his head and a sound like a child's wail or a stuck pig squeal was coming out of his clenched teeth. Eugenie raced to his side, grabbed him around the waist and that made him squeal louder. He grabbed her arms and she let out one hell of a pitched wail herself.

Scalia looked at them, opened his mouth and joined with his own gruff, deep roar and drew it out to at least five seconds. All three stopped at the exact same moment. Rodane looked from Eugenie to Scalia.

Eugenie jerked her head to Scalia and he said, "Now that we've all had our Banshee practice for the day, could we be maybe sittin' down quiet-like, have a nice cuppa and we could kinda talk soft and gentle and I'll clean out my ears from the blood that just pooled there."

"Hmpf!" Eugenie led Rodane to a chair near the bed and she sat on the edge of the mattress.

"Genie, I've got to get out of here. I've got to find Sabina and warn her. There's still that woman out there. I can bet you she knows where Sabina is and I have to warn her." he breathed heavily and his face was rigid with pain. The scratches on his face were beginning to ooze again.

"Ever hear of a phone Rodane, little slip of a thing that makes noise and carries conversation? Where are you going to start looking?"

He thought about that, looked at both of them and said, "Okay, what do I do? Help me out here."

"You are on injured reserve. I'm close to it myself though it causes me more pain just to admit it. Listen Boyo…" She proceeded to tell him what was planned and when it would happen. The look of relief on his face was palpable. They could actually see his shoulders and face relaxing.

"Now, do you want some food or some tea?" Rodane waved them off.

"No I want a shot of liquor, got any?"

Scalia said, "As a matter of fact…" he went to the kitchen reached above the sink and brought back the brandy and three glasses with ice.

"This should be the ticket, eh Eugenie?"

At her scowl he said, "What, you'd deny our patient the healing waters of the gods?"

She sighed deeply, took one of the glasses that Scalia had brought, put some ice in it, thought again and then took two more.

Scalia grinned impishly and said, "Now that's the ticket for sure!"

Naples Medical Center

The med center in Naples was a good one for the area. It was a heavily populated area filled with homeowners, renters, bars, shops, tenements as well as homeless people. Farther out, in the more trendy sections were where politicians, gang leaders, drug runners, local leaders and the wealthier citizens, hotels, stadiums and the Theater District enjoyed the services for which they paid. That being good doctors and nurses, comfortable rooms, good tech equipment and reliable emergency care.

Renata had slipped into that area and followed a stretcher in. The two attendants being too busy giving CPR to pay her any mind, she turned at the first corner she came to and found a supply closet. There were white and blue smocks and caps to cover her hair. She put them on and grabbed a pair of blue medical gloves out of a box, then she started down the corridor toward the emergency units where curtains were the only separation between beds. Machines beeped, respirators hummed and a buzzer squealed somewhere.

It smelled like a combination of vomit, bleach, blood and a fishy odor. {what's that all about}

Voices were everywhere. One nurse ran down and threw open a curtain and it was the man they had just brought in. One attendant was standing next to the squealing machine, while the other was doing CPR on his chest, pushing and pumping. She actually heard a rib crack. A blue cart was rushed into the room and a doctor went over and applied paddles. Renata saw her chance. She left them to their task and started checking each curtained area. There was no Tabor. That meant he had to be in surgery or Xray. She followed the signs and squeezed through the locked double doors as another nurse hurried out.

There were three surgical rooms and Tabor was in the third one with three people working on him. He had IVs connected, blood coming through hanging units, bloody pads all over the floor, soaked and tossed aside. One man was at his head administering anesthesia, the other two were bent over him cutting and suctioning. She backed away, her hand over her mouth. She started to feel dizzy as she walked to another hallway that was quiet. She leaned against the wall until she could get herself together. She couldn't stay here, it was too much but she couldn't leave until she knew if he would live or die. There was no way that much blood was a sign of life. More likely, it was ebbing away. She went back down the corridor and stopped short. At the glass window of the surgical unit was a cop. He waited on a chair brought over to him with his cap on his lap and a phone to his ear. She turned her head a little and walked to the first curtained unit that was empty. She began to gather up sheets, bandages, anything she could carry and she walked back to the corridor where she had gotten her smock and cap. She threw everything in the closet, left it, walking out slowly and made her way to their car. She was going to have to phone Mr. Gallo. Her mouth went dry and her stomach felt like lead. She sat there trying to decide how much to say and how to say it. Then with shaking hands, she took out her phone and pushed 'Contacts'.

Sorrento Farmhouse

The next morning Scalia showed up around 6 a.m. with a minivan which would carry them more comfortably than a car. They all ate breakfast in the kitchen though Eugenie had to wheel Rodane in since he was still too weak to walk the entire first floor. There were pancakes and soft bagels. Eugenie's teeth, some loose, were still giving her a lot of trouble when trying to chew. She was satisfied with hot coffee, a bagel to dip in and small bites. They sat down and took out the thin briefcase Eugenie had taken from Tabor Doukas in the alley.

At first, Eugenie was against even looking at the contents. She wanted to wait till they got to Sabina before they shared their information. Rodane was adamant that he hadn't gone through what he did to be kept in the dark. If he was going to be looking over his shoulder and be wary of all strangers who might look crooked at him, he wanted to know whatever he could about the Who's, the What's and the When's. Besides, if there was something in there he could use to find a way to put this to an end, wouldn't they all want to know and be able to use it to end this immediately?

In the top pocket there was a passport from Greece with Doukas' name. It was well stamped mostly from Mediterranean countries and some Eastern European countries. It appeared he had traveled often between France and Greece most often with some jaunts to Romania, Bulgaria and Macedonia. Interesting! There was a folder with a number of documents and photos enclosed. Rodane narrowed his eyes when he saw a picture of his family. He sucked in his breath and looked at it with dismay and complete anger. Who were these bastards and what did they want with him? How dare they delve into his family to get to him!

In the bottom of the case was a small digital camera a high-end one with good zoom, a thin wallet with two credit cards and over $1,000 in Euros. Whew! Man traveled heavy. There was a copy of the book, The Art of War.

{well-read or fixated}

Somehow there was something off, nothing here to awaken their 'aha' moment, nothing to give off vibes to satisfy their questions or explain their attacks on either Sabina or Rodane especially.

"Rodane" Eugenie hesitated, "wait a minute, the size is wrong."

"What size?" Rodane asked.

"The case, it's four inches wide. This pocket and this depth of case amounts to..." she used her fingers to do an eyeball measurement, "two-and-a-half. Where's the other one and three quarters?"

She felt around the case, probed and pushed. They heard a 'snap' when she pushed near the middle latch-lock. A little plastic tab popped up and she pulled up the stiff shelf to the hidden pocket. Scalia whistled through his teeth and Eugenie said a curse word in Hebrew. It was like something out of Sweeney Todd!

There was a set of instruments encased in velvet pockets, shiny and sharp and oh so ready for some action. There was also a serrated knife and a 22 caliber handgun with ammunition. The man was not only well traveled but packing. Each instrument was designed for its own particular form of torture. Pays to diversify; eyes, fingernails, small bones, teeth...

Rodane sat and looked in horror at what he should have been subjected to by now. He actually felt sick to his stomach.

Scalia bent over, examined it and said, "Looks like me Mum's good silver." It broke the tension as Eugenie snorted, Rodane chuckled and they took a good look at the documents, besides the picture of Rodane's family. There were some shots of Rodane by himself, Sabina, Rodane and Sabina on the parking lot, during the fire.

"Hold on!" Rodane looked closely at the next to last picture, "How did they get this? I'm not there so it had to be taken after I was arrested. Neither of these two were in the parking lot that close. I would have seen them. The only way they could get this close would be to have someone else working with them."

Scalia picked up the camera, "Lucky boy! This is one fine digital. It can get really good pictures from some distance away, sharp and clear and good zoom precision or someone else may be involved."

Rodane said, "Lucky boy? Where did that come from?" Eugenie and

Scalia exchanged looks and Eugenie said, "Someday Rodane, I'm bringing you back to Naples to meet a real guardian angel and a fantastic savior."

The documents were also eye opening. There was a complete rundown of Rodane's life from start up to the present. It included family members; names, dates, residences, education from kindergarten to the present jobs, taken jobs, jobs not taken, ex-wife, child, pictures of each.

{son of a bitch I need to bash someone}

His travels and digs were listed according to date and his awards were listed alphabetically for each find, countries' recognition awards and historical provenance. Eugenie looked at him and said "I didn't know I had a celebrity in my midst. I'm impressed!"

"Be more impressed at these people, whoever they are and the resources they must have to be able to obtain all this information and obscure facts," Rodane looked crestfallen.

"Roddy," Eugenie said, "You'd be amazed how little expertise it takes to be able to use the search engines out there and the different websites that can give you microscopic views of just about anybody on this Earth who has a birthday or death date."

Scalia added, "There are no secret lives anymore, Bucko. It's an open book for anyone who has an ounce of intelligence that knows how to click on a computer screen. Welcome to the new world!"

After breakfast they packed up whatever they needed. Eugenie took the briefcase and the meds for her and Rodane. She had convinced him after breakfast to take a pain pill. He didn't want to sleep but he finally gave in when Eugenie asked "What good will you be to Sabina when we get there if you are so tired you can't even think straight? We don't have a great deal of time here. We need you on your best game."

Rodane said, "I'll take one if you do the same. When she started to object he raised his eyebrows and wagged his finger in front of her. She took a pill.

"Goose, gander and all that." She looked confused at his words. The ride to Sorrento was therefore very quiet and smooth sailing. Scalia had packed Rodane in the back completely with seat belts and soft pillows. Without traffic it would have taken one hour. Since they encountered work traffic, they added another forty minutes to the commute. As they neared the outskirts of Sorrento, the sun was rising higher, the sky was clear and blue and the day promised to be a scorcher. Scalia had the address programmed into the GPS and had no trouble finding the small parking area near the road that carried them to the farmhouse.

They pulled up to a parking spot and Sabina was there pacing back and forth, looking from one side to the other, clearly anxious and nervous. Scalia opened the back doors and Sabina saw Rodane and Eugenie sound asleep, resting comfortably. She gasped at the sight of both of them, put her hand over her mouth, her shoulders shaking with quiet tears. Scalia went back to her and put his arm around her shoulders, "Think of the alternative Ms. Don't dwell on bruises and breaks. Dwell on the fact that they are healing and breathing. Me mum says that's really the test of a good life… breathing." She couldn't help laughing through her tears. He set up the wheelchair and took Rodane out of the back, helping him get into the chair, still groggy and half-asleep. Eugenie was struggling to be fully awake, chugging water to help her hydrate. She had cheated a little, taking only half a pill without Rodane realizing she had cut it.

Scalia pushed the chair up the winding path past lemon trees, blossoming with a citrus smell everywhere, filling the eyes and nose with color and pleasant scents. Cows were walking and laying in every available area mixed with chickens walking loose everywhere. There were olive trees just beginning to blossom with tiny, pea-sized olives that would grow and ripen and sweeten until harvest time. Every available inch of their land was used. No waste meant more products at harvest.

The farmer's wife was waiting for them in the enclosed patio, near the small open area with the milking room. Her daughter had a baby on her hip and a toddler hanging onto her leg. The large, wooden table was covered with flour and the buckets of milk and curd were waiting for processing by hand.

There were no tourists expected today. They had shifted all the tours around, to give themselves two days of quiet and privacy, healing time for both Rodane and Eugenie. That night, Sabina had stayed at the farm house next to Rodane's room. Eugenie slept on a cot in his room, because they were both on a pill schedule and it was easier for her to check on him. He was feeling much better and was starting to chafe at any restrictions. Here she ruled with an iron hand.

{men are terrible patients}

Sabina came in once, around two in the morning, walked over to Rodane's bed and stood there just watching him sleep. Eugenie was a light sleeper, heard her and came over,

"How in God's name did we get here?" Sabina shuddered.

"Not by our hand, that's for sure."

"Eugenie, I can't begin to repay you for…" she sucked in her breath.

"No need, it wasn't only my job, it was for a friend, friends…" she squeezed Sabina's shoulders.

"This man… seven days, it's hard to process."

"I'm only grateful he is still here for you to try and process. If I hadn't been so long, in hearing…"

'Eugenie, don't you dare take on any blame for what happened. Look at you! You…what… you risked… everything for him. We're going to find these people, find them and take them down and you're going to help me."

Eugenie looked at her confused. Sabina pulled her farther aside, afraid of waking Rodane,

"You're healing, Rodane is healing. After I meet with Nikos I'm going to have to go to Florence. Agatha has been given the job of inducting Rodane into our protector's cadre. Rodane is going to want to go there to complete his job for the travel company. There is no way I'm letting him go by himself."

"I'm going to be able…" Eugenie started,

"No, you're not. You're going to heal here and get ready to be my teacher."

"What?" Eugenie drew back and looked at her, "What are you talking about?"

"I'm talking about finally coming to the realization that for many years it has been smooth sailing for me and all the others who are charged with recovery, retrieval, or relocation. That time looks like it's over. We need to be prepared for whoever has changed the whole picture. Some, many, who knows… are playing a whole different game and are deadly serious, literally. Well, we need to get deadly serious too. No more dependence on others to protect us or fight for us" she looked over at Rodane, "or save us."

Eugenie said, "Sabina, I know I didn't …I wasn't there in time to keep this from happening but I swear…"

"No, you don't understand. This has nothing to do with your job. You're still invaluable to our protection but it's time to spread the wealth, Eugenie. It's time to teach us how to protect ourselves. You need to teach me how to fight, you need to teach all of us how to fight, how to give as good as we get."

"You want to fight? How?"

"Girl, what do you mean, how? The way you fight, that's how!" She raised her hand when she saw Eugenie's reaction "No not like you. I know I don't have the time or strength for that but I can do more than nothing. I don't want to use a flashlight to try to defend myself or hurl a little lamp at an intruder."

Eugenie said, "How much time are you willing to put into this? What about the others? What do you think they'll say about your idea?"

"I think you'd be surprised to realize we've all been thinking along these lines for some time."

"You have? Why haven't you said something before now?"

"Oh, I don't know, complaisance, embarrassment…"

"Embarrassment, what's to be embarrassed about?"

"Eugenie, if you had seen me going into my hotel room, knowing someone might be in there waiting for me, with an injured man I was trying to wrestle into the room... I had a flashlight! Like that was going to stop someone with a weapon! It was comical. Even I knew what it would look like. I was scared shitless! My mind was a blur. I need to be able to use my hands, or feet, or both, to defend myself and not be a hapless victim. I hate being a hapless victim!"

Eugenie recognized a possible rationale for Sabina's feelings, "You realize of course it involves a great deal of strength and conditioning...usually it takes years of practice and lots of training with Masters who are assigned the task of pushing you to the extremes."

"I would never hope to be as good as you or Helene but I think you could teach me enough to make it possible for me to be more confident in scary situations instead of looking over my shoulder for my rescuer. I could protect someone else and not react after the fact."

"Are you sure you're not just... reaching for a way to..."

"Make up for not being able to help Rodane? Yeah, I'll admit that's part of it but not the whole reason. We all feel we haven't done enough to be proactive in hairy situations. It all started five years ago when..."

"...when a team disappeared on a foray into El Salvador on a recovery mission?" Eugenie's voice lowered and her shoulders slumped,

"Yes, how did you know?" Sabina was surprised at her quick insight.

"Do you want to discuss this later or now? You could use sleep."

Sabina said, "If anyone could use sleep it's you but now if you can. I think this is important and the sooner the better." Eugenie pointed to the door and they both went out to the living quarters to continue the discussion. Rodane turned over and muttered, 'my girls' with unreserved admiration in his voice as he drifted back to sleep.

Chapter 22

Piazza Tasso, Sorrento

Sabina pulled up to the parking lot near Piazza Tasso, one of the most celebrated hotspots of Sorrento day or night. She was scheduled to meet Nikos by the statue of St. Anthony in the square and have breakfast. She had gotten the briefcase belonging to Tabor Doukas from Eugenie earlier and they had examined it together. Eugenie had made copies on the farm's computer/fax machine of all the photos and documents. She and Eugenie had poured over the documents looking for anything that could give them a glimmer of understanding as to why Rodane had now found himself in crosshairs and it had pulled him into their, up to now, very isolated, unique circle of 'family'. Either they were missing something here or it was hidden to them but known to others. Either way, Sabina now knew much about Rodane that very closely resembled her own path, just not in the same time frame.

His career was already starting to take off into the next level of his expertise. He was very circumspect and humble about his accolades and accomplishments but they couldn't be denied. He was most definitely an expert in his field of study. For one so young, he had many notches in his belt and feathers in his cap. She was proud of him and she expected him to go far if he could stay alive and get back home. She was going to make sure that was the case but then it seemed there were others who were even reaching there to accomplish their goals.

Nikos was waiting at the Statue of Saint Anthony and they went over to the closest shop that served breakfast. They each ordered their food and found a small table in the Piazza to eat and drink their cappuccinos.

Sabina said, "You picked a very interesting place to meet. Saint Anthony, the patron saint of lost or stolen items," she raised eyebrows.

"You know Sabina, no matter how many years I've been part of all this…," he waved his hands around the entire area including the whole wide expanse of… everything, "I can appreciate the beliefs and tenets of the people who picked holy, reverent people of their own to attribute these great miracles that helped us in our most turbulent times. It makes me have hope that those lost and stolen items will be found, maybe not by their owners, but still found and protected and used for good purposes. Think I'm too much of a Pollyanna? It's interesting because you never hear how many actually find their lost items. There should be a party for everyone involved when one is found, don't you agree? To find a precious sought after lost item should be cause for rejoicing and a festive occasion, don't you think so?"

Sabina sat quietly, thinking over his statement, wondering where he was headed but almost sure she knew where it was going, "Nikos, it's only been half my lifetime that you have been our guiding light, if you will. That's all I've been a part of it. I don't remember much of my life before you and Suri and all the others who found me helped to raise me."

She reached across the table and took his hand in hers as a surprised expression crossed his face. Sabina was not one to be overly emotional or to share it, with Nikos especially. Nikos remembered her as a timid, quiet, very observant child who was well-loved but also well-trained. It seemed like training her was the biggest part of what he could remember about her. Maybe a little more fun or affection would have a different person here in front of him now.

"What I can tell you Nikos, is I've never told you how grateful I am that you and all the others decided I was worth the time and trouble and your efforts to make me a part of your 'family'. I don't think I have made that clear to all of you. I've been remiss in showing you how important all of you are to me."

Nikos said, "I think you're about to tell me there is a caveat to that statement yes?" He gave her a rueful smile.

"Well, not exactly a caveat, but an amendment as it were."

"Okay Sabina, where are we here?"

She stood up and said, "You know I've never taken an open carriage ride around this town before. Would you care to do that?" She waited.

He was surprised but not shocked. Sabina was not one to do something spontaneously. He was sure she had something in mind. They walked to a line of carriages and horses waiting for customers. It was early for tourists but they took a tour of the Piazza and a good portion of the center of Sorrento. The carriage driver was very friendly and very knowledgeable about points of interest and historical facts that would have been charming to learn if not already known. When they drove down a small thoroughfare on the other side of town, Sabina leaned forward and told the driver to stop. She told him that she and her companion would be getting out here and going the rest of the way on foot. He offered to come back and pick them up but they declined. Nikos gave him a generous tip and they disembarked.

Nikos looked quizzically at her, "So, do you think we're being followed Sabina?"

She glanced at him from the side and quietly responded, "Don't know but better safe than sorry." The carriage drove off and Sabina and Nikos quickly left the street, walked down two blocks, looked around to spot any curiosity, turned again and disappeared into a narrow almost hidden gateway to a tiny, stone house. It looked so beaten down it resembled a small shack reserved for farm animals or an extremely poor family eking out an existence on the edge of town. They closed the door after entering and he reached for a lantern on the small table over on the side, lit it, and they moved through the short-hall. When they reached the back door, they both walked a few steps to another house that was more substantial, three floors high and appointed with colorful shutters, variegated flowers in boxes and a bronze knocker on the door. No need to knock, someone had been watching for them and opened the door as they approached. Once inside they all hugged. Sabina handed over the briefcase which was spirited away to another part of the house by a quiet, circumspect fourth party. All three sat down at the very old, very smooth- planed table, seasoned by a hundred or more years of use and scrubbing.

Sabina recounted all the events that Rodane and she had experienced. Nikos told of their efforts to have Rodane released from jail, his request for protection for them from Quimby and the conference they had in Capri. Both Sabina and Nikos told of the woman who met with Sabina, alerting them to the danger Rodane was finding himself a part of.

Nikos said, "It was very lax of us not to have more security on Rodane. It is a fault of ours that we do not intend to replicate. He is under close guard and scrutiny and we are awaiting DNA results from 'Doc' at any moment. If it confirms our suspicions, we will need to alter our plans to include Rodane and that will pose its own problems."

"So what is your plan at this stage?" their host asked.

Nikos waited a few heartbeats and said, "Rodane teaches at a University. We have someone who is set to take his place if we can convince him to allow her while we try to protect him and his family. If his DNA results are as expected, there will have to be an induction into some of our history without actually giving away information that would put us in some measure of danger. Sabina, do you trust his judgment? What do you think his response will be?"

"I would have to say…," she paused, "I think he is suspicious but patient, wary but open to reasonable suggestion. He may be shocked but I don't think it will throw him for a loop. I'm really not entirely sure Nikos. It could go either way. He could run or he could embrace it."

Their host said, "Okay, what next? What is the current thinking?"

Nikos laid out the next few days and where they would find themselves. He said he would arrange all the transportation, their lodgings and their protection. He gave them the names of those he had contacted in Virginia and Montana and those who were on standby if needed. Sabina laid out her schedule and they altered it right then and there to accommodate all the new events that had occurred in the last few days. Their host was in charge of observation and management of Rodane once he and Sabina had reached Florence. After that, depending on Rodane's reaction and reports from the US, they would plan their next steps.

Three new cell phones in packages were handed out, numbers programmed in and all three checked their pins for power and range. Nikos regarded Sabina, "One thing I want to hear Sabina."

"Yes" she said.

"What is your…amendment, as you said before?"

She hesitated, looked at her host and then said, "Whatever happens tomorrow or the next day, whatever you decide for Rodane, you have to allow him to return home to his daughter. That is not a matter for discussion or debate. We cannot expect him to absent himself from her even if he accepts his newfound role or persona or whatever you decide to tell him it is. I'll leave that to you."

They looked at her, exchanged nods with each other, minds attuned and agreed. She let out the breath she was holding. Nikos and Sabina got up and left by the front gate that opened on to an enclosed courtyard. There was a fountain in the middle, spitting water and exits on four sides leading to different parts of town. Nikos and Sabina hugged, and she left by one exit and he by another. She made her way back to the car and headed back to the farmhouse and to Rodane.

Sorrento Farmhouse

"That's ridiculous! I'm able to do my job. There's no reason for Sabina and Rodane to go to Pompeii without protection. That would be foolhardy after this." Eugenie looked around the table at Scalia, Rodane, and Sabina, her face pinched in frustration.

Sabina said, "Eugenie, no one said there would be no protection. It's just that I will be going with Rodane to Pompeii. Helene is going to come along with us and she won't let anyone near either of us."

Scalia spoke up, "I could always go with them Eugenie, kind of like a distraction to anyone watching."

Sabina looked at him, thinking of all he had done so far and spoke, "We have a job for you Scalia if you'll take it. It requires you to return to Naples and it may take some time. We want you to find a way to keep tabs on Renata Kappos and Tabor Doukas... if he's still alive. We really need to know where these two are as much as possible and also who they keep in touch with. They have someone much higher up helping them or feeding them info. If nothing else, you need to try and follow the money. That's going to lead somewhere higher, guaranteed."

"So... what, I sit here and twiddle my thumbs?" Eugenie was annoyed and hurt.

"Remember our recent conversation, Eugenie?" Eugenie nodded, still not mollified, "I have been in Sorrento this morning, meeting with Nikos." Eugenie's eyes popped open when Sabina said Nikos' name so casually.

Rodane realized she had let something slip, "Who's Nikos? Genie, you can pick your jaw up off the floor. I take it he's someone important in your 'family'?" Sabina nodded but continued, addressing Eugenie,

"I've arranged for you to meet some people today. I know what a stickler you are for organization and planning. Don't you agree we should get started on that right away?"

Now Eugenie was more than amazed. She was shocked that Sabina was talking so openly in front of Rodane about their ideas of setting up training and protection classes for all the R&R people. She nodded her head in slow motion, too cautious to say more out loud.

"It's okay, Eugenie," Sabina said, "I'm going to clue Rodane into this after you have your meeting. It will be in the reserved room for weddings and banquets, so quite private and quiet." She touched the pin on her lapel when she reached to smooth her hair.

Eugenie rose slowly, pale and seemingly somewhat in a daze. She looked at Rodane who just looked confused, then Sabina, who studied her reaction, then Scalia, who raised his head and then his hands and said, "Don't look at me, I'm just the hired help. I'm off to Naples, ladies. Cheerio! Rodane...,good luck, Boyo. I'll give your regards to Flossie."

"Who's Flossie" Rodane asked once again. They all laughed.

Scalia left and Eugenie went to her room to begin planning. Sabina knew that by the time they all met today, Eugenie would have a framework, schedule, a syllabus, with everyone divided into working teams. The only thing not covered would be a calendar for starting and stopping. That would depend on everyone's present location and what they were working on at the moment.

She and Rodane sat quietly for a moment. She reached across the table and took his hand, "I know the last two days have been a blur and painful for you. I can't tell you how sorry I am that…"

"Why are you blaming yourself?" he asked. He sounded annoyed.

"I'm not, I'm just sorry that you…that your trip wasn't what you expected and your plans with your daughter were all… upended and…"

"Stop, Sabina! Just stop!" she closed her mouth and sat back, waiting for the heat to dwindle. He slapped the table hard and then winced when it hurt his shoulders and his arms. He had the satisfaction of seeing her jump.

{calm down this is important}

He breathed in hard and lowered his voice, "I won't say sorry yet because right now, I'm not. I will be after I'm done venting. Maybe I'm taking it all out on you and you're the wrong one, so for that I'm sorry."

Sabina just waited, not sure how to respond to this sudden anger. She hadn't seen this much anger from him the entire time their lives had been in chaos over the entire seven days.

"Sabina, I'm not used to having my life out of control, having people tracking me, chasing me, attacking me. I'm not used to people accusing me of crimes and jailing me when I know I haven't done anything wrong. It sucks… it makes me angry… it… it scared me and I'm not used to being scared and not just for myself."

He took her hand. It was cold so he put it in both his hands and kneaded it till it was warm, "I want to tell you something but I don't want to frighten you."

Her blue eyes rounded and she leaned over and almost whispered, "Nothing at this point could scare me more than when they got you here and I saw you and Eugenie, and the shape you were both…" then she gulped and tried to talk through a choked voice.

"Rodane, I know you're going home. I know you'll see your daughter. I know we'll find a way to be together or at least to be with each other whenever we can. I came… no, **you** came so close to… not being able to do any of that. I've found you in such a short time, there's so much we could have ahead of us. I was terrified that would be taken away from us, that chance for both of us. How often do people get to find that? That's scary! I can take anything else as long as I don't lose that. So tell me," she said.

"Tell you what…Oh, okay," he was flustered but not angry anymore.

"When I was struggling on the ground and I thought my time was over here, that animal said to me, in my ear, 'Sabina Carter will be so much fun to question and..." play with...' it was a voice from hell and I just wanted to somehow take him with me. If we both were going out, I wanted to be the one to take him with me. Where is he? Is he still alive? I have to know. Who is he? Sabina, if you care for me..."

"Shush Rodane!" she put her finger over her own mouth, "I can tell you everything I know about Tabor Doukas. You'll know as much as I do before this day is over."

The phone rang, startling them both. They jumped! She hadn't brought her phone so it had to be Rodane's and no one had called them this entire trip. He had made calls to his mom, to Sophia, to the University, but no one else. He looked at the number and recognized Caroline's cell phone. He connected, "Caroline, what's wrong? Is Sophia okay? Because it's 10 o'clock there, right? Oh, right, it's nine. Are you in school now? I'm okay."

Sabina raised her eyebrows and shook her finger at him to go on,

"She had what? When? What did you do? Is she okay now? Yes, of course it's okay to call me on the job. I've been taking a break for a couple of days so you caught me... relaxing." He smiled at Sabina.

"I can call her tonight around 10. What? Okay, maybe it will make her feel better to know I'm good. What promise? I don't think I can use Skype tonight but I can call. Can't you just tell her you talked to me and I'm fine? No, I'm not hiding anything. So what did she say? She said what? No, I didn't say anything to her about my plans. Let me get back to you around... what time is your next break? Okay, I'll call you in three hours from now at lunch, 12 o'clock? Okay, Bye Caroline. Yes, please tell her." He hung up and sat back, mystified and somewhat dazed.

Sabina said, "I don't want to pry but is everything okay?" he told her Caroline was calling to make sure he was okay then he told her about Sophia's nightmare last night. He tried to remember every word that Caroline told him Sophia had spoken during her 'dream' and when she woke up this morning, Sophia had asked Caroline to call and make sure that he remembered his promise to Skype tonight.

"I told her... well, you heard my end of the phone call. When I tried to beg off Skyping, Sophia told Caroline I probably wouldn't want her to see me and that I shouldn't worry about all the bumps and bruises. She wasn't upset that I got in a fight. She was just glad I was ok and not to worry about showing her my battle scars. She said...," they looked at each other for a long moment and he was unable to continue.

Sabina felt such heartfelt sympathy for his feelings trying to handle all of this at once, "So what are you going to do? About tonight I mean?"

"I need something to… Sabina, do you have any makeup? Could we cover the worst of it?" Rodane admitted, "I don't think I can play innocent with my daughter but maybe we can cover it up enough that it doesn't look so bad." He gulped and looked beseechingly at her.

She beat him to the punch, "You have a lot to learn, Rodane, about yourself. It now appears you have a lot to learn about your daughter as well. I promise it's not as scary as you feel, okay?" Minutes passed and he finally breathed a heavy breath, "Okay?" She came around the table leaned down and kissed him on the one spot on his face that was not puffy and repeated, "Okay."

Chapter 23

Virginia

Zoe and Lexus had fought on Monday night when he told her how he had tried to befriend Sophia and then his attempt to get Caroline to give him Rodane's phone number or his location. "Do you always use this much finesse when looking for your 'dates'? I can't believe you cornered an eight year old and then scared her away when she didn't give you what you were trying to bully out of her. How dumb was that, Lexus, huh? And the wife yet, what did you expect?"

"She's his ex-wife. She was very clear about that."

"Whatever!" You think this woman was too dumb to know you were threatening her and her daughter? Christ, we'll be lucky if Belva doesn't tell you not to bother coming back tomorrow. I would."

"We're paying him too much money for him to do anything about this. Besides, I didn't do anything to Sophia or her mother. They can't point to anything I did now, can they?"

"Maybe not, but you certainly made sure they won't trust you as far as they could throw you."

"Okay, Zoe, our quite the perfect person" he sneered, "How would you go about doing this? I gave you the chance to do this instead of me and you wimped out."

She opened her mouth to answer then snapped it shut. She walked over to the file lying on the coffee table, and opened it, "Start looking at their daily routines. Find out where Sophia is after school, get me her schedule tomorrow and then let me try to get her to open up."

She handed over the file to him and then stood with hands on hips, scowling.

Tuesday Morning Lexus went into the classroom, prepared to get through the day, with all intentions to be friendly to Sophia and try to undo his clumsy attempt from Monday. Zoe dropped him off early and took off without even a word, heading for God knows where. The homeroom class was all in now, the Pledge recited, announcements made, breakfast had been eaten. He took attendance and asked the snotty kid in the back row to take it to the office. The bell rang and the kids moved toward the door.

"Sophia, could I please see you for a minute?" she looked over, a blank look on her face and walked over,

"I wanted to apologize to you for my third degree yesterday. You know what that means don't you?"

"Yes sir"

"I was just very interested in the wonderful places your dad has been. You're sure there's no way I could get in touch with him? I'd love to pick his brain!" he laughed out loud but she just looked at him

"No sir, none that I know."

{so we're playing dumb huh}

"Have you heard from him lately?"

"Mr. Fira, I'm going to be late for class or I'll need a pass from you. Can I go to class?" he looked at her with total disgust and he didn't care if it showed. He waved her out the door. She started out, looked back with her head tilted a little and a half smile on her face.

{little bitch I'll enjoy getting your dad}

He waved his hand at the door and without a word she turned and walked out and down the hall. How did an eight year old make him feel inept and guilty?

{oh if she were mine I would}

His class walked in dragging their feet and he opened his textbook and snapped his ruler on the desk, "Class, move along, you're slow as molasses in January." He smiled, they didn't. He turned to the board and began to write on the chalkboard, making it squeal. The students groaned and put their hands over their ears.

To be continued....

Insertion 3

Italy, 69AD, North of Sorrento at Mt. Vesuvius

She took one more measurement just for safety's sake. She had one chance to get this right and her hands were shaking terribly. Her stomach was twisted and threatening to heave into her throat and bring her lunch up at the same time. The afternoon was cooling and the high sun was at her back. Holding the laser wand up towards the sill of the window, she peered intently outward to the imposing site before her. The mountain rose hundreds, thousands of feet into a startlingly blue sky with few clouds. In her innermost thoughts there was a faint hope for rain, a pouring thunder cloud that would drench that boiling, rolling smoke hurtling upward. It wouldn't happen but the faint hope still existed, whispering to her deep in her mind like a sprite whispering teasing, tantalizing thoughts, to divert her from her task.

Their last meeting has been tumultuous, frenzied, many voices actually screaming in rage over each other trying to make their points and sway minds. Too late! The decision has been made by the High Council and it would not be undermined. A large number of enforcers were placed at each exit to keep order and prevent a possible riot. Their wands were fully charged and set not on stun, but kill, which those present found abhorrent and terrifying. They were very far from resigned though the methods had been announced and in place for well over a year. How can you resign your end to someone else's plans and decisions even if you recognize the necessity of that end?

Behind her and below the window where she hunkered down, she could hear people in the alleyway coming home from chores, going to market to shop for food or supplies, stopping at the fountain to fill their water containers to outlast the hot sun. With a few seconds of silence here and there, you could hear some of the younger children playing farther behind her, probably kicking a ball up and down the main street with a slapped together goal of some sort, from whatever recycled materials they could scrounge up.

She took three deep breaths to calm her racing pulse and to help still her hands. Out of the corner of her eyes she could clearly see Regis gazing out toward the south at the awesome site she was also viewing. She wondered what thoughts were sweeping across his mind at this moment. Did he feel at all helpless like she did? Did he want a different outcome as so many others did, knowing also, as they did, it was not possible but finding it difficult to accept the one about to happen? Almost as if he could read her mind, he spoke softly with just a hint of irony,

"You think we're wrong to do this, don't you?"

After seconds went by of tense silence, she gripped the laser wand tightly in her sweaty hand and turned slowly toward him, "It's not my place to question the decision of the High Council, nor their methods. I will do my job" she snapped. The last words were said by her with a little more strength and conviction than she actually felt.

"Oh come on Parsia, you can't tell me that you don't have a few qualms with what we're about to do in the next few moments. I can almost smell your fear."

"Of course I question it!" she snapped again, "I'm not averse to finding a way to hide our presence but at the expense of 20,000 people? How do you justify that?" she turned to the window, staring ahead to the smoking, rumbling mountain.

"Tomorrow, if this goes as planned, there will be a 6.5 earthquake and things will happen quickly. Is the council ready?"

Regis moved closer to the window, "We have sixty-six members preparing to move at our signal. Any idea how long this will take?"

"No more than a week. I'm guessing around August 24th or 25th". She looked up and met his eyes straight on, "Where do we go from here? What happens if we do survive this?"

"We'll be moved to a new location, given the means to continue on with solid jobs, enough money to live comfortably and a place to regroup and work on the next period of our lives."

Regis gazed out at that mountain again, "We had it pretty good for a long time" he said "kind of depressing to think of starting over."

Parsia went to speak then shut her mouth abruptly, looked back at the doorway and whispered, "Someone is out there listening. I can feel it."

Regis moved silently towards the door, stepping to the side to avoid direct confrontation. He looked at Parsia once more and lifted one finger, then two, then three. Parsia sighted on the mountain, let fly the beam of the laser pushing the fourth button on the wand and watched it bombard the side of the mountain with a thin line of the brightest red and white light combined. She blinked and then turned slightly to the side to avoid directly gazing at the light. Minutes passed, then more. Parsia realized she was holding her breath and let it out in a soft sigh. Regis leaned a little to the left and raised his staff.

As more minutes crept by, Parsia turned to lock eyes with Regis. They didn't say a word but looked down as the first wave of motion was felt like 1000 chariots driving down the street at once. The earthquake picked up steam and movement as they waited and stood against the wall and window for protection. The next week would determine if they lived or died. Thus began the start of the end of Pompeii, with the deliberate awakening of the giant, Vesuvius.

.

Chapter 23 (cont'd)

Pompeii—Present Time

It was after four when Rodane and Sabina had set out for Pompeii. He had been here once before but to examine and walk the ruins, not to see it from the perspective of a tour guide leaflet or a travelogue. She had put a thin but long--sleeved shirt on him even though it was going to be in the high 90s. According to weather reports, they were calling for showers in late afternoon or early evening.

{good people will leave early}

She bought him a Panama hat and a pair of sunglasses with side shades to cover his eyes. In the wheelchair, he looked like a mafia Godfather being escorted by his devoted nurse. She wore a long white smock over her dress and low comfortable shoes. She put her instruments in a cloth bag and put them on the small shelf under the wheelchair.

They headed out the winding road from Sorrento to Pompeii and after a drive of about thirty minutes, arrived at the ticket counter. The cashier took her money, handed her two tickets and let her through the turnstile. She said something to him, he nodded and they set off. They hooked up with a tour group... sort of, and followed them around to fountains, a gym, spa, the red light district and the open-air huge courtyard, where the temple ruins stood in front of a very clear open view of Vesuvius itself, still spinning smoke into the air.

Rodane was picture happy, somewhat of a reaction to doing nothing for hours on end that led to days. He was chafing to be more mobile and agitated that he still hurt everywhere and it cut down his mobility. Doc had removed his staples from the incident in Akrotiri and his scalp itched from the healing scabs and skin. He kept reaching to scratch without thinking and Sabina kept clearing her throat. It was driving him bonkers.

The flowering bushes and baby roses lent a soft, perfumed aroma on the pathway they walked. The path was steep and Sabina was huffing by the time they had made a short circuit around the area. Pompeii was surrounded by a black, wrought-iron fence around its entire perimeter. Rodane wasn't sure how Sabina expected to do her job here with all these tourists around. She stopped, checked her watch and began to push him back to the open stadium. Most tourists had moved on to other parts of the ruins and many had left an hour before when a shower opened up. It didn't matter. Ten minutes of a sprinkling did nothing to cool people off who were wishing for a downpour.

When she got to the long, partly-enclosed walkway, she stopped at a wooden door with heavy, thick, iron hinges and a large knob. She looked around her, up and down the walkway, saw no one and opened the door. She quickly wheeled him in, closed the door and felt around the wall to find a switch. There! There was a low bench against the outer wall and she sat down, wiping sweat from her face. Strangely, it was cool in here, even though it was enclosed. When he remarked on that she added, "Stone and vents."

He looked confused so she explained, "The walls are six inches wide, solid stone and there's a vent in the floor where cool air is piped in."

"What is this room for?" She answered tersely "Me." When he looked at her scowling, she continued, "I've arranged to stay here until the gates are closed and everyone except the night guard has left. Then we have time to check out our site." "Our site?" he chided, "ok, my site. It shouldn't take more than an hour to determine the method of safeguarding the ahh…"

"Sabina don't bother, too much to dance your way around. You promised I would be told all I needed to know. I'll take your word for it and just let you be about your business. What do I do here to help you?" He jumped in his seat when two short raps were heard on the door. Sabina didn't move but called out softly, "Be out in a second." She took the bag from under his chair and removed his sunglasses and asked if he wanted to change to a t-shirt. He thought about it a second or two, "No, actually I'm very comfortable."

She opened the door and Helene stepped in with barely enough room to hold her. "What is this room?" Rodane was curious.

Sabina said, "It was a waiting room for the actors or speakers for the amphitheater events. They stayed here until their role was announced, then came out and into the theater, with perfect acoustics."

"Can I get a couple of pictures of the temple courtyard and this Amphitheatre in the dusk?"

"Sure, we won't be disturbed until I take you out to the gate. Helene will take you." He was about to protest then saw her face. She was expecting him to do just that and attempt to stay with her to observe and maybe see whatever she was after.

"Good, ready to go Helene?"

"Yes sir, lead the way sir!" She saluted and they left, Helene pushing him with his camera on his lap, changing lenses, indicating which direction he wanted to be wheeled in.

She closed the door behind her, took the bag, opened it and pulled out a board of metal about 10 x 9 " with two rows of switches, the green button on the right, a red button on the left in the upper corner of the board. She pushed a switch and out popped a drawer. Inside was an isotope in a lead casing, to be handled with gloves and very gently. She checked to make sure it was secure then put it back in. She took out the EMS (electromagnetic spectrometer) she had used at Akrotiri, though much more advanced than today's type, and began walking through the side streets on the outskirts of the town, facing Mount Vesuvius; up one block, over and down the next, repeat. After about twenty minutes she saw the needle begin to move toward the end of the EMS in the positive range. She looked around, took her bearings and moved down the cobbled streets, watching the needle move slowly. When she reached the cross street and stepped over it, the needle jumped.

{good just where they said it was}

She was one block in from the perimeter of Pompeii, at a small house partly renovated that had a stone sill wide enough on which to place her tools and she undid the board, again pushed out the isotope and retrieved the small shovel with a folding handle. She began to dig small amounts out without rushing. Next week there would be three teams coming in to examine the ruins and start looking for a spot that showed promise. She stopped, picked up her small flashlight,

{gets dark fast here with no lights}

...and walked over a couple of blocks into the city center. She looked right and left and spied the bands of yellow tape to the right about three more blocks away. Okay, this was good news. She walked back to the digging spot and looked out the window. She saw a perfect outline of Vesuvius with the definitive curve to the middle where it had exploded those tons of ash and stone toward that river of hot, melted earth. It slid down the side of the mountain quickly, into this town and gave it a 'lights out' to almost 20,000 people, men, women, children, babies… she sucked in her breath, placed her hands on the sill and received a spark that tingled up her arm. She jerked her fingers off the sill.

"Oh my God, you stood right here! This window was your sight line!"

She felt her throat grow tight and unshed tears formed over her eyes.

She looked again and whispered, "I'm sorry" and began to dig in earnest. After another fifteen minutes and a check on the EMS, she reached the tip of silver. The needle was over to the very end, right before the red line of radioactivity overload. She had her gloves and no worries. She used the tip of the shovel to work out stones and loose dirt, dug more dirt to loosen, more stones, on and on and in ten minutes she had the wand out and packed in its leather casing. She put the isotope into the drawer...

{no need to destroy it now}

Closed it, covered over the depression from her dig, stomped on the loose dirt and used the shovel to pound it tighter and firmer. No one would be able to tell it had ever been dug up, after twenty or even two hundred people had walked and ridden over it in heavy feet, wheelchairs, kids running, stirring up the gravel, golf carts riding down, bringing water and tools. All of it would erase evidence of her efforts.

She pushed the top button on her pin and started toward the spot where Rodane and Helene had left for their photo shoot. Five minutes after she had reached the hall, Helene and Rodane showed up. Rodane looked pale and worn. Helene looked cautiously at her and she gave a slight nod to her.

"Well Rodane, let's get you out of here. I think there's been quite enough work for today agreed?" He nodded yes and gave her a wan, tired smile.

"You sound chipper. Everything go according to plan?" he looked up at her with a twinkle in his purple, bruised eyes.

"Roddy" Helene said, "You can be devilish, must be the Irish in you."

"Irish? I beg your pardon, it would be Scottish we're talking of now and me father takin us from the hills and heather down to the moors in bad weather."

"Really, you have Scottish Heritage?" Sabina asked.

"Don't know, sounded plausible. I'm hungry, let's go home." They left the ruins as quietly as they entered. The night watchman unlocked the gate, nodded to them and said

"Buona Notte. It is a good night, indeed!"

Virginia

School was over for the day. Caroline packed up her bag and made sure she had all the papers to grade for the following day. She was taking a day off tomorrow, unusual for her. The dentist had called and needed to switch her appointment. Caroline protested that this was the second time it had been changed. They found a cancellation last night and called her to see if she wanted it so she put in for a professional business day and rearranged her plans for a substitute. Adam was off tomorrow so they would get a very seldom taken day together. Maybe they could go to lunch or take Sophia out to dinner since she would be caught up on paperwork with a free afternoon. Nice break!

She had told Sophia her dad was going to try and Skype tonight and it really perked her up. This whole incident was so bizarre. When she and Adam questioned her in the morning when they were eating breakfast, she very honestly didn't know what they were talking about.

"No Mama, I don't remember any of that. I guess I fell asleep at the computer and you put me to bed, right?"

They didn't press her on any of it but then during the ride to school she had thrown Caroline for a loop when she made the statement about Rodane's bumps and bruises and a fight. She was adamant about letting Daddy know it was okay if he looked funny, she still wanted to see him. The phone call she made to him didn't quell her anxiety either. Rodane wasn't telling her something. She did know him well enough to know when his side-stepping was a way of avoiding unpleasantness. Ironically, she realized it was used mostly with her when she was badgering him or instigating a fight.

{I really was hell on wheels}

Not proud to go there, she told Sophia at lunch that Daddy would definitely be calling tonight. One problem solved.

She went out to the field where the soccer tryouts were being held and looked around to see where Sophia was. She spied her on the team bench lacing up her shoes. She waved and Caroline waved back.

{needs new ones growing so fast}

She sat down on the bleachers, took out a small stack of essays and began her grading and editing. Paperwork was the bane of her profession but still a necessary evil. A shadow crossed in front of her and shaded her light on her papers. She looked up,

"Hello Mrs. Arcos. Haven't seen you today. Had lunch in your room?"

"Why no, Mr. Fira, I skipped lunch today.

{if it's any of your business}

"Oh that's right. I heard you were taking a day off tomorrow. Hope everything is ok at home?" He waited for a response,

{you ignorant jerk what are you after}

"Everything's fine, thank you, it's just an appointment that needs to be kept. I think they can survive without me for a day."

"I'm sure they will. These children of this particular age seem quite independent for the most part.

{why are you even working with children}

"I noticed your daughter rides with you to and from school. Does that become an inconvenience on days when you need time off?"

A peculiar feeling had been rising in her since Fira had approached her. It started off with her being annoyed at his presence and ended with her fearing his presence and a growing anxiety at this unusual attentiveness he had to her and Sophia's doings and whereabouts. It was almost as if…

{you're keeping track you bastard}

"Not at all Mr. Fira. My daughter and I like to spend time with each other. I am always perfectly aware of her safety and security. It really helps my being here with her."

{why am I explaining myself}

Before he could say anything else she said, "You'll have to excuse me here. I'm getting a head start on my grading papers." She ended the conversation and looked down at her papers, willing him to just walk away. It took him a few seconds to do just that and she waited a few more before she glanced up. He was sauntering down the sidelines. He stopped and looked back directly at her. She didn't have time to turn her head and they looked directly at each other. A slow smirk appeared on his face. She shivered and felt ice in her veins.

She didn't know why but she immediately looked around for Sophia. She didn't see her, got instantly flustered and started to rapidly examine all the girls on the field. Then she checked the bench, no Sophia. She started to get up from the bleachers where she looked back and forth, pulse fluttering, eyes scanning the group again. She was about to go running onto the field when she saw her over at the far edge near the fence, talking with a woman she didn't recognize. Oh! There she was, but a niggling feeling still existed and her belly hadn't unclenched yet.

She walked down field till she passed the goal then she tracked across the field on her way to Sophia. As she got closer, Sophia laughed and turned and ran toward her mother and the lady walked away. Sophia came up to her, clothes wet with sweat, a smile on her face,

"Hi Mama, whatcha doin here?"

"Just came over to see if you were alright. I was wondering why you weren't on the field with the other girls."

"Coach gave me a ten minute break. I got my water bottle there" she pointed to the grass.

"Who were you talking to just now? I didn't recognize her."

Sophia said, "She said she lives back there…" she pointed to the neighborhood behind the fence "and she was on a walk. She stopped to ask me if I was ok when I sat down and got my water bottle. She was telling me some really interesting stuff about my Manga characters. She knew a lot of stuff that I didn't. Way cool for a..." she looked at Caroline, "older lady".

"Does she have kids? What's her name?"

"Mama, we only had three or four minutes to talk. I don't have her whole life story yet," she rolled her eyes.

"Sophia, honey, remember what we talked about… stranger danger?"

"Mama, look over there. The fence is about ten feet high. See? fence?… iron…? It would be pretty funny watching a grown lady climb over that to come and grab me, like I would stand there and let her."

Caroline hugged her, "Yeah, your mama is getting to be an old worrywart but just to please me…could you take your break closer to the bench?"

Sophia looked where the woman had been, looked down the street and didn't see her, "Yeah Mama, I can do that. Sorry if you were worried."

They both walked back to the bench and Sophia finished her tryouts. Caroline just had a feeling that somehow, this 'thing' was just beginning and it was scaring the shit out of her.

Chapter 24

Sorrento Farmhouse

When all three got back to the farmhouse from Pompeii, they found a wonderful homemade pizza waiting for them, ready to go into the outside brick oven. There was a luscious tray of antipasto which they devoured quickly. Rodane chewed, looked up at Helene chowing down, chuckled and kept eating. She snorted and took another slice. They drank unsweetened iced tea and then they all had cups of Cappuccino. Helene went off to spend some time with Eugenie but she and Sabina would talk later about her meeting with the other protectors.

Rodane looked up at Sabina and asked, "Same job as Akrotieri?"

"What? Same…jo…Oh" she took time to wipe her mouth stop chewing and placed her napkin on the table, "You know Pompeii is a story still being told? Over the years in fact, the story has started over, like a rewind with editing."

Rodane waited for her to continue,

"Have you read the recent excavation where they discovered fifty four people underground in a barrel-vaulted room, all joined as in a group, perhaps thinking to ride out the volcanic eruption?"

Rodane mused, "Yeah, big question was why they stayed. There was evidence some of them were wealthy merchants who could easily have paid their way out of the city. One skeleton, of a woman, the Green Lady, was found with her emeralds still on her. She was determined to be microwaved. Why hang around for that?"

"Well the room had air vents leading to the outside. They may have thought they had an air supply and if they hunkered down they could outlast it. After all, there had been other eruptions before that."

"Yeah, wasn't there one right before in late August? It even caused the water in their system to cease flowing. You'd think they might consider…"

"Getting out of Dodge?" Sabina finished.

"Exactly" said Rodane, "There was a seal discovered with one of the skeletons that identified him- Lucius Tertius, I believe. Again, why stay for that when he could have returned afterward? Of course it all would have been gone as it was proven but he didn't know that.

"They had seventy feet of packed, concrete-like ash to get through before they found those remains. I'm sure there are others there and other places that have yet to be unearthed. Hard to imagine this was a 1st Century town and a port city at that. Some of the paints on walls and floors were expensive pigments shipped in, like for the very expensive Villa Pontus."

"So," Rodane said, "question is, like I said…why did they stay? I think the earthquake was a 6.0 on the Richter. They had to have experienced others that would tell them this was much bigger, much badder."

"Just one of the reasons teams and groups are still coming to dig deeper and delve into those mysteries." He was into this and she sat back and pondered all they had discussed.

"You never know Rodane, one day soon we may be coming back here to do just that. A mystery kept for fifteen centuries is a very difficult story to solve and we're never sure when some of it is a story we make up as we piece it together and the real story is even bigger than our made-up one."

"Sure did put a damper on their Summer Games."

Sabina said, "Put a damper on an entire city of over 20,000 people."

"When the temperature rises up to 400 degrees incrementally as the ash cloud passes, it would be time to kiss your partner and say goodbye. If they had left earlier there would be more of their descendants to pass on the story of actual events."

Sabina looked at him and said, "Who's to say there aren't some of those descendants?"

He looked at her, a little confused. He knew there was the beginning of a message here.

Sabina looked a little sideways at him and seemed to study his face as she spoke, "You know, there's a theory that emeralds have very distinct properties that we're only beginning to figure out."

He was still thinking that over, when his phone rang. He was about to smack himself in the forehead when he remembered and stopped himself from self-inflicted pain, "Oh my gosh, I forgot my mom!"

"You forgot your mom? What?"

"Her birthday is the 26th. I always call her on the 26th of each month.

It's a good way to remember to stay in touch, no matter what else is going on."

"But yesterday was the 26th", she said.

"I know and I didn't, and now she's worried."

"Mom, Hi, how are you? No, I'm fine. Yes, I am. I forgot, we were so busy the time just…she what? Oh boy! No, there's nothing to worry about, honestly. We just got back from Pompeii. I know… still just as wonderful. Yeah, I'm almost finished with the tour. I got some great pictures of Pompeii at dusk. Well…we got permission to stay longer, that's all. So, tell me what's happening with you. You did? Cassie? No, she didn't call me. Ma, I'm fine! Honestly. How about I take a selfie and send it to you, will that help? I don't know how to Photoshop, Ma! What's going on? Ha ha! Yeah…"

His mom talked for a few more minutes. Rodane put in the requisite, 'really'? 'yeah' 'I know" ha ha' then, "I talked to Caroline today. I'm calling Sophia later, in an hour actually. I promise we're all fine. Tell Cassie I'm kicking her back to kindergarten when I see her."

Sabina took all the plates and dishes to the back room for washing while Rodane finished up his call from his mom and then she returned when he said his goodbyes.

"Did she buy your excuses? Are you in the doghouse?"

"He sat there looking around the room like he was trying to find a sign or a poster. He was definitely disturbed, "I'm getting more and more confused as things keep happening instead of less."

She sat down, folded her hands, looked at him and said, "What's up?"

"He was confused and frustrated, that was obvious from his wringing of his hands, "As I get closer and closer to getting some answers from you, I keep getting more and more questions to add to the list and they're… wacky… and odd… and…"

"Spooky?" Sabina asked.

"You know something don't you, you've figured it out already what my mom was asking or telling me. How do you do that?"

Instinct?" she asked.

"Don't even try. This is a hell of a lot more than instinct. This is tarot cards and tea leaves, palm reading, and crystal balls, and…" he huffed out a shaky breath and his hands were trembling,

"Tell me" she encouraged him "Voice it so I can help."

"Sophia has been calling my mom lately on the 26th also, just to talk and catch up on things. They decided, she and my mom, if I was going to call her on the 26th, she would be on the same schedule so it could be a Daddy's family thing. It has worked out well. Caroline agrees it's good for Sophia to keep in contact with her Oma. It helps my mom to go months without seeing her only grandchild."

"Did Sophia forget? 'Two peas in a pod' kind of thing?"

"No" Rodane said, "Quite the opposite. Sophia called her early this morning before she left for school and told her not to worry if she didn't hear from me because I was laid up. That was Sophia's word. My mom said Sophia told her I would be in touch soon and not to worry."

"Well, maybe Sophia just used the words incorrectly and she meant that you were… no, I know you're right. So is that it?"

"No, mom said yesterday she got a hurried call from Cassie. She told my mom she was going to 'bust my ass' when I got home and a few bumps and bruises would be nothing to the sore head **she** could give me. When mom wanted to know what she meant, she said, 'ask your son'. She wants my mom to find out what the hell I think I'm doing over here."

"A long silence stretched then Sabina said very slowly, "Rodane, I'm going to jump the gun just a little here," She put her two fingers close together without touching.

"Your family… some… all… we're not sure. They are, how to say this… exceptional. I would like to go to Florence with you tomorrow if you're up to it. I believe that's what your schedule said, am I correct?"

"Yeah, that was the plan before…" he waved his arms…"all this". He got up from the table, "I've gotten stronger over the last two days, lots of rest and nice nurses. He grinned at her "great hands-on care. I seem to have recovered nicely."

She watched him pace around the room, "I would say you've recovered remarkably, for someone who almost…" her words hung in the air, and he looked at her, looked at his bruises and bumps, sensed her thoughts and became more agitated,

"Died? "You're saying I almost died?" He did look shocked. "That couldn't be. I'd be in the hospital if that were the case. I only have bruises, some sore muscles and a few staples to show for that fight."

She raised her eyebrows and he continued, "well, maybe a concussion also, or two concussions…" he looked sheepish.

"Sit down Rodane, I want to enlighten you" she motioned to the chair when he hesitated. Once seated, she proceeded to give him a list of all the injuries and blood loss he has sustained and the shape he was in when he arrived in Sorrento two days ago. He rolled up his sleeves, examined his arms. He touched his face and feet, his shoulder.

"How can that be? That's not possible! If what you're saying is accurate, I'd be in a sling or in a hospital bed or hooked up to IVs or…" his voice drifted off when she just sat quietly and let him go on and on.

"Explain!" he said shortly and waited.

"I can tell you this. We are pretty sure you have some uncommon attributes to your immune system and it allows for some… rapid acceleration of healing."

"Hold on, you're talking about molecular regeneration and cellular restructuring."

"Well it sure helps to get to the nitty-gritty when we share the same background, saves us some time."

"So, being that you're crazy…" he waved his hands in the air and got back up and started pacing again, "There would have to be…cells don't act like that unless there is…" He started to sweat. "It requires either bioengineering or…"

Sabina interrupted, "Or…tissue engineering and regenerative DNA structure."

"Jesus Christ! What are you saying?" He was almost shouting.

"Rodane… Rodane… Rodane!" and he stopped and looked up, "Do you want honesty or do you want me to coddle your preconceptions? Which is it? You say you want answers. Do you? Do you really? If they don't fit your ideas and your scenario, do you want me to just let you go on as you have? Choose one. I'll abide by whatever that is."

She got up from her chair, came over to him in the middle of the room and went into his arms. He wrapped his around her and she laid her head on his shoulder. They stayed there quite a while until she felt his body trembling lessen so he could begin to listen and his sweating was cooling down the heat she could feel escaping from him. She looked up at him and he said to her in a tortured voice, "What am I Sabina? What the hell am I?"

"You're the man I've come to care about very deeply and you're the same person you were then and you are the same person now. You're just learning yourself a little more, kind of like a giant 'aha' moment after some deep introspection. You're lucky. Most people don't get a chance to learn themselves in a whole new light after an entire lifetime."

She saw his watch, "Uh oh, you have a half an hour if you want me to cover your bruises and make you presentable to Sophia."

"Oh God… Sophia! You…what about her? What about Cassie… and…

"One step at a time Rodane… one step at a time."

She took him to her bathroom, got out her makeup, and spent about fifteen or twenty minutes applying one or two different foundations until she found the one closest to matching his skin tone and then some powder to smooth out the recent deep gouges on his cheek. He looked fairly presentable when she was done.

"Stay in a little shadow if you can. Turn the screen to give her an angle on your better side. I have a feeling all this preparation was a little unnecessary…but we'll see."

The computer was on a table in her room. She went over to an easy chair, away from the screen. He had asked her to stay. She wasn't sure but she had agreed. At 11:10 he Skyped Sophia and held his breath. When it burped to open up the screen, Caroline was there.

"Caroline…hi, did I call at a bad time? I thought you had said eleven. I'm sorry."

"No, no, you're fine. Truthfully, Rodane, I wanted to talk to you before Sophia did." She leaned closer to the screen, "Could I see your face Rodane? You're in a dark shadow."

"Why do you want…?"

"So it's true. Something did happen to you." She put her hand over her mouth. "Sophia was right, I can see the purple bruises under your eyes. You think we girls don't know about covering deep shadows under their eyes? What happened to you? Don't lie! What the hell is happening here? I can't wrap my head around all the craziness that has happened the last few days, now this!" Her color had paled.

"Caroline, I was mugged on the way back to my hotel.

{well, mostly true anyway}

Someone came out of an alley and attacked me, did a nice number on me but I was taken to a doctor and I've been getting better each day. It looks worse than it is, honestly. That is the truth."

Caroline sat there and digested it. She breathed out slowly, "But what about Sophia's nightmare? How could she…"

"I don't know but since she can't remember any of it, wouldn't it just be as well to let it alone? You might not want to dredge up any ideas that might have her thinking about it before she goes to bed."

"I wouldn't worry if it weren't for the events that have happened around us and that stupid… never mind, that's on me."

"What's on you? Something else happened? I shared with you, how about equal time?"

She told him about Fira taunting her at the field, and her panic at not finding Sophia, and the strange woman who somehow just 'poofed' away, "but it's just a feeling and I make myself crazy when I dwell on those things."

"Have you talked to Adam like you said?"

"Yes, we discussed it this afternoon. He's going to come by school tomorrow… no wait…I have off tomorrow."

Rodane waited, "I have a dentist appointment so I took a business day.

Adam and I are having lunch afterwards so we can discuss it then. It's probably nothing. Somehow, I've taken a dislike to this asswipe and it's probably coloring my judgment."

"Caroline, don't second-guess your instincts. Just be careful around him."

"It's okay. He's going to be gone tomorrow. Mrs. Cooper is coming back from her cruise on Thursday so they'll be back to their normal routine. I'll get Sophia." She rose and left the room.

He turned to Sabina, "Did you get all that? I think she should be worried. Should I…"

Sophia plopped down in the chair "Who you talking to Daddy? Where are you?"

"Hi Sunshine, I'm at a wonderful farmhouse in the hills of Sorrento and it's a beautiful place. Even more importantly, they make the best pizza."

"Okay, so who's there with you? Can I meet them?"

He started to deflect then he thought, why not?

He turned and motioned to Sabina who was trying to slide down in her chair. She got up and reluctantly came to the screen.

Sophia said, "Hi, who are you?"

"Hi yourself, I'm Sabina, a friend of your dad."

"You have a pretty name. You're very pretty too but you're not the one who helped my daddy when he was fighting with that stupid man," Sabina glanced at Rodane and then said, "No, I'm not. That was a friend of mine. She's a good fighter and a good friend. She was there when your daddy needed her."

"Daddy, would you thank her for me… for helping you?"

"Sure Cupcake, I can do that. How was school today?"

Sabina left the room and Rodane and Sophia had a nice conversation for ten more minutes. They talked about Oma and her call to her earlier, and her soccer tryouts and eight year old interests. She told him about her Manga club and what they planned and mentioned the woman who she met earlier on the field.

"Yeah, Mom told me about your new friend. What does she look like?"

"She's little, almost as short as me, and real pretty. She reminds me of Tinkerbell."

"Tinkerbell, how so?"

"She flits, she's real… I don't know, kind of like a dancer. She knows a lot about Manga, some really cool things. She's going to bring me some Manga books she has but doesn't read."

"He sat up straight, "Really? When is she going to do that?"

"I don't know, she said soon. She's going to get my address from school.

She said Mr. Belva, she knew his name and all, and she are friends and she can even drop them off at my house. Cool huh?"

Alarm Bells were ringing and he was starting to sweat again.

{when will this all end)}

"Sophia, does Mom know about this? Did you tell her all that you just told me?" She squished her face and thought about it, "No, I didn't have a chance to. The coach called me back to the bench then I forgot. Why, Daddy?"

" Soph... I think it would be good for Mom to know that someone she doesn't know is coming by the house. She might not agree with the idea of taking things from someone you don't know. Might be a good idea to run it by her, okay kid?"

"Sure Daddy she's nice though. She said we might have the same things to like and she would love to get to know me better. She loves Manga."

"Okay sweetheart, I hope you make the soccer team."

"I hope so too, it's a lot of fun but boy, do you have to run a lot. My legs are tired."

"I'll talk to you in three more days when I'm almost ready to come home. Did Mom tell you?"

"Yes! Mama said you were coming here and you would spend the whole weekend and afternoon with me. Can we go somewhere special Daddy?"

"Why don't you think of a few places you'd like to go and then we'll pick. Goodnight Sunshine, can I talk to Mom for a minute?"

"Maaaamaaa! She yelled, then blew him a kiss and was gone. Sabina entered the room and was prepared to leave again, but he waved her over. She stood to the side while Rodane quickly told Caroline about the woman and Manga books. She looked surprised and fretful, just one more thing to worry over,

"Thanks Rodane, Adam and I have a lot to talk about. Please, take care of yourself. We'll be here two days from now. Make it eleven, in case Sophia is on the soccer team and she's at practice. Go Bears!"

They closed Skype. Sabina said, "You'll be home soon, you'll spend some time with Sophia, and all of you can get your feet back on the ground...unless you'd like to leave early. You could be home by tomorrow night if you wanted to return..."

"Oh no none of that. He looked at her, "We've just opened Pandora's Box or should I say 'Rodane's box'? I want to know what's in there. If I go home, when would I get answers?" he saw her face, "Aha! I thought so. My list of questions is so long it'll take us more time then I have to get answers. I'm going for as many as I can get in the next few days."

Sabina moved to him, "So…I can go with you to Florence? You're okay with that?" She rested her hands on his arms.

"Honey, wouldn't have it any other way," Rodane looked happy.

"Honey? Huh! No one ever called me Honey."

"I'm sorry, I was only…"

"No please, Honey. I like it. Let's make out a little Honey," she moved into his arms.

Virginia

"Look Zoe, you don't even have a job here. You're back up, so why aren't you backing me up, why the argument?" Lexus and Zoe were still arguing about how they would get their job done and Lexus was beginning to fume.

"Lexus, we've never had to strong-arm anyone or deliberately use any kind of violence to do our jobs. I don't see why you think it's necessary here."

"I've been the one out there dealing with the snotty brats, especially little bitch Sophia! I'm beginning to enjoy the thought of having Mommy be so scared for her little sweetheart, she'll sing like a bird. This is a perfect opportunity. She'll be home alone. Belva said she had a dentist appointment and that's why she's taking the whole day off. Sophia has to ride the bus. I have hours to get in there, get what I need from her and be out before her darling Sophia even makes it home. Job done, Miss Smart Cheeks, Caroline Arcos, put in her place and I'm out of there. I don't understand why they put me in the classroom."

She snapped, "Neither do I!" He shot daggers at her.

"Lexus let me go and try to get her cooperation. I did okay with the girl. I had her eating out of my hand before Mom came over. I know I could get Mom to see the benefit of giving me the information we want. I can convince her she needs to give me everything she has before her little girl gets home from school."

"Like that's not a threat?" Lexus sneered.

"Yeah it's a threat but one with a gloved hand."

"You're wearing gloves? See, even you know not to leave prints."

"Lexus…I can get the information without being too physical," she said as if to a child. He thought it over for a minute,

"No, it's my job, my payback to Mommy and her little smart and clever little girl. If mommy cooperates, all's good. If not…at least we'll have what we came for."

"Suppose the neighbor comes over or her boyfriend comes home or…"

"Stop making excuses!" he yelled. This is the plan so get on board. Just shut up and you be the driver. I'll get what we need and we'll get out of here without anyone being the wiser."

"What about Belva or Caroline? She won't go to the cops?"

"If she's smart she'll keep her mouth shut, her daughter safe and her ex-husband out of her life. If not then they all deserve whatever they get."

"Even the kid? What does she deserve? She's nice. She doesn't have a hateful bone in her body. I could tell just from our observations and my visit to school today. Why do anything to her, Lexus?"

He was riled, hateful and vindictive but she had never known him to go after a kid.

"Because I can and because she…she looks down on me."

"Who… Caroline? You scared her, you've threatened…"

"No not her, her brat of a daughter!"

She started to protest but Lexus was done, "We're going there tomorrow, done deal. When we see her get back from the dentist, I'm going in, you're waiting with the car running and I'll be out with the information we need. Case closed! Your job is set, understand?"

She stared at him, unable to come up with any other plausible excuse.

"Understand?" his eyes were wild and he looked like he was about to explode.

"Understood." she had a really bad feeling about this job, especially after her meeting with Sophia.

Chapter 25

Naples' Airport—Private jet to France

Renata was at the municipal airport at six that morning. She had left the medical center, not knowing if Tabor was alive or dead. She feared the latter, at the same time she felt a sense of relief. A plane had been arranged for, to pick her up at 6:30 and it was there on the tarmac by the plane hangars that accommodated the private jets. Nice little Lear jet to whisk her away to France, in a little over two hours. She would be meeting with Theras Gallo and had no idea what she could possibly tell him about the latest events. The sick feeling in her stomach and the turmoil in her mind, only added to her stress at flying back to France.

{two hours to figure out my life}

This whole job had been one fuck up after another. Everything they had tried, had either been thwarted by unforeseen events; Rodane Arcos, or bad judgment…

{both mine and Tabors}

or just plain stupidity and arrogance; Tabor's. She admitted to herself her own part in this. If she had stood up to him or when his paranoia had begun to adversely affect all their plans… but would he listen? If she had told Theras Gallo that day in his office when he had, thinking in retrospect now, begun to suspect that they were not the perfect, tidy little team everyone thought they were…

She battled these thoughts during the entire trip home. She came to no firm conclusions and still didn't have any idea what she was going to say to Mr. Gallo when she saw him. He had arranged for her to be there by 9 o'clock. The pilot had offered her a breakfast if she wanted anything on the flight home. She declined anything but coffee. She knew if she ate she would most likely vomit all over the leather seats and their gorgeous, butter-yellow color. She was going to be smart about that, at least.

{something I can still control}

When she landed, the pilot made sure she had exited the plane safely, showed her the office, doffed his cap to her, and walked off into another private hangar, talking on his phone. She was told the car would be there immediately, so she went outside to wait in the early, warm sun. She missed France when she went on assignment, but never more than this time. She had no family to be homesick for…

{not that I know of}

but she did miss the country itself, the orange cat in her apartment house complex, who waited for her outside the entrance and wrapped itself around her leg each time she came home, or went out. She had taken to keeping a little bag of treats in her carry on and he knew it as soon as she stepped out the door. A limousine pulled up to her.

Sometimes, like now, riding in the car with Franco, her childhood friend, to the boss who made her life what it was today, she thought of those words. She was no longer a naïve, poorly educated virgin who trusted in her church or her family for happiness or that peace Father Pietro was alluding to. She wondered if he had been paid or bribed or forced to give over some of his children to a cause he might not have understood. Perhaps he didn't even believe in it but he was long-deceased, gone on to his own peace and she was here where her fortunes led her and her choices were either acknowledged by her or bemoaned by her.

She went up the steps to the office and was met by the secretary who asked if she wanted tea, coffee, wine or water. She declined and was asked to seat herself for a few minutes.

"I'll let Miss Spiteri know you are here."

{miss Spiteri what's this}

In ten minutes of wondering and thinking, a tall, shapely woman came out from Mr. Gallo's office and greeted her. Her looks were stunning, she had the bearing of someone in a very commanding position and there was something about her. Renata couldn't put her finger on it but… she looked like… blue eyes! She'd seen those eyes before, that dark chestnut hair. Her brain was going full-tilt even as she shook hands and followed her into the office.

"Miss Spiteri, I'm a little confused here. I thought I was…"

"…to meet with Mr. Gallo, Renata? Yes, that is the plan but first…please call me Aldora, I insist," when she saw Renata's expression. "You and I are about to be very personal so I think it would make you more comfortable if we were on a first-name basis. First, welcome home. Please, have a seat" leading her to the same chair she had sat in when here with Tabor. God it seemed so long ago and it was only days. Seven days, how strange!

{very personal but I don't know you personally}

Aldora tilted her head and looked at Renata, waiting.

{waiting for what}

She was digging in her brain for where she'd seen this woman…the walk… the eyes…the eyes! Her face must have shown her revelation because Aldora Spiteri leaned in and said,

"What is it Renata? What have you just thought of?"

Renata felt a chill come over her like someone had walked over her grave as her mother was wont to say, "You remind me of… someone and I…was rather… surprised, that's all."

Aldora smiled, "Everyone has a double somewhere, it is said. Where might you have seen mine if I might ask? I hope it was a pleasant encounter.

"Actually, I never encountered her. I… was where she was and we… happened to…"

{Renata this is no time to lie}

Somehow she knew lying about this would be a big mistake which she would regret making. Aldora waited patiently as if expecting this reaction,

"It was the woman we were tasked with finding and retrieving an object from her. It was supposed to be an easy job but things didn't go as planned and…" her voice trailed off.

"Here we find ourselves, both of us in difficult positions and both knowing far more than we should about the vagaries of fate." Aldora smiled but it was sad.

"Renata, tell me about your search for Sabina Carter."

{there it's finally out}

For the next hour, Renata spilled her guts or at least it felt like it but it also felt like the lead was leeching out of her as she spoke and the weight of it all was lifted. It was hard to weave the search for Sabina Carter with the relationship with Tabor.

{if we can call that horror a relationship}

but that too became easier when Aldora actually cried with her and blew her own nose and held her hand while she sobbed out the disgusting, sordid details of the last months, almost years. When Renata reached the part of the attack in Naples, Aldora said, "You know of course it was not your fault at all when Tabor ruined any chance of coming out of this successfully? You realize that this result is all on him, yes? He almost asked for it n'est pas?"

Renata shook her head back and forth but couldn't tell herself if it was denial or torture. "But he may be…I owed him at least…"

You owed him nothing!" Aldora spit it out, "You were loyal, you were silent, you were degraded and controlled, you certainly didn't ask for any of that. No, don't say no. Not a one of us deserves to be used and demeaned and exploited! We don't ask for rape no matter what any man may tell you. We have brains and feelings and we give those to the one who we're supposed to work with, not to be used as punching bags or pieces of meat…" and her eyes glittered with anger and conviction.

{this woman has been there}

She leaned in again, "Renata, Tabor is alive." Renata covered her mouth and sucked in her breath, "You tell me if that is what you want."

Renata looked at her trying to process those words. "If…,

{if it's what I want}

"Yes, Renata. If you want him alive I will make arrangements to have him brought here alive. If not…"

"What, is he…Can he…?"

"He's in a coma at this time. We've moved him to a hospital from the med-center. He's lost a kidney and a great blood loss caused him to go into shock. He has some broken ribs and some nerve damage to his right arm that is most likely permanent. He will have some significant scarring to his face and his left eye…it was gouged…well, he'll be lucky if he can see from it."

"Rodane Arcos did all that? I would think that would be…"

"Impossible, yes, you would be right but it wasn't from Rodane."

"How…Who…I'm sorry, I'm babbling. I'm finding this out for the first time and it's hard to process."

"Renata, dear, you have to tell me what you choose for Tabor because there really isn't a big window here. Time is…of the essence."

"Who did this? Who could have inflicted that kind of damage on Tabor? He was, skilled…a trained fighter. He knew how to attack and…maim. How could anyone…," she felt a rage stirring in her. She realized the insanity of the feeling but it was still there. Someone would pay for doing this to him.

"It seems, from a witness, that Doukas attacked Rodane Arcos in the alley and was at the point of taking his life when someone witnessed the fight and alerted everyone around them. Then a…friend of Rodane's, a protector so to speak, I guess his guard, came to the fight and settled it to their advantage. This person was only interested in protecting Rodane so by the time any authorities or an ambulance arrived they were gone with help and Tabor Doukas was left in the alley. What did you see if I might ask?"

"By the time I got there the cops were all over trying to find any witnesses and the ambulance people were putting Tabor in and I followed it to the med center."

Her chest was tight and her breathing was short and she told Aldora what she did and saw when she got into the halls. The memory of the blood in the surgical unit had her panting and sweating, "Enough! That's all we need from you right now, Renata. Try to put it away from you."

She got up and got a bottle of water and brought it over for Renata to drink.

"Excusez-moi un instant." She left, and in minutes she returned with Mr. Gallo. He bent down and took her hand,

"I am so sorry I did not follow my instinct and remove you from this situation, Renata. I should have done so when I suspected and…heard rumors about…but never mind. That is all over for you now but Aldora needs to know what to do about Tabor because we need to make a decision. Now Renata…"

She looked up at him, "You want me to decide if he…" she filled up with tears of anger, fear and dread. Either way she decided, it was a life and how could she make that call?

Then a memory galloped into her brain of Tabor bending over a man at the dock pleading, begging for his life. Tabor had made a decision…"please allow him a chance to live and heal, to get better." Her voice was questioning, pleading for his life, even if it disgusted her and frightened her.

Mr. Gallo and Aldora looked at each other for long, hard seconds while Renata held her breath. Theras Gallo nodded to Aldora and she left the room and closed the door quietly.

"Mr. Gallo" Renata haltingly addressed him, "I want to find Rodane Arcos. I want to find him and his guard who put Tabor in hospital. I want to find Sabina Carter and finish the job you gave us."

When he began to respond she said, "Please Mr. Gallo, I know I can do this on my own. Tabor was my partner, he was more than that. I want to do this for both of us." She waited.

He sat down next to her and put his fingers together and though she heard the ticking of the mantle clock over the fireplace and the engines of vehicles outside the window, the silence was deafening.

"I'm sorry Renata but I can't allow that. This job has been difficult for everyone but especially for you. You've put so much into trying to accomplish it but it seems the fates have decided otherwise."

"But sir…"

"We need you to rest, recuperate. No, I know you're not physically hurt but you're hurting. You need to have time to recover, to reassess your role, your goals. I'm sending you to a wonderful facility where you can sleep, exercise, write home, take trips, whatever you want."

"I want to help...I want to pay these people back for what they've done... I want to do my job Mr. Gallo. I'll go anywhere, I'll study every last line of information on Rodane Arcos and Sabina Carter till I know them as well as I know myself..."

He stopped her with her hand on her arm, "Renata, take the time go and find yourself again. Find the Renata I am so proud of and want to see work again. I'm sorry, my dear but that's my decision. Franco will drive you to your apartment and I'll check in with you in a few days after you've gotten there." he handed her an envelope with money and instructions.

"Stay well and heal my dear. We really need you in strong, steady condition."

He got up and left a flabbergasted Renata sitting, trying to sort out all the many emotions warring with each other. She slowly got up and left the office and went to her driver for her next journey. She'd figure it out, she had choices to make.

After Renata had gone, Theras went to his desk and opened the bottom right drawer with his key. He brought out a list, looked at it and picked up the phone. He dialed a number, one of three which no one else had, not even Aldora. This entire thing was getting out of control, too many people involved, too many new factors introduced without any warning, a snowball in Hell, picking up speed with each new soul added to the storm. He couldn't remember a time this chaotic, at least not in this memory. The Holovids might be of some use but it upset him too much to watch them. It took him days to push it all away again,

"Hello, who is this? How did you get this number?" the voice on the other end was agitated, strong sounding, aggrieved at the invasion.

"Petrus, I hope you have a moment to speak with me, it's quite urgent."

"Oh, it's you." The tone had changed instantly still aggrieved but somewhat toned-down. Not polite by any means, civilly impolite if you would.

"You had some time to look over everything I sent to you? I was hoping we could come to some mutual arrangement."

"Arrangement of what, you call blackmail mutually arranged? I didn't arrange anything and I want to know how you got your information."

"I could tell you to use your investigators to find out but I don't think that's the way you want to go is it?"

"You know if you are ever found out and it isn't by me or my department, I can assure you there will be some consequences to you that are severe and who you must work for."

"You assume I work for someone else? That's not the case. I feel safe in telling you that you, however, are in a heap of trouble from the likes of

NSA, MI6 and a few others I could mention. Would you like to get down to business?"

"Suppose, hypothetically, I were to take these items you sent to me seriously. How do you think that's going to destroy me?"

"No one wants to destroy you Petrus. Where did you get that idea?" A long pause ensued but Theras knew they were still connected so he waited.

"Are you still there?"

"Well of course I'm still here. I'm the one who called you, Petrus."

"What do you want?" his voice dejected, wilted.

"I need information concerning a number of people you may or may not know. I need it sooner, like day before yesterday, and I need it delivered to an address that I will give you. Are we agreed?"

"What do I get from this? How can I do it safely?"

"You get your career, you get satisfaction knowing your life and fortune are secure and you get my thanks. What else might you want?" another long pause.

"How do I know you won't use this against me in any case?"

"You don't but rest assured it will be used if you don't. Are we agreed?"

"I need more time to mull this over. It's a serious offense we're talking about here. There are other people to consider."

"Why don't you talk it over with Egan tonight and I'll call you early tomorrow... or maybe not, your call Petrus."

Breath was sucked in harshly on the other end of the phone, "Is this being recorded, is it a secure line?"

Theras looked at the blinking red of his recording device and the blocking device on his phone that couldn't be traced.

"Now why would I stoop to that when I have already shown you the cards that I hold?"

Petrus choked out, "Where? Where do I send it and how do I get the list?"

"You have a burner phone for personal use do you not?"

"How do you know that, you son of a bitch? How...?"

"Now, now, Petrus, let's not stoop to insults and curses. After all, we're both educated, intelligent men who don't need to stoop to that. I'll send the list to your burner and you send the documents to the website that I will provide you with. Doesn't that sound easy and safe?"

With an abrupt end to that particular call, Theras made the next call to one Keifer O'Brien. This nut was a hard one to crack and he'd have to come down on him heavy. Even he felt anxious at the time they were losing. He made the call and received a message machine.

{okay let's use some real leverage}

"Mr. O'Brien, I have those figures I was telling you about. They're really quite substantial. If it's inconvenient for you to take my call I'll be happy to make a call to Acacia Mikel and she can pass it on to you. Thanks so much. Hear from you in 10?"

He waited exactly four and a half minutes and the phone spit out the tune for, "Oh what a beautiful Morning". Enough time to sweat and argue with yourself before you give in but not enough to appear anxious.

"Hello?"

"Hello yourself, I was wondering if you wanted me to send you those numbers, you know, the proof is in the pudding and all that?"

"You ridiculous upstart! Tying to blackmail me won't get you what you want. Didn't anyone ever tell you the victim needs to be frightened of you for it to work?"

"Oh, I have no desire for you to be frightened. That would be counter-productive to my goals."

"Which are what? You won't even tell me who you are, you yellow-bellied coward!"

"You know, Keifer, I'm not going to let you rile me with taunts and insults. It doesn't get either of us what we want."

"How the hell do you know what I want, and I really don't care what you want."

"You should Keifer. You've had it very good for a very long time and that could come crashing in a moment. I'm sending you a file," and he hung up.

He scrolled to documents, found the file he had secured on there, copied and sent it to the contact he had just spoken to. In five long minutes…

{for Keifer I'm sure it's an eternity}

his phone beeped and he saw Keifer's number. His number was blocked but you could redial any recent calls. He waited for five more minutes, went and got a drink from his bar. The phone rang again and he hummed along with the tune. He let him sweat through two more redials and then picked up.

{this should do it if I know my stuff}

Keifer's voice was hoarse, strangled, high-pitched, "What do you want? How did you get these figures and spreadsheets? How the hell do you know me?"

Theras sensed a growing panic and didn't want Keifer coming unglued so quickly,

"Keifer, listen to me. I don't care about your money. I don't want any of it, not a penny."

Silence from Keefer, then... a desperate, "Well then, what do you want?"

Theras said in a very short sentence, "I want you to work for me."

"Work for you? I have a job and it's a very good job. I have everything I could possibly want. Why would I work for you? I don't even know you."

"That 'everything you think you have' could be gone in an instant if I were to send these accounts to the right person or persons."

"It's a bluff, you're trying to bluff your way into a secure server and scam us of our funds."

"If I wanted to do that, it could have been done three years ago when you started skimming money off your funds."

"What the hell! Who are you?" he practically screamed over the phone.

"Hopefully your new boss and I'm pretty good at what I do. With your help we can be even more solidly in charge of all that we survey."

"What would I do for you?"

"Exactly what you're doing now, no difference, no new pay stubs, no interviews, no vetting. I know everything about you I need to know."

"Then... I don't understand...what do I...?"

"You send me copies of every report you make and copies of every request you get for funds or reservations to hotels or receipts for travel. You get the picture. You continue as you are, you keep skimming your thousands off the books and we don't tell a soul. You just keep me in the loop on everything. Soo, do you want to take on a new job and keep all the perks old boy?"

"At the end of this call Theras had given him a shop to go to and purchase a dozen burner phones to be used exclusively for contact with him and a secure website to email his reports and spreadsheets. Mission accomplished! The third call was a trifle more dicey. Here, he had to be friendly but not too much. He had to be jovial but sedate. He needed to compliment without being obsequious. The housekeeper answered the phone,

"Please tell her I'll call back."

"Let me see if she's available. I may hear her car now."

In a minute or two he heard heels clicking across the terrazzo tiles and a girlish voice close to giggling.

"Terry, so good of you to call, it's been ages. How are you?" like a breathless girl.

"Marian, I have been so remiss in touching base with you. I got up this morning and I told myself I would not make one more appointment to fill my calendar before I called you. So, here we are. Tell me about what has been going on with you and your wonderful family." They talked for a good ten minutes and he found a way to insert her husband's name into the conversation,

"So my dear, has Quimby been taking good care of you and the boys? I imagine all of you are very busy and active, with outings and vacations and such."

Her voice became whiny and strident, "Oh, Quimby is just so busy. We are left to our own devices, to have our own fun and diversion. The boys are in school, so that leaves me to fill my time… however," she trilled.

He said, "Don't tell me you're left in that rambling, huge, house by yourself with only your housekeeper for company."

"No, I couldn't bear to be stuck in here all the time. Quimby isn't one for dinners out, or shopping, or travels, so… well, I find my diversions. We have our little tiffs over my spending, but it all works out. I refuse to live like a pauper when I know we have… well, enough about me. I want to hear about your wonderful life over in France. It is still France, isn't it Terry?"

He plied her with compliments, he regaled her with made-up stories of his travels and adventures, he told her about art auctions and buying antiques, talked about her shopping for Christmas, and birthdays, for very special gifts. He could almost hear her salivating over the phone, "Oh, you devil, you must have a dozen women at your beck-and-call. How do I get on your shopping list?" she twittered.

"Just ask my dear, but I would hate to stir up any bad feelings with your Quimby."

"What he doesn't know won't hurt him."

They talked for fifteen minutes more and he almost felt her over the phone, talking breathlessly into his ear and reaching to touch him, anywhere at all.

Chapter 26

Virginia Suburbs

Willow took the call when she realized it was from Egan. Why in the world was he calling over here? She couldn't think of anything that was happening of any great concern right now, "Egan, is that you?"

"Yes, Willow, it's me. How have you been? It's been quite a while since we talked."

"Yes, it certainly has. Last time was about 18 months ago, that consult I was doing on the dig at Jamestown, I believe."

"Yep, that was it. Hope everyone is good on your end?"

"Very! The boys are almost grown and I have a lot of side ventures I'm expanding into. To what do I owe this call?"

"We have a problem that seems to be growing more difficult instead of stable and Suri entrusted me with the task of enlisting your help from your side of the pond."

Egan told Willow about the leak in their network, the team that almost took out Sabina. He explained, as well as he could, the incursion into their personnel files, the attack on Rodane Arcos, and their beginning of an investigation into his possible connection to the 'family'.

"It sounds like you have things well under control over there. I miss all of you. It seems we never get time away from all our instruction to visit. We'll have to do something about that. So... how can I help you over here?"

"Our Rodane Arcos is due to return to the states in a few days. We're trying to determine what role he will play, if it's proven he is a direct link to the core. It's already determined that the DNA component is there. He's from Virginia, by the way."

"Okay, this sounds promising. How did you find him?"

"He found us, or rather he found Sabina. It's caused quite a stir to know there are direct other selves still out here, after all this time."

"My, that is amazing. Wonderful for Sabina though."

"Here's the thing. The incursion seems to be taking place in teams and the information to fuel their searches seems to be coming from either New York or London. That might not be all. Rodane Arcos has his family in Virginia, his ex-wife and an eight year old daughter. We believe there might be a hunt going on by one team sent to gather facts and the whereabouts of Rodane so they can home in on him. They've made a few attempts here in just the last four days and it was getting pretty dicey. We're afraid for the safety of his ex-wife and child. Suri and Sabina have requested aid."

"So, our nemesis is at it again, is that what you're saying?"

"It's not possible but it seems that way."

"So what do you ask of me?"

"We'd like for you or those you might contact to go to Caroline Arcos' house and kind of be a perimeter guard for them just to keep things safe. It's only until Rodane goes home and back to his job at the University of Montana then we can have our Pacific cadre take over and we can focus on putting the chaos to rest once again. Do you have someone in mind?"

"Since there's a child involved I'm of the opinion that it might be well for me to go and I was thinking of having Philip help me out."

"That might be a very good way of giving Philip field experience. Is he good Willow?"

"Of course I'm a little biased but yes, he's a very strong empath and very quick to pick up on the undercurrents."

"Sounds like it might be a good fit" Egan said, "I'm forwarding all the info you will need to your phone and funds can be transferred to any bank of your choice."

"When does this happen?"

"That's the rub. We think you need to travel to their home this afternoon. We've just learned that the team sent to surveil has been in place since five days ago. We learned of their arrival in DC and then lost track of them for a couple of days."

"Wow! That doesn't give me much time to organize. Okay, Philip and I will be there by 3:30 at the latest, will that do?"

"It will have to. It's a two-hour drive from your home to theirs."

"We'll leave within the hour and I'll contact you once surveillance has begun."

"Thanks Willow, I appreciate the last minute effort."

"Not a problem. Okay, I'm getting your documents now. It looks like...

oh my... what a pretty little girl. Rodane Arcos looks...so familiar. I'll have to think on that one. Talk to you soon."

"Goodbye and good luck, I'll be in touch."

"Thanks Egan, let's let the stars align."

Willow had lived in Virginia for the last ten years since the boys had been twelve. They had made a very nice home for themselves since she and Leander had moved from Belgium for his position as attaché to the Ambassador from France. Willow worked in the Navy Jag office in Virginia and as a result of the excellent education they had received in Belgium, all spoke fluent German and French and the boys were both taking classes at Georgetown when the spirit moved them. Tegan was a little more focused and goal-oriented than Philip, but both were well-trained and entrusted with odd jobs that the 'family' needed done in the United States.

Philip came downstairs as Willow was perusing the faces on the phone that had been sent to her and she explained to him what the call was about.

"Think you might be interested in this job Phillip? It would be three or four days maybe, from what Egan tells me."

He was looking at her downloaded pictures and suddenly looked up surprised, "That's Rodane Arcos!"

"Who's he?" his mother asked.

"Just one of the best Archaeologists in the world. He is familiar with ancient sites all over the Mediterranean and the northern part of Africa. He finds artifacts people in his field would hand over their eye teeth for and be happy to gum their food for the rest of their lives."

"Philip" she laughed, "do you know him personally?"

"I wish! I'd just like to pick his brain for a couple of hours and learn one tenth of what he knows. How does he fit into this job you're talking about?"

Willow filled in the details from Egan and Phillip got more and more agitated.

"What is it Phillip? What's going through your head?"

"Sophia!" he answered. He scowled as he searched the pictures once more.

"That's her mother. It's bad and it's getting worse as we stand here talking about it." Philip paused, closed his eyes in thought, "We need to go now, we can't wait. We have to get to that house as soon as possible. We're probably already late but maybe not too late."

Willow said, "Philip it will take two hours to drive there no matter what. Are you sure it's that imminent?"

"It was eminent an hour ago and the time frame has narrowed to less as we speak."

"Let's go!" said Willow, "we'll come back and pack more things if we need them later. Call your brother and tell him what we're doing and we'll keep him in touch."

They grabbed their keys and phone and headed out to the car.

Lexus drove slowly and silently down the street and parked at the culvert at the end, behind an SUV. Their car was partially obscured by the size of it and Lexus turned off the car. They looked up the street and saw a white car parked in Caroline's driveway.

Her car was red Zoe thought and said, "Something's not right here. That's not Caroline's car."

"Well, there's no one else here, Zoe. It has to be her. Maybe she bought a new one, maybe it's a rental if hers is in the shop."

Zoe was astounded that he was ready to jump into this against all reason. She tried to talk calmly to him, "Lexus it's been two days since I saw her car and it was red. She had a dentist appointment this morning and she's been in school for two days. When could she have bought a new car?"

"Well it's not that guy she has living with her. He has a Jeep and that's not a Jeep is it? So why couldn't she have a different car, a rental or loner? Maybe she's got hers in the shop."

"Lexus, let's wait for tonight when it gets dark, late enough for the kid to be asleep..." Her stomach was getting more and more upset as she thought of how this could go..., "or let me try and talk to her tomorrow. I could bring those Manga books to her house and I might be able to get her alone and..."

"No! This is stupid, coming up with all these alternate plans. We don't have tomorrow. We should have done this the first day we were here."

"But suppose something goes wrong here, suppose it's not Caroline's car and someone else is in there? What if..."

"Shut up Zoe" he yelled at her, "just shut up and let me think, for Christ's sake!"

Adam had left the house that morning to work with a bodybuilder who was recovering from knee surgery. They had an 8 o'clock appointment and Adam spent an hour with him on rehab and weight training without the use of the knee. They talked shop for a while and then Adam went to teach his extreme step class to about eight stay-at-home moms and older women. No men this morning, they generally took the Yoga class on Mondays. When he went out to drive to the restaurant to meet Caroline there for an early lunch, his tire was flat and he didn't have a spare. That had been trashed riding through a construction site when two screws had torn it up and patches didn't hold. He had meant to get another one but...

{first thing tomorrow}

He had called Caroline and told her he was stuck. She had finished at the dentist, picked Adam up at the gym, taking him to the car dealership and they arranged for the Jeep to be towed there from AAA. They gave Adam a white loaner car to use till his was fixed and promised it would be done by early afternoon. They decided to go home, play around a little, make lunch at home and maybe play around a little more. Then they would take Sophia to dinner as a special treat. The day was turning out to be a fun day.

When they got home Caroline parked in the garage and Adam was going to have to go back to the dealership to get his Jeep and return the loaner car. It was turning out to be a very busy day and they would be home by the time Sophia got off the bus. Caroline's phone rang and she didn't recognize the number so she didn't pick up. They were very involved in each other at that point anyway, arms and legs entwined, coming down from a fantastic high. They both lay there for a few moments, hearts pounding, pulses racing and sweat oozing from both slick bodies.

"Who's that?" Adam asked.

"No idea…can't get it anyway."

"Why not?" Adam rolled over to her, "I need time to get my muscles moving again, they're Jello."

He put his hands over her breast and began to stroke her softly and slowly. She breathed in, "Feel like pudding to me, thick and creamy, lots of good flavor. He began to taste and she gave a little shudder and turned to him,

"Adam, you are in the wrong body. You should be a woman. I should be the man who needs a breather and a chance to rest before another round."

Adam laughed, kissed her tenderly and said, "Well, if I'm not going to get pudding, then let me eat cake." She laughed and they got up and Adam went out to the kitchen. Caroline went to her bathroom to clean up and get dressed then she started toward the kitchen.

A shadow passed by her window and she saw a shape outside, moving to Sophia's window further back. The back of their house faced the yard of the Moore's house or what was left of it. Part of the fence was still standing but the house had huge blue tarps covering the roof and there were boarded-up windows, all on the ground floor. She went to the window and looked down towards Sophia's room. Someone all in black was there with a screwdriver or a wedge or something, trying to pry up Sophia's window. Caroline's stomach dropped, bile filled her mouth and she hurried to the kitchen where Adam was starting to make grilled cheese sandwiches with bread and butter pickles and chips, one of his favorites.

"Adam, someone's trying to get in the house."

"What... Someone's...?"

"Someone's breaking into Sophia's room..." and they heard glass dropping, tinkling on the floor in Sophia's room. Caroline's heart dropped next. Adam went over to her and said low but clear, "Get to the den, go into the closet there, take your phone and call nine-one-one. Lock your door and don't open it and stay there until I tell you, understand?"

Caroline gripped his arm, "You too, you come. We'll call nine-one-one and wait till they get here."

"Caroline, he's here now. He's almost in. Do it! Call nine-one-one. This is our home, I'm not going to let someone come in here in broad daylight and chase us out of our own home," he grabbed her, kissed her hard on her trembling lips, turned her around and pointed to the hall, "Get your phone and go!"

She ran into her room, heard the wood splintering on the window frame, harsh grunts coming from broken glass. She ran out of her room, went to the den and locked the door. She moved into the small closet, shut the door, pulled the light cord and called nine-one-one. She was fuzzy-brained and muddled. It rang and rang... seeming like forever. Her hands were shaking trying to tap in 911.

{answer damn it answer the call}

Adam passed the door and another voice was heard...a different tone, guttural, loud, and angry. She heard Adam curse and a thud against the door.

The operator said "9-1-1, what is your emergency?" she tried to talk but could only listen to the grunts and thuds against the wall.

Her mind was blank... "An attack! Someone's being attacked! We need police here, now."

"Ma'am where is here? Where are you? Who's being attacked?" a yell from the hallway...another, more of a moan...more grunts and someone hit the wall, hard! It rattled the shelves in the den.

She heard Adam, "Bastard! You think this is easy pickings? Get the hell out of my house!"

"Too late!" someone else yelled out.

"Ma'am, ma'am, tell me where you are."

"I'm home, I'm in my home."

"Ma'am, tell me your address. Who is attacking you? Is there a weapon?"

"I don't know, I'm locked in a closet. Please, send someone now! Oh God, there's a scream!" She slid to the floor shaking so hard she couldn't hold the phone. She said her address and then repeated it over and over. Her voice was rising and choking her with fear.

"Ma'am we're sending someone, stay in your locked closet, we're on the way. Stay on the phone if you can, don't unlock your door."

"But Adam is being attacked. Oh God, they're shouting and yelling."

She couldn't think, couldn't move…"Please come… please come…" she was babbling and crying incoherently. The thuds were lessening but the breaking of glass and furniture being knocked over was louder. Then things were crashing around the kitchen. She heard pans crashing and bodies flailing and grunting. Her mind was a jumble of images, possible weapons with arms and legs tangling. She got up and reached for the closet door and stopped. Fear froze her but a need for Adam had her wanting to go to him. His words to her were there in her blurry mind and cold hands, 'stay there till I call you, don't open it until I tell you, understand?' She had said yes!

Minutes passed, a lifetime passed. Time stood still. She waited when she didn't hear anything. She heard the front door open and then slam shut. She heard what…? Gurgling water? Moaning? No, it was a far-off siren getting closer. There was a peeling of wheels outside, a car speeding off. She heard the siren pulling closer, nothing else.

She couldn't stay here. Adam was out there, he was down, maybe beat up. That was it, he was beat up. She needed to see to him. He was okay. He had scared off the guy so she needed to go out, *'stay there till I call, you understand'*? She couldn't, she just couldn't. She went to the door and put her ear to it… nothing. Wait, what was that? Moaning! That was Adam moaning. She opened the door, her heart in her throat, the phone in her hand, a man's voice somewhere in a background of other noises, a clock ticking, a single moan from the kitchen. She reached the door and saw his feet behind the kitchen table that was upended. There was blood on the floor, lots of blood. She couldn't step around it she had to get to Adam on the floor so she would have to step through it. She could wash her shoes later. She'd take them out to the slop sink in the garage and…

{see to Adam! worry about the shoes later}

She walked around the table and looked over at Adam. He was covered in blood beginning with his face and ending at the shoes, too much blood.

{some of it is the other guys, it has to be}

Adam lay there with his arm twisted in a strange, backward position. His face was chalk-white and blood was running down from his matted hair. His gym pants and shirt were red.

{Adam doesn't like red his clothes are white always white}

She knelt down on the floor and put her hands to his face,

{I've got blood on my hands}

"Adam… Adam, can you hear me? They're coming Adam, hang on, they're coming. Adam, open your eyes, please sweetheart? Open your eyes."

He tried, he really tried. He managed to get out, "Gone? He gone?"

"Yes, he's gone. It's okay Adam. The police are on their way."

"Stay in the closet Caroline, don't come out till I tell you to, you hear?"

"Yes Adam" she was crying uncontrollably, her nose was running and her throat was thick, so thick it hurt.

The police were knocking on the door, then hammering on it, "Police, open up it's the police! Open the door!" then it crashed open and two policemen,

{well one's a woman police}

…came into the kitchen with their weapons drawn, looking at Adam's prone form, looking at her half crouched over him, "Ma'am you okay? Are you alright? Ma'am?"

She couldn't talk, she was crying too hard. They came over and one helped her to her feet and one stooped down to feel Adam's pulse "He's alive" the policewoman said.

She reached for her phone and dialed nine-one-one. Caroline held up her phone and looked at it. The man on the other end was still talking, "Ma'am, are you safe? The police are at your house, you can come out of the closet now. Ma'am?"

She looked at Adam lying there, covered in blood. Two officers were looking at her as she stood there, lowered her arms and very slowly slid to the floor without knowing that was where she was going.

She looked up and one officer was bending over her on one side, a paramedic was checking her blood pressure and said, "It's okay, you're okay. We're taking you to the hospital, just lie still."

"Oh no, take Adam first. I'll get the next one. She closed her eyes "I'll be fine. Adam gets first turn."

"Shock" the paramedic said but no blood loss."

"Oh no, Adam has blood loss, see?" and she held up her hands, "That's Adam" and she began to cry, tears sliding down her face.

Things came back to her little by little. She sat up, looked over at them working on Adam. They had an IV in his arm, paddles on his chest, his shirt stripped from his chest and his pants. His shoes were on.

{they're going to be a bitch to clean with all that blood}

By the time she was back to a world of some clarity they had Adam's heart started again, his tubes were all in and they were lifting him onto a gurney.

Mrs. Floyd from next door was standing in her doorway, hands ringing, biting her lip and waiting for Caroline to recognize her. The cop helped her up and asked if she was going to the hospital.

"Yes, of course I'm going, I have to… change my shoes. They're red, I can't wear red shoes to the emergency room…" she trailed off.

Mrs. Floyd spoke kindly to her, "Dear, you go off to the hospital with Adam. I'll be here. Where is Sophia?"

Her heart clutched, "Oh God, Sophia! Mrs. Floyd, can you be here when Sophia gets home from school? Could you take her when she gets home?" she looked around the kitchen "It's a mess… there's… she looked at the blood on the floor, "I have to clean the floor and I don't want Sophia coming in here and getting her shoes all messy." She started crying again.

"Of course I'll get Sophia off the bus, no worries dear. You just go with Adam. I'll be right here when she gets home."

She watched Caroline being led to the ambulance and helped into the front seat. Poor Adam, he didn't look good at all. She checked her watch as they drove away with sirens blaring. It would be another half hour before Sophia was home. She'd go and check on her dinner in the oven and wait for the bus. She shuddered as she looked around the kitchen and then left, closing the door behind her on a horrific horror story.

Lexus came out the front door in a hurry, a big hurry. He limped to the car and got in the passenger seat, "Drive" he croaked, "drive now".

He pulled off his black ski mask and hunkered down in his seat breathing heavily. Zoe drove fast, heading out of the street and making the first left she came to. One minute after they had almost left the development, a police car came careening in the gates, lights swirling, siren blasting. Lexus leaned further down in his seat as it went past them at the intersection of their street, eyes straight ahead, focused on reaching Sophia's House. Zoe felt great relief.

{she's not there she's in school}

She was afraid to say anything and she knew very well it had gone badly when she heard glass breaking from the outside window. Their street was so quiet and there were no kids around or dogs barking. Those sounds inside echoed out to the street. She was so tempted to pull out and leave the idiot there. She was not going to go in there and join the circus. Her imagination couldn't be worse than what was going on inside. She was about to turn out of the development when Lexus said, "Pull over".

"What, you want to stay here? Lexus, we need to get out of here and…"

"No, pullover dammit!" he reached for the steering wheel.

"Lexus, stop!" she pulled to the curb, "You're crazy! We need to leave. Someone could have seen you, the cops are there."

"Yeah, I know that but they'll be leaving with the ambulance and no one else is in there."

Zoe looked at him flabbergasted, "So it's done, it's over, we can't go back there Lexus. What ambulance?"

Lexus turned and looked at her and then she saw blood on his black jacket and wet patches on his pants. She flung her hands to her face.

"You're hurt! We need to get you to a doctor." Lexus picked up his hands and she saw the long serrated knife in his hand, covered with blood on both his hands. She gulped, speechless.

"Not mine Zoe, it's not my blood! Dumb bastard had to face me down instead of getting out of there. Stupid crazy fucker had to fight me. Well look who walked out and who didn't." he sounded boastful, almost gleeful.

"So what do you intend to do? We have to leave here before anyone notices us."

"Oh no, we have to stay right here. We stay here until wonderful Sophia gets home and then we take her on a little ride and call Mommy and let her know we have her oh so darling, daughter and we need information about Arcos now!" He yelled the last word. His anger was so rabid he was spitting and dribbling and his face was so puffed with fury he looked inhuman.

Zoe took a deep breath, "Lexus, before you say anything else, listen to me, please!"

He stared at her and Zoe said, "This hasn't worked. It's going every which way including sideways. It's done and we need to leave here, contact our supervisor and find out what he wants us to do. I'm sure they don't want us to stay here, invite scrutiny, make ourselves an open target or try anything stupid with Sophia."

"So I'm stupid now!" Lexus sneered.

"I didn't say that. It's a bad idea to keep trying this after whatever happened in there." She stared at him and he was quiet for a minute, then she saw him make up his mind,

"Nope, we're not leaving here without trying to fix this. I need that girl to make her mother tell us everything she can about Arcos. However that happens, I'm not going home tomorrow without something to hand over to them. These jerks are not going to pull one on me!" He was panting,

{talk about rock and hard place}

"What do you want to do Lexus?"

"I told you, get Sophia when she gets off the bus and take her, then call Mommy."

"Take her where? What if Mommy refuses to believe we've got her, what if we can't reach her…"

"Stop coming up with arguments" he rubbed his bloody hands all over his sweating face and then looked at his watch, "We've got about ten minutes to wait. We drive down her street, park in front of the house and when she walks off the bus, we get her." She started to speak and stopped. At this point, with all their arguments, she knew it was a waste of time. What was she going to do, get out and hitch a ride back to New York? Hardly, but she was tempted.

They drove down to the outside of Caroline's house where the two of them sat in silence, lost in their own thoughts or worries. Zoe wondered what she would do when she actually saw Sophia get off at the corner and begin to walk home.

Mrs. Floyd was checking her meatloaf again in the oven. She looked at the clock and then looked out the window. Sometimes the bus was a few minutes early, sometimes a few minutes late. She didn't want Sophia going into her house and seeing that bloody mess all over. It would scare the child silly. She saw the car pull down outside of Caroline's house. It was one of those fancy cars, advertised on TV for lease, a Volvo, a Lexus, a BMW? That was it! Bored man's wish, that's what she called it. Too much money for four wheels to get you from point A to point B, used up too much gas.

Sleek though, nice looking car.

The longer it sat there, the odder she thought it seemed. No one got out, no one got in and after what just happened...? She picked up the phone, called Caroline's number. She answered on the 3rd ring, "Mrs. Floyd, what's wrong?"

"Nothing dear, I'm just waiting for Sophia. You weren't expecting anyone today were you dear?"

"Mrs. Floyd, I'm here in emergency! No, I wasn't expecting anyone today, why?"

"I was just wondering. A car is outside your house, and has been there a few minutes and I just was curious. It's a very pretty, expensive car. Thought maybe you had forgotten someone might be coming by today. I hope everything is alright with Adam."

"He's in surgery they're..." her voice choked, "Mrs. Floyd, please watch for Sophia. I'm going to call the police and have them check out that car. Probably someone pulled over to make a call, or check on a map but the day has been anything but normal so far, I'm not taking any chances. Please tell Sophia I'll be home as soon as I can. Watch out for my baby, please!"

"For sure Caroline, now, don't you worry, dear, Sophia will be just fine."

Mrs. Floyd ended the call and looked out the window. Sophia's bus was coming down the street. It pulled to the corner and Sophia got off, waving to the bus driver and laughing at him. At the same moment, the passenger door of the parked car opened and a man got out and leaned against the door. He was all in black and Mrs. Floyd didn't recognize him at all. The driver stayed in the car and the motor was running. She felt a little anxious but wasn't sure why.

At that same moment, another car came down behind the bus when it pulled out and left. The small, blue-toned car came up behind the BMW and parked. The man got out of the driver's side and a woman got out of the passenger side. They were about ten feet behind the other car and the woman waved at Sophia, who had hesitantly waved back, a puzzled look on her face. She kept walking down the sidewalk. The man in black, opened his door and climbed in. Mrs. Floyd saw him waving his hands, pointing down the street as the car pulled away, squealed wheels, went down to the end of the street and turned around and headed out.

The woman from the small, blue car stood with Sophia at the curb and watched the car leave. Sophia had a very confused expression on her face and her arm was raised as if to wave but she hesitated, watching the driver hurry past without looking over. Sophia looked at the woman watching her and said, "The woman at the fence… was she coming to bring me Manga books? I don't understand." Willow looked to Mrs. Floyd's house as she came out and walked over to them. She held out her hand to Mrs. Floyd, "Hi, I'm Willow Barbas and this is my son, Philip." He took her hand, "Hi, nice to meet you."

Mrs. Floyd looked at them, smiled and said, "Did Caroline call you to come and check on Sophia? Did she let you know who that car was for?"

Willow said, "No, she didn't but I think I know who they are. I've met them before."

She turned to Sophia and bent down, "Hi Sophia, I'm Willow and this is my son, Phillip. We live in Virginia too and came to see if you're okay. How is your mom?"

Sophia looked at Mrs. Floyd. She was biting her lip, not a good sign, "I don't know how my mom is…"

Willow said, "Mrs. Floyd, could I talk to you for a moment, please? Phillip…?"

"Yeah, right here, Mom." They walked a few steps away and Mrs. Floyd began to talk and picked up speed as she started pointing to the door, and the backyard, and the gouges left in the grass from the gurney going across the grass. Philip turned to Sophia and looked at her. She looked back, "I'm okay with you, right? I don't have to worry about stranger danger?"

He smiled at her, "No Sophia, there is no stranger danger here. We're good."

Both of them looked up the street where the car had gone.

"I think that was stranger danger" she looked frightened yet calm.

"You're quite a girl, Sophia." When she looked at him he added "in the nicest way possible."

She smiled, "I know and so are you."

Phillip thought of a way to take her mind off of all this for the moment, "I heard you say something about Manga. Do you like Death Note?"

Oh yes, that's one of my favorites! You know Death Note?" At his nod, she grinned, "Cool!" Then he smiled and shook his head in wonderment.

Mrs. Floyd took Sophia to her house, and told Willow and Phillip she wasn't letting her out of her sight for anyone. A police car pulled up in front of Caroline's house and two cops got out and came over to Mrs. Floyd's door and knocked. She talked to them out on the porch and told them about the BMW that came and left so quickly, and Caroline's two friends that had stopped by to visit. But of course, Caroline was at the hospital. She was keeping Sophia overnight, if necessary, and she was going to eat dinner there. Did they like meatloaf? Would they like to have some to take with them? There was plenty, she didn't need to eat leftovers for two days in a row. They left, minus the meatloaf, after getting as much of a description as they could. They gave her their card and asked her to call if she thought anyone unusual came by.

Sophia was very quiet through all this. She didn't seem frightened, just concerned. She asked questions about Adam, and asked if she could go into her house and get her computer. Mrs. Floyd had a surprise for her. Willow and Phillip had gone into her house and gone to Sophia's room. Willow had packed up her Frozen backpack with underwear and two clean outfits along with her Manga books and her laptop and charger. They brought a couple of them back to Mrs. Floyd's house and told her they were going home for some changes of clothes and they would return by around 9 o'clock in the evening.

"Now, never you mind about sleeping arrangements. I've been in this big, empty house since my husband passed away. I have three lovely bedrooms, all set up for an emergency. I guess you could call this an emergency. Sophia can sleep next door to mine, in case she needs anything during the night, poor child!" They reminded her to lock her doors and windows and call the police if they saw anything out of the ordinary.

"I'm going to be looking for that BMW that's for sure! I don't think those people were up to any good. It's a good thing you showed up when you did. Tsk, tsk!" She clucked like a mother hen and Philip wished it had been a half hour earlier.

"Well now, the important thing is, you were here when it mattered most, at least for Sophia."

Phillip came and took her hand, "You're a good neighbor Mrs. Floyd and you are a good woman. They're lucky they live next to you."

She blushed and stammered, "That's the way neighbors are supposed to be, least I think so."

Willow said, "I think you are absolutely correct Mrs. Floyd."

Phillip went back to the guest room to tell Sophia goodbye. She was sitting, looking at her manga drawings. Phillip walked over and bent down to her, "Sophia, are you concentrating on your book?"

She looked up, her eyes glistened with tears and her voice trembled a little when she said, "No, you know I'm not. I'm worried about Adam and my mama. It's not good, is it?" she watched him.

"I was going to say it will be 'fine,' Philip answered, "but I don't think you want me to lie, right?" Sophia put the book down and came into Phillip's outstretched arms. He held her gently and he could feel her little body trembling but she cried quietly. He looked up and saw his mom standing in the doorway. She nodded her head toward the front of the house and left them.

"Sophia, I'm not sure how things will be. We can hope for the best but I'm not going to lie to you if something bad happens. I think your mom is going to be fine from what Mrs. Floyd told us. We're leaving for a little while..." her arms tightened around him, "just a little while, and then I promise we'll be back."

Her tension eased, she sat back, blew her nose on a tissue and said, "The fence lady was in the car. She wasn't going to give me Manga books, was she?"

"No, Sophia she wasn't. I'm sorry you had someone who tried to do something mean and nasty and tried to be friends with you, but no, she was not being nice."

"I'll learn, I'll be better at stranger-danger next time."

"Tell me about the fence lady..." so Sophia proceeded to tell him about her meeting with her, and the fact that her mom had told her she wanted her to be very careful about who she met.

Philip assured her, "We're going to make sure there isn't a next time, Sophia, all of us." He got up and left her there with a promise to return before she went to sleep. Willow and Phillip left the house and started back home to pick up some things, make a couple of calls and get back there for Sophia and Caroline. Willow spoke, "It was the New York team. I got the license plate, Philip. I saw Zoe and Lexus, I recognized them." Philip looked over at her with a raw anger in his voice, "Let's hope they recognized us."

Chapter 27

Road to Florence

Sabina and Rodane left early the next morning to drive to Florence. He wanted to stop in Assisi on the way and then go to every museum he could walk to and get shots and take notes. He planned to work on his notes while Sabina went to see a colleague and he could get a good deal sent off to the company. When he got up that morning he couldn't see any bruises under his eyes and his scalp had stopped itching from the healing skin. His hair was growing back over the shaved spots but he kept the baseball cap on anyway.

They had eaten bagels with cream cheese and they drank coffee that morning, then they took long leisurely showers and dressed to leave for Florence. Eugenie and Sabina had met in her room late last night and Rodane heard Eugenie, Helene and Sabina talking late into the night before he went off to sleep like a rock.

Sabina wanted Eugenie and Helene to hear what she had accomplished in Sorrento and Eugenie had a lot to tell her about her meeting with the protector's cadre.

"Acacia sat in on our meeting" Eugenie said. Sabina raised her eyebrows. She was surprised that Acacia felt the need to be there.

"Oh wait till you hear" Helene widened her eyes and said, "She didn't feel the need. Quimby insisted she be there, strongly insisted."

"Why, what's happened?"

"We 'pinned' each other and we had everyone from the cadre there except for our North American team and one team that's on surveillance in the islands. That was interesting," she smiled with a slightly sly grin.

"How did they take my demands?" Sabina asked.

"Well, I used some polish Sabina. I didn't call them demands." Sabina narrowed her eyes at Helene...

"Hey girl, do you want this to work or not? It requires a little stroking and politicking if you want this to happen. I told them we had been talking about this for some time. Well..." seeing Sabina's look, "one late-night is some time isn't it? Well isn't it?" Helene waited.

"Hmph! So what did they say?"

"They asked us to provide a rationale for setting it up and investing time and money in something of that scope. We told them about the last six days and about you and Rodane... don't worry we left out the kissy huggy parts!" Sabina rolled her eyes at Helene.

Eugenie said, "Everyone was shocked at the increase of violence." she waited.

"Except Acacia... right?" Sabina asked.

"Yes! How did you know?" Helene asked.

"Something she said to me on Capri, right before we left. She asked me how I thought Egan and Petrus might handle this incursion. When I said I didn't know what to think, she asked me if I had ever had need to contact Keifer for extra funds or ask for more help with a job."

"What did you say, why is that important?"

Sabina scowled at Eugenie and raised her hands, waiting for the light to flash then she said "Acacia...requisitions...?"

She watched Eugenie still thinking about it. "Come on Eugenie, money to rent hotels rooms... get food for the job...requests for more money...?"

Eugenie's mouth dropped open, "You think someone's been faking requests or asking for too much?" Helene asked.

Sabina answered her, "I think... the leak may be coming from the security side of it. Perhaps someone is leaking info and then getting paid for it or maybe more than someone, working both sides against the middle."

Eugenie really was shocked, "Nooo! That wouldn't be. All our people are totally dedicated to the job. Serious!"

Sabina said, "Not if they wanted more and more money and had too few ways to get it... if it could be funneled without anyone being the wiser...if our own security was maybe...not so secure?"

Eugenie said, "You think that could actually happen to us?"

Helene said, "Yes!" too quickly.

"Eugenie, I'm fairly certain it's already been happening for a while now. Think about the last week. Tell me how all that could have happened to one unlucky man."

Eugenie and Helene thought over what was said, "Who? Who would you guess is that greedy or crooked or able to be bought? Wait, let me think." Helene looked over surprised, "Oh my God, you're talking our Security Head or our Financial Advisor?" Eugenie and Helene looked at each other,

"No, I'm not" Sabina answered with a grim expression, "I'm talking possibly our security heads or our financial advisor or all or maybe none!" Sabina said with new insight, "That's why Quimby wanted a list of all the team members who had security clearances for all the R&R teams!"

Eugenie said, "aaand he wanted the codes for the financial files and reports."

Helene was shocked, "Oh my God, who do you think it is?" she was actually shocked.

"Oh no, no guessing games here. I'm letting Acacia and Quimby handle this. They're the experts. I just want to know my back is covered and I have a bed to sleep in when I'm on the job."

"Oh come on Sabina, I bet you've got some ideas. You deal with all these people all the time."

"Nope...not going there, not until I have some proof. Now tell me about Quimby and his demands."

Eugenie retreated back to the fun and games, "I thought they were going to start fighting right there in the room. We had about... oh I don't know, maybe twenty to thirty people there and some of them looked positively eager to see feathers fly. It got loud and hot for a few minutes."

"So what was the end result? Did they agree to our ideas?"

Helene said, "What, you don't want to hear the gory insults?"

"No I do not. I want to know when we start and where and how many... yada... yada... yada..."

"You take all the fun out of these nasty get-togethers" Helene pouted.

"Eugenie! Helene!"

They stayed up until two in the morning talking and planning a new program that would be pleasure for Eugenie, hell for Helene and torture for Sabina. When they finally went to bed, Eugenie had her schedule, her teams and her long-range plans. She was a happy warrior.

Sabina was just tired. She woke up the next morning dragging and bleary-eyed. She came out to the kitchen where Rodane had coffee and bagels ready for her.

"You are my hero!" she said and sat at the table breathing in the hot steam of the coffee to open her stuffy head and awaken her sluggish brain. Then she went in and took a hot shower that made her feel a little more alive.

All three of them were dressed and ready to leave for Florence. Helene and Eugenie were driving in a separate car and Rodane was riding with

JOURNEY TO THE BLUE PLANET

Sabina in her car. Scalia had taken the minivan back to Naples and they hadn't heard from him yet. Rodane wanted to drive but Sabina said "No I'm driving. I'll hand over the car to you after you let me get you checked out in Florence." When he started to protest Sabina just looked at him with one hand on one hip and dangling the car keys in the other.

They set out around 10:30 and made good time to Assisi. They all climbed up the hill to the large, ornate cathedral that St. Francis would have avoided if at all possible. The people insisted that was what befitted their beloved Francis. He was satisfied with the simple, weathered, tiny chapel down the hill, as big as a large, walk-in closet.

They ate lunch at the hotel restaurant at the bottom of the hill and stayed inside for the cool air. In the open courtyard of the cathedral, Sabina was sure it was hot enough to fry an egg, or at least to soft boil one.

They drove down to the little church on their way out of town heading to Florence. Sabina and Rodane walked in and she saw the little, original chapel fitted into the church, like a box within a box. It was warm inside but she still walked up and knelt down in front and looked into the tiny space where one man had led thousands to a sense of greatness but more importantly, kindness. His statues always showed Francis blessing animals; foxes, wolves, rabbits…'and the lamb will lie down with the lion'. Birds sat on his fingers, nature applauded his tenderness… they could use a few thousand of Francis now, in this world of today.

They left the church and drove toward Florence. Rodane brought it up first,

"Tell me about my recombinant DNA or at least tell me why my recovery is so fast and easy if something regenerative is going on here." She wouldn't take her eyes off the road and her face scrunched a little in thought.

"There's so much to tell, I don't know where to begin." She heard him 'huff' in exasperation, "Okay, let's start with your attack in the alley. I've been somewhat suspicious of you since you first approached me at Akrotiri. No… not like that" she saw his frown,

"I trusted you, I believed you. Yet…there was something…'different' about you. I wondered if…"

"You can say it. I've begun to question it myself, if I was somehow connected to you and your 'family'. Did Lenny and Genie agree?"

She looked over and grinned, "Why do you do that?"

"Do what?"

"Think of them in terms of endearment."

He grinned back at her, "Is that what I'm doing? Are you sure you don't want a nickname too?"

"Like what?" She opened her eyes wider.

"Maybe Benny... or Sab or..."

"No thank you," she laughed at him, "I'm quite used to my full name. Sabina will do."

He reached over and touched her on her bare arm. The spark flew up in a blue zig zag and they both jumped. She sucked in her breath and glanced over quickly to see his expression of wonder and... shock! She drove along without speaking and Rodane broke the silence,

"Is this going to happen whenever I touch you? That's going to be a real drag."

"I don't know I've never been in this situation before, well... once." her voice drifted away,

"Really, someone else that lights your fire?" he was half-joking.

"No not exactly. I was about twelve and beginning to study certain specific lessons I needed to train for and he..." She again trailed off. But this time a flush rose up her neck and across her face,

"It's okay I won't put you on the spot... yet. I'll stick to 'honey' for now but only in private." his smile was a little less tense.

"To get back to our discussion...when certain changes occur in restructuring DNA, it's usually a natural 'tweak' over a long period of time due to... why am I telling you this? You probably already know all this."

"Maybe I do but I want to hear it from you. I'm asking for answers. I want your answers, not mine. I thought I knew mine. I'm way off base."

"Alright, you know how restructuring takes place; a virus, some human, endogenous retroviruses cause some degree of genetic reengineering but it happens over thousands or even millions of years."

"Yeah" Rodane said, "there was a re-awakening of a mutant strain of a retrovirus that triggered all kinds of change, like Herve-K, over two to five million years of gradual change."

"Exactly! Well, genetic engineering can be passed down through human populations over many generations. It's a natural, gradual thing. Eight per cent of the human genome can be found in codical and guinal neurons that date back to... "

"...to early man, even before. Yeah got it!" He was sitting up straighter.

"But chemicals and pollutants can also reactivate certain viruses or retroviruses that can happen almost overnight if you call years 'overnight'."

"Well" Rodane said, "Some of those could be traced all the way back to before humans were considered humans."

"Okay" Sabina looked at him and then turned her face to the road again. She took a deep breath, "Suppose, just suppose, that some of those were deliberately inserted changes into a population from areas of the land where genetics was tweaked. What if a restructuring could actually cause whole tribes or populations to experience changes that led to better survival rates, more immunity to the detrimental viruses working their way through that populace? What if it was possible to adjust their makeup for longer survival, a chance to enable the strong to stay strong, to battle infection, and stave off diseases that could wipe out their entire tribes or decimate whole populations? What if changes could be deliberately made in those subjects…?"

"Wait! Wait a minute! You're talking as if there were those around when humans were not even human that could affect these 'deliberate' changes. Where are these 'technicians' if you will, coming from that will take human test subjects…" he looked at her, "or 'inhuman' ones and make those changes?"

"Leap of Faith, Rodane, try and keep an open mind. If our multi-generations of early man or 'not man' as the case would be, were generous enough to share their allergies, their inherent weaknesses of bone and blood with anyone that they came in contact with, then how sensible would it be if these 'technicians', we are…just supposing…use the word 'suppose'…" she saw the look on his face.

"Go ahead. I am officially suspending disbelief till further notice."

"How sensible for our supposed 'technicians' to strengthen those immune systems with a host of antibodies that would save them from extinction and create more viable races and species that could thrive? They could then pass on those traits and they would contain the harmful ones and include the good as well as the not-so-good."

"What time frame are you…'supposing' here?"

"Would it matter how far back in time it went? Would it make a difference if these de-structured or re-structured makeup genes were say, one hundred thousand or ten thousand or even five thousand years? The changes would still be there over time, gradually performing the miracle that creates a better species, a stronger, more adept population? Wouldn't civilizations and societies benefit from even a small measure of recombinant DNA and restructured genes?"

"Are we doing this 'hypothetical' restructuring for all populations or just certain ones or certain percentages of certain ones? Wouldn't that be playing God? Don't different populations all need a bootstrap to pull themselves up to a higher level? Isn't that the whole premise behind the 'survival of the fittest' theory? "

He saw her face and recognized that his tone had become accusatory and negative but he also was becoming frustrated, angry at the assumptions that were being laid out as hypothetical, though they appeared to be much more than that. He needed to be true to his own thinking processes, "Who has the permission or the right to step in with their 'possibilities'? What about the civilizations that just disappeared without a trace who up and moved or died out or succumbed to a widespread disease?"

"All this is ethical and moral Rodane, but let's narrow our conversation to a more personal level. You…we…can discuss philosophical till a comet explodes but what about people like yourself, or myself? How do we fit into these populations with the edge we have? If there are many more than you might imagine, what do we do to fit into the civilizations we find ourselves a part of and become some of that fabric of the general population we are born into?"

Rodane paused, thought about her words, then spoke in a more conciliatory tone,

"I first have to know how I'm fitting into there now. I want to figure out how I am different. How different am I and how different do I want to be? Do I have a choice and how do I make use of this 'me' I'm just learning about?"

"You're being bombarded with ideas and facts and you haven't even gotten the report back from what we're looking at or dealing with. Perhaps we should lower your expectations somewhat and introduce you gradually to these strange, perplexing new ideas that you haven't even been able to process yet."

"You want me to go slower, to begin in small bites to accept an entirely different me than I have thought of for all these last years that I've been aware of being me. Is that it?"

Her hands were gripped on the wheel so tightly her fingers were white. She thought they were moving too fast with too many problems all coalescing at once. There wasn't time to sit, pore over reports, examine medical results and speak to all the elders who had a wealth of facts and experience and wisdom based on so many years of immersion and knowledge.

Rodane put his hands on the dashboard like he was slowing the car down, "I need to stop. Can we find a place to go find a bathroom?"

She looked over at him. He was sweating and his color was not good. He looked somewhat sick. She drove for a few minutes and took an exit to a rest station with facilities. He left the car and went into the rest stop while she sat there quietly, trying to calm her racing pulse and her heightened energy level. She felt her stomach doing flips and thought she might be right behind him heading for the toilets.

When he returned to the car he looked a little better but not great. He had bought two bottles of water and he gave her one,

"Tell me."

"Tell you what?"

"Tell me how I'm different. Forget the tests and the 'supposeds' and the 'possibles'. Tell me what I have that's different than the norm and what my daughter has to do with this and my sister."

"Okay, for starters… your eidetic memory. That's not just an anomaly, that's a trait found in a very small percentage of the entire population, usually male."

"Yes, I've done research on it through the years."

"Does Cassie have that in any degree?"

"No…well, sort of…not really." She raised her brows and waited.

She has gifts."

"What kind of gifts and in what area?"

"We don't spread or share it with anyone. It's something the family keeps close." They were coming up on Florence. The traffic had increased, the air was thicker, with buses passing, filled with dozens of tourists heading for Museums, Art Galleries, churches, leather goods shops, the marketplace and cafés. They parked as close to Central Market as they could on the other side of the cathedral.

"I would like a gelato, would you?" Sabina asked.

He looked around and saw two rows of shops in the center, busy with local art-school students, with their drawings spread out on the cathedral steps, bargaining for sales and trying to outdo those around them to get the final buy. He saw a shop to the left with a long line… that was it! Tour buses gave coupons to their passengers for free gelato in a consigned shop as a part of the tour. Most got off the bus 90% of the time and headed right for it so he looked to the right and saw another shop with no line.

"Yeah, over there…" and he pointed to the no line shop. They both ordered double dip and then walked back to the cathedral steps to eat them.

"So tell me about Cassie" Sabina said.

"I told you about her gift."

"You said 'gifts,'" Sabina interjected.

"We used to tease her. She knew all the answers to the homework math problems without even working them out. She aced every test without any review and she could convert huge numbers in her head. She counted cards! We used to tease her she was a savant and we would haul her away to Vegas and she would make us all rich."

"Was that it?"

"No, some of her talents we didn't talk about because they disturbed her too much. They were silly things that young girls thought were cool but Cassie found too close to her, like Ouija boards where the dial moved under her hands, dreams that she would wake up from crying and scared."

"The dreams you used to go to her room and calm her after your dad died?"

"Yes, they woke her in a sweat and she shook all over and babbled till I could help her get back to sleep."

"Why would you call that a gift?"

"Because many of the things she babbled about came true. It was like she was the telegram announcing an accident or a tragedy. Then a day or two or three later, it would happen. But she talked to me about them, babbled on about what would later be in the newspaper or on the web sites or on the radio. My mom was so frightened for her we just kept it to ourselves and didn't talk about it."

"Like she knew you had gotten attacked after it happened and she was so angry you put yourself in danger?"

"Yeah, like that. I wasn't surprised that Cassie had seen things but when Caroline told me about Sophia and her dream and what she said to you on Skype…"

"She sees things…she's there when it happens?" Sabina was almost whispering.

"Yes, it's like there were times when we thought she was dreaming but now looking back…"

"Do you, Rodane? Do you have any of those gifts, any secrets you keep? Maybe I could help you to recognize them or…how to say it…come clean about them."

Rodane looked directly at her, "You have some of those gifts don't you?" he waited till she lifted her eyes to him. She slowly nodded yes.

Rodane said, "My dad used to take me to the warehouse with him when he got new items in from all the companies he did business with. I spent my summers traveling with him."

"Yes, I remember you told me. You said you learned everything from him and after his death you kept the business going and learned a lot more."

"Yeah, that's true but what I didn't tell you was my dad took me on his trips and had me in his warehouse with him because he found me…valuable as well as helpful." he stopped and went silent.

"Okay, in what way? Why does it bother you?"

"How do you…oh, we're sharing gifts now, are we?"

She stood up, brushed off her pants from the dusty steps and took his hand to pull him up. She put her arm in his and said, "Let's walk to Piazza Michelangelo and you can get some shots. I want to look at leather in Toro's leather goods. I'm a sucker for a sale."

They headed to the Piazza to view the copy of Michelangelo's David and dozens of other marvelous marble and stone works of other artists open in the square for viewing and marveling at the art and the magnificence of their beauty.

"What traits do you have separate from the general population, Rodane, and why does it bother you?"

He looked down at her, bent his head and kissed her. She lent herself to the kiss and then poured more of herself into it to share equally. They stood on a hot sidewalk in the Florence marketplace, unaware of people passing, walkers walking and gulls swooping for food scraps. They just existed in their own sphere and their own time.

Rodane pulled away first. He cleared his throat and looked around at the crowds,

"We can't have me groping you in public with all these witnesses around. It wouldn't do well for your reputation or mine. Might get a minor orgy going and that would be scandalous to all the nuns and little old ladies."

"I think you'd be surprised how that would be a welcome distraction to all the nuns but especially to all the little old ladies." Her eyes were blue liquid like the sea.

As they walked, he explained how he could touch a crate when it had arrived and he would know if the item inside was really authentic or a copy. At first the workers and his dad would laugh it off or joke with him, rifle his hair and tease him for trying to be the next Howard Carter. When all his guesses turned out to be a lot more than just guesses, his dad brought in an appraiser and when new items arrived he would have read and identified each one as genuine or fake. Then his dad would have the appraiser go over them and the paperwork. A 100% accuracy rating had the appraiser offering him a job in the auction house as soon as he graduated high school, which of course, he never took after his dad had passed away. It was the gift of knowing provenance, recognizing authenticity and feeling the genuineness of each item that had his dad encouraging him to study Archaeology even before he started to really consider it as a career.

Now here he was, sharing electricity with a relative stranger, touching minds with a connectedness previously unknown to him and hearing about what his 'family' might be that he had never imagined in his wildest dreams. Some tour this was turning out to be!

They were walking through a museum of Antiquities in the Egyptian section when his phone vibrated and he stepped aside to answer it. What was 8 a.m. at home in the states was 2 p.m. here. It was Caroline calling from an unrecognizable number. He noted from the phone that this was the fourth time she had called him. The first call had been made at 4 a.m. in the morning. His heart sank. Something had happened, he had lost the calls and when he punched redial it went to message.

He took Sabina aside and told her about the call so they headed away from the museum and walked toward the car. He tried the number again and it still went to message. They decided to drive to the hotel where they were staying and try to contact her there. Sabina was going to meet a colleague in an hour and he was set to interview one of the travel companies in Florence, to arrange a cooperative venture with his travel company and their bus tours to Italy. It would be a lucrative joint effort for both and a very big residual for him if it worked.

They reached the car and drove to the Piazza Santissima Annunziata, where their hotel was located. They were staying in the Hotel San Marco, not considered one of the ten best, but well-regarded for clean rooms, good prices and easy access to just about everything in the city center. They had adjoining rooms and Rodane was tired but not exhausted. He and Sabina arranged to meet in the hotel dining room for dinner at seven.

"I'd suggest a light nap, Rodane. It's been a long day so far and if I know you, you'll want to go out and work at some photoshoot at night."

Sabina went to freshen up for her meeting and Rodane wanted to collate all he had done for his travelogue. It was coming down to the wire and he didn't want to be rushing the end and do a hasty final editing. He heard the door close to the hall and guessed that Sabina was leaving for her appointment. It took him one more minute to realize he had left all his papers and brochures in the car glove box. He hurried out to the elevator and just missed her. By the time he had gotten downstairs, he spied her out on the sidewalk. She stopped, pulled a scarf over her head and put on sunglasses. Antenna alert! It was obvious to him she didn't want to be recognized.

{oh ho, my girl what are you up to}

Forgotten were the brochures! He was on a hunt. If he let her know he was here would she lie to him? If he followed her, would he be embarrassed if it was a simple explanation and he would feel like a fool? He was about to find out one way or the other. He hung back but kept her in sight. She kept to side streets and narrow alleys and made her way toward the center then she headed for the National Archaeological Museum which they had just left.

{what the…}

When she reached the museum, she walked around the corner and he hung back or she would have seen him. When he turned the corner, she was gone. He tried the side doors, two of them, both locked. He was very tempted to turn around and return to the hotel. What was he doing here? If he were caught like a kid with his hand in the cookie jar, the trust they were building might be destroyed. If she were to really open up to him he had to show her he was actually investing in this new relationship. But if he ignored it and didn't investigate, how would he know if he could trust her? If she were somehow trying to pull the wool over his eyes and put one over on him, wouldn't he feel more the fool?

{in for a penny in for a pound}

He walked around to the front and tried to enter the ticket lines, "Sorry Signor, we will be closing in twenty-five minutes no more entrance today."

"But my friend is in there and I'm to meet her…"

"No sir, sorry, cannot let you…"

"It's okay Francis, he's with me."

He whipped his head around at the sound of Helene's voice. She was standing there watching his expression, seemingly wondering what he might do next.

"Helene, what are you…"

"I'm here because I was invited. I think the better question would be what are you doing here?"

"He looked at Francis who had turned as if to ignore both of them then he looked at Helene with narrowed eyes, "Where did you come from? Were you following me? How did you know I'm…"

"Rodane, you're a good guy, I have no doubt. If I'm wrong, I'll pay for it but you are so predictable." She laughed because he began to blush, "Well, are you ready to go find out what you seem to want to know?"

"And what would that be, do you think?" He was a little unsure of how to play this. An irate innocent, put upon by her? A sheepish, guilty person who was being sneaky? A totally innocent friend, attempting to catch up to his girl?

{just be yourself and give in you've been had}

"Okay Lenny, you got me. Lead the way." They walked hall after hall, a warren of rooms and doors, stairs down to the basement and finally to a locked door where Helene rapped two, then three short ones. A lock turned.

Chapter 28

Little Old Ladies Can be Deceiving

When the door opened, there stood a slim, diminutive, older lady around four foot eight inches, trim and straight as a rod. Her light blue eyes twinkled, her white hair was in a tight bun, and her eyeglasses were perched on her nose. Her eyes looked over the rims and she had a smile on her face as she looked up with her head tilted to the side. She stood back from the open door and motioned for them to enter.

They came into a very large room with shelves and baskets along all four walls, a large solid metal table that ran the length of the entire room, directly in the center. It was covered with items; small plastic bins, tags, labels, stickers, small pieces of pottery, larger chunks in the process of gluing. On the shelves were more baskets and bins with cataloging labels alphabetically, on one shelf. Under the bottom shelf about four feet above the floor were crates full of amphora jars; some with handles, some without, some with seals, some not. A string of pot lights covered the ceiling directly over the table.

Rodane knew old when he saw it. These were older than any he had ever handled or unearthed or studied. He was already hooked and he wanted to hunker down and find a pair of gloves and begin a thorough study of each one and every bin and basket. He could get lost in here for days.

He looked up from his observations and saw four women observing him. Eugenie was there as well as Sabina, sitting at the table. Sabina was seated on a bar stool at the end of the table and Helene was to his left, standing next to the little old lady. None of them looked surprised. He felt like he had become the White Rabbit who stumbled down into the hole and came upon a tea party in progress. Sabina just waited. He searched her face to try and determine her mood; angry, disappointed, surprised? None of the above and he realized, with a little shock of his own, that they all expected him, they were waiting for him and that was even worse than coming in and surprising them.

{some sleuth you are}

Sabina broke the silence, "Rodane, I'm guessing a nap was out?"

"Mr. Arcos is it? Welcome to my little corner of the world. Come in, come in." she twittered with a bird-like quality.

Helene closed the door and he reached out and took the hand offered to him, "I'm Agatha Anastos. I'm one of the curators here at the museum in charge of all artifacts connected to libraries, codexes and amphorae from all areas of the Middle Eastern and European cultural antiquities."

"That's quite an area to cover. I can see it is extensive and very diverse."

"Oh yes, it keeps me and my staff on our toes and leaves us with little time to waste. Please, have a seat." she led him to a stool on the opposite side of the table and she walked around to the other side and sat next to Sabina at the end. Helene took the seat over on the radiator against the wall next to Eugenie.

"So Mr. Arcos, how could I be of help?"

"Please, call me Rodane."

"If you will call me Agatha?" he nodded.

"Where would you like to start?" he looked puzzled and confused. They were way ahead of him here and if he ran, he still couldn't catch up. "Start with what? I'm not sure I…"

"Agatha, we didn't do any preparation here."

"None at all?" Sabina looked at her steadily as Agatha's face took on a frown.

"Oh dear, you've left it up to me? I might be flattered if I didn't know what a terribly complex task you've given me." Agatha seemed more than a little annoyed.

Eugenie interrupted, "Sorry Agatha, but both Sabina and I had a feeling that he might somehow try and follow her. We thought it might be best if we just let him come, brought him in and let you start his induction."

He looked alarmed, "Induction? What induction? What do you think I'm here for and…"

"Mr. Arcos, you haven't stumbled upon a secret meeting or a hidden agenda. We're not here to drag you into something dark or ominous, I can assure you. We're all friends here and I plan on being a little more than that to you, with time." he waited a few seconds, his thoughts trying to coalesce with everything he'd learned over the last few days.

{induction?time to lay all the cards on the table}

"Can I ask you a question Agatha?"

"Of course" she said, "that's a big part of why you're here."

Rodane said, "Are you part of Sabina's "family"? Is Helene? Is Eugenie?" he took a big breath as his color rose, "Am I"?

Agatha sat back in her chair, propped her arms on the sides and looked intently at him "Well, to answer specifically, I am most definitely a direct part of Sabina's 'family'. Helene and Eugenie are not, though they play a very important role in that family." Helene smiled at her and Eugenie blushed. Agatha stepped up from her chair, walked over to a folder on the table, extracted a sheet from it and handed it to Rodane.

"And yes, Rodane, it appears you are also a part of our 'family' as well, a very important part it would seem."

He looked at the sheets with red, green and yellow bars in different lengths, spreading across the sheet. "I'm not adept at molecular biology. I can see these are test results of a genome sequence and DNA results, but I don't know who I'm tracing here. What are all the red blocks?" Rodane scanned the pages again.

"Those are proof of direct-descendent, from those members of your own family and which side they are from, both maternal and paternal" Agatha let him absorb this.

"But…there are so many…how do I know these are my direct ancestors and my…?"

"I have an entire family tree being prepared for you, and it will be ready by tomorrow. It seems as if there are others who have been seeking and requesting the same documents and records that I have, for your search. Any idea of who might have immediate knowledge of your family?"

"Me? People have been researching me?" He was amazed and tense.

Sabina spoke up, "Remember Rodane, we told you they had files on you when we were still in Akrotiri? And the envelope that came to the ship?"

"But… that was to connect me to Sabina and they thought I might be able…"

Sabina said, "That was when the real search for you began because it had little to do with me at that point, and everything to do with you."

Agatha held up her hand, "We're getting away from the purpose of your being here Rodane. Your 'family', the one you know of, are subjects of concern and we want to assure their safety as well as yours, so that…"

Rodane slapped his forehead, "Oh! I have to make a call. I think something has happened to my…"

"Yes, it has. The basement here, this room in particular, will not allow for outside service. Would you like to go to my office upstairs to make your call?"

"What's happened? Is my daughter okay, my ex-wife? What!"

"They are safe and sound. You need to try to make your call. I think it much more necessary that you talk to them than to us."

Agatha led him upstairs to a large office with frosted glass and her name etched on the glass. Inside was a well-appointed office, professionally decorated. She had muted, neutral colors, a very comfortable-looking sitting area, mini-bar across the room opposite a huge teak desk shaped and cut from a single piece of wood and urethaned to a high-gloss. Her chair was a leather recliner/swivel chair, looking out on a quadrangle with a towering fountain displayed in a center area of stepping stones, surrounded by green grass. Her walls had reprints of some of the finest portraits and still pieces over thousands of years. The room itself was a mini-museum.

"I'll leave you here to make your call. Can you find your way back to my office? I could have Francis…"

"I'm pretty sure I can retrace my steps," he had his phone out.

"There's a bathroom connected there…" she pointed to a closed door next to the mini bar. She left and Rodane called Caroline's number once again, holding his breath, tense and anxious, "Rodane?" Her voice was low, raspy, with a leaden quality to it, like exhaustion.

"Caroline, what is it? What's happened?"

"Adam's dead, he killed him. I tried to get hold of you but…" she just stopped talking.

"Oh God, Caroline, I'm… I don't know what to say. Tell me if you can, are you okay? Are either of you hurt? What happened? Oh God, is anyone with you there?"

"We're okay Rodane. We're at Mrs. Floyd's, next door. My house is…" she took in a deep breath, and it allowed room for the grief to escape. He heard a gasp, choking sobs, and then the phone was in the hands of Mrs. Floyd.

"Rodane dear, it's been a fearsome afternoon and night. Caroline is so much in shock and grieving…she's like a walking robot herself. I'm so upset, we're all so upset.

"Who's all, Mrs. Floyd? What's happening?" He was beginning to feel frantic, adrift, scared. Mrs. Floyd proceeded to tell him all about the afternoon when she heard the sirens coming down the street. She described the state of the house and poor Adam being taken out by ambulance. She recounted the car with the couple that sat and parked then tried to approach Sophia as she came off the bus. She spoke to someone in the background and someone said, "Let him know Sophia is okay and well secured. Tell him we were sent by Sabina."

He was ready to tear his hair out, even if it was still mostly short stubble from his attack, "Mrs. Floyd, who are you talking to? Where is Sophia?"

"Rodane, dear, I'm going to let you talk to Willow. She'll help you understand all this, I'm sure. I am at a loss...oh, the poor man." Mrs. Floyd herself sounded close to tears. An unfamiliar voice came over his phone and he put it on speaker as she requested.

"Mr. Arcos", Willow began...

"Please, Rodane. Where's Sophia?"

"Would you like to talk to her? She's right upstairs with Philip."

"With Phil...? Willow, I'm sorry, I'm trying to process all this right now and I'm not doing a very good job of it."

Willow explained that Sabina had contacted one of her people, and they had contacted Willow, so she and her son had come to look out for Caroline and Sophia.

"I'm so sorry we were late. If we had just been twenty minutes earlier..." her voice drifted off.

"Oh God" Rodane said, "Don't apologize, please. If you hadn't come when you did, Sophia might..." He found himself choking up with a lump of lead in his throat.

"Let me put Sophia on the phone, to assure you she's OK."

As a minute or two passed, "Daddy, I'm ok. I'm here with Mrs. Floyd and we're baking cookies later. Phillip and I are drawing some of the characters from Sailor Moon. He draws really well. Daddy..." her voice grew softer and her tone became sad and quiet "Mama is very upset, and I miss Adam." She started to softly cry, "He's gone. Mama said we'll be sad for a long time, but I'm...I'm sad but I'm angry!" he actually heard her stamp her foot.

"Someone hurt Adam on purpose, now Mama cries a lot and knows that we won't have Adam anymore. We can't go in our house and the police are asking me all kinds of questions and it's making her sad all over again and mad, and it sucks!" her voice was angry now, not sad. His little girl was a real fighter and a trooper. Tears came to his eyes,

"Yes Sunshine, I can see where it would really upset you that someone would do that to Adam. I am so sorry for you and your mom. I wish I could be there with you, Pumpkin. It's hard to get through something like this but you and your mom have each other."

"Yes and I have Mrs. Floyd and you and Willow and Phillip... Mama said she doesn't have anyone now, except me. But I'm going to take care of her and help her feel better" she sniffled into the phone and Rodane felt tears fall down his face.

{this is on me all me}

Someone was handed the phone and he was told,

"Professor Arcos?" Automatically he said, "Rodane, please."

"Rodane, this is Phillip, I'm Willow's son and now I'm your daughter's friend." Sophia piped up in the background… "and Mama's too."

"Yes Sophia, your mama's too."

"You addressed me as Professor Arcos. Do I know you?" he couldn't keep from sounding suspicious.

"No sir you don't but I'm very familiar with your work, your accomplishments. I wish I could have met you under different circumstances. I want to tell you there was nothing you could have done to avoid this. There wasn't anything Caroline or Sophia could have done either. This was well-orchestrated, they were determined to find you and it didn't make a difference to them who got in the way. Please don't feel like this is your fault."

Rodane was shocked, "I didn't think…"and then he remembered his unspoken thought, "Did I hear your mother say she was contacted by Sabina?"

"Yes indirectly. We didn't know until yesterday afternoon there was a… immediate problem and we were two hours away. By the time we got here…"

"Ok, I won't try and take the blame if you don't… Phillip, is it?

"Yes sir, Phillip Barbas.

"I take it you and Sabina are 'family'?"

"Yes sir, we are. You're familiar with our 'family'?"

"…more and more each day. I think I'm getting to know it quite well, maybe even intimately."

There was a long pause then Phillip sounded almost happy. He was smart,

"Oh, that would be a fait accompli on your part, Professor. I have a wonderful 'family'!"

Sophia came back on the phone, still sniffling, "Daddy I miss you, I wish you were here with me." Sorry Philip, I'm having a good time with you but I…,"

"No worries Sailor, I know how much you miss your dad. I miss my dad when he's away too."

Rodane made up his mind, "I'm coming home Sophia. I'm going to get the first plane out of here tomorrow morning and I'll be there as soon as I can. Is that okay?"

"That's great Daddy. You can help me cheer up Mama so she doesn't feel so sad. Adam says…" she stopped and he heard the crying start again.

Caroline spoke up on the phone, "Are you really coming home?" It was the first sign of feeling or emotion that he had detected in her.

"Yes, if it's still okay to come there."

"Of course, but… the house is…I can't promise…"

"I understand. What are your plans?"

"Adam only had a sister. She's flying in from Utah this afternoon and we're going to make plans together after she and I go through his papers and see where he was with his wishes, if any. Mrs. Floyd insists we stay here until the house is cleaned and repaired. They're starting today. I can ask…"

"No, please, it's okay. I'm going to stay with my mom. She needs to see me too and it's not that far from you. I just have to settle some things at the University and make arrangements for my class. I'll give you a call when I land."

"Do you want me to pick you up at…?"

"No, Caroline, you have enough on your plate. I'll ask my mom to pick me up. I can fly into Richmond."

"Sophia will be so glad to see you but I'm not sure how she'll be feeling or…"

"It's fine Caroline. She's going to be very sad and upset. I'll expect nothing and we'll play it by ear. Is there anything I can do for you?"

"Can you turn back time? Sorry, I'm being maudlin. Adam always tells me…" her voice broke, "I have to be more positive." he heard more tears.

"Is Sophia there?"

"She and Phillip went back to their drawings. I'll get her…"

"No, that's okay. Let her do whatever takes her mind off of all this. I'll see her tomorrow"

He sat in this office for a few minutes and gathered his thoughts, used the bathroom, washed his face and found himself staring down into the sink, watching the water run down. He hung his head and couldn't help the flashes of the kitchen, and hall fight, with splashes of blood everywhere, and visions of poor Adam, fighting for his life. He sobbed once, and clenched his teeth to get himself under control. Thank God Sophia wasn't there. Where was Caroline? He didn't recall anyone telling him that. What did she see or hear? How frightened was she, that she might not be alive when it was all over? Life was so very fleeting and fickle.

Walking the corridors, finding his way back to the basement office, he began to make plans for his fall semester, thinking of a possible teacher aide who might take his class for a few days while he was in Virginia. Everyone that came to mind was there, already teaching, on maternity leave, had left for a new position, or… he couldn't think too straight now. He reached the basement room, rapped on the door and it was opened by Sabina. She looked anxious and sad. He walked into the room and they all hesitated to speak first. He went over to his stool, sat down, rubbed his hands over his face and looked up, "You all know?"

"Yes, Willow called us earlier right after you tried to contact Caroline the last time and couldn't get through. Willow had Caroline lying down and turned her phone off."

"Tell me."

They told Rodane how the doctors had tried to stop the bleeding, had performed surgery, that he had crashed during surgery and they spent forty five minutes trying to save him. He died at three in the morning from external and internal blood loss, organ damage and shock. Caroline had gotten a ride home from her best friend in Virginia, Cornelia from her college years. Willow and Mrs. Floyd had taken her to bed giving her a sleeping sedative and told Sophia about Adam. When Caroline had woken up she and Sophia had cuddled in bed and cried together and Caroline comforted her as best she could through her own haze of grief.

Rodane put up his hand to halt the telling. He slumped on his stool and scrubbed his face to try and erase it away. Sabina put her arm over his shoulder and held him, shaking. After a minute or two, he pulled himself together and faced them all,

"I'm going home tomorrow," he said, "I have to make arrangements for my class but I plan on staying with them till the worst is over, if they need me."

Sabina said "Rodane, Nikos was going to tell you after our meeting with Agatha but...this is..."

"Tell me what? He felt the tension in the air and hesitancy from them, to be the one to break the news.

"Ladies, how bad can it be after all this?" He looked at Sabina. She took a big breath... "Nikos has a friend at the University of Montana. It's the Provost, Edward..."

"...Tolson, I know him personally." He watched them all, then said, "Whatever you're afraid to tell me, just tell me. I can't tell you how I'll like it, but I can tell you I won't go ballistic. Spit it out!"

Agatha stepped up close to him, "Rodane, Nikos has asked one of us who is very well-qualified, to apply to the university. Her resume is impeccable, and she would be able to take your classes till further notice. Edward is satisfied she could do the job and she can start the first day of classes. Of course, when you are ready, you would step right into her place. Or back into your place, actually. There would not be any change in your position or salary while you are on 'leave'.

Helene said, "We thought, well...Agatha and Nikos thought that this would allow you to handle all of this...new information we've laid on you and now it would give you time to settle all the difficulties you've run into because of..." her voice drifted off.

Rodane sat there quietly for a long time. The three ladies looked at each other. Agatha stopped Sabina when she started to speak with her finger in the air. The atmosphere was one of patient waiting.

Rodane looked up, "Okay"

Sabina cocked her eyebrows and looked long and hard at him, "You're okay with this? You're not angry that we didn't tell you first?"

He smiled wryly at her with a twinkle in his eye, "I may be annoyed that you didn't ask me first…" he stressed ask vs. tell "…but you actually help me out here with a very difficult time. I was racking my brain trying to figure out how to juggle all this to be in two places at once so no, I'm not angry. I'm relieved and grateful that you can do these things. I won't appreciate it if it keeps happening but we can argue that point with your, Nikos is it?"

They shook their heads in acknowledgement.

"Any chance I may get a chance to meet your 'Nikos' anytime soon?"

"It's on the agenda as soon as you're squared away. Agatha spoke up, "we can suspend this conversation if…"

"Oh no Agatha, that's one thing I will be prepared to argue with you. This has been a fits and starts program. I'm not going home till I know more, as much as I can absorb. I've been abused, attacked and sacked. I deserve some answers, finally. Face it ladies, you owe me!" he said this with a smile and they smiled back, half-heartedly.

Agatha came over to him and put her hand on his arm, "Rodane Arcos, I am extremely sorry we did not have you in our fold many years ago. We have missed out on a possibly very enchanting relationship. It makes me a little sad to have missed it."

"Agatha, if things continue as they are, I'm pretty sure we have some healthy family reunions in our future so… where were we?" They spent the next three hours discussing Rodane's family history, his ancestor's and his parent's background. Rodane obtained more information about his grandparents and great-grandparents than he had known all the years he was growing up. They talked about Molecular Biology and the factors that allowed him to heal so quickly and avoid most childhood illnesses. They asked him lots of questions about his sister and her growing up years, about Sophia's and Cassandra's childhood.

Agatha called on the house line and Francis brought them food. They talked about ancient ruins, all the artifacts in this room while they ate pizza and drank cold beer. They discussed ancient civilizations, remnants of civilizations unknown on Earth, then possible civilizations. Rodane found himself totally immersed in fun, in-depth discussion of his field, with three ladies who kept him on his toes. He was bringing up information from brain reservoirs he hadn't accessed in a long time. It was refreshing and interesting.

They sparred over differing opinions. They unearthed opposing ideas and debated the validity and viability of those they disagreed with. They told personal stories of odd and funny and bizarre happenings on their digs and their assignments and their travels. The three hours went by so fast they didn't even realize the time until Francis came down to take away the trash and let them know he was locking up in a half hour. He also brought them a Strawberry Shortcake.

"Okay ladies, this takes the cake, literally!"

Sabina said, "We figured you might have a wish for something sweet."

"Oh yes, but why this out of all the deserts in the sugar case, why…?"

"You don't like it? I'm sorry…maybe we can find something…"

"Oh no you don't, this is my favorite of all times. This is my birthday cake bar none!"

"Ok then, dig in…" and they finished the entire cake.

Helene said, "Eugenie just wanted to have Strawberry Shortcake. She's addicted."

Eugenie looked at him and tilted her head as if in a quandary, "Rodane, I'd like you to think about something."

He looked up from scraping up the last strawberry with a gob of whipped cream. They all were sitting, waiting.

"Uh, ok. Will I like it?"

"I'd like to go with you when you leave tomorrow," she saw his face, "Now, think about it. You must know by now how lethal these people are who are trying to get to you. Why they are so hell bent on getting you has yet to be determined but there have been three known attempts in seven days. I'm going to be out front here…they have targeted your ex-wife and your daughter. They've used any means possible to obtain what they think is some golden ticket to reach you. They…"

Rodane held up his hands, "Eugenie?"

"What?" she took a breath, prepared to argue.

"Okay. Who makes the arrangements for the flight?"

"What? Yes? That's it, you're agreeing?"

"Are you disappointed I'm not arguing?"

"Well… sort of. I had all my points and reasons all prepared. It kind of takes the air out of all of it."

"If it was just me, you'd have a fight on your hands. I don't take well to babysitters." he watched Eugenie's face take on a flush of anger, not embarrassment.

"Genie, I'm not trying to insult you. I realize all of you are just trying to help here. I can't help that I feel the way I do. It's awkward and…damn it! I resent having to watch my back and see my ex-wife and child subjected to this horror that they're going through. But yes, I'm man enough to admit I would feel better having you there to help watch over them."

"Alright then, I'll make the arrangements for an early flight." Eugenie relaxed a little as Helene nodded.

"One question before you do, well, two really.

She hesitated, "Okay, what?"

"Can you fight as good as before with Doukas and who is going to watch out for Sabina?"

Sabina started, "Yeah" he repeated, looking directly at her, "You. You were targeted too and don't give me that look, you know we both were. Think they don't still want that little 'silver thingy' that they've been trying to get from you?"

Agatha peered sharply at Sabina who was now blushing in embarrassment.

"He knows about the 'silver thingy' and…?"

"Yes, I know about the silver thingy. Don't have any idea why it's so important but I'm hoping you feel like you can tell me." He raised his eyebrows.

"In due time Rodane, in due time." Agatha started gathering dishes and trash and the rest pitched in. Within five minutes they were ready to leave.

Agatha went to Rodane before they left the room. She took his hand and said,

"Rodane there's more going on in this one week then I have experienced in…well let's say decades. Be careful. For some reason our very unfriendly, curious subjects are going full speed ahead and it seems like anything in their path gets mowed down or at least they try. I look forward to meeting you soon when some things are squared away. I wish you luck going home. Please extend our condolences to your wife…" she saw Sabina flinch, "excuse me, your ex-wife, and if there's anything we can do to help you, you'll let us know, won't you?"

"That, I will. In times of crisis we need all our 'family' for support."

Rodane and Sabina walked down the streets, still busy, still noisy. All the cafes had tables outside and were all filled with late night diners, kids were running through the square and hawkers were selling selfie sticks, balloons and various cheap trinkets, at 'discounted' prices. Sabina had her hand through Rodane's arm and they strolled slowly down the open center and down the Palazzo Nationale on the way to their hotel. She looked up and saw the stars and pointed to them. They went down a small side street away from all the lights and noise. They were standing in a small courtyard with an old apartment building to their right, now renovated into a chick upscale hotel with exorbitant prices for a room the size of a matchbox. Sabina found

Orion and the Seven Sisters and the Little Dipper. Rodane found the Bear and Cassiopeia and the North Star. They were relaxed and enjoying the evening and having fun with each other.

If Rodane had known what was coming he might have wanted to go to his hotel room, get in bed and pull the covers over his head to shut out the whole world.

Helene and Sabina drove Rodane and Eugenie to the airport at six the next morning. Their flight out would be ten hours from Italy to Philly, then a connecting flight to Hampton Roads Airport where his mom was scheduled to pick him up. He hadn't seen her since April, during spring break and their visits were always very pleasant, but built around her schedule. He had been trying to convince her for two years to either retire or at least slow down and hand over the reins to someone else but she was driven. It's hard to argue with someone whose largest part of life is spent running a multimillion-dollar business that encompasses countries all over the world.

Cassie never made him feel guilty for not being the one to take over Dad's role in their enterprise but he felt it anyway. While Mom was putting in twelve-hour days and spending weekends catching up on paperwork and accounts, he was in his dorm, sometimes in someone else's, maybe studying, possibly partying but enjoying his college experience. When he would come home, Cassie would ask him to spend time with them and convince his mom to go out to dinner or go and see a concert or anything to give her a break.

Her response was always, "I'll have plenty of time to relax and do things when you two are on your own and ready to give me grandchildren."

When Rodane and Caroline got married, she threw a weekend party to celebrate their wedding for all the family and friends that Caroline couldn't or wouldn't have at the wedding. Caroline didn't complain or at least not to him because she was certain there would be quite a few very expensive gifts and if not, money was always something to be grateful for.

When Sophia was on the way, Caroline did manage to spend some time with his mom. At first he was grateful and happy they got to be together until he realized that each time they met for lunch or a girl's afternoon out, Caroline would come home with receipts for the crib or the nursery furniture or the paperwork for a savings account for Sophia and… on it went. When Sophia was due, it was Iona who gave her the shower with Caroline's friend Cornelia, and the guest list was given to Cornelia by Caroline. There were four people on it for Rodane; his mom, his sister, Iona's sister who was to be her godmother and the personal secretary who worked for his mom in the warehouse offices. The insult would have made anyone else crazy but his mom said, "That baby deserves a wonderful party and a chance to start her life with good things to make her a happy baby." No recriminations, no personal hurt feelings.

It was a small miracle that Caroline had allowed Oma (Sophia's name for Iona) to be a part of her life even after Rodane and Caroline divorced. Rodane was able to see Sophia two nights during the week, Saturday one week and Sunday the next. His mom and his sister were invited for each of Sophia's birthdays and during the holidays, they could see her for a couple of hours to bring presents and visit. He celebrated her birthday with just the two of them. If Rodane had to be open and honest, it rankled on him. He resented it, held it against her and he found it so difficult to be civil to his ex-wife when he thought of the first years after the divorce. The anger still boiled over inside even though he made a supreme effort to be courteous and flexible. He rearranged his schedule whenever she requested it, he put up with cancellations at the last minute. He worked very hard at not rolling his eyes at the statements supposedly made by Caroline, as told by Sophia. He was pretty sure those statements were spot-on.

Oma was in heaven last year when Caroline was planning a spring cruise with Adam and she allowed Iona to take Sophia for the seven days she was gone. That was the beginning of a wonderful friendship of his two most favorite girls. They had a marvelous time together and it was the first time he could ever remember his mom putting work aside, putting the projects into the hands of her most able secretary and just plain having fun with her grand-daughter. Both of them enjoyed the time they spent with each other; baking cookies, going on little shopping trips, visiting the Navy ships in harbor at Hampton roads. They went on picnics to state parks and spent the whole day at Busch Gardens. Oma and Sophia slept in and stayed up late, ate ice cream every day, and spoiled each other royally. Oma was in love and Sophia felt very much loved. When it was time to go home, Caroline was quite annoyed at Sophia for hanging on to his mom and crying when they had to leave. She never let him forget that she blamed his mom for spoiling his daughter and making so much over her that Sophia preferred to spend time with his mom instead of her Grammy in Alexandria.

Sophia started calling her up on the 26th of each month. Usually they spent a long time on the phone giggling, telling silly jokes. Oma sent her jokes on email and a package every once in a while of a new graphic novel which she loved. He had called his mom to ask about staying there after they had decided on the quickest way back to the states. Iona said, "Of course you will stay here. I wouldn't consider it any other way. What about Caroline?"

"What about her?"

"What can I do for her, how can I help?"

"Can I get back to you on that once I get back home and have a chance to see them?"

"You're going there?"

"Well yes... I think Sophia is a little lost right now. Caroline may be a little too much into her own loss to have the energy or the will to put it aside and look to Sophia's loss as well."

Flight to Hampton Roads

"Now here they were, on a plane bound for Hampton Roads to make it to Virginia and help with funeral plans for Adam. The flight gave him plenty of time to converse with Eugenie and discuss what they had talked about with Agatha and Sabina.

{was it just yesterday}

"Eugenie," Rodane said, "there's something I'd like to say before we reach Virginia."

"Yes, what is it?" she sat there snacking on three bags of pretzels and two bags of peanuts,

"When I was in that alley with Doukas...,"

She shivered, ""Do we have to revisit that night?" her voice was tremulous and plaintive, "Rodane, I want to apologize for not getting...,"

"No, you saved my life. I'm not going to complain because you showed up a few seconds late."

"Those few seconds, if only a few more added, would have been your death..."

"Yet here I am... and still alive and... well, besides, that's not what I wanted to talk about so..."

"It's not? What else could you..."

"Eugenie, it was about what you said earlier about Sabina and what he intended to do with her."

She took a breath, puffed it out with her question, "Okay, what did he say?"

"He said he was going to enjoy hurting her, and making her pay. What would she have to pay for to him, do you know?"

"No, I don't, but Doukas is... not able to hurt anyone now."

"What, you mean he's dead?"

"Not dead, just... not able."

"Not able?" What? I don't understand."

Doukas won't be hurting anyone for a long time... if ever."

"I'm not sure how I feel about that."

"Relieved, you should feel relieved. His pattern of behavior is somewhat... torturous. We're not losing anything by losing him."

Rodane said, "I'm going into a situation I don't know anything about and don't understand. I'm leaving a situation I know less about and also don't understand. I have so little control here, I'm holding on by my fingernails. Can you help me?"

She chewed on her peanuts for a few seconds in silence then turned to him.

"Rodane, do you believe in destiny or fate?"

"Do I ...no, well, I don't know, I haven't thought of that too much."

"You're a scholar. Let me ask you a few hypotheticals, those that concern your field of study."

"Sure."

"How long have homo sapiens thought to have been here on Earth?"

"Uh, around 200,000 years, right?"

"Ding Ding. Right!Next question, when was Easter Island thought to have been colonized or inhabited?"

"A little harder...about...1500 CE?"

"Ding ding! Now, how about the Sphinx?"

"...in Egypt?"

"No, Manhattan! Of course Egypt!"

"Well, that's an ongoing debate, still. Lately, some scholars have said 7000 years. Before, it was supposedly 2500 years."

"Then how about the French cave paintings at Lascaux? How old?"

"About 18,000 years at last estimate"

"Ding again! One more, okay?"

"Fire away."

"Any idea about how long strange losses and happenings have occurred in the Bermuda Triangle?"

"I think plus or minus about five centuries."

"Now, want to know why we were playing Jeopardy on a plane flight to the US?"

"I don't know...take my mind off of some serious questioning?" he looked at her with a grim expression bordering on sarcasm.

"Actually...I plan on using our time to begin to answer some of your questions."

"What?"

"We have seven hours left in this flight. I'm going to begin to answer some very vexing questions that have been asked for a long time. I just need you to try and keep an"

"…open mind, I know, been there before. I'm listening."

"What do you think about the time between Earth 200,000 years ago, with the beginnings of homo sapiens and the age of the earth, 4.5 billion years?"

Rodane rubbed his hands over his face, "What do I think about what?"

"Let's talk about 'what if' in the time when Earth was calming down from its birth pangs and four-footed animals began to walk upright. It's going to be a long flight." Rodane's induction was just beginning.

Chapter 29

Hampton Roads, Va.

The airport at Hampton Roads was labeled as International but what that meant in actual terms was larger international flights came into major airports such as Dulles or Philly and then people caught smaller planes to outlying airports. Hampton Roads was not an extremely busy airport but it was busy none the less. Iona Arcos had arrived a half hour before and waited at baggage to greet her son. He needed to collect his baggage so he would be coming straight down to the arrival belts. Iona was a people watcher, always had been. With time on one's hands, watching people and observing their interactions, reactions and just actions, you could try and deduce a lot about someone. Most would just be guesswork.

Iona was a tall woman, holding at least an extra twenty pounds on her straight frame of 5'10". She wore her hair longer, shoulder length but usually up in a loose bun or at least in a ponytail. The color was nondescript, a soft brown mixed with some gray. Her walk was confident and her dark brown eyes swept the airport baggage carousels for signs of her son. She wore little to no makeup but she looked at least ten to fifteen years younger than her stated age of sixty one. She was a woman of simple ways even though she had a great deal of independent finance and many connections with people of enormous wealth.

Being the head of her very successful company and doing much of it largely by herself even by today's standards, was not the burden some would expect. She had employees who had been with her since their first days of seeking employment and they were fiercely loyal and dependable. During the first years after her husband Addy's death, they had been protective and constantly observing to make sure she ate and slept and had free time to herself and her two children. When Rodane went off to college and beyond, he knew she was in good hands. Cassie was doing well and Iona never allowed Rodane to worry about the business or household concerns. Having money didn't change her habits of having a spotless house or keeping up with painting and house repairs. It did however, allow for being able to live worry-free and give her children excellent educations and home life without her children being aware she gave enormous amounts of money to local and state charities and causes.

The hospital in their area had a new wing for cancer research from an anonymous donor; the college had a Chair in the Science Department named for Addy and at least four students each year were given full scholarships in a field of either Anthropology or Paleontology. The food bank in the town was restocked every month by 'donors'. The death of Addy had awakened something in her she had not been aware of. Well... that was not quite true. She had always believed she was more than a housekeeper and a baby maker but she had been contented and looking forward to her grandchildren and her golden years with Addy.

That had all been taken away from her so suddenly on one grey, rainy Thursday morning when someone had knocked on her door. He was sweating, trembling and white-faced, tears mixing with the rain, standing on her front porch wringing his hands, delivering the news to her that Addy had been found dead from a stabbing. How? What? Those first few days were like a living nightmare, going through the motions of a viewing, a funeral, a wake and an internment with police hovering over her throughout and her children in shock, bereft, clinging. Well, Cassie, Rodane not so much. He was angry, so very angry, at everyone and anyone, even her. He felt that somehow she should have, could have prevented that death and that loss. At least that was the feeling she got from him.

They had never talked about that. She had found in herself the strength to go to the offices each day and home to the children each night. She felt like an automaton running on pure energy, moving as if programmed, pouring herself into accounts and invoices. She went home each night and spent sleepless nights going through bank accounts and insurance papers. She sometimes cursed her beloved Addy for leaving her here to take care of all this without any warning or preparation. She slept in their bed each night, all these years, missing his warmth and his love-making, his strength and his kindness to his children.

She looked up as she heard her name and there was her son coming toward her with a wide grin on his handsome face, his arms out to enfold her and his huge hug. It was a good day. She looked over to the woman at his side, waiting. Iona opened her arms and went to Eugenie, "Welcome to our town. Welcome to my home." Eugenie, not used to overdoses of affection was nonetheless hugged and made to feel welcome. They made their way to the parking lot and her car. On the way to Iona's house, Rodane tried to let her know what had happened without causing her concern or fear for him. It was tricky to let her know about the attack at the ruins, the fire, the assault on him in Naples. Hearing himself tell it all, he was amazed at how it sounded like a thriller novel in the making. Yet here he was, going to a funeral for Adam who was protecting Caroline from enemies from across the ocean, using them to get at him… for what? He was overwhelmed, no other way to put it. Iona looked over at him, made a decision, turned the car toward downtown and parked in the garage.

"Where are we going Ma?" Rodane asked.

"We're having an early dinner or late lunch, take your pick. I need food."

Rodane looked at Eugenie and nodded with a smile toward his mother, "Whenever Ma has to process a difficult problem or handle stress she needs food. It's her answer to all life's vagaries." Eugenie looked appreciatively at Iona from the back seat, "Works for me!"

They went to one of Iona's favorite restaurants, right on the main artery to a table outside. As they waited for their appetizers and their drinks, Iona spoke first, "Now Rodane, fill in the missing spaces in your story," giving him the stern 'Ma's look' that Rodane and Cassie knew not to challenge and were so familiar with.

"What do you…?"

"Don't even try dear. My 'people watching' has given me a great penchant for observing undercurrents and recognizing deflection when I see it or hear it. Please fill your mother in Rodane, on what's really been happening here." She waited patiently. He wasn't sure how to begin with the whole truth. He couldn't hazard a guess how she would take it or how she would react to what he considered as life-threatening. She knew his consternation was in trying to protect her and keep her from suffering more fear and stress for her children.

"Rodane, try telling me what you think the reason is that you have been targeted because that's what it looks like to me."

Eugenie spoke up, "Mrs. Arcos…"

"Please Eugenie, I am Iona or if it makes you more comfortable, Oma, as Sophia's grandmother.

"Okay, Iona… it's taken Rodane some time to process this whole situation. I would like to tell you one or two things before Rodane begins to open up to you if that's okay?" Iona looked from one to the other and realized it was a lot more complicated than she had first thought. She nodded to Eugenie to continue.

What followed next was an explanation of a family that had been in existence for many generations, equitable to the Medicis, the Bourbons, the Tudors, the Changs... or a dynasty of a royal family where the descendants were still very much connected and very involved in the activities of the 21st century. Eugenie told Iona about their members, who were inserted into all areas of science and medicine, politics and religion, business and even entertainment. They had connections of a high-level, to universities and hospitals, research labs, military and industrial complexes. They ran businesses, had members in countries all over the globe in international banking and commerce, they were placed in corporate offices of finance, sports franchises, food industries and chemical plants. They existed in leadership roles in the energy industry and controlled large agricultural combines and textile industries. They owned or ran construction companies, recycling and trash removal, pharmaceutical companies and tech industries.

Eugenie said, "We're placed everywhere, we're global and we're trained in all fields and we have some of the best minds working in every country to develop and promote health and medical advances, military advances in weaponry and technological breakthroughs... the reason I'm telling you all this is because Rodane is part of this. Iona sat back and took a deep breath and then asked her, "He's one of the members of this 'family' you are a part of?"

"Actually, I don't know. I'm not a member of this 'family'. Well, I am, but it's in a purely employee capacity."

Rodane cut in, "Ma, I've only recently found out that I am a descendant of these... I don't know how to describe them, but..."

"Rodane," his mother spoke consolingly and with a degree of what could only be heard as sympathy, "I know this."

She watched his and Eugenie's face show shock and surprise, "Your father was a descendant of this line of 'family' members. I always knew, I just didn't think it affected our lives. It was a part of his history I thought, something that didn't matter to our family. We were here; you, Cassie, your father, and myself. It was like having an uncle or a great-grandfather who was a hero, or a rebel, or a member of the royal family ancestry, yes, not something that would make a difference in our present lives."

Eugenie spoke up, "Iona, your daughter, Cassie...I think you already know she has some very strong traits that we look for, in searching out direct descendants to the original 'family' lines. She hesitated..."all the things that have happened to Rodane... and his ex-wife... and your granddaughter..."

Iona put up her hand, "Stop! I know what you're going to say. I'm just not sure this is the time to consider that. Rodane, you have a funeral to attend, possibly a death of someone who was killed as a result of some people attempting to get to you through them. I can't tell you how frightened that makes me." They stopped discussing this as their food was brought to their table. All three had lost some of their appetites. Iona asked for three boxes, they took their food and left the restaurant and headed for Iona's house where they would be staying. The ride was much quieter than the earlier part. When they pulled up to the house, Eugenie looked over at the warehouses and the Navy yards in the distance. She and Iona looked at each other for a long quiet moment, "I'll bring up all the things from the car." Rodane walked away to the trunk.

"Things are going to change, aren't they?" Iona asked.

"Yes, they are," Eugenie's expression was somber and sad, "I'm afraid whether we like it or not, we are embarking on a very dangerous journey that will pull in those you love and want to protect. I can't promise you it won't be hard on people or that they won't be hurt, but I can promise you I'm here to look out for Rodane and you… your daughter… your granddaughter… and I'll do everything in my power to keep you all safe and protected from those who have very different ideas," she was leaning forward in the car with her hand on the driver's seat. Iona reached back with her hand and covered Eugenie's.

"Well, Eugenie, you won't be doing it alone. I may be old, so…" Rodane had returned to them and overheard her remark, "Don't bother with that look, I am old but I'm not powerless or stupid. I haven't actually seen this day coming but I'm not surprised it's here. Deep down, I've been expecting something like this since I lost… since we all lost our Addy." A fierce note of pride and protection shaded her voice, "No one is going to harm my loved ones as long as there is breath in me and they'll have to go through me to get to them." Her gray eyes had a glint of steel in them.

They went into the house, unaware that a camera was snapping pictures of all three of them. The top floor of the warehouse had a visitor, unseen and unnoticed by everyone below, working hard at keeping a thriving business going smoothly. One part of their lives was closing, a new part, very unique, very challenging, was opening up.

Caroline was supervising the remaining work crews, the painters and the cleaning crew, that were putting finishing touches on the house repairs. Sophia and Hallie were in her room playing Minecraft and the giggles coming from there made her smile a little. She hadn't been able to get a giggle or smile from Sophia since the morning she had come home and given her the news about Adam. She swallowed hard and directed the men to move the furniture, working around the ladder and the sounds of shampooers and sandpaper, smoothing new drywall to prepare for painting.

When the work trucks showed up at her house, she was reluctant to let them enter. They showed her the worksheet with the signed order to repair walls and shelves and a cleaning crew right behind them to tackle the kitchen. They brought all their own supplies and were at work within the hour. That was two days ago, the day Adam died. They had just moved back into the house last night.

{oh God what am I doing here}

She took a call from Cornelia and found out it was she who had contracted for the work done, the hiring and scheduling. All Caroline had to do was make arrangements for Adam. She had picked up Tara at the airport from Utah and they cried in each other's arms and then went to the funeral parlor to make arrangements for Adam's cremation and internment. Tara told the funeral director Adam wanted no viewing, no service, and the remains after cremation were going home to Utah to be buried on top of his mom's grave. But Tara, in talking to Caroline, realized Adam had made many friends here and among them some pretty influential people. She and Caroline decided that they would hold the wake at her house to have anyone who cared to, attend. The notice on Adam's death had been published yesterday as a result of the police investigation into his death. The phone calls had not stopped coming into the house.

Caroline had taken bereavement leave from the school and Sophia was not attending classes. She and Sophia had hunkered down at Mrs. Floyd's house and consoled each other after Willow and Phillip had gone home. They promised to return for the wake and Philip checked the house for secure windows and doors.

{something Adam used to do each night}

She shuddered and fisted her hands to gain control. She wasn't sure what the future held but she knew it would feel empty and dark for a while. Her life seemed so secure in the last months, full and happy, surrounded by love and a sense of fulfillment, a sense of Adam as the other part of her and Sophia as well. Gone in one horrific event she had heard every second of, but not seen. It would live with her forever, mostly at night when she was attempting to go off to sleep. Her phone rang at the same time as the chime of the doorbell. She called out to Sophia, "Honey, could you answer the door? I'm on the phone." She saw Cornelia's number.

"Cornelia. Hi, it's a madhouse here and the noise is making me frazzled."

"Hon, want to come here for a little till they're done?"

"No, they'll be done in the next hour, they promised me. The house smells like paint but it's clean and there's no evidence of…" her voice hitched, and her throat lumped.

"Oh Caro, I'm so sorry, so, so sorry. I wish I didn't have my meeting with Lori but I already rescheduled once and…" the doorbell chimed again.

"No worries Corny, I'm surrounded by chaos and… Sophia! Please answer the door!"

"Okay, Mama." Sophia went past her,

Cornelia asked, "Is Hallie behaving herself?"

"Daddy!" Sophia shrieked.

"I'll call you back in a couple, okay Corny?"

"Sure, just checking in. No need to call me back, I'll be there first thing in the afternoon, three o'clock, right? I'm sending over someone to serve for you, so set your mind at rest. Oh and a few covered dishes."

"Corny, you've already done too much. We'll be…"

"…fine… I know, but let me do this for you, Caro. I know you would do it for me if I was in the same boat. Okay hon?"

Caroline almost lost it, "Yes" she whispered, "you know I would."

Rodane moved into the family room, where Caroline was seeking a moment's peace, with Sophia wrapped around his neck. She had buried her head in his shoulder and her small frame was quietly shaking with soft sobs. He had his arms tightly around her protectively and he murmured into her ear. It struck Caroline as such a tender moment, so much a picture of Daddy and his little girl, that the tears came unbidden to her own eyes.

{they really love each other so much}

He came over to her and placed his arm around her shoulders and she turned into him and let herself give in to those tears for a moment. They made a sad tableau for no one else except themselves to witness. Caroline gathered herself together and looked up at him, "Thank you for being here… for Sophia…and me."

His mother walked into the room at that moment and put her arms out to Caroline. She moved to them like a ship to a safe harbor, "Oma" and she stood sobbing in her arms.

"You loved him." It was not a question it was a clear statement of fact. Oma held her and whispered to her, "Sophia loved him too. He was very good for both of you Caroline. You will get through this but not easily. Your grief will also be your loss and that will last a long time dear but it will lessen and you both will be ok," Oma fought her own tears to give comfort to Caroline.

Rodane sat down on the sofa with Sophia and just held her and rocked a little. Sophia's tears quieted and she looked up at Oma and her mother and smiled tremulously,

"Oma loves Mama doesn't she?" She watched her dad's face.

Rodane said, "Yes honey, she does. I don't think there's anyone that Oma doesn't love."

"Oma hates the man who killed my Poppa." she said it so calmly and matter-of-factly that Rodane paused a moment to process that statement. She was still watching his face as if to gauge whether he was telling her fact or fancy.

"I'm not sure if the word 'hate' is the right one to use here, Pumpkin, but I would guess that Oma feels a lot like your mom and you feel right now, losing Adam."

"I'm mad as hell!" Sophia spit out and her eyes glittered. His arms tightened around her and he kissed her on her forehead, "It's okay to be mad, just don't go around using potty-mouth with a lot of people you might not know. Put your best foot forward, right?"

Caroline walked over to them and gave Sophia a hug, "That's right Sophia. This house is going to be overflowing with politeness in a little while so we need to remember our manners, okay hon?"

"What's that mean," Rodane raised his eyebrows, "overflowing with politeness?" Sophia waited for their response.

"There are a lot of people coming to visit, to pay their respects to Adam and many of them are very important people so they expect…" Caroline paused and then said, "You know what Sophia? It doesn't matter who they are important to, if you're mad as hell, you have a right to say that so don't worry about being angry or not having perfect manners. I'm mad as hell too, Sugar. We'll be mad together until we feel better, okay?"

"Good for you," Oma said at her elbow, "Best way I know to grieve. Go after the one who did this and it will make you feel better. Never did deny something like 'eye for an eye' or 'tooth for a tooth' anyway."

Rodane sat there, more surprised than shocked. Here were three of his favorite people in the world instinctively knowing that to bear this grief, they needed to turn that to anger and avoid being ineffectual and overcome by a feeling of lack of control or fear. Here were three generations of strong women who made up most of his world, all on the same page, dealing from strength instead of weakness. He was so proud of all of them.

Once Rodane had been assured that Sophia and Caroline were Ok and handling everything as well as could be expected, he and Oma headed home to settle in until the wake tomorrow. They drove out behind the painters who were finally finished and before the serving crew that was just arriving could block them in. They would set up everything including dishes, glasses silverware, and do all the clean-up. Caroline would have one less thing to take care of.

Oma said, "It's time for you to catch me up on what has been going on Rodane. Don't give me that look. Now that I know what you've been through in the last week or so, I need to know what you intend to do about it."

Rodane said, "Do about it? What should I do about it? I have a job in Montana that I'm absent from, a daughter grieving over a man who was almost certainly going to be a stepfather or at least a role model for her. By the way, I liked him, I really did. I think he was very good for both of them and this makes me so mad."

"What about your job at the University?"

"Someone has been placed there temporarily to sub for me until I can get back there, hopefully at the end of the week.

"Your travels... and your... new friend, Sabina?" she raised her eyebrows but didn't elaborate.

"You don't miss much, do you Mom?" Rodane looked sheepish yet happy, "She is just wonderful, smart, funny, open..."

"Can I surmise that you have found someone you might be seriously considering having a permanent relationship with?"

"I'm considering it but long-distance relationships...?" he said with a sense of unease.

"Relationships meant to be have a way of working out despite our best efforts to torch them."

When they arrived back at Iona's house, Eugenie was waiting with some information about the team that Willow and Phillip had identified, "They've been here since the day after Rodane was arrested. It seems Lexus Fira was placed in the school where Caroline works, as a substitute teacher and...,"

"Holy hell! You've got to be kidding me!" Rodane exploded out of the kitchen chair he was sitting in, "That asshole had access to my daughter and frightened Caroline half to death. He was there? He was outside their house! How could that happen?"

"Funny you should ask that. Seems the principal, Mr. Belva..." Eugenie looked for affirmation, "has disappeared. When the police were looking into an 'anonymous' phone call about a suspect possibly working with Caroline, they went to the school looking for Lexus Fira and were told no one could answer their queries because their principal was not there and he was the one who hired this sub. Ordinarily it went through the office but this particular hire was totally handled by Mr. Belva."

"Anything there that might lead them to him?"

"Even stranger... when Belva's office was searched, the only thing found was a name under the desk mat and a phone number. When the number was called, a phone rang in a file drawer and it was erased, all contacts, all numbers..."

"Now what, how can my daughter and her mother be kept safe?"

Eugenie said, "That's where I come in. I've called for some backup and when you leave they'll be here to make sure no one gets near Sophia or Caroline." she looked over at Iona, "your mother as well."

"Me? Iona was surprised, "What's going on here that I should be involved?" she looked at Rodane and shook her finger at him, "and don't you dare try and keep the truth from me or even one fact you might think I won't like." Her cheeks were flushed with anger even though her voice was still level and quiet.

Eugenie reached across the table and placed her hand gently on Iona's arm.

"Oma, as honest as I can be, the people who are spearheading this whole incursion... are after Rodane because we've only just discovered ourselves that he is quite necessary to our whole 'family' unit. He has remained in hiding, so to speak, for too long...,"

"In hiding?" Rodane sputtered, "I haven't even known I was... whatever you..."

"Rodane, you've been hiding from yourself. I think your whole family has in a way. You didn't know the stakes. You weren't aware of the consequences. You were attempting to juggle two selves, the familiar and the unknown"

Now Iona spoke up, "She's right! No Rodane, she is. You didn't deliberately hide or ignore this, I did."

"Ma!"

"Listen son, I knew. Not everything but I knew your father was... different. I told you, as you and Cassie were also. Then I realized Sophia was just part of it, earned it from him and you. Tell me you didn't realize Cassie was so very open to the unknown, a penchant for foretelling just as I realized. I loved you, I loved your father and would have married him even if I hadn't known the peculiarities he presented to me over our entire married life but we both loved each other and he tried very hard to overcome any peculiarities. There were friends, relatives, guests in our lives, who were more than they appeared on the outside. Your father's trips to Europe and the Mediterranean...they were often taken without notice or preparation. He'd get a phone call, pack a bag or a small suitcase and leave the next day. He'd be gone two or three days then back home without a word about his trip. Shipments and merchandise, delivered within two or three days, that only Addy would handle or he allowed to be handled by those who would show up at our front door instead of the office, then leave after visiting with your father behind closed doors until late into the night."

"How did you handle all that, Ma? How come you never told me any of that?"

"What was to tell? I never heard the conversations, or saw what was in the shipments. That was your dad's world. I had two babies I was caring for and a house to keep..." she stopped and took a deep breath, "No, that's not entirely true. I realized there was something big going on, but only infrequently. I closed my eyes and ears to that part of your father's business. I was afraid to ask, so I just ignored it and went on with the life we had and just pretended those things didn't concern me." Her color heightened and then she placed her hands to her flushed cheeks. There was silence in the room for minutes, while the clock ticked quietly on the wall above the kitchen sink.

"Oma, what did you do about that after your husband died? Did your books reconcile?"

"Eugenie, they were the strangest part of it all. When I started checking the books and balancing the spreadsheets, it was as if those things didn't exist, like there had been no shipments or buyers or trips to overseas. Everything balanced perfectly, no fudging the missing funds, no private accounts, no second set of books...it was just as if all that was part of a dream, not reality. I was so worried they wouldn't. All the merchandise was accounted for, sold and unsold."

Rodane asked, "Everything? Every piece was accounted for?"

"Nothing there that wasn't listed but there was not one person who could remember that merchandise, who was there for the shipments being delivered. I've puzzled over that all these years."

"Let's get back to the reason we need to secure you and your family Rodane," Eugenie was business again, "We know some of them, we've dealt with some of them from long before...," she hesitated as if she were juggling her words, "They have never before used this level of violence. It's like they have...,"

"Inside information, someone who knows your schedules, your itineraries...a leak?" Rodane waited for her answer.

"Yes" Eugenie said, "We discussed this and we all feel like that is a distinct possibility. It makes it that much more difficult to protect everyone and keep our movements under wraps. They seem to have a larger organization with more resources available than in the past. Nikos is sure we can uncover these leaks in a short time." Rodane watched his mother take all this in and he hated to be the one to bring all this to her on such short notice. This was hard on her and she was handling it more calmly than he expected.

She asked, "Who is this Nikos you speak of? Can he find this leak or does he have someone who can?"

"We have many people in our group who are capable and able to investigate all this information we are compiling. We too, have our resources and our organization. It's made up of some of the sharpest, brightest and best trained people we could find from all over the globe."

"Does this Nikos have plans for my son?"

"Nikos is one of the members," Eugenie looked surprised at Rodane's remark. She added, "He's very adept at keeping us all together and very wise in knowing where our talents are most useful. We owe a lot to his direction over many years."

"He performs magic and got me a temporary replacement at the University to free me up here. I owe him one for making my life less complicated, for now."

Iona rose from her chair, "It's always good to eliminate complications from your life whenever possible," she went to Rodane and enfolded him in an embrace, "You are safe, that's what's important…to keep Caroline and Sophia… and Cassie…," Iona's voice hollowed out.

Eugenie added, "Yes…and Cassie. To keep them safe is my most pressing priority. How do we do this?"

"Tomorrow we go to Adam's wake. We need to find a way to protect Caroline and Sophia first. Whoever wants me is using them as bait. Or they are attempting to either take them or find me, whichever. We can't leave them alone now. So how do we do this Eugenie?"

"Let me think on this for a time. We'll come up with something by tomorrow I promise. I have a couple of ideas percolating."

Two hundred yards away, Lexus Fira was monitoring their conversations from the attic floor of the warehouse. He had fled there trying to locate Arcos' mother, not really knowing what he would do if he found her. He had left Zoe back at their apartment without a word once they had gone back from the bitch's house and their failed attempt to snatch that brat. He would not be in touch with her till he had a solid plan in place. She wasn't going to argue him out of this and he wasn't going to listen to her whining about getting caught and failing their mission. He stopped in the town at a local tech store and bought all the equipment he needed to do eavesdropping or bugging of phones and her computers. He had been monitoring Iona Arcos for two days and downloaded all her files from her computer and had even managed to put cameras into hidden places around her house in the dark hours of last night. He had a place to be tomorrow and he had someone to deliver to his bosses by the end of the day. Maybe he wouldn't be in great shape but Rodane Arcos would be delivered none the less and a bonus was he would be alive. That galled him to no end but he wanted his money. If he could take out Caroline Arcos in the bargain, it would be doubly rewarding. He thought of what he should do with Sophia but he hadn't come to a decision yet.

Meanwhile he would hunker down here, leave by his manufactured exit to get food, use the bathroom, and check out Caroline Arcos' house. He felt jazzed, excited, thinking of the wake for her boyfriend, Adam. A grin crossed his face, a feeling of euphoria at his conquest. He had no idea you could get such a rush from taking someone down, permanently. Usually it was a case of surveillance, obtaining information, taking pictures, taping conversations, sending out blackmail letters and photos that might get their subject to fold and pay up. This was a whole new ball game.

Taking someone down was a thrill, a high, the reason why he loved what he did so much, with the added plus of showing his prowess, his control. He planned on asking for a significant increase in his payments once this particular assignment was completed. He moved down a back stairs to a closed closet and exited that to a narrow hallway to a delivery loading area. Looking around, he saw old ships being welded on off hours, sparks flying into the warm night air, hearing the buzz of saws and drills. He moved off into the dark toward the main road and a fast food 24/7 joint to finally have his one meal a day that he allowed himself.

He wondered what Zoe was thinking by now as to where and how he was. He might even give her a call later. He'd have to let her know soon, what they would be doing to end this assignment and head back to New York. He felt the need to 'party'. His gut was beginning to hurt again. Since he had fought with Adam, he had been pissing blood in the toilet and everything he ate managed to either give him the runs, or bring acid up his throat and he was in constant pain. He would have to buy more Anti- acid at a convenience store while he was out. It would just have to work itself out and he would be fine. After the wake was over and all the guests had left he would have the chance to finally put this all to rest and head home. He sauntered out of the lot with a grin on his thin, wan face.

Zoe, meanwhile, was where he had left her, too afraid to wander far from the apartment, too cautious to make any phone calls, except to their superior. She had called him as soon as it was evident Lexus wasn't returning anytime soon, if ever! She thought that might be a good thing. If he didn't show up in the next twenty-four hours, she was instructed to return home and report in. Her superior hadn't been too happy when she explained all the events that had recently occurred. He looked up the assault online while they were talking, and saw the death notice and the police rendering of Lexus. It was actually quite good. It left Zoe wondering why there wasn't one of her. She still saw that face, watching her as she drove away from the house, recognition springing to her expression, and her eyes following them to the end of the street. Willow! What the hell was she doing there? If she remembered correctly, that was one of her sons with her, Paul… Peter …Philip… that was it! Philip! He was older of course, but unmistakable. When they were still in Belgium, he had been what…ten…eleven years old? How long ago was that? Ten years, more?

Since that afternoon, she had a knot in her belly all the time, and a persistent tension headache that threatened to become a full-blown wrecking ball, kind of like what they had been using since they had come here. This whole assignment was fucked up. Nothing has gone right and what had gone wrong had gone straight to hell two days ago.

She kept the TV on all day and night, ears tuned to anything that seemed to be connected to the murder of Caroline's boyfriend, Adam. She even went so far, as to visit his gym on the pretext of joining. She met with a counselor, and in the course of her tour, broached the subject of all the trainers huddling together and talking continuously.

Marty told her about the death of one of their trainers and how hard it had been on all of them. "He was good?" she asked innocently.

"He was more than good. He was a good trainer. He was an example to all the other trainers and made them want to up their game. He was smart and funny, and so dedicated to helping his clients actually make a change in their lives."

"Sounds like you really liked him. Anything romantic there?" she asked impishly.

"Me?" Marty laughed out loud and then lowered her voice, "No luck there, not that I wouldn't have minded, but he and his girlfriend were a total item and it was getting very serious. They were an awesome couple. Talk about changing someone's life!"

They entered the pool area and the smell of chlorine was strong at the hot tub. Zoe listened, while Marty explained the lap pool, the kiddie pool, the lanes reserved for a swim club that practiced there each day religiously, and the physical therapy pool and rehabilitation center, for anyone who needed water therapy for surgery or rehab, or just to keep old bones moving. Zoe interrupted her, "Well, my bones are just fine and I don't need kiddie pools or rehab." She laughed, "I guess his girlfriend is pretty torn up over all this. Was she a client of his, so to speak?" Marty lowered her voice almost to a whisper,

"Let's say she chased him until he caught her."

"What do you mean?" Marty smiled at her with a Cheshire Cat grin,

"Caroline was a tough customer, went through men like her training outfits, a new one for each season. Then her eye caught Adam, and he wasn't interested in being her new conquest. She even admitted that was what she called them. She was a total bitch, saucy and sailor mouthed and demanding...had a great body though. Had! What am I saying, she still has."

"Don't like her much? Zoe felt bad for Sophia, "Did she have kids? I pity them."

"Oh, no pity necessary there. She's an awesome mom, protective, but didn't spoil that child. Sophia is a wonderful little girl, just as smart and funny as Adam." Marty teared up, "He used to bring her to the gym when her mom had appointments or teacher conferences. She was so good with the little kids in the nursery. They adored her"

They moved to the weight section of the gym and Zoe chafed with impatience but hid it well while she was listening to the spiel about weights and muscles and machines for every muscle group God had invented. She had to show an interest in all this stuff or Marty would perhaps wonder why she was here except to gossip,

"Did Sophia like her mom's new conquest?" Marty smiled sadly, "She loved him, they were such a cute threesome and Adam's presence in Caroline's life really helped her to open up and be so much nicer. The bitch is gone...or was. I'm not sure what happens after Adam has been taken away."

"What exactly happened? " They were over at the mats, balls, and bosu balls. Everyone seemed to be in a talking mood, small twosomes or threesomes, quietly discussing, what, his murder? She felt ashamed, of all things. Then, she felt guilty and embarrassed, for feeling ashamed. This was her job!

{not to kill someone innocent and ruin three lives}

"Some bastard, and maybe a sidekick, broke into their house and didn't know anyone was there. Stupid dope head probably. The car was right in the driveway for any idiot to notice someone was probably home. They attacked Adam but he managed to get Caroline to a hiding spot and thank God Sophia was in school. It was awful... well from what I hear... there are rumors all over and no one here is really sure of what happened. I can tell you we're all going to the funeral if they have one. The owner is even willing to close for a couple of hours. They were good friends."

"Did they catch who did it?" she held her breath not knowing what to expect.

"They think they might know who it is. They interviewed every one of us here but I don't think they have him or his accomplice. Don't worry, they'll catch them both and put them where they won't see the light of day, ever again."

Zoe felt sick, literally felt her breakfast coming up from her stomach. She breathed deeply and turned to Marty, " I'm so glad I stopped in. You've been great showing me around. I think I'll bring my boyfriend by and we can talk again. I'm sure he will love this place. It's been great." she smiled with a false effort then turned and headed out and left as fast as she could without sending smoke under her tires. Marty watched from the entrance.

Chapter 30

Small town in Italy

The sun came in through the little window above her bed and reflected off the mirror above the one bureau in the bedroom. Actually, 'her bedroom' was not quite apt. It was as if she were a guest in this house because her mother had insisted she take her bedroom and her sister and brother were in the living room on the pull-out sofa and on the floor. It was one of the few things that her mother had allowed her to buy for this house over the years.

For whatever reason, she would not accept money from Renata and it was done with a gentle refusal, a patient denial of the need for such an offer. At first it angered Renata. She tried to reason with her, then she argued with her, then she accepted the fact that her mother was adamant in her stance and would not give in. Yet over the years she came to see that it was not so much refusing to accept anything from Renata but as a kind of penance for whatever sins she felt she had committed, and reparation for them. When her younger sister refused to stay in the tiny house as long as she had to sleep in the one-bedroom for all four children, she unwillingly accepted the pull-out sofa as a solution.

Now here she was, waking up with the sunrise as she had for so many years long ago. It seemed like an entire lifetime ago but today no crying babies to wake her, no mother calling for her to make breakfast so they could get to their chores.

Instead of going to the country villa that Theras had asked her to consider and expected her to attend, she had traveled on impulse back to her old village and back to her old home where the walls were bursting with two teenagers, a toddler and her younger sister Isabel, who was 20 years old and who was the mother of the toddler. Her two-year-old Marco, was a sweet boy, smart and ornery, a giggler who kept everybody on their toes and brought sunshine into the house, even on rainy days. Remarkably or maybe not so much, Marco had attached himself to Renata. Whenever she was in the house, he cried and clung to her leg when she was about to leave. It brought back a lot of not so pleasant memories, of other babies vying for her attention when that was the last thing she wanted then.

The first day there she slept the entire day. Her mother checked on her, anxious and concerned that she might be ill. She finally emerged the second day and when she went for a walk to escape the strangled feeling she had when inside, was greeted by every woman on the street and some of the men eyed her with recognition but did not approach her. Just as well. She didn't think too much of or welcome the attentions of any man just now.

The third day she pulled out the small box given to her so many years ago by Father Pietro and went down the hill to the village church. It was open, dark and cool inside and blessedly empty. She kept asking herself why she was pulled to come here. She had no answer but she gradually gave in to the pull of the place. She sat there and tried to clear her mind and reach a place of calm and peace. Minutes passed and all she could do was watch as images and faces appeared in her tortured mind, Tabor on the surgical table, blood-soaked and hooked to tubes, Rodane Arcos lying on stones of the ruins of Akrotiri, bleeding from his head wound, a man looking up at Tabor and begging for his life right before that life ebbed away with his own blood. Her mind was flooded with bloody images and men of her past who seemed to bleed so easily and freely. What was the point? Was there a message here? Was she trying to face something important, or pushing it to the depths of her subconscious to evade the ugly parts of her?

She looked at the small box she had kept for all these years since she had left her village and gone to work for Theras Gallo. Opening it, she took out the small pin that rested in a velvet cushion and the gold of the pin gleamed up at her. The mountains rose to tiny points. In the foreground was a tangle of vegetation and dunes, strange but somehow compelling. Why did Father Pietro give this to her?

{what does it have to do with me}

Why did she keep it? What was she to do with it? She sat there for a long time, how long she wasn't sure. If she was seeking answers here she wasn't getting any new messages from God. No voices to put into words what was expected of her, no guidance to put her on a new path. Those saving graces were not forthcoming in this building. She would have to be the decider of her own fate, the voice that would tell her what to do and where to go.

She was tempted to curse this Being who had led her to this point, brought her through terrible, horrible assaults on her life, her body, her very soul. No being could be benevolent or kind who seemed to relish the evil of so many men. No God who ruled over an entire species would expect worship or glory, while controlling those very humans that he proposed to love and protect.

The back door opened and she heard steps slowly walking up the center aisle. Those steps stopped at the pew where she sat wasted, wilted, a plant that could grow and thrive if given new life. She felt like she had been denied sun and water for so long she was wilting away until all that life was drained from her. Yet she had returned to her roots, come home again to try and make sense of all the past years, to decide if it was worth trying to grow again, to reach for sun and sustenance, to heal and thrive in this awful place where she found herself.

"Renata, what can I do to help you child?" her mother's voice was trembling, soft and sad. Renata moved over, looked over her shoulder and motioned for her mother to sit with her. Flora sat down slowly, her tired bones stiff and achy. She looked to Renata and caught sight of the gold pin nestled in the red velvet cushion. She gasped out loud and her eyes widened in shock as her hand flew to her mouth to cover it.

"Where did you get that? Who gave that to you?" Her body trembled all over and her hands reached for it and then hovered over it, afraid to touch. At the last second, she snatched her hand back as if burned, her breathing rapid and shallow.

Renata looked at her, went to put her hand over her mother's to calm her then she too, paused, "Tell me Mama, why can I not just dispose of this as a trinket, a little piece of jewelry given so long ago? Why do I feel the need to keep this? It must be important. You obviously know it, you seem to fear it. What? Tell me." she waited, afraid to speak again. Even in the darkness of the church Renata could see her mother's pale color and watch her wringing her hands in her lap.

"You will hate me. I have feared this day for all of your life. Somehow I knew it would come and I could see in your face that something awful has been weighing you down and this might be the time I would be called to account…," she crossed herself.

"Whatever it is, it can't be any worse than where I am now, in this hole, this painful place where I drown with self- hatred and anger and…,"

"No Renata, not you, me. Why do you hate your life so much that it makes you eat at your own soul, devour your own dreams? That is my task in this life, not yours. Tell me what has brought you to this terrible place, let me help you."

"My insides have died Mama. I feel little, I believe in less, and I want for nothing yet I have nothing." She saw the lack of understanding in her mother's eyes, "It's okay, I'm just tired. Let's go home."

"First, I have to tell you something. It may be what will send you away again. You may never speak to me again but I must tell you…" her mother's voice was filled with despair and torment.

Renata took her hand and spoke softly to her, "Whatever it is, I feel it must be said if I am to survive this earth any longer and find a better reason to be here, to breathe this air, live in this world where I find myself trapped."

"Father Pietro is your father." She left out a breath and her shoulders slumped, "There, I have finally said it."

They both sat in silence, Renata trying to piece together all the mysterious, curious, pieces of her life, her mother, crying silently and finally telling her the story. It wasn't surprising to Renata. The affair that led to her birth gave Renata her sister and brother as well. Her other sister was born much later by a different man her mother had taken up with for a few years and then he had left to go and look for work and had never returned.

"For Pietro to give you this was an acceptance of you as his daughter, something we both kept in strictest secrecy from everyone. Did he explain it?"

"Explain it? It's a pin. He said he wanted me to have it." She remembered his plea for her to come home if she needed peace and comfort.

"I'm home but I don't feel peace or comfort. I feel lost."

"That pin is not just a pin. I've seen that pin become something…fearful. It terrified me and I've never seen anything like it. He made me swear to never talk of it to anyone for any reason. I never did but I remember…"

"Tell me Mama, I swear to you it will go no further. Somehow I know I need to learn this."

She stayed for two more days. For the first time in days, she had a meal. She woke early in the morning when the gold light of sunrise was touching the hills with fingers of soft light and myriad colors. The village was quiet and she listened to the small songbirds waking each other up and greeting the day with unending joy and exuberance. She still found none for herself. Knowing the story of her birth and her mother's secret life didn't affect her in any way other than to make her aware of what she had been, what she now was and how she decided to fix herself. She was going to complete her assignment. She was as responsible as Tabor had been in causing the events which led her here. She needed to make it right with herself and those who had taken a chance on her and given her a new life, apart from a tiny, poverty-stricken town in the hills of Italy.

She hated her life, she hated Tabor. She thought she might hate all men but she would not rest until she had exacted revenge on Rodane Arcos. It was his appearance and presence that had driven them to where only she remained now. He was the catalyst of all the horrible, shitty things that had followed them on this job from the very beginning. If she couldn't get Sabina Carter she would settle for Rodane Arcos and she would settle all the scores that she had with him. She made some calls to her contacts, got her information and arranged to leave Saturday morning on an early flight.

Va. apartment

The knock on the apartment door made Zoe jump at least six inches off the sofa. She was finishing a TV dinner minus the TV. She couldn't let herself get any more paranoid than she already was.

{maybe Lexus left his key here}

She hadn't even checked. She was afraid to open the door and there wasn't even a peep-hole to see who it was or a chain on the door.

"Who is…," her voice squeaked. She cleared her throat and tried again.

"Theras Gallo sent me" It was a woman's voice but not familiar, "Could we not play twenty questions in the hallway? It's stifling out here."

Zoe summoned her courage and opened the door. Before her was a small, trim, dark-haired woman with a pixie haircut dressed in black from head to toe. She reminded Zoe of an elf. She was empty-handed except for a clutch purse and carried one bag.

{no suitcases can't be too dangerous I can always box her ears}

"I am Renata Kappos from the Med Team and I need to speak with Lexus." Short, clipped, dry words without much inflection, this person was unknown.

"Lexus is not here right now. I'll give him a message when I hear from him."

"The woman pushed past her and entered the apartment.

"Hey! You can't come in here! This is my place and Lexus…"

"…is in serious trouble!" Renata spit it out, "as are you if you helped him a few days ago." She decided to bluff her way through this.

{can't hurt I got nothing}

"Theras Gallo sent me to clean up your mess and take care of things… permanently."

Zoe said, "Fine, I'll call my Superior and you can have this assignment. I want to go home so that makes it good for both of us." she turned to get her phone, "Don't." Renata's voice was low but it brooked no argument. "Your superior knows nothing of this change of plans. Mr. Gallo took care of this himself, that's how serious it is."

"Well then, I'll call my superior and tell him to call Mr. Gallo and make sure this is on the up-and-up," she turned again and a hand gripped her arm above the elbow and in a split second she was in a vice grip with an arm crossing her windpipe and tightening. She ducked and flipped Renata over her shoulder and onto the floor. Renata swept her feet instantly and took Zoe across the knees and down. They spent about five minutes doing what they could to hurt the other. Zoe gave out some solid punches to midsection and nose and Renata gave Zoe a fractured finger, a kick to the ribs and a pulled tendon in her left leg. They were in a grappling hold when Renata said, "If you don't let go, I'm prepared to snap your neck or your leg, it doesn't make much difference to me." Zoe was immobile, her nose bleeding as was Renata's, her sore ribs were constricting her breathing and she realized this woman could do what she threatened. She relaxed and Renata's grip loosened a fraction. They moved away from each other very slowly, both calculating the risks of continuing this free for all.

"I have complete authority to handle this my way and you are to follow my orders. When this is done, feel free to run to Mr. Gallo and complain all you want. We'll both get paid and problem solved."

"What about Lexus?"

"What about him? Where is he?" Renata had her eyes on Zoe when she was silent, "You don't know, do you? He's run off after fucking up this whole job and left you high and dry. Am I right?" she smirked at Zoe still standing there silent and gritting her teeth with each breath she took.

"Look I'm sorry about the ribs but you didn't give me much choice. You fight like a cat in heat." When she saw Zoe stiffen, she added " That's a compliment by the way."

Zoe looked over at her, "Yes he left and I haven't heard from him. I have instructions to leave tomorrow if he doesn't show up."

"Well then, you're in luck. I take over, we finish the job then I'll go back with you to your place, New York, right? Then you get paid and we both go our separate ways. Sounds like a better plan than the fiasco you've been playing at the last week or so."

{I'm not liking you much girl}

"Don't give me that look! What? I can't tell you want to rip my face off and feed it to the rats in here? Are there rats in here?" she jerked her head up as if the thought just occurred to her, as Zoe shook her head.

Renata continued, "Sit down and let me look at your finger." she reached for Zoe's hand and Zoe jerked it away. "Fine! Live with it or take care of it yourself but you better get some ice." Zoe looked down and saw a swollen little finger, her pinky finger, twice its size.

"Now tell me about Lexus' plan if you ever had one. That man sounds like a total screw-up with half brains." Zoe laughed, she couldn't help it. She had been thinking that very thing right before Renata had shown up.

She went to get ice, made a pack of a sandwich bag with ice wrapped in a dish towel. They sat and Zoe told Renata what had been planned for this assignment and how it had actually gone down. She joined Zoe in laughing when she heard her play out the scene where Lexus found out he was teaching kids in school as a cover. She grimaced when Zoe recounted what had occurred at Caroline Arcos' house where the boyfriend was attacked and killed. Now here they sat like rabbits in a warren, afraid to venture out and more afraid to sit and do nothing. Renata hopped up,

"Okay, tell me what you were set to do."

"Go home."

"That's it? Girl, you got nothing better than that? I thought you were the East Coast team." She snorted, "Huh"

Zoe was offended, "We are... well we're supposed to be...It's hard to be..."

"...working with a dork like Lexus? This guy is a walking grenade. How have you managed to keep your finger on the pin for so long? I would have pulled it long ago.

{like I wouldn't with Tabor}

Zoe saw her snap her mouth shut and a look passed over her face of disgust, anger, dejection.

"Look Renata..." she handed her the ice, "Your eye is beginning to swell shut. I'm sure you are awesome at what you do but..."

You too girl! You're a Hellcat." she sounded like she was actually praising her.

"Thanks. You don't know Lexus. You're right, he's a real piece of work and I've never seen him go off like this on any of our assignments. This one seems to have gotten under his skin so much he's just..." she couldn't find the words.

"Letting his dick do his thinking for him?" Zoe shook her head yes, very slowly.

"Well since we don't have dicks..."

"Thank God for that!" Zoe exclaimed.

"Yeah you got that right but now we can make plans using our brains and finish this. What are your orders... what were your orders?"

Zoe explained their mission and Renata said, "Oh I got that. You get information on Rodane Arcos and you get it through his ex-wife and daughter. Guess you didn't count on her boyfriend in the mix huh? Well, we'll fix that. We still have the ex-wife and it should be a cinch to get hold of the kid."

"That's not necessary. Sophia can't tell you anything. I've already talked to her and she's a typical eight year old who has no idea what her daddy is up to."

"You have no idea how fast her mom will squeal all she knows and then some when she knows we have her little girl."

"You would traumatize that little girl who knows nothing just to use her as bait for her mother?" Zoe was flushed and getting angrier as she listened to Renata and the cold, calculating way she was planning this.

"You seem to forget that you've been at this for days and accomplished nothing. I don't plan on being here till I age gracefully. We do this, we get out, we head to New York and by the time we arrive there, our trails are stone cold and we don't leave anything behind to point to us. What's not to like?" Renata seemed satisfied with herself.

"What if Lexus shows up and disagrees with this?"

"You really think he will object to pay back? That's what this is, right? He failed, so he wants revenge for his incompetence. Typical?"

"...except for Sophia. I'm not after revenge and I don't think harming a little girl is in your file either." Zoe waited, determined to get an answer.

"Okay how about this? We get Mom out of the house, take her somewhere we can determine now and let the kid alone. She's eight. She'll be fine and probably run to a neighbor. Does that salve your conscience enough?"

Zoe looked at Renata for a long moment of silent observation. Renata began to feel like a bug on a slide and uncomfortably inspected.

Zoe said, "How long have you been doing this?"

"Why, what does that have to do with anything?"

"Actually, I think everything. There's a window of time where you can shove all your ethics and morals aside and go for the gold. You try to grab the ring while you're on the Merry-Go-Round and if you can hold on long enough you get the free ride. After a time you don't have the stamina to keep riding the incessant, never ending circle. You begin to wish fervently for a way to get off the horse. You're all in and it becomes your most ardent wish to get off the merry-go-round. In order to do that you have to give up any desire to go for the ring and begin to gather the morals and ethics you have shoved aside before. It becomes your one clear goal; get your life back and all obstacles be damned and you'll try anything, attempt anything, sacrifice anything to try and get your life back. That's it, no big secret or mystery. I think we all go through it."

"You sound like you're speaking from experience."

"Like I said, there's a window of time. How long do you think you have left?"

Renata was about to answer and the phone rang on the coffee table. Zoe picked up the phone and looked at the screen.

"It's Lexus."

Renata said, "Put it on speaker" she looked at Zoe, "Please."

Lexus said, "I'll be there in the next forty minutes. Be ready to go to Caroline Arcos' house. We're doing this tonight and I need your stuff packed and ready to head out immediately. Don't leave anything in the apartment that can be traced back to us, got that Zoe? You follow?"

"Yes Lexus, I follow. There's someone he..." the call ended. Lexus had disconnected.

"Should I call him back?" she looked to Renata.

"No, there'll be time enough to explain when he gets here. Let's clean up the apartment."

They went from room to room, wiping down door knobs and handles, cleaned out the traps on the two sinks for hair and fibers, vacuumed and emptied the contents in a garbage bin and emptied all the trash cans and washed them out. Then Zoe went around using bleach on every surface she could think to wipe. They washed the filter on the vacuum and packed up all Zoe's things and then wiped out the drawers and cabinets. Just as they were finishing up Lexus walked in and did a double take when he saw Renata standing there. He pulled out his knife and held it loosely in his hand,

"Who the hell are you and what are you doing here?"

"I guess I could ask you the same thing. We were told by a reliable source you had left Zoe here to take a fall and headed out to parts unknown. I was sent to clean up your mess. Lexus, where's your report? It was due yesterday."

{may as well go for broke}

He stepped back like he had been slapped. He didn't look good. His skin was sallow, had a yellow tint to it and his cheeks were sunken in. The man was ill, that was evident. He looked around the apartment, sniffed and motioned to the door,

"Let's go, I've got the engine running."

"Lexus, maybe we should sit down and go over..."

"I said let's go!" he screamed at them and his eyes were practically bulging out of his head now.

Renata looked at Zoe and she nodded. They left the apartment. Renata turned out the light and they got in the car, Zoe in front. The drive to Caroline's house took about twenty minutes and there was not one word spoken the entire ride. Zoe had a very bad feeling about this. She looked back at Renata and she shook her head 'no' very subtly and then looked straight ahead.

Virginia

The entire afternoon had been not only physically exhausting, but mentally as well. Caroline couldn't believe the number of people who had come through the house to pay respects to Adam. It was as if she hadn't known this Adam at all. There were doctors and chemists, politicians and policemen, secretaries and surgeons. They had known Adam as their trainer or client and each one couldn't praise him enough for being a dedicated trainer as well as a fine young man. Housewives and Human Resources people all thought he was perfect father material, told Caroline how often he told stories of Sophia and how smart and cute she was. It brought her to tears. Mechanics and ministers all let her know what a sincere, honest man he was. She felt like she was being bombarded with goodness and it made her feel very small and insignificant until one hairdresser came up to her and said,

"Adam loved you so much and was so proud of you."

"Me?" Caroline said in wonder, "what could he be proud of me for?"

"He thought you performed miracles in your classroom. He saw you when you held assemblies and worked after school with failing students. He thought no one could reach those kids like you did. I want you to know the stories he told me while we were working out convinced me to go back to school and I'm going into education. I want to make a difference in kids too and I think I might be pretty good at it so, thank you for being such a good example to me and your students."

She had to leave the room for a few minutes, lock herself in her bathroom and sob out her grief for having such a wonderful man and loving him and losing him too soon. Rodane knocked on her door to check on her, "Caroline, are you okay?"

"Yes, just needed a few minutes to feel sorry for myself." she opened the door and stood with tissues in hand. He saw a wan, white-faced, red-eyed vestige of the woman he had known, drowning in grief and trying so hard to hold it all together. He opened his arms and she moved into them.

"You know, Caroline, you can ask everyone to go home now. You've done your duty, the crowd has slowed down and you can…you are allowed, to grieve in private, you and Sophia. If you want, I can ask everyone to make their way out."

"No. But thank you. I had no idea of the impact Adam had on so many people. It's humbling and so rewarding to have had him, if only for a little while."

A knock on the bedroom door had Caroline wiping her face and blowing her nose. She opened the door to a strikingly beautiful, tall woman with a thick head of strawberry blonde hair, dressed fit to kill and holding a glass of wine. Caroline's face had a rare smile on it when she saw her and let her into the room to meet Rodane.

"Rodane this is 'Corny'...Cornelia, my best friend from college. I think you might have met her once or twice." she grinned and said, "I kept you away from each other because I was a jealous bitch and I guess I thought if you saw her it would be all over for me. Lord, how stupid I was in those years."

"Well I'm not sure that I wouldn't have taken a second look at you, Cornelia. Glad to meet you where no one minds if I do or not."

They shook hands and Caroline spoke up, "Well you're too late Corny. It seems as if Rodane has taken up with a foreigner in an exotic country and... what was her name, Sabrina?"

"No, Sabina, but I wouldn't call it exotic, maybe just mysterious and challenging."

Caroline smiled a little, "So, he's had a time of it. Sophia tells me he really, really likes her and she likes him too. They've been examining ruins, Rodane has gotten mugged, they escaped a hotel fire...it's like a novel. Let me wash my face and use the bathroom and we can chat for a few minutes before someone comes searching for me."

When she went to the bathroom, Cornelia walked over to Rodane and reached out with the wine. Rodane declined and she sat on the edge of the bed while he took the recliner in the corner.

"Sabina is it? Are you two an item?" Cornelia said it as if she expected him to really bare his feelings.

He thought for a moment and decided to be forthcoming rather than be coy, "She's a wonderful woman. We became very friendly on our trip and I think I would like to pursue it further if distance doesn't kill it first."

"What does Suri think about it?" Her question had him jerking his head up and looking at her in shock,

"Suri? How do you...what do you know about..."

"Rodane, we have two minutes at best." She leaned closer and spoke softly, "Let me be very clear and very frank and listen closely. Eugenie is downstairs with your mother. That means she is with you, correct?"

Rodane stood up and started toward the door, "Wait! This is important! Suri and I are...connected, we're part of each other's growing-up years and I am..."

He halted at the door, "Part of her 'family'? Seriously?" He had his hand on the knob like that rabbit, ready to run.

Now it was Cornelia's turn to be shocked, "Family? That's an odd way to describe a friendship. What makes you think we are related?"

"What makes you think I'm not?" Rodane said. She stared at him in silence as she took in his words and then processed them, "Oh good Christ with his mother Mary!" She rose and went over to him and took a good long swallow of her wine, "Rodane, Sabina is in a good deal of danger and I need you to be aware of that. I'm going to ask Eugenie to return to France and get in contact with everyone to let them know what has happened here and…"

"They already know."

She jerked, startled, "Wow, seems you've become very close to my 'family' and in such a short time. How did that happen?" she drank the remainder of her wine after one last swallow and placed the glass on the bureau with trembling fingers "I feel like Rip Van Winkle who just discovered she's been asleep for years and had everything passing her by. We need to talk."

Caroline came out of the bedroom, stood there and looked from one to the other.

"What! What did I miss? Something's going on here, what did I miss? Come on guys, what's the deal here?"

"Rodane and I have found we have some friends in common and we were exchanging some memories, right Rodane?"

"Corny I…" Caroline was struck silent for a minute and then she shuddered and said, "I'm going downstairs and see to my guests. You can catch up on your…'friends'" she stressed the word with sarcasm.

Cornelia and Rodane shared confidences for over fifteen minutes and connected the dots between what had been going on here and what had happened in Greece and Italy. They arrived at the same conclusion: Rodane was on someone's 'A' list and there were quite a few people interested in getting to him that included using his family and his contacts, even new ones, to find a way to accomplish that. He told her about his visit to Agatha and that got a laugh from her.

"Agatha is a treasure trove and I can't imagine what we would do without her."

"So what about Sabina, what do you know about these threats?"

Cornelia considered if she could share the info she had with Rodane since he was only now learning of his heritage and history. Not to share it would possibly put him in more danger and his immediate family under more scrutiny.

"I've been having meetings with the first lady, she's a friend" he raised his eyebrows in surprise, "She's helping me lay the groundwork for some examination of suspicions that we have concerning fraud and embezzlement of funds earmarked for science and research grants. We're working on presenting her husband with enough proof to begin an investigative committee to search for any evidence of that and more. It reaches far and deep and we can't go into him with accusations unless we can provide some substance. It sounds simple but we're talking about illegal activities that reach all the way to the space program, and all the hiring of scientists and researchers around the world."

"Think it's all connected, don't you?"

"Don't know dude, what would you think?"

He laughed at her terminology, "I guess. So, where do I fit in?"

"Not sure but I am sure you are somewhere in the equation and only recently. We have to make sure you're not stopped in your tracks. You seem to bring out the…"

"…best in people?" he grinned at her and she was charmed.

"Let's just say their hidden impulses haven't been this busy for… well, a long time."

"What is it about my…'family' that they are so circumspect about giving me dates and times?"

"Whatever do you mean?" Cornelia looked at him in confusion.

"You skirt whole decades and life histories, you hesitate to pin down dates and times, you make illusory comments or references to long ago, many decades, a long, long time, more years than I can count… what is it? You hoard time and refuse to let it loose on the rest of us? It's like you have a lock on time and we have to fit into your time constraints."

"Rodane, want to know what will settle all your concerns and qualms?"

"What? I'm looking forward to it."

"Time" he opened his mouth to retort, couldn't help but laugh and they both laughed together and she looked at her watch,

"Oh Lordy, I've got to get Hallie home to get her to sleep for school tomorrow. I've already let her stay two days with Sophia so she needs to make up a lot. I will talk to you more Rodane. I think it is imperative we keep in touch but stay in contact with Sabina. Tell her and Suri I'm working on getting some answers and solving some riddles. I'll meet with her this week sometime."

"You'll meet with her? You're going to Italy?" she looked embarrassed that she had let something slip.

"I'll meet with her online and get some answers from her and share our conversation. She's in France by the way, not Italy."

"France? What's she doing... never mind I know... with time."

"Ghrrr", he almost growled. Cornelia moved to hug him, surprising him for a few seconds, "Welcome to the 'family' Rodane." she took her wine glass and left as quickly as she had come.

When Rodane went downstairs, most people had left and the servers were moving through the rooms cleaning up, collecting glasses and food trays. Noise from the kitchen let him know the place was being cleaned and organized and before long Caroline and Sophia would be here alone and he wasn't sure if he should leave or not. He saw two people sitting in the family room with Sophia so he moved to join them.

"Daddy" Sophia ran to him and practically jumped into his arms, "Philip brought me some new books. Look!"

"Let's take a look Pumpkin. He went over and put out his hand to Phillip and apparently Willow, his mother. They shook hands and everyone sat down together while Rodane shared Sophia's new books with her. He looked over and saw two suitcases next to the door. Philip saw him looking and said, "Caroline is okay with us staying here for a few days and we thought we could be of some help in giving her some peace of mind about being here alone. Is that okay with you Professor Arcos?"

"If you call me Professor Arcos one more time Phillip, we're going to…" he was about to say come to blows but he saw the look on Sophia's face and said, "have you sitting in my class and listening to my lectures."

Sophia snorted at that, "Philip, you would be asleep before the lecture was over. I know I've gotten a few lectures from my dad and they're… awful. Sorry Dad." He smiled at her and tousled her hair.

Willow said, "We won't be in anyone's way but we have something we need to discuss with you."

"Let me get Caroline" Rodane said. "Philip I'm very happy you're staying here. I was wondering how I could juggle all the…"

"Consider all the balls in the air. We'll stay as long as we need to but we had a couple of ideas we wanted to run by Caroline."

As he said that, she entered the room carrying Max, "Oho, who do we have here" Philip asked.

Sophia bounded over to her mom and gathered Max into her arms. He began instantly to purr, "Mrs. Moore brought Max over for Sophia so she would have some familiar company for a few days. They're tightly squeezed into two motel rooms for a while so it was a relief to her. Max is delighted, as you can see."

"Willow said, "Max is a good judge of character." he was lying in Sophia's arms like a baby and his purring could be heard across the room.

Philip said, "Excuse me, something to attend to..." and left the room. Caroline spoke to Rodane, "You're going to think I'm not in my right mind but I've agreed with Philip and Willow to...," she looked over at Sophia, "get a dog". Sophia's eyes grew large and round and glistening. Her color heightened then a smile slowly grew on her face until it covered her whole shining self. She must have squeezed Max because he leapt from her arms with a loud protest and sprang to the carpet. He kneaded the carpet and Caroline suppressed a cringe but then he moved to the front door and planted himself in front of it like a Praetorian Guard.

At that moment, lights went on outside, two on the front and one over the driveway, above the garage. They were bright and lit up the window like daylight. Caroline moved to shut the blinds as Phillip came in from the kitchen with a small, remote controller in his hand. He gave it to Caroline, "We've put lights out back and front and a new security system is being installed tomorrow. It's a motion sensor system as well as camera, mounted between the lights over the door and over the garage. I'll set up the monitors in your room, Caroline and we"ll both test them out later to make sure you can use them correctly."

Rodane breathed a sigh of relief and he saw Caroline's face register the same expression as what he was feeling. The lights went off outside.

"They'll only go on if there is motion up to twenty feet away from the house. It's also hooked up to an outside alarm which makes a hell of a noise, if activated. Tomorrow it will all be connected to a security service that will be alerted if lights, siren, or monitor activity is spotted or should they spot something suspicious and be tripped."

"Well Philip, I do believe you've thought of everything," Rodane said. "I'm very grateful to you and your mom for being here."

Culvert—9:30 p.m. Virginia

Down at the culvert, a car sat, motor silent, while the three people inside of it listened to the conversation taking place inside the house. The electronics Lexus had purchased worked well and he felt great satisfaction in knowing exactly what was going on in the house and who was there.

Zoe said, "Lexus, Willow and Phillip are in there. They know us. There won't be any chance to get in there tonight and they'll be on guard for us."

"If we don't go in tonight, we fail. There will be an alarm when we even approach that house by tomorrow and we lose any advantage we still have and now there might be a dog there, by tomorrow maybe, who might bark or alert."

Renata spoke up, "Not necessarily. There's always a time slot when new security service has glitches to iron out false alarms and power surges. That can knock out service for minutes or longer. If we can cause one or two false alarms, it will make them complacent when they go off tomorrow. Willow and Phillip should be gone by then, probably too far to return at each glitch as it occurs. I can handle Sophia, Lexus if you can handle Caroline. Zoe can be prepared to take over with Sophia while we get what we need from Caroline…" she looked at Zoe, staring at her with a good deal of animosity.

"Don't worry. Nothing is going to happen to Sophia. Don't get your panties in a bunch about it."

"Oh yeah, what about Caroline?" Zoe asked. "Is she on your DND list or are there no restrictions in getting what you want?"

"That's going to depend on her, isn't it Zoe?" Lexus snapped.

Renata said, "Wait here and don't get out of the car." She left the car and made her way in the dark toward Caroline and Sophia's house. Zoe sat back and felt her stomach shift and her brain begin to muddle with confusion as to what she truly felt.

Chapter 31

Soleux, France

Across the pond, otherwise called the Atlantic Ocean, outside of Amiens, France, six of the fifteen council members had gathered for their council meeting. The small town of Soleux in France had a few things to make it remarkable for people to visit but only those who knew the obscure draw of Soleux. It was close to four miles north of Paris and not a usual site for tourists or strangers. There existed a commune on the river, known to all who lived within a twenty mile radius of Soleux itself. They arrived at a chateau that claimed to be built in the fifteenth century with room enough for at least two hundred people in the château itself, together with all the outlying buildings. The draw to outside tourists is the Museum Picardie, which carries collections of artifacts and antiquities from prehistory to the 19th century.

Unknown to the locals, the Chateau had a unique feature known only to the Council and those they trusted. Over the last few centuries design changes had occurred slowly, and largely by hand, that enlarged the dungeon and gave over to renovations that went down rather than up and out. It encompassed four floors with a mechanical elevator on a pulley system that would function despite loss of electricity or any generated power. There were meeting quarters with every convenience for a lengthy stay, separate bedrooms, similar to monastic cells for one or two people. There were meeting rooms small and large, where soundproofing kept all outside interference stymied, where lead- lined walls prevented use of any electronic devices, even satellite tracking.

There were kitchen facilities, communal bathrooms with showers, where water was supplied by a gravity flow system and heating was geothermal and solar powered to produce light. Fresh air was gathered from generators spaced in sheds around the chateau with an energy system that was silent and not dependent on fossil fuels. A huge pantry held food reserves and liquids that could span decades.

There was a research lab that covered the entire second level below the dungeon. The latest and best equipment was purchased from European companies whose excellent equipment brought the highest prices for the best results. There were contamination, detoxification and contagion facilities to prevent any crossovers from one experiment leaking results or being affected by others that were not connected. Half of the fourth underground floor was given over to a huge meeting room with a round table that had chairs for up to twenty people. Each place had an Ergonomic chair for comfort, a computer setup complete with backup and face to face camera inset. There was a built in light system as well as a mini fridge at each station between two places where they had access to drink and food throughout long conference sessions. The other half of the floor contained an in ground lap pool, a hot tub, a sauna and a massage center, holding five tables. There was a holographic room with chairs and headphones and the capability with eye visors and wire hook ups to transport the ones using it to any of a dozen different geographic and holographic scenarios for programed time limits up to sixty minutes.

This was not the only place built for the 'families' where security was beyond anything any company or government agency had, or could even hope to have, in the near future. These fortresses were found all over the globe, some more advanced than others based on when their particular 'family' had arrived in that region and had begun to set up housekeeping. Each secured location had been specifically designed to be a part of the landscape, blend in with their present surroundings with their own unique features that hid their advanced technology and avoided scrutiny of those living there at that time.

The 'family' in Soleux, having taken possession of this particular habitat since 1340, had arrived right before the spread of the black plague through Europe from 1342 to 1346. As the disease spread over the next few years, knowing they had to save themselves from contagion and interaction with the villages and manors around them was a dicey proposition. They had built three simple houses each, to house a total of thirty people in three spots as close to the river as they could chance. They took in food reserves to avoid market places in the town. They put in a gravity flow water system and rain water barrels, designed traps around the entire compound to catch rats and burned out any nests they found. By June of the Year 1348, the plague had invaded the entire valley where they lived and no matter what precautions they had in place, they lost three of their own before they had grown and reproduced a stable vaccine against it with many fails and finally success.

The plague burned itself out generally by 1353 and in their locale, with a vaccine created by them, by 1350. All the people in their village and surrounding countryside had been vaccinated, with the cure having been put into their drinking water from the town well in the center. The women in the compound were exhausted from treating all of the sick with the entire town's death toll limited to sixteen people; ten adults and six children.

Somehow the villagers had come to the conclusion that the 'family' that lived near the river was responsible for their welfare and their own safety. They were eternally grateful that they had escaped the same ravages as other villages they had heard about being totally decimated. For the next three centuries, the villagers, their future generations and the 'family' had shared a close-knit partnership where loyalty was sacrosanct and the lives of the villagers were inextricably connected to the 'families' descendants.

Their children were groomed to act as their gardeners, cooks, secretaries, their lawyers in time of legal difficulty, their bankers, accountants, daycare providers, and teachers. The family paid for their education, training in medicine, or business, culinary arts, landscaping, computer technology, University degrees, anything needed to make sure their partnership was based on cooperation and trust.

No one outside of their villages and then their towns over a period of time understood the links but were jealous they couldn't experience the same benefits. Over time it was forgotten what had pulled them together but they never lost the underlying trust that bound villages or townspersons now with the 'family' members they saw so infrequently. 'Family' had only to ask and all things were done to help them, work for them, look out for their safety and provide security and surveillance to protect their secrecy and their persons.

Four people hovered around the doorway leading into the main conference room. Evangela, Egan, Acacia and Nikos were catching up on events and life milestones they hadn't had time or opportunity to keep up with for quite some time. Inside at the table, Suri and Alysia had a stack of folders and binders in front of them and were going over spreadsheets spilled all over the table. Their computers were opened with the same spreadsheets open on screen and projected on a whiteboard on the wall across from them.

Alysia looked over at the group chatting in the doorway, "Should we let him know what we found?" She waited for Suri to think it through,

"Who… Nikos? He already knows what we've uncovered. He helped me download all the files that pertained to our budget and their assets, took us over an hour to unlock them. We're not even sure we identified all of them. There are hundreds to go through. "No, not Nikos," Alysia looked over to her, "I was talking about Egan."

Suri glanced at him and away again, "I don't think we have to do that just yet. It could all be a miscommunication or a flaw in the program. We need time to find proof and eliminate any chance of jumping to conclusions. There's too much riding on this."

Egan looked over their way, saw them looking and waved to them. Suri smiled and waved back. He walked over, "Hi, just got here, had a delayed flight out of Heathrow. I went on standby and took the next plane and had to change planes in Frankfurt but still made good time. Suri got up and gave him a hug. Alysia stood there and smiled shyly.

"Hello, Alysia. I understand we have you to thank for getting help to our latest find in Greece. Good work."

"Glad you didn't think I was overstepping my bounds and encroaching on your jobs, Petrus' and yours."

"Good Heavens no, we were so swamped with MI6 that we didn't even get the request till you had already done your magic. Just happy you were able to keep them safe and sound, especially the newest member of our family."

"I don't know how you and Petrus manage to do your job in London and still are able to juggle all of our concerns. It was a real headache taking care of just one problem"

"Alysia, if you want to come to our offices, we'd be happy to have you intern with us and learn the ropes. What say you?" he gave her a half salute.

Suri stepped in, "Oh no you don't. I've just now gotten her adapted to her new position in finances. She's not going anywhere for a while. She smiled at Alysia to soften the edict. Evangela and Acacia came over and hugged Suri,

"How's the setting up going? Need any help?"

"I thought you'd never ask. We have two people making up fifteen rooms over the next two days and the chef hasn't arrived so we need a cook.

Acacia smiled, "What, you want me to cook? You must be desperate!" Evangela laughed.

Nikos and Egan joined the group and Nikos looked up at the whiteboard and then to Suri, "We're ready to start sharing information?" he asked frowning.

"Oh, good heavens, no! Alysia and I were just going over some files we were confused about before. I wanted to make sure I wasn't missing anything."

Nikos said, "And were you? Missing anything? I could help you if you like. I have loads of free time for the next two or three days until everyone else arrives."

"Well, now that you mention it…" Suri paused and Nikos smiled,

"You can put all the folders together and get the conference carols all set up. There's a great deal to do for fifteen individuals between now and when everyone else arrives. I'll give you a list and you have free reign on the mini-fridge to put in snacks and drinks."

Nikos looked crestfallen for an instant and almost annoyed. Suri quickly said,

"But that's fine if you have something else in mind. I don't want to burden you with all these tasks of minutiae."

"No" Nikos answered with a smile, "That's fine. Just give me your list and I'll have Egan help me, right Egan?"

8 a.m. Virginia

The next morning, Phillip and Willow were up early, made coffee and Willow made pancakes and bacon for everyone. She made Sophia's pancakes in the shape of Mickey Mouse and Donald Duck. She had done the same for her two boys while they were little till they complained it took too long and they were starving. Philip looked over and smiled at her, "Still got the knack?"

"Something you never lose Phillip while there are still children around."

Philip said, "I could have slept in this morning. How many times did those alarms go off? I stopped counting after three and slipped into a coma."

"Three was all but then the police showed up to make sure everything was okay. They got a phone call from two neighbors who complained they couldn't get any sleep because the alarms were worse than if they were actual burglars. They claimed there were people crawling all over the yards."

"I checked everything over twice after the second time they tripped and I couldn't find a thing wrong. Maybe I've got the signal too strong and it was sensing a rabbit or a deer or something else moving around."

"Well after you get home with Sophia and her new friend, we'll go over the diagnostics with a fine-tooth comb and try tonight to make sure the hookups are functional before we send the direct signal to the security service."

Sophia came into breakfast almost skipping, a bounce in her step and a grin on her face.

"A dog and Mickey Mouse pancakes all in one day, I've died and gone to heaven…" her face fell, "I didn't mean that. I wasn't talking about Adam…" and she burst into tears. Willow put down the spatula and walked to her and pulled her into her arms,

"Honey, no one would think that. We all know how much Adam and you loved each other. I think he would have liked Mickey Mouse pancakes too."

Sophia looked at her and gave a small smile, "Yeah he would. He even made them for me."

"Well, I don't know if I like to be in a competition with another pancake maker."

Sophia sat down and started in on her first pancake, "No competition here, you win!" she smiled for real this time.

They finished their breakfast and headed out to a kennel in Arlington to check out their newest family member. Phillip, Caroline and Sophia all crowded anxiously into the car, equipped now, with a blanket and some treats for puppies on the back seat. Sophia was immersed in her tablet with her earphones for the whole trip. They kept up small talk and Caroline was airing her reservations in having a dog in the house for the very first time. Phillip finally said after all the complaints had been lodged, "Mom, you know don't you, that having a dog in the house increases Serotonin and also allows the children in the house to develop their social skills more easily and sooner?"

"You made that up!" Caroline said.

Philip answered, "Well I'm not sure about the Serotonin..." he looked sideways at her..."but I can attest that social skills are definitely, positively, affected by the presence of a dog in the family. Caroline was silent for a moment and then said, "Huh!"

When they reached a dusty, rural road that opened up to a small, tidy farmhouse and a small barn turned into kennels, they were shown to the back of the kennels to a room reserved for 'meet and greet' of possible adoptions. The door opened and a tech brought in a thirty pound bundle of black and tan fur, with long floppy ears and even longer legs. Caroline gaped and said, "This is a puppy?" The tech said proudly, "Six weeks old today!"

Sophia walked up to him and said, "You have a long nose."

He looked at her, dropped to the floor and sat gazing at her, turning his head from side to side as if trying to translate her words into dog.

She sat on the floor next to him and put out her hand, "Hi I'm Sophia."

This solid, quivering bundle of fur reached out his paw to her, gazing up at her with liquid brown eyes and an actual grin on his muzzle.

"I've never seen anything like this..." the tech whispered.

"You've never seen my daughter at work and she is definitely working here" Caroline spoke with pride in her voice, "I think we have a dog."

They took him home with Sophia sitting in the back, and her friend next to her, lying on the back seat atop the blanket, with a treat between his paws, like a small toy. He put his head between his paws, gave out a loud sigh and promptly fell asleep with his head butted up against Sophia's leg. She placed her hand on his head and both of them slept the whole way home. Philip drove silently the entire way home, lost in his own thoughts. Every once in a while he viewed all of them from the rear view mirror.

Virginia

The motel was a seedy, dilapidated row of rooms next to the highway, advertising room rates for the day or week to make up for little traffic from the highway. It was cheap, not too dirty, definitely off the beaten track and anonymous. Renata, Zoe and Lexus spent a stressful, tense day in the motel room with the AC giving off minimum cool air and their paranoia heating up by the hour. Little conversation led Zoe to go for two long walks during the day, despite warnings by Lexus to stay hidden. Lexus was getting sicker by the day. His skin was yellow, his cheeks sunken but red from fever, and his gate was wobbly at times. When he went to the bathroom to relieve himself, they could hear his groans from outside.

Renata's plans seemed to pose a possible solution to getting into the Arcos house. She had tripped the alarm twice and crawled away into the Moore's backyard where there was little to no light to expose her. Then she made her way back to the car. They would doze a little for a short time and then she would repeat her reconnoitering. The third time she was almost seen by the young man who raced out the door from the house, fast. She barely got around the garage and out of sight across the street. Lights went on and she had to climb fences and crawl through the drainage ditch to reach the car. They waited an hour before they left and made their way to the motel that Zoe had scoped out on her laptop. They paid cash, ate energy bars and had bottled water for the last seventeen hours. They took turns napping throughout the early morning so they would be functional for the evening.

At dusk they would set out for Caroline's house and a final showdown where Lexus was determined to extract all the information he needed to send a complete file back to Theras Gallo. He wanted to be paid, he wanted recognition for the good work he had done and he wanted to make Caroline and Sophia Arcos pay for the three most miserable weeks he had experienced during his entire career with the Gallo organization.

Surprisingly Renata was totally on board with all this even though Zoe was silent then derogatory toward him. The bitch! She didn't understand how they all looked down at him because he hadn't had what they had. He couldn't help where he came from, who he had lived with. It was unfair and he would show them he was as good as them, even better.

{I'll show all of you}

They went in two cars, the one Renata drove that she had rented when her plane landed and Lexus' car with all their things loaded in his trunk. Lexus planned to get out of the neighborhood with Caroline and take her to the warehouses near the docks where noise would not be noticed. Depending on how it went, he could leave her there after they had gotten her to give them all she knew about Rodane or just leave her there. Either way she would no longer be a problem. As far as Sophia went, who cared? He wouldn't hurt her on purpose but if she became a problem, who knew?

Zoe was silent, nauseated, fearful and so angry that their assignment had gone so badly and their partnership had become so toxic and the outlook so precarious. She looked out the window, watched the streets become an open road, past small developments, some horse farms, with open fields and few stores or businesses on either side of the road. They came to a crossroads and it all began again, a few small stores here and there, then developments, an industrial park with warehouses and the view of the water off to the left near piers and boat houses. The air had become colder and noise was lessoned with lack of houses and businesses.

Lexus slowed down as they came close to Caroline's neighborhood and when they turned down her street he coasted the last block to the culvert and turned around and stopped. Renata pulled in behind him.

Renata took in a deep breath, opened her car door and moved quietly over to Lexus' car. She leaned in his open window, "When I get to the yard and trip the alarm, wait till the lights go back off and then move to the backyard. I'll meet you there and get us into the house. It will be completely dark inside so remember the layout of the kitchen and the hallway. Lexus, you remember?"

"Yes, I remember it well."

"Then we go to the master bedroom, put the sedative into Caroline's neck, hold her down and quiet till she's out, then we get her to your car and you take her to the industrial park. I'll follow and then I go to New York to your condo, you do your thing and then meet me there, agreed? Are we clear?"

Lexus growled, "Am I stupid?" his breathing was heavy and his voice was guttural, "you do your part…I'll take care of the rest."

Zoe spoke "Are you sure about this? What if they don't turn off the alarm system like you're figuring?"

"I'm willing to bet that no one wants to antagonize their neighbors two nights in a row or lose a night's sleep themselves. We've done this before and it's a charm."

{third time's a charm or an unlucky number}

Inside the house, Caroline had tucked Sophia and Beaker in bed. She smiled at the fur ball with a nose the size of the Muppets creature he was named for and closed the door over. Beaker whined and she pushed the door open a little and looked at him sitting up on the bed.

"Shush Beaker, time for sleep. She went to close the door and he woofed softly at her, "He wants the door open a little mama."

"No trouble going to sleep if you hear talking Sophia?"

"No Mama, I'll be fine." Caroline shook her head gently but left the door open a smidge.

Philip was in the family room watching a soccer match On Demand. Willow had gone to her room to make some calls. Caroline headed to the kitchen to set things out for breakfast to save time the next morning. They planned on going to the vets to register Beaker, get him microchipped and register him for behavior training. Sophia had objected to the behavior training saying, "If I'm his owner and his leader, shouldn't I be the one to train him Mama?" Willow had explained that she would be the trainer with other owners and their dogs in a group, led by a licensed trainer who would teach Sophia how to use hand signals as well as voice commands.

Time passed as each person in the house relaxed from the long day and went about their business. Caroline was the first one to see the lights go on from the back and then the sirens went off and the lights tripped in the front as well. They were so bright you could see into the living room of the house across the street. Philip jumped off the sofa, went to the monitors in Caroline's room and looked at three screens and saw nothing, not even a squirrel. He then checked doors and windows throughout the house and again found nothing. He came out of Caroline's room and almost tripped over Beaker sitting in the hallway facing the kitchen and whining. Sophia was standing in her doorway rubbing her eyes from sleep.

Philip looked to where Beaker was looking and back at Beaker and said, "Yeah you think so too, don't you boy? I'm with you. Think we'll turn off the noise though, huh?"

He used the controller to turn off all security functions and took a walk around the house and yard to check it out. He stood for a moment in the backyard, looking toward the Moore's house where ladders were still against the house and the shadow looked like a stairway going to the roof and beyond. He heard a noise near the property line and even took a step toward it but stopped when a cat ran out from under the ladder and took off across the lawn. "Damn cats!" he said loudly then walked back to the house. Caroline waited at the door and Willow stood behind her and Sophia was tucked in again.

"Philip, we can't let the system do this for another night. The neighbors will have a conniption and a for sale sign on our lawn in the morning. Can you blame them?"

"Okay, we'll leave it off for tonight and tomorrow I'll get the installation company out here first thing and we'll do what we need to and fix it. I've tried everything I can to spot a flaw but no luck."

"Well I'm certainly ready for a good night's sleep." Caroline took the controller and headed for her room.

She turned and said, "Come on Beaker, let's go to bed." He sat there in the hallway and looked at her and looked at Phillip then he plopped down in the hallway, put his head between his paws and let out of sigh.

Philip said, "Maybe it's cooler here in the hall."

"Okay pup, you sleep here tonight."

An hour went by and the clock ticking on the mantelpiece and a gentle whir from the refrigerator was the only sound heard then Beaker lifted his head, gave out a low wine and then stood up. The lock on the kitchen door clicked then began to ease open. A low, guttural growl started in his throat and he gave off a shiver. A dark form, small and compact, entered the kitchen and a taller form followed behind. They moved easily as if knowing where furniture might impede their progress. Then a third, small form came last and hesitated in the doorway. The lights stayed off. No siren to be heard, the door didn't squeak, the tile was solid with no creaks heard. Two of them began to move toward the hall and Caroline's bedroom.

Beaker stood straight up and let out one bark, high and sharp. They froze in their tracks. The form in front took the flashlight in hand and raised it up as if holding a club. Beaker backed away… two steps, then three and began barking in earnest. A light went on in Caroline's bedroom and footsteps sounded on the steps.

Without warning, Sophia appeared sleepily in her doorway, rubbing her eyes and talking to Beaker as if to a child, "Now you know you'll get in trouble if Mama doesn't get her beauty sleep, right Beaker?" she looked at the two dark shapes in the hall, "and you know you shouldn't be here." she looked straight at Lexus, dressed in black with a face mask on and taller than the other two in a child's voice with an adult's wisdom.

She said, "Is this what that TV show means by 'returning to the scene of the crime?' "

Caroline came out of her room at that minute, saw the two figures in the dark from the back light in her bedroom. Philip appeared at the base of the stairs at that same exact moment and had a baseball bat in his hand. His mother was on the step behind him, eyes narrowed, lips thinned and Phillip spoke first, "So, you decided to see what more damage you could do?"

Lexus had his mask over his face and all that could be seen were his two eyes, feverish and manic. He pulled out his knife, the form behind him gasped, said 'No' so softly it might have been missed. Renata came two steps closer and Caroline jerked her arm out, stepped from the room and stood in front of Sophia, "Don't you come one step closer, bitch!"

Renata jerked still. She was covered head to foot in black with no discernible telltale traits that showed. She laughed softly and it raised the hair on Beaker's body. He moved one step toward her and put his head down and growled deep in his throat, his eyes positively glittering. Renata stepped back a step...that was her mistake. Beaker sprang without warning, grabbed her in a vice grip between his sizable jaws and bit down on the inner part of her thigh. She squealed and swung her flashlight at Beaker's head. It hit with a resounding 'thud'. Beaker yelped and let loose. Lexus took his knife and raised it high toward Caroline but the narrowness of the hallway impeded his forward move.

Phillip came up behind him and swung the baseball bat, cracking it across his right forearm and the break could be heard distinctly by all of them. He let out a yell and turned to face Philip.

Sophia yelled, "Don't you dare hurt him, you jerk!" and she started screaming.

Lexus' right arm was hanging uselessly down by his side. He switched the knife to his other hand and started toward Philip again, rage and pain evident from his groans. Willow turned to Renata and snapped out, "I've called 9-1-1, they're on their way" and they could hear sirens moving toward the house. The figure in the doorway turned abruptly away, and ran out the kitchen door. Sophia watched her leave without a word. Renata and Lexus looked once at each other, turned and followed close behind. The door slammed on their exit. Beaker was laying in the hallway whimpering.

Caroline bent down over him, "It's okay boy, you did an awesome job!"

She stood up and said, "There's an emergency vets five minutes down the road. I can't go and leave Sophia.

Willow spoke up, "I'll go, just tell me where. We have to go before the police get here." They heard a car blow past the house and then another, peeling out and racing up the street. Philip and Willow got Beaker into the back seat of Caroline's car and Sophia stood in the front doorway, anxious and trembling. Caroline put her arm around her and spoke "It will be okay Sophia, it will be okay."

"Mama, it will be okay for Beaker. He'll be fine but the lady he bit...she won't be fine and I'm glad."

JOURNEY TO THE BLUE PLANET

6 a.m.—France

Aldora heard the phone through a thin fog. Her usual rising time was 7:30 but she and Theras had attended a political function the night before and stayed out late. Then when they had returned home he had been in an amorous mood so they stayed up even later. He wasn't always eager for sex but when he was, she never put him off or begged off. She had to admit he was a good lover. That was one of the perks she received to have convinced her to work for him for so long. She reached out to the other side to jostle Theras and the sheets were cool. She opened her eyes and then heard the shower. He was up early and she had to think of what day it was for a second or two. Her momentary confusion told her it was not a work day or she would not have accepted the tickets for last night. She received quite a few free gifts; to concerts, benefits, fundraisers, parties. She knew it was all because she worked for Theras and the complimentary gifts were a way to try and obsequiously get money from him through her. If he thought the entire city was unaware of their personal relationship, she would let him go on thinking that. It made it that much easier to control those who thought they were using her and for her to control Theras.

She picked up the phone just as Theras came out dripping from the shower. For a man his age he was solid, muscular and very fit. She smiled at him as he walked over to the bed, kissed her softly on the lips and reached for the phone and pushed speaker. There was never any fear or reason for him to keep anything from her. She had become inextricably bound up with all his affairs and businesses, personal and public. He had no idea she was aware of the other women he gifted with his charms and his wealth and she planned on keeping it that way.

"Speak" One word and it would be enough to make even her quake.

"Mr. Gallo, we contacted the rest home as you asked and there is no record of Renata Kappos being in residence there or even having registered. We're not sure where to begin tracing her whereabouts now."

"Goddammit, I've given you people enough business over the years for you to figure out where she is. How could you not know where she is? That's what I pay you for."

"We've got two people on it now and we'll..."

"You'll find her, that's what you'll do and within the hour or there will be your heads everyone is looking for!"

"Yes sir, we'll call you as soon as we've located her."

He threw the phone across the room and it hit the wooden French doors and bounced on the carpet. He stood there naked, taking deep breaths to calm himself, glaring at nothing.

{you're close to losing it aren't you}

She pushed the cover back and went to him, keeping her face inscrutable. She stood in front of him, touched his cheek gently then went over and picked up the phone. She looked at it and tapped a contact.

"It's Aldora," Theras looked over at her questioningly.

"We have a problem Security seems unable to solve." She talked for a few seconds, giving whoever was on the phone a very rapid run down of the situation, said 'yes' a couple of times and disconnected.

"Who was that Aldora?" He sounded accusing and he frowned at her. She tilted her head and raised her eyebrows.

Theras, his face relaxed, said, "Acteon" and she nodded.

"He went to her and folded her against his still wet body. The moisture seeped through her thin nightgown.

"This is getting out of hand. Rodane Arcos has been quite the challenge to me lately. It's like the gods got together and decided it was time for one huge joke to be played on me.

She stepped back, "Theras, Rodane is one man and this…"

"This is mine. That's what this is!" His voice rose to a low roar, "I've worked too hard to have any young upstart come in and wipe it all away. I'll be damned if I allow him and I'll die making sure I have done anything to protect what's mine!"

{you may have to}

"Are you sure he even wants to? He may not even know that he's…"

"He knows! Good Christ how could he not? He's been with that bitch and there's no possibility he hasn't been told."

"What, you think Sabina would…"

He roared, "No for Christ's sake! Not Sabina, Agatha!"

He spit the word out of his mouth. His skin was now dry from the anger and rage he was exhibiting.

{need to calm you down}

She put her hands on his arms and said softly, "What can I do to help? Tell me love." He gripped her shoulders, his eyes glazed and dark, his breath slowing down but deeply whistling out his nose. She felt his erection against her and she knew what help that would be. He clamped his hand around the back of her neck, pulled her face to his and locked his lips over hers, pushing his tongue like a knife into her mouth. He walked her backwards a few steps to their bed and pushed her onto it with himself gripping her nightgown and ripping it off from the shoulders, hurting her. She found herself and her body answering him. His kisses were then all over her warm body and she felt the warmth reaching from inside through her belly. She opened her legs willingly and gripped him tightly around the shoulders and pulled him in. He took both breasts, one after the other, squeezing until she was panting as he thrust rapidly, hard, harder and she arched her neck and cried out at the same time as he made one final thrust and collapsed against her, his heart hammering against her as much as her belly was clenching and unclenching with her own orgasm.

His climax seemed to be equal to the climax of his rage and anger. It expelled with his own fluid into her, the brunt of his rage, masqueraded as love or sex. Quite funny actually! Love and rage were now tied together no matter what the philosophers might quibble about.

{another meltdown avoided}

They lay there for only seconds till she felt his heart slow down and then he rolled off of her and lay quietly. He spoke just as quietly "I have a very hard decision to make Aldora. It's not one I look forward to having to make but all this…" He spread his hands as if measuring the room, encompassing all of his businesses, his wealth, his minions, his world…

"All this is at stake. I won't have him be the successor to what I have. I won't! I can't! It would all be for nothing.

{this is not the time to ask you who}

She took her hand and rubbed it soothingly over his chest, twined her fingers into the abundant patch of dark and graying hair he was enormously proud of,

"Acteon will have this sorted out very soon. You know you can trust him."

Almost as if Acteon was privy to their conversation, the phone rang and startled them both.

"Well, at least I don't have to get a new phone," he said sheepishly and grinned at her. He connected and said,

"Yes? Oh, Acteon. Yes." He listened for a few seconds. She couldn't hear the conversation and she chafed at the fact that he didn't put it on speaker.

"Well, thank the gods for that. Now what will… of course I do. You get word by any means to her to get her ass back here to France on the very next flight out. Nope! She flies by paying her own way. Our little Miss Independent is going to learn very quickly that when I want something done, there is no other response except to do it. Call me as soon as you know."

He hung up, walked to the French doors and stood looking out at the courtyard and the fountain. He opened the door and walked out onto the balcony, buck naked. His lack of self-consciousness had charmed her at first, until she realized it was just one more example of his arrogance and his understanding that he stood above all moral or social restrictions that mere mortals, in his estimation, were guided and controlled by those same mores.

She got up from the bed, walked over to him but stood behind, away from sight. She rested her hand on his shoulder and leaned her face against his back, soothing him like a pet. He spoke with more calm,

"It seems our young protégé Renata, has taken it upon herself to ignore my wishes. She did not go to the rest home I told her to and instead returned to her village and stayed there for five days."

Aldora chanced to comment, "Wouldn't that be just as restful, for her to be with her family?"

"Not when it opens Pandora's Box and makes her privy to information we've kept hidden from her all these years. Now she's decided to fix our problem herself and has flown to Virginia to take care of it on her own with no permission to do any such thing."

"How did you learn of this?"

Aldora still, after all this time with Theras, didn't have enough knowledge of his doings and his people that he could count on and she needed to know.

"Acteon has many contacts in a great number of places where no one could possibly believe they could be a threat or a spy. They fit in quite nicely in areas where I have my concerns. As you might guess Aldora, I keep tabs on my daughter and my granddaughter, as well as anyone who is an integral part of their lives. I couldn't do that if I didn't have an extensive network of my people in all the different places where they live and work. The same can be said for Rodane and his new 'family' now."

{I've got to find out where and who}

Aldora showered and dressed and when she came out of the bedroom Theras had left for the office. She gathered all her things and started out. She had one last thing to do though. She took out her own phone, coded and encrypted, and made a call.

Not more than an hour away, the Council members were having a late breakfast or brunch. They had convened around 9 o'clock and started working out a schedule for the upcoming meeting. It had been forty-nine years since the council had been in session. They hadn't lost anyone to death since then from sickness or natural death but they had added a few younger people to replace two members lost five years ago in the El Salvador incursion. A great deal happens on a planet the size of Earth over a span of forty-nine years.

Each member on the Council, fifteen in all, with Agatha being an honorary sixteenth, had been given a particular segment of the family's holdings and fortunes to present to them. It included Science and Technology, communication, finance and Investments, 'family' member's status, especially their employment and their skill levels. One segment was to be presented by Raul from Spain concerning their descendants and the possible names and locations of 'family' members heretofore not identified or newly identified. Another segment was devoted to alerting the council to recent discoveries in Archaeology and Anthropology so they could plan the upcoming travels and employment of the R and R's they had among them, the recovery or removal experts. Sabina was scheduled to be there for that sometime after they had all settled in and done a great deal of sharing and investigating using all their information. A report was to be presented sharing all the demographics that had changed the 'family's lives and situations over forty-nine years, an enormous task with the growth of countries and cities all over the world.

There was one member whose job it was to present the topographical and geological happenings over the years; natural earthquakes, tsunamis, plates shifting studies, Arctic and Antarctic studies of climatological significance and ocean studies also. There were other reports as well but among the most important would be scientific breakthroughs in medicine and pharmaceuticals. Everyone was pretty much up-to-date on surgical advancements and genetic testing but it was the smaller breakthroughs they were interested in, those done by private companies with no connection to any 'family' business. It wouldn't be wise to not investigate every possible new tool or organism that might lead to vaccines or immunizations against some of the worst raging diseases left on this planet.

This new century was not the time to introduce anything that could not possibly be related to present methods and materials. There was too much scrutiny and too many conspiracy nuts Skyping and tweeting and pinning. They shared every detail of every happening, large and small as if the world turned on knowing the smallest details of what you had for breakfast or your dog's latest trick. People instagrammed every possible event and happening, cameras invaded every corner of buildings and roads and streets, hackers leaked all kinds of confidential information out to the whole world on media.

Putting something new into the present system, that earth's own scientists could not possibly replicate or duplicate was asking for investigation, questions, accusations and theories that might hit too close to their own holdings or labs or their own scientists in those labs. All work had to be done by the book, with evidence and measurements. They needed proven results, transparency in the testing and qualified people whose work could not be disputed or discounted. So far so good up to now.

But fifty years of time apart from each other took them back to mid and late 1960's, the still early days of the Space Program, the days and decades when artery bypasses were new and just beginning to be tried like stents and shunts. The first heart transplant was done in December of 1967 in South Africa by Dr. Christiaan Barnard, at Groote Schuur Hospital, Cape Town and began a series of enormous changes in heart care.

Brain mapping was created, the means to perform this skill by a neurosurgeon having theorists warn against creating robotic people or brainwashed idiots. Palliative care started instead of useless experimentation of drugs that kept someone comatose until dead. Naysayers wanted to end the space program before it actually accomplished its goal because of a fire in a capsule that killed the three astronauts inside. A probe landed on the moon and a Russian cosmonaut was killed in the landing because they were foolishly racing without tested equipment to catch up to the United States.

They had a very real scare of discovery when Pulsars were discovered by a physicist in Cambridge and it was pure luck they were able to insert themselves into the research and lead them toward rotating neutron stars, rather than radio waves. Everyone agreed at the time that with political positions of warring countries heating up, introducing any alien attempts to communicate would cause widespread panic and chaos. Forty nine years hadn't made the possibility anymore viable. Actually, the times were worse now than improving.

The book, 'The Naked Ape' posed some interesting platforms that hit a little too close to 'families' ensconced all over the globe but like most of the eye opening theses that Earth's people produced, only a small segment of the thinking population read anything groundbreaking or earthshaking into it. Like all written words that created a major stir, it lasted for a while then others books became the next best thing and thinking minds moved on. Everyone breathed a sigh of relief and felt they had dodged a bullet.

They sweated out the writings and studies of Tilly Edinger, but she passed away in May of that year and the council collected all her missing research. As of now, it was well-preserved but well-hidden. Paleo-neurology could be traced all the way back to the explosion of tools and weapons at the time of the first 'family's' arrival on the North American continent in the caldera at Yellowstone. They had warned her against posing questions in seminars and working on studies with her students and her interns. They held their breath every time she won a prize in her field because that gave rise to interviews, and TV appearances, as well as other scientist's queries. But with her passing, that became a moot issue, at least for now.

Forty-nine years ago, everyone was still fighting polio in many countries and trying to find antibiotics that could save a person with a bug bite from certain death. Bacterial infections were responsible for most deaths of the youngest and the oldest. High risk death from childbirth was becoming a thing of the past and you didn't die when you picked up a common staph infection.

Scientists in this world were helped by scientists of the 'families' placed in research labs to lead them by the nose without their realizing it to induce fertilization production by manipulation of sperm and ova.

The most impressive success they had among the 'families' was getting the scientific community to the research level where they were able to actually sequence the genome and make rapid advances in Genetics. This would serve them very well for the next fifty years. There were plans for some of their research labs to inculcate a sense of urgency to find cures for some of the most horrific diseases among men and women here, like Parkinson's disease, Alzheimer's, cerebral palsy, ALS and others. It was time to take them to the next level of giving the current human race a good chance of having a pleasant, disease-free, productive life to an old age, lots longer than sixty five or seventy at least.

Virginia

Lexus was screaming at both women in the industrial park behind a closed warehouse. The darkness was complete, the clouds hid a fingernail moon and there were no lights anywhere except on the dashboard of their cars.

"Why didn't you tell us about the others staying there? You didn't say one word about a dog already there. What's wrong with you bitch? You just fucked up any chance of getting anywhere with these people. You're an idiot!"

He had been ranting for the last ten minutes since they had high tailed it out of their development. His arm was in a made-up sling from a rag found in a trash bin and he had taken pain meds, at least four, since they had left the house where everything had gone straight to hell in just minutes.

Renata was even worse off than he was. She had been bleeding steadily since she had been bitten by Beaker, the dog from hell as she thought of him. They had tied a makeshift tourniquet around her leg but it was still seeping constantly, her color was beginning to pale and she was becoming gradually weaker and woozy.

Zoe was so undecided as to what she should do, her first impulse was to get out of there and leave them both to figure out how to fix this clusterfuck, but her feelings of loyalty to Lexus and her inbred sense of loyalty to her team kept her there listening to Lexus rant and watching Renata get steadily worse. She made up her mind on the spot and pulled out her phone,

"Who are you calling?" Lexus stopped talking and looked at her. His eyes were glittering and glazed from all the pain meds. She tapped in her contact and it rang three times. When it was answered by her superior, the inspector in the trench coat, she explained what had happened then and what the situation was now; two injured, one just along to assist with no orders. He told her where to go by car to have them picked up and by whom. Right before he hung up he told her Renata was to go immediately back to France on the first flight out.

"You realize that's impossible now?" Zoe said.

"I'm only giving you the instructions sent to me from Mr. Gallo but you do what you need to, remembering the results are on you." He disconnected, literally.

"Lexus, do you have a place where we can go? The motel is out…too many eyes around and a chance to be noticed with the shape we're in."

He thought for a minute, looked up at her with a wolfish grin on his skeletal face. He definitely was in worse shape in just the last two hours. He and Renata made it almost impossible to go out among people right now.

"Yes, I have just the place but we meet there. I'm not following you and that… idiot can't drive." Renata bared her teeth at him.

"Renata, listen to the directions or we leave you behind."

Lexus had Zoe drive and he gave directions. It took approximately an hour to wend their way to the section of Virginia where Iona had her business and her house. They parked a short way down the road and Zoe went to check out if there was anyone there at this late hour. Renata pulled in behind them with everything quiet and locked up tight. Zoe went back to the car and told Lexus it would be impossible to get in any of the buildings. Lexus just smirked at her and dragged himself out of the car.

Between the two of them they got Renata around the back of a small shed buttressed against the larger warehouse. He lifted the rake leaning against the door and they realized it was there to hold the old decaying door closed. Inside, he moved a number of long-handled gardening tools and reached to pry open an already detached plywood backing. It led into the warehouse but with a rickety set of stairs behind the walls reaching up to the loft area. It took a few minutes to get Renata up the stairs and into the small low ceiling area Lexus had been using for a few days of hiding out after he had murdered Adam.

Zoe had followed the news about Adam's death, the police investigation, the wake at Caroline's house and she thought she had learned as much about Caroline as she had Adam when she visited the gym. She kept beating herself up mentally because it only made her feel worse to think about the tragedy they had inflicted on a perfectly normal, innocent family. Sophia had to be traumatized with everything that had happened. She still saw Sophia in her mind, watching her. Her eyes had burned a hole through her when she had turned and fled their house right before the police had arrived.

How did she know it was her? Did she? Zoe thought she did.

{it was like I didn't even have on a mask}

Here they were now, stuck in a dark, dusty, sweltering hidey-hole in a warehouse; two sick people, one severely injured, pissing blood and the other having it leak out of her legs slowly but surely, her life's blood.

Lexus had one sleeping bag, a handful of fiber bars and bottles of water. He had a stand set-up at a tiny window toward the roof with an empty wooden crate to stand on. From there Zoe could see into the small house about two hundred yards away over a fence. It was a small rancher, tidy with shutters and a small garden planted out front. Looking to the left she could just catch a glimpse of the water from the marina near the river. She couldn't see anything in the dark of the other side except for the shadowy outline of a huge navy boat, maybe a destroyer, maybe a cruiser. She didn't know much about big Navy boats except they had Navy personnel on them and they probably carried guns. She climbed down and walked a few steps to Lexus sitting on the floor with one candle lit and leaning against the beam holding up part of the roof.

"Whose house is that Lexus?"

"Why ask me? It's a house."

"No, it's never that simple with you. You found this place for a reason. It's nowhere close to our assignment and you don't deviate, ever, unless there's a reason so whose is it?"

He looked at her for a few seconds but she refused to back down. He blinked first, "It's Arcos' mother's house. She lives by herself but Rodane and another woman have been staying there while he's in town and I've been monitoring all her communications to see if she will give me any info on Rodane."

"Annnnd..." Zoe asked.

"Just shit! Talk about his sister, the business, his daughter. It got so boring I gave up and ignored them. Spent a bundle on all this equipment," he waved his hand around all the monitoring equipment, "and I got squat!"

"Now what?" She looked out the window, "what do we do now? You need medical care, Lexus. You're getting sicker each day. Renata needs medical care. I don't know what to do for the bleeding and she's getting weaker. We can't leave her up here even if she were to..." she stopped.

"Die? He asked.

"Yeah, die. Any investigation into a dead body up here will send us right onto a suspect list and we'll be on the ground running."

He thought about that for a minute then he said, "What if Renata could help us get to Rodane Arcos without using Caroline or Sophia? What would you think of that?"

He watched her closely, "How?"

"Suppose we could get to Rodane without them being involved? We'd have him and not just info about him. What could be better?"

"What do we do with him? We were sent for information only. We were never instructed to hurt him or his family" she said accusingly.

Renata spoke up for the first time in hours, "We were to find a way to stop him in his tracks. I don't think Mr. Gallo will care if we use the opportunity to stop him… permanently." She stopped speaking and closed her eyes.

"Renata, you're in no shape to take down Rodane Arcos. Lexus, who else is in the house? Who else would we have to worry about besides Arcos? I don't want another repeat of our last adventure."

A phone rang. They looked at each other, surprised and anxious if anyone might be nearby, "That's my phone" Zoe said. She took her large, cloth bag and routed through it until she pulled it out. She took the call and moved away to talk without any eavesdropping. She really had no idea who it could be and if it was a surprise she didn't want two others aware of her reactions, one thing she could have control of. She turned around and spoke to Renata, "There's someone here who wants to talk to you."

Renata's eyes widened then. She felt a hot flush moving up her neck to her face as she took the phone from Zoe,

"Mr. Gallo, I know you said to come back but I…"

"Renata, listen to me, listen carefully" It was Aldora, "I have one or two minutes to talk to you, clear? Are we clear?"

"Ms. Spiteri, what do you want? Why are you…?"

"I'm calling you because I need you to back off of this, Renata. I've talked to Zoe. I know how badly things have gone in this particular assignment from the very beginning. Lexus has not done us any favors the way he has handled this whole thing but you and Zoe can still redeem yourselves and salvage some of your job. Renata, come home and I will personally explain everything to you but you cannot, let me repeat myself, you cannot kill Rodane Arcos. Do you understand? Tell me you're not stupid or foolhardy to do that."

Renata took a deep breath. Her thinking was not clear and Aldora's voice was so far away and hard to hear.

"Aldora, I keep seeing Tabor. I can't get his face out of my mind. I feel like I owe…"

"You owe him nothing! I told you that before. He brought that on himself just as Lexus is making the choices that will destroy him in the end.

Renata, come home, save yourself here and your career. You have an opportunity to do great things. Come home and let me talk to you and explain what is at stake here, please. I have to go, I'll be missed. Just think about it but don't wait too long. Here is where you go if you come home. I can meet you there. Someone will get in touch with me." She gave her the address she was to report to and then hung up. Renata stood there hurting, weak and confused.

Lexus called her and Zoe over, "Here's what we do. Rodane Arcos is not here now, I've been watching. We get his mother to call him and get him back to here. When he arrives, we finish this once and for all, take all his personal info, get out and go back to New York. We leave there to lay low for a while and send all the personal items to our inspector, whoever he is, in the trench coat. After everything blows over, we start over with a new assignment, richer and getting credit for taking down Arcos, maybe go to another state, one by the ocean.

"No one else...just Rodane Arcos and his mother, that's it? No one gets hurt?"

"Did I say that? I don't remember saying that."

Lexus limped over to the windowsill, reached underneath and pulled out a burlap wrapped bundle. When he opened it up, it was a small-caliber gun, probably a 22. Zoe sucked in her breath and Renata looked at it as if it were a living writhing snake in his hand. He looked at his watch and said, "One hour. Zoe, you need to go to the convenience store and get some stuff for me and Renata."

Reluctantly, Zoe went out and drove a quarter mile to the store where she bought gauze pads, surgical tape, more pain pills over the counter, and some snack foods and water. She drove back to the loft and thought the whole way back as to how she could extricate herself from this boondoggle. She looked at the car when she came out of the store. It was her car. She could just get in it and go. It had all their things in it. She could drive to New York by herself, clear out the condo with the rest of her things and just move out. She had enough money to buy her own place anywhere she wanted. A picture of her mother on the porch, and her brother crossing from the stables flashed across her mind. She could go home. She could make amends to her brother and help her mother out on the ranch in her old age. She shook her head. What was she thinking? How could she possibly throw away everything she had worked for years to get, walk away and return to what she had fled from so willingly?

She filled up the car with gas and reached the loft where a crazy, dying man and a severely injured renegade from the very company she worked for, were waiting for her to aid in another attack on innocent people. How did they ever get here?

They changed Renata's bandage. Her tourniquet had to be loosened every twenty minutes or so or blood clots would form and one could easily be her quick death. As soon as they loosened the tourniquet, the jagged wound would begin oozing again and in just a few minutes, would be open and they would have to apply it again. It led to a great deal of swelling and she was having trouble walking on her own.

Lexus sneered at her, "Not so great is it?"

"What's not so great?" Renata asked.

"…having something be totally out of your control and bringing you down. I heard you were a real firecracker, not so much now, huh?"

What are you talking about," Zoe asked.

Lexus' head snapped to her, "I called our wonderful 'Inspector Clouseau' and he gave me a rundown on our little spitfire. It appears our cute young whippersnapper is AWOL from France and Mr. Gallo's generous hand. His advice to us was to send Renata on her way with a ride to the nearest airport and watch as the plane takes off. Right, Renata? Do I have all of this down correctly?"

Renata looked at him sideways, "You've got a case, Fira. We got a report on your asswipe mistakes at the school. Belva has been sent to a very anonymous place to 'retire' in comfort, like keep his mouth closed if he wants to stay on this side of the dirt. You managed to bring so much attention to yourself they'll probably never hire another male substitute at that school. The police had to hush up the evidence found at Caroline's house that linked you to Adam's murder and your license plate number was seen and reported and they had to hide that too, so you and Zoe wouldn't have an APB out on you. Could you have screwed it up any more than that?"

Lexus flexed his fist once or twice and his jaw was closed so tight his mouth was one thin line and the muscles in his throat were distended.

"Bitch" he sputtered it out.

"Bastard" she rejoined.

"Kids" Zoe said, exasperated, "This will not get us anywhere. Is it true? Are you on your own and not just circumventing Mr. Gallo's direct orders?

"I don't answer to you or him" she waved her hand at Lexus, "As long as the job gets done I don't think Mr. Gallo will have a problem when I return home. You however, Lexus, may not find yourself in a good position when this is all over."

Lexus snarled, "Watch your back, bitch, you might not make it back to France."

He handled the gun and Renata looked at him with narrowed eyes of anger. At that moment, they heard a car door open and close. Lexus made his way to the high window where his binoculars were trained on the house.

"They're here. His mother had a friend staying with her I think. I thought at first it was someone from our files but then Rodane left without either of them and hasn't been back since. She's by herself and now we have both of them."

Chapter 32

Soleux, France

In the bunker of the compound in Soleux France, the six members were wrapping up the day's work and heading to their various accommodations. It would be another week before all the rest of the fifteen committee members traveled here prepared to stay until all was covered, consensus was agreed to and everyone received a flash drive, a memory stick with the notes and results of their conferences and their future endeavors. They would touch base often throughout the next fifty years but never all at once or all at the same time. If anything extraordinary were to happen in that time that required all fifteen together, it would be holographically done in a secret location, imparted to them by using their pins and their R&R crew.

Egan received a phone call and he left to take it in private. Suri nodded to him as he left and went over to Acacia and had words with her. Nikos went over to Alysia and engaged her in conversation and everyone took a few moments to just relax and go over their own personal notes. When Egan came back to the room, he was pale-faced and shaken. He looked over at Nikos, seemed confused and then walked around the table to where Suri and Evangela were still talking. He approached Suri and the two of them moved away from the group and Evangela went over to Nikos and asked,

"Has Raul contacted you in the last few hours Nikos?"

"Why no, he hasn't. Was he supposed to? I don't recall requesting a meeting."

"No it's just that I haven't heard from him either and usually he will touch base at least once a day."

Nikos smiled wryly, "You two lovebirds are very assuring to watch. So much time together and still you love each other so much that apart, you both seem somewhat… adrift."

Evangela blushed and said, "It sounds like love struck, but when you find yourself in another, it's like leaving yourself behind whenever you're separated, you know?"

Nikos grimaced, "Actually, sadly, I don't but someday I hope to." Evangela touched him on the arm and he recoiled, startled her and then apologized.

"I'm sorry I'm very tired and need a rest from all this." He looked around the room, "I think I'll go and catch a nap before we go out of here to return home." He left the room and Evangela looked after him, somewhat confused. It didn't seem like Nikos was quite himself. She wondered if she should mention it to Suri. At that thought, Suri spoke up loud enough for all to hear.

"I'm afraid our day is not over yet. We've gotten word that our presence here has been divulged and there are some very nasty people who should be arriving about…" they heard the elevator in the hall moving upward…"now". She turned to the monitors and they all started talking at once and moving to see what the surveillance cameras were seeing.

They watched in horror as two of the help came out to the wide porch and were gunned down immediately. Blood erupted and so did about eight or ten men from two Jeeps that roared to the steps and they climbed out, heading for the front door. It snapped closed with a loud thud and the men brought out a battering ram of steel and approached the door.

"Well that won't help them!" Acacia said. The door was self-manufactured in the lab made of tensile Iridite that could withstand approximately a kiloton of explosives. When the battering ram hit the door, the four men handling it were thrown backward from the concussion where they lay dazed and definitely confused. One had a nosebleed and the other held his head in his hands, moaning. The two closest to the door were still. The others moved to surround the building and all had very expensive toys, assault weapons that held many rounds of armor-piercing bullets.

Two small apertures opened up above the windows and a canister was ejected from each, on either side of the door. They were flashbangs and even though it was late afternoon, they lit up the area like broad daylight. Two men, soldiers, watching them fly out, screamed as they took the full brunt of the blinding light. Then gunfire took over and all four men in front were taken down. The same thing held true for the back and sides of the house. The smoke hid the ones closest to the open apertures and when gunfire erupted there, it took three more down. They fired over and over at the windows but made not one dent in the lab-manufactured glass. The remaining men took cover against the bushes at the side of the house and the ones around back raced up and to their jeep for cover. Just as they got there, a projectile flew out of the opening in front and hit the two Jeeps square on one side. They both exploded in balls of flame. One soldier bounced out of the Jeep on fire, batting with his hands at the fire and tearing at his clothes. Liquid, petroleum, LPG, gas didn't respond well to most fire retardants for some time.

The front door opened, two men raced down the steps while covering fire came from behind them. They each picked up one of the two assailants who were blinded, flung them over their shoulders and raced with them back in the front door as if they were carrying a sack of potatoes. The door slammed shut again and all they could hear on the monitors were moans and crackling fire and the wind whistling through the gutted remains of the two Jeeps. Only about twenty minutes had passed from start, to what was obviously a finish. The man who had tumbled from the Jeep on fire was curled in a tight fetal position, his muscles and tendons constricted into knots, like hot wire. He had a phone clutched in his hand, curled like a claw. There was not a sound in the room where the committee was standing in shock and misery, watching so many lives all at once snuffed out so quickly and so mercilessly. No one wanted to be the first to speak then Suri took charge quickly.

"Evangela, check the monitors in the rooms upstairs. Make sure no one got into the house. Alysia, take all the files and spreadsheets to the vault and lock them in until it's time for us to leave." she looked around, "Where's Nikos?"

Evangela said haltingly, "He said he was going to his room for a short nap. He wasn't too clear but he seemed anxious and very tired. Want me to check on him?"

Suri looked around the room, "Is everyone else accounted for?" They all took stock and shook their heads in agreement, "Fine, let's wait till we get the all-clear signal from upstairs. Egan and Acacia, you go to a safe room and make calls to Quimby and Petrus..." she stopped and said, "No, just call Quimby and report what has happened. Acacia, you call Cornelia and have her contact all our friends in Virginia and make sure everyone is okay. Tell them we'll call them tomorrow with news and details..." she looked around, "From now until we're told differently by Quimby, we consider ourselves under direct attack. No one leaves here until we're all prepared to go together. I'll call...no, Acacia, you call and have a small plane fueled and ready at the Amiens airport for..." she looked at each one, "Can you all be ready by eight tomorrow morning?" They all shook their heads yes, "Okay we'll leave here at eight tomorrow and each one will be flown directly to their home destination."

She saw all the lifted eyebrows, "You need to phone all your residents and make sure they secure your homes and take account of each one's schedule and movements. No one goes out alone even to the corner grocery store and they are to be carrying. Make sure they and you are 'pinned' at all times from here on out till further notice. Alysia, can you have copies of everything onto flash drives by tomorrow morning?"

"Yes" it was terse and confident.

"Okay everyone, I'm going upstairs…" they all started protesting and arguing.

"People, they are taken care of. You watched it play out. I'm checking with Franco and Pierre. I want to know why they ran out and collected two of them. Don't you want to know why?"

They all stopped, silent and then grumbled and assented.

"Okay when I know, you'll know. Get some rest tonight, looks like we might be getting less pretty soon if we're preparing for all-out battle." She left and they heard the elevator start down.

"Okay folks, you heard the woman, let's get to it." Egan and Acacia left to go and make calls, Evangela and Alysia went around the table collecting each person's portfolio and their flash drives, then headed to the safe.

On the way up in the elevator, she leaned against the wall and gave into a moment's heavy breathing, almost panting. She felt weak and scared but not helpless, never helpless. They were all the help each other needed. So… it had begun. She would face it head-on and try to finish it once and for all.

"Damn you Theras, damn you to the netherworld and all your sheeple with you." she pulled out her secured phone,

"Quimby, Suri here. You heard?" the elevator rose higher and the red light inside gave the all secure. She felt anything but.

Virginia

At that same moment, when everything seemed to have gone to hell in France, Eugenie was talking on the phone to Cornelia. She went to her drawer, opened it and pulled out the Swiss knife and the brass knuckles. She checked the locks on the windows and just as she put the brass over her fingers, she heard a car coming, quiet, one of the drawbacks of a hybrid. Any hybrid vehicle, under thirty miles per hour, came in silent unless it was riding on gravel.

She and Iona had just come home from a quick dinner at a local franchise. Seafood! She could eat it twenty-four seven and twice on Sunday. She was part fish it seemed, and part wild woman. Rodane was coming shortly and she remembered all too well that night in Naples a week ago, where everything almost came apart at the seams and Rodane almost… stopped…

{stop don't revisit this again}

She moved to the kitchen, hoping Iona had gone to bed or at least to her room. She was at the stove heating water for tea, "Want a cup Genie?" Iona asked. Eugenie smiled at the nickname Iona had taken to calling her along with Rodane. It made her feel…part of his family.

She felt the brass knuckles in her pocket, "Iona, listen carefully. There are some, one or two I hope, who'll be trying to get in here soon and I would like you to…"

"…stay the hell right here with you" Iona snapped, "Call the police, where's my phone?" Iona looked around.

"Mrs. Arcos, that won't do. These people have been playing Russian roulette with your family. It's time they pulled the trigger at their own head. The police would haul them off and in an hour or two they would be in their car and back to surveilling you."

"What are you going to do, take them on by yourself?" Iona looked like a stern mother correcting her child.

"I want this to stop here and now. I want Rodane to come home to peace and quiet and know his ex-wife and daughter are safe when he leaves." Iona looked at her, focused and thinking for a long minute, "Okay, what do you need from me?"

"I want you to go into your room, stay there until…" the kitchen door knob turned slowly… Iona stood firm, "Too late, now what?"

"Get behind me and when you can, head for your room and lock yourself in."

"I will not! What about you?" Iona was frightened but indignant.

"Mrs. Arcos…" the door flung open and two people came in dressed all in black, wearing ski masks, and the taller one had a knife in his hand, a long, serrated, ugly thing that looked sharp.

"Get down on the floor, now!" the man said in a low, guttural voice. Eugenie saw his eyes through the slits in the mask. She put up her hands in mock surrender.

{step closer sucker just another two steps}

He gestured to the shorter one (obviously a woman) "Look for their phones," she hesitated, "Now!" Lexus yelled and Iona flinched. A third person entered the kitchen door leaning against the door frame and one hand free, just standing there as if waiting for something.

{I know you bitch, I do}

Eugenie took a big risk…in for a pound… "Lexus, do you really

{ha saw you flinch jerk}

…want to try this again? Haven't you learned anything from your last attempt? Having trouble remembering?" she saw his eyes glitter at her through the slits in the mask and felt the venom he was waiting to spew.

"Get her hands tied behind the chair," he motioned to the one at the door and she produced a roll of duct tape and moved toward Eugenie.

{this won't do}

"No idiot, the old woman! I want to question her and I don't want to hold her down. Tape her!" Iona's chin came up in defiance. She looked over to Eugenie who shook her head subtly.

Renata took the tape, pushed Iona roughly into a chair and proceeded to tape her hands together and over her mouth, then wrapped tape around the back rungs of the chair to further inhibit her movement. Then she turned to Eugenie.

"Oh no," Lexus said, "this one I want to take care of." So it was him after all. At that moment when Lexus moved toward her, the other one came from the hallway holding two phones and stepped in front of Eugenie.

{now}

She grabbed her around the neck and had her in a chokehold when the girl did a shoulder curl and dipped down. Eugenie went over her shoulder but bounced deliberately into Lexus who went down like a bag of beans. She flipped over and at the same time took her hand out of her pocket with brass knuckles on. She went for his face, he jerked, and she got him in the neck instead.

{better yet}

Again, Fate has a way of intervening at the most auspicious moments. Renata moved to cover Lexus while he choked and sputtered, looked up at Eugenie directly and stood up but had trouble balancing. She swayed and Iona took that opportunity to lean over in her chair and tumble into her. Renata groaned, grabbed her leg and went down under the chair and the weight of Iona combined. She was struggling to get out from under when the front door opened and Rodane came in calling "Oma… Genie, I'm home!" and walked into the kitchen and saw a fracas taking place that seemed like a living nightmare.

Lexus reached into his pocket and pulled out the snub nose 22. Zoe was bending over and chanced to look directly into his eyes. She saw murder, clear as day. He pointed it directly at Rodane and cocked the trigger. It was like slow motion. Zoe saw his finger clearly pressing back on the trigger and saw the flash when he released it. She stood up in front of Rodane and put out her hands. It hit her square in the chest and Rodane grabbed for her as she folded then stepped up and kicked Lexus in the head. The gun flew out of his hand and he shoved Rodane to the floor and rolled over to get to it.

Eugenie was on him in a second. They tussled and grappled until Eugenie had gotten enough leverage to kick him in the side. The scream in the kitchen muffled any sounds made by all the people involved. Lexus used the gun to bash her in the head.

Renata, freed from the chair, went to Zoe to try and stop the bleeding flowing from her chest with kitchen towels. Lexus got up from the floor, left the gun, and ran out the door. Rodane went to his mother on the floor and was righting it to get off the tape she had over her mouth. He then went over to Eugenie as he heard the car peeling out of the back and heading north. He couldn't be bothered with that, Eugenie was more important. He bent over her, not sure if he had heard a gunshot or not. Her head was bleeding but not profusely. He lifted her head gently, "Genie open your eyes, look at me." She did and one side of her face was beginning to swell, blood was seeping from under her hairline. She asked, "Gone? Are they gone?" she tried to rise. "Oh, no you don't, stay still, I'm calling for help."

He grabbed a phone from the floor where Zoe had dropped them and pressed 911. Renata was holding towels against Zoe's chest and groping for the ones hanging from the stove. Rodane talked as he moved to get the knife left on the floor by Lexus. He went to his mother, cut her tape and she quickly moved off the chair and went to the pantry and pulled out more towels. She tore the tape brusquely off her hands and went to Renata on the floor, "Here," she handed her two or three towels and then went to the freezer and got ice, "This will slow down the flow till the ambulance gets here." They put ice in a towel, wrapped it tight and pressed it over Zoe's chest. Her eyes were moving back and forth and then slipped up into her head, "No" Renata yelled, "Zoe, no, hold on!" The ambulance came up the driveway and a police car followed close behind. Their headlights shone brightly into the kitchen and two cops showed up at the open door with drawn guns and stood there a second, taking in the site. They motioned to the ambulance guys and they came in with their med kit and went to Zoe's side.

Renata moved away. She looked around like a deer in headlights and Rodane could almost hear her thinking how she could get out of there, "Don't even try" Rodane said under his breath, close to her ear. She started and looked up at him, "If I have to grab you in front of these cops it's all over for you. Stay still and stay quiet, don't say anything until I've talked, got it?" He glared at her with steeled resolve on his face and Renata stood there.

One cop spoke up, "What happened here?" He looked to Rodane while Renata watched silently.

{typical man thinking another man has all the answers}

Renata held her tongue and watched them working on Zoe. She felt dizzy, nauseated and her stress level most likely had her blood pressure going through the roof. Her pulse was rapid and adrenaline was still flowing freely. She was already figuring out which door to head for, to run out and try to hit the grounds of the warehouse. She thought she might be able to hide for a few minutes to get to Zoe's car and get out the other end while everyone else was busy here. Then reality set in; she could barely stand much less run. She remained silent, watching Rodane and calculating what might come next.

Rodane said, "We had a break-in and my mother and my friends here were in the kitchen." Renata's mouth dropped open, she goggled at Rodane, her eyes widening till he looked over at her and frowned. She got hold of herself and tried to mask her face. She still had on all black as did Zoe. Wouldn't that raise suspicions? "When I came into the kitchen, he had taped my mother to the chair and Eugenie tried to defend her and got hit with his gun."

{true as far as it goes}

"He had turned it on me when I surprised him at the door and he fired at me. I'd be on that floor now if it weren't for..." he hesitated and Renata said quickly, "Zoe just reacted when the gun was raised and she stepped away and got hit instead." She was watching Rodane as she said it.

{now how do you play this}

"Yeah, Zoe was just in the way and took the shot meant for me," He nodded his head at her.

"Anyone here recognize this guy?" the second cop said. She looked at Iona, standing silently close by Zoe's side, while the attendants continued to work on her.

"Any idea why he would only tie you up and not these three?" she motioned at the three.

Iona spoke for the first time, moving to the table, sitting down heavily, and watching Renata closely, "I guess he was coming to my house to get back at us for the other break-in he had tried at my daughter-in-law's house. He must have found out where I lived."

"You're telling us this guy follows you and your family around, doing break-ins and getting revenge for one gone bad?" He looked skeptical as did the other officer.

"Officers, I believe Renata..." she looked for her acknowledgement, needs some medical attention. She was wounded in the other break-in and it appears all this trouble has her bleeding again."

Renata's head snapped downward and saw her pants leg was soaked in blood and had run down to her black shoes and onto Iona's white stone floor. She looked up at Iona in amazement. The ambulance attendants came over to the police, pointed to Zoe on the floor and said, "We need to move her right now. Her blood pressure is all over the place and her skin is getting clammy, probably still internal bleeding."

The cop said, "Take this one too. She has an old injury that has apparently reopened. We'll follow you to the hospital as soon as we're finished here."

Three of them watched as the attendants took one gurney out and Renata followed after refusing to be put on another gurney. Eugenie had refused to go with them for her head wound, despite all Rodane's attempts to persuade her. The patrol cops questioned them for at least a half-hour on the break-in at Caroline's house and then tonight's attempt. They were familiar with Adam's death and while they were there, they called into the precinct to check on the investigation,

"Well…" the female officer said, "everything you've told us pans out. We have all your information and if we need you downtown for some more questions we'll be in touch. You got yourselves a real mess in here…" She looked around the kitchen, "but it could have been much worse. You folks have a good rest tonight and maybe this will all make sense to you in the morning."

They headed out to the patrol car and Rodane said to Iona, "Mom, I'm going to the hospital to keep tabs on your two 'friends'. At her look he added, "…wouldn't do for either one to disappear to…'wherever' now, would it?"

"Are you going to tell me why you told the police those two women were with me? Whatever were you thinking?" she looked quizzically at him.

"Same reason that I guess you decided not to give over… who was it? Renata?"

She looked confused, "It was strange, I just had…"

"…a gut feeling?" Rodane said wryly, "Same here and you always told me to follow my gut. Somehow I got the feeling that…" he searched for a name, "Zoe wasn't really invested in this fiasco and after she took a bullet for me, I was sure."

"Something about her hesitation from the other encounter has me thinking she's not a willing participant with Lexus," Eugenie said.

They both looked at her surprised, "Yeah I know. I wasn't sure at first after Adam's murder and Caroline's description but when they broke in at her house, I was sure. Caroline saw his eyes and when I looked at him, he recognized me, I could tell by his reaction. That's why he didn't want to tie me up. He wanted a confrontation where he could get the best of me."

Rodane said, "Caroline heard him murder Adam. I thought…"

"No, Caroline was told by Mrs. Floyd that two people tried to get Sophia and Willow saw them and recognized Lexus and Zoe."

"Tried to get Sophia…? Lexus… Zoe? Why?" He now looked more

confused than ever. Eugenie spoke up, "Cornelia called me this evening around six and told me there was an attack at their Château, to be on guard to everyone we didn't know or trust. I didn't expect anything here or this soon, they surprised us."

Rodane asked her, "How did Renata get here and what is she doing with Lexus and Zoe? How did Cornelia know?"

Iona spoke up, "Doesn't matter. We have to decide now what to do and if the police call us in for more questioning what do we do then? We have to be on the same page here. Rodane, you know Renata?"

Rodane brushed it off, "She's the one who attacked me in Akrotiri. She was with Tabor Doukas the night they tried to kill me." Then he realized what he had said when his mother blanched and her hand flew to her mouth.

"Mom, I'm here, I didn't get killed. See?" He spread his hands out over his person.

"Oh, ok then, everything's fine, right? Nothing to worry about, it's all peachy keen!" Eugenie broke out laughing and both of them turned to her in surprise,

"Are you okay?" Rodane asked.

Iona got up and walked to her, "Genie, come sit down. You took a good hit to the head."

"I'm laughing Oma. I'm good...really. I just find the two of you amusing, how you handle a traumatic event and take everything in stride. It's very refreshing to have people able to function after something like this or even planning ahead. The only two people I know who send their enemies to the hospital to make sure they're tended to and are prepared to shelter and protect them."

Iona started to object, looked at them, grinned and then chuckled, "Keep your friends close..."

Rodane completed it, "and your enemies closer."

Rodane left to go to the hospital, Eugenie took a long walk around the warehouses to check them out, making sure Iona was well locked in and everyone else locked out. When she reached the back of the warehouse she saw a glint above from the reflected light of one of the security spotlights so she searched and eventually discovered the shed and the back stairs to the loft. She climbed the stairs to where the three had been holed up. Bloody rags were scattered, bags and trash were strewn everywhere and there were binoculars set up at the window looking directly into Iona's house and the kitchen. No sign of Lexus. She took pictures on her phone and sent them directly to Suri. She found a set of car keys on a makeshift stand and left to see if they fit the car outside the shed. They did. She started the engine and it turned over smoothly.

{why leave their car and take a rental}

She guessed Lexus had escaped and driven off in the rental car and this belonged to him, or Zoe, or both. She had already gotten a download of information on those two and it seemed they were very successful at their snooping job and putting flies in the ointment, or not. It was somewhat of a mystery but Zoe and Lexus had very detailed dossiers that would help her when she had to interrogate them.

{first thing tomorrow}

She went around to the trunk and opened it. She saw two suitcases and one carry-on duffel bag. When she opened the carry bag, she saw a faint pulsing light within and stopped short. Gingerly, she dug in the bag and removed each item one by one. She laid them on the seat; comb, brush, tablet, one file, a couple of pens, wallet, packets of tissue, a book, dog-eared and worn, a small square box, with a slight opening tilted on its side, a picture of a young, blonde-haired toddler about two, and a bottle of water. She took the box where the light was coming from, lifted it up to the light and saw three letters inscribed on the top, RPK. She lifted the lid and saw what was in it. She sucked in her breath, let out a gasp and a curse and snapped it shut. She took a few seconds to calm her racing blood and thoughts, opened it once again, used her phone camera to get a picture of the little triangular pin, lying on the velvet packing, with water and sand for a tiny, front relief and a mountain spewing smoke with jungle below it. The pulsing light was coming from the top-center of the pin's mountain, as if there were a working volcano there. She snapped the box shut and put it in her jacket pocket. This was turning out to be a great deal more complex than first thought.

Eugenie had come back to the house, told Iona what she had found and then they made a trip to the warehouse together where they found it was dark and empty. They decided to remove the suitcases and duffel, locked the car to let the police take care of finding it, and returned to Iona's home.

Iona had been busy with phone calls when she left; Caroline, checking on Rodane, Sophia wanting to talk to her Oma, even the night watchman at the warehouse, informing her of an unknown car parked behind it and what should he do about it. She had hired him on a monthly basis, three nights a week, just to give one of her manager's sons a temporary job and also to check for any serious abnormalities or activities that might require attention from her. She had a feeling she might know what the presence of the car meant. Their story could only be better verified, if everything fell into place, naturally. She told the watchman to log in the discovery, call the local police and have it towed. They took the suitcases and duffel to the house, put all the things in the attic, into an old steamer trunk and locked it. Then they hauled it into the storage area in the eaves. The rest was up to Virginia's finest.

Iona had brewed some tea and had brought out some small scones and biscuits. They sat at the table till late in the evening, going over the recent events of the last few days; Rodane's recent travels in Greece, which took them to the attack in Naples and his recovery, the break-in at Caroline's house and Adam's death, the next break-in that proved all were targets and in their sights, to the attack tonight. Eugenie asked about Cassie, and her career, about Iona's journey from Greece to Hampton Roads and about Sophia and all her funny adventures and her mom.

When they turned out the light to go to bed, Eugenie stayed up for a long time, sitting in bed with the box in her hands, debating about what to do with it and planning how she would get it back to Suri and the committee without anyone knowing she had it. Would it pass security at the airport? It must, because Renata must have brought it with her to here. Whose was it? Who from? How did she fit in this picture? Finally, she was so tired, her eyes were gritty and her head drooped, so she turned out the light, put the box under her pillow, and went off to sleep, her nagging headache finally drifting away into her dreams.

Chapter 33

Hampton Roads General Medical Center

Rodane arrived at the hospital and parked in the underground garage. When he went to the front desk of emergency, of course he had to wait until finally, after an hour, a nurse walking briskly, holding a clip board came directly to him and asked, "Are you a relative?"...she checked her chart..."Mr. Arcos?"

"No, I'm a friend and their injuries took place in my house. I'm feeling kind of responsible."

"I understand." Again, she checked her chart, "Well, it won't be possible for you to see her this morning, she's still in surgery, but Ms. Kappos has been asking for you, and she's in room 208."

She looked carefully at him before she spoke again, "That surprises you?" She didn't wait for an answer, "I understood it was your mother's house where the break-in occurred?" She waited for an answer.

"Well yes, but I'm staying there for a while and the girls were there to visit me."

{just won't say what for}

"Please don't stay long, Mr. Arcos. Ms. Kappos has been doing quite a bit of damage to herself, walking around on a pretty serious injury. How did she do it again?" she tilted her head and waited.

He decided to go with as much of the truth as he could and said Renata had been bitten by Beaker, when she went too close to his daughter and Beaker reacted out of instinct and since he was only a puppy, he really didn't realize what he had done."

She scowled at him, "Doesn't that give you pause Mr. Arcos, that he might not be a good fit for a young child?"

I think if you check with Ms. Kappos she will tell you Beaker is a wonderful protector and very good with Sophia and she is with him."

"That's interesting. Ms. Kappos said pretty much the same thing. Enjoy your visit." She turned on her rubber-soled shoes and hurried away.

{nurse ratched in dr scholl's.}

When he got to room 208 by elevator, he walked in and found Renata asleep. He turned to go and heard a soft, "Please, come in, I'm awake."

She had her leg in some kind of elastic leg bandage, raised up on two big pillows with a pulley and cable attachment. She had an IV in her arm with dripping fluids, and a BP machine keeping track as well as heart rate.

{how sick is this girl}

"I find myself drifting asleep every time I close my eyes." She examined his face and took a minute to gather her thoughts.

"How badly were you hurt, Ms. Kappos? I thought that Sophia's dog had just bitten you. This looks pretty serious."

"Yeah, that would have been nice if that were all." He waited, observing her manner and her tone. She chuckled, "My friends… you've met them… tried to use some emergency first-aid and it seems they did more harm than good with their tourniquet."

He scowled at her, "How so? Why wouldn't they just get you to a doctor?"

"Well, I'm pretty sure you can figure that one out for yourself. You pretty much experienced the same thing for yourself" he looked puzzled. He **was** puzzled. "Sabina Carter? Akrotiri… at night? …A treasure hunt in the dark?" She waited for it to all connect.

"So, it **was** you that night at the ruins! I find myself confused, as to why I don't just turn you in, spill everything to the cops, and let you take your best shot with our legal system."

She used her controller to bring up the bed to a sitting position. She sat with her hands in her lap, the only sound in the room, the AC clicking on and off from the antiquated radiator system and the sounds of the machines. Then she looked up at him and her expression was part courage, part defiance, mixed with a feeling of guilt.

"I don't either… Boy Scout training?"

He shook his head and grinned, just a little.

"Here's the thing…" she coughed a little and he handed her some water, "I hope you can let me say this but you can stop me anytime you want…" she seemed to have come to a decision, "I've fucked up my life for so long it was only a matter of time before it caught up with me." She caught his surprise… "this is not an apology, Mr. Arcos or should I say Dr. Arcos?"

"Either Ms. Kappos" she was startled at the use of her name,

{I can give as good as I get woman}

"…and I'd like to think that if we had managed to get to you in your mother's house, that you would have been no worse for the wear, just roughed up a little, to get what we came for."

"And… what would that be?"

"See, that's the thing, I'm not sure what you have that's gotten us into so much trouble the last three weeks. I have no idea why so many people want you so badly that they're willing to go to extreme lengths to get to you by any means."

"My daughter, my ex-wife, her boyfriend, my mother…? Were there any lengths you would not go to?"

He watched a flush creep up her darker skin, and saw that guilty look intensify, "I'm not going to apologize for doing my job!"

He went to reply and her hand raised, "Please, but I am going to apologize for what Tabor Doukas and Lexus Fira have done to your family. It was unnecessary, mindless, reckless, and just plain wrong. You may not believe me, but I'm hoping I would have stopped at deliberately hurting anyone or even going after them. I found it distasteful and abhorrent, what Tabor did to you, what he did in that alley. I was a coward. I am a coward, for not standing up to him and refusing to stalk and track you."

Her voice was hoarse, and the BP machine showed a steady rising, along with her heavy breathing, "Ms. Kappos, why don't we take this up at a later time? Are they keeping you here overnight?"

"Maybe" She heard her own voice and saw his reaction and his frown, "I'm not going to try to escape. I couldn't if I wanted to. My leg is the least of my problems."

He looked at her, feeling alarm, concern. She saw his look and said, "Oh no, there's nothing life-threatening or anything like that. They took tests when they saw my wound and then they gave me a blood workup. I'm waiting for the results."

"What, if you don't mind my asking, seems to be the problem?"

"Your guess is as good as mine. Nurse Ratched is…what, I said something funny?"

He was laughing softly and her expression just caused him to laugh more and louder.

"What? Share the laugh. I could use one right about now."

"It's just that a few minutes ago, I said the same thing to myself about the nurse who came to me and let me come to see you."

"Tall?" He nodded his head and she said, "Rubber soled shoes?" He laughed. "Tweetie Bird prints on her Smock?" He laughed harder. Renata almost whispered,

"I'm waiting for the cops to show up here. I think she believes I'm a menace to old dogs and children." Then her face fell and her voice changed, "Maybe I am."

Silence enfolded them both.

"I didn't mean to hit you that hard at the ruins." He looked up, surprised, "I needed to try to get to Sabina Carter and I didn't want to take a chance on someone who might recognize me, so I probably swung too hard. I thought Dr. Carter was coming out."

Her face crinkled with disgust, "My cohort…took off …and I lost my nerve and scooted out of there and then later, in Naples…I… avoided the alley. I was…a coward."

Rodane shuddered slightly that she could relay this so quietly and so easily.

"I swear to you I did not know what he had in mind. I thought that he would…" she squirmed around on the bed, rose up a little against the pillows, stopped and took a deep breath… "No, that's not true. I didn't know how he was going to get to you but I knew he didn't have any compunction about hurting you…or even worse." He looked up at the catch in her voice and was astonished to see her eyes glistening with tears.

He found himself talking hoarsely and feeling…

{what sympathy}

"Apology accepted, I think!" A few more long seconds of silence then… "What do we do now? " They both spoke the exact same words, at exactly the same moment. They stopped, and both looked sharply at each other. "Let's talk about…" The same thing happened. Their eyes widened, Rodane waved her on to speak, and she swallowed and said, "Let's talk about where we go from here and what we do next."

Rodane grinned and said, "My thoughts exactly!" She smiled, not broadly but a smile none the less. He sat down in the corner chair and asked her, "What do the doctors say? Can you leave soon or… what?"

"No one will tell me anything. When I ask what they're testing for, they hem and haw. What? You never heard that expression? I get tired of all the men in my life beating around the bush…" She looked at him, "with exceptions of course."

"If you can leave tomorrow, where will you go?"

"I'm not sure, but I have enough money to go anywhere I want, I guess." She watched him… "If you're not interested in pressing charges, I should go home."

"Where would that be?" He really was curious.

"See, that's the thing. I'm really not sure about that, either." She looked at him, "I guess you think I'm a real nut case, huh?"

He thought about that, examined his own feelings, and said, "No, I think you've come to a crossroads of some sort and you're trying to figure out where you go from here, and I'm not talking about a place."

She pursed her lips and then said, "That Golden Ring doesn't appeal to me anymore. Noting his look of confusion, she added, "Sorry, it's an inside joke, sort of. How is Zoe?"

The change in subject threw him for a moment then he said, "She's in surgery…I'm not sure. I hope she makes it."

"Me too" Her face was thoughtful, sad, worried…"

"Do you two work together often, on your jobs?"

"I just met her two days ago, really."

"I was under the impression you were both good friends."

"I think we would have been, under other circumstances. Now… just don't know where I'm headed."

At that moment, a tech or nurse or doctor… someone, showed up at her door with a chart in his hand and a tray with vials and tubes. He saw Rodane sitting there and he was obviously surprised and annoyed.

"I'm sorry. I didn't know you had company. Tina said you were here from overseas and didn't know anyone. I'll come back later."

He turned to leave very quickly. Rodane and Renata looked at each other in tandem. Rodane thought quickly, "Yeah, where is Nurse Tina now?"

"She had to leave early tonight, I think. She'll most likely be back on day shift tomorrow." He shuffled his eyes and his feet.

{wanna lay bets, fellow}

"You work with her, uh,.." he looked at his tag, "William?"

"No, I work in the lab downstairs… over in the hospital section… over…" and he was definitely flustered.

{what's up guy and who are you really}

"It's okay, you can come in. What do you need? Dr. Arcos is going to be here a while, right?" she looked at Rodane hopefully.

"Sure, come on in, you need something?"

William, definitely uncomfortable now, said "I was instructed to get some blood samples to take to the lab but I can come back later after your visit."

"Is my doctor requesting that? I wasn't told anything about more blood. I think I've lost quite enough already, don't you Dr. Arcos?" she actually grinned at him.

They turned to look at William and he was already gone. Rodane moved quickly to the door and caught the swinging of the stair's exit door as it was closing. He came back to Renata's bed, puzzled out something in his own mind, "I do believe it's either time for me to set up my sleeping arrangements here or else it's time for you to ask for discharge, even against doctor's orders. What do you think?"

Eugenie had answered the phone and had gotten the lowdown on what was happening at the hospital. She and Iona decided to go together and spell each other until Zoe was out of surgery and be there for the night. Iona was not about to brook any opposition. She was groggy from only four hours of sleep when he had called and told them about William and Nurse Tina, aka Nurse Ratched. She took the phone out to the kitchen and Iona was there. They put it on speaker so they could all listen together. After some hasty discussion and a call that Eugenie made, they headed out to the hospital in the middle of the night.

When they arrived, Rodane was waiting for them at the front lobby, with Renata sitting in a wheelchair, her leg propped up, wan and weary. He took them aside and explained in more detail. What they had first believed was Renata's desire to get out of the hospital and take off on them, was clearly a desire on Rodane's part to possibly stave off some kind of attack on Renata, maybe Zoe too. Eugenie's phone sang, 'Eye of the Tiger'. When she answered, she put it on speaker for all of them to hear together.

"Eugenie, can you talk?"

They all looked at an empty lobby, not even someone at the information desk.

"For right now, yes, is this Philip?"

"Nope, it's Tegan."

She raised her eyebrows and her voice, "I didn't know you were…"

"Mom has quickly brought me up to date on the 'event' Philip and mom have been busy with lately. I was away at a seminar when this all started to go down over here but that's ended. Philip and Willow would be more than happy to follow up, but they're in the process of getting Caroline and Sophia off to an undisclosed location until this either concludes or we're sure they are off the radar. They thought you might require some muscle." Rodane stepped in, "What do you mean an undisclosed location? Who are you?"

"Is that Dr. Arcos I'm speaking to?"

"Yes it is and…"

"Good to hear from you Dr. Arcos. Sabina has been calling every fifteen minutes or ten as of now, to find out if you are safe or found or…"

"Well, I'm fine but I want to know where you intend to take my daughter and her mother to stay."

"I'll let Sabina know when she calls in, should be in the next few minutes.

His tone held some levity and Rodane blushed.

"I'm on my way now about fifteen minutes out. If I don't get a ticket, that is. Where do I find you?"

Iona spoke into the phone, "Young man, do you have 'muscle' as you young folks put it?" Rodane sputtered and they could almost hear the restrained laughter in Tegan's voice, "Sorry, who am I speaking to?"

"It's Iona Arcos, and I want to make sure you understand why you're coming here or are you?"

"Am I...muscled?" Now he didn't bother to mask his laughter, "Well, I'm not the Hulk or Captain America but I do manage to take care of myself, but there will be others coming who are...you know...muscled."

Eugenie said, "Who's on your list again? When can we expect them?"

"They're already there. Mom called the hospital, talked to her friend in Finances and Billing. She's sending two security personnel; one to Recovery and one to room 208."

"That won't be necessary." Rodane looked over at Eugenie, and then to Renata. "I will be taking Renata to my mother's house for however long she needs to stay there. She looked at him fiercely, still not quite trusting the man she tried to kill or at least maim slightly, "Or, until she decides where she wants to go." Renata relaxed again.

"Okay, that's fine. We play this however you want. Look for Ofc. Flint when you go to recovery. He will probably be with Ofc. Cochran. Both have photo ID's so you can be sure. I should be pulling in around five minutes. Good luck." he disconnected.

Rodane asked Eugenie what he had been thinking about all the time during the phone conversation, "Tegan...who's that."

"Philip's twin, but he's seldom called on for assignments. His school schedule keeps him extremely busy but this is an emergency and I can vouch that he's okay."

"Genie, Philip's brother is good enough testimony for me, if he's anything like his twin."

"Peas in a pod!" Eugenie quipped.

A woman came out of the hallway, saw them all standing, except for Renata. She looked at the clock and then walked around the information desk to sit. Rodane walked over to her and asked about the status of Zoe Martin. She checked her computer, looked back at him over her glasses and said, "May I know who's asking, please?"

Iona stepped up, "Mrs. Iona Arcos and her son, Rodane Arcos."

"May I see your IDs please?" Then her shoulders visibly relaxed and her smile seemed more genuine.

"Thank you. Miss Martin is out of surgery and in recovery with a red flag. I'm sorry, but only one person at a time can visit and only two people are listed on the visitor's list at this time. Mr. Arcos, you are listed but Mrs. Arcos, I'm sorry but your name is not there. Who would be the second name?" Iona asked.

"I'm sorry but since it's red-flagged, I can't give out that information." She saw his look, "Security Mr. Arcos, for her safety."

He couldn't fault that. He turned to his mom, and she spoke first,

"Over here" and led them away out of earshot.

"Here's what we do, Roddy." Eugenie raised her eyebrows and smiled,

"I will take Renata back to our house, with Genie. We will be fine, don't give me that look. All the drama is done for the night, I'd lay bets. You visit with Zoe and see if you can find out who that second name is for visitors. It might give us some insight. Then you return home and do some research. Genie and I can come relieve you if she's awake and allows our names to be put on the list of visitors."

He thought for a moment and then said, "Okay."

Eugenie said, "Never ceases to amaze me how he is the most stubborn man I know, but full of surprises." Rodane couldn't help grinning and quipped, "Keeps you on your toes."

"Sure enough, Roddy" She grinned at his expression.

Renata seemed okay with the move, but looked somewhat askance at Eugenie.

"Don't worry Renata…Genie's bark is worse than her bite." They both scolded him.

He helped Iona and Eugenie get Renata to Iona's car and Eugenie assured him they could handle it well by themselves. A young man walked in at the same moment Rodane was heading to Recovery. He walked over to Rodane and held out his hand smiling.

Rodane said, "If I hadn't talked to you, I would think Philip was standing in front of me. They shook hands and Tegan said, "Excuse me for a sec."

He walked over to the desk and he and the staff member talked for a couple of minutes. Rodane watched her hand signal point out the signs overhead, which included surgical recovery. Tegan returned to Rodane's side, "Ready?"

They followed the signs around the lobby to a hallway, passing vending machines, a spiral stairs that Rodane had skipped in favor of the elevator and then around a semicircle to an admitting station. The nurse in charge asked for photo ID when they requested Zoe Martin, and examined them carefully. Apparently, the red flag extended everywhere here. The double doors whirred quietly open and they went to the third cubicle. They knew which one immediately because the security guard was sitting directly in front of the closed curtain and his gun was un-holstered, with his hand on the grip.

Tegan spoke, "I'll wait out here if that's okay?" Rodane nodded.

The security guard stood up and asked to see their IDs again, nodded at Tegan and sat down. Tegan stood by him and the two began chatting. Rodane pushed the curtain aside and entered the tight space with machines buzzing and beeping.

Zoe Martin lay there still, hooked up to three IVs and a heart and BP monitor, pale, small. Her body under the sheet and blanket looked like a child sleeping peacefully, hands at her side, BP 80/ 50.

{just about conscious}

Her blonde hair was matted to her head, a thin sheen of sweat on her forehead and her upper lip. Her eyes under the closed lids were also still, no dreams to break her sleep, no sounds registering in her ears. He sat down on a straight-backed chair and waited. He watched the slow drip of glucose into her arm with a morphine drip into her other arm. A third IV was inserted into one hand. He saw her pinky finger taped to her ring finger and all taped down to the bed railing while a slow drip of a blood transfusion made its way into her.

{must have almost bled out}

He lost track of time, leaned his head back against the chair and dozed. He saw a gun pointed at him, a bullet moving in slow motion toward him right before it hit. He saw a hand reach out and grasp the bullet and smoke escaped from the hand that held it. The hand reached out and held the bullet toward him, offering it as a gift. He started awake and looked into those amber eyes, open wide and looking at him. He slid forward and without considering, took her hand, telling her, "You're okay Zoe, you're in the hospital. You had surgery and you're going to be fine…"

{don't make a liar out of me }

She tried to talk but nothing came out. Her voice cracked and her hand tightened in his, "Don't talk yet, there's plenty of time to talk, just rest. Know that I'm here, we're here and you're going to be okay." She closed her eyes, her breathing softened, her hand relaxed in his and he sat back wondering.

{why did you save me and take a bullet}

This was the one who hesitated at Caroline's house (had to be) when the bastard Lexus, tried to take Sophia. She had met Sophia and his daughter felt safe and friendly with her. She almost died protecting him and here she was, surviving the whole thing and except for him, seemingly alone, to recover and recuperate.

The last three weeks had certainly had its ups and downs; danger and assault, excitement and love. Yes, he would admit that he felt love for Sabina, excitement about someone who made him feel…complete. The two times he had talked to her since he had returned home made him ache to hold her, kiss those soft, yielding lips of hers, see the sparkle in her eyes when she laughed and the crinkle in her nose when she was confused or intensely concentrating. He missed her sorely and was anticipating the time when he could see her again. Not knowing when that might be, he was eager to get back to some normalcy, spending time with Sophia but then going back to Montana to take over his courses and get back to what he loved to do. He hadn't had any time to work on getting his travelogue completed and was ignoring about ten messages and emails from the travel company. Tough! This was more important. He felt like he needed to be here for Sophia, for Caroline… now for this woman lying in a post-operative stupor, a shade off of losing her life while protecting his.

It was such a mess but such an adventure. Exciting and disturbing, happy but anxious… too many different moods to hit him in too short a time. He felt overwhelmed and angry, frustrated and yet alive. The tug on his hand pulled him out of his reverie. He opened his eyes and saw Zoe looking at him. She tried again to talk, "Ducky"

"Yeah everything's ducky, you're good Zoe."

"No" she licked her lips, cracked and dry, "Brother…Ducky."

He paused, thought about what she might be saying, "Your brother is Ducky? That's his name?"

She tossed her head from side to side, "Arizona… mom…"

"Zoe, don't talk .You need to build up your strength. You've been through a lot."

{don't scare her to death}

She still had his hand and she closed her eyes again and drifted off. A nurse came in, took her blood pressure, her temp and her pulse, checked her tubes then left without a word.

Tegan stuck his head in the curtain and Rodane told him what Zoe had managed to say. Tegan said, "I have time to look. I'll get on to some of my friends in Arizona and ask them to start doing some investigating of Zoe Martin. It may take a while. You okay with that? I can spell you if you want to go out where the sofa is softer."

"No, I'm good. I told her I'd be here when she's stronger." Tegan looked as if he was going to say something, changed his mind, shook his head slightly and disappeared through the curtain.

The hours went by and Rodane managed to doze a little but he felt lethargic, woozy, very sluggish and his lower back hurt and his legs tingled but every time he tried to rise and stretch his legs, Zoe's hand tightened on his. The security guard looked in once, asked if he wanted coffee and he declined. Then Tegan brought him a cup of hot tea.

"How did you know I'd want tea instead?"

"When you declined coffee, I figured 'tea drinker'. It didn't take a Doctor Watson to figure that one out." Rodane laughed and shook his head.

"What?" Tegan asked.

"Our 'family' has some very interesting connections and it still startles me, when it all comes together." Tegan looked at him in confusion. It finally dawned on him what Rodane meant after he remembered the 'our family' and he watched Tegan's face register understanding, then shock, then pure enjoyment. Without thought, he said loudly, "Dude, you serious, you pulling my leg? Wow! This is wonderful!"

"Shhhh" A nurse put her head in and shook her finger at Tegan, "Young man, there are some seriously ill people in here who need calm and quiet." She left, frowning.

Tegan was sufficiently chastised, "Your mother didn't tell you or Phillip?"

"No, they were rushed and anxious to get Caroline and Sophia out of the house until they could move them to…" he stopped himself.

"Why the secrecy, I'm her dad, damn it!"

"Should I let you figure that out for yourself, or do you really want an answer?"

Rodane was on the edge of snapping at him and then calmed himself,

"I know the answer, sorry for jumping at you."

"You've had more action from the cabal than all the rest of us have had for years. Now, we want to make sure we compartmentalize until we know all the whos and whats involved in this incursion."

"What cabal? What 'incursion'? This has happened before? By who? When? Why wasn't I warned?"

Tegan flushed, smacked himself on the forehead and clamped his mouth shut, to gather his thoughts.

Rodane gently disengaged his hand from Zoe's and stood up to try and relax the cramps he was getting in his shoulders and back. The tension from the conversation had finally caused the physical reaction he was beginning to feel, from sitting or lounging on a hard chair without respite. Tegan took a step backward and looked at him, surprised.

"What? You think I'm going to hit you?"

Tegan looked leery, "I don't know you well enough to answer that but if it was me in these circumstances and I discovered all those working for me and with me had kept me in the dark, I'd..." Tegan shook his head and shut up. They both started at the frog-sounding voice that whispered, "Arcos."

Zoe was looking at them both. Rodane took three steps to her bed side, "Here, I'm right here."

"Water" he looked on the small table, took a cup with ginger ale with a straw in it "Will this do?"

She nodded, he helped her sip through the straw and then she asked to be let up on the bed. He pushed the bed controls and raised her up a foot.

"More"

He hesitated and she whispered, "Yes."

She drank a little more and whispered again, "I'm sorry."

Rodane looked askance at her and said, "You saved my life so what are you sorry about?"

One hand free of tubes waved shakily in the air, "All this...our attack, Sophia's..." Her voice cracked, her face crumpled and her eyes spilled tears, "All of it."

He sat back down and took her hand again, "Me too but don't take all the blame. You helped."

When she started to shake her head he said, "You did. When push came to shove you stood up. You helped. I'm standing here, I should know."

Her throat was clogged her nose was running and Rodane took care of tissue and ginger ale. Then she looked at Tegan, "Tell him"

Tegan again looked puzzled, "Tell him what?"

"The cabal...the whos and the whats" Silence became as a living thing in the room, waiting for a response from Tegan.

He asked "Do you know who... and what's?" He cleared his throat, watching Rodane and then her,

"Not all, some" her blood pressure was rising and her pulse as well.

{nurse should be here soon}

"Why do you think I would know?" Tegan was watching the monitors closely,

"...Because...you teach the children," Zoe closed her eyes again.

It was as if he had been slapped soundly. Tegan whipped his head around and his eyes were wide, shocked, and his mouth dropped open. It took a few seconds for him to gather his wits about him. Rodane was in the middle, looking between Zoe and Tegan with a sense of watching through a window. The atmosphere almost crackled with the ricocheting emotions and reactions.

Tegan had folded his arms together. He gazed at Zoe for a long silent period, seeming to try and get into her head, "Where do you fit in all this, Zoe?

What makes you say that just now? Where's your information coming from?"

The nurse came in looking grim and stoic, "Gentlemen, it's time for your visit to end for now." When Tegan started to protest, she held up her hand, "We've been monitoring her vitals from the nurse's recovery center and it seems your visit is disturbing her. We can't have that right now. You can come back of course, but now, she needs some rest."

Rodane turned to her, "Can I please ask Zoe one question before we go?" The nurse looked at Zoe who nodded her head, yes.

"Okay thanks, one question." He leaned down by Zoe, took her hand and asked, "Would you allow my mother, and my friend Eugenie, to visit with you? They'd like to thank you in person for… everything." He searched her pale face, "You'd have to request that they be placed on your visitor list."

She looked at Tegan for a few seconds, looked at Rodane, squeezed his hand and nodded yes. The nurse gave him a withering look but said, "You'll have to stop at our center and give us their names, Mr. Arcos."

Both Tegan and Rodane returned to Oma's house, each in their own vehicle, thinking their own thoughts. Rodane kept thinking 'what children could he teach'? Tegan was going over a cabal, the whos and whats, and getting more worried by the mile.

Chapter 34

Lyon, France

Two in the morning in Virginia was 8 a.m. in Lyon France. It was also the same from DC to Madrid Spain and it was also the same six plus hours difference of New York and Paris, France. That wouldn't matter to anyone who either wasn't traveling to those places or anyone who didn't consider any of them a point of interest or a need for communication. There were a number of entities however, who were directly involved in making use of that time difference to their advantage and others who missed a vital chance to make good use of that time difference.

When Rodane called Sabina in Lyon France, he used the number she had given him over a secure line on a phone she used that was encrypted and password protected. It also contained an unknown and undeveloped device that would track anyone who was trying to break that encryption or pinging any towers, trying to follow it to its source. That was a very good thing because at that moment in Virginia, when Rodane was calling Sabina, Gallo was having his team of cryptographers attempt to gain access to both phones. One purpose, to listen to their conversation, the other and more important as far as Gallo was concerned, was to detect the location from which Sabina was calling.

They had lost her! The idiots had been assigned to follow and stay with Sabina and not to let her out of their sight. That was over twenty four hours ago. They hadn't even bothered to notify the communications lab until 9 o'clock last night. Acteon had only been able to gather a handful of lab techs to work on searching for her through the night. Everyone there was tired, tense and anxious and fearing the reaction of their top boss when they had to tell him the result; zip, nada, nothing.

Acteon came into the room, himself haggard with bloodshot eyes, shirt mussed, tie missing, a very unusual fact for Acteon, a growth of beard on his tired face. He told them all to go home since the day crew was about to come on. He instructed a short report be submitted from each person as to what and where they had worked on during the night and their results.

"Sir, there's a call being made by Rodane Arcos coming out of Virginia. It's logged in at eight seconds ago."

"Who to…?" He looked up sharply.

"That's unknown at this time, sir. Contact is blocked and towers are unresponsive."

"How the hell…" He stopped and took a breath, "how is that possible?"

"We don't know, sir, we've only recently experienced this kind of security network. Our people are trying non-stop to break their blocks and rewrite the program for encryption, to find a backdoor into their communications." The man was white-faced and sweating as he watched the myriad expressions running over Acteon's face.

"Where are we with active feet on the ground?"

"Uh…nowhere, sir. We had three people on scene and all three at this time are awaiting your instructions. They've lost all sight lines of Sabina Carter since 6:30 yesterday."

He went to speak then thought better of it. His anger would not control him, he would control it. After all, shit happens!

He, of all people, was well aware of that, he had all the scars and after effects to attest to it. He turned and exited the room and went directly to Gallo's office. He never put off anything unpleasant he was faced with. Better to tackle it, get it over with, suffer the consequences and then move on to a solution.

Aldora was at her desk and looked up as he entered the room. She smiled faintly, anticipating something negative and disturbing. Acteon was not prone to visits to the inner sanctum unless something really great had happened or in her opinion, more likely when something not so great was occurring.

"Morning, Acteon. Something I can help you with?"

"Afraid not Ms. Spiteri, I need to see Mr. Gallo if he's free. I'm prepared to wait."

{which means you'll take root here if necessary}

"I'll call into him and let him know you're here."

Strange, that at that moment, Theras Gallo was on the phone to one of his sources whose job it was to keep him advised of operations only he was aware of. The call had come in ten minutes earlier and Theras was just getting down to checking all his mail. He had come across one mail that concerned scheduled meetings for the President of the United States and the NABSG.org.

As he read the email, he became more and more focused. At first he wasn't sure why this particular email found its way into his private account. On reading it however, he found himself becoming more and more agitated, reading between the lines. His blood pressure was rising. He could almost feel it doing so. He had called his lab research assistant who had been planted in the NABSG.org for over a year.

The National Board of Science Grants had been developed a few years before, as a result of the president in office at the time, attempting to find ways to reduce the deficit as well as get a handle on all the various science organizations that were insulated and uncoordinated. So far it looked promising, because they had already cut down over sixty million in duplicated grants, awards, monetary supplements to smaller science labs and independent labs that depended on grants and scholarships to perform well.

What the directors of this board were unaware of was the fact that Theras Gallo, with all his associates in their cabal, were responsible for rewarding and placing certain scientists and scholars in various positions and in varied institutions where they could, almost with carte blanche, guide and subvert, divest, focus, and otherwise control all of the major scientific labs and programs in the country. They also had much influence on other programs outside the US as well; coercing cooperation, removing those who became obstacles and shutting down any experiments or research they found as threats to their global efforts. Those efforts had been going on for very many years, under various cabal members and leaders.

This organization was almost as old as the 'families' that inhabited all corners of the globe, all cities and developed countries, and all governments, even those that were not quite as developed. Their existence and agenda were always the same over many generations; to unmask and uncover all others of 'family' as dangerous, labeling them as terrorists or criminals, using their technology for their own means and… to use others they could corral or corrupt for their own purposes and finally, control of any and all other futuristic technology that might or would appear.

The present cabal was broken into two distinct groups. One group believed they had amassed enough evidence and documentation to submit proof to the highest leaderships on earth to prove the existence of 'others' but were still unsure of whether they had uncovered all of the 'others' still out there.

The second group was somewhat more aggressive; looking for patterns in all areas of the world to identify whoever, over time, seemed to possess the abilities or knowledge that would identify them as those 'family' members seen as fearful 'others'. Then they would seek them out or keep surveillance on them, keeping tabs and sending reports back to their bosses located in France and other locales.

Theras was only one of those bosses but had become the most powerful with the strongest alliances and supporters. He had amassed a fortune over much more time than just the last fifty years, funneling and liquidating other assets to acquire tons of money to accomplish his goals. Revenge was the driving force behind his success; 'family' loyalty was forgotten, 'family' members were dead to him, even if they still walked on this Earth. He had developed a mental and emotional armor that shielded him from any compunction or sympathy toward those he had once paid allegiance to and protected at all cost. He had developed a thick skin that neither blood relationship or the deepest friendship from so long ago had any effect on his plans or his direction and orders to those who worked for him.

He was not a patient man. He had become less so as years had passed and he had not met his goals. Now here he was on the phone with a man who was informing him of some very different plans being laid by the president of the U.S. and all the other NATO nations, to investigate most of the scientific communities responsible for furthering his own agenda to upend the 'families'.

"What do you mean they're all involved? We're talking about NABSG. org. They don't own the world, for Christ's sake!"

"No sir that's true but they're only one organization. I'm afraid they have sent out feelers to quite a few more and are trying to consolidate the investigation into one large umbrella organization."

"Who" he asked, tingling and sweaty, sitting in his desk chair. He was staring out the window at the fountain in the center of the Quad. Usually it relaxed him.

"Well sir, as far as I know, they've sent out queries to USNSF, NIH, Student Aid grants and scholarships, USDA…"

"USDA! What the hell does the Department of Agriculture have to do… never mind… seeds, hybrids, pesticides… okay, who else?"

"There are all the organizations that study cancer; Women's Cancer Foundation, Susan B Comen Foundation…that's most of the ones in the US. But then you have …" he cleared his throat on the other end of the line.

{you should sweat you incompetent ass}

"Why wasn't I told of these efforts before? Why am I only learning about this when the cat is already out of the bag?"

"Sir, we've only learned of it ourselves a few hours ago. It's apparently all been under wraps, and just released to committee appointments."

"Okay, give me the global science groups involved."

"There's college scholarships.Org; Australia.gov; Human Frontier Science Program and…" he hesitated a few seconds.

"Spit it out damn it! Couldn't get much worse, could it? Who else, damn it!"

"NASA sir, in concert with the Russian and Chinese space program."

"For Christ's sake, why don't we just include every government organization in existence and let them all fight over all the money and the notoriety?"

"That's all we know about sir, but there may be more as it's made public."

"Who the hell is spearheading this clusterfuck?"

"That's the only thing we haven't been able to determine, sir."

Theras took a deep breath and said, "Okay, keep me informed of every development or heads will roll!"

"Yes sir" Theras would bet his next million the man needed to change his pants.

This entire screw-up could be the undoing of the interests of the cabal with over centuries of expansion and domination, an investigation that could lead to the collapse of his entire business, his fortunes and his efforts to destroy the 'families' he had been working toward for too long.

A knock at the door startled him and started his pulse racing. Aldora stepped into his office and looked at him, searching his face for a moment.

"Are you ok Theras?" he waved her away.

"Acteon would like a few words with you if you have time. Should I send him in?"

"Sure why not? More the merrier!" she looked at him again and walked over to the desk, "Theras is there anything you want me to do?" he looked at her steadily for a long silent moment then he shook his head slowly, "Not unless you can send us back about two hundred and fifty thousand years and we get to start over." She digested that, turned and walked out to send Acteon into his office.

International phone call

Rodane spoke softly to Sabina, "I'm sorry I'm not there with you. I know it must be very stressful. Is everyone okay?"

Sabina gave him a very quick rundown of the attack at the compound in Soleux, France. They had two survivors who were being interrogated by the staff at Soleux and the 'family' meeting had been very rapidly moved to another secure location not known to anyone except the committee. They had left the compound within hours of the attack and no one had been in touch with them since then or at least not that they were aware of.

Sabina had been on her way to Soleux when she got a message from Acacia to go to ground. The next day was chaos, with all the members of the family dealing with the unknown, questions as to how this could be happening with no warning and not knowing the outcome of their present condition. It was indeed, a very stressful two days.

Sabina heard the wistfulness in Rodane's voice and said,

"I know, I feel exactly the same way. I'm getting a lot done and I've completed my work, all my recoveries and I only had to relocate one item that I had to remove out of a ruined temple site in the heart of Tuscany. But something was…missing. I didn't have anyone to celebrate with."

"Where's Helene? She's with you, right? You have protection?"

"I'm surrounded by 'family' Rodane. No one could get to me with the phalanx of protectors I have at the moment.

{unless they get to the entire committee}

"Where are you?"

"Someplace safe, that's all I can say."

"Can you tell me what you've learned from your 'interrogation of the two survivors?"

Sabina sounded frustrated, "We're at the same place we were before, names being thrown around and no one of any high level interest to trace all these subversive acts back to. We have gotten names of people we already know, about, planning to disrupt and destroy the entire 'family' network. I'm talking global here."

"Let me guess. They gave up Tabor Doukas and Renata Kappos in a split second."

Yeah…and also Lexus Fira and Zoe Martin then they clammed up and we couldn't lose them as assets so we eased up and are at a standstill."

"What about global efforts to eat into their agenda?"

Sabina huffed, "They know more than they're saying but there's no action in any other part of the world except here, and at your end. We think their plans are incremental and we're waiting for something else unanticipated to break out."

"Is your committee still planning on having their 'reunion'?

"I can't tell you anything about the committee. We're taking no chances on another outright attack on the elders. We're spending time on examining each safe house and compound and pulling up all records of occupancy and travel destinations."

"You're searching for a mole!"

"Damn right we are and we're narrowing it down quickly. I kind of hope there's a way for him…or her… to know we're on their ass. It might cut down on some of our losses and their violent attacks on us."

Upstate New York

Quimby and Egan began an inquiry from locals and all the surrounding small towns and found enough information that they could piece together the attack and the final results. Neither of them could tell where the committee was now in hiding but had begun the process of identifying the dead, tracing them back to whomever had hired them or controlled them and were attempting to find out who had paid for or sponsored the attack.

All they knew at the moment was they were in danger, their movements were being accurately monitored and at this point it was definitely a fact that there was a mole in their midst, one who was high enough up in their ranks that they had access to the deepest movements of the entire global group. Their most pressing need now, was to find out how much had already been handed over to the cabal and the second most pressing need was to try and identify the mole or moles and halt their access. It would be too much to ask that they give themselves away from any paper trail that might exist. Egan had his investigators on it from European sources and Quimby would be working from here in the US to try and uncover anything that would lead them to their source.

Quimby was very aware of Rodane Arcos, his mother, sister and daughter. He had been in touch with Agatha as well as Suri on a number of occasions over the past weeks. At first he was only concerned that he had helped to avert a possible theft of one of their recoveries. Sabina Carter was not an alarmist and he had no doubt that she and Rodane had happened upon each other by chance but it was also evident there was much more at work here. Agatha had apprised him of the DNA results of the blood work done on Arcos. Suri had clued him in on the background of Rodane's family, especially the sister and daughter.

He had taken time from his busy schedule to do personal research on the mother and Rodane's deceased father, Addison Arcos. He had done it on his own time without anyone else's involvement and it looked as if that was quite fortuitous, even though he hadn't realized it at the time. What he had learned from past news accounts in public records had not only piqued his interest but raised several alarms in his mind. For now, he was keeping all that under wraps. He placed all the printouts and copies of documents in his own personal office safe to which very few people had access. He had to help squelch this latest incursion but there was something niggling at the back of his mind that wouldn't come, even when he sat and relaxed and just let his mind and memories wander.

He was extremely tired and needed a break from this and some R&R with Alysia. It had been months since they had seen each other and Skype didn't count in his opinion. He wanted skin-to-skin, mouth-to-mouth, as necessary to him as CPR. A picture of Marian came into his mind. He cringed as if she had walked in the door at that moment. He felt no guilt for his continued tryst with Alysia. Did she know? Was Marian able to find anything at all to link him with Alysia and their house in South Carolina?

He didn't see how she could. They hadn't been down there in over a year and there was no paper trail to lead Marian to Alysia or any other evidence to show her connection to Rodane other than a long-term renter who faithfully paid her rent on time and Quimby faithfully deposited it into their joint account which Marian made short work of very quickly.

How many shoes and pocketbooks could one woman use at a time or even own in a lifetime? She could supply a soup kitchen for a year or more from selling some of her designer outfits if she cared to. The sad thing was, she didn't care. Over the thirty two years they had been married and in raising their sons for thirty of them, he had finally admitted to himself that he really didn't like his wife that much. She was a very cold, calculating, greedy woman who was only expert at subterfuge. He hadn't realized it at first, being in a stupor at the beginning, beguiled by her beauty, lulled by her sexual exploits and her curves.

{no doubt they were still beautiful}

They were definitely good in bed… and on the table tops… at beaches behind sand dunes… in library reading rooms, even elevators. If he made a list there weren't too many areas where they hadn't had sex. It aroused him, he would admit. He anticipated her needs and desires, he bought all the toys she squealed over and screamed during their frequent exploits in making use of them. She seemed insatiable and it buoyed his ego, piqued his appetite and he gloried in her body and his… until the twins came. Maybe something had happened he wasn't aware of, maybe she had a medical condition they were both unaware of that caused that cold curtain to come crashing down like glacial ice sliding into their bed, crushing his desire and freezing his very testicles when attempting to awaken her to him again.

She was forcing herself to meet his needs, she made that very clear. Her systematic schedule of which night she was available would have been laughable if not for the fact that the schedule became more and more crowded.

Headaches became more frequent, the boys' activities just tired her out to the point of 'non-functioning' as she put it, so days became weeks then months, followed by separate bedrooms and now years. He smiled to himself. He didn't miss anything. If she thought she was punishing him by withholding herself and her body he wasn't going to enlighten her. They seemed to have come to a manageable parting of the ways. As long as the money kept coming she was affable, friendly to all his business associates and very self-absorbed in her shopping, her endless luncheons and her soirees. He was also aware of her many lovers.

They saw each other as little as possible. She was only around when the boys were there and they both felt very comfortable with that arrangement. A cook came in each week to make five dinners and freeze them. If Marian wanted to host something at their house, a caterer was called and all the details were gone over and paid for with a check. Sometimes she would ask him to make an appearance depending on who it was for. He readily agreed to put in a showing, stay for perhaps an hour and quietly extract himself with the excuse of work or overseas phone calls etc. So far it had worked out very well.

He snapped to, realizing he drifted off into a reverie of the past and found himself wondering why he was revisiting this scenario of himself and Marian. There were no negative vibes coming from her except…over two weeks ago, he had come downstairs while she was on the phone to… he didn't know. She had whirled around at his step and blushed brightly as if caught in the act.

He remembered very well that afternoon… "What are you doing home Quimby?" It came off like an accusation.

"I had some personal papers I needed to put in our safe and I stopped long enough to grab some leftover chicken and rice from the fridge. Is that okay?" he hated how he sounded in his own ears, snappish and combative.

She smiled and walked over to him. She surprised him by kissing him on the cheek and patting his arm. He couldn't recall when she had last done something like that.

"Of course it's alright, silly. I've been so busy I haven't had time to clean out the refrigerator. Feel free to use all of it up or take it into the office. I know your staff loves when I send our party leftovers to them." she looked up at him coquettishly and said…

{what you're flirting with me}

"I've been thinking we really ought to do something special for your staff. They are so very loyal to you and I think they need to be reminded how much we value that loyalty. What do you think?"

Now that he thought about the whole incident he realized she had deflected the phone call, her embarrassment and had turned the conversation to inanities. He sat and thought, trying to bring up that niggling thought at the back of his mind that kept getting louder and louder. He took out his phone to place a call.

Chapter 35

Madrid, Spain

July in Madrid is Al Caliente! It only receives an average of *10*mm of rain in the summer. When you look out your window from El Escorial, close to Madrid City, you have a clear or sometimes hazy view of rocky hills, brown-yellow grass, meandering out to the stale, stark dryness of the mountains. This city lies sheltered in the shallow valley between them, and at night you can stand on the hillside and see thousands of twinkling lights, like stars that landed in a shallow ditch when they fell, with Lake Casa de Campo close by. Because of the interminable summer heat, most shops opened early, schools and universities opened early as well for classes and study, then went to Siesta for the worst heated part of the afternoon.

Looking out the wide kitchen window of their hacienda, Raul de Acevedo watched the haze dissipate from the sultry waves of heat rising from the scrub bushes and mounds of rocks covering the hillside. He was sipping on a very hot cup of expresso, readying himself for morning classes at the University of Madrid. He could just make out a few of the little buildings, sprawling along the valley floor that made up the University, as well as the cathedral-like buildings posted in every campus brochure.

There were universities from all over the world with Madrid as simply one of those campuses. Raul had been very lucky in obtaining his position in the Saint Louis University of the Jesuits, on the Madrid campus. He taught various subjects, some in the sciences, Aerospace and Engineering, as well as undergraduate courses in Biomedical Sciences and Computer Science. His back was strong. It had to be in carrying all the degrees and accolades he had accumulated over the years. He was proud that Madrid was one of the top countries listed for students desiring to study abroad.

New students signed up well in advance of his semesters or they were frozen out after the second day of registration. They flocked to his lectures, filled his electives instantly, signed up for tutorials with his aides and begged him to have informal group discussions on his subject areas in the quads, and on the campus park areas, of which there were many.

He was funny! They loved when he cracked his knock knock jokes. His quips during lecture found their way onto Youtube sites posted by the students, of course without his knowledge, and quickly went viral all over the campus. He spoke four languages and was able to reach every student easily, especially those with a language barrier. He had no inkling he was one of the most revered professors at the Institute.

He heard the phone in the den,

{forgot it again}

…rushed to answer and saw Evangela's face, switched to messenger and went facetime with her.

"Secure?" He searched her face.

"As secure as I can be without your arms around me." She blew him a kiss.

"Mi preciosa esposa! I miss you. What are you doing awake at two in the morning? Has something happened?"

She smiled, "No more than usual, a few gunshots, some kidnappers floating around…a couple of terrorist threats that closed school for an afternoon… pretty boring day yesterday!"

"If you had said everything's fine then I would have known something was wrong. All settled in Evangela?"

Evangela had the same protective devices as everyone on the committee. They blocked searches, re-rooted pinging towers, cut off 'exploits' trying to find back doors to their proprietor's server, and pretty much made it impossible to be traced. However, their conversations were still somewhat coded, just in case.

Raul hadn't heard from her since the attack in Soleux and he let out a sigh and blew her kiss back to her, "Coming home soon?"

"Maybe not, depends on the weather at sea."

{that means events across the ocean}

"Any luck with reaching your friends? It's been so long they might have forgotten you."

"People from years ago in DC and England, so… I still have my contacts and they still practice law.

{keeping up with the court cases Quimby's legal staff and Cloe's mom as well as Leander through Willow}

"What's your schedule for today, courthouse caricatures?"

"No, sun and fun but watching my cash flow".

{examining finances tracking and hunting their moles}

"Have enough money to see you through?"

{committee's finances are being investigated for embezzlement and skimming}

"Maybe…found a few extra Euros in some unique places, more to spend on drinks by the poolside."

He paused, narrowed his eyes and watched her softly nod her head and make like a wave.

{Cayman Islands, our sheltered accounts}

"Well, at least it's warm where you are."

"Yes" That was it.

{Switzerland funds are untouched, that leads to only one source}

"Is Acacia having fun with you on this trip?"

"Yep, she's broadened her horizons with all this travel and finding it very educational."

{our finance advisor is getting close}

"Sorry my love but I have to get to my classes. Can we touch base later today?"

She shook her head no, "Maybe after I catch some extra sleep."

{more days in silence}

"Take care my love, be safe. Vaya con Dios." Raul didn't fear for his own safety but then again he hadn't feared for Evangela or the entire committee until a few days ago. Everything was happening so fast, it had to be coordinated and well planned out long before this had occurred. He could only think of one reason for all of it happening now. They were working in a cabal, to take over or take out the 'family' heirs and the finances that kept them all afloat. What had happened? Some event, some unknown occurrence must have happened to make them attempt all this so brazenly and so publicly. Who attacked an entire 'family' network that has the knowledge and skills they had and had resources to follow them globally? His eyes widened with sudden awareness.

{someone with the same knowledge skills and resources}

Someone or ones… working an agenda, rooted and founded in jealousy, insecurity, and resentment. Someone like their old enemy from so long ago, who hadn't been heard from in years and years.

He picked up his satchel for school, threw the straps over his shoulder and headed for his car. While he walked, he used his phone to connect to three very important people investigating this and who needed to talk with him today. This had to end one way or another. Their entire way of life depended on it. He looked up at the clear sky.

{definitely too late to go back home now}

Somewhere in France

"What the hell are you telling me Acteon? They're broadcasting all over the whole goddamn earth and no one can track them or decode them? What the fuck do I have all this for..." he swept his arms around, "if you can't use it to find fifteen tiny little people who can just disappear without a trace?" he took a tape dispenser off his desk and threw it across the room. It hit a bookshelf with glass and metal and glass shards flew everywhere at that end of the room. Acteon winced,

"Mr. Gallo, they're going to ground. We can't get near Renata or Zoe. They have a twenty-four-hour guard on them. Lexus is in the wind and..."

"I know!" He screamed, "Tabor is useless, might as well be dead. He still may be."

"We've eyes on a number..." Acteon continued with his report.

Theras Gallo was not the only person who was totally frustrated by the events unfolding so rapidly.

Six family committee members had left Soleux by private van at two in the morning. The caretakers of the compound were moving the two survivors of the attack to a different location known only to Suri. They were quiet, dosed high on pain meds and sullen. Mercenaries did not like having the tables turned on them. They were in charge, not the other way around.

There was a quick memorial for the two men killed from the initial attack. The caretakers were shaken and solemn. Never had they been asked and required to provide actual physical protection yet it spoke to their loyalty that they were willing to die if need be in keeping everyone safe here.

Suri wanted no more bloodshed if it could be prevented. They were going to a new meeting place and she was not disclosing it to anyone until they all arrived there. Their business jet would go to each location, pick up the committee member and bring them directly to their new compound. Only then, under strict protocols, would they know where they were and then they could begin their deliberations but it would take time to set everything up once again. She had decided to take Alysia and no one else to help her with all the arrangements. The others protested they could be of service and she shouldn't have to bear the burden alone so she had picked Alysia at random from their names placed in a bowl. Nikos made it clear he was very concerned about her safety and Egan told her if anything were to happen he expected to be notified at once.

Disgruntled members left and headed to the airport lounge. Suri and Egan hung back for a time.

"You've tried all his contacts, even throughout MI6?"

Egan frowned, "Every last one. No one has heard from him in days and all his files have been commandeered and placed in secure storage. The Commanding General has sworn everyone to silence and now I can't reach anyone. No one will return my calls."

Suri looked hard at him, "Has he ever done anything like this before Egan or anything close?"

Egan and Petrus had been partners in work and love for over ten years. It was totally hidden and surreptitious for the first five but rumors swirled and whispers continued under the radar. It was not as shocking a situation as it might be in another country. Englishmen and women were not quite as staid as movies and books made them out to be. Most British accepted others as they were, not as they might want them to be.

Petrus had risen in the MI6 faster than Egan but Egan didn't owe Petrus anything for his eventual promotions. He was a brilliant analyst in his own right and everyone knew there was no unwritten contract, no clandestine meetings set up to feather Egan's cap. Petrus allowed Egan to rise on his own. He made his own reputation and the benefit was allowing the two of them to share the workload after sufficient training had taken Egan to the same building and the same floor as Petrus. Suri thought through how she could pose her next question without Egan feeling interrogated or just distrusted.

"What was the last conversation you had with him Egan? Was he himself, do you think…anything different?"

Egan raised his eyes to Suri and looked long and hard at her. He made up his mind even though he quivered inside and his belly carried lead in it and his throat threatened to close entirely from tears that appeared,

"Something was off. He wasn't sleeping, he was irritable and short. That wasn't like him, you know?"

"No, it wasn't. Petrus is one of the most affable, flexible people I know and more prone to laugh off the other pressures the rest of us give into."

"Suri I want to say something but I'm not sure how it will be taken," Egan took a deep breath.

"Egan, you've known me for practically my whole life. You were the one who took over my tutoring and got me through those teenage years when all I was interested in was rocks and bugs and didn't want to hear anything about children's classes and history lessons. If you don't know me by now…" she petered off.

"It's not that, it's just…" he rubbed his hands through his hair and scrubbed at his face.

She noticed he hadn't shaved for a few days and put it down to relaxing away from the job and letting himself bend a little.

"Okay" he blurted out, "I think Petrus was being blackmailed and I think he was giving in to whatever demands were being made on him." His shoulders slumped and his face crumpled. Suri waited a few seconds to gather her thoughts even though they were swirling around right now as if on a Merry-Go-Round.

"Tell me what makes you think that." Did Petrus let you think…?"

"No nothing like that. He was too introspective the last couple of months. Didn't engage in serious conversations, was busy all the time, no time for us, no time to vacation or travel or enjoy each other's company…"

"Then why?"

"That's why! It was as if he was afraid I was glass and had to be handled with kid gloves or hands off, more like it. Bugger it! We had a wonderful relationship, open and happy, relaxed, no need to keep anything hidden anymore. Then he closed up, shut down, went all hush-hush with me about everything; our jobs, our home life, our families." He looked at her and she could actually see the pain flicker through his eyes and his mouth tremble.

Egan spoke softly, "I heard him on the house phone a couple of weeks ago. He was almost whispering, had his back to me and didn't hear me come in. He was angry and upset but trying to be calm and quiet. I brushed against the lamp and the shade rattled. You know those little crystals we have on them?"

Suri nodded but kept very quiet. She was afraid to interrupt.

He took another long breath, "I thought he might have a lover…for a minute, just a minute. When he turned to me I saw a terrible, terrible pain go through him and he stood there dejected, hopeless almost, looking utterly lost. I… he came to me and… he folded into my arms and cried like an infant, kept saying over and over, 'I'm sorry, I'm so sorry I tried to hold out, I did.' Suri, I wanted to come to you talk to you but… everything that happened at the compound and all the events we've been investigating, I just…"

Suri took both his arms, "Egan, dear Egan it's going to be okay. I'm sure of it. Petrus is a good man, honest, loyal and whatever's going on we'll find him and we'll find out what is happening to him and we'll fix it, I promise."

He looked up at her and then they both hugged each other tightly and she stepped away.

"What else did he say? Did he tell you who he was talking to?"

"No, he said I was not going to have to pay for his indiscretions. He was going to make sure he could protect us both and if not, I was not going to suffer as a result of us loving each other. Then he left. He just walked out and didn't come home till much later. I had gone to sleep, finally. When I woke, he had left a note on my night table and gone into work. Except when I got to work, he wasn't there and he hasn't come home since." His voice trembled again, "His note gave me access to his safety deposit box and instructions on where his sister was living. He told me to trust no one and especially to say nothing to Nikos."

Suri's eyes widened, "Nikos? Why would he say…I don't understand," Suri felt like heaving her last meal. Her gut tightened and her mind fuzzed over for a few seconds.

"Suri, are you okay? Do you want to sit down? Suri!"

She waved him off, "I'm okay. I'm tired and stressed. It's okay, I'm good." She shook it off.

"Have you spoken to anyone else about this?" Her heart hammered in her chest.

"What, are you nuts? Sorry that just… came out of its own accord… brain freeze!"

Suri smiled, "You and me both. Can you keep this between us for the time being while I contact Quimby and get him in on this?"

Egan eagerly accepted without a qualm. He trusted her explicitly and a weight was shared with someone else he could depend on no matter what. They agreed to touch base with each other in two days or if Suri discovered something sooner. Then they joined everyone else in the airport lounge.

Evangela looked up as they entered and everyone else followed suit. Nikos stood and came over to them.

"Are you okay? You two both look like you've seen a ghost of our ancestors… Is anything the matter?"

"Suri spoke up, "We were just reviewing the last day's events and both of us were a little overwhelmed in talking about it, so sad and so worrisome." She looked at Egan for reassurance, "I promised her I would be there in a flash if she needed me and I made her promise to call me if that were the case."

"Good Man, Egan. Suri, you will call us if you need help with anything, right my girl?" Nikos smiled at her.

It took everything in her to smile back at him right then. Her skin crawled as if a snake was finding its way across it and she gave a little shiver,

"Now, now Suri, it will be alright. We're all here for you, aren't we folks?" Nikos looked around to the others. Suri looked to Egan and nodded her head slightly. His lips were thinned together and his eyes took on a glitter. He lowered them and went to sit down by the window. Evangela moved over and patted the seat next to her and Suri went and sat down and put her head back against the seat. She closed her eyes and everyone looked at her with concern. Nikos clucked his tongue like a mother hen concerned for her chick.

Suri 'pinned' Quimby when she got on the plane. She went to the small lounge in the back and asked them to give her some privacy to make some calls and lineup her agenda for their meeting. Everyone was exhausted, stressed out and happy to have time for their selves. Evangela was messaging Raul, the rest were dozing or listening to music, lights low, some on the movie channel, just zoning out. The flight would take them to three airports in three different countries, with little time to deplane, then refuel and take off again. They would all be home by dawn or shortly after. His form was in front of her on the table, his shirt cuffs undone, his tie askance and his face haggard. He paced and he paced in front of the screen. Suri laid out the conversation she and Egan had shared. Her mind was jumbled and now Quimby had laid another jolt on her and she was grappling with it.

"No, you can't be sure Quimby. It's a hunch. What proof do you have?" He reached over to his desk and held up a sheaf of papers, "This…and phone records going back two years." He threw the documents onto the table and they slithered across and lay jumbled on the floor.

"Maybe it's only a flirtation. Maybe she's just using it to make you…"

"Suri, it's obvious you haven't kept up with events in my life. Marian and I are in a 'compatible' arrangement, devoid of the actual niceties of a marriage. We are, however, satisfied with the arrangement and we both have found what we need to be happy.

"Who is it Quimby? Where are the calls coming from?"

"…France…almost every one of them except for the last two. They were placed to the Cayman Islands and to a small shire in the north in England. I don't know how it was done but the numbers were redacted."

"How is that… who could… sorry, I'm rambling. Let's figure this out."

"Suri, my wife is consorting with our enemies, I'm certain of that. What's to figure out? I'm going to push these papers into her face and she will tell me what and who she is involved with." His figure actually shimmered with his anger and body heat.

"Quimby wait! Don't do anything rash that would send her scurrying… possibly to whomever she's in touch with. We need time to figure out how to uncover this tangled mess and do it without these people knowing we're aware. If you face her down now with this, we'll lose any advantage of her not realizing you are on to her. Please think!" She waited.

"Thirty two years" he mumbled, "I knew we didn't have much anymore, but I thought we at least had…"

"What, trust?" Suri lowered her voice, "Quimby, on a much more personal note, does Marian know about Alysia? Before you say 'no way', is it possible she does and this is her way of getting even? Marian is far from dumb you know?" He paused, thought it over.

"I guess she could have found out but I don't know how. I never keep anything here that would lead to Alysia or... Wait! Oh my sweet gods...!" He slapped himself upside the head. "How could I be so stupid? Now I know what I was trying to remember. Shit, shit, shit, double shit on a stick!" He paced in front of her.

"What is it Quimby? I don't have much time here..."

"I put them in my safe. I didn't even consider she would want to look at papers I put in the safe. She never takes an interest in my business except to spend the money I make with it. Christ! How could I be so stupid?" he slapped himself again.

"Quimby, please stop! Tell me what you did."

He looked over at her, "I arranged for supplies and transportation for Caroline and Sophia Arcos to be taken to my beach house for safety with Philip Barbas until we had all this sorted out and either tabled or permanently fixed. All the papers were sent to Alysia for her signature and copies were in the safe. So yes...to answer your question, Marian knows about Alysia and yes, she is probably a bit upset, if you will. She might not want me but she'll be damned if she would want someone else to have me." He ceased his rambling and stood there abject, "This is my fault, I caused this."

"No you didn't, Marian did. If she is giving information to anyone against us, it's her, not you that is responsible."

"What do we do now? Why couldn't she just pitch a fit or throw my clothes out on the lawn or file for divorce or ..."

"Quimby, what do we do now? Focus! You're good at this. We have two people off the reservation here, Petrus and possibly Marian. How do we handle this and what do we do about Philip, Caroline and Sophia? They won't be safe there now."

"How bad do you think this head of the cabal now, with the moves they are making, want to get to Rodane Arcos and his family?" Quimby waited for her thoughts.

He looked at Suri's expression and said, "Never mind I know the answer to that. Is the pope Catholic?"

"What? Is the..." Suri finally smiled and then chuckled, "Good one Quimby. At least you still have your sense of humor."

"Okay, let me put a halt to the move and get them out of their house. I'll put them up in a hotel if necessary until you and I figure out what we're doing. I'll contact you in..." he looked at his watch..."five hours with a plan on this end and we work it together. Do we deal with anyone else about Petrus… or Marian?" He winced at the thought.

"No definitely not. This stays between you and me until we make a move." Suri was firm.

"Get some rest Suri you look like hell. Talk to you soon."

Outside the door to the lounge, a silent figure turned slowly and softly tread on the plush carpet to make as little noise as possible and made their way back to the seats via the bathroom.

{much to do and little time to do it}

Suri had no sooner disconnected with Quimby than a soft knock at the door had her startle up in her seat. She invited whoever in, but dreaded having to face anyone with the news she now had under her hat at the moment. Alysia slipped in, looked out the door and down the hall and closed it. She put her finger to her ear and tilted her head at Suri who took a slim tablet and turned it on. The red line showed no fluctuations and no anomalies of sound.

She said, "We're secure Alysia."

"Suri, I didn't have time back in Soleux to talk to you before… well, I didn't get a chance to talk to you. All of us were kind of… busy" she smiled weakly.

"What is it Alysia? I hope not bad news or anything amiss. I'm feeling like a flash drive that's overloaded and about to crash." She looked worried and pale and very tired. The deep circles under her eyes bespoke a few sleepless nights.

"It's okay. I can talk to you after we land and before I'm dropped off at my…"

"No, I'm sorry. That came off as very self-serving. We have time now. Please, sit down. Tell me now."

"You gave me all the printouts of travel and accommodations. I had looked them over but this morning something occurred to me that I overlooked at the last meeting we had."

"What was that?"

"Well, I can account for all the money that was spent down to the penny for all the R&R teams. I also have a clear and concise record of all the travel made by every committee member over the last forty-nine years and it's extensive to say the least but…"

"Whose is missing?" Suri held her breath.

"Not missing just inaccurate. I cross-checked travel dates with destinations and then did a computer spreadsheet of all trips and air flights over the last twenty five years. If I hadn't reconciled I was going to backdate to thirty or more years and go as far as it took to reconcile them. I didn't have to go back. All the anomalies and inaccuracies only went back to twenty one years."

"Is it bad?" Suri prepared herself and her pulse increased to a fluttery runaway.

"I'm not sure what it means. They're maybe just errors in bookkeeping, something we could review and recalculate." She looked so very uncomfortable.

"But you don't think that's the case, do you Alysia?" Suri sounded resigned and dejected.

Alysia let out a long sigh, "No I don't. The numbers have been checked and cross-checked and the dates are on signed invoices. These don't seem to be errors."

"Okay, give me the name please."

Alysia started, "Name? You know…? Did you already know…?"

"No I didn't, but some things have been falling into place lately, some very disturbing connections and I'm beginning to make out some very distinct patterns. I wish I could say the same; that it's errors, mistakes in invoices or receipts but I don't think we have that luxury. Who is it?"

Alysia's voice hitched and choked when she answered, "Nikos Kostas." She didn't dare add anything to that one answer. Alysia sat in silence and the muted noise of the plane's engines was muffled. It sounded to their ears like a prolonged knell. Suri sat in silence with her hands clasped so tightly her fingers were bone white. "Did you share this with anyone else? Does Nikos know?"

"Oh good gods, no! I've been so frantic trying to figure out how to tell you, then…the attack and…"

"It's okay" Suri reached over and covered her hands, "Has anyone been to the safe to look them over that you know?"

Alysia looked chagrined and self-conscious, "I changed the password and combination. I thought if we were injured or worse, the attackers would have access to all our paper trail and our passcodes to banks and financial houses. I thought if anything happened to me, one of you could crack the code I left in my room with my 'pin'."

Suri laughed out loud, "How very clever of you! Your promotion has been long overdue and well deserved." She hugged Alysia and the girl blushed scarlet. "I'm going to leave you here and I want you to 'pin' with Quimby and relay all of this to him. Give him the new passcodes and combinations and when you go back to your things, destroy the codes where you placed them."

"You don't want them? I thought…"

"Nope, too close to the solution of this incursion. I won't take a chance on all the bad guys slipping away into the night after they force me to give them up."

Alysia paled, "You think he'd… they'd… oh good gods, what's happening here?" She burst into tears.

Chapter 36

White House, DC.

The plane moved through the skies, delivering its passengers to their destinations while others across the vast ocean of the Atlantic gathered together for an early morning meeting in the Situation Room of the White House. The president's Science Advisor was present as were Senator Jackson Lovett, Co-chairman of the Science Investigative Committee, the chairman of the Science, Space and Technology committee, and the head legal counsel of the president. Fifteen minutes after they had convened, they were joined by the Chairman of the Joint Chiefs and the Secretary of State. The president's wife had made good on her commitment to Cornelia Lovett. She had her team do research, request documents and collate all the scholarships and grant applications going back at least five years. It was a daunting task, but they were up for it.

Once the cat had scratched a hole in the bag, everyone felt the tension and excitement of a true mission; find the fraud, locate the source of all the embezzlement and trace all of it back to the source. They were on a mission that would uncover some of the most egregious malfeasance and misuse of government funds since the Watergate scandal of years past. Millions, perhaps billions of dollars had been funneled and misdirected to sheltered and hidden accounts in many places all over Europe and the islands. The president was legitimately enraged that he had to hear these facts from his wife's team. His Science Advisor and the entire Science Investigative Team had no idea or any inkling of the lengths to which this fraud and theft of funds had reached.

Now, research had determined that 24% of the scholarships granted to science researchers and labs all over the globe were devoid of legitimate contact information or background resume information. Small labs that filed for grants and listed their research projects were found to be non-existent. Money was already distributed, grants had already been signed over and the procedures were well underway. Even NASA could not account for the scholarship funds that had been dispersed to addresses that were non-existent and checks had been cashed at banks all over the country by untraceable persons and fake accounts. It amounted to well over twelve billion dollars.

"What the hell do I even have a Science Investigative Committee for if nothing is investigated and money is flowing through a sieve of hackers and frauds? How could you people call yourselves learned men in science and technology when hackers and frauds have managed to pull this off on you with a minimum of technology and apparently better hackers than anyone you have in service?"

"Mr. President, as soon as this was brought to our attention, we put our best cybersecurity experts on finding and tracking resources. They're working very hard to have some leads soon. We'll..."

"You'll give it 'all your attention since it's your job and you have absolutely no idea how this happened'. Yeah, I get that. I'm directing you to join with the HSA and the CIA to share information and put a team together comprised of at least two hackers and two CSC, ASAP. I want a daily report on my desk by 6 a.m. tomorrow and I want it started now. Dismissed!"

The president's military background sometimes made him forget that his civilian staff wasn't as quick to salute as he might be used to, but salute they did, turned smartly and exited the room red-faced and sweating, with some low mumbling under their breath.

"Logan, I heard that. If jackasses you act like, jackasses you are. Now get to work." Logan Potter paled and said, "Yes sir!" and left quickly.

"Margo, stay... and Cornelia... have your team meet with you immediately after this session."

"Yes sir" She turned to leave.

"Mr. President" the Secretary of State spoke, "Could Cornelia remain for this discussion? I think what she has accomplished already is invaluable and I'd like to keep her in the loop if I may, and my assistant as well, if that's okay?"

He looked from Cornelia to Cloe and narrowed his eyes at Cloe, "Cornelia I know of course, from Senator Lovett. Good man that, and you are...

"Cloe Kostas uh...Mr. President, I'm..."

"I know what your title is. I was just trying to place where I've seen you before. Any ideas?"

She was somewhat taken by surprise. Those in higher offices usually give little notice to the underlings and she would have liked to keep it that way. She grimaced with the thought then said, "No sir, afraid not."

"That's okay, I'll remember. I got a mind like a trap. Not good cuz it keeps me awake at night but it will come to me."

They discussed the findings of the evidence his wife and her team of researchers had uncovered and passed along to her. It wouldn't do for the First Lady to be tied into decisions made by the president that were going to get a great deal of attention soon. A few big companies and some mighty wealthy donors were in for a bumpy ride and President McAndrew was not averse to rattling their cages even if they roared at him. This was money and lots of it, that was finding its way to Lord knows where, and he was on to it like a lion tamer. If he could have his people find millions, perhaps billions of dollars in theft and fraud, and if any of those wealthy donors or companies were complicit in funneling those millions or billions, it would give him a very substantial gain in the polls and a foot up the ladder for reelection.

{always an upside to every negative event}

Lori McAndrew and Cornelia Lovett had been friends since college. They had rooms in a Quad together with Caroline Arcos, nee Bigelow for the first year of college. They had become best friends, along with Trudy McCarty. Their foursome went everywhere together and watched each other's backs at dorm and frat parties and dates that met in bars and concerts. No one of them ever had to ask for help but the whistles were there none the less. The friendship lasted even when Lori transferred to Georgetown in her third year, where she met Seamus McAndrew while he was studying at the War College in DC at an interparty get together of a frat and their sorority.

Cloe had been groomed by Cornelia from her freshman year, when Cornelia had been asked by Suri to take her under her wing and teach her what she needed to learn to achieve a high position in the next elected government. That was six years ago, and Cloe was a gem. She was bright, had a gift for song, had two well-known parents in DC in the high court system, and was sweet in the bargain.

When Cloe had shared her knowledge with Cornelia about Rodane Arcos and Sabina, and the events in Greece and Italy, Cornelia had asked her to share that with her parents who were both well-respected lawyers. Her father was a judge in DC. Cloe's mother was Isabel Kostas, a lawyer in the US District Court, under review for a promotion to the US bankruptcy court on Constitution Avenue. Her father was Nikos Kostas, currently a judge on the US Court of Federal Claims on Madison Place Northwest, in the heart of DC. He was also a longtime member of the present committee of the 'family'. All three of the ladies tried to meet during the day, sometimes for breakfast, sometimes lunch. She and her mother had met for lunch at the Old Glory Barbecue Place on M Street in downtown DC. It was close to the Potomac River and afforded breezes on the hottest of days, up on the rooftop deck. The best ribs in all of DC, as far as Isabel was concerned.

Nikos was on his way home and Cloe was leaving soon for a trip to Myrtle Beach with Andrew, her boyfriend of ten months and a real 'hottie' as Isabel told Cloe. She laughed when her daughter covered her red face and said, 'Mom, please' She would be gone for three days and when she got back, there was certain to be a pile of folders on her desk with URGENT stamped across the file covers. Everything was urgent in DC until they got their answer back. Then they dragged their feet for days or weeks or even months before all the 'Urgent' information was released to the public.

President McAndrew and these three very astute women shared all their information, all of it! Seamus McAndrew was well aware of the abilities of Cornelia and Lori, his own wife, in getting things done when they worked together. It was scary to him what odds they consistently beat, what people they advised him to avoid, which turned out to be spot-on and spooky; how Lori knew what he was thinking before he did and the effect she had, even with his enemies, in coming to a bipartisan agreement using her advice. He liked Cornelia but he adored her daughter, Hallie. He and his wife had been blessed with two wonderful boys, now almost grown men, but never a daughter who they had wished for avidly. Hallie was a treasured, adopted goddaughter, the girl they never had and so doted on her, along with her mother, but never in public. President McAndrew looked up sharply and said, "Trudy McCarty!"

They looked at him in confusion for a few minutes and then Cornelia put it together and said, "Her brother?"

"Yes!" he slapped his knee and chuckled, "I go around in a maze but I find my way out eventually."

"Sir?" Cloe said, still confused.

"You were at a White House dinner we gave six or seven months ago to the Journalists' Conference of DC and I presented awards and gave a speech… should have handed out prison sentences to those bastards that are always twisting my words and trying to make me out an idiot."

The Secretary of State raised her eyebrows and pursed her lips.

"Don't look at me like that Margo. You have to put up with it too. Can you tell me you wouldn't want to meet them in a dark alley some night?"

"No sir, there's always cameras somewhere."

He returned his attention to Cloe, "You were dressed in that royal blue color that made your eyes look like Sapphires and you were with…who's that guy from The Eagle Margo? Some…"

"Andrew McCarty, Mr. President."

"Yeah, his older sister and Lori are friends and he pussyfoots around saying nasty things about me in a nice way. Trudy is nice, I like her. Her brother… he narrowed his eyes and asked, "You serious about that young man, Clarisa?"

"Cloe, sir"

"Well, never mind, none of my business, but watch how he treats his mother before you get serious. Always can tell how they'll treat you by how they treat their mother. Save yourself some grief."

"Thank you sir, I'll remember that." She was two shades of red and flustered.

The president said, "Okay Corny, come clean. How did you get on to this? It's me now. I'm not some congressional committee trying to trip you up. Don't claim the fifth on me."

Cornelia laid out the events that had dragged her into the tragedy of Adam's death and the attack at Iona Arcos' house. That led them to Rodane Arcos and his attacks at Akrotiri and Naples. It slowly took shape and formed a pattern that was becoming clear, even to the president, who generally took little notice of personal events that crossed oceans or country's borders unless it created an International incident. He left that to his staff and his Secretary of State with their daily briefings of International events of more newsworthy happenings. He was a very compassionate man but only one man. He couldn't take on the entire globe and extend sympathies from the Office of the President for each person who died or became ill.

Cornelia looked at him, taking notes rapidly and chanced a statement, "Your wife and I shared notes…we researched these events which led her to have her staff do extensive research on…"

"No, don't tell me." he looked up, "I don't want any connection coming out from Lori's staff that will have the hyenas circling and attempting to breach the perimeter of White House confidence. Let's just say that Madam Secretary and her staff were led to uncover some irregularities in the… what's that called Margo?

"NABSGr.org Mr. President."

"Yeah, that. We just lead them to the end result of the investigation without revealing their 'sources' as they are so fond of saying. Let's give some back to them," he chuckled, "let them know it was done because of concern for the International and Global repercussions that we could all experience if we don't get a handle on this. We'll stress how much money is involved and how we intend to see our taxpayers are not duped and blah, blah, blah. That should have them looking at the reports under investigation instead of the investigators. What do you think of that, Margo?"

"Well sir, do you think we can rely on your wife's staff to keep it under wraps?"

"Most definitely, I can assure you."

"Then I think it's a very good way to proceed Mr. President, quite clever but entirely true also"

He basked in the praise but also knew they were in a tricky spot.

"Not a word spoken here by anyone, got it?"

They all nodded, "Calinda…no, Cloe, right?" she smiled and nodded her head.

"Watch out for that reporter of yours. They're always digging for… whatever. Tight lips, right? Loose lips… scuttle boats… or something."

"Mr. President, sir…I…" Cloe's hands were sweating and she felt a little dizzy.

"My mother is a lawyer in the DC courts and I asked her to…"

"She knows about all this?" He narrowed his eyes, "Anyone else?" He didn't sound pleased at all.

"Her paralegals were the ones to do all the research and follow up on…"

"Read them in as National Security Margo. Get someone to their offices to give their oaths. He turned to Cloe, "Anyone else missy, the janitors…any of the kitchen staff?"

Cloe colored red and answered "Not that I know of sir." She felt like sinking into the plush carpet under her feet. His bearing had stiffened and straightened, "We need to contain this to as few people as possible. Are we done here?" They looked at each other and nodded assent. "Okay, we'll keep on this and Margo, give me any updates that you feel are necessary. Good day ladies."

Virginia

Caroline was cleaning and scrubbing the stove and trying to take out her nervous energy cleaning and scrubbing anything not held down. The doorbell chimed and she ignored it. She didn't want to talk to anyone, didn't want to see anyone and didn't want to bring one more casserole into her kitchen. She wanted, as Greta was fond of saying, 'to be alone.' The bell over the door chimed again and held.

{idiot! I'm not home can't you tell}

The last few days were busy but frenetic for her. She had plenty to do and when that was done, she found things to do. Then she redid what she had already done. All the drawers were sorted and organized, all the furniture polished to a high sheen, all the closets cleaned out and donations made to several organizations. The kitchen was the last thing she was tackling to take her mind off anything real or present. It didn't really help the perpetual ache she had in her gut and the knot in her throat. When she stopped to sit down, she toppled into a chair and looked around as if she found herself in a strange place, even a strange land. Then she was up and at it again. Curtains! She could wash them or go buy new ones and replace them. The bell chimed again.

She threw down the cloth and tore her gloves off as she walked toward the front door, a string of curses escaping her lips. Beaker got up immediately and nudged his way in front of her. She reached over and opened the door, prepared to tell whoever, 'don't want any' and slam the door in their face. She stopped and looked at a trim, silver-haired, very distinguished man in a seersucker suit

{who still wears seersucker}

…holding a briefcase and looking at his watch.

"Am I keeping you up from your next appointment? It's fine if you want to move on, I'm not interested." She went to close the door.

"Mrs. Arcos, please. You've had us running in circles trying to get in touch with you. I'll only take a few minutes of your time. Please, time is of the essence." He hadn't cracked a smile, not even a smirk.

"Do I know you? What are you selling and how do you know my name? Beaker sat there, head cocked to the side, content to simply listen.

The man in the seersucker suit reached across to hand her a business card and Beaker was on his feet in a split-second, a low rumble in his throat. The man flinched, took a step back and stood ramrod-straight.

"Beaker, still!" Beaker stopped and sat back and watched Caroline put her hand out for the business card,

"Lafferty, Cork and Caine, Attorneys at law: Wills, Estates and Trusts. Okay Mr. Lafferty…"

"Mr. Cork, ma'am, my name is Fuller Cork."

"Well now Mr. Fuller Cork…" trying hard not to laugh,

{are you fuller wine too}

"What can I do for you?"

"I'm here to do something for you Ms. Arcos. It won't take long, I promise."

"How about we do this? I'll call your law office and if you don't mind waiting, we'll see what you can do for me."

She closed the door, leaned against it and thought... 'What now?' Okay, she was game. He looked reputable.

{shows you what looks count for}

Instead of calling the number on the card he had given her she pushed 3-1-1, and asked for the number for Lafferty, Cork, and Kane. Surprised, she saw the number was the same as the card.

"Well, Beaker, it seems we have a verified lawwwyer here." she drew out the word. Beaker tilted his head and appeared to listen to her. Opening the door, she smiled, extended her hand and spoke, "Mr. Cork, please come in. Sorry for the rude welcome. Can't be too careful now, can we?"

"No Miss Arcos...definitely can't be too careful, especially with what happened with Mr. Porter." She flinched and drew back, "Adam...you knew Adam? How..."

She was on guard again, "Could we please talk inside or I can have you come to the office if you care to and if it makes you feel more comfortable. It's quite... confidential."

She made a gut decision and stood to the side and motioned him in. She picked up her phone again and called Mrs. Floyd next door.

"Mrs. Floyd, I have a visitor from Lafferty, Cork, and Caine with me now, so I'll be over as soon as we are finished our business." Without his being aware, she snapped a photo of him sitting on the sofa and disconnected with a message sent. She couldn't believe she had become so paranoid in such a short time but Sophia would be home soon with Phillip from soccer practice, and she didn't want this man here when she walked in.

She had become very jumpy and suspicious of anyone who walked by the house. Truth be told, Caroline felt likewise but she was trying her damndest to tamp down her feelings and relax around her daughter.

He opened his briefcase and pulled out a sheaf of papers and handed them to her silently. She looked at him quizzically, took the papers and got her reading glasses off the mantle. She read, her eyes widened, her mouth dropped open and her pulse picked up speed. She looked up at him, he nodded to her and she went back to the beginning and read them all over again. It didn't help. The words remained the same on the pages and her mouth was still open in shock.

"Mr. Cork, I don't understand. Adam was... you know... Adam..." He nodded.

"He was a trainer at the gym. He didn't have a career or a job, outside of... how could this say..." She stopped and swallowed. Her throat was dry, her chest felt tight and her head was light.

"Mrs. Arcos are you all right? Should I call someone or get you some water or…" he looked very flustered to be alone with her now, when she was obviously in some distress.

"No, I'm Okay. Please…give me a minute here. You can't just drop this in my lap and expect me to be calm and collected."

"You didn't know? I assumed that you knew…"

"Mr. Cork, you know what they say about people who assume… sorry that was supposed to be clever. I meant…"

"Quite, quite, you're exactly right. Well, here is where we are. Your Mr. Porter was very well off in his own right. He had substantial shares of stock in several high-end companies, very aggressive companies. He also had an insurance policy with Double Indemnity in case of accidental or homicidal death. He also had treasury bonds to the tune of $250,000 when they mature. It appears that will be when your daughter reaches eighteen years of age or college whichever comes first."

"My daughter… what does she have to do with…?"

"The treasury bonds list her as the beneficiary with you as the holder of entitlement to disperse those funds as you see fit until she reaches twenty one."

"He has his sister…she lives in…"

"We are quite aware of his sister…Tara is her name, correct?"

"Yes, she was here for the funeral and she…"

"She is quite aware of the provisions of his will. We met with her the day she flew back to Utah. She was most understanding of her brother's wishes, especially after she met you and your daughter, Sophia."

"Right"…she rose from the sofa, "Excuse me Mr. Cork I'll be right back."

She went to the bathroom, emptied her bladder before she peed her pants and used cold water on her flaming face. She looked into the mirror and saw Adam's face bending to her and felt his lips so close to her, it was as if he were there in the bathroom with her. She let out one hard sob then grabbed the sides of the cool sink, took a couple of deep breaths, a drink of water and returned to the sitting room.

Mr. Cork was sitting as ramrod-straight as he had when she left, with one exception. Beaker was lying across his feet with his head between his paws, eyes closed, relaxed and happy.

Caroline said, "Beaker! I'm sorry Mr. Cork. Usually he doesn't do this with strangers. Beaker, come."

Mr. Cork put up his hand, "Please…let him stay? I recently lost my dog and he…seems to be in tune with me at the moment, if you don't mind?" His look was supplicating and she got a totally different vibe from him now.

She smiled broadly, "Of course. You know Mr. Cork, I thought I was able to handle surprises but you've handed me one humdinger of a total surprise. I'm not quite sure…" her voice trailed off.

"We can do all this at the office if you would like some time to assimilate it. I'd be happy to arrange an appointment at your convenience…" the door opened and Sophia came tripping in and threw her book bag on the floor in the foyer and yelled,

"Momaaa, are you home? There's a car in our driveway…, oh hi, who are you?"

Sophia stood in the doorway looking from Caroline to Mr. Cork, gauging whether she should be concerned or not. She looked at Beaker across his feet and said, "But you're okay, because Beaker feels safe with you, right mom?" she looked steadily at her mother.

"Yes honey, he does. Mr. Cork is here to bring me some papers to read and go over. We were just talking about Adam…" Sophia's face went slack for a moment and Phillip came into the doorway at that moment, hearing Caroline's comment and he looked directly at Mr. Cork with a wary look and a stiff posture putting his arm around Sophia's shoulder.

Mr. Cork said, "It's okay young man, we're just wrapping this up and I'll be out of here in a few moments, nothing to worry about here."

Philip looked at him, made a judgement and went over to him and extended his hand, "Philip Barbas…you are…?"

"Simon Cork of…"

Sophia giggled, "I'm sorry Mr. Cork, I didn't mean to laugh but I've never met a cork before…" then she blushed and giggled some more.

"Quite so Miss Sophia, I'm sure. My family name comes from a part of Ireland where my parents came from when they set out for the land of the free." he smiled at her.

"Ireland" Sophia said, "they have leprechauns there, don't they?"

Caroline went over to Sophia put her arm around her shoulder, "Sophia honey, you know that leprechauns are pretend?"

"I know Mama but you can pretend if it makes you happy and doesn't hurt anyone, Dad said so."

Caroline looked in her innocent eyes, squeezed her shoulder and said, "Dad's right. Leprechauns are meant for little girls to believe in. Would you please go put your school things away and you can use the computer for a half hour before you do homework."

"Cool… thanks Mr. Cork. He looked up at her remark and smiled at her, "I usually have boring homework as soon as I get home. Mama, can I get a snack?"

"Something small, don't…"

"…spoil my dinner, right?" She skipped out and Phillip turned to follow her.

Caroline said, "Philip I'd like it if you could stay." She turned to Mr. Cork, "That's okay, right? I can use his advice?"

Mr. Cork looked questioningly at Philip, then back to Caroline. She thought she could almost read his mind, "Yes, I know he seems such a young man and I could be his mother…"

He put up his hand and said "No, no. I wasn't thinking that. Actually Mrs. Arcos, I was hoping you had someone at hand who could be of help to you in deciphering all this.

"He is definitely able and clever enough to help me 'decipher' this, as you put it."

They both sat down in separate chairs and Mr. Cork began to once again, go over the papers in front of them while Caroline looked at the surprised expression on Philip's face but the calm manner in which he listened and followed the instructions left by Adam for the care and support of his sweet Caroline and his girl, Sophia.

Chapter 37

Oma's home—Virginia

People were moving all over the place; some in secret, some definitely leaving a trail and some being moved despite their wishes and the wishes of others.

It was a busy travel week for at least seven people and a dog. Renata was healing nicely and Rodane had made it his business to make sure she took it easy and concentrated on getting better. Zoe was another case. She was healing slowly but it was surprising she was healing at all. By all accounts she should have died but she didn't and Rodane was making sure she healed as well. His mother insisted on them staying in her home, though Eugenie was more adamant that they find somewhere else to heal, away from prying eyes and curious inquiries.

Renata had gone home with Eugenie and Iona and found her room pleasant and sun filled. She was healing exceptionally well and quickly. Most mornings, she came in from her room on the first floor, usually early, and asked to help with breakfast or coffee or just sat and talked with Iona while she fixed breakfast for everyone.

Rodane had brought Zoe home three days after surgery with a long list of diet restrictions and an exercise regimen designed to make her heal faster. She had follow-up doctor's appointments in two days and a schedule of physical therapy, but was not happy about them. Iona was using her mom's skills to feed and care for both women despite their assurances they could fend for themselves. Truth be told, they were grateful for the concern, the Mickey Mouse pancakes, the soft sheets, the conversation with a woman of much knowledge and a great sense of humor.

Eugenie came downstairs and watched the interplay between the two women for a few seconds. It was surprising, the feelings of relief and compassion she felt for Renata. Usually when someone deliberately tries to kill you not once but three times, you have a tendency to hate their guts or at least distrust them a lot. But that hadn't turned out to be the case. Renata was bright, quick to discern subtle meanings in their conversations, and very adroit at deflecting the conversation to other avenues when she felt like she was being interrogated, which was exactly the problem.

She was being interrogated. They all knew she had a treasure trove of knowledge and inside information. It was very necessary to uncover the highest levels of those responsible for the latest attacks and incursions into all they held dear and secretive and they knew she knew. They tread softly but surely, trying to be kind and unobtrusive but most definitely attempting to intrude into her background and her personal space. It resembled something like a masquerade, people dancing around each other, masks on but flirting around the true motives that were masked, as it were.

Renata seemed to sense Eugenie's presence and said, "Come on in, pancakes are almost ready."

Eugenie placed a smile on her face and entered the kitchen, sat at table, poured herself some orange juice and looked over at Iona,

"Grocery shopping today? I imagine we are beginning to eat you out of house and home."

"Nonsense" Iona quipped, "I love feeding invalids who have to eat whatever I give them and no bones about it."

Renata chuckled, "If I eat any more of what you force me to eat, I'll have to buy a new wardrobe when I get back to…" she stopped suddenly and looked from one to the other, "Not that easy," as she looked down into her coffee cup.

Eugenie spoke hesitantly, "Renata, I have some news for you. I'd like to explain our travel plans for the next few days…" her hesitation made Renata bristle.

"Whether I like it or not… is that what you're leading up to?"

Iona stepped in but gently, "Renata, you are in more than a little of a tough situation here. The police officers who were here that night…" Renata winced, "are calling every day wanting to know when they can talk to you…"

Renata broke in, "How did they know I'm here? You told them?" she looked hurt and sullen.

"No, the hospital did. We don't know who but someone there called them when we were leaving and they checked with the nurses on duty and found out who had been to see you and then called here."

Renata started to get up from her chair and cringed at the lingering pain in her leg. All the infection was under control and it was healing but the damage and tears to the muscles and the swelling still gave her some discomfort.

Iona said "Renata, before you try and collect your things and head out for parts unknown, why don't we at least listen to Genie and then you can decide your next move?"

Zoe appeared at the doorway, her arm in a sling, walking slowly but upright and a grim expression on her face. She had lost some weight just over the few days of the shooting, her surgery, and her recuperation in the hospital and here in Iona's house. It was a struggle to get her to eat and Iona and Genie both, thought there was a lot more going on than just the shooting itself. She was reticent to even join them during the day and when she was there, her silence was pronounced.

There was a separate war going on in her, as there was with Renata but they both had their own ways of handling it. Zoe was introspective and Renata was fragile but defensive. Her actions were those of a feisty little vixen, holding her ground when faced with stronger and more threatening adversaries.

Iona was determined to make her see they were not her adversaries. Hard for someone who spent the last weeks searching, finding, and attacking those perceived adversaries. She smiled inwardly. She was actually beginning to like Renata. She saw the strength in Renata that transcended that aggressive, alpha-like attitude she displayed to everyone around her. She also saw a very hurting, angry, young woman who was struggling with some inner demons Iona couldn't even begin to imagine but she sensed their presence.

Renata looked at Genie, "You talked to them? You told them how this all went down?" It was Eugenie's turn to bristle, "If that were the case Renata, you wouldn't be here. You'd be in court or in jail." Then she held up her hand to forestall a verbal attack on her comment, "Let's look at this logically. You can't leave the country, your name is sure to be on the watch list till this investigation is completed, you said yourself you didn't know where you were heading, you're not in great physical shape yet, and you have no transportation. Suppose you let all those sink in, and then possibly calm down?"

Renata looked at Zoe, "You know what they're planning? Genie's talked to you already?"

Zoe walked to the table and took a seat. She leaned in and said calmly, "Since it involves me and my family, I think it was sort of necessary to run it by me first, especially when both of us are under a cloud here."

Renata looked at her a long time then said, a little less angry, "What is it, tell me. I can't promise I'll like it or agree but I'm kind of in a bind here, aren't I?"

Iona put down her spatula, turned off the stove and walked over to her and squatted down in front of her, "Renata" she reached out her hand, placed it on Renata's knee and was surprised when Renata didn't jerk away. Progress!

"We know you a little now. We've spent enough time and conversation with you to say we know you. You need a safe place to stay and…, you need to feel like someone has your back and is just looking out for you. You can decide to accept it or reject it…your choice. I'm hoping you will make the right one for you."

"Okay let's talk." Renata relaxed and Iona got up to serve a good breakfast while they hatched out their less than desirable travel plans. Eugenie looked at her, nodded her head slightly, and sat down to attack the crisp bacon sitting on the table.

Rodane and Philip had stayed up till the wee hours discussing so many topics they had lost track of time. Both were avid devotees of Archaeology and the latest discoveries in that field as well as Paleontology. Rodane took note of Phillip's vast, extensive knowledge in fields seldom followed by one so young. He suspected that his youth was not the only thing to be unusual for him. His education seemed to encompass all the historical facts, the evidentiary proof of facts and figures, the past and present grants in these fields and an extensive travel experience that had taken him to most of the places that Rodane was personally familiar with. Phillip was definitely much more than what was perceived by someone based on first impressions and perceptions.

The barking from the downstairs hall startled him out of his reverie and he bounded out of bed and raced to the door, a little disoriented but adrenaline flowing. The events over the last weeks had kept him on constant alert, even when sleeping. His body was at once both exhausted and wired, even without coffee. He felt himself always looking out for abnormal behaviors, constantly reviewing everyone around him and examining his surroundings for anything the least suspicious.

He jerked open the door and made it to the top of the stairs. He and Philip were staying in Caroline's house until it could be determined where she and Sophia would be moved or until all the chaos could be brought to a close and they would be truly safe. He looked over the stairwell and saw Eugenie tussling with Beaker on the floor. He was ready to vault the stairs to protect Eugenie when he heard her laughing… laughing! Sophia ran from the kitchen and joined the fun and ended up on top of Beaker and Eugenie with arms and legs all tangled together.

Then Phillip came in from the kitchen also and he grabbed Beaker by the collar and pulled him away from two girls rolling on the floor having a case of the giggles. Eugenie rolled up, brushed herself off and looked upstairs to Rodane.

"Hi, need to get some things moving…if that's ok with you?"

"Sure, I'll be right down. Then he looked at his pajamas and grinned.

"Why don't you shower and join us for breakfast" Caroline said from the doorway. She had a big spoon in her hand and Beaker was trying to worm his way out of Phillip's hand to lick the spoon. A half hour later they were all eating a hearty breakfast and Beaker was lying across Eugenie's feet under the table, mooning up at her with a love-struck eye.

"What is it about you and animals?"

"What, you don't think I should be good with animals?" Genie looked semi-insulted at Rodane,

"Well maybe foxes, or wolves but dogs…?"

She narrowed eyes at him, "Is that supposed to be placating me, because you're stepping deeper and deeper into the muck, Boyo."

Caroline interrupted, "Genie, get it over with, what's happening?" They all stopped eating with forks raised to their mouths or chewing. Eugenie looked around the crowded table. Her eyes became misty, "It's strange…sitting with people I've only known at most a few weeks, some less, and I feel as if we've been together for a very long time and have a tremendously strong connection, crazy, huh?"

Caroline said, "Genie, if Sophia were here, I know what she would say 'Ohana'. We're family. I would trust you, I have trusted you, with my life, and Sophia's as well." Her eyes filled with unshed tears.

Rodane, confused, said, "She is here Caroline. I saw her…" he looked at her as if she were having a senior moment.

"I sent her in to get her shower and get ready for school." She looked at the clock, "Whoa, the bus will be here in three minutes. Genie, make it quick, I don't want Sophia walking in while we're discussing this."

"Won't matter much Caro, they want you safe today, this afternoon. You were too much easy access to anyone who knows where to look and we're pretty sure you haven't kept that hidden."

Caroline's expression hardened, "Who's they and why this afternoon? We need time…"

Rodane tried to speak with a patient tone, "Caroline, think of Sophia. She's an active, little girl, that can't be kept in a bubble forever. We have no way of knowing if there could be more attempts or by whom."

Caroline's face became rigid, her chin lifted and Rodane recognized the signs,

"Caroline are you prepared to pick her up every day and keep her with you 24/7 for the years to come? Is she never to go to birthday parties, or sleepovers, or prom night, or graduation ceremonies? Can she play soccer games away or go to concerts with her friends? Can she take vacations to a crowded beach or go on field trips? Can she walk a college campus by herself?"

He came over to her and placed his hands on her shoulders, "Do you intend to build a wall around her and a bubble too?" His voice lowered and he looked at her with concern and real affection, "Caroline, how about listening and then we can both agree. If not both of us, it doesn't happen. I'll stay here with you if you want."

She studied his face very carefully. She must have recognized the truth of what he said and also the sincerity. Her face crumpled and she hid it with her hands, tears leaking through. He reached for her and raised her to his arms and wrapped them around her while she regained her composure. She turned around and looked at everyone around the table…her family, her protectors for her and Sophia, without a doubt, to the death if necessary.

Phillip came over and whispered something in her ear. Her eyes widened and she paled even more. She reached out and took both hands he held in front of him. They stood very still and time seemed to do the same. Sophia came into the kitchen at that moment, looked around the room, walked over to Philip and her mother and placed her hands on both of theirs. The silence became more pronounced if possible and the air stilled. Beaker padded over to them and placed his body flush up against Sophia. The sound of the ceiling fan stopped and the kitchen felt as if it were encased in a cocoon. Beaker's huffing breath was even muffled and he uttered neither a whimper nor a whine. Sophia turned a little to the side, held out her one hand to her dad and Rodane reached out and covered her hand with his. It was a mystifying moment, one that could not be defined or explained but inexplicably moving and ethereal.

Caroline wavered and Rodane reached out and took hold of her arm to steady her. The small, connected group broke apart and Caroline sat down with a plop on the chair in front of her, eyes somewhat glazed over. Sophia moved to her lap, wrapped her arms around her mother's neck and murmured, "It'll be okay Mama, it's going to be okay. Mama, do you believe me?"

Caroline nuzzled her neck and replied, "Yes, I believe you Sunshine."

Rodane rubbed his face with both hands as if he were waking up from sleep and Beaker sat next to Caroline's chair and looked up at her expectantly. She reached out, stroked his fur and took hold of his ear, tugging gently on it. He lowered himself and laid peacefully across her feet.

Philip pulled up another chair and Eugenie gave everyone another moment and then broke the silence, "I think we need to determine whether we can agree on…"

"It's okay" Caroline smiled weakly at everyone around the table, "Genie, whatever they have planned, we're prepared to go along with it, at least for the time being. Sophia, honey, get your book bag and lunch in the fridge. I'll walk you to…"

Phillip stepped up to her, "Caro, I'll see her on the bus. You stay and get the details for your…" he looked at Sophia getting her lunch…"adventure."

Sophia giggled, "Better than any adventure I could dream up. Come on Beaker, time for the bus." He followed them out of the kitchen, tail swishing and a sparkle in his eyes.

Rodane started toward the stairs and Genie put a hand on his arm, "Roddy, this concerns you as well. Stay and listen? She asked.

{I don't think I will like this}

Genie started right in on the travel plans. Rodane was going to go to the airport with them and they would all fly to France. Caroline opened her mouth wide and shocked, but remained quiet. The house would be on private security surveillance and they would check on it sporadically so as not to establish a pattern. Willow would come once a week and dust, water the plants, and collect the mail from a P.O. Box. Caroline raised her eyebrows at that and put up her finger, thought better of it, lowered her hand to her lap and continued her quiet. Rodane watched her and wondered when the shoe would drop for him.

When they would finally arrive in France at Orly Airport south of the city, they would be picked up by private limousine or take the train; to be determined. Anonymity would be more possible by train. They would be picked up and taken to their safe house where they would remain until the primary instigator could be determined or eliminated, didn't much matter to them which one was the solution. They were just interested in putting an end to it. They had five hours to get ready, have Sophia come home from school, act naturally, have them drive to the airport and leave within the early evening at seven and arrive at Orly, France at eleven p.m. at night.

"Any questions so far?" Eugenie asked.

Caroline fluttered her hands, "Only just a few dozen. Let's see…" she ticked them off on her fingers which were shaking, "Sophia and school, Sophia and soccer, Mom and Sophia leaving home and hearth, Mom's teaching career…and I've just begun to scratch the surface." She sounded ready to go off the rails.

"Any thoughts on how I can give my daughter a normal life in Lyon? Is that it, Lyon, France? With a strange house, strange people, strange language…I could go on and on but…" She stopped and fluttered her hands again, "it's a start."

Philip was back from the bus stop and he lounged in the doorway listening to the burgeoning plans for Caroline and Sophia. He could imagine how daunting this was to Caroline after what she had just gone through. It was time to come clean or at least assuage some of her deepest fears.

"Caroline, you and Sophia will be met by the caretaker at the cottage where you will be staying." He looked over at Eugenie and she nodded, "It's a lovely little three bedroom cottage on Lac d'Aiugelbette, near some curative hot springs, in the community of Novalaise, very near Lyon, about an hour away. There's a bus, train and good roads to Lyon where all of your shopping can be done. The lake is very private and quiet but with many activities Sophia can be involved in… you too. It provides a wonderful eco-system of wildlife and migrating birds. There are fishing and swimming activities, rowing, there's walking and hiking, cycling, mountain terrain and climate…"

"That's all well and good but what about schooling? What about my job, my house, our daily lives and routines? How do we solve those problems and the language, not to mention that barrier?"

Phillip looked to Genie, and she spoke up, "Caroline, I will be there with you as your protector, Sophia's teacher, and the all-around gopher." Caroline raised her eyebrows and said to her, "Sophia's teac… you? I don't mean that as…"

"No worry, I can assure you. I've been in these situations before. I am quite capable of getting her through third grade and teaching her French to acclimate herself to the town and the people."

Caroline studied Eugenie like a strange foreign object or an unusual animal in front of her, determining if it was to be trusted or petted… cute, but strange.

"And me? How do I make money to live? How do I leave my job here and just show up in Lyon France…excuse me, Lac d'Aiugelbette. Did I say that correctly?"

"You'll be busy working all day in town, for a very nice salary, if I may add."

"What? You can't be serious. I don't know the system, the curriculum, the standards, the language…,"

"All taken care of now. You will be teaching American students whose parents are placed in Lac d'Aiugelbette and there is a school on the grounds of their military encampment. It's a joint effort between the United States and France and includes a hefty competition on the lake for rowing championships and inter-country competitions. We owe them for 1997 when we took away their title."

"How… what will I be…I can't believe this is happening and so quickly."

Rodane had been very quiet through all of this. He thought if he asked any questions whatsoever, he would be next to get the falling bomb and he wasn't ready for it.

{too much too soon}

But then he looked at Caroline and realized what she had gone through without any preparation or forewarning whatsoever and mostly on her own.

"Caroline, I'll help you through this. We can make it successful and a real adventure like Sophia is thinking. A new school, French lessons, activities on the lake, summer in the Mont Blanc region…a dream for an eight-year-old. It won't be for long, I have faith we can get a handle on this and put it to an end."

"But my house, my job at home…" her voice petered out on a note of mild hysteria.

Eugenie hesitated but said, "Roddy, you won't be staying there." He looked sharply up at her, "You have a different assignment and it requires you to be somewhere else. You'll certainly be able to come see them in free time and spend time with them, but we need you somewhere else for now." She hurried to say, "It's not far, only an hour's drive…"

He crooked his fingers, "…and my job? What do you need my presence so badly for?"

"There is some… instruction you need to have access to, and you have to be instructed by one of our teachers with experience in genetic markers and genealogy."

She tilted her head at him and he could almost feel her begging him not to argue the point. He decided to let this play out for a while as they wished, or until he got tired of the secrecy and the deflection. Caroline was wringing her hands and looking around her kitchen, as if she was in a strange place, far away, and she didn't recognize it.

"Genie" she said, with a tremble in her voice, "I have to tell you I'm scared shitless with all this and I really don't give a fuck about learning French, or fishing… or fucking birds running away from home for the winter…" She stopped and they all looked at each other. Caroline heard herself, broke out laughing and all three ended up chuckling and the tension was broken with simple truth.

"How about rowing on the lake?" Genie waited, and they laughed again. It was going to be okay, she was sure. She had her gut feeling working here.

Renata and Zoe made their way to the kitchen when they heard a strange voice, deep and mellow. A man was standing in the hall, with Iona blocking the way to the sitting area. They looked at each other and then moved to go around and come from the other end of the house.

The man looked up and said, "Renata, Zoe, you ready to go? We have a three o'clock flight to Tucson.

Iona asked, "You're the one taking them to Arizona?"

"Yes Ma'am, I'm already late getting here due to god-awful traffic around DC. I even left an hour early to avoid it." He shook his head in exasperation.

Iona turned around and faced Renata and Zoe, "Are you ready? We can always book another flight, maybe tomorrow, we could…" her face fell and she clamped her lips tight shut.

Renata came hobbling over to her and put her arm around her shoulder. Iona hesitated then put her head down on her shoulder. Zoe walked up to the man and said,

"Who are you? I'd like some ID." she stared at him in silence.

"I'm sorry. I thought my father had spoken to all of you earlier. He told me…"

Quimby? You're Quimby's son and one of his twins?'" Iona snapped too, "Why didn't you say so? We've had a few little incidents here lately, can't be too careful. You even look something like Phillip."

"Cousins, but most people do say we look like each other."

"Phillip's cuter!" Renata blurted it out then realized what it sounded like, and a rush of blood filled her face and her darker skin glowed. He opened his mouth to respond, thought better of it and said, "Yes, are you both ready?"

"Young man, they're not going anywhere without some food in their stomachs. You may as well sit and join in too" she saw his hesitation "and no arguments. You have plenty of time to make your flight to Arizona. Don't see why they can't just stay here and heal, we've been doing fine so far." They ate what was put in front of them and talked.

"Mrs. Arcos…"

"Iona" she insisted, "or Oma, but not Mrs. Arcos."

"You know the offer is still open for you to come along. You could make it a nice vacation."

"For how long?" she waited.

"I'm not sure exactly."

"No thank you. I have a business to run and a home with plants that need care and… she broke off and looked at the two girls, "I would, girls, you know I would, but…

"Oma" Zoe said gently, "we want you to be safe but we'd never dream of tearing you away from here. We understand and we'll miss you." Zoe hugged her tightly but winced and backed off.

"None of that girl, you save those hugs for when you are healed and fit. You'll call me when you get there?"

"Mrs. Arc..." He saw her face, "uh...Oma, we can't. We need an element of secrecy here as much as possible. Zoe has afforded us that and we have to take advantage of it."

"You're sure no one knows Zoe? They can't tail you or know where you're going?" Oma was fretful.

"Oma, if they do, we'll be prepared for them."

Oma said, "I didn't even ask you your name. What you must think of all of us."

"I'm Tyson ma'am and I plan on keeping both of them as right as rain, whatever it takes. If it makes you feel better, I'll keep in touch with my dad and he can relay some very brief messages."

"It will have to do. Lord, I want this over with. Life can't be all chaos and gloom...it doesn't do a body good."

They finished lunch, got their bags loaded into his Jeep and Iona stood at the door. After more hugs and her giving them snack bags to take, she pressed something into each woman's hand and then waved as they drove away till she couldn't see them anymore. Then she went inside, picked up the phone and tapped her contact list.

Cayman Brock, Cayman Islands

Farther out in the Atlantic, south of Cuba and North East of Costa Rica, Acacia sat on a covered deck at the top of a little neighborhood, overlooking the small town of Brock Reef Beach Resort. She had been there two days and was already itching to get to work. When she had flown into Grand Cayman and then taken a hired boat to Cayman Brock, she had managed to break into Keifer's office around 2 a.m. without being seen and placed a plug into his computer that would allow her to copy his password off site as soon as he logged on, without detection.

The advantage to her arriving unnoticed and undetected would end when she had to appear at Keifer's office, unannounced. That would stir the hive and she really wanted to avoid getting stung. She was pretty good at being politic but with all that had been happening, any small surprise should have suspicious and astute observation kick in if everyone was really on their best game. If he accepted her rationale for being there with no warning or notice, then she had the opportunity to uncover what would become glaringly obvious if their research was accurate. Having access to computers wouldn't do a bit of good if his computer was not the site where he kept his second set of books. Time would tell.

She sipped her Mimosa, stretched out in her lounge chair, soaking up the hot, dry sunshine to get that wonderful tan. She even had an excuse for that. If he took notice of the tan and her flight was recorded out of Miami and he checked up on her, it would reaffirm her story of a vacation cut short at Quimby's request. If he accepted that, the rest should fall into place.

She went over all the events that had occurred since her trip to France and the attack on their compound. In her mind, she tried to recall every conversation she had with each member present in the mansion. She closed her eyes and tried to bring up a facial memory for each person talking to her. Did they appear uncomfortable? Did they use direct eye contact when discussing the records and files before them? Did anyone try to obtain information from her during their… yes! From all her memories and recollections of body language, two people stood out as subtly 'grilling' her on names and numbers. Why couldn't she sense it then? Was she reaching? Could it just have been simple curiosity or concern for the people who they now knew were being targeted? A knock on her door had her jump a little and her drink spilled over onto her bare legs.

{damn sticky alcohol now I'll have to shower again}

She rose, walked across a plush white carpet and went to the door. Looking through the peephole, she sucked in her breath. Fuck! This was not coincidence nor was it welcome. She considered not answering the door. Stupid! He must know she was here. How?

"Acacia don't let me stand out here and have people walking by. It will be easy to remember and we need to keep this to ourselves." The voice of Petrus was even and low but very firm. She opened the door and they stood silent, eyeing each other, like two wild animals assessing the danger of the other and deciding whether to pounce first.

Acacia spoke first, "Does Suri know you're here? Does Egan?" She waited tensely, trying to keep her voice calm.

"No one knows I'm here except you." Petrus returned her gaze, and lifted his eyebrows. She turned a little and motioned him into her suite. She closed the door softly, never taking her eyes off him. He remained standing and reached into his pocket. She tensed her arms, bent her knees and was prepared to go full frontal to take him down.

"Wait" he squeaked out. He held up in his hand holding his 'pin' and his other hand in supplication, "I want to call Suri so you can talk to her with me, together. I just had to be sure you were here and alone. I swear, I mean you no harm."

A parrot flew by her deck and squawked, startling them both. It startled other birds in the palms as well and they all set up a raucous squabble for a few seconds. Acacia never took her eyes off Petrus, "How about we use my pin instead?" She walked slowly to the table, reached for her carry bag and felt inside for her 'pin'.

"I don't blame you for being suspicious. I could call anyone couldn't I, good or bad?"

"Then you're okay with my 'pin'?

"Yes, go ahead. Can we sit down first? I'm tired from the sun and climbing your damned hill to get here. It's been a very long night"

She looked at him and now she noticed the deep shadows and bags under his eyes, his sweat soaked clothes and his heat- mottled skin. "Would you like some cold water or a drink?"

"Yes! Let's get Suri on board and then you'll feel more comfortable. I wouldn't say no to a stiff drink either."

They sat opposite each other on both sides of the table and put their pins together. A fine, silver sheen appeared above them, shimmered into the shape of a woman. Then her face grew clearer. She was looking from Acacia to Petrus, quickly asking,

"Acacia, are you okay?"

"Yes Suri, I'm fine. I just wanted to call you so you wouldn't be worried… no… actually… no. I'm going out on a limb here. Petrus showed up without my knowledge, scared the shit out of me, and wants to talk to you about…I don't know what."

Suri looked at Petrus, cleared her throat and asked, "Are you okay Petrus? We've been…worried about you."

Petrus's face hardened and he took in a deep breath and said, "Let me guess. Egan is worried I went off the farm, and you've both been trying to figure out where I am. Correct?"

Suri looked bewildered, "Why do you think Egan is looking for you? Should he be worried about something Petrus?"

"I don't think you should be worried about me Suri. I'm as loyal as I ever was but I'm sure Egan is worried about me and my location as well as worried about who I might be in contact with…" He stopped and breathed deeply again, "Acacia, could I have that drink now, the strong one if you don't mind, maybe a double?"

Acacia got up to fix his drink but kept her ears attuned to the conversation between Petrus and Suri. His tone was calm and easily heard. He wasn't trying to hide anything or prevent her hearing his sordid tale of betrayal and blackmail. He sucked down half his drink in one gulp when Acacia set it before him, and continued almost without a pause, "So you see, everything Egan told you was true except it was me who was being kept in the dark while he was taking our private conversations and sharing them with a third party, a very nasty, vengeful, third-party. When I found out he was divulging all the information I was sharing with him to the cabal, I was shattered. We had a terrible argument the night I heard him talking on the phone to some unknown. When I confronted him he said he'd take care of it. We would be okay and no one could be hurt. I left, that part was true. I walked until almost dawn trying to figure out how I could tell you that..." He stumbled for the first time, his voice hitched and his face was tortured.

Suri said, "Petrus, why? Why did he do this? What possible reason could he have for betraying his own family so totally? Did one of us hurt him, anger him, turn on him somehow that…"

"Money, Suri, position. It's tawdry… cheap…it's unforgivable. He was ashamed of our relationship, worried it would hold him back and angry that he had to scrabble his way up while I had it so easy according to him. Those were his words. He was so angry, so vengeful. I've never seen him so resentful, so vindictive so…mean." His face fell and his voice clogged up, "It was not the Egan I thought I knew. It was someone else, a stranger."

Suri looked over to Acacia, "Does any of this make sense to you? Do you see any… proof of what Petrus has said?" I'm sorry Petrus, but I have to…"

"Don't, please don't apologize. I would feel exactly the same way if I were in your shoes."

Acacia thought for a few minutes while Suri stayed silent and attentive. The cool air blew towards the open deck and she was caught between hot and cold just as Petrus was feeling at the moment.

"It makes more sense than what Egan was alluding to, the inaccuracies and errors and all the financials couldn't have been done by Nikos' hand. It would have to go through Finance. The books could only be cooked by someone who had daily access to everyone's schedules and travels. Nikos didn't have that but Egan did and he and Keifer have been very close for a long time. The travel records showed lots of vacations and trips to this island from Egan's accounts. Keifer has been given a free hand for decades, to present whatever reports he felt were germane to the whole family. He could easily have altered Nikos' records to hide the inconsistencies, the transfer of funds from one system to another. It would be simple to do."

Suri closed her eyes and sat still until finally she said, "Acacia, do you have access to Keifer's computer?"

"Yes."

"Can you copy files and send them?"

"Not yet, but I'm hoping soon, when Keifer gets on his computer this morning…" she looked at her clock, "in about twenty minutes, actually, if his password is correct. I'll be into his files in three minutes and we can start printing in four but if he notices a login by me at 2 a.m. he'll know we're monitoring him."

"So what do we do now?" Suri said, frustrated but determined.

"We distract him. I'll call you back in five after I've done my assault okay?"

Suri looked at her closely, "Be careful, we could be dealing with cornered rats here. They have a tendency to bite."

"Oh I can bite right back. Talk to you in about a half hour"

They turned off their 'pins' and sat in silence for a few minutes. Acacia, without a word, got up from her chair, fixed another drink for Petrus and one for herself, sat down again and told him what was happening next. She had to leave there in five minutes, ride her rented scooter into town and show up at Keifer's office as soon as he was in there. The rest was up to the luck of the gods or the chaos of the cabal. Time would be the deciding factor here.

Petrus was put in charge of setting up the new printer to her laptop and printing out enough paper of thousands of pieces of priceless information.

"If Keifer bites at my story and allows for an audit without preparation, I'll be knee-deep in accounts for hours. Will you be okay by yourself for a time?"

"How will we be able to copy all those records if you have to transport them here? Is it safe here?"

"That's why I've been making plans the last couple of days and purchasing materials and the printer. It had better work or all of it is very, very iffy. The copying will come from my hacking Keifer's files and moving them by flash drive to here. It will begin transfer automatically when I hit a certain key on the computer and Keifer doesn't have any knowledge of its placement. It's built into the computer itself as of two o'clock this morning. All of the files will be sent here where we can work safely and without notice or detection. Cross your fingers…" and she was out the door.

Petrus stood in the middle of the floor, partly bemused, mostly confused. In such a short time, his world had tumbled, his partner was gone, his job might be in jeopardy and his 'family' was in danger. What else could go wrong? He reached into his pocket and pulled out the tablets he took for all his exacerbated heartburn. As he told Acacia, this job would be the death of him yet. He started pulling boxes apart and unpacking reams of paper. He looked up at the clock over the TV and pictured Acacia tooling down to Keifer's office. Sweat broke out on his forehead.

Chapter 38

Brock Reef Beach town, Grand Caymans

Keifer's office was in a small two-story building, with a canvas overhang providing shade for the hot humid days. He occupied the ground floor of five rooms and overhead, a real estate company had a carbon copy footprint of these rooms. There was no elevator and an outside stairway went up to the second floor. The outside of the building was nondescript and a plain brass nameplate was nailed to the door; Plutus Enterprises.
 {god of wealth cute}
 Acacia had never been here before. When she was being trained by Quimby and his staff, she was only beginning to handle the 'family's' accounts and assets and she had done everything over phone or Internet. She had met Keifer exactly once, when she and her then current lover were on vacation some years back. Quimby had let Keifer know they were at the resort and he had come to introduce himself and meet her.
 {probably check out the newbie}
 It went well, drinks were had all around, and Keifer asked her questions about her other assignments and their mutual acquaintances. She was going to use that right now to get in the door and do her dirty deeds. Hopefully, Suri had told Quimby what was up by now. She looked around, straightened her shoulders, took a breath, reached for the door knob and walked into the cool outer office. No one was there, the shade produced a shadowed, cooling atmosphere and a bell tinkled over the door.
 A tall, thin man with balding head and a sharp aquiline nose with a sparse sandy-colored goatee came out from the adjoining room. He wore glasses perched lower on his nose and looked over them at her with a half-smile on his face. It fell flat when he recognized her but only for a second.

Then he put out his hand and smiled "Acacia, my goodness, what a surprise! To what do I owe this surprise visit? It is Acacia, right?"

She took his hand and was surprised at how cool it felt and lax. He wore summer shorts and a flower patterned shirt with a small shell on a gold chain around his neck. She gripped his hand, gave it a fair shake and released it slowly,

"Hello Keifer, I'm sorry to come unannounced. I told Quimby we should at least give you a day or two to prepare your staff for a visit. He was sure you wouldn't mind the unexpected audit, even if it was the height of the summer. Suri agreed it might surprise you, but she said your office was so organized and your staff was so professional, they would probably have everything ready for me within minutes if she knew you."

She looked curiously around the room "Is your staff expected soon?"

Keifer's face had a faint sheen of sweat on it now and his eyes had widened with her explanation, "What? Quimby sent you here for an audit? I don't understand...we aren't due..."

"Yes, I know! Exactly what I told him. You're due for an October audit but when he found out I was on vacation here and I would be here for a few more days he called and asked me to apologize for the change of schedule but it would be so convenient for everyone if I could do it while I was here and then send him an early report. He was sure you would be up for it. He said your mind was a tightly coiled calculator that could adapt to anything."

"Oh, how nice of him, but I wouldn't want you to take your vacation time to do an audit. That would be a terrible way to spend your time..."

She interrupted, "Actually it's a perfect time. I've had enough sun as you can see, and I hate being footloose for too long. It makes me antsy. I won't be in your way, I promise. I brought along my laptop to work on so you wouldn't be inconvenienced. All you have to do is use your computer to open your books and I can move them to my laptop... I can even do it from my hotel room if that would be easier. Then I can give you a report at the same time I send it to Quimby and Suri. She says hi, by the way..."

{please please say no or I'm cooked}

His eyes narrowed, and he hesitated long enough to let her know his mind was working furiously to come up with a seemingly tight excuse, "Oh, I'm afraid taking files off site would be impossible... security and all that. You have to do them here and I'm afraid I don't have any extra place for you to work..." his hands came up as if in abject apology.

"Well, where does your auditor work on an announced audit?" She waited, while she heard the gong of a clock. He looked around the room as if looking for a spot, "They generally have a desk brought in next to mine but it's quite cramped and... we don't have a good deal of free space. Maybe by October I could..."

"Nonsense I don't take up much room. I'll just take my things if you don't mind..." and she started toward the door to the back office.

"No wait!" he put his hands up like a traffic cop handling traffic, "I'm just not prepared. I mean...I wasn't expecting..." with his voice dwindling off into a tense silence. She pulled her final card,

"Okay Keifer, I can appreciate that. I work with companies all the time where unpreparedness can happen. Just let me call Quimby." She pulled out her phone and pushed a contact. He stood there and wrung his hands watching her, then stepped forward and lay one hand very timidly on her arm, "No, let me see. I don't think it's necessary to cancel it. I'm sure Quimby was right when he said my staff was up for anything."

"Suri" she interrupted and he looked at her in confusion "It was Suri who said your staff was very organized and prepared. Quimby just thought you had a mind like a calculator" she smiled at him innocently.

{Keifer time to give in}

"Quite, quite," He put his hand to his chin, thought for a few moments, "Let's see where we can get you set up while I call my staff. They can be here in minutes."

"Your staff? They don't work today? Oh, that would be a shame to do it here and not be able to interview staff. I'd have to come back in October again and do it all over."

Keifer's glittery eyes took on a sharp intense look, "Well, perhaps you could call Quimby and explain the difficulty and we could put this off till October as planned."

She could see his body relax and his face take on some relief.

"Of course Keifer, Quimby did say that if it became a problem, he would have to start transferring all your files up to New York. He's already scheduled a committee meeting for your reports. He would have to notify all of them we're not ready. It might raise a few eyebrows, but what the hell, it's happened before. Remember that debacle in the law offices in Paris, when we found all that money missing and... who was it, Mikel? He got canned and his mistress, who was acting as accountant and was as dumb as a box of rocks?" she tittered, "that was one hell of an audit. It kept people at it for months and heads rolled over on that one. I'm sorry. What were you suggesting? I do tend to keep on once I get hold of something unsavory," she waited again, as a drop of sweat rolled down his hairline.

{gottcha sucker}

He fluttered his hands and said, "No matter, it will just work out fine. It will take me a few minutes to contact my staff and have them here. Let me show you to the office." He gestured to the back room and Acacia picked up her laptop and bag and walked down a short hallway.

Keifer's office was plush, very concealed and different from the front room. A large teak desk, highly-polished, had not one item on its surface, the room smelled of apples and his computer was off to the side at a computer center and turned off. His phone was dinging and he moved to shut it down. "Oh Kiefer, I'm sorry, I've kept you from your call."

He picked it up and said, "Not anything important, I can always call back" he turned it off.

{got to get that computer on}

"Would you mind if I use your computer to log in and announce myself before we begin?" he narrowed his eyes and stared at her,

"But you've got your laptop. You said…"

"Of course I can work from my laptop but I need your files up so I can disseminate them to different folders for a segmented report. You know, accounts payable…accounts overdue…receipts and invoices…all the nitty-gritty they are expecting with my report. She stood there almost holding her breath, hoping against hope he would buy it all.

He paused and then sat down and turned the monitor toward him and away from Acacia's eyes. She laid the laptop down on the edge of the desk and flipped the tiniest of switches and saw it blink blue, once. Then she averted her eyes and pretended to examine his wall hangings while he logged into his password and username.

{doesn't matter doofus I've got you}

Then he left to call his 'staff'.

{and I'm a rocket scientist too}

She opened her laptop, looked to the far left corner an the top of the open file, and saw it spinning on 'load'. It was copying every file he had, even the secure ones, faster than his outdated computer could bring them up. Her laptop had been built by one of the lab techs in one of their unknown and unadvertised tech centers. The flash drive was built incognito into the rim of the computer case and it automatically used an algorithm to unlock secure files and folders as fast as numbers on a casino slot machine. Within seconds, it had broken the codes, lifted the material and transposed it to her laptop then locked them in, where no one else could get to them except with her thumb print. It also had voice recognition to lock out anyone even attempting to access her information.

She carefully walked around the desk, opened her case and took out the useless computer that held innocuous fake files of other audits and imaginary reports and reviews. Meanwhile her case was copying at more than a zettabyte a minute or an optimally compressed network equivalent to every person on earth receiving the total information of one hundred different newspapers every day. Even her mathematically enhanced brain couldn't grasp the enormity of that, yet it was here in front of her, like an out of control gyroscope, doing the work of hundreds of thousands of machines in minutes.

She was bringing up a trove of fake audits and files along with false spreadsheets when she heard the door open and Keifer appeared at the office door with two people in tow. One was a young, blonde, buxom girl of perhaps twenty-five, twenty-six, who had a pasted smile on her pasty skin. She had wide, frightened eyes and a big smile for effect. The other person was a man of about forty to fifty, with scruffy, close, scraggly hair and an overgrown beard. He had an insolent grin as he looked her over, really looked her over. Her skin crawled and she checked her first impulse to scowl or sneer at him. She was introduced to Taffy, of all things precious, and Simon.

{Bambi and Simon Legree how clever}

Keifer said, "I totally forgot that I had given the day off to Taffy for her to look after her brother. He's been ill for a time but if you really need her here we can arrange a time for her to come in for your evaluation."

Simon spoke up with a slur, "but I can stay pretty lady, as long as you need me." He looked straight at her and licked his lips. She felt nauseated and chilled. "Thank you Simon. What do you do here? For your job, I mean?"

Simon looked at Keifer for a second, "I look over all the weekly totals and tabulations and check them against past and future expenditures, for tax purposes."

{huh, maybe the real deal}

"I really don't need your help right at the moment but perhaps tomorrow you could come in and we could have our chat about those expenditures and future taxes owed. I can see you both here at…" she looked up to Keifer, "What time do they generally leave?"

Keifer shuffled his feet, looked over at Taffy and said, "We're not big about set schedules here on the island. How about you name a time convenient for you and I'll make sure they're here." Keifer looked at her open laptop, making his way around the desk. She pushed a key, the esc tab, and shut it down just as the button blinked blue again, once… done!

"I'm taking a break to get some water. It's a hot one today isn't it?"

He looked at her for a space and said, "Yes it is that. It has a way of either exciting some people or making others take it easy." His eyes flicked to Simon and he nodded his head, so little she wasn't sure if she had actually seen it.

She rose from the desk to go to her bag to get her phone and water bottle just as he moved slightly to her right so she had to brush past him. He very slowly twisted his body, and she was caught between the desk and his body. He moved a little toward her and she found herself bending slightly backward, his breath close to her face and the alcohol stench filling her nose. She swallowed the hot phlegm rising in her mouth and at that moment, her phone rang. Simon jerked his head back and took a backward step. She opened her bag, felt for her phone and grabbed her bottle. She held the phone and said, "Hello?"

Quimby's voice had her legs feeling loose and like jelly as she leaned against the desk for support. He spoke softly, "Everything okay? You pushed the panic button."

On each phone and laptop belonging to a 'family' member, there was a blank key below the number pad that alerted Quimby or his staff to a possible need for help, for security. At least they would be aware of where she was and who she was with.

She pushed speaker, "Hi Quimby. I was just here at Keifer's office, meeting with his staff. Taffy, Simon, this is Quimby, our business partner in New York. Keifer and I were just arranging a time for me to do evaluations tomorrow after I finished my audit."

{please know about this Quimby or I'm toast}

"About that...I've checked our calendar. It seems as if I have double booked you for audits this week. I do apologize for messing up your vacation. Keifer, I must also apologize to you for this unnecessary intrusion into your work week for nothing. Acacia is needed back in Miami so I've sent a boat to pick her up and take her to Grand Cayman for a flight out. I'm really sorry to have this happen, Keifer. I must be having a senior moment before senior hits. Ever had that happen to you Keifer?"

Keifer stuttered, "Uh...Quimby, I totally understand... happens to all of us I'm sure. Should we postpone the audit until our October date or do you want Acacia to finish here first?"

"I'll arrange things with Acacia and I'll certainly put off your audit till a later date. I will personally check with our Accounting Bureau to contact you and set up a convenient date and time for you and your staff. Taffy and Simon...nice to meet you. Perhaps next time, we can face time and really meet each other. Simon, I understand you own and operate a very popular bar on the island?"

Simon's face showed surprise and his jaw dropped, "Oh yeah, it's the Beach Bum. Seems like a good venture."

Quimby said, "Yes, I hope the tax guys and Department of Permits and

Licenses are not riding you. I've heard they can be very intrusive at times. Has that happened to you?"

Simon looked to Keifer, narrowed his eyes at him, glanced at Acacia and said,

"Why, no, we've always managed to be on friendly terms with them and they appreciate a good water hole."

Keifer spoke up, "Quimby, so good of you to give us a little leeway to make sure we have all the necessary up-to-date accounts for our businesses. I appreciate that. We'll see that Acacia gets to her boat on time, what flight is she booked on?"

{It looks like I've been made}

"Not necessary. I should have someone by your office in the next few minutes and they will accompany her. It's all taken care of. Acacia, call me when you are done with your calendar changes and we'll both check for duplicate audits or conflicts in your dates. Till then, I hope you've enjoyed what vacation time I've managed to mess up for you. I owe you a couple days. We'll talk soon."

Quimby broke contact and at that moment the bell over the door in front tinkled and a booming bass voice sang out, "Mz Acacia…hello, anyone here?" Before they could move toward the front waiting room, a hugely built, muscled man, dark as the teak on Keifer's desk, filled the doorway. His arms were saplings growing thick and smooth, his head was immense, gleaming without one hair to be seen. His torso was more compact and muscled than any pro football tackle and they already knew he had a voice that needed no megaphone to be heard. His eyes went straight to Acacia, "Mz Acacia, Mr. Papadakis gave me direct orders to see you to the boat and make sure you took everything with you so you could catch your flight out tomorrow. You ready ma'am?"

She leaned against the desk to try and keep her balance with her lifeless legs, or so it seemed. She felt sweat under her armpits and realized her face must appear flushed and sweaty. She gathered up her things, made quick goodbyes to everyone there and moved outside to her scooter parked in front.

{and good riddance}

They started their scooters and took off down the small street. She followed her guide around the twisting road for a few hundred yards then he pulled over and she stopped behind him. He walked over to her and looked at her closely, "You okay to ride? You look a little shaky. Smart thing you did, pushing that esc key. Quimby got in touch with me immediately. Good thing I was eating my second breakfast and not out on the boat. Sure they didn't pull anything?"

She finally found her voice, stilled the trembling, and wiped her face with a towel in the side pack, "Thanks to you, no. I'm not sure what would have happened in there but I didn't want to stay and try to prevent it all. Thank you." she heard her breath hitch.

He handed her a card, "Here's my number if you need anything before you leave or if they try to find you. Call it and I'll be there or my cousin will. We look alike. She smiled at him, shook his huge hand and they parted. He went down the hill toward the beach and she rode up to her room and let herself in.

Petrus was on the sofa, spread out and asleep with a soft gurgle coming from his throat. She looked at him for a minute, shook her head and walked to the printer humming in the corner of the kitchen. There were piles of paper spread across the counter on both sides of the tiny kitchen and the printer was continuing to belt out sheet after sheet. The machine was hot and she could smell the ink that produced the print so she put it on pause and went to get a drink of water. She held on to the sides of the sink and hung her head, gathering her thoughts together.

{he wouldn't hurt me or I don't think so}

She really wasn't that sure anymore. She felt as if she might have dodged a bullet back there and she was grateful for the reprieve. She began piling the printed forms into the empty boxes that held the paper and was filling the third one when Petrus came to the counter and she turned the printer back on.

"How long do you think we have to stay here? How many boxes still have to be filled?"

"Petrus, you don't have to stay. You could go back to... where? England? We'll try and sort this out if we can find Egan."

He paced back and forth over the small area and took turns breathing heavily and wringing his hands, "I don't want Egan to get hurt. I'm not ready to give up on him and I don't want the 'family' to either." his voice rose and his face flushed.

"Isn't that up to Eagan? You can't take the blame for his treachery."

"If I just knew where he was, what he was thinking. I could..."

"You could try but I think he has already chosen his side and we're not on it with him. I'm sorry Petrus, but this is beyond us now and in the hands of our Committee."

Petrus started to answer her and his voice choked up, he grabbed his left arm, and his face went ash gray. His eyes glazed over and he dropped where he stood. Acacia dropped the box she was holding and rushed to him. His eyes rolled up and his breathing became shallow. She checked his pockets feverishly, found a pill bottle in one marked Nitro, "Dammit Petrus, why didn't you let me know?" She remembered his pasty color, his shallow breathing, his rubbing of his arm and chest. This man was not going to die here, on this isolated island apart from his loved ones. She placed a tablet under his tongue and gently closed his mouth. She held his hand while he gradually came around and his breathing became more regular. His pulse was steady though weak and he opened his eyes and looked up at her, "I didn't really mean it you know?"

She was confused, "Mean what? What are you talking about Petrus?"

"…that this job would be the death of me." He closed his eyes again.

"And it won't!" She stood up, took out the card she had been given and pushed in the numbers. She looked around the room and stood listening to the flip flop of the pages spinning out of the printer. Then she looked at Petrus on the floor, tired, ill, dejected in betrayal and desertion. It was going to be a tough few days ahead for all of them.

"Damn you Egan, you will be held accountable for this, along with your traitorous cronies."

Chapter 39

Flagstaff—Pulliam Airport, Az

When the plane landed in Flagstaff, they left their seats and walked down the steps of the private jet that didn't have a flight plan anywhere near where they actually landed. They got their luggage from the steward and walked across the tarmac to the little, low ceilinged building that was the airport waiting room, big enough for about fifty people at a time. Tyson brought up the rear and walked them to a side building where a seven passenger minivan was gassed and ready. All three of them climbed in. Tyson started the engine, turned on the A/C and they left the airport and headed out to the highway.

Renata spoke up first "It's so hot but it doesn't feel that hot. How is that possible?"

Zoe said "No humidity. It's dry but it still feels hot and no doubt it will be hotter as the day wears on."

They sat in virtual silence as Tyson used his GPS to follow the easiest, quickest route to their new digs. They had rented a house through the owner, paying up front in cash for a small rancher, only seven miles down the road from Zoe's old homestead. They drove farther and farther up into the hills and all of it was familiar to Zoe. She kept quiet and eventually eased her head back to the seat and dozed off. Renata looked up and caught Tyson looking at her in the rearview mirror. The expression on his face was… different, calm, curious yet cautious. She looked at him in silence and his eyes returned to the road.

"I don't want to be here you know." He drove quietly and then responded, "What, in this van, or in this state, or in this position?" "Yes" she answered.

He chuckled, "Good to meet someone who knows their own mind and isn't afraid to spell it out." She sat silently and finally looked out the window and said, "I'm not part of this. I don't belong with all of you. I should be going back to my own place, not traveling to your secret hideaway. I wouldn't trust me if I were you. I don't trust me and I'm me."

She looked up, away from the dry hills, the tall stately pines interspersed with a few Saguaro cacti and the reflection of a strong hot sun on red brick hills that made them look as if they were on fire. She saw his face and said, "Don't give me that look. I'm not spouting crazy. I'm telling you, I don't belong here with all of you."

He slowed down and looked back at her, "Where do you belong? What do you consider to be your place? Who do you belong with?"

She crossed her arms over her chest, turned her head and looked out at the passing landscape, heat coming off the road in a shifting, ephemeral being, moving, undulating above the black top, dissipating into a cloudless blue sky the color of azure. She felt his eyes on her but refused to look back at him. He shrugged his shoulders and concentrated on driving. Renata leaned back and closed her eyes. It was a long ride out to 'their' place where she would be taking up some of the space for herself.

Tyson looked back at her once again, pursed his lips and let his mind go off into his own thoughts while the road went off into the distance and left a black ribbon behind them that seemed to drift off the horizon into nowhere. Both girls woke when the tires ran over loose gravel and pulled to a stop. They looked out the front of the van at the small, rectangular ranch house, sand-colored with a Mexican tile roof and a long, narrow porch running its length. There were four white rockers spaced across it and a table between each one with an outdoor fan blowing hot air around. A large dog came loping around the right side of the house, between it and a long, low stable with small closed sheds attached on each end. His fur was a mixture of black, white and tan, his tail switching rapidly back and forth, and he was alternating between whining and yelping at them.

Zoe looked out surprised and said, " Is that... it couldn't be...is that Gunny?"

Tyson answered, "I couldn't tell you. I wasn't told anything about a dog. Hope he's friendly."

Renata smirked, "Ever seen a tail in motion like that to enemies or hostiles? Don't think so."

Zoe opened the door, got down from the mid passenger section and bent down to ruffle the floppy ears of the mutt in front of her. He rolled onto his back, splayed his paws and demanded attention. She rubbed his belly and he let out soft whines and accompanying wiggles in the dirt.

"Gunny, you come here right this minute or I'm getting a gun and putting an end to that foolishness. Them sheep had better be in that pasture, you hopeless excuse for a herd dog. Gunny! Here, now!" The voice had him on his feet and lowering his belly almost to the dirt while he shuffled toward the porch, head bent in submission and apology.

They all looked up to a stout woman standing on the porch with a ladle in her hand, a wide multicolored apron across her front and a mop of silver white hair to accent her round, tanned face. She peered at all three of them with an examining expression on her face of...part curiosity, part familiarity.

"Okay you three, time to get yourselves in here to chow down. I assume your flight was long and boring, been there before, and your car ride has dust up your nose and down your throat. Time's a wastin'. I take it you're Tyson", looking directly at him.

"Yes ma'am, I thank you for your meal and your welcome." Renata looked between the two of them, assessing the greeting similar to a welcoming rancher's wife and a rancher returning from a long, dusty cattle drive. She shook her head gently. This might take some getting used to.

The screen door pushed out with a grinding squeak and Zoe stopped in her tracks. The man walked to the edge of the steps, tall, arrow-straight, hands in both pockets, his thick heels clumping on the wooden porch, his cowboy hat pushed lazily back on his head. Renata realized Zoe wasn't following, turned around to see her standing there tense, white-faced, hands almost balled into fists. She tensed herself, ready to run or attack or...

"Ducky" Zoe's one word came out as almost a whisper, her voice vibrating with fear... no, with amazement.

"Zoe" she asked, "Are we okay? Is he okay? Zoe, look at me!" She shook her gently. Zoe turned to her and said, "It's okay, it's my brother."

"Your brother? I thought they said no one would be able to track us here. How could... should we be...?"

Zoe removed Renata's hand gently off her arm, looked at Ducky again, standing on the porch just... waiting. She turned to Tyson who was also looking at her but with a calm, relaxed face. She felt like she was caught in a thin spider web, her feet rooted to the ground, her voice absent, the strands winding around her head, preventing her brain from processing what was in front of her... who was in front of her.

She croaked out two words to Tyson, "You knew?" He nodded.

She had to move, she had to act. They couldn't stay in this overwhelming state of limbo until the winter rains came and filled the arroyos. She broke the strands around her head with a shake of her lengthening hair and turned back to Ducky, still silent on the porch, waiting for her move and her reaction. She took the remaining steps to the porch and looked up at the face she had loved for all of her years and probably before that.

She said more calmly than she felt, "Hello Ducky." He grinned or winced, she couldn't tell. He waited. Zoe found some words from somewhere, she wasn't sure where.

"We didn't know you would be here. We were expecting a refuge, if you will. Are you here in your work clothes or your brother clothes?" She just looked at him.

Tyson took a step closer. Ducky held up his hand and stopped him cold. More silence. Renata looked around at the hills and the farmhouse, to the woman on the steps, to the man standing ramrod still, and to Zoe. She felt her old angers coming over her after such a period of rest and quiet, of making some good friends and trying to bury her wounds. Not again, she wouldn't be helpless again, ever.

She stamped her feet in the dust and it blew up in little dust devils around her and she let out of string of curses, every one she could think of in Italian. Then she switched to French and spewed quite a few of them as well. Her eyes were shut tight and she looked to the others like a little pixie, arms swinging, hair blowing with the dust, face grimaced in torture, not physical but torture none-the-less.

When she finally wound down and stood there with arms akimbo, breath heaving and her face streaming with tears, she saw the people in front of her staring as if at an apparition. The woman came down from the steps, dropping her ladle on the porch and walked slowly up to her, "Hi, I'm Myrna. I take it you had a pretty rough trip to get here?"

Somehow Renata knew she wasn't just referring to the plane or car ride. She rubbed the tears off her face, smoothed her hands over her jeans to dry them, took a deep, wobbly breath and put out her hand, "Yes, it's been quite the trip. I'm Renata Kappos. Thank you for your welcome."

Mryna took the hand offered to her in both of hers and said, "We aim to make your stay safe and restful. Let's see to some chow, shall we?"

She turned around, glowered for a second at Ducky and began to lead the still silent Tyson and Renata to the porch. Ducky came down two steps and reached one hand toward Zoe, stopped… then walked the remaining steps toward her, "Aw hell, bugger it!" He took Zoe by the shoulders and pulled her to his very ample chest and wrapped her in the biggest bear hug she could remember getting from him, ever. The strands of the web were broken, dissolved, just as she dissolved into sobs so big her whole body quaked in his arms. He rested his chin on top of her head, cradling her and rocking gently back and forth on the driveway.

Myrna led them around the sad tableaux and up the steps to the house. She opened the screen door and gestured for them to go in. She turned back to the two still out there and a faint smile appeared on her flushed face, "It's going to be just fine." She picked up the ladle, followed them in and closed the door gently as it squeaked softly.

Lyon France

In France, a private jet touched down at Orly Airport with no notice and no fanfare. The late hour of 11 p.m. this time, had everyone jet-lagged and feeling hyper yet exhausted. Rodane carried a sleeping Sophia off the plane and into the large van waiting for them at the private office. Caroline came down the steps of the plane with Eugenie, holding a leash, helping her entice Beaker down the steep steps with a treat after each step. After the 5th step Beaker bounded down the remainder of them, pulling Eugenie with him, who almost tumbled down the remaining steps. At the bottom he sat and waited for his sixth treat.

"No you don't, you clever clown. You had no trouble on those stairs you fluffy cheat." He looked at Caroline and lay down on the plane's tarmac. Eugenie tugged on his leash and he lowered his head and settled in with a 'whoof!' for her trouble. The two women looked at each other. Eugenie held out her hand with a treat, "You win. Let's go big boy. Don't want to give anyone a good view of four, very tired Yankees entering France, and a big galoot of a dog, who could be remembered for sure."

He bounded up, seized the treat and ambled at her side to the van and jumped in the back. "Deliver me from intelligent, controlling men, and that includes Beaker" Eugenie said, with frustration but dark humor in her voice.

The van drove off immediately toward Le Lac Aiguebelette, their 're-treat'. Sophia had her head in her mother's lap and Rodane had the shotgun seat in front. The driver was French and he and Eugenie kept up a conversation of sorts. That was when she wasn't yawning or staring sleepily out at the landscape around them. They couldn't make out much in the dark, but Caroline could tell it was countryside and could make out rows and rows of grape arbors at farm houses from a few lights scattered here and there. Then it was all black, as if they had entered a tunnel.

"Madame, there is 'Le lac' on your left. It is most beautiful at dusk and in a full moon's light." There was pride in his voice and wonder at its beauty.

She was testy and tired, not a good companion for appreciating this strange, foreign life she was taking on, "I'll let you know after I've had a chance to test it out."

He looked confused. She put her hand on Sophia's head and leaned back and closed her eyes. They were gritty from the afternoon's crying bout and the strain that comes from being overtired.

The door slammed and she jumped. She had been sound asleep for all of twenty minutes but it made her feel much better. Sophia was sitting up looking out the window and talking to Beaker, "You know you're going to have to leave the ducks and geese alone, don't you Beaker? They're not for play but I'll take you for long walks around parts of the lake and you'll love the hikes into the hills. We can learn all the flowers and all the things you can't eat that could make you sick. I'm going to teach you commands in French and you'll be the best watchdog around. Maybe you can meet some other dogs or cats."

Beaker whined softly then 'woofed' as if he understood her every word, "Don't worry, they'll love you. Daddy will come on weekends and we'll go fishing and boating on the lake. Wait till I show you the raft I'm going to build so we can paddle on the lake. We'll be just as strong as the ones who want to win that trophy." She stroked his fur and continued, "I'll miss some of my friends but not too many. They were all dumb, into weird music and trying make-up. Can you imagine an eight-year-old girl looking like a streetwalker?"

Caroline put her hand over her mouth to stifle her laughter.

"But Daddy and Mama and Genie will be here, so I'm not worried or scared. We're going to have a wonderful time."

Caroline could not detect any effort on Sophia's part to exhibit any fear or lack of confidence in this move. She would be a wimp to show her own fears if Sophia could be so upbeat and positive. She steeled herself to have half the bright outlook her wonderful daughter had. She could do no less.

Rodane opened their door and ushered them out of the van. The lights had been turned on in the house and Rodane hefted two suitcases, while Genie grabbed the handles of two more. They trudged up the stone walkway and entered through a doorway at least six to eight inches wide of solid wood. Beaker bounded in the door and ran to the huge fireplace in the middle of the wall, flopped down by the edge of a gray slate hearth, put his face on his paws and closed his eyes with a huge sigh. Sophia looked up at Rodane first, then her mother and said, "This will be the most wonderful place I will remember the rest of my life. Daddy, you'll always have this time to remember no matter what happens." She went over to the large, overstuffed sofa, stretched out and instantly went sound asleep. Caroline walked over slowly, pulled an afghan off the top of the sofa and gently laid it over her. Beaker took up residence at her feet.

Rodane and Eugenie stood under the overhang, softly talking in the dense blackness of the late night. Caroline and Sophia were settled in the cabin, Beaker was on 'watch' and Rodane was preparing to take off with directions to his next stop. He wasn't happy about it. One light from inside allowed them some half vision, "My place is here with my family Genie."

She could only imagine how torn he was in wanting to protect his family but also wanting to join the Committee, to finally learn all the answers to his growing list of questions, "Nikos said if you were adamant about remaining here, then you should stay."

He lifted his head…"but Suri requested that you really think about joining them even for a day or two so you could finally put all your major concerns to rest."

Genie looked hard at him and decided she had to offer the final enticement…"and Sabina is very anxious to see you and be a part of the discussion."

Rodane looked sideways at her and mumbled, "Not fair, Genie, not fair."

"I'm sorry Roddy but there's so much at stake here."

He pointed to the cabin, "Like in there?" She nodded and answered, "Like in there."

"You're sure you will be okay here by yourself? Can't Nikos give you…?"

"No I'll be fine. Our resources are spread thin right now. You trusted me in Naples and in Virginia," she narrowed her eyes, questioning him.

"Yes I did, and I do." He unexpectedly reached out to her, took her into a hug and whispered, "I'm leaving my whole world here Genie, and that includes you. Take good care." She choked up and just nodded her head. He got into the van and drove off down the rutted road toward the highway and another hour's drive to the mountains, his headlights stabbing into the dark surroundings.

New York City

Marian felt the little tremors in her belly. She always did when she was close to starting an affair and feeling the excitement and the anticipation of making the physical connection, after the opening salvos of flirting and cajoling the other party into realizing she wanted to take this to the highest level. She sat at the antique table in the hall where she could see the driveway as well as the stairs. No one was home so she had tapped in her International card number and placed a call to Terry. He had finally called her back after an hour's wait. She had gone to her room, piddled in her jewelry, looked in her closet for her travel bags and totes and run down the stairs at the ringtone of the phone, like a schoolgirl meeting her teen date for the first time.

"Terry you naughty man, I've been sitting here for over an hour, waiting for you to return my call." He heard the giddiness in her voice, the tremor of emotion he was expecting and hoping he could now take advantage of.

"Marian my dear, I've been so busy, it's a wonder I can get two minutes to myself for personal calls but I had to make this one. I've been so looking forward to talking to you. I've missed your calls. Have you been out of the country?"

"Why no, just right here, bored and lonely, and to tell you the truth, a little angry."

"You're angry... at me? I'm so sorry...I told you..."

"No Terry, not at you my dear. Why would I be angry at you? You haven't betrayed me, have you?"

"Tell me Marian, what has you angry? I find it helps to talk these things out."

So Marian proceeded to tell her most embellished tale of Quimby's mistress in South Carolina, who had no idea she was aware of her. She sighed and added all the indignities she had to suffer when she found receipts and overheard plans to meet in South Carolina and his plans to hide some of his clients away in her house where they would be safe from some wicked plan to do them harm or something.

"Savior of every woman he fancies. Her house…the bitch! "It's my house! And Quimby wants to have his cake and eat it too. I'm beside myself…"

She let loose a little sob and tried hard to tear up but couldn't quite get there. Damn!

"Marian, I'm so sorry you're going through this alone. What can I do to help? He lowered his voice to a sympathetic enticing offer, without offering anything.

"I just need to get away from this place and him. I can't stay here and be shamed and laughed at by probably everyone at his work. I can't very well go to our summer house even though it would be empty."

"I thought you said he was sending…"

"No, that fell through. He's working on somewhere else now, for heaven knows what reason. You'd think he and his associates were playing spy games and intrigue for amusement." She waited.

"Marian, would you like to come here for a visit, to get away from all the unpleasantness and the tense situation? I would be more than happy to put you up in a villa for as long as you wanted and I would promise to carve out some time for the two of us. We could just pretend it's a short vacation and you could stay on if you cared to. I so want to help you. I've grown quite eager to meet with you and I think this would be a perfect time."

JOURNEY TO THE BLUE PLANET

"Terry, you realize Quimby and I have nothing left? We've been non-communicative for some time and the only reason I'm so angry is not that he's screwing someone else, but that he considers his love life more important than our boys and everything we've built here."

"Marian, my dear, I'm sure we will have enough to do and talk about that I can make you forget all about Quimby and his mistress, as well as all the upheaval he has caused you. I'll make sure of that. I'm becoming quite excited, thinking about finally getting to see you and spend time with you. I'm pretty sure I can make you forget all about Quimby and everything else unpleasant there. Please say you'll come."

She heard a door slam and startled, she heard a car peel off down the driveway. She saw her son Tyson's car, roaring down the driveway. She felt the heat rising through her skin. He couldn't have... where had he been... why didn't he stay to say hello?

"Marian, are you there Marian?"

"I'm sorry Terry. I've had a situation come up. I'll have to call you back. I'll think very hard about your offer. Thank you so much for being there for me. I'll call soon."

She hung up and tried Tyson's phone and it went to message. She sat and thought for a moment then she called her husband's office and asked his secretary to ask Tyson to call her if he should show up at his dad's office. Then, she began to construct the story to tell her son if he had heard her call to Terry.

Across the ocean in Paris, Aldora knocked on Theras' door and entered just as he threw the phone across the room. It hit the wall, knocked the picture off the wall and landed on the hearth of the fireplace, where it shattered into pieces.

"God damn it to hell! I almost had her. One more minute and she'd have been swimming to get here."

Aldora raised her eyebrows at him and waited patiently. She walked over to the fireplace, stooped and began to pick up the pieces of phone, "Leave it there." She paused, "I said leave it!" She half turned in a stoop and slowly stood up to face him.

His face was flushed, his hands were fisted and he looked as if he just needed to swing at something or someone, "Where is Acteon?" and he stared at her, glaring.

"I'm not sure. You sent him out to the Grand Caymans and we haven't heard from him in over a day. Would you like me to try and contact him?"

"No, never mind. I have to do this myself. I want a plane ready in an hour and I'll be going to the states for a day or two. I'll be back tomorrow and perhaps I will have a guest with me. See that the second penthouse suite is ready. I'll call you from the airport before I return." He went to his desk, dismissing her out of hand. She looked at him for a moment then turned and walked out, closing the door softly behind her. "Goddamn women, bitches, all of them, made just to torture and plague me."

Chapter 40

DC, Georgetown

Andrew McCarty finished dressing, came over to the bed where Cloe was still snuggling beneath the covers. Andrew liked the room very cool in her apartment but she found it uncomfortable to make love outside the covers when the air from the fan was blowing off 65 degrees. They had been testy with each other their first night back from the beach. The weekend had been lovely and Andrew had been so attentive, even giving up golf that Saturday. He had taken her out dancing at a trendy club and they had been relaxed and joking Sunday night, before they left to drive back to DC.

He had taken a call and his entire demeanor had changed. He became short with her, accused her of delving into his business and told her that her parents were a real stumbling block to their continuing relationship. When she tried to get him to talk to her, he stomped off to the car with his bag and waited there while she heaved her own things out of the room they were in and came down in the elevator. On the way home he was stone silent, and she didn't give him an opening to start on her again.

This was not like Andrew. He was usually very laid-back and taciturn, very jovial and good-natured. She was hurt, confused and a little angry. What right did he have to attack her for her parents and his work? She never interfered with his work and her parents were nothing but civil to him. She knew her mother didn't like him much but she was always gracious and welcoming whenever she had them together. Who was that phone call from? Why did everything change badly, and so quickly?

He stood at the bed, looking down on her. She had her arm over her head and her face was hidden from him. She liked to block out the light. She lay still deciding whether to roll over and kiss him or pretend to be asleep. Just as she was about to roll over, he let out a huge sigh and whispered, "I guess this is it. It's been fun but now the real work starts." He turned and she heard the front door close and a minute later the garage door went up and his car left. She rolled over, sat up against the headboard and her jaw clenched.

{*what the hell what real work wasn't this real enough for you Andrew*}

A tear slipped out and she wiped it angrily away. She looked at the clock and it was a half hour earlier than his usual time. He was like clockwork, scheduled and routine oriented, actually a little anal. She sat and thought for a few minutes. She didn't know what was going on, but she suspected she was about to be dumped.

{*let's see what are the signs*}

He received a phone call that agitated him,

{*another woman a lover waiting in the wings*}

…he started an argument over her parents, trust issues…a diversion? He said some really rude things about her mother. How could she find out what phone number and person he was talking to? She picked up her phone and tapped her contacts. She knew someone she could count on not just being up at this hour, but could also do a little delving on the fly, "Cornelia, hi, I've got a huge favor to ask you so just say no if it bothers you."

After her conversation with Cornelia she got up, showered, dressed and headed out to work for the day. On the way out the door, she went over to the wall and flicked on the temp gauge and changed it to 71 degrees, "Finally, I'll be warm at night!" she said out loud. She was surprised at how light she felt and free.

While Cloe was heading to work, her mother, Isabel, was already at her desk. She was on the computer scrolling through documents from a flash drive she kept locked in her bedroom safe. She hadn't reviewed these for years. She had gotten the floppy disks transferred to hard disks years ago and then destroyed the floppies. There was at least thirty years' worth of information on here that no one's eyes should see except for those most trusted by her and that was a scant handful of people.

Dozens of names and flagged references came up quickly, moving upward and she followed them just as quickly. She took notes just as fast, speaking into her Android and reciting page and details that she saw and dates. Nothing yet, at least nothing she was looking for. The interns in her office had handed her a folder on Friday with the results of their search on one Lexus Fira. She had immediately recognized two names on there. She wasn't shocked or disappointed. Seeing her husband's name was surprising but not unexpected. Their families carried their names through many generations and they were numerous. To see Nikos' name connected to Lexus Fira, was not as daunting as she might have supposed.

Isabel realized she had lost track of the documents scrolling in front of her and lost track of where she was. She halted the program and looked at the pages handed to her yesterday. She knew one thing for sure and she would bet her career on it. She could trust Nikos beyond a doubt, with her life if necessary. These records were going to provide her with the proof she needed to take this to Suri, Egan and Quimby...and Agatha, to the whole Committee if she had to. She just had to find all the pieces and connect the dots. She started back to the place she had drifted off in thought and began reading and dictating names and numbers. She looked up at the clock.

{it's going to be a long morning}

She made a late-morning call to Cornelia and invited her for lunch for 1 p.m. then she called Cloe at work and did the same. It was a beautiful day; early fall, with cool mornings, warm afternoons close to 85 and then cooler nights. Both she and Nikos welcomed the chance to open windows and enjoy fresh air and the sounds of tree frogs in the pond out back. Their sounds reminded her of the time they spent in the mountains before Cloe was theirs and they had traveled to their home in Virginia to begin a life, with the three of them settling into their new home. It was the beginning of a very different experience. The years had flown, her happiness was overflowing and she and Nikos had been eternally grateful to be allowed to raise such a wonderful child who was so smart, funny and sweet. Before they knew it, Cloe was off to training, becoming the person she was today. She and Nikos were busy being high-level professionals, busy juggling the pressures of their different jobs and helping out wherever and whenever called to do so.

She reached the barbecue joint early, got a table up on the open deck and was sipping tea when Cornelia and Cloe came to the table from different directions at the same time. They laughed at each other and ordered a half rack of ribs each, and iced tea. Cornelia handed a folder to each one and they settled in to eat a very satisfying lunch. They talked of the last few days and each seemed lost in their own thoughts, trying to make connections and find a common thread that joined everything together.

Isabel spoke first, "Have either of you heard from Caroline or Sophia?" She looked up to see them both squirming and glancing at each other sideways, "What? What's happened?" She took her daughter's hand, "What's wrong?"

"Nothing's wrong Mom, really." She patted her mother's hand then she looked at Cornelia "Corny?" The pause was long and Isabel searched each face for some insight.

"If one of you doesn't talk in the next five seconds I'm calling your offices and asking for myself. I do still have some pull in this town."

Cornelia raised her palm, "Hold on Isabel, nothing drastic has happened. We wanted to wait a few days till everything was sorted out."

"What do you mean, 'sorted out'? I'll ask again, what's happened? I can't get them on my phone and their numbers are disconnected. Tell me!"

Cloe looked at Cornelia and she nodded for her to continue, "Mom, Caroline and Sophia have left for a while and it was done quickly and quietly. They'll be away for... a little while and they'll be fine, I promise. It was safer for them."

"Where did they go? Who's with them? What about school for Sophia... and Caroline's job at school?"

Another pregnant pause ensued. She stared at both for a heartbeat, "You can't tell me." It was not so much a question as a statement of fact.

"No" they both said at the same time.

"For how long?" Cornelia answered, "We don't know. It depends on what happens with this Committee and the results of the investigation into these teams of assassins that have been sent out..." she lifted her palms in a gesture of uncertainty.

Isabel took a breath, "Okay, I get it. But let's put that aside for now because I have to tell you both something important."

"Should we talk here mom?" Cloe seemed agitated even before Isabelle began.

"Why not, who's to hear?" she tightened her gaze on Cloe, "What is it? Why are you so..."

"Upset?" Cloe took a breath, "Andrew left this morning after an argument last night and I don't think he's coming back."

Cornelia said, "Oh I'm sorry Cloe. Maybe he will cool off and..."

"No, I don't want him to come back." They both sat back and waited for her, watching her color heighten and her voice dropping to a lower volume.

"Corny, did you get what I asked you for?" Her mother turned to Cornelia and narrowed her eyes between the two, "It seems we all have our secrets to share today," she sat back in her chair.

Cornelia handed Cloe a manila folder with one sheet of paper inside filled with what looked like phone numbers.

"This is it?" Cloe stared at the numbers from yesterday, "all these?" She sounded confused.

"Well..." Cornelia fiddled with her silverware, waited while their rib platters were brought and the waitress had walked away, "There were two phone calls but they were rerouted all over the place so all of them showed up as a conference call."

"All of this from one call? How is this possible?" She went down the list and saw New York, Virginia, Italy, Romania, France… small towns and big cities, Shanghai, Beijing, Puerto Rico, South America, the Andes… Isabel took the paper out of Cloe's hands and put up a hand to her protests,

"Can we unravel this all now, this minute?"

Cloe said, "I don't see how. I have no idea what's going on here," her hands were actually shaking.

"I do" Cloe stared at Isabel her eyes wide, "No, not now. We eat. I'm hungry, I'm on edge. You're both on edge. We eat, we talk…about lovely things and then I tell you what I have as a secret and we discuss all of this shit at once." She picked up her fork…

"Mother!" Cloe exclaimed.

"Not another word unless it's something pleasant….It also must be accompanied with good ribs and delicious coleslaw." She looked up to find them both grinning at her "Yes ma'am" they chorused and picked up their forks and tucked into the best ribs in DC.

Lyon France

It was 5 a.m and Rodane was over on a side street in the town of Lyon, having driven for two hours to arrive close to the town of Quais de Pecherie around 3 a.m. He was parked between two box trucks at a small warehouse and had dipped down into his seat and gotten in a couple hours of sleep. The flight, the drive to the lake cabin, the settling-in of Sophia and Caroline had truly whipped his ass. Leaving Eugenic in the driveway, he had driven straight from there to Lyon and could hardly keep his eyes open. A deer crossing the highway from the woods had almost put him over the embankment. After his heart stopped racing and the stirred gravel had stopped cascading over the edge, he crept his way into town and found a quiet space, closed his eyes and was out like a light.

He woke to a soft, gray edge to the sky and birds sitting on telephone wires and beginning their morning songs or screeches, or whatever the early birds did to announce dawn. He drove down the road and found one Pasticherie open or in the process of opening. He gestured to the owner filling urns, and was let in to get a pastry and a cup of coffee. He tipped him double the amount and rode over the Pont Bonaparte Bridge and up the drive to the Cathedrale St. Jean Baptiste, and on to La Basilique Notre Dame, perched on the hill like a squat wrestler with two muscled arms reaching to a now lightened sky, a nineteenth-century monolith, escaping wars and bombings and pillages.

Parking his car by the side door, he called to the sacristan inside as instructed and a side garage opened up to an empty bay in a few minutes. The sacristan waved him in and he parked the car, exited and handed the keys to him as the doors closed.

"Monsieur Arcos, do you have a gun with you, sil vous plais?" He reached out his hand, "Felix I'm surprised at you…" and he grinned, "you know I always carry two. He handed them over and Felix grinned back, "Yes, the times they change. Good to be sure, oui?"

They entered the front nave and walked to the huge, towering vestment case against the wall and pushed it easily on the rollers to the side. Rodane walked softly next to Felix down a darkened hall, parallel with the back of the altar and the dim lights flicked on as they moved. After a few minutes, they came to the seven foot door encased in stone and with a keyhole where Felix inserted an antique key intricately carved with land and mountains and trees interwoven, the very same design on Sabina's pin he had yet to determine.

Chapter 41

Le Basilique Notre Dame

Rodane walked into a room about nine feet tall, narrow, about fifteen feet long that felt damp and chilled. A stout wooden table was centered halfway and had five chairs around it. Three people at the end of the room were somewhat hidden with the dim light and the shadows. They surrounded a service table with pastries, coffee urns, and fruits in a bowl. They turned and Rodane couldn't help but smile as one stepped forward and walked toward him. Felix turned and left as silently as they had entered.

"Rodane my dear, how nice to see you so soon again. It is indeed a pleasure."

"Agatha, good to see you again as well…I think." She reached him, took both arms and kissed him on the cheek,

"You know Suri?" Agatha waved behind her.

"Only by reputation and through Sabina" he looked to the gentleman present. The man stepped forward, extended his hand and they shook.

"Leander…I believe you know my wife and sons…"

His face lightened, "Willow and Phillip! Yes, you have a fine son there and I've just recently met the other one, also a great kid! Willow is lovely."

"You flatter us… I'm very aware of how wonderful they are but thank you for noticing" and his handshake was firm and warm.

A door opened from what appeared to be paneling and Sabina stepped through. She turned, saw him and stopped. He looked at her, couldn't say anything, didn't want to say anything…couldn't do more than just look…at her wavy, dark hair, her topaz eyes that he couldn't really see from here but could envision. She did the same with him as if they were caught in a photo frame, still engaged, mesmerized, painted with dim shadow, dark colors and absorbing all the energy and the vibrations in the room. A fork or knife dropped and the spell was abruptly broken. An awkward silence ensued until Sabina lowered her eyes.

Suri stepped to Rodane, "Welcome Rodane and I think it's about time we actually met in person and then did some talking. I know you have lots of questions and I have some of my own.

"You're darn right I do. Hello…?"

"Suri, just Suri is fine. Would you care for some breakfast?" She waved to the serving table behind her,

"Just some coffee if you don't mind. Leander moved to get him a mug and Suri pointed him to an empty chair. He looked toward Sabina and she smiled at him, glowing but subdued, "Hello Rodane, it's been a while."

He smiled broadly at her, "Too long Sabina, how are you?" It sounded so trite and ineffectual for what he was feeling.

She sat down across from him and he could hear the silence in the room as clear as if there were no one else there. But there were a few…'someones'!

"I'm fine and we're all somewhat anxious to hear from you about all the events you've been part of for the past few weeks. Have Caroline and Sophia settled in nicely?"

"Yes they have, thank you. I guess all of you are pretty much aware of what's been happening then." He was taken aback by the question and how blithely it was posed and he answered the question just as forthrightly, "I'm not sure if I should thank all of you or sue your asses off." She raised her eyebrows, everyone sat still and Leander folded his hands and leaned forward, "Rodane, may I call you Rodane?" At his nod Leander continued, "I know you'll find this hard to believe but I understand how you feel, exactly."

He must have seen the unspoken response from Rodane's eyes.

"I know you find that hard to swallow, but I have been in your shoes…" he paused.

"Why do you think so?" Rodane was surprised and intrigued.

"You've had your entire family uprooted, attacked, uprooted again, taken away from everything they know and love and…" he paused.

"I'm sorry but I find it difficult to believe that you have experienced what I've gone through these last few weeks and…had my family put through… my mother… he stopped, swallowed hard, waited a few seconds and went on "My mother has been through hell in just a couple weeks, my ex-wife and daughter are thousands of miles away from their comfort zone and their friends and home…" His voice rose, "My job is in jeopardy and my career, my…" he stopped again and sat still, heart beating fast, sweat forming on his brow, his fingers cold and tingling, his gut in turmoil, "What the hell!" He looked up and they were all still statues, attentive and silent, waiting for him to wind down, like a musical toy box playing discordant notes.

Sabina came around from her seat and sat next to him in the empty chair. She leaned in, took his trembling hands lightly in hers, "Breathe, Rodane, slowly… breathe… with me." They sat hand-in-hand breathing shallow, light breaths, then slower, evenly, slower still. His heart quieted and his hands warmed. He looked slowly, hesitantly around the room at each one in turn. Leander sat with hands still folded, a look of curiosity on his face, gazing back and forth, rotating from him to Sabina. Suri was leaning back on her chair, taking in his physical appearance and tilting her head as if watching her experiment in action. Agatha sat, arms on the table, eyes narrowed, absorbing… what? Him? Sabina and him together? What did they see, what were they looking for? He took a deep breath and extricated his hands from Sabina, "I'm sorry, I guess I'm tired and stressed. I don't mean to take it out on you."

He stopped again, wondered if he had the courage to say what he truly felt, "Actually yes, I do. Well, not exactly take it out on you but I want answers, damn it! I deserve answers! Somehow I have to get my family squared away and safe. I need to know they are safe, not just for now, but for good."

"That's why we're here now Rodane…" Agatha spoke up, "Finally, we have your answers. We have just as much of an investment in keeping your family safe as you do… Yes, we do" seeing his expression, "I think you'll see that as we talk, you and us, together."

"Okay, can we start with why am I here and not with my family? Why couldn't Sabina come to us, and we could discuss this entire thing and I could still be there for them?"

"Because we wouldn't have access to the tools we need to allow you access to records and files that help to explain all this… thing you've been going through. Sabina?" she waved her to the computer monitor at her station.

Sabina rose and squeezed his shoulder before she walked back to her seat. Rodane stared as a panel rose in front of him, hidden in the folds of a design in the table; scrolls and figures carved from mahogany and walnut. An exact similar panel rose up at all the seats except the empty one to his left. The screen lit up and a box appeared for a password.

"Rodane, please place your hand flat on the screen." Suri turned her screen to show him her five fingers splayed directly over the box. He did so and a second smaller box appeared inside, his hand now displayed on the monitor. "Now tilt your screen as I do" she showed him how…"look directly into that smaller box for three seconds without blinking, if you can."

He did so and after four seconds the image beeped and his hand and eye were displayed in the boxes, in 3D. They were amazingly clear and he could even see the flecks in his pupil. His hand showed all the lines and cracks in his skin, a small scar on his palm from a scissors cut when he was ten and his fingerprints were clearly visible. Amazing! It was as if his real hand and eye were there in front of him.

"Thank you" Suri nodded to him, "Now I am going to put some short files in front of you and ask if you recognize them. The screen showed two pages, spreadsheets with varied lines and numbers. "Do you recognize them?"

"Yes, those are the papers Agatha showed me in Florence, at the museum."

"Do you remember what they showed?

Rodane answered, "Supposedly, they are my DNA results and a hereditary lineage report on my family background going back hundreds of years, I think.

"Would you like time to study them or use the computer to research any of the names to provide verification? We could arrange for that, if you'd like." Suri watched him.

"I guess it's because I used the term 'supposedly' that you're asking me if I want to verify them now."

Leander spoke up, "Rodane, I live and work with results, facts, and data. I would suspect this info as well as you so if you find it hard to believe this, you'll find it even more difficult to accept the knowledge we're about to impart to you. It's very important you satisfy the facts to yourself, as well as your curiosity."

"Otherwise" Agatha said, "we may as well call it a day and send you back to your family." She sounded agitated and short. He was surprised at the tone then he thought about all the times he had demanded answers and information and was so disturbed when it was lacking. After he was finally brought to the very edge of getting those answers, he was now questioning the very possibility of their validity.

"I'm not going to say sorry for this because it's my life we're contemplating here and not just mine, but I apologize for not attempting to hear you out and not keeping an open mind." He looked at each one in turn.

"How do you think these results of your DNA and the events you've been embroiled in are somehow related? Or do you think that's not the case?" Agatha asked him with a touch of asperity. She continued, "Suppose I were to tell you that you are a member of a dynasty of sorts, grown to the age and the point in time where you are next in line to become one of the most powerful people on…" she hesitated and looked at him with her hands folded…" the planet?"

"Well…! Hahahah!" He guffawed and coffee spouted out his mouth and he sputtered it over his shirt. Mff! Then he choked, snorted some more coffee out his nose and accepted a thick napkin from Sabina who had hurried around the table. She slapped him on the back a couple of times and let him cough until he cleared his throat and put up his hands to show he was okay. After a few minutes, he looked around at each of them. What he saw made him pale and his pulse start speeding up again, "You're serious? You're not kidding? You all believe this?"

"It's not important if we believe it Rodane" Agatha said, "It's important that you believe it or we're done here."

Suri said, "What we're about to tell you is shared with no one, not one soul, outside of this 'family', not your mother, your ex-wife, your child, your friends or co-workers, your priest or your bartender. We need to establish that right now before we go any further, clear?" she sat back and waited.

"Do I have to sign something? Take an oath or something?" he still felt shaken by this turn in the conversation.

"No need..." Agatha pointed to the computer, "you just gave us all we need to ensure your silence or your termination if you break it." Rodane watched her especially. He had a feeling she was the Dowager Empress so to speak, among the 'family' or at least the closest thing to it.

"What, you're serious aren't you, about my termination?"

"Serious as an interrupted heartbeat," she was talking with a cold, level tone that sent a shiver up his back and his neck hair stood on end.

He leaned in, placed his hands on either side of his terminal and spoke calmly, "Let's say, hypothetically, that I accept your theory. I'm some kind of royalty or... I don't know, 'dynastic influence'. Why isn't my mother living in the lap of luxury and I still have to work for my living? Why doesn't Mom know she is a part of this... dynasty?"

"...because she isn't...part of the dynasty that is." Agatha continued, "Your father Addy was an invaluable and long-lived member of the 'family'. However, he married outside the 'family' so she is not privy to what we are about to tell you. It is why you must absorb the imperative of your secrecy concerning everything we say here for your safety, your family's safety and because anything you divulge could put every single member of the 'family' at risk and our entire future in jeopardy."

Suri added, "Hypothetically, you and Sabina might have helped to uncover a longtime nemesis that we thought had been terminated and seems to have been working among us for some time. We might say you have 'hypothetically' helped us to avoid a crisis in the works and allowed us to uncover a very singular attack before it actually got off the ground."

"Huh! Eugenie and Helene part of this hypothetical scenario?"

"Very much so" she touched her screen, pictures popped up on Rodane's screen, among them Tabor Doukas and Renata Kappos, who he instantly recognized. He sucked in a breath like a sharp, low whistle at the next person shown, "Are you kidding me? Zoe is a part of this? Who else?"

An entire page of photos appeared in three rows across the screen. Rodane slapped the table with his hand and the clap shook the table. The monitors and the screen jiggled for a few seconds then settled again, "Hah!" he chortled, "Bellboy! Who would have thought?"

Sabina smiled, "Only recently Rodane. We sent our people to question him, to see how secure his promise was to you not to reveal your trip and to get more details on the team that tried and failed to take you out twice. Seems there is a genetic connection to us he's never been aware of. Now we're taking advantage of that. We've eliminated that problem."

"What!" he exclaimed, "You've terminated him?" His face showed shock and anger. "No...of course not, silly!" Sabina put her hands in the air to hold his thoughts. "We've sent him to training and education. He's over the moon with the opportunities we shared with him."

"Oh well then... that's okay." He smiled back at her, "Wait a minute, education training? What kind of training? He's almost a kid."

Leander spoke for the first time in a while, "That's the next step for you, education at least. Training may take longer to accomplish."

"You know my background I take it?" Rodane looked at all four of them. "I teach at a university and I have numerous degrees in various fields. Not to sound a braggart, but what else could I study and how could I if I have my job and my Photo journal business?"

Leander replied, "There's a lot more to a specialized education besides degrees and subject matter. Our 'education' will be more like an extended period of enlightenment and 'family' history. You don't have books for that my boy, at least not books you can get here" he said the last word, encompassing the room and the outside and...'everywhere'.

"Here, the cathedral? What books?" he was overwhelmed with question after question popping into his head, no time for thought, no chance to force them into coherent thought processes.

"Yes, let's get on to it." Agatha spoke with that touch of asperity, "Rodane, forgive me but I can't afford to dilly-dally around all this 'hypothetical' stuff when time is of the essence, so..."

Suri looked at her in alarm, "Agatha, do you think it's wise to lay all..."

"What, you don't think he has intuited some, maybe a great deal, of what he's about to have put into words? Seems we should give our Rodane some credit for being what we're telling him he is, letting him have a chance to deconstruct it and make sense of five hundred thousand years of education, don't you all think so?" She examined Suri's face and then Leander's and then Sabina's quiet countenance, with a more critical look. Sabina looked at her a few seconds then spoke with a hint of irony, "You know already, don't you, mother?"

"Mother?" Rodane sputtered with shock and confusion on his face, "She's your mother?"

Sabina laughed at the same instant as Agatha did, "No Rodane, just in the sense of a wise woman, a granny of tales, a historian in charge of records kind of mother, a protector of us all."

"Okay...." he said in a long drawn-out breath, "like my Oma is to everyone, related or not!"

Agatha and Sabina said at the same instant, "Exactly!"

"Look, we've been at this awhile and it's going to be a long day if Rodane is ready for it. Are you ready for it Rodane Arcos, son of Addison, Arturo, Emmanuel, Andreas, Lucius Arcos?" His eyes widened, he took in a deep, sustained breath, looked around the table and let it out in a huff, shook his head as if he was clearing cobwebs from his thoughts and said, "Let's do it."

Suri rose, started around the table and lightly remarked, "Let's eat something. It's been an exhausting morning already. The afternoon may prove to be... somewhat more so. We need to keep up our energy, all of us. She looked to Rodane, "Does that appeal to you, to have some late lunch and then continue?"

"I'm always up for a late lunch, or an early one. Let's eat!"

Barbecue joint in DC

Isabel took a Wet One from the pack, wiped her fingers thoroughly, took her napkin from her lap, folded it carefully and placed it beside her empty plate. Cornelia was on the phone and disconnected.

She looked at them and turned to Cloe, "Andrew is nowhere to be found. He didn't show up at the paper this morning, but that's not unusual. He's a Stringer, who's often out on the streets looking for events or talking to a source for a burgeoning story. The Senior Editor is going to call me the minute he shows up. I've talked to Lori and he won't be admitted to the White House Press Corps or any other government building if he attempts to show up at one. Lori is having her staff run down every story he's been on for the last... Cloe, how long have you been dating Andrew?"

Cloe stilled her entire body, gathered her breath, drew it in and then she expelled it slowly and deliberately, "What are you saying Corny? This was a set up? I was duped by a cute guy who is now in the wind with state secrets?" Two bright spots formed on her cheeks. Isabel reached over to take her hand and Cloe snatched it away, "No, tell me Corny. What do you and Lori think…I gave away information as pillow talk and under the influence?"

"Cloe!"

"No Isabel," Corny watched the hurt girl's expression, "Cloe's got a right to be angry. I would be too but I'd be angry at the person who is taking advantage of me and put me in a precarious position. I wouldn't be angry at my closest friends who always, always have my back." She looked straight at Cloe and simply waited. Both women stared across at the other while Isabel looked from one face to another and back again, also waiting.

Cloe blinked, "You're right, I'm sorry. To think I might have endangered us and our…"

"No" Isabel broke in, "Don't go there and don't feel sorry for yourself either." Cloe looked over toward her mother…abashed. "This was in no way your fault. You're here, are you not? Attempting to make things right?"

Corny added, "If you hadn't found this out, not only would he be in the wind but he could be playing havoc with information, files, sources… don't blame yourself for having feelings, blame him for apparently having none. And he's not going anywhere. Airports have his name and passport photo, train stations have camera surveillance working on face recognition, taxis have a red flag over their radios and even bus stations are on alert. If he attempts to drive out of town, police have his license plate and are instructed to inform but not follow. Just go up the chain. He'll come out somewhere soon, for food or money or… just because he doesn't know we're on to him."

Cloe looked concerned "I don't want him to be hurt Corny. She saw her face "I know, I know, but he does mean… did mean…oh I'm so confused at all this happening so fast," Tears slid down her face and Isabel handed her a napkin. Isabel's phone chimed to the theme from 'Dr. Zhivago' and she picked it up, then exhaled quickly, "Where are you? When are you coming home? No, I want to know!" Isabel snapped, unlike her.

"Is that Daddy?" Cloe asked. Isabel waved her off and Cornelia and Cloe looked at each other both with raised eyebrows. It was very unlike Isabel to snap at other people and in particular her husband. Whatever he responded to her, it served to agitate her even more. "So why can't you? It's important Nikos, that's why. I won't discuss it over a phone, not even a secure one. Come home!" she almost shouted the last and then amazed them as she cut him off and ended the call. She sat for a minute or two getting her breath, calming her pulse and gathering her thoughts.

It was as if the other two women were not even there. Then she looked up from one to the other, came to a decision from the look on their faces and spoke, "Nikos is my husband, has been for almost my entire life or it feels like it. I love him dearly but I know I'm not his whole world as he is mine."

"Mother! You can't be saying that Daddy has... is..." Isabel laughed long and hard, "No Cloe, your father is not unfaithful, has never been and I think I would know if he were. No, the other part of his world is the part I can't share, never could and the part you two are also wrapped up in, to the exclusion of all else. Am I right?" She examined each face carefully as they looked to each other. Corny folded her hands, sat back, crossed her legs, and pinched her face as if tasting something sour or bitter. Cloe looked at her long and hard and then turned to her mother,

"Mom I... can't... can we talk about this at some other time? I'm not sure this is the place or..."

"No Cloe your mom's right. This is the perfect time, so we'll have to make do with the place. They're all connected, aren't they Isabel? The boyfriend, the phone calls around the world, Nikos' business and his work?"

Cloe, surprised, asked her mother, "Are they? Is Daddy part of the reason Andrew has been duping me and gathering information? Where is he? Does he know about Andrew?"

"Whoa there Cloe, one mystery to solve at a time, one crime to solve, then move toward the other." Corny was sitting on the edge of her seat and looking around at mostly empty tables and chairs.

Isabel decided it was time for her to come clean as she was so wont to tell others.

"Cloe, I may not be in the same 'league', she pointed her fingers, "as you and Corny but I'm not totally clueless. Never in all the years I've known your father, have we kept things from each other." She saw their faces, "I'm not talking about 'family' history or what he does for his other business. Other than the fact that we pretty much know what the other is up to, you get my drift? It's never hampered our relationship or put either of us in a compromising position. I can't talk to you about this until your father is home and we have a chance to examine all of this... and put the clues together. I will say this. I know a lot more than I should, but less than it would take to become a problem myself. Does that make sense? Do I now have to go and turn myself in somewhere?"

Corny chuckled, "No Isabel, Cloe and I are not going to turn you in for being the intelligent and sensitive soul you are. It's no wonder Nikos was willing to go through hoops to marry you, no matter what."

Now Isabel was shocked, "What? Corny, how could you possibly know how Nikos and I got married? You had to be hardly more than a child yourself."

"Family history, it's about 'family' history. Our entire 'family' takes each other very seriously and studies our history very carefully, every last one of us." She rested back against the seat, "You get my drift?"

Isabel smiled sardonically and then grinned at Corny, "I think I do, thanks for clearing that up." Corny gathered her things and stood up, "I have an appointment with Lori and I don't want to be late. I think we may end up having to brief her husband on how things stand now, in case more shit is thrown at the fan."

"You mean if more shit hits the fan!" Isabel chuckled.

"…gets thrown at the fan. We don't intend to let one little bit of this shit actually hit the fan, too much at stake. We have to stop it before it hits and stinks! I'll call you soon"

Cloe spoke up, "Do you have to tell the President about Andrew? I mean about me and Andrew?" Corny looked at her as curiously as her mother did, "I mean, he has a mind like a trap he said, and he knows Andrew and I are… an item. He… warned me…" she looked down and her face was flaming.

Corny laughed, "If he remembers, it will hardly be something he brings up, considering why we're meeting with him and the complications of the investigation and now the current activities… if he does bring up the subject of Andrew, I'll try my best to keep it as professional as possible."

"Whoa boy," was all Cloe could manage.

Chapter 42

Lyon, France

It was late afternoon in Lyon, France. The members in the room had been working hard since early afternoon with no breaks and plenty of coffee; heated, reheated, re-brewed and reheated again. Rodane sat at his console, with piles of papers spread all around him, a dual screen open on his monitor and his printer spitting out one sheet after another, which he grabbed up and placed on a new pile alongside all the others.

He had lost his sense of time quite a while ago and his stomach was knotted up so that even food didn't even call out to him His eyes were gritty, his nose was stuffy and his shoulders ached as if he had lifted weights for a long time, beyond his comfort level.

Every once in a while he would sputter something under his breath and then look up to see if everyone else was aware of his 'outburst'. He would stop and circle something on a sheet or use his highlighter to cover lines of print, and then move on to another sheet. His eidetic memory had never absorbed so much information at once that he could remember. His head felt heavy, sluggish, but then another piece of information would come up in front of him and he would read, exclaim, wring his hands through his hair or whistle under his breath. Then another sheet would print out.

Much of what he read was known to him or at least the first flow of info he could grasp that could connect to other pieces of knowledge he was more familiar with. Slowly, oh so slowly, yet seeming like a speeding train, he was beginning to put the pieces together. His brain was starting to assimilate what all the connections were and his psyche was beginning to butt up against his sense of reality. These pieces felt like little punches to the gut, small hits and runs on his previously held beliefs that were now under attack, a bombardment of the impossible meets the possible, shakes hands then comes out swinging. His monitor went blank and his printer closed down, beeped once and slept... he could just put down his head and do the same. He looked up as he heard a throat cleared, and saw three of them watching him.

{nothing like being a bug on a tray}

Leander spoke, "Would you care to take a break or perhaps stop for coffee and a bathroom break? Do you think you've reached a point where you have some questions you might like to ask?"

"Yeah, well folks... see...it's like this..." he stalled, cleared his own throat and tried again, "I know I asked for my questions to be answered and I really think I do... want to know that is... but I'm at a loss as to where to start. There's so much here in front of me...there's so little organized thought in my head right now it's..." he shook his head as if to clear his ears or chase away a gnat, no, a giant mosquito.

The other three people had been in closed conference at the end of the table sharing one computer, reviewing whatever it was they were studying and speaking in low tones that resembled the hum of bees in a hive undisturbed. Agatha had left the group about an hour before when Felix had come and spoken quietly to her. She had flowed up and out of her chair and out of the room. Only once had they spoken so hurriedly and so vociferously that the hive was stirred and the bees threatened to erupt and go on a stinging spree. They looked up as Leander asked his question.

"A little overwhelming?" came from Suri, "You're at a disadvantage. You're quite a bit older to be taking this all in at once. Usually it's a timeline of years, gradual lessons, education and exposure. You're also at a disadvantage because you now have in front of you, a very expansive compendium of information and scientific fact that totally throws much of what you have believed your entire educated career, into a grinding wheel. Like some of our older, somewhat more mature later subjects, you are in a quandary as to what to let go and what to hold onto for your life and sanity."

"I couldn't have said it better myself" he said. He took a deep breath, "All of you, including the committee members not here... do you all have this knowledge from long ago? Are you all... how do I put this..." he was so intense it was like hearing his anguish out loud, as clear as a bell, "I have a few hundred questions at this point but what I'm more interested in is whether you can prove to me any of the information I have read up to now. If you can, I believe my 'education' is more like a re-education and a startling one at the least, a stupendous one at best. I'm trying my best to wrap my head around it and getting more flabbergasted by the page."

Sabina asked, "Do you remember the conversation we had while driving some time back? You had a very difficult time then of understanding what I was telling you at that point about yourself and your abilities as well as your family's unique abilities?"

"Yeah I do. I remember almost every word of that but this... this is...1000 times more than that...isn't it? Or am I missing the whole message here and ..."

"You're not missing anything..." Agatha stepped into the room, "You're only just beginning and I'm sure you have some of those questions about our purpose on this earth and why it is so important to go back to the beginning. Are you ready for some hard facts?"

Suri spoke up as he searched Agatha's face for a sense of her mood, "We're placing an enormous amount of trust in you, someone we don't know well... no, think about it. We've only allowed you into our...'family' for a very short while. With everything that's happened in such a short time, how much do we really know of your part, your trustworthiness, the possibility that all we tell you might not remain among us...?"

"So how do I earn that trust? What would have to happen before I am privy to this information that concerns me and my family...?" he sounded petulant, annoyed, dejected.

Agatha said definitively, "Isn't the fact that you're here now, some of that proof? The fact that we are sharing some of the most secretive and protected files we have kept from all eyes, except those we trust with our own lives? You want it all, you want it now! Is that realistic or even possible? You've been introduced to facts and statistics that our own children never see until they have proven themselves to us, many times over." She stood up and walked over to him, "I understand how you feel trapped in the moment Rodane, but we can't expose the past to you except in increments your psyche can absorb, and we can't tell you what's going on, because we're only learning it ourselves. As for the future...please don't make us regret our decision to involve you in this. We've come very far. I don't think you want to stop now and I know I don't, how about the rest of you?" She looked from one to the other.

Leander started his query again, "Any questions pop immediately into your head Rodane? We can start anywhere... well, within reason. Most of us are well-versed in all those files your printer has been pumping out."

"Take me back to your beginning here, if you can. That really interests me and it's as good a place as any."

Leander paused, looked around the room at each person and stated, "In the beginning, there was light." They all tittered.

Rodane rubbed his hands over his face and gazed at the group with some frustration, "Okay, okay, I get it. I have a feeling this goes way beyond the age of the Bible or any written document for that matter.

"You're absolutely right!" Suri added, "Are you in a frame of mind to begin accepting a few conspiracy theories that are not conspiracies?"

"I think I told you, I'm keeping an open mind!"

"Well it's going to have to be a lot more than open-minded. You're going to have to face some very unbelievable information and where it leads you. Annnnnd (she drew the word out) you're going to have to regroup all that knowledge you've learned to practice for your whole career, because we're going to unearth some very oppositional opinions as well as facts, that your professors would never dream of presenting in your classes. Many years ago, they'd be hung or burned as witches."

"Lead on!" He was feeling excited to actually begin his quest no matter where it led him.

{what if it's all a hoax a giant lie}

His indecisiveness must have registered on his face. Sabina spoke up, "Suppose we start with about two to five million years ago…?" She saw his face, "No not us, but it was the start of the efforts we made to 'interfere' as you say, in your world. We discovered a virus that triggered the Herve K once again. It was a human, endogenous retrovirus which created our need for genetic engineering. It was being passed down through generations. 5 - 8% of the human genome was found in the cortical and guinal neurons. We found a way to bring it to a period of stasis, a very long period, to help those neurons to develop and expand. All this was way before humans were considered humans. Our engineering was done well beyond their beginning, but we thought we had it under control."

"Now we've recently reached a point in time…" Leander grimaced, "where chemicals and pollutants in excess quantities are activating them once again. We won't interfere but we can surreptitiously lead them to some positive conclusions, with the possibility of beginning to corral them."

Suri added, "Conditions like allergies to simple foods, to grass, to medicines, even holistic ones, to neurological conditions in the unborn and children, but we can't make them accept the science, we can only help them see it."

"That's a tall order with some of the skeptics we have today in every field that think they have the answer to everything and other's opinions count for nothing." Rodane knew his politics, bureaucracy and infighting. He had experienced it often enough over the years, "I've read about these retroviruses. Scientists believe they have existed for millions of years. Is that still the case?"

"Even we can't account for millions of years…" Sabina snuck in her piece, "but we can tell you solid information that goes back at least a hundred and fifty thousand years."

"Why did you... your 'family'... what do I call them?"

"Family is appropriate. We are all of one 'family' broken into many familial lines."

"So why did you interfere in natural, biological evolution? Why not let nature take its course?"

Sabina looked at him quizzically, "If Sophia... forgive me for hitting close to home, but... if Sophia were being examined for a cold and the Dr. found suspicious leanings toward a serious infection or disease that could only get worse with time, would you want him or her to sit back and tell you to keep an eye on her and then give you an appointment for a year later if it turned deadly?"

"Of course not but we're talking about people trained in medicine, experienced... and..." He stopped, put his chin in his hand, thought it over and then said, "Why do something that can compromise healthy people, change their makeup and perhaps cause a disruption that could be unknown or unexpected?"

"That conversation we had..., about your DNA and the differences you possess outside of a whole population all over the world, that do not possess those factors?"

"Yeah that's me, but the 'family'... what about people who might not want their DNA tweaked, might be happy with a natural evolution over time for their descendants?"

Sabina turned on the Whiteboard, turned to Leander and said, "Pull up G 17 for me, please. Graphs showed on the screen of spirals, circles, bar graphs, line graphs, and columns of data.

"Rodane you have a series of files labeled with a letter of the factors we'll be discussing. G files take you to Genetics and Genomes as well as others. You can refer to them whenever you like. Let's look at these for just a moment, okay?"

"Sure, this is where I can get comfortable with facts and data and square them away."

"Okay, DNA 'flows' can make the incredible happen to any species. Tweaks of DNA can alter your makeup to produce disease resistance, sharper instinctual nerve response, better, stronger eyesight, more muscle mass with the response time to danger..."

"Okay, I can add in more interbred species of birds, or lizards etc."

Sabina smiled at him, "Now you're connecting the dots! You might want to look up M5 at your leisure to study Mitochondrial Replacement

Techniques, MRT, which are being used now in our time, to understand the similarities and the progression of three-parent Genome structure. It's being used to eliminate defective gene presence and alter the end results."

"So how do I reconcile what this 'family' did with their science, to your ancestors? Did you use any of this tweaking on your own people?"

Suri responded, "As science advisor for our Committee, I would recommend you read the files on... Sabina, what file is reconstruction under?"

Sabina tapped her tablet and on the Whiteboard a line of files marked 'A', stopped at A-4, Ancestral Protein Reconstruction. "All the A files concerning ancestry of our people will give you some insight into modern descendants and even the DNA from past genomes of long-dead and extinct creatures and organisms, as well as their use of reconstruction of protein links to our own people. There are many connections, both from species to species and subspecies, with links to humans and ...us."

She had groped to find a word then stopped. Rodane's eyes widened considerably, "You're intimating you're not human?"

Chapter 43

Basiliique Notre Dame, underground

Rodane squinted, rubbed his face and remained silent for a time then… "I want to do something spontaneously if you let me" he was addressing each of them.

Agatha had a half smile, "Now you're being the Archaeologist and scientist I was expecting to see and hoping to observe. Please feel free."

"I'm going to ask each one of you without references or files open in front of you, to provide me with a different example of something your family was involved in producing, or causing something otherworldly to happen, as a result of your intervention from your earliest days."

"Is this a test?" Agatha looked amused and Rodane smiled back, "There's always a test!"

"Lead on then. Who do you want to hear from first?"

Each computer beeped offline and the Whiteboard was blanked. Rodane looked at Agatha, "I'd like to pick your brain for hours…" they all laughed "but you for now, if you please."

"I'll refer you to the European Stone Age tunnels if you're familiar with the subject?"

"Yes! They stretch for many miles from Scotland and Europe all the way to Turkey." he didn't look really surprised at her choice, "They have been recorded as approximately 12,000 years old and scientists are still not sure of their purpose or their creation."

"I believe it's found in the A files…" Sabina broke in "Around A- 22-25 I think. Sorry!" She looked embarrassed.

Agatha continued with a nod to Sabina, "It was a system of transportation in those early days of wars between factions of sub humanoids and early humans, a way to avoid disease and geological events as well, such as floods, droughts, and violent storms. But it had a more important use as well. Those tunnels allowed for continued communication from one family to another, an exchange of medicines and supplies for many years. Science will eventually record they are far older than 12,000 years, more like a 120,000. I have no doubt they also haven't found the other tunnels built across North America or Asia, definitely not those in Antarctica. 'Family' provides for any eventuality, or at least the ones they could foresee."

Rodane did look surprised at that, "North America? Don't you think we would have found those by now with all the universities sending out teams to…Montana, Wyoming…the Dakotas, all through the west, the places we've discovered artifacts, the mountains…"

"Not if you don't search what's in front of your face!" Agatha looked a trifle smug "How do you think we've managed to avoid detection for so long even with all your scientific expeditions? How about, just for one example, your own cave systems, reaching through each and every mountain range in the US all the way through South America?"

"Wow! I never considered what we are still beginning to seriously investigate. Do you have 'family' working for Nat'l Geographic and the Spelunker Society of America?"

Her only answer was a slight shrug and a smile.

He took a minute to digest all she had just given him, twitched his shoulders then, "Okay Leander, I'd like to hear from you."

"I'm going to relate some thoughts for consideration that I personally am very interested in investigating, simply to learn more about my ancestors, kind of like delving back through Ancestors.com." Rodane sat back, prepared to remember as much as he could for his own later research.

"Gobekli Tepe is…"

Rodane cut in, "Oh for heaven's sake, you're going to deflate all I've studied about one of my favorite places?"

"No, quite the contrary. I'll probably just reinforce your own understandings. Gobekli Tepe is in Turkey… sorry…would you like me to choose a different event, rather than one you may probably know already?"

"No!" he was very curious as to what new facts he was about to learn.

"There were actually several millennia of activity through the Mesolithic period. And that site is actually 7,000 years older than Stonehenge. What you may not know is there are several layers of an underground city buried under Gobekli Tepe. We've allowed for incursion into uncovering a few of those stratified layers, but there's much more to be seen if it continues on. Those layers of the city not yet uncovered, show a level of organization more complex than anything otherwise known of the entire Paleolithic era."

"You've allowed? What does that mean?"

Agatha spoke with determination in her voice, "We'll get into that very soon Rodane, but not today. We still have so much introductory information for you to mull through, we'd really like you to stay on that track if you wish to discuss your own family with us."

He thought about that for a moment, shrugged and said, "Okay Agatha, why don't I go to Sabina as my next contestant?" He smiled over at her.

Sabina began hesitantly, "My choice is closer to your home Rodane, because I'm very interested in American artifacts and finds. I've spent relatively all my time investigating our European finds and sites for so long. London Texas is known for…" she began…

"…the Hammer! How did you know?" Rodane was astounded.

"How did I know what?" She looked confused and uncertain.

"I've submitted all my paperwork for an extended fall dig at London Texas, to go deeper and send results back to the university, if they'll fund the research and a small team."

She looked carefully at his excited face and asked, "Why?"

"Why what? Why do I want to do a dig? It's my job, and I'm good at it!"

"Why did you choose London, Texas of all the places you could travel and… why the hammer? It's a really suspect find for one of your record and reputation."

He had the grace to blush. "That's why! I've become very interested in studying Ooparts. They not only tickle my curiosity but so few people have even come up with any rational explanation. I wanted to break the stalemate."

Sabina continued, guarding her words and framing her thoughts. "I'm going to tell you that the Hammer is dated to 400 million years…" she noted his stunned expression. "That's why the Out Of Place artifacts designation."

"How is that possible? It can't…"

"It can and it was. As you might know, it was found encased in Ordovician rock and that was deliberately done. To answer the question you're going to ask, it was because at that time, they believed where it was planted would never be discovered until much more time had elapsed, centuries…if ever.!"

"Planted by whom? Why was it planted?"

"…because the Hammer was used 100 million years ago by us but they planted it much deeper and in a place they thought would keep it concealed much longer. They didn't account for the land shifting and eroding so rapidly in that area of your country."

"So you're saying they planted it on purpose to be used later, much later? For what"?

"I... we don't think... she looked around at everyone, "At this point I'm going to leave it to your research to prove or disprove what I don't care to gift to you." she was resolute and determined. "You asked for one example, that's mine."

He sat back brooding then sighed, "Yes ma'am, I recognize that look." The rest laughed under their breath and she looked annoyed.

"Suri, I guess that leaves you. I saved the best for last." He grinned at her and she smiled back, "I think my choice will be the best after all." They all looked at her, skeptical, "I choose to enlighten you about some unknown facts wrapped around the Baigong Pipes in the Qinghai province of China."

"Oh good, that's where I would love to be able to do a dig, but the fact that it's in China... and the paperwork is a nightmare and... sorry, please go on." He was excited and those around the table were looking at Suri with one of warning.

"If you know anything about that site..."

"Yes I do, but not a lot. It's near a lake apparently. Most think the artifacts are at least 150,000 thousand years old. Some however, try to place them only up to 1000 BCE."

"Good. Do you know how they were first discovered?"

"I believe a plane flying off the grid and out of its legal airspace spotted it."

"Yes, in 1939 to be exact. Gales and sandstorms in the desert have covered most traces so deep they could only be seen by air. Expeditions proved treacherous and very expensive. They managed to uncover the fact that all the lines of the pipes led to a convergence with the winter solstice. The pipes, hundreds of them, besides the ones above ground, led under the lake with a very few protruding above the surface."

She stopped and Rodane waited... and waited... he hesitated, not wanting to sound critical, "That's it? I thought there would be more."

"So there is, but not that can be proven yet."

"I'll bite. What do you know that they don't know?"

"That the three caves they were found in are not the only place to find more; that the pipes lead from caves to under the lake and that many of the pipes are radioactive. Oh yes AND that the salinity levels in the lake based on shells and deep lake bones show levels rose, dropped and rose again, to alarming highs and lows."

"Okay, that is interesting and very confusing."

There was a long pause as each person seemed lost in their own thoughts.

Rodane was no exception. Minutes ticked by until Agatha cleared her throat and said, "Did we pass your test Rodane, or are you more skeptical now?"

"Either you folks are students and experts of Archaeology, Paleontology, Genetics, and a host of other subject areas beyond reason or..." he paled a little at his next remark..."You are who you say you are and I would like to know so much about where you're from, why you're here, why you haven't announced yourself, and so much more."

"Rodane, there's a saying among lawyers, 'Don't ask a question you don't know the answer to'. That applies partly to you and to us."

Sabina looked at her and added, "and there's another saying that you'll never know the answer if you don't ask the question."

Rodane looked up, "There's also the saying; 'if you think you know the answer be prepared to be proven wrong'. I bet I could pose any question about any site or dig or recent discovery and you'd all be able to explain in detail, am I right?"

Agatha answered him, waving at all those seated, "I would venture to say yes, but that's our history and knowing is our job. We'd be pretty piss-poor at our jobs if we didn't know our own history."

"Okay, the $64,000 Question. Who are you and where are you from and why..."

Leander said teasingly, "That's three my boy, pick one." When Rodane started to respond, Leander said, "To be clear Rodane, we can't, under the strictest confidentiality, answer any of them right now, security and all that, need-to-know basis."

Rodane was annoyed as well as frustrated, "How many questions that I want answered will get that response? If my sister...my daughter... my father...are all 'family', don't you think some of that confidential stuff should be waived for... his son... her brother... her father... the dynastic heir?" He sat still, petulant and frowning. The last was said with mild anger and sarcasm. Agatha sat and composed herself, the rest were silent, and she could feel the agitation building.

Finally she stated, "I am prepared to offer you any explanation you ask for concerning just about any subject, but I cannot share confidential and highly classified information until..." She looked directly at him..."until we are..." and she raised her hands to indicate everyone..."**they** are convinced that you have our best interests at heart and you are convinced our family is worth that trust. You must show us you believe we have your best interests at heart as well, you and your family."

"Oh, is that all? Doesn't seem to be too much to ask now, does it?" he was still angry.

Suri stepped in, adding her own comment, "I could offer you another example no one has approached, to begin to answer just a little of what you're asking without exposing any confidential or classified info. Interested?"

He was trying to see himself from their point of view. He realized he must seem like an agitated, sulking young man who was being given reliable information, amazing at that, yet wanted more... and more... and more...

{greedy bastard for just beginning}

He breathed deeply, looked across at Sabina and saw her expression of... what? Was it hope? Begging him to understand? Fear it would all come to nothing? Quiet desperation, hoping he would reach out for the Olive Branch?

"Sure why not? We've come this far."

Suri raised her brows. She probably was seeing him as a very sulky, discontented child, who wanted the whole candy jar, not satisfied with a few pieces, unable to handle his own anger management.

"Some of the most mystifying Archaeological drawings are geoglyphs around 8,000 years old in Kazakhstan. They can only be seen from space."

Now he picked up his head and showed renewed interest. He knew this one!

"Yes! They're over 400 miles above Earth and there's a swastika and a cross and..."

"They haven't even uncovered all of them."

"But the symbol of the swastika has been around for over twelve thousand years as a sign of prosperity and power."

"Yes, just one reason why Herr Hitler was so eager to adopt it as his Legion's most respected sign of his time in power, and why that same sign is one of the most hated and feared among rational people on Earth," She sat up straighter.

"Rodane, those alignments track the movement of the sun. They provide views to a part of earth that was uninhabited and difficult to reach, except for those arriving and needing some hidden, encased, safe places to land. Even some scientists from all over the globe theorize that."

"So... you're throwing me a treat that answers where but not when... or why... or even how?"

Suri was now annoyed as well, but kept her voice level, "Yes, and it's up to you how you take it."

Rodane took all this in, spread his hands and remarked to all of them, "Have you ever had this kind of situation before? Where you had someone who should be a part of your 'family' but lacks the knowledge of it, being brought in and given what I've been given here?"

Three of the five shook their heads. "No!" Agatha said immediately and

JOURNEY TO THE BLUE PLANET

Sabina seemed to be offended as she spoke, "Are you trying to push each person's button one at a time? Is it my turn?"

He opened his eyes wide and leaned back to absorb the blow.

"I'm not trying to offend you Sabina. I..."

"Rodane, except for confidential and classified information, I have never given you anything but complete truth. As far as bringing you to the Committee...the other choice was to let you... be killed!" her eyes stabbed at his face and he found himself cringing inside and staring openly at her.

"In fact, a number of times I questioned my own decisions to safeguard you, to warn you, to divert attention from you to... put myself in danger! It would have been so much easier to... she stopped and there was a hitch in her voice.

"Let me die? Or be killed? How about my own family and their loved ones? Did you question protecting them too?"

Agatha stood up and pointed to the door, "Professor Arcos, there's the door! If you feel we've somehow betrayed you or yours or lied to you for our own purposes... please use it, and return to your own place, your own family, your own... bubble! Feel free!" Her words stopped, her mouth snapped shut and her eyes actually crackled with electricity.

He ignored her and looked at Sabina, "Why did you choose not to? Please..."

Now it was him reaching out an olive branch. Tears leaked from Sabina's eyes and everyone was emotionless, silent, afraid to move it seemed.

"Because you and I..." she looked up at her 'family' around the table, "you and I... are... in synchronicity! That's all I can explain. I can't expect you to know...but..."

"But I do" he almost whispered, "I understand. It's one of the things I've lost sleep over, thought constantly about, been sick over, since we met. I do understand. I just find it difficult to explain..." They both just looked across at each other and everyone else lowered their eyes to avoid the naked feelings being exposed at that moment, the charged atmosphere. If he touched her now, he thought he might suffer electrocution.

Agatha sat down next to him, "Is that it Rodane? Are you afraid? Do you doubt us because you doubt yourself?"

He didn't even answer. He just sat quietly and averted his eyes.

Suri said hesitantly, "Mother, I was concerned that it might be too..."

"Balderdash! I listened to you Suri, we all did. We don't have the time or the means to slow this process down or ignore him and send him on his way."

"But... but you just said..."

"I'm doing a 'when push comes to shove' moment. There's your shove

Rodane. What are you going to do with it?" She looked at her watch and said, "We need a recess, Meeting's adjourned, back here in one and a half hours. Rodane, if you want to remain here, you may. Felix can bring you food or drink. If you want to go, I can let you out and you can drive back to La Lac. We owe you that choice!" She turned and walked out, but she did close the door softly behind her.

Chapter 44

Iona's kitchen in Va.

The kitchen was bright with all the lights on, the tea kettle was still whistling in a soft whine, Iona and Nikos sat at the table finishing a light lunch she had prepared of fruits, cheeses, and an antipasto tray. Nikos had brought dessert, a fresh peach cake from the farmer's stand on the highway near her house. He also brought a bottle of ouzo which they were sipping as they talked.

"This is a fine pickle we find ourselves in, isn't it Nick?" Iona was tired, her face was shadowed with puffy eyes, and her eyelids felt heavy all day from a broken, restless night's sleep.

She had dropped weight since well before all the events that began with Rodane's trip to Santorini. She thought at first it was just due to overwork at the warehouse and spending her Saturdays in cleaning house and pouring over invoices and orders. She began taking vitamin C and B12 to try and kick start an immune response but she still felt fatigued all the time and she'd been battling a long-lived cold for over a week now.

Nikos, 'Nick' to Iona for over 40 years, looked in fine shape, greater than the last time she had seen him, his skin a little wrinkled from all the sun he craved. Otherwise he could have said he was twenty years younger and people would easily have believed it.

"You're sure it's him?"

"It's him all right even without laying eyes on him. When all this started back in Naples, when I got a call from Teddy Scalia asking permission to take an injured man to see Doc…"

"Goodness, Doc is still alive? He'd be what, eighty or ninety now?"

"Maybe older, I can't tell. But he'll probably outlive us all."

"So how does this tie into…"

"The injured man was Rodane." She sucked in her breath, placed her hands on the table and said in clipped tones, "Doc doesn't take cases lightly. He won't expose Flossie to any chance whatsoever of being…"

"It was Doc and Rodane was in very bad shape. He and Flossie worked on him a good while before he was stable and then they took him back up the hills to our farm in Sorrento." Iona's hands were trembling and her face had lost color. Nikos placed his warm ones over hers and then handed her the glass she had of ouzo, "Take a sip."

She took a swallow, not a sip, then she chugged the rest down and he poured in another finger full, "Iona, this was weeks ago. You know he's fine now, right?"

"Doesn't make it go down any easier. I knew that twit of a son of mine was hiding something, just knew it and Cassie… she called here and now I know it was the next morning and gave me an earful of what she'd do to him when she saw him next time."

She saw Nikos' facial expression, "Don't worry yourself, Nick. I know Cassie has some…shall we say…'different skill sets' than us…" she quirked her fingers, " 'normal folks', known it almost all her life. Addy didn't ever refer to them but we both knew she got his genes instead of mine. It does run in the 'family' doesn't it?" She quirked a crooked smile at him and he averted his eyes.

"Oh don't pull that 'I know nothing' act on me! It's way too late for that."

"After Scalia called me and told me about the attack in more detail I started looking into it. I called the two hospitals in Naples and found a patient suffering from a beating and stab wounds but he wasn't there. He had been airlifted out in the early morning. No witnesses, no records, no medical files to examine."

Iona said, "Nick, it could have been a robbery… a mugging… a fight gone bad…"

"Not when one of my best agents…uh, employees… was in charge of following and keeping him safe. She saved his life.

"If she hadn't been close…"

"But she was!" Nikos took her hand, "Iona she was, and he's ok."

"That still doesn't explain how you traced it back to…"

Nikos wrinkled his brow, "The way it went down and the reports following from my… employee, it was the exact methodology of Theras from the beginning; send out a team, surveil, corral and destroy. If you can't get them the first attempt you don't give up until the job's done. Never let anything or anyone stand in your path to success. You better than anyone should know that."

"So when Rodane came back home…"

"Oh it had gone farther even before Rodane came home. Theras sent out a secondary team to find him, get to him and obtain all the information he wanted, to see if Rodane was who he feared he was."

Ione couldn't stay still anymore. She got up and paced her kitchen, back and forth, back and forth, "Iona please sit down. You're making me nervous as a pregnant bunny!"

"She laughed out loud, "How in the world would you even know how a pregnant bunny acts?"

"Ever seen one? I have!" he chuckled.

He rose from his chair and went to her, wrapped his arms around her and she laid her head on his shoulder for a minute or two. Then she sighed and spoke, "Tell me the rest. Better to hear it now then later when Rodane comes back home. I might rap him upside the head with a skillet!"

They sat back down after Iona had put on the kettle. Too much ouzo, they needed clear heads. Nikos said, "Does he look any worse for the wear Iona?"

"No he doesn't but that doesn't surprise me. He came by his genes the same way Cassie does… honestly! But the chance, the possibilities…" she shivered and folded her arms tight against her. "…because I have to ask, why now? Why are you here now telling me all this? It's not that I'm not glad to see you, or have this time but what's happening for me, of all people, to be getting the story from the horse's mouth?"

He chuckled at that, "You're not so far removed from 'us' as you might think. You're not being spied on, believe me, but you do have people checking up on you every so often and making sure you want for nothing."

She really laughed out loud at that statement, "I haven't wanted for anything for quite some time Nick. I'm doing very well and Rodane is having a wonderful career. He now has a girlfriend…don't spill the beans… and Cassie is really loving her life. My granddaughter… well…" Tears showed in her eyes but she held them back.

"I'm not sure when I'll see her again but I'm hoping all this is over soon. What would it take Nick, for this to be over?"

Nikos wondered the same, looking around her neat, friendly kitchen wondering when he might be back here again. The kettle began whistling for them to take notice.

They had spent many nights here after Addy's death, commiserating, crying, holding and calming the other one when they took turns breaking down. Nikos continued trying to put those nights way back in his memory.

"Theras sent a team here to get to Rodane through you…. he sent…"

{there it's almost all out in the open}

"Are you saying all this shit with Adam and Sophia was…"

"Yes, it was him, I'm sure."

"Do you have proof? I'll kill him with my bare hands if I can get to him!"

"Not proof positive but we're getting there. We had a few… incidents that we're sure all tied together to lead back to him."

"Where is he, after all this time…?" she seemed to look back to past lives.

"Okay I need to give you the rest. Think you can handle it without pacing the floor?"

"Go on…" she narrowed her eyes at him, "get it all out now so I can figure out what kind of reactions to have."

"Rodane was targeted in Naples by Renata Kappos and Tabor…" he watched her,

"I know, I know but she was not involved in his physical attack, okay?"

"Oh, ok then, that's good to know!" she raised her voice, "and after all…"

"Iona no, let me finish. You can melt down after I'm done. Okay, the team that was sent here was Lexus Fira and…"

"Zoe? Zoe was part of Adam's death? Oh, good God, how could I…"

"No, no she wasn't! She almost died not being a part of this whole thing. She had no idea Lexus had a knife or planned on taking Adam down like he did… she and Renata…" he saw her face, "Want me to stop?"

"No, finish it. 'In for a penny…'"

"She and Renata both were almost unwilling victims here as much as you and Caroline were secondary victims as bystanders, not really victims, but horribly affected never-the-less."

Iona sneered as she spoke, "Theras was always good at using women as victims and then enmeshing them in situations where they got to be the fall guys. Damn him! Why couldn't he just die and be done with it and do all of us a favor?"

For the next hour they talked over all the events of the last few weeks. Nikos tried to set her mind at ease, that they were well on their way to finding Theras, isolating him in some way, and removing him from their lives. Iona knew it was better said than done, in her heart as well as her mind. She knew Theras was acting out of pique as well as a desire for revenge. Many years ago in Greece, Theras, Nikos and Addy, her Addy, had been close friends. Addy and Nikos however were the closest, best of friends, and the entire island population knew this.

Theras worked very hard to insinuate himself into their sports, their games, and their close relationship between families. As they grew older, Theras was constantly looking for ways to best his brother, Nikos, and his brother's closest ally, Addy. A part of it was a feeling of jealousy that Nikos preferred the company of Addy over his own brother. Another issue, much more hateful, reared its ugly head when Iona came to Greece on vacation with her parents and a good friend of hers for company. They spent a month on the island and Theras fell head over heels for Iona but Iona only had eyes and feelings for Addy. A wash of memories came to her as it would an unexpected flood. She was not sure how long she had thought of these relationships but it was cutting close to home and in very dangerous ways as of now, both for her and her family.

Nikos broke her reverie and she started at his fixed stare. "Where in the world were you Iona? It's like you took off and left your body here. You okay?"

Looking at Nikos, she realized even though she had known and loved him almost all her adult life, there was an untold story here that she didn't think she wanted to know or hear. Touching his face with her hand gently she said, "It's late Nick. I think we should call it a night and maybe finish this conversation at another time."

"Right, that seems sensible. Have you decided when you'll tell Rodane about…"

"No!" she whipped out the word so fast, Nikos reared back, "I only meant…"

"I know what you meant. I'm not going to be the one to tell him anything about this. He's moved beyond me now. I'll let someone else bear the burden of giving him whatever information he may need or want, about other parts of his life. I may not be a part of…" she saw his look and sympathized with his feelings but she couldn't help resenting them. … "your life but I will leave it to you because I respect your position, I really do. I love you and Isabel, you know that. But I'm also filled with anger at times that you and your 'family' have brought me misery and anguish along with the love you have for Isabel and the love I have or had, for Addy. No, let me finish. I've never kept too many things from Rodane or Cassie. The ones I have… well let's just say I'll believe to my dying day they had to be kept, at least by me. Someone else will have to be either the bearer of bad news or bring him glad tidings, whichever. I think I don't want to witness it happening, either now or later. We both know it was probably Theras that was responsible for…"

"No Iona, please don't go there. There's no proof, no reason to…"

"Oh come on Nick you're more rational than that. I know how your mind thinks, all of you! I've known for some time that Rodane, Cassie, even Sophia, would move past me and on to a different future. I'm okay with that truly, but I won't let you try to avoid what is 99% sure and certain. You owe me more than that!"

Nikos rose from his chair, kissed her gently on the mouth and softly touched her face, "I know Iona, I know. It's hard for me too with Addy…even Theras, gone for so long. Every day I think about…" He shook his head… "no, never mind what I think. It's too long, too much…"

Iona gripped his hand "Nick, if I ever need help you know you'll be the first one I come to. You know that, don't you?" In answer, he stroked her hair and went out the kitchen door into a black night. She sat for a very long time, thinking, sometimes crying.

"Addy… Addy, how could you have left me like that without telling me? I loved you so, and I'm so angry at you!"

Chapter 45

Basilique Notre Dame

Night had fallen but one couldn't tell, being in various conversations in a room with no windows and everyone gathered around the table. They were awash in printed documents, the hum of more documents rolling out of every printer from each computer station. They all looked tired and had eaten little of what was put before them; the risotto and seafood platters, the pasta dishes and fruit baskets remained, almost none eaten. The coffee pot however, gurgled and hissed, producing more caffeine and hyped nervous systems. Time to crash would come later, much later. The knock on the door caused everyone to look up at once, and silence descended like a blanket covering them.

Sabina went to the door and opened it to Rodane. He was standing there with shoulders slumped, head lowered, and a look of utter exhaustion and bewilderment on his face. Sabina put her hand on his arm. He bent close to her and their murmuring went on for some minutes. Sabina said something to which he shook his head 'no', back and forth and then he motioned behind him and into the room. She stepped aside and he straightened his shoulders, rubbed his face once or twice and entered the room. He walked directly to the spot he had been working from all morning, and turned to face all of them. "I want to begin by saying…" he swallowed, "I'm afraid I've been acting like a total ass but that shouldn't surprise you!" They laughed, just a little.

"I asked for answers, I practically begged for information about myself and you gave me both. I threw them back in your face!" He looked over at Agatha, standing stiff and straight, hands folded across her chest like a shield.

"If I'm…Mother, I'd like a chance to prove to you that asses are good for carrying heavy loads and plodding through some pretty heavy storms and floods." He tightened his lips and stood quietly waiting for an answer from… someone.

"Rodane…" Sabina said with a touch of compassion, "anyone who is going through what you… and I… if I may, have gone through in such a short time, with events of such import, might be expected to lash out and retaliate…" she looked briefly at Suri and Agatha, "in the face of the information we've shared here today. You're being quite normal in your reactions and pretty normal in your anger and frustration. At least that's how I feel." She colored with a rosy blush and she sat quietly. The silence stretched on for some seconds then Agatha cleared her throat, "Okay folks, what's next? Rodane, do you have a question? Please feel free to ask any of us."

"Can I start with an observation first?"

"You can start with anything you care to. That's why we're all here to help you understand. What one of us can't answer, another might."

"I'm wrapping my head around this 'tinkering' or 'experimentation' or however you call it, of man's DNA. For what purpose, to improve, expand, mutate? How would you describe something done so long ago, that our scientists are not prepared to believe or accept it?"

"That's exactly why so much of our history is classified and confidential…" Leander pointed to his pile of documents next to his computer, "I've taken the liberty of delving back into early history way before recorded history to explain some of the 'tweaking' that was done and can't be revealed for obvious reasons."

Rodane sat up straighter, "Yeah, about that. I know from my own knowledge and study that sometime between 150,000 and 20,000 years ago, power tools changed radically besides sharpened rocks and sticks. The human toolkit exploded to include bone, needles, hooks, arrowheads… it's like a light went off in our ancestor's heads about all things useful as tools and at the same time as that wondrous movement, humans were also creating remarkable works of art in the form of cave paintings, sculpture, instruments to create music, the very soul of humanity. Was that you?"

"Yes Rodane. Most scientists are ready to accept that explosion but without really understanding the impetus behind it. It's already long established that approximately 50,000 to 80,000 years ago there was a technological explosion that caused man as he was then, to use the untried and untested part of his brain, to evolve to a path of innovation. They needed that boost we gave them to address all the social conditions; population, resources, specialization of tools, all the things necessary to evolve, improve and make leaps and bounds into a new order of humanity. That couldn't continue forever. There had to be a cut-off time or a period where we removed our help, our 'tweaks' and left man to develop independently."

"So you're saying you just kind of left him to his own devices after you had given him such a boost that he stumbled all the time…?"

"Not at all" Sabina interrupted, "These were parochial limitations and they were profoundly relational in nature but early man didn't have the concepts necessary to organize them for a long period of time. It took many, many, many, more years for any of that organization to come to a point where you started to move ahead instead of three steps back, one step up. Does that make sense?"

"If I accept the thesis that 'family' was in charge of these revolutionary 'awakenings' way before science gives credit to their own ingenuity, yes. How do I posit all the natural things that moved us into such times of survival, destruction, innovation, survival and the cycle continues on and on…?"

"Are you referring to natural disasters and cyclical, destructive events that changed the shape and foundation of earth and with it the need to use our brain power to overcome them?" Agatha seemed…intent and tense.

"I guess I am. What about volcanic activity, earthquakes that forced migration and habitat construction? How about the need to escape floods and fire, drought, disease which led to starvation… all the factors that forced man to create and believe in new means and methods? That's you?"

"Of course not… at least…not always." She almost grinned at him but not quite.

"Rodane, if you had it in your power to take primitive man with all his plights and trials, all his disease and sickness, all his loss of life of children and fathers, mothers, whole tribes,…if you could change the earth to make it easier to live there and eat, survive, procreate and see your children to adulthood, would you?"

"Would I …interfere…? Make it different…? Cause things to turn out my way instead of letting nature…?"

"No Rodane, not interfere, become part of the solution to man's evolution rather than let him wander, unknowing, into extinction. Our own survival was tied up intrinsically and irretrievably with theirs. They died, we died. They were diseased, we were diseased, except we had the ability to prevent their deaths and along with that, our deaths as well. Would you not make use of your knowledge and your advanced skills to save them, as well as yourself? Would you watch while they wiped themselves out?"

"But…aren't we talking about the entire population of early man in the entire world? There's an enormity there that I can't …fathom…accept…"

"Then you'll find it even harder to accept that it didn't just affect man himself. It was tied into the food he ate, the clothes he wore, the animals they either befriended or hunted. If there was no evolution of plants and animals along with man, it would have come to nothing but starvation and poisoning."

Leander interrupted with a brief nod to Agatha, "We have in our world today Rodane, the means to do exactly what our 'family' did so long ago and for exactly the same reasons. Powerful gene-editing tools like CRISPR/Cas9 have made it relatively easy to alter the DNA sequences that serve as the genetic code of plants and animals, including humans. We may be on the brink of a major revolution in health care. It's not all due to our 'assistance' any more. We can afford to step back.

These new-found tools may make it possible to cure genetic illnesses like Cystic Fibrosis…and Sickle-cell Anemia… Cerebral Palsy…Parkinson's Disease… and to eradicate Malaria, a disease that kills hundreds of thousands of people each year. They may also bring cures for certain forms of cancer. Our scientists, working with mice, have shown that CRISPR can rid the body of HIV, the virus that causes AIDS. Which of those would you resist using, to make those profound changes if you could? Which ones would you eliminate from the pool of advanced care for man?"

Rodane had a very somber expression on a face that also registered awe in some form. "Some of our most intelligently trained, experienced scientists worry that gene editing could change our DNA in unintended ways, triggering unknown health problems. Since the same tools that make it possible to fix faulty genes can be used to insert genes to enhance desirable traits, some foresee the rise of so-called "designer babies" engineered to have, say, the 'right' color of eyes or an advanced IQ or… any other of a myriad of sought after traits not now available to all of us. How can this be good for all of mankind? We are so….flighty, so…precariously unstable at times…so possibly and predictably violent…" He looked totally bemused.

"We reached a time not so long ago…," Leander spoke up again with real surety in his voice, "when we resisted the urge to fix all those 'undesirable' traits of man as well as animals and plants. It was too much like creating a zombie civilization with no heart or soul. It's been difficult to parse out our skill sets to cause some of these more recent changes in man and his nature, without being observed and recognized for bringing finds to the table that would not be considered 'finds' but…something else. We have to tread very lightly to avoid detection. After all, there are dozens of scientists working now who are only a few steps away from what we could accomplish long ago, using our advanced knowledge.

Rodane narrowed his eyes and thought about all that had been said. Then he asked, "If you had the power to do all the things I think you are alluding to, in those so long ago times, then why do we even have these diseases you mentioned just now? Why not 'assist' the scientists of any age to find faster and safer cures for these illnesses when they had the chance?"

Sabina interjected, "I don't want you to think that all of these changes were done without lots of thought and experimentation on our own and much discussion about whether or not we felt we had the right to act as gods would do. We don't make ourselves out to be gods. From the beginning of our explorations, when mammoths and men began to meet each other, your populations have undergone explosive increments, then deaths of millions, hundreds of thousands, through plague, disease, and wars... to explosive again with medical advances and biological and chemical inroads to increase health and life span."

Agatha spoke kindly to him for the first time in a while, "We did not always interfere or interject our own skills and techniques. That would not have been our idea, our aim, nor would it have been our goal. It takes time, lots of time, before we can introduce new techniques and developments into this world of yours. Years, decades have to pass just for small inventions to be discovered. The lightbulb wasn't just an 'Aha' moment! It was the result of introducing one step at a time, over time. Otherwise we put ourselves and all of our people at risk of discovery. But if we didn't accomplish it that way, we'd still be using whale oil (if there were any whales left) and walking miles instead of discovering new methods of transportation."

Suri spoke up and startled Rodane since she seldom entered into the discussions,

"Today it's learning how acoustic tractor beams can use ultrasound to levitate objects and someday we'll take it to the next level with large objects and people. Those ultrasound vibrations affect air molecules and form shapes and manipulate particles. We already have it today in smaller form, when people get kidney stones blasted or laser surgery and cauterization. Can you imagine what would happen if those inventions were introduced all together, or too soon? The Salem Witch Trials would now be many governmental investigative committees around the globe. Eventually, someone will figure out how to remove those boxes with sound emitting surfaces and use this ultrasound technique to make rapid advances in medicine and particle physics. Your space program isn't a winding down, it's just getting started. But baby steps Rodane, baby steps or we'd all be on our way out."

Rodane asked, "Then you're telling me all the inventions that we have are a result of...?"

"No not nearly all, just some notable ones that impacted the entire world, not just certain portions for the good of all mankind, not just for profit and not just for small numbers in certain places." Suri watched for his reaction.

Thinking through what he had discussed, Rodane came to a conclusion. "You must have enormous resources, manpower and ingress into every field of science as well as every government and political power on the globe. The money required alone…"

"There's no doubt that what we have accomplished comes at a huge price in many different ways." Agatha chose her words carefully, "Man is a fickle creature, 'we' being part of that statement. We are all most familiar with the quote from Lord Acton, a British politician in the nineteenth century, "Power corrupts, absolute power corrupts…"

Rodane finished it, 'absolutely'. I've always believed in that completely and history bears it out."

"Well…" Agatha continued, "there is one part of that quote that is seldom mentioned in tandem with those words. It is; 'Great men are almost always bad men, this idea has been tested in laboratory settings.' Think about the second part of his quote. I believe he is referring to the laboratory of our entire earth. Rodane…in order to do good, you have to have the means to protect and defend against all the 'bad men' and women too by the way, that seek to obtain power for its own sake and not for the good it is able to accomplish. So yes, we have the means and the resources, and the money to do all these things and it has been acquired over many centuries. Hopefully it won't run out any time soon, because there is still much work to be done to keep this home of ours safe and stable. …To answer the question you are not asking, there are always bad people, even among our own 'families', that seek to acquire that power by any means necessary and use it for their own devices. To deny that would be self-effacing and a lie. Fortunately they have come to nothing, and most have failed miserably to have any lasting effect on your entire history, but they are there nonetheless."

Rodane sardonically quipped, "I can attest to that, can't I? Were these people…bad men…and women… the ones who are after me and my family? What do they want?"

"Some bad, some misinformed but well- intentioned, some just greedy and some very badly twisted and scarred from past slights and their own psychotic, delusional attempts to keep and use power to their own advantage and the disadvantage of all others. Evil lives, Rodane, in the hearts of some men and women and many leaders are overcome with its draw and mesmerizing hold on them."

Sabina was hesitant to intrude but found the courage to interject, "They want you Rodane, you and all you hold dear." He was astounded at her statement.

"But…what did I…how am I and my family…," he was overwhelmed.

Suri continued, "They want us gone from the equation so there are no stumbling blocks to deter them. They want total control over all the technology we brought with us as well as created here, so they can more easily accomplish those goals. You are the next one in the direct line of our ancestors, to guide us and present goals that we all agree on.

To allow that would be to thwart all their plans to be in charge and take advantage of all we have done over many, so many, years of trial and error. If you are removed as well as your family, the danger of that happening is minimal and they are free to reign terror and control over too much, entirely too much. No war could stop the devastation that would cause."

Rodane got up from his seat and started pacing back and forth in front of his computer workstation. No one felt the need to speak or add anything to the conversation at this point. He seemed to need the time to piece all of the information he had been given into some composite of a whole. It would be difficult under any circumstances. In Rodane's case, it was doubly difficult. Many of the theories and premises he had been working under as an Archaeologist were now upended or suspect. It's impossible to believe that a trained scientist in any field, but especially one of tracing man and his accomplishments back thousands, maybe hundreds of thousands of years, is based on faulty or incorrect assumptions and information. It would make one question their entire careers and education.

He turned, picked up his empty coffee mug and headed for more. He grabbed a pastry from the tray and almost shoved it whole into his mouth. Sabina watched him and smiled circumspectly. When anxious or tense or working through an important puzzle, she found her appetite increased exponentially to the seriousness of the issue. Eugenie was the same in that respect. She felt so much tenderness and sensitivity to this man she had only known a few weeks. This had to be one of the most conflicted times in his life filling him with doubt and confusion.

She remembered the first months of that first year when she had been found, reeducated and trained in the 'family's' history and her own past. She didn't take it nearly as well as Rodane was doing. She didn't act out, she did the opposite. She withdrew into herself, into her books, away from all those around her, learning the same history but under such different circumstances. They belonged. They had parents to support them, to study with them, to introduce the information in small bites, small portions, very much more comfortable to swallow. They had a childhood to remember, of laughter and fun and pleasant vacation times…

Then she looked over at Suri and then to Agatha. She felt somewhat ashamed, thinking her quiet thoughts while Rodane ate donuts and the members present gave him space to work out his own thoughts. Except for them and Nikos, and so many more, those who saw her potential and worked with her, she would be… where would she be? Good question, one she could honestly say she hadn't thought of.

"Sabina!" The strength of the voice had her starting up in her chair, looking at Agatha who was standing over her, bending low but speaking earnestly to get her attention without alerting Rodane.

"Sorry Mother, I was off in la-la land, I guess."

"Oh I think you were definitely somewhere but not la-la land. It's okay dear. We all have our pasts to reconsider and reflect on."

"How did you know… never mind, that was a thoughtless remark I was about to make." She smiled tenderly at an old woman who could have been her… great-grandmother? Maybe farther even than that.

Agatha spoke quickly and softly, "You must go and see about the break-in at Rodane's Secure Area in Montana for his artifacts and before anyone else finds out she has stolen them. Leander is now tracing Eliana's movements for the last weeks. He'll see if we can get a lead on where she's been and who she's contacted. It will take a while."

"Who should I contact?

"The Provost at the college is the first one. If you can't reach him, go to the Registrar of Classes. He knows all about Rodane's digs and whatever he brought home with him. Under no circumstance do you approach the Dean of the University. It was he who was so adamant about hiring Eliana in the first place. There's going to be some hell to pay from our West Coast team!"

Sabina looked to her in total surprise, "You think someone in the R&R teams out west is…"

Agatha was livid, "I don't know what to think right now except we're going to find out how this happened and where the responsibility lies. Theras may think he's outsmarted all of us and can do as he pleases, but he has no idea of the people who owe me big-time and very soon!"

"Should I wait for…"

"No, go now, while people are still up in Montana. I have a feeling Tegan is going to need to stay in Arizona for a while, maybe even do some traveling."

Sabina quietly looked over at Rodane, sighed and rose from her chair, leaving the room as unobtrusively as possible. Agatha looked after her as she left, forehead creased in concern, and letting out a sigh of her own.

Chapter 46

New York City

Marian pulled up her pantyhose, trying not to cry. Her hands were shaking, her throat was dry and she tasted the salt of those unshed tears. She dressed over by the window, looking out at 3rd Street and 8th Avenue. To her right she saw what looked like a huge tank but must have been pretty at night, all lit up. Below her she saw all the scaffolding that wrapped around the hotel to the next street. People were walking out in the street and under the planks, hurrying to go home at the end of the work day.

{maybe I should hurry home too}

"Are you ready Marian? Our table is reserved for seven. We don't want to be late now, do we dear?"

{dear how dare he}

She looked around the room, a quite adequate space with a king bed, decent appointments, clean and well-regulated for temperature control. Not what she would have chosen. The rooms ranked at the low end of the scale and the hotel was smack in the middle of a busy retail area. A McDonald's and a camera shop were her direct views. She would have preferred a larger suite and a view of Central Park. She tugged her skirt up over her hips and a flash of that same skirt being pulled down raced across her memory. The hands that gripped her shoulders and threw her on the bed still left their hot rough feeling on her skin. She shivered and swallowed hard, afraid she would be sick. This experience was not anything like what she had imagined or thought about. It was a far cry from the intense, emotional, pleasurable encounters she was looking forward to having.

{what did you expect you don't know him}

Terry had called her on his cell that afternoon, asking her to meet him in the lobby of the hotel. He had sounded sweet, eager and ready to be her shoulder and her confidant. She was so surprised to know he was in New York and he explained he had some very important business to hammer out. She had bathed in bubbles, used all the marvelous lotions she treasured, spent a long time in packing her overnight case at his suggestion and dressed carefully in some of her prettiest lingerie and a revealing skirt and blouse but not too revealing, and her enormously expensive slingback heels.

Sizing herself up in the mirror, her dark hair glinted with russet highlights and her makeup was flawless. Now? Now her makeup was smeared, her blouse was missing buttons and her underwear was torn beyond repair. She gulped and sucked in another breath to keep from breaking down.

{I was a fool}

What began as one of her exercises in getting even with Quimby and having her flings with other men had become scary and felt almost like she had been...

{no don't go there}

It was her idea, she asked him over drinks in the lobby, if he wanted to go somewhere more private to discuss her anger and her disappointment in her marriage to Quimby. He was so observant, so sympathetic, letting her bare all her slights and insults from what she saw as a loveless marriage. When he suggested they go to his room and have drinks sent up, she agreed almost immediately. Normally she would make them ask and almost beg, then give in and get what she really came for...

{and was that what you got fool}

He made a reservation at the desk for dinner, ordered drinks sent up to his room, took her up to the 6th floor on the express elevator and showed her to his rooms. He closed the door, locked it, after placing the Do Not Disturb sign on the outside, and walked over to her with a broad smile on his face. Her stomach shifted and she tingled all over as he put his hands around her face and leaned in for a slow lingering kiss, tasting her as she did him. In an instant it changed. He tightened his grip on her face till she tried to talk through his lips. He walked her backwards and she tripped in one of her heels. He bent down to pick it up and threw it across the sitting area, then he kept going through the bedroom door as he took his hand and thrust into her blouse and squeezed her breast till she cried out. Then he...

{I don't want to remember}

She did remember though. She played it over and over in her mind, try as she could to block it out; the torn blouse, the ripped bra, the hands that groped and pulled her skirt down in one sharp tug, the bed...

{oh don't forget the bed}

She didn't remember all of it. She only knew when it was over, she laid there in shock, surprise, shame, while he went to the bathroom and told her, "Don't forget, we have a dinner reservation. I absolutely hate to be late for reserved tables."

She had no idea what he thought. How was he with other women? What had he expected from her?

"Marian, our drinks are here. Five minutes more, alright my dear?"

What would he expect after dinner? Could she beg off dinner? a headache?... a previously forgotten appointment?... a call from a friend that needed her? She found herself afraid to make excuses to this man. He seemed overbearing, unstoppable.

{face it he's scary and you're scared}

What if she did beg off dinner? How would he react? Well, it was only dinner. After that she could ask him to get her a cab and go home. It would be a memorable night, just not one she would choose to consign to memory.

{let it go put it behind you}

She left the bedroom and Terry was sitting facing her door, drinks on the movable cart as he looked her over with a measured eye and gave her an expression of puzzlement..., "That's what you brought to wear for dinner?" She looked down at herself to check if it was soiled or torn, "why yes, I wasn't thinking of..."

"Apparently not but no worry, there are plenty of shops around to buy you something a little more appropriate for tomorrow."

She was confused, "Tomorrow? What are you talking about? I'm only here for..."

"Oh come now Marian, we talked about this over the phone. You wanted an escape, I'm providing you with one. You asked for a way to forget all the shitty things Quimby has put you through, well I aim to please." He pointed to the cart and asked for a martini, dry. Her eyes widened and she stood there rooted in place, while the shock of being ordered to make his drink set in,

"I'm not... I don't..." she began stuttering and flushing shades of red.

"Oh, for Christ's sake, don't tell me you don't know how to make a martini? Good God woman, what can you do?" he glared at her, rose from the sofa and walked to the cart. He slammed the shaker and bottles around, whipped up his martini and poured two of them, then offered her one, "Here Marian, let's forget all about who makes what drinks and enjoy each other's company."

She didn't drink martinis. Why was she taking one? She didn't want to be here, why was she staying? Her feet wouldn't move, her mouth wouldn't speak, and her hands had to be grasped together to avoid shaking.

{what am I going to do here}

He started a conversation about her boys. He relaxed and leaned back to admire her shoes. He continued talking until she felt more comfortable and he poured both of them second drinks. They were very strong ones. She tried to listen and just not utter a one-word response. She let him talk, he was very good at it. He remembered all she had told him in their phone conversations, she gave him that. He really was interested in her and it made her relax a little.

{maybe he's just a rough lover}

To one who had been given an easy marriage, easy children to raise, easy living for most of her marriage, she had little experience with rough sex, even from the lovers she had taken over the years. They were extremely attentive and thoughtful, even Quimby.

{wondering now what you've rejected}

Oh, this night was going to be a long one. During dinner he was attentive, very patient with the servers and very personable to those near them, ordering a bottle of wine for the near table and inviting them to join them for drinks and dessert, which they declined. Both of them were a little tipsy after leaving the restaurant and Terry suggested they go for an evening stroll. The weather, for once, was clear and the temperature was just right to walk outdoors. She thought the night air might be good for her lightheadedness. They walked about a block and Marian began to feel somewhat sick and more than a little dizzy. Terry stopped a cab and they returned to the hotel as her mind became more and more muddled. She remembered getting into the elevator and she seemed to remember him carrying her into the bedroom then try as she might, it all went blank.

She dreamed of seeing people around her carrying her by the arms, into a limousine, carrying her back out again. She saw planes flying overhead, heard the roar of engines, felt Terry tightening her waist, tighter, tighter, his face next to hers, close enough to kiss, hissing at her that she'd find out what she wanted wasn't what he wanted. He would show her soon.

"Marian dear Marian, I've waited a long time to have all of you in the palm of my hand. I'll just have to start with you." His fingers dug into her arm and the pain cleared the fog enough to see his face clearer, hear his final words before she dipped back into that thick gray fog, "When I'm done, you can all go to hell."

Epilogue

Somewhere in the Indian Ocean, off the coast of Africa and close to Madagascar, Terrence Gurlow had purchased an island. It only cost a few million and he was moving all his people into the labs that had been developed over the last eighteen months. His staff was made up of dozens of full and part-time workers who occupied the living quarters on that small island. The underground bunkers had been carved out and built with a handful of loyal, single, skilled, vetted and studied to the nth degree, people who signed confidentiality contracts, non-disclosure agreements, and had all the money they could ask for in using their skills in those pristine avant-garde labs. Outside of the workers, those bunkers had only been visited by 'Terry'.

Terrance Gurlow was a trifle thinner than his previous persona. He was trim and fit and looked about twenty years younger than his last visage. That one was a hell of a lot older than either of the other ones he had used in this wretched hole he called home. Now he was about to use what resources he had accumulated (and they were massive) and begin to put his long-delayed plan into action. Enough of the little skirmishes he had been monitoring and effecting the last few years. Those responsible for his being holed up here all this time were in for a shit storm and it was about to collide with all the do-gooders and the noble Nellies he was now prepared to take on and take out.

Marian was due on the next skiff that transferred personnel to his island and the medical team assured him she would be ready and presentable for the video session he had planned. Her quarters were all prepared and ready for her.

He wrung his hands in anticipation and grinned alarmingly. He reached into his pocket and pulled out the pin he kept with him at all times. He would find a way to make it connect to those of the others around him. His researchers and technicians and computer wonks were close to having it hook up with the communication towers that he could feed into. But first, he would have to make a return trip to the base camp and the resting ship that lay quietly beneath four miles of Pacific waters. He needed some of the tools that were left there deliberately (fools, all of them). He needed to pick his travelling crew very carefully for that adventure and he knew it had to be soon. He wondered who he should take with him for pleasure and relaxation besides Marian...maybe Cassie Arcos? It would take some thought. It actually looked as if his face had taken on a rictus that only came with death. Well he had plenty of that in his pocket also. This was going to be such fun.